Fantasy Masterworks

'Rudyard Kipling is one of the finest writers of fantasy in the last one hundred years.' Ray Bradbury

'Kipling has taught me more about writing technique and hit me with more real emotional shocks than any other short story writer.' David Drake

'I grew up in love with Kipling. My mother read the *Just So Stories* to us when I was a kid. We begged her to read them again and again. Phrases still haunt me. "The great, grey, green, greasy Limpopo" river. I'm happy to welcome him back.' Jack Williamson

'As of what Kipling wrote about nineteenth-century Anglo-India . . . it is not only the best but almost the only literary picture we have.' George Orwell

'I once bought in a second-hand bookshop in mid-Wales a "rupee dreadful" published for the Indian Railway Library of *The Phantom 'Rickshaw & Other Eerie Tales*, which turned out to be seriously strange in an enjoyable way. C. S. Lewis reckoned that such Kipling stories "may be his best work, but they are not his most characteristic", and it is excellent news to see them back in print in this collected edition.'
Sir Christopher Frayling

'The idea that I or, for that matter, any living writer of fantasy, should offer a quote to persuade readers to try Rudyard Kipling is akin to the notion of a garage band recommending the work of the Rolling Stones.'
Lucius Shepard

'He has seen a perfect Odyssey of strange experiences.'
Andrew Lang

ALSO BY RUDYARD KIPLING

Fantasy Masterworks

THE MARK OF
THE BEAST
and Other Fantastical Tales

RUDYARD KIPLING

Edited with an Afterword by Stephen Jones

The right of Rudyard Kipling to be identified as the author
of this work has been asserted by him in accordance with the Copyright,
Designs and Patents Act 1988.

This edition published in Great Britain in 2006 by
Gollancz
An imprint of the Orion Publishing Group
Orion House, 5 Upper St Martin's Lane,
London WC2H 9EA

A CIP catalogue record for this book is available
from the British Library

ISBN-13 9 780 57507 791 1

ISBN-10 0 57507 791 3

1 3 5 7 9 10 8 6 4 2

Printed in Great Britain by Mackays of Chatham, plc

Typeset at The Spartan Press Ltd, Lymington, Hants

The Orion Publishing Group's policy is to use papers that
are natural, renewable and recyclable products and made
from wood grown in sustainable forests. The logging and
manufacturing processes are expected to conform to the
environmental regulations of the country of origin.

www.orionbooks.co.uk

CONTENTS

ACKNOWLEDGEMENTS

Grateful acknowledgement is made to the following individuals for their help and inspiration in the compiling of this volume: Jo Fletcher, Mandy Slater, Peter Haining, Sara and Randy Broecker, Kim Newman and The Kipling Society (www.kipling.org.uk). Very special thanks to Mike Ashley.

Introduction: Neil Gaiman copyright © September 2006.
'The Vampire' from *The Vampire* (1897).
'The Dream of Duncan Parrenness' from *Civil and Military Gazette*, December 25, 1884.
'The City of Dreadful Night' from *Civil and Military Gazette*, September 10, 1885.
'An Indian Ghost Story in England' from *Pioneer*, December 10, 1885.
'The Phantom 'Rickshaw' from *Quartette*, December 1885.
'The Strange Ride of Morrowbie Jukes' from *Quartette*, December 1885.
'The Unlimited Draw of Tick Boileau' from *Quartette*, December 1885.
'In the House of Suddhoo' from *Civil and Military Gazette*, April 30, 1886.
'The Bisara of Pooree' from *Civil and Military Gazette*, March 4, 1887.
'Haunted Subalterns' from *Civil and Military Gazette*, May 27, 1887.
'By Word of Mouth' from *Civil and Military Gazette*, June 10, 1887.
'The Recurring Smash' from *Civil and Military Gazette*, October 13, 1887.
'The Dreitarbund' from *Civil and Military Gazette*, October 22, 1887.
'Bubbling Well Road' from *Civil and Military Gazette*, January 18, 1888.
'The Sending of Dana Da' from *The Week's News*, February 11, 1888.
'My Own True Ghost Story' from *The Week's News*, February 25, 1888.
'Sleipner, Late Thurinda' from *The Week's News*, May 12, 1888.
'The Man Who Would Be King' from *The Phantom 'Rickshaw & Other Eerie Tales* (1888).
'The Solid Muldoon' from *The Week's News*, June 2, 1888.
'Baboo Mookerji's Undertaking' from *Civil and Military Gazette*, September 1, 1888.
'The Joker' from *Pioneer*, January 1, 1889.
'The Wandering Jew' from *Civil and Military Gazette*, April 4, 1889.
'The Courting of Dinah Shadd' from *Macmillan's Magazine* and *Harper's Weekly*, March 1890.
'The Mark of the Beast' from *Pioneer*, July 12 and 14, 1890.
'At the End of the Passage' from *The Boston Herald*, July 20, 1890.

Your Gods and my Gods –
do you or I know which are the stronger?

— Native Proverb

INTRODUCTION

Years ago, back when I was just starting to write *Sandman*, I was interviewed, and in the interview I was asked to name some of my favourite authors. I listed happily and with enthusiasm. Several weeks later, when the interview had been printed, a fan letter arrived at DC Comics for me, and was forwarded to me. It was from three young men who wanted to know how I could possibly have listed Kipling as a favourite author, given that I was a trendy young man and Kipling was, I was informed, a fascist and a racist and a generally evil person.

It was obvious from the letter that they had never actually read any Kipling. More to the point, they had been told not to.

I doubt I am the only person who writes replies to letters in his head he never sends. In my head I wrote many pages in reply, and then I never wrote it down or sent it.

In truth, Kipling's politics are not mine. But then, it would be a poor sort of world if one were only able to read authors who expressed points of view that one agreed with entirely. It would be a bland sort of world if we could not spend time with people who thought differently, and who saw the world from a different place. Kipling was many things that I am not, and I like that in my authors. And besides, Kipling is an astonishing writer, and was arguably at his best in the short story form.

I wanted to explain to my correspondents why 'The Gardener' had affected me so deeply, as a reader and as a writer – it's a story I read once, believing every word, all the way to the end, where I understood the encounter the woman had had, then started again at the beginning, understanding now the tone of voice and what I was being told. It was a tour de force. It's a story about loss, and lies, and what it means to be human and to have secrets, and it can and does and should break your heart.

I learned from Kipling. At least two stories of mine (and a children's book I am currently writing) would not exist had he not written.

Kipling wrote about people, and his people feel very real. His tales of the fantastic are chilling, or illuminating or remarkable or sad, because his people breathe and dream. They were alive before the story started, and many of them live on once the last line has been read. His stories provoke emotion and reaction – at least one of the stories in this volume revolts me on a hundred levels, and has given me nightmares, and I would not have missed reading it for worlds. Besides, I would not have told my correspondents, Kipling was a poet, as much a poet of the dispossessed as he was a poet of Empire.

I said none of those things back then, and I wished that I had. So when Steve Jones asked me to write the introduction to this book, I said yes. Because I've said them now, to you. Trust the tale, not the teller, as Stephen King reminded us. And the best of Rudyard Kipling's tales are, simply, in the first rank of stories written in the English language.

Enjoy them.

Neil Gaiman
September 2006

THE VAMPIRE

A fool there was and he made his prayer
(Even as you or I!)
To a rag and a bone and a hank of hair,
(We called her the woman who did not care),
But the fool he called her his lady fair—
(Even as you or I!)

Oh, the years we waste and the tears we waste,
And the work of our head and hand
Belong to the woman who did not know
(And now we know that she never could know)
And did not understand!

A fool there was and his goods he spent,
(Even as you or I!)
Honour and faith and a sure intent
(And it wasn't the least what the lady meant),
But a fool must follow his natural bent
(Even as you or I!)

Oh, the toil we lost and the spoil we lost
And the excellent things we planned
Belong to the woman who didn't know why
(And now we know that she never knew why)
And did not understand!

The fool was stripped to his foolish hide,
(Even as you or I!)
Which she might have seen when she threw him aside—

(But it isn't on record the lady tried)
So some of him lived but the most of him died—
(Even as you or I!)

'And it isn't the shame and it isn't the blame
That stings like a white-hot brand—
It's coming to know that she never knew why
(Seeing, at last, she could never know why)
And never could understand!'

THE DREAM OF DUNCAN PARRENNESS

Like Mr Bunyan of old, I, Duncan Parrenness, Writer to the most Honourable the East India Company, in this God-forgotten city of Calcutta, have dreamed a dream, and never since that Kitty my mare fell lame have I been so troubled. Therefore, lest I should forget my dream, I have made shift to set it down here. Though Heaven knows how unhandy the pen is to me who was always readier with sword than ink-horn when I left London two long years since.

When the Governor-General's great dance (that he gives yearly at the latter end of November) was finisht, I had gone to mine own room which looks over that sullen, un-English stream, the Hoogly, scarce so sober as I might have been. Now, roaring drunk in the West is but fuddled in the East, and I was drunk Nor'-Nor' Easterly as Mr Shakespeare might have said. Yet, in spite of my liquor, the cool night winds (though I have heard that they breed chills and fluxes innumerable) sobered me somewhat; and I remembered that I had been but a little wrung and wasted by all the sickness of the past four months, whereas those young bloods that came eastward with me in the same ship had been all, a month back, planted to Eternity in the foul soil north of Writers' Buildings. So then, I thanked God mistily (though, to my shame, I never kneeled down to do so) for license to live, at least till March should be upon us again. Indeed, we that were alive (and our number was less by far than those who had gone to their last account in the hot weather late past) had made very merry that evening, by the ramparts of the Fort, over this kindness of Providence; though our jests were neither witty nor such as I should have liked my Mother to hear.

3

When I had laid down (or rather thrown me on my bed) and the fumes of my drink had a little cleared away, I found that I could get no sleep for thinking of a thousand things that were better left alone. First, and it was a long time since I had thought of her, the sweet face of Kitty Somerset, drifted as it might have been drawn in a picture, across the foot of my bed, so plainly, that I almost thought she had been present in the body. Then I remembered how she drove me to this accursed country to get rich, that I might the more quickly marry her, our parents on both sides giving their consent; and then how she thought better (or worse may be) of her troth, and wed Tom Sanderson but a short three months after I had sailed. From Kitty I fell a musing on Mrs Vansuythen, a tall pale woman with violet eyes that had come to Calcutta from the Dutch Factory at Chinsura, and had set all our young men, and not a few of the factors, by the ears. Some of our ladies, it is true, said that she had never a husband or marriage-lines at all; but women, and specially those who have led only indifferent good lives themselves, are cruel hard one on another. Besides, Mrs Vansuythen was far prettier than them all. She had been most gracious to me at the Governor-General's rout and indeed I was looked upon by all as her *preux chevalier* – which is French for a much worse word. Now, whether I cared so much as the scratch of a pin for this same Mrs Vansuythen (albeit I had vowed eternal love three days after we met) I knew not then nor did till later on; but mine own pride, and a skill in the small sword that no man in Calcutta could equal, kept me in her affections. So that I believed I worshipt her.

When I had dismist her violet eyes from my thoughts, my reason approacht me for ever having followed her at all; and I saw how the one year that I had lived in this land had so burnt and seared my mind with the flames of a thousand bad passions and desires, that I had aged ten months for each one in the Devil's school. Whereat I thought of my Mother for a while, and was very penitent: making in my sinful tipsy mood a thousand vows of reformation – all since broken, I fear me, again and again. To-morrow, says I to myself, I will live

4

cleanly for ever. And I smiled dizzily (the liquor being still strong in me) to think of the dangers I had escaped; and built all manner of fine Castles in Spain, whereof a shadowy Kitty Somerset that had the violet eyes and the sweet slow speech of Mrs Vansuythen, was always Queen.

Lastly, a very fine and magnificent courage (that doubtless had its birth in Mr Hastings' Madeira) grew upon me, till it seemed that I could become Governor-General, Nawab, Prince, ay, even the Great Mogul himself, by the mere wishing of it. Wherefore, taking my first steps, random and unstable enough, towards my new kingdom, I kickt my servants sleeping without till they howled and ran from me, and called Heaven and Earth to witness that I, Duncan Parrenness, was a Writer in the service of the Company and afraid of no man. Then, seeing that neither the Moon nor the Great Bear were minded to accept my challenge, I lay down again and must have fallen asleep.

I was waked presently by my last words repeated two or three times, and I saw that there had come into the room a drunken man, as I thought, from Mr Hastings' rout. He sate down at the foot of my bed in all the world as it belonged to him, and I took note, as well as I could, that his face was somewhat like mine own grown older, save when it changed to the face of the Governor-General or my father, dead these six months. But this seemed to me only natural, and the due result of too much wine; and I was so angered at his entry all unannounced, that I told him, not over civilly, to go. To all my words he made no answer whatever, only saying slowly, as though it were some sweet morsel: 'Writer in the Company's service and afraid of no man.' Then he stops short, and turning round sharp upon me, says that one of my kidney need fear neither man nor devil; that I was a brave young man, and like enough, should I live so long, to be Governor-General. But for all these things (and I suppose that he meant thereby the changes and chances of our shifty life in these parts) I must pay my price. By this time I had sobered somewhat, and being well waked out of my first sleep, was disposed to look upon the matter as a tipsy man's jest. So, says I merrily: 'And what price shall I pay for this palace of mine, which is but twelve feet square, and my five poor pagodas a month? The devil take you and your jesting: I have paid my price twice over in sickness.' At that moment my man turns full towards me: so that by the moonlight I could see every line and wrinkle of his face. Then my drunken mirth died out of me, as I have seen the waters of our great rivers die away in one night; and I, Duncan Parrenness, who was afraid of no man, was taken with a more deadly terror than I hold it has ever been the lot of mortal man to know. For I saw that his face was my very own, but marked and lined and scarred with the furrows of disease and much evil living – as I once, when I was (Lord help me) very drunk indeed, have seen mine own face, all white and drawn and grown old, in a mirror. I take it that any man would have been even more greatly feared than I; for I am, in no way wanting in courage.

After I had laid still for a little, sweating in my agony, and waiting until I should awake from this terrible dream (for dream I knew it to be), he says again that I must pay my price; and a little after, as though it were to be given in pagodas and sicca rupees: 'What price will you pay?' Says I, very softly: 'For God's sake let me be, whoever you are, and I will mend my ways from to-night.' Says he, laughing a little at my words, but otherwise making no motion of having heard them: 'Nay, I would only rid so brave a young ruffler as yourself of much that will be a great hindrance to you on your way through life in the Indies; for believe me,' and here he looks full on me once more, 'there is no return.' At all this rigmarole, which I could not then understand, I was a good deal put aback and waited for what should come next. Says he very calmly: 'Give me your trust in man.' At that I saw how heavy would be my price, for I never doubted but that he could take from me all that he asked, and my head was, through terror and wakefulness, altogether cleared of the wine I had drunk. So I takes him up very short, crying that I was not so wholly bad as he would make believe, and that I trusted my fellows to the full as much as they were worthy of it. 'It was none of my fault,' says I, 'if one-half of them were liars and the other half deserved to be burnt in the hand, and I would once more ask him to have done with his questions.' Then I stopped, a little afraid, it is true, to have let my tongue so run away with me, but he took no notice of this, and only laid his hand lightly on my left breast and I felt very cold there for a while. Then he says, laughing more: 'Give me your faith in women.' At that I started in my bed as though I had been stung, for I thought of my sweet mother in England, and for a while fancied that my faith in God's best creatures could neither be shaken nor stolen from me. But later, Myself's hard eyes being upon me, I fell to thinking, for the second time that night, of Kitty (she that jilted me and married Tom Sanderson) and of Mistress Vansuythen, whom only my devilish price made me follow, and how she was even worse than Kitty, and I worst of them all – seeing that with my life's work to be done, I must needs go dancing down the Devil's swept and garnished causeway, because, forsooth, there was a light woman's smile at the end of it. And I thought that all women in the world were either like Kitty or Mistress Vansuythen (as indeed they have ever since been to me), and this put me to such an extremity of rage and sorrow, that I was beyond word glad when Myself's hand fell again on my left breast, and I was no more troubled by these follies.

After this he was silent for a while, and I made sure that he must go or I awake ere long; but presently he speaks again (and very softly) that I was a fool to care for such follies as those he had taken from me, and that ere he went he would only ask me for a few other trifles such as no man, or for matter of that boy either, would keep about him in this country. And so it happened that he took from out of my very heart as it were, looking all the time into my face with my own eyes, as much as remained to me of my boy's soul and conscience. This was to me a far more terrible loss than the two that I had suffered before. For though, Lord help me, I had travelled far enough from all paths of decent or godly living, yet there was in me, though I myself write it, a certain goodness of heart which, when I was sober (or sick) made me very sorry of all that I had done before the fit came on me. And this I lost wholly: having in place thereof another deadly coldness at the heart. I am not, as I have before said, ready with my pen, so I fear that what I have just written may not be readily understood. Yet there be certain times in a young man's life, when, through great sorrow or sin, all the boy in him is burnt and seared away so that he passes at one step to the more sorrowful state of manhood: as our staring Indian day changes into night with never so much as the grey of twilight to temper the two extremes. This shall perhaps make my state more clear, if it be remembered that my torment was ten times as great as comes in the natural course of nature to any man. At that time I dared not think of the change that had come over me, and all in one night: though I have often thought of it since. 'I have paid the price,' says I, my teeth chattering, for I was deadly cold, 'and what is my return?' At this time it was nearly dawn, and Myself had begun to grow pale and thin against the white light in the east, as my mother used to tell me is the custom of ghosts and devils and the like. He made as if he would go, but my words stopt him and he laughed – as I remember that I laughed when I ran Angus Macalister through the sword-arm last August, because he said that Mrs Vansuythen was no better than she should be. 'What return?' – says he, catching up my last words – 'Why, strength to live as long as God or the Devil pleases, and so long as you live my young master, my gift.' With that he puts something into my hand, though it was still too dark to see what it was, and when next I lookt up he was gone.

When the light came I made shift to behold his gift, and saw that it was a little piece of dry bread.

THE CITY OF DREADFUL NIGHT

The dense wet heat that hung over the face of land, like a blanket, prevented all hope of sleep in the first instance. The cicalas helped the heat, and the yelling jackals the cicalas. It was impossible to sit still in the dark, empty, echoing house and watch the punkah beat the dead air. So, at ten o'clock of the night, I set my walking-stick on end in the middle of the garden, and waited to see how it would fall. It pointed directly down the moonlit road that leads to the City of Dreadful Night. The sound of its fall disturbed a hare. She limped from her form and ran across to a disused Mahomedan burial-ground, where the jawless skulls and rough-butted shank-bones, heartlessly exposed by the July rains, glimmered like mother o' pearl on the rain-channelled soil. The heated air and the heavy earth had driven the very dead upward for coolness' sake. The hare limped on; snuffed curiously at a fragment of a smoke-stained lamp-shard, and died out, in the shadow of a clump of tamarisk trees.

The mat-weaver's hut under the lee of the Hindu temple was full of sleeping men who lay like sheeted corpses. Overhead blazed the unwinking eye of the Moon. Darkness gives at least a false impression of coolness. It was hard not to believe that the flood of light from above was warm. Not so hot as the Sun, but still sickly warm, and heating the heavy air beyond what was our due. Straight as a bar of polished steel ran the road to the City of Dreadful Night; and on either side of the road lay corpses disposed on beds in fantastic attitudes – one hundred and seventy bodies of men. Some shrouded all in white with bound-up mouths; some naked and black as ebony in the strong light; and one – that lay face upwards with dropped jaw, far away from the others – silvery white and ashen grey.

'A leper asleep; and the remainder wearied coolies, servants, small shopkeepers, and drivers from the hack-stand hard by. The scene – a main approach to Lahore city, and the night a warm one in August.' This was all that there was to be seen; but by no means all that one could see. The witchery of the moonlight was everywhere; and the world was horribly changed. The long line of the naked dead, flanked by the rigid silver statue, was not pleasant to look upon. It was made up of men alone. Were the women-kind, then, forced to sleep in the shelter of the stifling mud-huts as best they might? The fretful wail of a child from a low mud-roof answered the question. Where the children are the mothers must be also to look after them. They need care on these sweltering nights. A black little bullet-head peeped over the coping, and a thin – a painfully thin – brown leg was slid over on to the gutter pipe. There was a sharp clink of glass bracelets; a woman's arm showed for an instant above the parapet, twined itself round the lean little neck, and the child was dragged back, protesting, to the shelter of the bedstead. His thin, high-pitched shriek died out in the thick air almost as soon as it was raised; for even the children of the soil found it too hot to weep.

More corpses; more stretches of moonlit, white road; a string of sleeping camels at rest by the wayside; a vision of scudding jackals; ekkaponies asleep – the harness still on their backs, and the brass-studded country carts, winking in the moonlight – and again more corpses. Wherever a grain cart atilt, a tree trunk, a sawn log, a couple of bamboos and a few handfuls of thatch cast a shadow, the ground is covered with them. They lie – some face downwards, arms folded, in the dust; some with clasped hands flung up above their heads; some curled up dog-wise; some thrown like limp gunny-bags over the side of the grain carts; and some bowed with their brows on their knees in the full glare of the Moon. It would be a comfort if they were only given to snoring; but they are not, and the likeness to corpses is unbroken in all respects save one. The lean dogs snuff at them and turn away. Here and there a tiny child lies on his father's bedstead, and a protecting arm is thrown round it in every instance. But, for the most part, the children sleep with their mothers on the housetops. Yellow-skinned white-toothed pariahs are not to be trusted within reach of brown bodies.

A stifling hot blast from the mouth of the Delhi Gate nearly ends my resolution of entering the City of Dreadful Night at this hour. It is a compound of all evil savours, animal and vegetable, that a walled city can brew in a day and a night. The temperature within the motionless groves of plantain and orange-trees outside the city walls seems chilly by comparison. Heaven help all sick persons and young children within the city tonight! The high house-walls are still radiating heat savagely, and from obscure side gullies fetid breezes eddy that ought to poison a buffalo. But the buffaloes do not heed. A drove of them are parading the vacant main street; stopping now and then to lay their ponderous muzzles against the closed shutters of a grain-dealer's shop, and to blow thereon like grampuses.

Then silence follows – the silence that is full of the night noises of a great city. A stringed instrument of some kind is just, and only just audible. High over head some one throws open a window, and the rattle of the woodwork echoes down the empty street. On one of the roofs a hookah is in full blast; and the men are talking softly as the pipe gutters. A little farther on the noise of conversation is more distinct. A slit of light shows itself between the sliding shutters of a shop. Inside, a stubble-bearded, weary-eyed trader is balancing his account-books among the bales of cotton prints that surround him. Three sheeted figures bear him company, and throw in a remark from time to time. First he makes an entry, then a remark; then passes the back of his hand across his streaming forehead. The heat in the built-in street is fearful. Inside the shops it must be almost unendurable. But the work goes on steadily; entry, guttural growl, and uplifted hand-stroke succeeding each other with the precision of clock-work.

A policeman – turbanless and fast asleep – lies across the road on the way to the Mosque of Wazir Khan. A bar of moonlight falls across the forehead and eyes of the sleeper, but he never stirs. It is close upon midnight, and the heat seems to be increasing. The open square in front of the Mosque is crowded with corpses; and a man must pick his way carefully for fear of treading on them. The moonlight stripes the Mosque's high front of coloured enamel work in broad diagonal bands; and each separate dreaming pigeon in the niches and corners of the masonry throws a squab little shadow. Sheeted ghosts rise up wearily from their pallets, and flit into the dark depths of the building. Is it possible to climb to the top of the great Minars, and thence to look down on the city? At all events the attempt is worth making, and the chances are that the door of the staircase will be unlocked. Unlocked it is; but a deeply sleeping janitor lies across the threshold, face turned to the Moon. A rat dashes out of his turban at the sound of approaching footsteps. The man grunts, opens his eyes for a minute, turns round, and goes to sleep again. All the heat of a decade of fierce Indian summers is stored in the pitch-black, polished walls of the corkscrew staircase. Halfway up there is something alive, warm, and feathery; and it snores. Driven from step to step as it catches the sound of my advance, it flutters to the top and reveals itself as a yellow-eyed, angry kite. Dozens of kites are asleep on this and the other Minars, and on the domes below. There is the shadow of a cool, or at least a less sultry breeze at this height; and, refreshed thereby, turn to look on the City of Dreadful Night.

Doré might have drawn it! Zola could describe it – this spectacle of sleeping thousands in the moonlight and in the shadow of the Moon. The roof-tops are crammed with men, women, and children; and the air is full of undistinguishable noises. They are restless in the City of Dreadful Night; and small wonder. The marvel is that they can even breathe. If you gaze intently at the multitude you can see that they are almost as uneasy as a daylight crowd; but the tumult is subdued. Everywhere, in the strong light, you can watch the sleepers turning to and fro; shifting their beds and again resettling them. In the pitlike courtyards of the houses there is the same movement.

The pitiless Moon shows it all. Shows, too, the plains outside the city, and here and there a hand's-breadth of the Ravee without the walls. Shows lastly, a splash of glittering silver on a house-top almost directly below the mosque Minar. Some poor soul has risen to throw a jar of water over his fevered body; the tinkle of the falling water strikes faintly on the ear. Two or three other men, in far-off corners of the City of Dreadful Night, follow his example, and the water flashes like heliographic signals. A small cloud passes over the face of the Moon, and the city and its inhabitants – clear drawn in black and white before – fade into masses of black and deeper black. Still the unrestful noise continues, the sigh of a great city overwhelmed with the heat, and of a people seeking in vain for rest. It is only the lower-class women who sleep on the house-tops. What must the torment be in the latticed zenanas, where a few lamps are still twinkling? There are footfalls in the court below. It is the *Muezzin* – faithful minister; but he ought to have been here an hour ago to tell the Faithful that prayer is better than sleep – the sleep that will not come to the city.

The *Muezzin* fumbles for a moment with the door of one of the Minars, disappears awhile, and a bull-like roar – a magnificent bass thunder – tells that he has reached the top of the Minar. They must hear the cry to the banks of the shrunken Ravee itself! Even across the courtyard it is almost overpowering. The cloud drifts by and shows him outlined in black against the sky, hands laid upon his ears, and broad chest heaving with the play of his lungs – 'Allah ho Akbar'; then a pause while another *Muezzin* somewhere in the direction of the Golden Temple takes up the call – 'Allah ho Akbar.' Again and again; four times in all; and from the bedsteads a dozen men have risen up already. – 'I bear witness that there is no God but God.' What a splendid cry it is, the proclamation of the creed that brings men out of their beds by scores at midnight! Once again he thunders through the same phrase, shaking with the vehemence of his own voice; and then, far and near, the night air rings with 'Mahomed is the

Prophet of God.' It is as though he were flinging his defiance to the far-off horizon, where the summer lightning plays and leaps like a bared sword. Every *Muezzin* in the city is in full cry, and some men on the roof-tops are beginning to kneel. A long pause precedes the last cry, 'La ilaha Illallah,' and the silence closes up on it, as the ram on the head of a cotton-bale.

The *Muezzin* stumbles down the dark stairway grumbling in his beard. He passes the arch of the entrance and disappears. Then the stifling silence settles down over the City of Dreadful Night. The kites on the Minar sleep again, snoring more loudly, the hot breeze comes up in puffs and lazy eddies, and the Moon slides down towards the horizon. Seated with both elbows on the parapet of the tower, one can watch and wonder over that heat-tortured hive till the dawn. 'How do they live down there? What do they think of? When will they awake?' More tinkling of sluiced water-pots; faint jarring of wooden bedsteads moved into or out of the shadows; uncouth music of stringed instruments softened by distance into a plaintive wail, and one low grumble of far-off thunder. In the courtyard of the mosque the janitor, who lay across the threshold of the Minar when I came up, starts wildly in his sleep, throws his hands above his head, mutters something, and falls back again. Lulled by the snoring of the kites – they snore like over-gorged humans – I drop off into an uneasy doze, conscious that three o'clock has struck, and that there is a slight – a very slight – coolness in the atmosphere. The city is absolutely quiet now, but for some vagrant dog's love-song. Nothing save dead heavy sleep.

Several weeks of darkness pass after this. For the Moon has gone out. The very dogs are still, and I watch for the first light of the dawn before making my way homeward. Again the noise of shuffling feet. The morning call is about to begin, and my night watch is over. 'Allah ho Akbar! Allah ho Akbar!' The east grows grey, and presently saffron; the dawn wind comes up as though the *Muezzin* had summoned it; and, as one man, the City of Dreadful Night rises from its bed and turns its face towards the dawning day. With return of life comes return of sound. First a low whisper, then a deep bass hum; for it must be remembered that the entire city is on the house-tops. My eyelids weighed down with the arrears of long deferred sleep, I escape from the Minar through the courtyard and out into the square beyond, where the sleepers have risen, stowed away the bedsteads, and are discussing the morning hookah. The minute's freshness of the air has gone, and it is as hot as at first.

'Will the Sahib, out of his kindness, make room?' What is it? Something borne on men's shoulders comes by in the half-light, and I stand back. A woman's corpse going down to the burning-ghat, and a bystander says, 'She died at midnight from the heat.' So the city was of Death as well as Night after all.

AN INDIAN GHOST IN ENGLAND

The following story is appropriate just now, apart from the fact of the ghost's land of birth, in the first place, because the event narrated occurred just before the last General Election, and, in the second, because Christmas approaches, when, ghosts, like oysters, are in season.

A lonely horseman – what better, or more hackeneyed, opening for a tale of blood and horror, could there be? Yet in this case the loneliness of the horseman was as undeniable as it was, for him, uncomfortable – a lonely horseman, then, was making the best of his way – and between the best and the worst of it there was very little difference: it was all so uncommonly bad – from Chester to Tarporley. Persons who know that part of England will at once acknowledge that a better line of country might be chosen for a long ride on a misty, dripping afternoon in February; and our lonely horseman, just returned from India, found affairs anything but pleasant. After splashing mile after mile along straight, unhedged roads, between stretches of sodden heather and gloomy pine-woods, past ponds and reed beds, patches of gorse, and wildernesses of alder, without meeting a single soul since he rode out of the withered, leafless landscape of the salt district, – where the sheep are as black as ink and the grass they eat gritty with soot from the salt-mine fires, – when at last the road divided and on one side of the signboard he read 'Tarporley 6 miles', and on the other 'Budworth 1/2 mile', he not unnaturally glanced longingly up the Budworth road. Through the gathering dusk he could see the twinkling lights in the village windows, could hear the cheery shouts of boys at play, and, better than all, the red glow of a fire in what was evidently the Inn of the village. This decided him, and he turned his horse's head towards 'The George'. A dinner, a fire, a bottle of wine; and after these, in true novel style, our lonely horseman sits musing alone. Perhaps the chill of his ride made him dismal; perhaps he regretted having failed to carry out his intention of dining at Tarporley. He was restless, any way, and often got up and looked out of the window.

It was a chill, cold night, with the rain-sodden mists lying white and thick over mere and glebe. A wind, rising fitfully, fills the old house with uneasy sounds, and ever and again brings the rain with a pattering rush upon the window.

The handmaid of the Inn looks in before going to bed, 'just to see if you wanted anything, sir.' Finding he does not, she wishes him good-night, and retires hesitatingly to the door, then turns; 'I would no sit up to-night, master. 'Taint good to keep awake o' nights now. Maybe ye'ld sleep and hear naught of it.' 'Naught of what?' 'Eh? 'tis more than I can tell and maybe ye'ld say 'tis the wind.' The door closes abruptly and she is gone.

'I wonder', muses our cavalier, 'what the deuce the woman is thinking there will be to hear!' Somehow he feels attracted to the window again, and after walking once or twice across the room stands and looks out into the dark.

The rain has ceased, and something like moonlight showed faintly through the racing clouds. The wind wailed mournfully across the silent village, swinging the signboard of the Inn till it groaned like an uneasy spirit of the dead in the churchyard opposite. Beyond, the square outline of the mill rises black, but vague, above the long expanse of mere with its fringe of reeds. As the wind reaches them the alders by the mill shudder together. They almost seem to be stopping to whisper something to each other and to the willows beneath, whose weeping branches toss their weird arms down to the black water's edge. The long ripples on the mere plash mournfully under the bank, and there is a wash and rustle among the reeds; and they, too, seem to be bending all together and to be whispering: 'It is coming! Listen'. Far out in the dark water the giant pike splashes suddenly to the bottom; and the eerie voice of some wild water-bird wails into the distance, as though it fled on swift wings from the haunted place. Then the wind itself seems to stoop and listen, with hushed breath – and far over the seep of the mere, where that ruined cottage stands, a mere speck at the edge of the waste of shimmering water, there rises fitfully through the drifting mist a long, low, melancholy echo. Not altogether unfamiliar it sounds to the listener's ear, and carries his mind, by some connection of ideas, straight back to lonely jungle nights in India. He throws open the window and looks out. The echo swells and dies into the distance round the furthest water's edge where the road winds into the village. 'It is coming!' Then the wind shudders and leaps from among the reeds and passes on, hurrying over the grass fields in their winding sheet of mist, to the open moor, to the pine-woods, anywhere away from that ruined cottage by the mere, from the churchyard with the withered yew tree at its gate.

Once, so the landlady had told our traveller as he alighted at the door, that yew had been a splendid tree, and used to toss its dense green branches in the wind like other trees; but years ago, they said, a curse had come upon it. It drooped and shrunk; and when the boughs were bare of leaves, a black and mouldering rope became apparent hanging, straight as though a heavy body hung from it, from the biggest branch. 'Murder will out', the villagers said, and though an old man did aver that he had himself as a small boy fixed a swing up there and thought this might be the rope, his neighbours would have none of it. Old Cowp, they said, who used to ill-use his daughter and lived in the cottage, now a ruin, by the mere, could tell more about that rope and the use it was put to than most of us would like to hear. But Old Cowp and his daughter had long ago disappeared, none knew why or whither, suddenly, and no one took his cottage; and when the yew tree withered and the rope was seen, a moral certainty grew in the village that Cowp had done the deed of horror, and his cottage acquired an evil name and fell into a ruin. None visited it even by day. So with the yew tree. Children used to play merrily in its branches by day, and the wind sung in it cheerily by night; but for years, so they say, the wind has swept by and stirred neither twig nor rope, and the children in the evening pass it quickly. For the last month or more, too, the 'Devil's Dog' had been heard in the village almost every night, coming from Old Cowp's cottage and yelling as it rushed past the yew tree into the churchyard where it would try, and try, to dig a grave. So all the neighbours were agreed that Old Cowp was dead, and his wicked spirit had come back to haunt the scene of his former wickedness and try to dig a grave for his victim's bones in the churchyard.

All this our traveller recollects now as he hears the wailing echo coming nearer, and he stares, not altogether comfortable in mind, out into the night. A dead silence had fallen upon the water and the land, like an oppressive, suffocating cloak. The ghostly wail grows louder and nearer. The cottagers crouch in their beds and whisper: 'The Devil's Dog! it is coming!' And now, distinct and suddenly near, the howl breaks out, and, just as his door is burst open and the terrified landlady rushes in with an 'Oh? sir, it is coming!', our traveller recognises the unmistakeable screeching of an Indian jackal. 'It is no ghost, my good woman, it's a fox or some sort of wild dog. If I was in India again, I should call it a common jackal.' 'Jack 'All did you say? Why, here, Tom', who, more frightened than his mistress, was hovering at the door, 'what was the name they gave to that furrin kind of wolf that got out of the wild-beast show at Tarporley last August and has never been seen since?' 'Jack 'All, they called him, mum!'

Subsequently our traveller went peacefully to bed; and next morning an investigation of Cowp's old cottage revealed not only master Jack's comfortable lair, but the fragments of an old letter addressed to Cowp, telling him that he had come into his brother's farm in another county; where letters addressed by curious neighbours found him afterwards living in comfort if not in peace, with his daughter, who, so far from being murdered, had developed all her mother's vixenish qualities and gave the old man – so his new neighbours averred – a terrible bad time of it.

THE PHANTOM 'RICKSHAW

'May no ill dreams disturb my rest,
Nor Powers of Darkness me molest.'

Evening Hymn

One of the few advantages that India has over England is a certain great Knowability. After five years' service a man is directly or indirectly acquainted with the two or three hundred Civilians in his Province; all the Messes of ten or twelve Regiments and Batteries, and some fifteen hundred other people of the non-official castes. In ten years his knowledge should be doubled, and at the end of twenty he knows, or knows something about, almost every Englishman in the Empire, and may travel anywhere and everywhere without paying hotel-bills.

Globe-trotters who expect entertainment as a right, have, even within my memory, blunted this open-heartedness, but, none the less, to-day if you belong to the Inner Circle and are neither a bear nor a black sheep all houses are open to you and our small world is very kind and helpful.

Rickett of Kamartha, stayed with Polder of Kumaon, some fifteen years ago. He meant to stay two nights only, but was knocked down by rheumatic fever, and for six weeks disorganised Polder's establishment, stopped Polder's work, and nearly died in Polder's bed-room. Polder behaves as though he had been placed under eternal obligation by Rickett, and yearly sends the little Ricketts a box of presents and toys. It is the same everywhere. The men who do not take the trouble to conceal from you their opinion that you are an incompetent ass, and the women who blacken your character and misunderstood your wife's amusements, will work themselves to the bone in your behalf if you fall sick or into serious trouble.

Heatherlegh, the Doctor, kept, in addition to his regular

practice, a hospital on his private account – an arrangement of loose-boxes for Incurables, his friends called it – but it was really a sort of fitting-up shed for craft that had been damaged by stress of weather. The weather in India is often sultry, and since the tale of bricks is a fixed quantity, and the only liberty allowed is permission to work overtime and get no thanks, men occasionally break down and become as mixed as the metaphors in this sentence.

Heatherlegh is the nicest doctor that ever was, and his invariable prescription to all his patients is 'lie low, go slow, and keep cool'. He says that more men are killed by overwork than the importance of this world justifies. He maintains that overwork slew Pansay who died under his hands about three years ago. He has, of course, the right to speak authoritatively, and he laughs at my theory that there was a crack in Pansay's head and a little bit of the Dark World came through and pressed him to death. 'Pansay went off the handle,' says Heatheriegh, 'after the stimulus of long leave at Home. He may or he may not have behaved like a blackguard to Mrs Keith-Wessington. My notion is that the work of the Katabundi Settlement ran him off his legs, and that he took to brooding and making much of an ordinary P & O flirtation. He certainly was engaged to Miss Mannering, and she certainly broke off the engagement. Then he took a feverish chill and all that nonsense about ghosts developed itself. Overwork started his illness, kept it alight, and killed him, poor devil. Write him off to the System – one man to do the work of two-and-a-half men.'

I do not believe this. I used to sit up with Pansay sometimes when Heatherlegh was called out to visit patients and I happened to be within claim. The man would make me most unhappy by describing in a low, even voice the procession of men, women, children, and devils that was always passing at the bottom of his bed. He had a sick man's command of language. When he recovered I suggested that he should write out the whole affair from beginning to end, knowing that ink might assist him to ease his mind. When little boys have learned a new bad word they are never happy till they have chalked it up on a door. And this also is Literature.

He was in a high fever while he was writing, and the blood-and-thunder Magazine style he adopted did not calm him. Two months afterwards he was reported fit for duty, but, in spite of the fact that he was urgently needed to help an undermanned Commission stagger through a deficit, he preferred to die; vowing at the last that he was hag-ridden. I secured his manuscript before he died, and this is his version of the affair, dated 1885: –

My doctor tells me that I need rest and change of air. It is not improbable that I shall get both ere long – rest that neither the red-coated orderly nor the mid-day gun can break, and change of air far beyond that which any homeward-bound steamer can give me. In the meantime I am resolved to stay where I am; and, in flat defiance of my doctor's orders, to take all the world into my confidence. You shall learn for yourselves the precise nature of my malady; and shall, too, judge for yourselves whether any man born of woman on this weary earth was ever so tormented as I.

Speaking now as a condemned criminal might speak ere the drop-bolts are drawn, my story, wild and hideously improbable as it may appear, demands at least attention. That it will ever receive credence I utterly disbelieve. Two months ago I should have scouted as mad or drunk the man who had dared tell me the like. Two months ago I was the happiest man in India. To-day, from Peshawar to the sea, there is no one more wretched. My doctor and I are the only two who know this. His explanation is that my brain, digestion and eyesight are all slightly affected; giving rise to my frequent and persistent 'delusions'. Delusions, indeed! I call him a fool; but he attends me still with the same unwearied smile, the same bland professional manner, the same neatly-trimmed red whiskers, till I begin to suspect that I am an ungrateful, evil-tempered invalid. But you shall judge for yourselves.

Three years ago it was my fortune – my great misfortune – to sail from Gravesend to Bombay, on return from long leave, with one Agnes Keith-Wessington, wife of an officer on the Bombay side. It does not in the least concern you to know what manner of woman she was. Be content with the knowledge that, ere the voyage had ended, both she and I were desperately and unreasoningly in love with one another. Heaven knows that I can make the admission now without one particle of vanity. In matters of this sort there is always one who gives and another who accepts. From the first day of our ill-omened attachment, I was conscious that Agnes's passion was a stronger, a more dominant, and – if I may use the expression – a purer sentiment than mine. Whether she recognised the fact then, I do not know. Afterwards it was bitterly plain to both of us.

Arrived at Bombay in the spring of the year, we went our respective ways, to meet no more for the next three or four months, when my leave and her love took us both to Simla. There we spent the season together; and there my fire of straw burnt itself out to a pitiful end with the closing year. I attempt no excuse. I make no apology. Mrs Wessington had given up much for my sake, and was prepared to give up all. From my own lips, in August 1882, she learnt that I was sick of her presence, tired of her company, and weary of the sound of her voice. Ninety-nine women out of a hundred would have wearied of me as I wearied of them; seventy-five of that number would have promptly avenged themselves by active and obtrusive flirtation with other men. Mrs Wessington was the hundredth. On her neither my openly-expressed aversion, nor the cutting brutalities with which I garnished our interviews had the least effect.

'Jack, darling!' was her one eternal cuckoo-cry, 'I'm sure it's all a mistake – a hideous mistake; and we'll be good friends again some day. *Please* forgive me, Jack, dear.'

I was the offender, and I knew it. That knowledge transformed my pity into passive endurance, and eventually, into blind hate – the same instinct, I suppose, which prompts a man to savagely stamp on the spider he has but half killed. And with this hate in my bosom the season of 1882 came to an end.

Next year we met again at Simla – she with her monotonous face and timid attempts at reconciliation, and I with loathing of her in every fibre of my frame. Several times I could not avoid meeting her alone; and on each occasion her words were identically the same. Still the unreasoning wail that it was all a 'mistake'; and still the hope of eventually 'making friends'. I might have seen, had I cared to look, that that hope only was keeping her alive. She grew more wan and thin month by month. You will agree with me, at least, that such conduct would have driven anyone to despair. It was uncalled for, childish, unwomanly. I maintain that she was much to blame. And again, sometimes, in the black, fever-stricken night watches, I have begun to think that I might have been a little kinder to her. But that really *is* a 'delusion'. I could not have continued pretending to love her when I didn't; could I? It would have been unfair to us both.

Last year we met again – on the same terms as before. The same weary appeals, and the same curt answers from my lips. At least I would make her see how wholly wrong and hopeless were her attempts at resuming the old relationship. As the season wore on, we fell apart – that is to say, she found it difficult to meet me, for I had other and more absorbing interests to attend to. When I think it over quietly in my sick-room, the season of 1884 seems a confused nightmare wherein light and shade were fantastically intermingled – my courtship of little Kitty Mannering; my hopes, doubts and fears; our long rides together; my trembling avowal of attachment; her reply; and now and again a vision of a white face flitting by in the rickshaw with the black and white liveries I once watched for so earnestly; the wave of Mrs Wessington's gloved hand; and, when she met me alone, which was but seldom, the irksome monotony of her appeal. I loved Kitty Mannering, honestly, heartily loved her, and with my love for her grew my hatred for Agnes. In August Kitty and I were engaged. The next day I met those accursed 'magpie' *jhampanies* at the back of Jakko, and, moved by some passing sentiment of pity, stopped to tell Mrs Wessington everything. She knew it already.

'So I hear you're engaged. Jack dear.' Then, without a moment's pause: 'I'm sure it's all a mistake – a hideous mistake. We shall be as good friends some day, Jack, as we ever were.'

My answer might have made even a man wince. It cut the dying woman before me like the blow of a whip. 'Please forgive me, Jack; I didn't mean to make you angry; but it's true, it's true!'

And Mrs Wessington broke down completely. I turned away and left her to finish her journey in peace, feeling, but only for a moment or two, that I had been an unutterably mean hound. I looked back, and saw that she had turned her rickshaw with the idea, I suppose, of overtaking me.

The scene and its surroundings were photographed on my memory. The rain-swept sky (we were at the end of the wet weather), the sodden, dingy pines, the muddy road, and the black powder-riven cliffs formed a gloomy background against which the black and white liveries of the *jhampanies*, the yellow-panelled rickshaw and Mrs Wessington's down-bowed golden head stood out clearly. She was holding her hand-kerchief in her left hand and was leaning back exhausted against the rickshaw cushions. I turned my horse up a byepath near the Sanjowlie Reservoir and literally ran away. Once I fancied I heard a faint call of 'Jack!' This may have been imagination. I never stopped to verify it. Ten minutes later I came across Kitty on horseback; and, in the delight of a long ride with her, forgot all about the interview.

A week later Mrs Wessington died, and the inexpressible burden of her existence was removed from my life. I went Plainsward perfectly happy. Before three months were over I had forgotten all about her, except that at times the discovery of some of her old letters reminded me unpleasantly of our bygone relationship. By January I had disinterred what was left of our correspondence from among my scattered belongings and had burnt it. At the beginning of April of this year, 1885, I was at Simla – semi-deserted Simla – once more, and was deep in lover's talks and walks with Kitty. It was decided that we should be married at the end of June. You will understand, therefore, that, loving Kitty as I did, I am not saying too much when I pronounce myself to have been, at the same time, the happiest man in India.

Fourteen delightful days passed almost before I noticed

their flight. Then, aroused to the sense of what was proper among mortals circumstanced as we were, I pointed out to Kitty that an engagement-ring was the outward and visible sign of her dignity as an engaged girl; and that she must forthwith come to Hamilton's to be measured for one. Up to that moment, I give you my word, we had completely forgotten so trivial a matter. To Hamilton's we accordingly went on the 15th of April, 1885. Remember that – whatever my doctor may say to the contrary – I was then in perfect health, enjoying a well-balanced mind and absolutely tranquil spirit. Kitty and I entered Hamilton's shop together, and there, regardless of the order of affairs, I measured Kitty's finger for the ring in the presence of the amused assistant. The ring was a sapphire with two diamonds. We then rode out down the slope that leads to the Combermere Bridge and Peliti's shop.

While my Waler was cautiously feeling his way over the loose shale, and Kitty was laughing and chattering at my side – while all Simla, that is to say as much of it has had then come from the Plains, was grouped round the Reading-room and Peliti's verandah – I was aware that some one, apparently at a vast distance, was calling me by my Christian name. It struck me that I had heard the voice before, but when and where I could not at once determine. In the short space it took to cover the road between the path from Hamilton's shop and the first plank of the Combermere Bridge I had thought over half-a-dozen people who might have committed such a solecism, and had eventually decided that it must have been some singing in my ears. Immediately opposite Peliti's shop my eye was arrested by the sight of four *jhampanies* in black and white livery, pulling a yellow-panelled, cheap, bazar rickshaw. In a moment my mind flew back to the previous season and Mrs Wessington with a sense of irritation and disgust. Was it not enough that the woman was dead and done with, without her black and while servitors re-appearing to spoil the day's happiness? Whoever employed them now I thought I would call upon, and ask as a personal favour to change her *jhampanies'* livery. I would hire the men myself, and, if necessary, buy their coats from off their backs. It is impossible to say here what a flood of undesirable memories their presence evoked.

'Kitty,' I cried, 'there are poor Mrs Wessington's *jhampanies* turned up again! I wonder who has them now?'

Kitty had known Mrs Wessington slightly last season, and had always been interested in the sickly woman.

'What? Where?' she asked. 'I can't see them anywhere.'

Even as she spoke, her horse, swerving from a laden mule, threw himself directly in front of the advancing rickshaw. I had scarcely time to utter a word of warning when, to my unutterable horror, horse and rider passed *through* men and carriage as if they had been thin air.

'What's the matter?' cried Kitty; 'what made you call out so foolishly, Jack? If I *am* engaged I don't want all creation to know about it. There was lots of space between the mule and the verandah; and, if you think I can't ride – There!'

Whereupon wilful Kitty set off, her dainty little head in the air, at a hand-gallop in the direction of the Band-stand; fully expecting, as she herself afterwards told me, that I should follow her. What was the matter? Nothing, indeed. Either that I was mad or drunk, or that Simla was haunted with devils. I reined in my impatient cob, and turned round. The rickshaw had turned too, and now stood immediately facing me, near the left railing of the Combermere Bridge.

'Jack! Jack, darling!' (There was no mistake about the words this time: they rang through my brain as if they had been shouted in my ear.) 'It's some hideous mistake, I'm sure. *Please* forgive me, Jack, and let's be friends again.'

The rickshaw-hood had fallen back, and inside, as I hope and daily pray for the death I dread by night, sat Mrs Keith-Wessington, handkerchief in hand, and golden head bowed on her breast.

How long I stared motionless I do not know. Finally, I was aroused by my groom taking the Waler's bridle and asking whether I was ill. I tumbled off my horse and dashed, half fainting, into Peliti's for a glass of cherry-brandy. There two or three couples were gathered round the coffee-tables discussing the gossip of the day. Their trivialities were more comforting to me just then than the consolations of religion could have been. I plunged into the midst of the conversation at once; chatted, laughed and jested with a face (when I caught a glimpse of it in a mirror) as white and drawn as that of a corpse. Three or four men noticed my condition; and, evidently setting it down to the results of over many pegs, charitably endeavoured to draw me apart from the rest of the loungers. But I refused to be led away. I wanted the company of my kind – as a child rushes into the midst of the dinner-party after a fright in the dark. I must have talked for about ten minutes or so, though it seemed an eternity to me, when I heard Kitty's clear voice outside enquiring for me. In another minute she had entered the shop, prepared to roundly upbraid me for failing so signally in my duties. Something in my face stopped her.

'Why, Jack,' she cried, 'what *have* you been doing? What *has* happened? Are you ill?' Thus driven into a direct lie, I said that the sun had been a little too much for me. It was close upon five o'clock of a cloudy April afternoon, and the sun had been hidden all day. I saw my mistake as soon as the words were out of my mouth: attempted to recover it; blundered hopelessly and followed Kitty, in a regal rage, out of doors, amid the smiles of my acquaintances. I made some excuse (I have forgotten what) on the score of my feeling faint; and cantered away to my hotel, leaving Kitty to finish the ride by herself.

In my room I sat down and tried calmly to reason out the matter, Here was I, Theobald Jack Pansay, a well-educated Bengal Civilian in the year of grace 1885, presumably sane, certainly healthy, driven in terror from my sweetheart's side by the apparition of a woman who had been dead and buried eight months ago. These were facts that I could not blink. Nothing was further from my thought than any memory of Mrs Wessington when Kitty and I left Hamilton's shop. Nothing was more utterly commonplace than the stretch of wall opposite Peliti's. It was broad daylight. The road was full of people; and yet here, look you, in defiance of every law of probability, in direct outrage of Nature's ordinance, there had appeared to me a face from the grave.

Kitty's Arab had gone *through* the rickshaw; so that my first hope that some woman marvellously like Mrs Wessington had hired the carriage and the coolies with their old livery was lost. Again and again I went round this tread-mill of thought; and again and again gave up baffled and in despair. The voice was as inexplicable as the apparition. I had originally some wild notion of confiding it all to Kitty; of begging her to marry me at once; and in her arms defying the ghostly occupant of the rickshaw. 'After all,' I argued, 'the presence of the rickshaw is in itself enough to prove the existence of a spectral illusion. One may see ghosts of men and women, but surely never of coolies and carriages. The whole thing is absurd. Fancy the ghost of a hill-man!'

Next morning I sent a penitent note to Kitty, imploring her to overlook my strange conduct of the previous afternoon. My Divinity was still very wroth, and a personal apology was necessary. I explained, with a fluency born of night-long pondering over a falsehood, that I had been attacked with a sudden palpitation of the heart – the result of indigestion. This eminently practical solution had its effect; and Kitty and I rode out that afternoon with the shadow of my first lie dividing us.

Nothing would please her save a canter round Jakko. With my nerves still unstrung from the previous night I feebly protested against the notion, suggesting Observatory Hill, Jutogh, the Boileaugunge road – anything rather than the Jakko round. Kitty was angry and a little hurt, so I yielded from fear of provoking further misunderstanding, and we set out together towards Chota Simla. We walked a greater part of the way, and, according to our custom, cantered from a mile or so below the Convent to the stretch of level road by the Sanjowlie Reservoir. The wretched horses appeared to fly, and my heart beat quicker and quicker as we neared the crest of the ascent. My mind had been full of Mrs Wessington all the afternoon; and every inch of the Jakko road bore witness to our old-time walks and talks. The boulders were full of it; the pines sang it aloud overhead; the rain-fed torrents giggled and chuckled unseen over the shameful story; and the wind in my ears chanted the iniquity aloud.

As a fitting climax, in the middle of the level men call the Ladies' Mile, the Horror was awaiting me. No other rickshaw was in sight – only the four black and white *jhampanies*, the yellow-panelled carriage, and the golden head of the woman within – all apparently just as I had left them eight months and one fortnight ago! For an instant I fancied that Kitty must see what I saw – we were so marvellously sympathetic in all things. Her next words undeceived me – 'Not a soul in sight! Come along. Jack, and I'll race you to the Reservoir buildings!' Her wiry little Arab was off like a bird, my Waler following close behind, and in this order we dashed under the cliffs. Half a minute brought us within fifty yards of the rickshaw. I pulled my Waler and fell back a little. The rickshaw was directly in the middle of the road: and once more the Arab passed through it, my horse following: 'Jack! Jack dear! *Please* forgive me,' rang with a wail in my ears, and after an interval: 'It's all a mistake, a hideous mistake!'

I spurred my horse like a man possessed. When I turned my head at the Reservoir works, the black and white liveries were still waiting – patiently waiting – under the grey hillside, and the wind brought me a mocking echo of the words I had just heard. Kitty bantered me a good deal on my silence throughout the remainder of the ride. I had been talking up till then wildly and at random. To save my life I could not speak afterwards naturally, and from Sanjowlie to the Church wisely held my tongue.

I was to dine with the Mannerings that night and had barely time to canter home to dress. On the road to Elysium Hill I overheard two men talking together in the dusk – 'It's a curious thing,' said one, 'how completely all trace of it disappeared. You know my wife was insanely fond of the woman (never could see anything in her myself) and wanted me to pick up her old rickshaw and coolies if they were to be got for love or money. Morbid sort of fancy I call it; but I've got to do what the *Memsahib* tells me. Would you believe that the man she hired it from tells me that all four of the men, they were brothers, died of cholera on the way to Hardwár, poor devils; and the rickshaw has been broken up by the man himself. Told me he never used a dead *Memsahib*'s rickshaw. Spoilt his luck. Queer notion, wasn't it? Fancy poor little Mrs Wessington spoiling any one's luck except her own!' I laughed aloud at this point; and my laugh jarred on me as I uttered it. So there *were* ghosts of rickshaws after all, and ghostly employments in the other world! How much did Mrs Wessington give her men? What were their hours? Where did they go?

And for visible answer to my question I saw the infernal thing blocking my path in the twilight. The dead travel fast and by short-cuts unknown to ordinary coolies. I laughed aloud a second time and checked my laughter suddenly, for I was afraid I was going mad. Mad to a certain extent I must have been, for I recollect that I reined in my horse at the head of the rickshaw, and politely wished Mrs Wessington 'good evening'. Her answer was one I knew only too well. I listened to the end; and replied that I had heard it all before, but should be delighted if she had anything further to say. Some malignant devil stronger than I must have entered into me that evening, for I have a dim recollection of talking the commonplaces of the day for five minutes to the thing in front of me.

'Mad as a hatter, poor devil – or drunk. Max, try and get him to come home.'

Surely *that* was not Mrs Wessington's voice! The two men had overheard me speaking to the empty air, and had returned to look after me. They were very kind and considerate, and from their words evidently gathered that I was extremely drunk. I thanked them confusedly and cantered away to my hotel, there changed, and arrived at the Mannerings, ten minutes late. I pleaded the darkness of the night as an excuse; was rebuked by Kitty for my unlover-like tardiness; and sat down.

The conversation had already become general; and, under cover of it, I was addressing some tender small talk to my sweetheart when I was aware that at the further end of the table a short red-whiskered man was describing, with much broidery, his encounter with a mad unknown that evening. A few sentences convinced me that he was repeating the incident of half an hour ago. In the middle of the story he looked round for applause, as professional story-tellers do, caught my eye, and straightway collapsed. There was a moment's awkward silence, and the red-whiskered man muttered something to the effect that he had 'forgotten the rest'; thereby sacrificing a reputation as a good story-teller which he had built up for six seasons past. I blessed him from the bottom of my heart and – went on with my fish.

In the fulness of time that dinner came to an end; and with genuine regret I tore myself away from Kitty – as certain as I was of my own existence that It would be waiting for me outside the door. The red-whiskered man, who had been introduced to me as Dr Heatherlegh of Simla, volunteered to bear me company as far as our roads lay together. I accepted his offer with gratitude.

My instinct had not deceived me. It lay in readiness in the Mall, and, in what seemed devilish mockery of our ways, with a lighted head-lamp. The red-whiskered man went to the point at once, in a manner that showed he had been thinking over it all dinner time.

'I say, Pansay, what the deuce was the matter with you this evening on the Elysium road?' The suddenness of the question wrenched an answer from before I was aware.

'That!' said I, pointing to It.

'*That* may be either *D.T.* or eyes for aught I know. Now you don't liquor. I saw as much at dinner, so it can't be *D.T.* There's nothing whatever where you're pointing, though you're sweating and trembling with fright like a scared pony. Therefore, I conclude that it's eyes. And I ought to understand all about them. Come along home with me. I'm on the Blessington lower road.'

To my intense delight the rickshaw instead of waiting for us kept about twenty yards ahead – and this, too, whether we walked, trotted, or cantered. In the course of that long night ride I had told my companion almost as much as I have told you here.

'Well, you've spoilt one of the best tales I've ever laid tongue to,' said he, 'but I'll forgive you for the sake of what you've gone through. Now come home and do what I tell you; and when I've cured you, young man, let this be a lesson to you to steer clear of women and indigestible food till the day of your death.'

The rickshaw kept steadily in front; and my red-whiskered friend seemed to derive great pleasure from my account of its exact whereabouts.

'Eyes, Pansay – all eyes, brain, and stomach; and the greatest of these three is stomach. You've too much conceited brain, too little stomach, and thoroughly unhealthy eyes. Get your stomach straight and the rest follows. And all that's French for a liver pill. I'll take sole medical charge of you from this hour; for you're too interesting a phenomenon to be passed over.'

By this time we were deep in the shadow of the Blessington lower road and the rickshaw came to a dead stop under a pine-clad, overhanging shale cliff. Instinctively I halted too, giving my reason. Heatherlegh rapped out an oath.

'Now, if you think I'm going to spend a cold night on the hillside for the sake of a stomach-*cum*-brain-*cum*-eye illusion . . . Lord ha' mercy! What's that?'

That was a muffled report, a blinding smother of dust just in front of us, a crack, the noise of rent boughs, and about ten yards of the cliffside – pines, undergrowth and all – slid down into the road below, completely blocking it up. The uprooted trees swayed and tottered for a moment like drunken giants in the gloom, and then fell prone among their fellows with a thunderous crash. Our two horses stood motionless and sweating with fear. As soon as the rattle of falling earth and stone had subsided, my companion muttered: 'Man, if we'd gone forward we should have been ten feet deep in our graves by now! "There are more things in heaven and earth" . . . Come home, Pansay, and thank God. I want a drink badly.'

We retraced our way over the Church Ridge, and I arrived at Dr Heatherlegh's house shortly after midnight.

His attempts towards my cure commenced almost immediately, and for a week I never left his sight. Many a time in the course of that week did I bless the good fortune which had thrown me in contact with Simla's best and kindest doctor.

Day by day my spirits grew lighter and more equable. Day by day, too, I became more and more inclined to fall in with Heatherlegh's 'spectral illusion' theory, implicating eyes, brain, and stomach. I wrote to Kitty, telling her that a slight sprain caused by a fall from horse kept me indoors for a few days; and that I should be recovered before she had time to regret my absence.

Heatherlegh's treatment was simple to a degree. It consisted of liver-pills, cold-water baths and strong exercise, taken in the dusk or at early dawn – for, as he sagely observed: 'A man with a sprained ankle doesn't walk a dozen miles a day, and your young woman might be wondering if she saw you'.

At the end of the week, after much examination of pupil and pulse and strict injunctions as to diet and pedestrianism, Heatherlegh dismissed me as brusquely as he had taken charge of me. Here is his parting benediction: 'Man, I certify to your mental cure, and that's as much as to say I've cured most of your bodily ailments. Now, get your traps out of this as soon as you can; and be off to make love to Miss Kitty.'

I was endeavouring to express my thanks for his kindness. He cut me short:

'Don't think I did this because I like you. I gather that you've behaved like a blackguard all through. But, all the same you're a phenomenon, and as queer a phenomenon as you are a blackguard. Now, go out and see if you can find the eyes-brain-and-stomach business again. I'll give you a lakh for each time you see it.'

Half an hour later I was in the Mannerings' drawing-room with Kitty drunk with the intoxication of present happiness and the foreknowledge that I should never more be troubled with Its hideous presence. Strong in the sense of my new-found security, I proposed a ride at once; and, by preference, a canter round Jakko.

Never had I felt so well, so overladen with vitality and mere animal spirits as I did on the afternoon of the 30th of April. Kitty was delighted at the change in my appearance, and complimented me on it in her delightfully frank and out-spoken manner. We left the Mannerings' house together, laughing and talking, and cantered along the Chota Simla road as of old.

I was in haste to reach the Sanjowlie Reservoir and there make my assurance doubly sure. The horses did their best, but seemed all too slow to my impatient mind. Kitty was astonished at my boisterousness. 'Why Jack!' she cried at last, 'you are behaving like a child! What are you doing?'

We were just below the Convent, and from sheer wantonness I was making my Waler plunge and curvet across the road as I tickled it with the loop at my riding-whip.

'Doing,' I answered, 'nothing, dear. That's just it. If you'd been doing nothing for a week except lie up, you'd be as riotous as I.

'Singing and murmuring in your feastful mirth,
    Joyful to feel yourself alive;
Lord over nature, Lord of the visible Earth,
    Lord of the senses five.'

My quotation was hardly out of my lips before we had rounded the corner above the Convent; and a few yards further on could see across to Sanjowlie. In the centre of the level road stood the black and white liveries, the yellow-panelled rickshaw and Mrs Keith-Wessington. I pulled up, looked, rubbed my eyes, and, I believe, must have said something. The next thing I knew was that I was lying face downward on the road, with Kitty kneeling above me in tears.

'Has it gone, child?' I gasped. Kitty only wept more bitterly.

'Has what gone? Jack dear: what does it all mean? There must be a mistake somewhere, Jack. A hideous mistake.' Her last words brought me to my feet – mad – raving for the time being.

'Yes, there *is* a mistake somewhere.' I repeated, 'a hideous mistake. Come and look at It!'

I have an indistinct idea that I dragged Kitty by the wrist along the road up to where It stood, and implored her for pity's sake to speak to It; to tell It that we were betrothed; that neither Death nor Hell could break the tie between us; and

Kitty only knows how much more to the same effect. Now and again I appealed passionately to the Terror in the rickshaw to bear witness to all I had said, and to release me from a torture that was killing me. As I talked I suppose I must have told Kitty of my old relations with Mrs Wessington, for I saw her listen intently with white face and blazing eyes.

'Thank you. Mr Pansay,' she said, 'That's *quite* enough. Bring my horse.'

The grooms, impassive as Orientals always are, had come up with the recaptured horses; and as Kitty sprang into her saddle I caught hold of the bridle entreating her to hear me out and forgive. My answer was the cut of her riding-whip across my face from mouth to eye, and a word or two of farewell that even now I cannot write down. So I judged, and judged rightly, that Kitty knew all; and I staggered back to the side of the rickshaw. My face was cut and bleeding, and the blow of the riding-whip had raised a livid blue weal on it. I had no self-respect. Just then, Heatherlegh, who must have been following Kitty and me at a distance, cantered up.

'Doctor,' I said, pointing to my face, 'here's Miss Mannering's signature to my order of dismissal and . . . I'll thank you for that lakh as soon as convenient.'

Heatherlegh's face, even in my abject misery, moved me to laughter.

'I'll stake my professional reputation' – he began. 'Don't be a fool,' I whispered. 'I've lost my life's happiness and you'd better take me home.'

As I spoke the rickshaw was gone. Then I lost all knowledge of what was passing. The crest of Jakko seemed to heave and roll like the crest of a cloud and fall in upon me.

Seven days later (on the 7th of May, that is to say) I was aware that I was lying in Heatherlegh's room as weak as a little child. Heatherlegh was watching me intently from behind the papers on his writing table. His first words were not very encouraging; but I was too far spent to be much moved by them.

'Here's Miss Kitty has sent back your letters. You corresponded a good deal, you young people. Here's a packet that looks like a ring, and a cheerful sort of a note from Mannering Papa, which I've taken the liberty of reading and burning. The old gentleman's not pleased with you.'

'And Kitty?' I asked dully.

'Rather more drawn than her father from what she says. By the same token you must have been letting out any number of queer reminiscences just before I met you. Says that a man who would have behaved to a woman as you did to Mrs Wessington ought to kill himself out of sheer pity for his kind. She's a hot-headed little virago, your mash. Will have it too that you were suffering from *D.T.* when that row on the Jakko road turned up. Says she'll die before she ever speaks to you again.'

I groaned and turned over on the other side.

'Now you've got your choice, my friend. This engagement has to be broken off; and the Mannerings don't want to be too hard on you. Was it broken through *D.T.* or epileptic fits? Sorry I can't offer you a better exchange unless you'd prefer hereditary insanity. Say the word and I'll tell 'em it's fits. All Simla knows about that scene on the Ladies' Mile. Come! I'll give you five minutes to think over it.'

During those five minutes I believe that I explored thoroughly the lowest circles of the Inferno which it is permitted man to tread on earth. And at the same time I myself was watching myself faltering through the dark labyrinths of doubt, misery, and utter despair. I wondered, as Heatherlegh in his chair might have wondered, which dreadful alternative I should adopt. Presently I heard myself answering in a voice that I hardly recognised:

'They're confoundedly particular about morality in these parts. Give 'em fits, Heatherlegh, and my love. Now let me sleep a bit longer.'

Then my two selves joined, and it was only I (half crazed, devil-driven I) that tossed in my bed, tracing step by step the history of the past month.

'But I am in Simla,' I kept repeating to myself. 'I, Jack Pansay, am in Simla, and there are no ghosts here. It's unreasonable of that woman to pretend there are. Why couldn't Agnes have left me alone? I never did her any harm. It might just as well have been me as Agnes. Only I'd never come back on purpose to kill *her*. Why can't I be left alone – left alone and happy?'

It was high noon when I first awoke: and the sun was low in the sky before I slept – slept as the tortured criminal sleeps on his rack, too worn to feel further pain.

Next day I could not leave my bed. Heatherlegh told me in the morning that he had received an answer from Mr Mannering, and that, thanks to his (Heatherlegh's) friendly offices, the story of my affliction had travelled through the length and breadth of Simla, where I was on all sides much pitied.

'And that's rather more than you deserve,' he concluded pleasantly, 'though the Lord knows you've been going through a pretty severe mill. Never mind; we'll cure you yet, you perverse phenomenon.'

I declined firmly to be cured. 'You've been much too good to me already, old man,' said I, 'but I don't think I need trouble you further.'

In my heart I knew that nothing Heatherlegh could do would lighten the burden that had been laid upon me.

With that knowledge came also a sense of hopeless, impotent rebellion against the unreasonableness of it all. There were scores of men no better than I whose punishments had at least been reserved for another world; and I felt that it was bitterly, cruelly unfair that I alone should have been singled out for so hideous a fate. This mood would in time give place to another where it seemed that the rickshaw and I were the only realities in a world of shadows; that Kitty was a ghost; that Mannering, Heatherlegh, and all the other men and women I knew were all ghosts; and the great, grey hills themselves but vain shadows devised to torture me. From mood to mood I tossed backwards and forwards for seven weary days; my body growing daily stronger and stronger, until the bed-room looking-glass told me that I had returned to everyday life, and was as other men once more. Curiously enough, my face showed no signs of the struggle I had gone through. It was pale indeed, but as expressionless and

common-place as ever. I had expected some permanent alteration – visible evidence of the disease that was eating me away. I
found nothing.

On the 15th of May I left Heatherlegh's house at eleven
o'clock in the morning; and the instinct of the bachelor drove
me to the Club. There I found that every man knew my story
as told by Heatherlegh, and was, in clumsy fashion, abnor-
mally kind and attentive. Nevertheless I recognised that for
the rest of my natural life I should be among, but not of, my
fellows; and I envied very bitterly indeed the laughing coolies
on the Mall below. I lunched at the Club, and at four o'clock
wandered aimlessly down the Mall in the vague hope of
meeting Kitty. Close to the Band-stand the black and white
liveries joined me; and I heard Mrs Wessington's old appeal at
my side. I had been expecting this ever since I came out; and
was only surprised at her delay. The phantom rickshaw and I
went side by side along the Chota Simla road in silence. Close
to the bazar, Kitty and a man on horseback overtook and
passed us. For any sign she gave I might have been a dog in
the road. She did not even pay me the compliment of quickening her pace; though the rainy afternoon had served for an
excuse.

So Kitty and her companion, and I and my ghostly Light-o'-
Love, crept round Jakko in couples. The road was streaming
with water; the pines dripped like roof-pipes on the rocks
below, and the air was full of fine, driving rain. Two or three
times I found myself saying to myself almost aloud: 'I'm Jack
Pansay on leave at Simla – *at Simla!* Everyday, ordinary Simla.
I mustn't forget that – I mustn't forget that.' Then I would try
to recollect some of the gossip I had heard at the Club; the
prices of So-and-So's horses – anything, in fact, that related to
the work-a-day Anglo-Indian world I knew so well. I even
repeated the multiplication-table rapidly to myself, to make
quite sure that I was not taking leave of my senses. It gave me
much comfort; and must have prevented my hearing Mrs
Wessington for a time.

Once more I wearily climbed the Convent slope and entered
the level road. Here Kitty and the man started off at a canter,

and I was left alone with Mrs Wessington. 'Agnes,' said I, 'will you put back your hood and tell me what it all means?' The hood dropped noiselessly and I was face to face with my dead and buried mistress. She was wearing the dress in which I had last seen her alive: carried the same tiny handkerchief in her right hand; and the same card-case in her left. (A woman eight months dead with a card-case!) I had to pin myself down to the multiplication-table, and to set both hands on the stone parapet of the road to assure myself that that at least was real.

'Agnes,' I repeated, 'for pity's sake tell me what it all means.' Mrs Wessington leant forward, with that odd, quick turn of the head I used to know so well, and spoke.

If my story had not already so madly overleaped the bounds of all human belief I should apologise to you now. As I know that no one – no, not even Kitty, for whom it is written as some sort of justification of my conduct – will believe me, I will go on. Mrs Wessington spoke and I walked with her from the Sanjowlie road to the turning below the Commander-in-Chief's house as I might walk by the side of any living woman's rickshaw, deep in conversation. The second and most tormenting of my moods of sickness had suddenly laid hold upon me, and like the prince in Tennyson's poem, 'I seemed to move amid a world of ghosts'. There had been a garden-party at the Commander-in-Chief's, and we two joined the crowd of homeward-bound folk. As I saw them then it seemed that *they* were the shadows – impalpable fantastic shadows – that divided for Mrs Wessington's rickshaw to pass through. What we said during the course of that weird interview I cannot – indeed, I dare not – tell. Heatherlegh's comment would have been a short laugh and a remark that I had been 'mashing a brain-eye-and-stomach chimera'. It was a ghastly and yet in some indefinable way a marvellously dear experience. Could it be possible, I wondered, that I was in this life to woo a second time the woman I had killed by my own neglect and cruelty?

I met Kitty on the homeward road – a shadow among shadows.

If I were to describe all the incidents of the next fortnight in their order, my story would never come to an end; and your patience would be exhausted. Morning after morning and evening after evening the ghostly rickshaw and I used to wander through Simla together. Wherever I went, there the four black and white liveries followed me and bore me company to and from my hotel. At the theatre I found them amid the crowd of yelling *jhampanies*; outside the club verandah, after a long evening of whist; at the birthday ball, waiting patiently for my reappearance; and in broad daylight when I went calling. Save that it cast no shadow, the rickshaw was in every respect as real to look upon as one of wood and iron. More than once, indeed, I have had to check myself from warning some hard-riding friend against cantering over it. More than once I have walked down the Mall deep in conversation with Mrs Wessington to the unspeakable amazement of the passers-by.

Before I had been out and about a week I learnt that the 'fit' theory had been discarded in favour of insanity. However, I made no change in my mode of life. I called, rode, and dined out as freely as ever. I had a passion for the society of my kind which I had never felt before; I hungered to be among the realities of life; and at the same time I felt vaguely unhappy when I had been separated too long from my ghostly companion. It would be almost impossible to describe my varying moods from the 15th of May up to to-day.

The presence of the rickshaw filled me by turns with horror, blind fear, a dim sort of pleasure, and utter despair. I dared not leave Simla; and I knew that my stay there was killing me. I knew, moreover, that it was my destiny to die slowly and a little every day. My only anxiety was to get the penance over as quietly as might be. Alternately I hungered for a sight of Kitty and watched her outrageous flirtations with my successor – to speak more accurately, my successors – with amused interest. She was as much out of my life as I was out of hers. By day I wandered with Mrs Wessington almost content. By night I implored Heaven to let me return to the world as I used to know it. Above all these varying moods lay the sensation of dull, numbing wonder that the seen and the unseen should mingle so strangely on this earth to hound one poor soul to its grave.

August 27th – Heatherlegh has been indefatigable in his attendance on me; and only yesterday told me that I ought to send in an application for sick-leave. An application to escape the company of a phantom! A request that the Government would graciously permit me to get rid of five ghosts and an airy rickshaw by going to England! Heatherlegh's proposition moved me to almost hysterical laughter. I told him that I should await the end quietly at Simla; and I am sure that the end is not far off. Believe me that I dread its advent more than any word can say; and I torture myself nightly with a thousand speculations as to the manner of my death.

Shall I die in my bed decently and as an English gentleman should die; or, in one last walk on the Mall, will my soul be wrenched from me to take its place for ever and ever by the side of that ghastly phantasm? Shall I return to my old lost allegiance in the next world, or shall I meet Agnes loathing her and bound to her side through all eternity? Shall we two hover over the scene of our lives till the end of time? As the day of my death draws nearer, the intense horror that all living flesh feels towards escaped spirits from beyond the grave grows more and more powerful. It is an awful thing to go down quick among the dead with scarcely one half of your life completed. It is a thousand times more awful to wait as I do in your midst, for I know not what unimaginable terror. Pity me, at least on the score of my 'delusion,' for I know you will never believe what I have written here. Yet as surely as ever a man was done to death by the Powers of Darkness I am that man.

In justice, too, pity her. For as surely as ever woman was killed by man, I killed Mrs Wessington. And the last portion of my punishment is even now upon me.

THE STRANGE RIDE OF
MORROWBIE JUKES

Alive or dead – there is no other way

Native Proverb

There is as the conjurors say, no deception about this tale. Jukes by accident stumbled upon a village that is well known to exist, though he is the only Englishman who has been there. A somewhat similar institution used to flourish on the outskirts of Calcutta, and there is a story that if you go into the heart of Bikanir, which is in the heart of the Great Indian Desert, you shall come across not a village but a town where the Dead who did not die but may not live, have established their head-quarters. And, since it is perfectly true that in the same Desert is a wonderful city where all the rich money-lenders retreat after they have made their fortunes (fortunes so vast that the owners cannot trust even the strong hand of the Government to protect them, but take refuge in the waterless sands), and drive sumptuous Cee-spring barouches, and buy beautiful girls and decorate their palaces with gold and ivory and Mintol tiles and mother-o'-pearl, I do not see why Jukes's tale should not be true. He is a Civil Engineer, with a head for plans and distances and things of that kind, and he certainly would not take the trouble to invent imaginary traps. He could earn more by doing his legitimate work. He never varies the tale in the telling, and grows very hot and indignant when he thinks of the disrespectful treatment he received. He wrote this quite straightforwardly at first, but he has since touched it up in places and introduced moral reflections, thus:—

In the beginning it all arose from a slight attack of fever. My work necessitated my being in camp for some months between Pakpattan and Mubarakpur – a desolate sandy stretch of country, as everyone who has had the misfortune to go there may know. My coolies were neither more nor less exasperating than other gangs, and my work demanded sufficient attention to keep me from moping, had I been inclined to so unmanly a weakness.

On the 23rd December, 1884, I felt a little feverish. There was a full moon at the time, and, in consequence, every dog near my tent was baying it. The brutes assembled in twos and threes and drove me frantic. A few days previously I had shot one loud-mouthed singer and suspended his carcass *in terrorem* about fifty yards from my tent-door. But his friends fell upon, fought for, and ultimately devoured, the body; and, as it seemed to me, sang their hymns of thanksgiving afterwards with renewed energy.

The light-heartedness which accompanies fever acts differently on different men. My irritation gave way, after a short time, to a fixed determination to slaughter one huge black and white beast who had been foremost in song and first in flight throughout the evening. Thanks to a shaking hand and a giddy head I had already missed him twice with both barrels of my shot-gun, when it struck me that my best plan would be to ride him down in the open and finish him off with a hog-spear. This, of course, was merely the semi-delirious notion of a fever-patient; but I remember that it struck me at the time as being eminently practical and feasible.

I therefore ordered my groom to saddle *Pornic* and bring him round quietly to the rear of my tent. When the pony was ready, I stood at his head prepared to mount and dash out as soon as the dog should again lift up his voice. *Pornic*, by the way, had not been out of his pickets for a couple of days; the night air was crisp and chilly and I was armed with a specially long and sharp pair of persuaders with which I had been rousing a sluggish cob that afternoon. You will easily believe, then, that when he was let go he went quickly. In one moment, for the brute bolted as straight as a die, the tent was left far behind, and we were flying over the smooth sandy soil at racing speed. In another we had passed the wretched dog, and I had almost forgotten why it was that I had taken horse and hog-spear.

The delirium of fever and the excitement of rapid motion through the air must have taken away the remnant of my senses. I have a faint recollection of standing upright in my stirrups and of brandishing my hog-spear at the great white Moon that looked down so calmly on my mad gallop; and of shouting challenges to the camel-thorn bushes as they whizzed past. Once or twice, I believe, I swayed forward on *Pornic's* neck and literally hung on by my spurs – as the marks next morning showed.

The wretched beast went forward like a thing possessed, over what seemed to be a limitless expanse of moonlit sand. Next, I remember, the ground rose suddenly in front of us, and as we topped the ascent I saw the waters of the Sutlej shining like a silver bar below. Then *Pornic* blundered heavily on his nose, and we rolled together down some unseen slope.

I must have lost consciousness, for when I recovered I was lying on my stomach in a heap of soft white sand, and the dawn was beginning to break dimly over the edge of the slope down which I had fallen. As the light grew stronger I saw that I was at the bottom of a horse-shoe shaped crater of sand, opening on one side directly on to the shoals of the Sutlej. My fever had altogether left me, and, with the exception of a slight dizziness in the head, I felt no bad effects from the fall overnight.

Pornic who was standing a few yards away was naturally a good deal exhausted, but had not hurt himself in the least. His saddle, a favourite polo one, was much knocked about, and had been twisted under his belly. It took me some time to put him to rights, and in the meantime I had ample opportunities of observing the spot into which I had so foolishly dropped.

At the risk of being considered tedious, I must describe it at length; inasmuch as an accurate mental picture of its peculiarities will be of natural assistance in enabling the reader to understand what follows.

Imagine then, as I have said before, a horse-shoe shaped crater of sand with steeply graded sand walls about thirty-five feet high. (The slope, I fancy, must have been about 65°.) This crater enclosed a level piece of ground about fifty yards long by thirty at its broadest part, with a rude well in the centre. Round the bottom of the crater, about three feet from the level of the ground proper, ran a series of eighty-three semi-circular, ovoid, square and multilateral holes, all about three feet at the mouth. Each hole on inspection showed that it was carefully shored internally with drift-wood and bamboos, and over the mouth a wooden drip-board projected, like the peak of a jockey's cap, for two feet. No sign of life was visible in these tunnels, but a most sickening stench pervaded the entire amphitheatre – a stench fouler than any which my wanderings in Indian villages have introduced me to.

Having remounted *Pornic*, who was as anxious as I to get back to camp, I rode round the base of the horse-shoe to find some place whence an exit would be practicable. The inhabitants, whoever they might be, had not thought fit to put in an appearance, so I was left to my own devices. My first attempt to 'rush' *Pornic* up the steep sand-banks showed me that I had fallen into a trap exactly on the same model as that which the ant-lion sets for its prey. At each step the shifting sand poured down from above in tons, and rattled on the drip-boards of the holes like small shot. A couple of ineffectual charges sent us both rolling down to the bottom, half choked with the torrents of sand; and I was constrained to turn my attention to the river-bank.

Here everything seemed easy enough. The sand-hills ran down to the river edge, it is true, but there were plenty of shoals and shallows across which I could gallop *Pornic* and find my way back to firm ground by turning sharply to the right or the left. As I led *Pornic* over the sands I was startled by the faint pop of a rifle across the river; and at the same moment a bullet dropped with a sharp '*whit*' close to *Pornic*'s head.

There was no mistaking the nature of the missile – a regulation Martini-Henri 'picket'. About five hundred yards away a country-boat was anchored in midstream; and a jet of smoke drifting away from its bows in the still morning air showed me whence the delicate attention had come. Was ever a respectable gentleman in such an *impasse*? The treacherous sand slope allowed no escape from a spot which I had visited most involuntarily, and a promenade on the river frontage was the signal for a bombardment from some insane native in a boat. I'm afraid that I lost my temper very much indeed.

Another bullet reminded me that I had better save my breath to cool my porridge; and I retreated hastily up the sands and back to the horse-shoe, where I saw that the noise of the rifle had drawn sixty-five human beings from the badger-holes which I had up till that point supposed to be untenanted. I found myself in the midst of a crowd of spectators – about forty men, twenty women, and one child who could not have been more than five years old. They were all scantily clothed in that salmon-coloured cloth which one associates with Hindu mendicants, and at first sight gave me the impression of a band of loathsome *fakirs*. The filth and repulsiveness of the assembly were beyond all description, and I shuddered to think what their life in the badger-holes must be.

Even in these days, when local self-government has destroyed the greater part of a native's respect for a Sahib, I have been accustomed to a certain amount of civility from my inferiors, and on approaching the crowd naturally expected that there would be some recognition of my presence. As a matter of fact there was; but it was by no means what I had looked for.

The ragged crew actually laughed at me – such laughter I hope I may never hear again. They cackled, yelled, whistled, and howled as I walked into their midst; same of them literally throwing themselves down on the ground in convulsions of unholy mirth. In a moment I had let go *Pornic*'s head, and, irritated beyond expression at the morning's adventure, commenced cuffing those nearest to me with all the force I could. The wretches dropped under my blows like nine-pins, and the laughter gave place to wails for mercy; while those yet untouched clasped me round the knees, imploring me in all sorts of uncouth tongues to spare them.

In the tumult, and just when I was feeling very much ashamed of myself for having thus easily given way to my temper, a thin, high voice murmured in English from behind my shoulder: '*Sahib! Sahib!* Do you not know me? *Sahib*, it is Gunga Dass, the telegraph-master.'

I spun round quickly and faced the speaker.

Gunga Dass (I have, of course, no hesitation in mentioning the man's real name) I had known four years before as a Deccanee Brahmin lent by the Punjab Government to one of the Khalsia States. He was in charge of a branch telegraph-office there, and when I had last met him was a jovial, full-stomached, portly Government servant with a marvellous capacity for making bad puns in English – a peculiarity which made me remember him long after I had forgotten his services to me in his official capacity. It is seldom that a Hindu makes English puns.

Now, however, the man was changed beyond all recognition. Caste-mark, stomach, slate-coloured continuations, and unctuous speech were all gone. I looked at a withered skeleton, turbanless and almost naked, with long, matted hair and deep-set codfish-eyes. But for a crescent-shaped scar on the left cheek, I should never have known him. But it was indubitably Gunga Dass, and – for this I was thankful – an English-speaking native who might at least tell me the meaning of all that I had gone through that day.

The crowd retreated to some distance as I turned towards the miserable figure, and ordered him to show me some method of escaping from the crater. He held a freshly-plucked crow in his hand, and in reply to my question climbed slowly on a platform of sand which ran in front of the holes, and commenced lighting a fire there in silence. Dried bents, sand-poppies and driftwood burn quickly; and I derived much consolation from the fact that he lit them with an ordinary sulphur-match. When they were in a bright glow, and the crow was neatly spitted in front thereof, Gunga Dass began without a word of preamble:

'There are only two kinds of men, Sar. The alive and the dead. When you are dead you are dead, but when you are alive you live.' [Here the crow demanded his attention for an instant as it twirled before the fire in danger of being burnt to a cinder.] 'If you die at home and do not die when you come to the ghât to be burnt, you come here.'

The nature of the reeking village was made plain now, and

all that I had known or read of the grotesque and the horrible paled before the fact just communicated by the ex-Brahmin. Sixteen years ago, when I first landed in Bombay, I had been told by a wandering Armenian of the existence, somewhere in India of a place to which such Hindus as had the misfortune to recover from trance or catalepsy were conveyed and kept; and I recollect laughing heartily at what I was then pleased to consider a traveller's tale. Sitting at the bottom of the sand-trap, the memory of Watson's Hotel with its swinging pun-khas, white-robed attendants and the swallow-faced Armenian, rose up in my mind as vividly as a photograph, and I burst into a loud fit of laughter. The contrast was too absurd!

Gunga Dass, as he bent over the unclean bird, watched me curiously. Hindus seldom laugh, and his surroundings were not such as to move Gunga Dass to any undue excess of hilarity. He removed the crow solemnly from the wooden spit and as solemnly devoured it. Then he continued his story, which I give in his own words: –

'In epidemics of the cholera you are carried to be burnt almost before you are dead. When you come to the riverside the cold air, perhaps, makes you alive, and then, if you are only little alive, mud is put on your nose and mouth and you die conclusively. If you are rather more alive, more mud is put; but if you are too lively they let you go and take you away. I was too lively, and made protestation with anger against the indignities that they endeavoured to press upon me. In those days I was Brahmin and proud man. Now I am dead man and eat' – here he eyed the well-gnawed breast bone with the first sign of emotion that I had seen in him since we met – 'crows, and – other things. They took me from my sheets when they saw that I was too lively and gave me medicines for one week, and I survived successfully. Then they set me by rail from my place to Okara Station, with a man to take care of me; and at Okara Station we met two other men, and they conducted we three on camels, in the night, from Okara Station to this place, and they propelled me from the top to the bottom, and the other two succeeded, and I have been here ever since two and a half years. Once I was Brahmin and proud man; and now I eat crows.'

'There is no way of getting out?'

'None of what kind at all. When I first came I made experiments frequently and all the others also, but we have always succumbed to the sand which is precipitated upon our heads.'

'But surely,' I broke in at this point, 'the river-front is open, and it is worth while dodging the bullets; while at night—'

I had already matured a rough plan of escape which a natural instinct of selfishness forbade me sharing with Gunga Dass. He, however, divined my unspoken thought almost as soon as it was formed; and, to my intense astonishment, gave vent to a long low chuckle of derision – the laughter, be it understood, of a superior or at least of an equal.

'You will not' – he had dropped the Sir completely after his opening sentence – 'make any escape that way. But you can try. I have tried. Once only.'

The sensation of nameless terror and abject fear which I had in vain attempted to strive against overmastered me completely. My long fast – it was now close upon ten o'clock, and I had eaten nothing since tiffin on the previous day, combined with violent and unnatural agitation of the ride had exhausted me, and I verily believe that, for a few minutes, I acted as one mad. I hurled myself against the pitiless sandslope. I ran round the base of the crater, blaspheming and praying by turns. I crawled out among the sedges of the riverfront, only to be driven back each time in an agony of nervous dread by the rifle bullets which cut up the sand round me – for I dared not face the death of a mad dog among that hideous crowd – and finally fell, spent and raving, at the kerb of the well. No one had taken the slightest notice of an exhibition which makes me blush hotly even when I think of it now.

Two or three men trod on my panting body as they drew water, but they were evidently used to this sort of thing, and had no time to waste upon me. The situation was humiliating. Gunga Dass, indeed, when he had banked the embers of his fire with sand, was at some pains to throw half a cupful of fetid water over my head, an attention for which I could have fallen on my knees and thanked him, but he was laughing all the while in the same mirthless, wheezy key that greeted me on my first attempt to force the shoals. And so, in a semi-comatose condition, I lay till noon. Then being only a man after all, I felt hungry, and intimated as much to Gunga Dass whom I had begun to regard as my natural protector. Following the impulse of the outer world when dealing with natives, I put my hand into my pocket and drew out four annas. The absurdity of the gift struck me at once, and I was about to replace the money.

Gunga Dass, however, was of a different opinion. 'Give me the money,' said he; 'all you have, or I will get help, and we will kill you!' All this as if it were the most natural thing in the world.

A Briton's first impulse, I believe, is to guard the contents of his pockets; but a moment's reflection convinced me of the futility of differing with the one man who had it in his power to make me comfortable; and with whose help it was possible that I might eventually escape from the crater. I gave him all the money in my possession, Rs. 9-8-5 – nine rupees, eight annas and five pie – for I always keep small change as *back-shish* when I am in camp. Gunga Dass clutched the coins, and hid them at once in his ragged loincloth, his expression changing to something diabolical as he looked round to assure himself that no one had observed us.

'*Now* I will give you something to eat,' said he.

What pleasure the possession of my money could have afforded him I am unable to say; but inasmuch as it did give him evident delight I was not sorry that I had parted with it so readily, for I had no doubt that he would have had me killed if I had refused. One does not protest against the vagaries of a den of wild beasts; and my companions were lower than any beasts. While I devoured what Gunga Dass had provided – a coarse cake and a cupful of the foul well-water, the people showed not the faintest sign of curiosity – that curiosity which is so rampant, as a rule, in an Indian village.

I could even fancy that they despised me. At all events they treated me with the most chilling indifference, and Gunga Dass was nearly as bad. I plied him with questions about the terrible village, and received extremely unsatisfactory answers. So far as I could gather, it had been in existence from time immemorial – whence I concluded that it was at least a century old – and during that time no one had ever been known to escape from it. [I had to control myself here with both hands, lest the blind terror should lay hold of me a second time and drive me raving round the crater.] Gunga Dass took a malicious pleasure in emphasising this point and in watching me wince. Nothing that I could do would induce him to tell me who the mysterious 'They' were.

'It is so ordered,' he would reply, 'and I do not yet know anyone who has disobeyed the orders.'

'Only wait till my servants find that I am missing.' I retorted, 'and I promise you that this place shall be cleared off the face of the earth, and I'll give you a lesson in civility, too, my friend.'

'Your servants would be torn in pieces before they came near this place; and, besides, you are dead, my dear friend. It is not your fault, of course, but none the less, you are dead *and* buried.'

At irregular intervals, supplies of food, I was told, were dropped down from the land side into the amphitheatre, and the inhabitants fought for them like wild beasts. When a man felt his death coming on he retreated to his lair and died there. The body was sometimes dragged out of the hole and thrown on to the sand, or allowed to rot where it lay.

The phrase 'thrown on to the sand' caught my attention, and I asked Gunga Dass whether this sort of thing was not likely to breed a pestilence.

'That,' said he, with another of his wheezy chuckles, 'you may see for yourself subsequently. You will have much time to make observations.'

Whereat, to his great delight, I winced once more and hastily continued the conversation: – 'And how do you live here from day to day? What do you do?' The question elicited exactly the same answer as before – coupled with the information that 'this place is like your European Heaven; there is neither marrying nor giving in marriage'.

Gunga Dass had been educated at a Mission School, and, as he himself admitted, had he only changed his religion 'like a wise man,' might have avoided the living grave which was now his portion. But as long as I was with him I fancy he was happy.

Here was a Sahib, a representative of the dominant race, helpless as a child and completely at the mercy of his native neighbours. In a deliberate lazy way he set himself to torture me as a school-boy would devote a rapturous half-hour to watching the agonies of an impaled beetle, or as a ferret in a blind burrow might glue himself comfortably to the neck of a rabbit. The burden of his conversation was that there was no escape 'of no kind whatever,' and that I should stay here till I died and was 'thrown on to the sand'. If if were possible to prejudge the conversation of the Damned on the advent of a new soul in their abode, I should say that they would speak as Gunga Dass did to me thoughout that long afternoon. I was powerless to protest or answer; all my energies being devoted to a struggle against the inexplicable terror that threatened to overwhelm me again and again. I can compare the feeling to nothing except the struggles of a man against the over-powering nausea of the Channel passage – only my agony was of the spirit, and infinitely more terrible.

As the day wore on the inhabitants began to appear in full strength to catch the rays of the afternoon sun, which were now sloping in at the mouth of the crater. They assembled in little knots, and talked among themselves without even throwing a glance in my direction.

About four o'clock, as far as I could judge, Gunga Dass rose and dived into his lair for a moment, emerging with a live crow in his hands. The wretched bird was in a most draggled and deplorable condition, but seemed to be in no way afraid of its master. Advancing cautiously to the river-front, Gunga Dass stepped from tussock to tussock until he had reached a smooth patch of sand directly in the line of the boat's fire. The occupants of the boat took no notice. Here he stopped, and with a couple of dexterous turns of the wrist, pegged the bird on its back with outstretched wings. As was only natural, the crow began to shriek at once and beat the air with its claws. In a few seconds the clamour had attracted the attention of a bevy of wild crows on a shoal a few hundred yards away, where they were discussing something that looked like a corpse. Half-a-dozen crows flew over at once to see what was going on, and also, as it proved, to attack the pinioned bird. Gunga Dass, who had lain down on a tussock, motioned to me to be quiet, though I fancy this was a needless precaution. In a moment, and before I could see how it happened, a wild crow who had grappled with the shrieking and helpless bird, was entangled in the latter's claws, swiftly disengaged by Gunga Dass, and pegged down beside its companion in adversity. Curiosity, it seemed overpowered the rest of the flock, and almost before Gunga Dass and I had time to withdraw to the tussock, two more captives were struggling in the up-turned claws of the decoys. So the sport – if I can give it so dignified a name – continued until Gunga Dass had captured seven crows. Five of them he throttled at once, reserving two for further operations another day. I was a good deal impressed by this, to me, novel method of securing food, and complimented Gunga Dass on his skill.

'It is nothing to do,' said he. 'Tomorrow you must do it for me. You are stronger than I am.'

This calm assumption of superiority upset me not a little, and I answered peremptorily: 'Indeed, you old ruffian! What do you think I have given you money for?'

'Very well,' was the unmoved reply. 'Perhaps not tomorrow, nor the day after, nor subsequently; but in the end, and for many years, you will catch crows and eat crows, and you will thank your European God that you have crows to catch and eat.'

I could have cheerfully strangled him for this; but judged it best under the circumstances to smother my resentment. An hour later I was eating one of the crows; and, as Gunga Dass had said, thanking my God, that I had a crow to eat. Never as long as I live shall I forget that evening meal. The whole population were squatting on the hard sand platform opposite their dens, huddling over tiny fires of refuse and dried rushes. Death having once laid his hand upon these men and forborne to strike, seemed to stand aloof from them now; for most of our company were old men, bent and worn and twisted with years, and women aged to all appearance as the Fates themselves. They sat together in knots and talked – God only knows what they found to discuss – in low equable tones, curiously in contrast to the strident babble with which natives are accustomed to make day hideous. Now and then an access of that sudden fury which had possessed me in the morning would lay hold on a man or woman; and with yells and imprecations the sufferer would attack the steep slope until, baffled and bleeding, he fell back on the platform incapable of moving a limb. The others would never even raise their eyes when this happened, as men too well aware of the futility of their fellows' attempts, and wearied with their useless repetition. I saw four such outbursts in the course of that evening.

Gunga Dass took an eminently business-like view of my situation, and while we were dining – I can afford to laugh at the recollection now, but it was painful enough at the time – propounded the terms on which he would consent to 'do' for me. My nine rupees eight annas, he argued, at the rate of three annas a day, would provide me with food for fifty-one days, or about seven weeks; that is to say, he would be willing to cater for me for that length of lime. At the end of it I was to look after myself. For a further consideration – my boots – he would be willing to allow me to occupy the den next to his own, and would supply me with as much dried grass for bedding as he could spare.

'Very well, Gunga Dass,' I replied; 'to the first terms I cheerfully agree, but, as there is nothing on earth to prevent my killing you as you sit here and taking everything that you have' (I thought of the two invaluable crows at the time), 'I flatly refuse to give you my boots, and shall take whichever den I please!'

The stroke was a bold one, and I was glad when I saw that it had succeeded. Gunga Dass changed his tone immediately, and disavowed all intention of asking for my boots. At the time it did not strike me as at all strange that I, a Civil Engineer, a man of thirteen years' standing in the Service, and, I trust, an average Englishman, should thus calmly threaten murder and violence against the man who had, for a consideration it is true, taken me under his wing. I had left the world, it seemed, for centuries. I was as certain then as I am now of my own existence, that in the accursed settlement there was no law save that of the strongest; that the living dead men had thrown behind them every canon of the world which had cast them out; and that I had to depend for my own life on my strength and vigilance alone. The crew of the ill-fated *Mignonette* are the only men who would understand my frame of mind. 'At present,' I argued to myself, 'I am strong and a match for six of these wretches. It is imperatively necessary that I should, for my own sake, keep both health and strength until the hour of my release comes – if it ever does.'

Fortified with these resolutions, I ate and drank as much as I could, and made Gunga Dass understand that I intended to be his master, and that the least sign of insubordination on his part would be visited with the only punishment I had it in my power to inflict – sudden and violent death. Shortly after this I went to bed. That is to say, Gunga Dass gave me a double-armful of dried bents which I thrust down the mouth of the lair to the right of his, and followed myself, feet foremost; the hole running about nine feet into the sand with a slight downward inclination, and being neatly shored with timbers. From my den, which faced the riverfront, I was able to watch the waters of the Sutlej flowing past under the light of a young moon and compose myself to sleep as best I might.

The horrors of that night I shall never forget. My den was nearly as narrow as a coffin, and the sides had been worn smooth and greasy by the contact of innumerable naked bodies; it smelt abominably. Sleep was altogether out of question to one in my excited frame of mind. As the night wore on, it seemed that the entire amphitheatre was filled with legions of unclean devils that, trooping up from the shoals below, mocked the unfortunates in their lairs.

Personally I am not of an imaginative temperament – very few Engineers are – but on that occasion I was as completely prostrated with nervous terror as any woman. After half an hour or so, however, I was able once more to calmly review my chances of escape. Any exit by the steep sand walls was, of course, impracticable. I had been thoroughly convinced of this some time before. It was possible, just possible, that I might, in the uncertain moonlight, safely run the gauntlet of the rifle shots. The place was so full of terror for me that I was prepared to undergo any risk in leaving it. Imagine my delight, then, when after creeping stealthily to the river-front I found that the infernal boat was not there. My freedom lay before me in the next few steps!

By walking out of the first shallow pool that lay at the foot of the projecting left horn of the horse-shoe, I could wade across, turn the flank of the crater, and made my way inland. Without a moment's hesitation I marched briskly past the tussocks where Gunga Dass had snared the crows, and out in the direction of the smooth white sand beyond. My first step from the tufts of dried grass showed me how utterly futile was any hope of escape; for, as I put my foot down, I felt an indescribable drawing, sucking motion of the sand below. Another moment and my leg was swallowed up nearly to the knee. In the moonlight the whole surface of the sand seemed to be shaken with devilish delight at my disappointment. I struggled clear, sweating with terror and exertion, back to the tussocks behind me and felt on my face.

My only means of escape from the semi-circle was protected with a quicksand!

How long I lay I have not the faintest idea; but I was roused at last by the malevolent chuckle of Gunga Dass at my ear. 'I would advise you, Protector of the Poor,' – the ruffian was speaking English – 'to return to your house. It is unhealthy to lie down here. Moreover, when the boat returns, you will most certainly be rifled at.' He stood over me in the dim light of the dawn, chuckling and laughing to himself. Suppressing my first impulse to catch the man by the neck and throw him on to the quicksand, I rose suddenly and followed him to the platform below the burrows.

Suddenly, and futilely as I thought while I spoke, I asked:

'Gunga Dass, what is the good of the boat if I can't get out anyhow?' I recollect that even in my deepest trouble I had been speculating vaguely on the waste of ammunition in guarding an already well-protected foreshore.

Gunga Dass laughed again and made answer: They have the boat only in daytime. It is for the reason that *there is a way*. I hope we shall have the pleasure of your company for much longer time. It is a pleasant spot when you have been here some years and eaten roast crow long enough.'

I staggered, numbed and helpless towards the fetid burrow allotted to me and fell asleep. An hour or so later I was awakened by a piercing scream – the shrill, high-pitched scream of a horse in pain. Those who have once heard that will never forget the sound. I found some little difficulty in scrambling out of the burrow. When I was in the open, I saw *Pornic*, my poor old *Pornic*, lying dead on the sandy soil. How they had killed him I cannot guess. Gunga Dass explained that horse was better than crow, and 'greatest good of greatest number is political maxim. We are now Republic, Mister Jukes, and you are entitled to a fair share of the beast. If you like, we will pass a vote of thanks. Shall I propose?'

Yes, we were a Republic indeed! A Republic of wild beasts penned at the bottom of a pit, to eat and fight and sleep till we died. I attempted no protest of any kind, but sat down and stared at the hideous sight in front of me. In less time almost than it takes me to write this, *Pornic*'s body was divided, in some unclean way or other; the men and women had dragged the fragments on to the platform and were preparing their morning meal. Gunga Dass cooked mine. The almost irresistible impulse to fly at the sand walls until I was wearied laid hold of me afresh, and I had to struggle against it with all my might. Gunga Dass was offensively jocular till I told him that if he addressed another remark of any kind whatever to me I should strangle him where he sat. This silenced him till silence became insupportable, and I bade him say nothing.

'You will live here till you die like the other Feringhi,' he said coolly, watching me over the fragment of gristle that he was gnawing.

'What other *Sahib*, you swine? Speak at once, and don't stop to tell me a lie.'

'He is over there,' answered Gunga Dass, pointing to a burrow-mouth about four doors to the left of my own, 'You can see for yourself. He died in the burrow as you will die, and I will die, and as all these men and women and the one child will also die.'

'For pity's sake tell me all you know about him. Who was he? When did he come, and when did he die?'

This appeal was a weak step on my part. Gunga Dass only leered and replied: 'I will not – unless you give me something first'.

Then I recollected where I was, and struck the man between the eyes, partially stunning him. He stepped down from the platform at once, and, cringing and fawning and weeping, and attempted to embrace my feet, led me round to the burrow which he had indicated.

'I know nothing whatever about the gentleman. Your God be my witness that I do not. He fell in here to this place. He was as anxious to escape as you were, and he was shot from the boat, though we all did all things to prevent him from attempting. He was shot here.' Gunga Dass laid his hand on his lean stomach and bowed to the earth.

'Well and what then? Go on!'

'And then – and then, Your Honour, we carried him into his house and gave him water, and put wet clothes on the wound, and he laid down in his house and gave up the ghost.'

'In how long? In how long?'

'About half an hour after he received his wound. I call Vishnu to witness,' yelled the wretched man, 'that I did everything for him. Everything which was possible that I did!'

He threw himself down on the ground and clasped my ankles. But I had my doubts about Gunga Dass's benevolence, and kicked him off as he lay protesting.

'I believe you robbed him of everything he had. But I can find out in a minute or two. How long was the *Sahib* here?'

'Nearly a year and a half. I think he must have gone mad. But hear me swear, Protector of the Poor! Won't Your

Honour hear me swear that I never touched an article that belonged to him? What is Your Worship going to do?'

I had taken Gunga Dass by the wrist and had hauled him on to the platform opposite the deserted burrow. As I did so I thought of my wretched fellow-prisoner's unspeakable misery among all these horrors for eighteen months, and the final agony of dying like a rat in a hole with a bullet-wound in the stomach. Gunga Dass fancied I was going to kill him and howled pitifully. The rest of the population, in the plethora that follows a full flesh-meal, watched us without stirring.

'Go inside, Gunga Dass,' said I, 'and fetch it out.'

I was feeling sick and faint with horror now. Gunga Dass nearly rolled off the platform and howled aloud.

'But I am Brahmin, *Sahib* – a high-caste Brahmin. By your soul, by your father's soul, do not make me do this thing!'

'Brahmin or no Brahmin, by my soul and my father's soul, in you go!' I said, and seizing him by the shoulders I crammed his head into the mouth of the burrow, kicked the rest of him in, and, sitting down, covered my face with my hands.

At the end of a few minutes I heard a rustle and a creak; then Gunga Dass in a sobbing, choking whisper speaking to himself; then a soft thud – and I uncovered my eyes.

The dry sand had turned the corpse entrusted to its keeping into a yellow-brown mummy. I told Gunga Dass to stand off while I examined it. The body – clad in an olive-green shooting-suit much stained and worn, with leather pads on the shoulders – was that of a man between thirty and forty, above middle height, with light, sandy hair, long moustache, and a rough unkempt beard. The left canine of the upper jaw was missing, and a portion of the lobe of the right ear was gone. On the second finger of the left hand was a ring – a shield-shaped bloodstone set in gold, with a monogram that might have been either 'B.K.' or 'B.L.'. On the third finger of the right hand, was a silver ring in the shape of a coiled cobra, much worn and tarnished. Gunga Dass deposited a handful of trifles he had picked out of the burrow at my feet, and, covering the face of the body with my handkerchief, I turned to examine these. I give the full list in the hope that it may lead to the identification of the unfortunate man:—

1. Bowl of a briarwood pipe, serrated at the edge; much worn and blackened; bound with string at the screw.

2. Two patent-lever keys: both broken.

3. Tortoise-shell handled penknife, silver or nickie name-plate, marked with monogram 'B.K.'.

4. Envelope, post-mark undecipherable, bearing a Victorian stamp, addressed to 'Miss Mon—' (rest illegible) —'ham' —'nt'.

5. Imitation crocodile-skin note-book with pencil. First forty-five pages blank; four and a half illegible; fifteen others filled with private memoranda relating chiefly to three persons – a Mrs L. Singleton, abbreviated several times to 'Lot Single' or 'Mrs S. May' and 'Garmison,' referred to in places as 'Jerry' or 'Jack'.

6. Handle of small-sized hunting knife. Blade snapped short. Buck's horn, diamond cut, with swivel and ring on the butt; fragment of cotton cord attached.

It must not be supposed that I inventoried all these things on the spot as fully as I have here written them down. The note-book first attracted my attention, and I put it in my pocket with a view to studying it later on. The rest of the articles I conveyed to my burrow for safety's sake, and there, being a methodical man, I inventoried them. I then returned to the corpse and ordered Gunga Dass, to help me to carry it out to the river-front. While we were engaged in this, the exploded shell of an old brown cartridge dropped out of one of the pockets and rolled at my feet. Gunga Dass had not seen it; and I fell to thinking that a man does not carry exploded cartridge-cases, especially 'browns' which will not bear loading twice, about with him when shooting. In other words, that cartridge-case had been fired inside the crater. Consequently, there must be a gun somewhere. I was on the verge of asking Gunga Dass, but checked myself, knowing that he would lie. We laid the body down on the edge of the quicksand by the tussocks. It was my intention to push it out and let it be swallowed up – the only possible mode of burial that I could think of. I ordered Gunga Dass to go away.

Then I gingerly put the corpse out on the quicksand. In doing so, it was lying face downward, I tore the frail and rotten shooting-coat open, disclosing a hideous cavity in the back. I have already told you that the dry sand had, as it were, mummified the body. A moment's glance showed that the gaping hole had been caused by a gun-shot wound: the gun must have been fired with the muzzle almost touching the back. The shooting-coat, being intact, had been drawn over the body after death which must have been instantaneous. The secret of the poor wretch's death was plain to me in a flash. Some one of the crater, presumably Gunga Dass, must have shot him with his own gun – the gun that fitted the brown cartridges. He had never attempted to escape in the face of the rifle fire from the boat.

I pushed the corpse out hastily, and saw it sink from sight literally in a few seconds. I shuddered as I watched. In a dazed, half-conscious way I turned to peruse the notebook. A stained and discoloured slip of paper had been inserted between the binding and the back, and dropped out as I opened the pages. This is what it contained: – *'Four out from crow-clump; three left; nine out; two right; three back; two left; fourteen out; two left; seven out; one left, nine back; two right; six back; four right; seven back'*. The paper had been burnt and charred at the edges. What it meant I could not understand. I sat down on the dried bents turning it over and over between my fingers, until I was aware of Gunga Dass standing immediately behind me with glowing eyes and outstretched hands.

'Have you got it?' he panted. 'Will you not let me look at it also? I swear that I will return it.'

'Got what? Return what?' I asked.

'That which you have in your hands. It will help us both.' He stretched out his long, bird-like talons, trembling with eagerness.

'I could never find it,' he continued. 'He had secreted it about his person. Therefore I shot him, but nevertheless I was unable to obtain it.'

Gunga Dass had quite forgotten his little fiction about the rifle-bullet. I received the information perfectly calmly. Morality is blunted by consorting with the Dead who are alive.

'What on earth are you raving about? What is it you want me to give you?'

'The piece of paper in the notebook. It will help us both. Oh, you fool! You fool! Can you not see what it will do for us? We shall escape!'

'His voice rose almost to a scream, and he danced with excitement before me. I own I was moved at the chance of getting away.

'Don't skip! Explain yourself. Do you mean to say that this slip of paper will help us? What does it mean?'

'Read it aloud! Read it aloud! I beg and I pray to you to read it aloud.'

I did so. Gunga Dass listened delightedly, and drew an irregular line in the sand with his fingers.

'See now! It was the length of his gun-barrels without the stock. I have those barrels. Four gun-barrels out from the place where I caught crows. Straight out; do you follow me? Then three left— Ah! I remember when that man worked it out night after night. Then nine out, and so on. Out is always straight before you cross the quicksand. He told me so before I killed him.'

'But if you knew all this why didn't you get out before?'

'I did *not* know it. He told me that he was working it out a year and-a-half ago, and how he was working it out night after night when the boat had gone away, and he could get out near the quicksand safely. Then he said that we would get away together. But I was afraid that he would leave me behind one night when he had worked it all out, and so I shot him. Besides, it is not advisable that the men who once get in here should escape. Only I, and *I* am a Brahmin.'

The prospect of escape had brought Gunga Dass's caste back to him. He stood up, walked about and gesticulated violently. Eventually I managed to make him talk soberly, and he told me how this Englishman had spent six months night after night, in exploring, inch by inch, the passage across the quicksand; how he had declared it to be simplicity itself up to within about twenty yards of the river bank after turning the flank of the left horn of the horseshoe.

In my frenzy of delight at the possibilities of escape I recollect shaking hands effusively with Gunga Dass, after we had decided that we were to make an attempt to get away that very night. It was weary work waiting throughout the afternoon.

About ten o'clock, as far as I could judge, when the Moon had just risen above the lip of the crater, Gunga Dass made a move for his burrow to bring out the gun-barrels whereby to measure our path. All the other wretched inhabitants had retired to their lairs long ago. The guardian boat had drifted downstream some hours before, and we were utterly alone by the crow-clump. Gunga Dass, while carrying the gun-barrels, let slip the piece of paper which was to be our guide. I stooped down hastily to recover it, and as I did so, I was aware that he was aiming a violent blow at the back of my head with the gun-barrels. It was too late to turn round. I must have received the blow somewhere on the nape of my neck. A hundred thousand fiery stars danced before my eyes, and I fell forward senseless at the edge of the quicksand.

When I recovered consciousness, the Moon was going down, and I was sensible of intolerable pain in the back of my head. Gunga Dass had disappeared and my mouth was full of blood. I lay down again and prayed that I might die without more ado. Then the unreasoning fury which I have before mentioned laid hold upon me, and I staggered inland towards the walls of the crater. It seemed that some one was calling to me in a whisper, 'Sahib! Sahib! Sahib!' exactly as my bearer used to call me in the morning. I fancied that I was delirious until a handful of sand fell at my feet. Then I looked up and saw a head peering down into the amphitheatre – the head of Dunnoo, my dog-boy, who attended to my collies. As soon as he had attracted my attention, he held up his hand and showed a rope. I motioned, staggering to and fro the while, that he should throw it down. It was a couple of leather punkah-ropes knotted together, with a loop at one end. I slipped the loop over my head and under my arms; heard Dunnoo urge something forward; was conscious that I was being dragged, face downward, up the steep sand slope, and the next instant found myself choked and half fainting on the sand hills overlooking the crater. Dunnoo, with his face ashy grey in the moonlight, implored me not to stay but to get back to my tent at once.

It seems that he had tracked *Pornic*'s hooves fourteen miles across the sands to the crater; had returned and told my servants, who flatly refused to meddle with any one, white or black, once fallen into the hideous Village of the Dead; whereupon Dunnoo had taken one of my ponies and a couple of punkah ropes, returned to the crater, and hauled me out as I have described.

To cut a long story short, Dunnoo is now my personal servant on a gold mohur a month – a sum which I still think far too little for the services he has rendered. Nothing on earth will induce me to go near that devilish spot again or to reveal its whereabouts more clearly than I have done. Of Gunga Dass I have never found a trace, nor do I wish to do. My sole motive in giving this to be published is the hope that someone may possibly identify, from the details and the inventory which I have given above, the corpse of the man in the olive-green hunting-suit.

THE UNLIMITED DRAW OF TICK BOILEAU

He came to us from Naogong, somewhere in Central India; and as soon as we saw him we all voted him a Beast. That was in the Mess of the 45th Bengal Cavalry, stationed at Pindi; and everything I'm going to write about happened this season. I've told you he was an awful Beast – old even for a subaltern; but then he'd joined the Army late, and had knocked about the world a good deal. We didn't know that at first. I wish we had. It would have saved the honour of the Mess. He was called 'Tick' in Naogong, because he was never out of debt; but that didn't make us think him a beast. Quite the other way, for most of us were pretty well clipped ourselves. No, what we hated about the fellow was his 'dark-horsiness'. I can't express it any better than that; and, besides, it's an awful nuisance having to write at all. But all the other fellows in the Mess say I'm the only man who can handle a pen decently; and that I must, for their credit, tell the world exactly how it came about. Everyone is chaffing us so beastly now.

Well, I was saying that we didn't like Tick Boileau's 'dark-horsiness'. I mean by that you never knew what the fellow could do and what he could not; and he was always coming out, with that beastly conceited grin on his face, in a new line – 'specially before women – and making the other man, who had tried to do the same thing, feel awfully small and humble. That was his strong point – simpering and cutting a fellow out when he was doing his hardest at something or other. Same with billiards; same with riding; same with the banjo; he could really make the banjo *talk* – better even than Banjo Browne at Kasauli you know; same with tennis. And to make everything more beastly, he used to pretend at first he couldn't do anything. We found him out in the end; but we'd have found him out sooner if we'd listened to what old Harkness the Riding-Master said the day after Tick had been handed over to him to make into a decent 'Hornet'. That's what the bye-name of our regiment is. Harkness told me when I came into Riding School, and laughed at Tick clinging on to the neck of his old crock as if he had never seen a horse before. Harkness was cursing like – a riding-master. He said: – 'You mark my words, Mr Mactavish, he's been kidding me, and he'd kid you. He *can* ride. Wish some of you other gentleman could ride as well. He is playing the dark horse – that's what he's doing, and be d – – d to him!' Well, Tick was as innocent as a baby when he rolled off on to the tan. I noticed that he fell somehow as if he knew the hang of the trick; and Harkness passed him out of Riding School on the strength of that fall. He sat square enough on parade, and pretended to be awfully astonished. Well, we didn't think anything of that till he came out one night in the billiard line at Black Pool, and scooped the whole Mess. Then we began to mistrust him, but he swore it was all by a fluke. We used to chaff him fearfully; and draw him about four nights out of the seven. Once we drugged his chargers with opium overnight; and Tick found 'em asleep and snoring when he wanted to go on parade.

He was a trifle wrathy over this; and the Colonel didn't soothe him by giving him the rough edge of his tongue for allowing his horses to go to sleep at unauthorised hours. We didn't mean to do more than make the chargers a bit bobbery next morning; but something must have gone wrong with the opium. To give the Beast his due, he took everything very well indeed; and never minded how often we pulled his leg and made things lively for him. We never liked him, though. Can't like a man who always does everything with a little bit up his sleeve. It's not fair.

Well, one day in July Tick took three months' leave and cleared out somewhere or other – to Cashmere I think. He didn't tell us where, and we weren't very keen on knowing.

We missed him at first, for there was no one to draw. Our regiment don't take kindly to that sort of thing. We are most of us hard as nails; and we respect each other's little weaknesses.

About October, Tick turned up with a lot of heads and horns and skins – for it seemed that the beggar could shoot as well as he did most things – and the Mess began to sit up at the prospect of having some more fun out of him. But Tick was an altered man. Never saw anyone so changed. Hadn't an ounce of *bukh* or bounce left about him; never betted; knocked off what little liquor he used to take; got rid of his ponies, and went mooning about like an old ghost. Stranger still, he seemed to lay himself out in a quiet sort of way to be a popular man; and, in about three weeks' time we began to think we had misjudged him, and that he wasn't half such a bad fellow after all. The Colonel began the movement in his favour. Said that Tick was awfully cut up about something or other, and that we really ought to make his life more pleasant for him. He didn't say all that much at once. Don't believe he could if he tried for a week, but he made us understand it. And in a quiet sort of way – Tick was very quiet in everything he did just then – he tumbled to the new *bandobust* more than ever, and we nearly all took to him. I say nearly all, because I was an exception. He had a little bit up his sleeve in this matter, too.

You see he had given all his skins and his heads to the Mess, and they were hung in trophies all round the wall. I was seeing them put up, and I saw in one corner the Cabul Customs mark, in a sort of aniline ink stamp, that all the skins that come from Peshawar must have. Now I knew Cashmere wasn't Peshawar, and that bears didn't grow with Customs marks inside the hide. But I sat tight and said nothing. I want you to remember that I suspected Tick Boileau from the first. The fellows in the Mess say I was just as much taken in as the rest of 'em; but in our Mess they'd say *anything*. One of Tick's new peculiarities just at this time was a funk of being left alone. He never said anything about it. He used to be always coming over to fellows' quarters in the afternoon though, just when they were trying to put in a little snooze and he'd sit still or *bukh* about nothing. He was very queer altogether in that way; and some of us thought he'd had D.T.; others that he was engaged and wanted to get out of it; and one youngster, just joined, vowed that Tick had committed a murder and was haunted by the ghost of his victim. One night we were sitting round the table smoking after dinner, and this same youngster began *bukhing* about a Station dance of some kind that was coming off. Asked old Tick if he wasn't coming and made some feeble joke about 'ticks' and *Kala Juggas*. Anyhow it fetched Tick awfully.

He was lifting a glass of sherry up to his mouth and his hand shook so that he spilt it all down the front of his mess jacket. He seemed awfully white, but perhaps that was fancy; and said as if there was something in his throat choking him – 'Go to a ball. No! I'd sooner rot as I stand!' Well, it isn't usual for a fellow to cut up like that when he's asked if he's going to a hop. I was sitting next to him and said quietly – 'Hullo! what's the matter old man?' Tick was by way of being no end of a dawg before he took leave, and that made his answer all the queerer. 'Matter!' said Tick, and he almost screamed. 'You'd ask what was the matter if you'd seen what I have!' Then he turned on the youngster, 'What the this and the that do you mean, you young this and t'other thing' (It's no use putting down the words he used. They weren't pretty) 'by asking me a question like that?' There would have been decanters flying about on the wings of love if we hadn't stopped the shindy at once; and when Tick came to himself again he began apologising all he knew, and calling himself all sorts of hard names for raising the row. And that astonished us more than anything else. Tick wasn't given that way as a rule. Said the Colonel from his side of the table; 'What in the name of everything lunatic, is the matter? Have you gone mad, Boileau?' Then Tick chucked up his head like a horse when it's going to bolt, and began to speak. Goodness knows what he said exactly; but he gave us to understand that if he wasn't off his head, he was next thing to it, and, if we cared to listen, he'd tell us all about it. You bet we *did* care, for we were on needles to know the reason of the sudden change in the fellow. Tick half filled his peg-tumbler with port – it was the nearest decanter – and told us this story. I can put it down word for word as he said it, not because I've got a good memory, but because – well, I'll tell you later. This is what Tick said in a shaky, quivery, voice, while we smoked and listened: – 'You know I took three months' leave the other day, don't you? And that I went to Kashmir? You mayn't know' – (we didn't) – 'that I put in the first month of my time at Mussoorie. I kept very quiet while I was up there, for I had gone up on purpose to follow a girl that you men don't know. She came from Pachmarri; and she was the daughter of a doctor there. I used to know her very well when I was stationed out Naogong way, and from knowing her well I got to falling in love with her.'

He pulled up half a minute at that, and glared all round the table to see how we took it. We aren't whales exactly on falling in love with unmarried girls in our Mess. The Colonel doesn't hold with it, and he's quite right. But none of us moved a finger, and Tick went on.

'She was absolutely the most perfect girl on the face of this earth; and I'd knock any beggar's brains out who denies it' – (None of us wanted to, I give you my word) – 'Upon my soul, I meant marrying her if she would only he' taken me. And she did. O Heaven, she did! She has accepted me!' Tick covered his face with his hands and went on like a lunatic. I fancied he'd got a touch of the sun, or that the peg-tumbler of port was beginning to work. Then he started off on a fresh tack, while we were staring at one another and wondering what on earth was coming next.

'Do any of you fellows recollect the Club Ball at Mussoorie this year?' Curiously enough not one of us had been up of the Mess; but you may be certain that we knew all about the Ball – (By the way, take us all round and we're the best dancers in India; but that's neither here nor there.) Some one said 'Yes'; and Tick went on again – 'It happened there! It happened there! I had arranged beforehand that she was to give me four or five dances and all the extras. She knew long before that, I think, that I loved her; and I as good as told her before the dance began that I intended proposing. It was the first extra – there were going to be three that evening – that I had arranged to sit out with her and tell her how I loved her. We had been dancing together a good deal that evening, until she began to complain of a pain in her side, and then we sat out in the verandah.'

Tick shovelled his hand through his hair and rolled his eyes about, more like a maniac than ever, and we sat tight and filled up our glasses quietly without saying anything.

'At the end of the last *pukka* waltz she went into the cloak room, because her slipper-elastic had become slack – I heard her explain that to the man she was dancing with – and I went out into the verandah to think over what I had got to say. When I turned round I saw her standing at my side: and before I had time to say anything she just slipped her arm through mine and was looking up in my face. "Well, what is it that you're going to say to me?" said she. And then I spoke – though honestly I was a little bit startled at the way she herself led up to the point, as it were. Lord only knows what I said or what she said. I told her I loved her, and she told me she loved me. Look here! If a man among you laughs, by jove, I'll brain him with the decanter!'

Tick's face was something awful to look at just then – a dead white with blue dimples under the nostrils and the corners of the mouth. He looked like a corpse that had been freshly dug up – not too freshly, though. I never saw anything more beastly in my life – except once at the front. Then he brought his hand down on the table in a way that made the dessert plates jump, and almost howled – 'I tell you I proposed to her, and she accepted me. Do you hear? She accepted me!'

Well, that didn't strike us as anything particularly awful. I've been accepted once or twice myself; but it didn't turn me into more than an average lunatic for the time being.

Tick dropped his voice somewhere into his boots – at least it sounded awfully hollow and unearthly – 'Then as the extra stopped she got up to go away from the sofa we'd been sitting on, and I asked her to stay. She told me that she was going to her next partner. I said, "Look here, darling, who *is* your next partner if it isn't me, for ever and ever? Sit down and let us wait till your chaperone is ready!" "My chaperone *is* ready, dear", said she, "and I must go to her. But remember that you are my next partner for ever and ever. Amen. Good-bye."

'Before I could say anything she had run out of the verandah and into the ball-room. I stopped to look at the moon and to thank my stars I was so lucky as to win her. Presently a man I knew hurried by me with a rug out of one of the dandies. My heart was so full I just pulled him up where he stood, and said: "Congratulate me, old boy! She's accepted me. I'm the happiest fellow on earth!" Now everyone in Mussoorie knew pretty well that I meant business with the girl; but instead of congratulating me the man just let the rug drop and said, "O my God!"

'What's the matter?' said I. 'Were you sweet on her yourself, then? All right, I'll forgive you. But you'll congratulate me, won't you?

'He caught me by the arm, and led me quietly into the ball-room, and then left me. Everybody was clustered in a mob round the cloak-room door; and some of the women-folk were crying. A couple of 'em had fainted. There was a sort of subdued hum going out, and everyone was saying: "How ghastly! How shocking! How terrible!" I leant up against a door-post and felt sick and faint, though I didn't know why. Then the fellow who had taken the dandy-rug came out of the cloak-room and spoke to one of the women.'

Tick had nearly emptied the decanter by this time; and I looked up and down the Mess. I could see two or three of the men looking awfully white and uncomfortable. My hair began to feel cold, as if draughts were blowing through it. I don't mind owning to that. Tick went ahead: –

'The women – she was an utter stranger – came up to speak to me, and she told me that my little girl had gone into the cloak room at the end of the last dance before the extras came on, complaining of a pain in her side. She had sat down and died of heart disease as she sat! *This was at the end of the last pukka waltz. Do you hear me? I tell you it was at the end of the last pukka waltz.*'

(I don't know much about printing presses; but if you printer fellows have got any type big enough and awful enough to give any idea of the way in which Tick said that, you are seven pounds better than I thought.)

I felt as if all the winds in the Hills were crawling round my hair. You know that cold, creepy feeling at the top of the scalp, just when the first dropping shots begin, and before the real shindy starts. Well, that was how I felt – how we all felt, in fact – when Tick had finished and brought down his hand again on the table.

We shifted about as if our chairs were all red-hot, trying to think of something pleasant to say. Tick kept on repeating: '*It was at the end of the last pukka waltz!*' Then he'd stop for a bit, and rock too and fro; and ask us what he was to do. Whether 'a betrothal to a dead woman was binding in law,' and so on – sometimes laughing and sometimes chucking his head about like my second charger when the curb-chain's tighter than it should be.

It may sound awfully funny to read now; but I assure you sitting round the Mess table with Tick's white and blue face in front of one, and Tick's awful way of laughing and talking in one's ears, the fun did not dawn on us until a long while after. And even then we weren't grateful.

Our Colonel was the first to move. The old man got up and put his hand on Tick's shoulder, and begged him, for his own sake, not to take it to heart so much. Said that he was unwell and had better go to his own quarters. Tick chucked up his head and regularly yelled – 'I tell you I have seen it with my own eyes. I wish to Heaven it had been a delusion.' All this time the Colonel was soothing him down, just as you or I would gentle a horse; and the other Johnnies stood round and mumbled something about being awfully sorry for his trouble, and that, if they had known it, they would have dropped pulling his leg like a shot. Whether it was too much liquor, or whether Tick really had seen a ghost, we didn't stop to think. He was so awfully cut up no one could have helped being sorry for him.

Well, I and another Johnnie went with him over to his quarters, and Tick chucked himself down on the charpoy and buried his face in the pillow; and his shoulders shook as if he were sobbing like a woman. The other Johnnie turned the lamp down, and we left him and went back to Mess. There we sat up the rest of the night, the lot of us, *bukhing* about ghosts and delusions, and so on. We were all pretty certain that Tick hadn't got the 'jumps' or anything foolish of that kind, because he was as steady as a die in these things – couldn't have played to win unless his head had been fairly cool, you know. Finally we decided that there was no need to tell anyone outside the Mess about the night's business, and that we were all awfully sorry for Tick. I want to remind you that *I* was sitting tight all this time. I thought of the Custom's mark on the bearskins and browsed quietly over a peg. About parade time we went to bed. Tick turned up awfully haggard and white on parade.

He took the down train to Lahore that day and cleared out, he didn't tell us where to, on a few days' leave. We did not look at his quarters. Three of us went over to the Club that afternoon, and the first thing a man asked us was 'What we thought of it?' Then all the Johnnies in the smoking-room began to laugh, and then they began to roar. It seems that that blackguard Tick had been over to the Club directly after parade and told all the men there about his yarn overnight, and the way we'd sucked it in from the Colonel downwards. It was all over Pindi before nightfall; and you may guess how they chaffed us about 'pukka waltzes' and men with 'dandy rugs' and whether a 'betrothal to a dead woman was binding in law'. Just you ask one of the 45th that question and see what happens! When we three rode back to Mess I can tell you we didn't feel proud of ourselves. There was a regular indignation meeting on, and everybody was talking at the top of his voice. Fellows who had just come in from polo, or from making calls, had all been told of it; and they wanted Tick's blood.

The whole blessed business was a *berow* from beginning to end, and we had believed it! We moved over to Tick's quarters to begin by making hay there. Nothing except the chairs and the charpoy (and those belonged to Government) had been left behind.

Over the mantelpiece a double sheet of notepaper had been pinned, and above this, in letters about two foot high, was written in charcoal on the wall – 'The Unlimited Draw of Tick Boileau'. The Beast had carefully written out the whole yarn from beginning to end, with stage directions for himself about yelling and looking half mad, in red ink at the sides. And he had left that behind for our benefit.

It was a magnificent 'sell'; but nothing except Tick's acting would have pulled it off in the perfect way it went. We stopped dead, and just pondered over the length and the breadth and the thickness of it. If we'd only thought for a minute about the improbability of a woman dying at a Mussoorie ball without the whole of Upper India knowing it we might have saved ourselves. But that's just what we didn't do. And if you'd listened to Tick you'd have followed our lead.

Tick never came back. I fancy he had a sort of notion it wouldn't have been healthy for him if he had. But we've started a sort of Land League – what do you call it? Velungericht? – in our Mess; and if we come across him anywhere we're going to make things lively for him. He sent in his papers and went down to Pachmarri; where it seems he really was engaged to a girl with money – something like two thousand a year, I've heard – married her, and went home. Of course he had spent his three months' leave at Pachmarri too. We found that out afterwards.

I don't think I should have taken all that trouble and expense (for the Mess room is full of those horns and heads) to work out a sell like that, even if it had been as grand a one as 'The Unlimited Draw of Tick Boileau'.

P.S. – Just you ask any of us if 'a betrothal to a dead woman is binding in law', and see what happens. I think you'll find that I have written the truth pretty much.

IN THE HOUSE OF SUDDHOO

A stone's throw out on either hand
from that well-ordered road we tread,
    And all the world is wild and strange:
Churel and ghoul and *Djinn* and sprite
Shall bear us company to-night,
For we have reached the Oldest land
    Wherein the Powers of Darkness range.

From the Dusk to the Dawn

The house of Suddhoo, near the Taksali Gate, is two-storied, with four carved windows of old brown wood, and a flat roof. You may recognise it by five red hand-prints arranged like the Five of Diamonds on the whitewash between the upper windows. Bhagwan Dass the grocer and a man who says he gets his living by seal-cutting live in the lower story with a troop of wives, servants, friends, and retainers. The two upper rooms used to be occupied by Janoo and Azizun, and a little black-and-tan terrier that was stolen from an Englishman's house and given to Janoo by a soldier. To-day, only Janoo lives in the upper rooms. Suddhoo sleeps on the roof generally, except when he sleeps in the street. He used to go to Peshawar in the cold weather to visit his son who sells curiosities near the Edwardes' Gate, and than he slept under a real mud roof. Suddhoo is a great friend of mine, because his cousin had a son who secured, thanks to my recommendation, the post of head-messenger to a big firm in the Station. Suddhoo says that God will make me a Lieutenant-Governor one of these days. I daresay his prophecy will come true. He is very, very old, with white hair and no teeth worth showing, and he has outlived his wits – outlived nearly everything except his fondness for his son at Peshawar. Janoo and Azizun are Kashmiris, Ladies of the City, and theirs was an ancient and more or less honourable profession; but Azizun has since married a medical student from the North-West and has settled down to a most respectable life somewhere near Bareilly. Bhagwan Dass is an extortionate and an adulterator. He is very rich. The man who is supposed to get his living by seal-cutting pretends to be very poor. This lets you know as much as is necessary for the four principal tenants in the House of Suddhoo. Then there is Me of course; but I am only the chorus that comes in at the end to explain things. So I do not count.

Suddhoo was not clever. The man who pretended to cut seals was the cleverest of them all – Bhagwan Dass only knew how to lie – except Janoo. She was also beautiful, but that was her own affair.

Suddhoo's son at Peshawar was attacked by pleurisy, and old Suddhoo was troubled. The seal-cutter man heard of Suddhoo's anxiety and made capital out of it. He was abreast of the times. He got a friend in Peshawar to telegraph daily accounts of the son's health. And here the story begins.

Suddhoo's cousin's son told me, one evening, that Suddhoo wanted to see me; that he was too old and feeble to come personally, and that I should be conferring an everlasting honour on the House of Suddhoo if I went to him. I went; but I think, seeing how well off Suddhoo was then, that he might have sent something better than an *ekka*, which jolted fearfully, to haul out a future Lieutenant-Governor to the City on a muggy April evening. The *ekka* did not run quickly. It was full dark when we pulled up opposite the door of Ranjit Singh's Tomb near the main gate of the Fort. Here was Suddhoo, and he said that by reason of my condescension, it was absolutely certain that I should become a Lieutenant-Governor while my hair was yet black. Then we talked about the weather and the state of my health, and the wheat crops, for fifteen minutes, in the Huzuri Bagh, under the stars.

Suddhoo came to the point at last. He said that Janoo had told him that there was an order of the *Sirkar* against magic, because it was feared that magic might one day kill the Empress of India. I don't know anything about the state of the law; but I fancied that something interesting was going to happen. I said that so far from magic being discouraged by the Government it was highly commended. The greatest officials of the State practised it themselves. (If the Financial Statement isn't magic, I don't know what is.) Then, to encourage him further, I said that, if there was any *jadoo* afoot, I had not the least objection to giving it my countenance and sanction, and to seeing that it was clean *jadoo* – white magic, as distinguished from the unclean *jadoo* which kills folk. It took a long time before Suddhoo admitted that this was just what he had asked me to come for. Then he told me, in jerks and quavers, that the man who said he cut seals was a sorceror of the cleanest kind; that every day he gave Suddhoo news of the sick son in Peshawar more quickly than the lightning could fly, and that this news was always corroborated by the letters. Further, that he had told Suddhoo how a great danger was threatening his son, which could be removed by clean *jadoo*; and, of course, heavy payment. I began to see exactly how the land lay, and told Suddhoo that I also understood a little *jadoo* in the Western line, and would go to his house to see that everything was done decently and in order. We set off together; and on the way Suddhoo told me that he had paid the seal-cutter between one hundred and two hundred rupees already; and the *jadoo* of that night would cost two hundred more. Which was cheap, he said, considering the greatness of his son's danger; but I do not think he meant it.

The lights were all cloaked in the front of the house when we arrived. I could hear awful noises from behind the seal-cutter's shop-front, as if someone were groaning his soul out. Suddhoo shook all over, and while we groped our way upstairs told me that the *jadoo* had begun. Janoo and Azizun met us at the stair-head, and told us that the *jadoo*-work was coming off in their rooms, because there was more space there. Janoo is a lady of a free-thinking turn of mind. She whispered that the *jadoo* was an invention to get money out of Suddhoo, and that the seal-cutter would go to a hot place when he died. Suddhoo was nearly crying with fear and old age. He kept walking up and down the room in the half-light, repeating his son's name over and over again, and asking Azizun if the seal-cutter ought not to make a reduction in the case of his own landlord. Janoo pulled me over to the shadow in the recess of the carved bow-windows. The boards were up, and the rooms were only lit by one tiny oil-lamp. There was no chance of my being seen if I stayed still.

Presently, the groans below ceased, and we heard steps on the staircase. That was the seal-gutter. He stopped outside the door as the terrier barked and Azizun fumbled at the chain, and he told Suddhoo to blow out the lamp. This left the place in jet darkness, except for the red glow from the two *huqas* that belonged to Janoo and Azizun. The seal-cutter came in, and I heard Suddhoo throw himself down on the floor and groan. Azizun caught her breath, and Janoo backed on to one of the beds with a shudder. There was a clink of something metallic, and then shot up a pale blue-green flame near the ground. The light was just enough to show Azizun, pressed against one corner of the room with the terrier between her knees: Janoo with her hands clasped, leaning forward as she sat on the bed; Suddhoo, face down, quivering, and the seal-cutter.

I hope I may never see another man like that seal-cutter. He was stripped to the waist, with a wreath of white jasmine as thick as my wrist round his forehead, a salmon-coloured loin-cloth round his middle, and a steel bangle on each ankle. This was not awe-inspiring. It was the face of the man that turned me cold. It was blue-grey in the first place. In the second, the eyes were rolled back till you could only see the whites of them; and, in the third, the face was the face of a demon – a ghoul – anything you please except of the sleek, oily old ruffian who sat in the daytime over his turning-lathe downstairs. He was lying on his stomach with his arms turned and crossed behind him, as if he had been thrown down pinioned. His head and neck were the only parts of him off the floor. They were nearly at right angles to the body, like the head of a cobra at spring. It was ghastly. In the centre of the room, on the bare earth floor, stood a big, deep, brass basin, with a pale-green light floating in the centre like a night-light. Round that basin the man on the floor wriggled himself three times. How he did it I do not know. I could see the muscles ripple along his spine and fall smooth again; but I could not see any other motion. The head seemed the only thing alive about him, except that slow curl and uncurl of the labouring back-muscles. Janoo from the bed was breathing seventy to the minute; Azizun held her hands before her eyes; and old Suddhoo, fingering at the dirt that had got into his white beard, was crying to himself. The horror of it was that the creeping, crawly thing made no sound – only crawled! And, remember, this lasted for ten minutes, while the terrier whined, and Azizun shuddered, and Janoo gasped, and Suddhoo cried.

I felt the hair lift at the back of my head, and my heart thump like a thermantidote paddle. Luckily, the seal-cutter betrayed himself by his most impressive trick and made me calm again. After he had finished that unspeakable triple crawl, he stretched his head away from the floor as high as he could, and sent out a jet of fire from his nostrils. Now I knew how fire-spouting is done – I can do it myself – so I felt at ease. The business was a fraud. If he had only kept to that crawl without trying to raise the effect, goodness knows what I might not have thought. Both the girls shrieked at the jet of fire and the head dropped, chin-down on the floor, with a thud; the whole body lying then like a corpse with its arms trussed. There was a pause of five full minutes after this, and the blue-green flame died down. Janoo stooped to settle one of her anklets, while Azizun turned her face to the wall and took the terrier in her arms. Suddhoo put out an arm mechanically to Janoo's *huqa*, and she slid it across the floor with her foot. Directly above the body and on the wall were a couple of flaming portraits, in stamped-paper frames, of the Queen and the Prince of Wales. They looked down on the performance, and to my thinking, seemed to heighten the grotesqueness of it all.

Just when the silence was getting unendurable, the body turned over and rolled away from the basin to the side of the room, where it lay stomach-up. There was a faint 'plop' from the basin – exactly like the noise a fish makes when it takes a fly – and the green light in the centre revived.

I looked at the basin, and saw, bobbing in the water, the

dried, shrivelled, black head of a native baby – open eyes, open mouth, and shaved scalp. It was worse, being so very sudden, than the crawling exhibition. We had no time to say anything before it began to speak.

Read Poe's account of the voice that came from the mesmerised dying man, and you will realise less than one-half of the horror of that head's voice.

There was an interval of a second or two between each word, and a sort of 'ring, ring, ring,' in the note of the voice, like the timbre of a bell. It pealed slowly, as if talking to itself, for several minutes before I got rid of my cold sweat. Then the blessed solution struck me. I looked at the body lying near the doorway, and saw, just where the hollow of the throat joins on the shoulders, a muscle that had nothing to do with any man's regular breathing twitching away steadily. The whole thing was a careful reproduction of the Egyptian teraphin that one reads about sometimes; and the voice was as clever and as appalling a piece of ventriloquism as one could wish to hear. All this time the head was 'lip-lip-lapping' against the side of the basin, and speaking. It told Suddhoo, on his face again whining, of his son's illness and of the state of the illness up to the evening of that very night. I always shall respect the seal-cutter for keeping so faithfully to the time of the Peshawar telegrams. It went on to say that skilled doctors were night and day watching over the man's life; and that he would eventually recover if the fee to the potent sorcerer, whose servant was the head in the basin, were doubled.

Here the mistake from the artistic point of view came in. To ask for twice your stipulated fee in a voice that Lazarus might have used when he rose from the dead, is absurd. Janoo, who is really a woman of masculine intellect, saw this as quickly as I did. I heard her say '*Asli nahin! Fareib!*' scornfully under her breath; and just as she said so the light in the basin died out, the head stopped talking, and we heard the room door creak on its hinges. Then Janoo struck a match, lit the lamp, and we saw that head, basin, and seal-cutter were gone. Suddhoo was wringing his hands, and explaining to any one who cared to listen, that if his chances of eternal salvation depended on it, he could not raise another two hundred rupees. Azizun was nearly in hysterics in the corner; while Janoo sat down composedly on one of the beds to discuss the probabilities of the whole thing being a *bunao*, or 'make-up.'

I explained as much as I knew of the seal-cutter's way of *jadoo*; but her argument was much more simple – 'The magic that is always demanding gifts is no true magic,' said she. 'My mother told me that the only potent love-spells are those which are told you for love. This seal-cutter man is a liar and a devil. I dare not tell, do anything, or get anything done, because I am in debt to Bhagwan Dass the *bunnia* for two gold rings and a heavy anklet. I must get my food from his shop. The seal-cutter is the friend of Bhagwan Dass, and he would poison my food. A fool's *jadoo* has been going on for ten days, and has cost Suddhoo many rupees each night. The seal-cutter used black hens and lemons and *mantras* before. He never showed us anything like this till to-night. Azizun is a fool, and will be a *purdahnashin* soon. Suddhoo has lost his strength and his wits. See now! I had hoped to get from Suddhoo many rupees while he lived, and many more after his death; and behold, he is spending everything on that offspring of a devil and a she-ass, the seal-cutter!'

Here I said, 'But what induced Suddhoo to drag me into the business? Of course I can speak to the seal-cutter, and he shall refund. The whole thing is child's talk – shame – and senseless.'

'Suddhoo *is* an old child,' said Janoo. 'He has lived on the roofs these seventy years and is as senseless as a milch-goat. He brought you here to assure himself that he was not breaking any law of the *Sirkar*, whose salt he ate many years ago. He worships the dust off the feet of the seal-cutter, and that cow-devourer has forbidden him to go and see his son. What does Suddhoo know of your laws or the lightning-post? I have to watch his money going day by day to that lying beast below.'

Janoo stamped her foot on the floor and nearly cried with vexation; while Suddhoo was whimpering under a blanket in the corner, and Azizun was trying to guide the pipe-stem to his foolish old mouth.

*

Now, the case stands thus. Unthinkingly, I have laid myself open to the charge of aiding and abetting the seal-cutter in obtaining money under false pretences, which is forbidden by Section 420 of the Indian Penal Code. I am helpless in the matter for these reasons. I cannot inform the Police. What witnesses would support my statements? Janoo refuses flatly, and Azizun is a veiled woman somewhere near Bareilly – lost in this big India of ours. I dare not again take the law into my own hands, and speak to the seal-cutter; for certain am I that, not only would Suddhoo disbelieve me, but this step would end in the poisoning of Janoo, who is bound hand and foot by her debt to the *bunnia*. Suddhoo is an old dotard; and whenever we meet mumbles my idiotic joke that the *Sirkar* rather patronises the Black Art than otherwise. His son is well now; but Suddhoo is completely under the influence of the seal-cutter, by whose advice he regulates the affairs of his life. Janoo watches daily the money that she hoped to wheedle out of Suddhoo taken by the seal-cutter, and becomes daily more furious and sullen.

She will never tell, because she dare not; but, unless something happens to prevent her, I am afraid that the seal-cutter will die of cholera – the white arsenic kind – about the middle of May. And thus I shall be privy to a murder in the House of Suddhoo.

THE BISARA OF POOREE

Little Blind Fish, thou art marvellous wise,
Little Blind Fish, who put out thy eyes?
Open thy ears while I whisper my wish –
Bring me a lover, thou little Blind Fish.

The Charm of the Bisara

Some natives say that it came from the other side of Kulu, where the eleven-inch Temple Sapphire is. Others that it was made at the Devil-Shrine of Ao-Chung in Thibet, was stolen by a Kafir, from him by a Gurkha, from him again by a Lahouli, from him by a *khitmatgar*, and by this latter sold to an Englishman, so all its virtue was lost; because, to work properly, the Bisara of Pooree must be stolen – with bloodshed if possible, but, at any rate, stolen.

These stories of the coming into India are all false. It was made at Pooree ages since – the manner of its making would fill a small book – was stolen by one of the Temple dancing-girls there, for her own purposes, and then passed on from hand to hand, steadily northward, till it reached Hanlé: always bearing the same name – the Bisara of Pooree. In shape it is a tiny square box of silver, studded outside with eight small balas-rubies. Inside the box, which opens with a spring, is a little eyeless fish, carved from some sort of dark, shiny nut and wrapped in a shred of faded gold cloth. That *is* the Bisara of Pooree, and it were better for a man to take a king-cobra in his hand than to touch the Bisara of Pooree.

All kinds of magic are out of date and done away with, except in India, where nothing changes in spite of the shiny, top-scum stuff that people call 'civilisation.' Any man who knows about the Bisara of Pooree will tell you what its powers are – always supposing that it has been honestly stolen. It is the only regularly working, trustworthy love-charm in the country, with one exception. [The other charm is in the hands of a trooper of the Nizam's Horse, at a place called Tuprani, due north of Hyderabad.] This can be depended upon for a fact. Some one else may explain it.

If the Bisara be not stolen, but given or bought or found, it turns against its owner in three years, and leads to ruin or death. This is another fact which you may explain when you have time. Meanwhile, you can laugh at it. At present the Bisara is safe on a hack-pony's neck, inside the blue bead-necklace that keeps off the Evil Eye. If the pony-driver ever finds it, and wears it, or gives it to his wife, I am sorry for him.

A very dirty Hill-coolie woman, with goitre, owned it at Theog in 1884. It came into Simla from the north before Churton's *khitmatgar* bought it, and sold it, for three times its silver-value, to Churton, who collected curiosities. The servant knew no more what he had bought than the master; but a man looking over Churton's collection of curiosities – Churton was an Assistant Commissioner by the way – saw and held his tongue. He was an Englishman, but knew how to believe. Which shows that he was different from most Englishmen. He knew that it was dangerous to have any share in the little box when working or dormant; for Love unsought is a terrible gift.

Pack – 'Grubby' Pack, as we used to call him – was, in every way, a nasty little man who must have crawled into the Army by mistake. He was three inches taller than his sword, but not half so strong. And the sword was a fifty-shilling, tailor-made one. Nobody liked him, and, I suppose, it was his wizenedness and worthlessness that made him fall so hopelessly in love with Miss Hollis, who was good and sweet, and five-feet-seven in her tennis-shoes. He was not content with falling in love quietly, but brought all the strength of his miserable little nature into the business. If he had not been so objectionable, one might have pitied him. He vapoured, and fretted, and fumed, and trotted up and down, and tried to make himself pleasing to Miss Hollis's big, quiet, grey eyes, and failed. It was one of the cases that you sometimes meet, even in our country, where we marry by Code, of a really blind attachment all on one side, without the faintest possibility of return. Miss

Hollis looked on Pack as some sort of vermin running about the road. He had no prospects beyond Captain's pay, and no wits to help that out by one penny. In a large-sized man love like his would have been touching. In a good man it would have been grand. He being what he was, it was only a nuisance.

You will believe this much. What you will not believe is what follows: Churton, and The Man who Knew what the Bisara was, were lunching at the Simla Club together. Churton was complaining of life in general. His best mare had rolled out of stable down the cliff and had broken her back; his decisions were being reversed by the upper Courts more than an Assistant Commissioner of eight years' standing has a right to expect; he knew liver and fever, and for weeks past had felt out of sorts. Altogether, he was disgusted and disheartened.

Simla Club dining-room is built, as all the world knows, in two sections, with an arch-arrangement dividing them. Come in, turn to your own left, take the table under the window, and you cannot see any one who has come in, turned to the right, and taken a table on the right side of the arch. Curiously enough, every word that you say can be heard, not only by the other diner, but by the servants beyond the screen through which they bring dinner. This is worth knowing; an echoing-room is a trap to be forewarned against.

Half in fun, and half hoping to be believed, The Man who Knew told Churton the story of the Bisara of Pooree at rather greater length that I have told it to you in this place; winding up with a suggestion that Churton might as well throw the little box down the hill and see whether all his troubles would go with it. In ordinary ears, English ears, the tale was only an interesting bit of folklore. Churton laughed, said that he felt better for his tiffin, and went out. Pack had been tiffining by himself to the right of the arch, and had heard everything. He was nearly mad with his infatuation for Miss Hollis, that all Simla had been laughing about.

It is a curious thing that, when a man hates or loves beyond reason, he is ready to go beyond reason to gratify his feelings; which he would not do for money or power merely. Depend upon it, Solomon would never have built altars to Ashtaroth and all those ladies with queer names, if there had not been trouble of some kind in his *zenana*, and nowhere else. But this is beside the story. The facts of the case are these: Pack called on Churton next day when Churton was out, left his card, and stole the Bisara of Pooree from its place under the clock on the mantelpiece! Stole it like the thief he was by nature. Three days later all Simla was electrified by the news that Miss Hollis had accepted Pack – the shrivelled rat. Pack! Do you desire clearer evidence than this? The Bisara of Pooree had been stolen, and it worked as it had always done when won by foul means.

There are three or four times in a man's life when he is justified in meddling with other people's affairs to play Providence.

The Man who Knew felt that he was justified; but believing and acting on a belief are quite different things. The insolent satisfaction of Pack as he ambled by the side of Miss Hollis, and Churton's striking release from liver, as soon as the Bisara of Pooree had gone, decided The Man. He explained to Churton, and Churton laughed, because he was not brought up to believe that men on the Government House List steal – at least little things. But the miraculous acceptance by Miss Hollis of that tailor, Pack, decided him to take steps on suspicion. He vowed that he only wanted to find out where his ruby-studded silver box had vanished to. You cannot accuse a man on the Government House List of stealing; and if you rifle his room, you are a thief yourself. Churton, prompted by The Man who Knew, decided on burglary. If he found nothing in Pack's room . . . but it is not nice to think of what would have happened in that case.

Pack went to a dance at Benmore – Benmore was Benmore in those days, and not an office – and danced fifteen waltzes out of twenty-two with Miss Hollis. Churton and The Man took all the keys that they could lay hands on, and went to Pack's room in the hotel, certain that his servants would be away. Pack was a cheap soul. He had not purchased a decent cash-box to keep his papers in, but one of those native imitations that you buy for ten rupees. It opened to any sort of key, and there at the bottom, under Pack's Insurance Policy, lay the Bisara of Pooree!

Churton called Pack names, put the Bisara of Pooree in his pocket, and went to the dance with The Man. At least, he came in time for supper, and saw the beginning of the end in Miss Hollis's eyes. She was hysterical after supper, and was taken away by her Mamma.

At the dance, with the abominable Bisara in his pocket, Churton twisted his foot on one of the steps leading down to the old Rink, and had to be sent home in a rickshaw, grumbling. He did not believe in the Bisara of Pooree any the more for this manifestation, but he sought out Pack and called him some ugly names; and 'thief' was the mildest of them. Pack took the names with the nervous smile of a little man who wants both soul and body to resent an insult, and went his way. There was no public scandal.

A week later Pack got his definite dismissal from Miss Hollis. There had been a mistake in the placing of her affections, she said. So he went away to Madras, where he can do no great harm even if he lives to be a Colonel.

Churton insisted upon The Man who Knew taking the Bisara of Pooree as a gift. The Man took it, went down to the Cart-Road at once, found a cart-pony with a blue bead-necklace, fastened the Bisara of Pooree inside the necklace with a piece of shoe-string and thanked Heaven that he was rid of a danger. Remember, in case you ever find it, that you must not destroy the Bisara of Pooree. I have not time to explain why just now, but the power lies in the little wooden fish. Mister Gubernatis or Max Müller could tell you more about it than I.

You will say that all this story is made up. Very well. If ever you come across a little, silver, ruby-studded box, seven-eighths of an inch long by three-quarters wide, with a dark brown wooden fish, wrapped in gold cloth, inside it, keep it. Keep it for three years, and then you will discover for yourself whether my story is true or false.

Better still, steal it as Pack did, and you will be sorry that you had not killed yourself in the beginning.

HAUNTED SUBALTERNS

So long as the 'Inextinguishables' confined themselves to running picnics, gymkhanas, flirtations and innocences of that kind, no one said anything. But when they ran ghosts, people put up their eyebrows. Man can't feel comfy with a regiment that entertains ghosts on its establishment. It is against General Orders. The 'Inextinguishables' said that the ghosts were private and not Regimental property. They referred you to Tesser for particulars; and Tesser told you to go to – the hottest cantonment of all. He said that it was bad enough to have men making hay of his bedding and breaking his banjo-strings when he was out, without being chaffed afterward; and he would thank you to keep your remarks on ghosts to yourself. This was before the 'Inextinguishables' had sworn by their several lady loves that they were innocent of any intrusion into Tesser's quarters. Then Horrocks mentioned casually at Mess, that a couple of white figures had been bounding about his room the night before, and he didn't approve of it. The 'Inextinguishables' denied, energetically, that they had had any hand in the manifestations, and advised Horrocks to consult Tesser.

I don't suppose that a Subaltern believes in anything except his chances of a Company; but Horrocks and Tesser were exceptions. They came to believe in their ghosts. They had reason.

Horrocks used to find himself, at about three o'clock in the morning, staring wide-awake, watching two white Things hopping about his room and jumping up to the ceiling. Horrocks was of a placid turn of mind. After a week or so spent in watching his servants, and lying in wait for strangers, and trying to keep awake all night, he came to the conclusion that he was haunted, and that, consequently, he need not bother. He wasn't going to encourage these ghosts by being frightened of them. Therefore, when he awoke – as usual – with a start and saw these Things jumping like kangaroos, he only murmured: 'Go on! Don't mind me!' and went to sleep again.

Tesser said: 'It's all very well for you to make fun of your show. You can see your ghosts. Now I can't see mine, and I don't half like it.'

Tesser used to come into his room of nights, and find the whole of his bedding neatly stripped, as if it had been done with one sweep of the hand, from the top right-hand corner of the charpoy to the bottom left-hand corner. Also his lamp used to lie weltering on the floor, and generally his pet screwhead inlaid nickel-plated banjo was lying on the charpoy, with all its strings broken. Tesser took away the strings on the occasion of the third manifestation, and the next night a man complimented him on his playing the best music ever got out of a banjo, for half an hour.

'Which half hour?' said Tesser.

'Between nine and ten,' said the man. Tesser had gone out to dinner at 7:30 and had returned at midnight.

He talked to his bearer and threatened him with unspeakable things. The bearer was grey with fear. 'I'm a poor man,' said he. 'If the *Sahib* is haunted by a Devil, what can I do?'

'Who says I'm haunted by a Devil?' howled Tesser, for he was angry.

'I have seen It,' said the bearer, 'at night, walking round and round your bed; and that is why everything is ultra-pulta in your room. I am a poor man, but I never go into your room alone. The bhisti comes with me.'

Tesser was thoroughly savage at this, and he spoke to Horrocks, and the two laid traps to catch that Devil, and threatened their servants with dog-whips if any more 'shai-tan-ke-hanky-panky' took place. But the servants were soaked with fear, and it was no use adding to their tortures. When Tesser went out for a night, four of his men, as a rule, slept in the veranda of his quarters, until the banjo without the strings struck up, and then they fled.

One day, Tesser had to put in a month at a Fort with a detachment of 'Inextinguishables.' The Fort might have been Govindghar, Jumrood or Phillour; but it wasn't. He left Cantonments rejoicing, for his Devil was preying on his mind; and with him went another Subaltern, a junior. But the Devil came too. After Tesser had been in the Fort about ten days he went out to dinner. When he came back he found his Subaltern doing sentry on a banquette across the Fort Ditch, as far removed as might be from the Officers' Quarters.

'What's wrong?' said Tesser.

The Subaltern said, 'Listen!' and the two, standing under the stars, heard from the Officers' Quarters, high up in the wall of the Fort, the 'strumpy, tumty, tumpty' of the banjo; which seemed to have an oratorio on hand.

'That performance,' said the Subaltern, 'has been going on for three mortal hours. I never wished to desert before, but I do now. I say, Tesser, old man, you are the best of good fellows, I'm sure, but . . . I say . . . look here, now, you are quite unfit to live with. 'Tisn't in my Commission, you know, that I'm to serve under a . . . a . . . man with Devils.'

'Isn't it?' said Tesser. 'If you make an ass of yourself I'll put you under arrest . . . and in my room!'

'You can put me where you please, but I'm not going to assist at these infernal concerts. 'Tisn't right. 'Tisn't natural. Look here, I don't want to hurt your feelings, but – try to think now – haven't you done something – committed some – murder that has slipped your memory – or forged something . . . ?'

'Well! For an all-round, double-shotted, half-baked fool you are the . . .'

'I dare say I am,' said the Subaltern. 'But you don't expect me to keep my wits with that row going on, do you?'

The banjo was rattling away as if it had twenty strings. Tesser sent up a stone, and a shower of broken window-pane fell into the Fort Ditch; but the banjo kept on. Tesser hauled the Subaltern up to the quarters, and found his room in frightful confusion – lamp upset, bedding all over the floor, chairs overturned and table tilted sideways. He took stock of the wreck and said despairingly: 'Oh, this is lovely!'

The Subaltern was peeping in at the door.

'I'm glad you think so,' he said, 'Tisn't lovely enough for me. I locked up your room directly after you had gone out. See here, I think you'd better apply for Horrocks to come out in my place. He's troubled with your complaint, and this business will make me a jabbering idiot if it goes on.'

Tesser went to bed amid the wreckage, very angry, and next morning he rode into Cantonments and asked Horrocks to arrange to relieve 'that fool with me now.'

'You've got 'em again, have you?' said Horrocks. 'So've I. Three white figures this time. We'll worry through the entertainment together.'

So Horrocks and Tesser settled down in the Fort altogether, and the 'Inextinguishables' said pleasant things about 'seven other Devils.' Tesser didn't see where the joke came in. His room was thrown upside down three nights out of the seven. Horrocks was not troubled in any way, so his ghosts must have been purely local ones. Tesser, on the other hand, was personally haunted; for his Devil had moved with him from Cantonments to the Fort. Those two boys spent three parts of their time trying to find out who was responsible for the riot in Tesser's rooms. At the end of a fortnight they tried to find out what was responsible; and seven days later they gave it up as a bad job. Whatever It was, It refused to be caught; even when Tesser went out of the Fort ostentatiously, and Horrocks lay under Tesser's charpoy with a revolver. The servants were afraid – more afraid than ever – and all the evidence showed that they had been playing no tricks. As Tesser said to Horrocks: 'A haunted Subaltern is a joke, but s'pose this keeps on. Just think what a haunted Colonel would be! And, look here – s'pose I marry! D' you s'pose a girl would live a week with me and this Devil?'

'I don't know,' said Horrocks. 'I haven't married often; but I knew a woman once who lived with her husband when he had D.T. He's dead now and I dare say she would marry you if you asked her. She isn't exactly a girl though, but she has a large experience of the other devils – the blue variety. She's a Government pension now, and you might write, y'know. Personally, if I hadn't suffered from ghosts of my own, I should rather avoid you.'

'That's just the point,' said Tesser. 'This Devil will end in getting me budnamed, and you know I've lived on lemon-squashes and gone to bed at ten for weeks past.'

' 'Tisn't that sort of Devil,' said Horrocks. 'It's either a first-class fraud for which some one ought to be killed or else you've offended one of these Indian Devils. It stands to reason that such a beastly country should be full of fiends of all sorts.'

'But why should the creature fix on me,' said Tesser, 'and why won't he show himself and have it out like a – like a Devil?'

They were talking outside the Mess after dark, and even as they spoke, they heard the banjo begin to play in Tesser's room, about twenty yards off.

Horrocks ran to his own quarters for a shot-gun and a revolver, and Tesser and he crept up quietly, the banjo still playing, to Tesser's door.

'Now we've got It!' said Horrocks, as he threw the door open and let fly with the twelve-bore; Tesser squibbing off all six barrels into the dark, as hard as he could pull the trigger.

The furniture was ruined, and the whole Fort was awake; but that was all. No one had been killed and the banjo was lying on the dishevelled bedclothes as usual.

Then Tesser sat down in the veranda, and used language that would have qualified him for the companionship of unlimited Devils. Horrocks said things too; but Tesser said the worst.

When the month in the Fort came to an end, both Horrocks and Tesser were glad. They held a final council of war, but came to no conclusion.

' 'Seems to me, your best plan would be to make your Devil stretch himself. Go down to Bombay with the time-expired men,' said Horrocks. 'If he really is a Devil, he'll come in the train with you.'

' 'Tisn't good enough,' said Tesser. 'Bombay's no fit place to live in at this time of the year. But I'll put him in for Depôt duty at the Hills.' And he did.

Now here the tale rests. The Devil stayed below, and Tesser went up and was free. If I had invented this story, I should have put in a satisfactory ending – explained the manifestations as somebody's practical joke. My business being to keep to facts, I can only say what I have said. The Devil may have been a hoax. If so, it was one of the best ever arranged. If it was not a hoax . . . but you must settle that for yourselves.

BY WORD OF MOUTH

Not though you die to-night, O Sweet, and wail,
    A spectre at my door.
Shall mortal Fear make Love immortal fail –
    I shall but love you more,
Who, from Death's house returning, give me still
One moment's comfort in my matchless ill.

Shadow Houses

This tale may be explained by those who know how souls are made, and where the bounds of the Possible are put down. I have lived long enough in this India to know that it is best to know nothing, and can only write the story as it happened.

Dumoise was our Civil Surgeon at Meridki, and we called him 'Dormouse,' because he was a round little, sleepy little man. He was a good Doctor and never quarrelled with any one, not even with our Deputy Commissioner who had the manners of a bargee and the tact of a horse. He married a girl as round and as sleepy-looking as himself. She was a Miss Hillardyce, daughter of 'Squash' Hillardyce of the Berars, who married his Chief's daughter by mistake. But that is another story.

A honeymoon in India is seldom more than a week long; but there is nothing to hinder a couple from extending it over two or three years. India is a delightful country for married folk who are wrapped up in one another. They can live absolutely alone and without interruption – just as the Dormice did. Those two little people retired from the world after their marriage, and were very happy. They were forced, of course, to give occasional dinners, but they made no friends thereby, and the Station went its own way and forgot them; only saying, occasionally, that Dormouse was the best of good fellows though dull. A Civil Surgeon who never quarrels is a rarity, appreciated as such.

95

Few people can afford to play Robinson Crusoe anywhere – least of all in India, where we are few in the land and very much dependent on each other's kind offices. Dumoise was wrong in shutting himself from the world for a year, and he discovered his mistake when an epidemic of typhoid broke out in the Station in the heart of the cold weather, and his wife went down. He was a shy little man, and five days were wasted before he realised that Mrs Dumoise was burning with something worse than simple fever, and three days more passed before he ventured to call on Mrs Shute, the Engineer's wife, and timidly speak about his trouble. Nearly every household in India knows that Doctors are very helpless in typhoid. The battle must be fought out between Death and the Nurses minute by minute and degree by degree. Mrs Shute almost boxed Dumoise's ears for what she called his 'criminal delay,' and went off at once to look after the poor girl. We had seven cases of typhoid in the Station that winter and, as the average of death is about one in every five cases, we felt certain that we should have to lose somebody. But all did their best. The women sat up nursing the women, and the men turned to and tended the bachelors who were down, and we wrestled with those typhoid cases for fifty-six days, and brought them through the Valley of the Shadow in triumph. But, just when we thought all was over, and were going to give a dance to celebrate the victory, little Mrs Dumoise got a relapse and died in a week, and the Station went to the funeral. Dumoise broke down utterly at the brink of the grave, and had to be taken away.

After the death Dumoise crept into his own house and refused to be comforted. He did his duties perfectly, but we all felt that he should go on leave, and the other men of his own Service told him so. Dumoise was very thankful for the suggestion – he was thankful for anything in those days – and went to Chini on a walking-tour. Chini is some twenty marches from Simla, in the heart of the Hills, and the scenery is good if you are in trouble. You pass through big, still deodar forests, and under big, still cliffs, and over big, still grass-downs swelling like a woman's breasts; and the wind across the grass, and the rain among the deodars say – 'Hush – hush – hush.' So little Dumoise was packed off to Chini, to wear down his grief with a full-plate camera and a rifle. He took also a useless bearer, because the man had been his wife's favourite servant. He was idle and a thief, but Dumoise trusted everything to him.

On his way back from Chini, Dumoise turned aside to Bagi, through the Forest Reserve which is on the spur of Mount Huttoo. Some men who have travelled more than a little say that the march from Kotegarh to Bagi is one of the finest in creation. It runs through dark wet forest, and ends suddenly in bleak, nipped hillside and black rocks. Bagi dâk-bungalow is open to all the winds and is bitterly cold. Few people go to Bagi. Perhaps that was the reason why Dumoise went there. He halted at seven in the evening, and his bearer went down the hillside to the village to engage coolies for the next day's march. The sun had set, and the night-winds were beginning to croon among the rocks. Dumoise leaned on the railing of the verandah, waiting for his bearer to return. The man came back almost immediately after he had disappeared, and at such a rate that Dumoise fancied he must have crossed a bear. He was running as hard as he could up the face of the hill.

But there was no bear to account for his terror. He raced to the verandah and fell down, the blood spurting from his nose and his face iron-grey. Then he gurgled – 'I have seen the *Memsahib!* I have seen the *Memsahib!*'

'Where?' said Dumoise.

'Down there, walking on the road to the village. She was in a blue dress, and she lifted the veil of her bonnet and said – "Ram Dass, give my *salaams* to the *Sahib*, and tell him that I shall meet him next month at Nuddea." Then I ran away, because I was afraid.'

What Dumoise said or did I do not know. Ram Dass declares that he said nothing, but walked up and down the verandah all the cold night, waiting for the *Memsahib* to come up the hill, and stretching out his arms into the dark like a madman. But no *Memsahib* came, and, next day, he went on to Simla cross-questioning the bearer every hour.

Ram Dass could only say that he had met Mrs Dumoise, and that she had lifted up her veil and given him the message which he had faithfully repeated to Dumoise. To this statement Ram Dass adhered. He did not know where Nuddea was, had no friends at Nuddea, and would most certainly never go to Nuddea, even though his pay were doubled.

Nuddea is in Bengal, and has nothing whatever to do with a Doctor serving in the Punjab. It must be more than twelve hundred miles south of Meridki.

Dumoise went through Simla without halting, and returned to Meridki, there to take over charge from the man who had been officiating for him during his tour. There were some Dispensary accounts to be explained, and some recent orders of the Surgeon-General to be noted, and, altogether, the taking-over was a full day's work. In the evening Dumoise told his *locum tenens*, who was an old friend of his bachelor days, what had happened at Bagi; and the man said that Ram Dass might as well have chosen Tuticorin while he was about it.

At that moment a telegraph-peon came in with a telegram from Simla, ordering Dumoise not to take over charge at Meridki, but to go at once to Nuddea on special duty. There was a nasty outbreak of cholera at Nuddea, and the Bengal Government being short-handed, as usual, had borrowed a Surgeon from the Punjab.

Dumoise threw the telegram across the table and said – 'Well?'

The other Doctor said nothing. It was all that he could say.

Then he remembered that Dumoise had passed through Simla on his way from Bagi; and thus might, possibly have heard first news of the impending transfer.

He tried to put the question and the implied suspicion into words, but Dumoise stopped him with – 'If I had desired *that*, I should never have come back from Chini. I was shooting there. I wish to live, for I have things to do . . . but I shall not be sorry.'

The other man bowed his head, and helped, in the twilight to pack up Dumoise's just opened trunks. Ram Dass entered with the lamps.

'Where is the *Sahib* going?' he asked.

'To Nuddea,' said Dumoise softly.

Ram Dass clawed Dumoise's knees and boots and begged him not to go. Ram Dass wept and howled till he was turned out of the room. Then he wrapped up all his belongings and came back to ask for a character. He was not going to Nuddea to see his *Sahib* die and, perhaps, to die himself.

So Dumoise gave the man his wages and went down to Nuddea alone, the other Doctor bidding him good-bye as one under sentence of death.

Eleven days later he had joined his *Memsahib*; and the Bengal Government had to borrow a fresh Doctor to cope with that epidemic at Nuddea. The first importation lay dead in Chooadanga dâk-Bungalow.

THE RECURRING SMASH

In himself, Penhelder was not striking. His worst enemies did not call him ugly, and his best friends handsome. But friends and enemies alike were interested in his Fate, which was unique. When he was three years old, he interrupted some moving operations with a pair of mottled chubby legs and bled, as his nurse said at the time 'all round the hay-field in quarts'. In his sixth year, he started on a voyage across the horse-pond: his galley being a crank hurdle, which, in mid-ocean, turned turtle, and but for the pig-killer, who happened to pass that way, he would certainly have been drowned. At nine years of age, he sat upon a wall like Humpty-Dumpty – a high wall meant to protect an apple-orchard – and like Humpty Dumpty, fell, fracturing his collar bone. About this time, his family noticed the peculiarity of his Fate and commented upon it. Three years later, being at a Public School, Penhelder dropped from the trapeze in the gymnasium and broke one of the small bones in his leg. It was then discovered that every one of his previous accidents had occurred between the months of May and June. Penhelder was apprised of this and bidden to behave more seemly in the future. His conduct was without flaw or reproach till his fifteenth year, when the school dormitories caught fire and Penhelder, escaping in his nightgown, was severely burnt on the back and legs. He enjoyed the honour of being the only boy who had been touched by the flames. This saddened him and his family, but more especially his old nurse, who maintained that 'her boy', as she lovingly called Penhelder, was 'cast' – a provincialism for bewitched. At eighteen he found himself in London. What he did then does not come into this story.

The end of a thirsty summer night, and indulgence in waters, to Penhelder, of entirely unknown strength, was, for some hours, a felon's cell and 'forty shillings or a month'. With the guilelessness of youth Penhelder had given his real name, and had the satisfaction of seeing it not only in the police reports of *The Times* but – and here the type was used much larger than his modesty demanded – in the market town weekly newspaper as well. It may be mentioned that Penhelder was the only one caught of a riotous gang. At one and twenty, Penhelder set foot in India, a solemn and serious boy, whose mind had been darkened by the shadow of his Fate. He was overheard by a man who afterwards came to know him intimately, muttering, as he set foot on the Apollo Bunder in the blazing May sunshine: 'I hope it won't be anything *very* serious'. It was not, but the Doctor said that it might have been *most* serious; and that young men who paraded Bombay in small hats deserved instant death instead of severe sunstroke merely.

Penhelder crept up-country to his station, and, in a weak moment told the story of his Fate even more circumstantially than has been set forth here. From that day he became an object of unholy interest to the gilded youth of the Army within a two hundred mile radius. They looked, like the islanders of Melita, that he should 'fall down dead suddenly', but their watch was in vain.

Late June of his twenty-fourth year saw Penhelder almost the sole occupant of a deserted station. But there were witnesses to attest the strange tale that follows. At dinner at the Club, one of the glass shades of a hanging lamp cracked with the heat, and a huge fragment fell hatchetwise across Penhelder's left wrist, cutting it to the bone. 'I told you so', said Penhelder drearily, as the blood spurted over the tablecloth. The rest of the Company held their peace, for they remembered that for the past month Penhelder had been prophesying disaster of some sort to himself. The wound was a serious one and nearly ended in blood poisoning.

Three years later, Penhelder took warning in time, and as May drew near, retired into his own house and lived then the life of an eremite. 'If anything happens now', said he, 'it will be the roof falling in, and I don't mind that. It will put me out of my misery'. But Penhelder had miscalculated. In summer it is necessary to drive to office. Penhelder hired an enormous ticca-gharri of dutch gallest beam, and unquestioned solidity, and yoked thereto the soberest horses that he could find. The turnout something resembled an ambulance in search of wounded, but Penhelder was deaf to the voice of sarcasm. What he demanded was safety. He secured it. It took him half an hour to reach his office, but he secured it. June had nearly ended and, in his delight, he stopped, ere going into his office, to pat the neck of one of the horses. There is a hideous description in *Lorna Doone* of great John Ridd tearing out the muscle of his enemy's arm as though it had been orange pulp. The horse, indeed, tore out nothing, but he clung like a leech to the inner arm of Penhelder, high up and close to the armpit. A lighted match forced him to open his jaws, but Penhelder had fainted, and it was then months before he mixed with his friends – a moody, melancholy man, perplexed with the fore-shadowing of his next visitation. 'It's not murder I object to', said Penhelder, 'it's mangling'.

Time, chance and the Government parted me from Penhelder for many years, and he gradually faded out of my mind. But we met at Bombay a few weeks ago. I was introduced to Mrs Penhelder, a large lady. My friend's face was drawn and haggard. I learnt that he was going Home for his health's sake. 'Have you – have you', I whispered 'had any return of – broken your run of bad luck that is to say?' Penhelder hesitated for a moment. Then he drew me aside, 'I've broken it', he said, 'But I married *her* on my thirtieth birthday. May the twenty-second it was'. And since that date I have in vain been trying to discover what on earth my friend Penhelder meant.

THE DREITARBUND

As a conspiracy it was infamous, and in the hands of un-scrupulous men might have been dangerous, seeing how foolish women-folk are.

But, worked with circumspection, as Houligan, Marlowe and Bressil worked it, it secured to three dear sweet girls with money, the right of paying Houligan's, Marlowe's and Bressil's bills for the rest of their days; and, as every one knows, all is fair in love or war. Houligan claimed and was allowed the honour of the Inspiration; Marlowe put fifty rupees into the pool, because he chanced to be the millionaire of the month; Bressil, like Mr Gigadibs, was a 'literary man' with no morals but exquisite tact, knowledge of fitting opportunity, which was more than the money or the idea. He was the Napoleon of the Bund, and his contribution was a book, in two volumes, called *Phantasms of the Living*, written by some of the members of the Psychical Research Society. Houligan had an Indian Tele-graph Guide, and on this library and the fifty rupees, the Bund opened the campaign. Two men united can do a great deal, but a threefold cord can draw Heaven and Earth together.

The Bund was desperately poor, and, collectively, had not enough good features in it to make up one handsome count-enance to go wooing with. It was unlucky in its love-affairs, for it failed to interest young women; and, even when it did, the parents said that it had better work and earn twelve hundred a month before calling again. On occasions like these, the Bund used to smoke vehemently and arrange for a revenge. Houligan's ambition was to drive over Miss Norris's father in his dogcart; Marlowe desired to poison Miss Emmett's mamma; and Bressil, like Job, wished that Miss Yaulton's brother-in-law had written a book. But what they wanted most was honourable matrimony with Miss Norris, Miss Emmett and Miss Yaulton. All their angry feelings died away when the Bund was formed, quietly and without ostentation, on strictly practical lines and in thorough accordance with the principles laid down in *Phantasms of the Living* – Vide the chapter on Thought Transference, Brain-waves, Percipients and people of that kind. Houligan said that it was one thing to tell a girl that you were fond of her, when you were by her side, but that it was quite another, and a much more startling thing to prove, that you were fond of her when you were miles away. Once started, at Bressil's instigation the Bund quarrelled violently and in public, broke up its chummery, and was dead cuts to the great interest of the Station. Everything, even down to the perverted English to be used for the communications, was cut and dried, and there was no further need of personal intercourse. The Bund devoted itself to laying siege to its chosen maidens in a dark and mysterious sort of way that made the latter laugh.

Houligan was transferred to a Station three hundred miles away, and Miss Norris laughed when she said goodbye. The type of Houligan's love-making has not been made public. Miss Norris said that he used to talk strangely. She held to her opinion till she was attacked by a rather severe fever, after over-exertion at tennis, on a Friday afternoon. Twenty-four hours later, being then in bed, she received a hurried letter from Houligan, explaining that an 'overmastering presentiment' – that was the wrong word, but Houligan could never make head or tail of *Phantasms of the Living* – compelled him to write to her and ask if any trouble had overtaken her on Friday evening. He had had a feeling, an idea that she had suddenly fallen ill – had put the feeling from him as absurd, &c., but it had returned, &c. He was her devoted slave, and apologised for thus troubling here. From that date onward, Miss Norris never referred to the strangeness of her lover's talk. She only wondered; told her parents, who wondered too, and thought a great deal of Houligan. Miss Emmett was of a different type from Miss Norris. She was nervous and hysterical by birth, and Marlowe always thought that her parents might have been won round in time. But another man appeared and began to make love to her – he was a man from the North-West – and the Emmetts were going to spend the summer at Naini Tal. Time and propinquity in a case like Miss Emmett meant everything. By this time, it should be explained, the pool stood at nearly four hundred rupees – the result of monthly contributions. There had been a drain upon it for Houligan's benefit, in 'private deferred' wires sketching the daily life of Miss Norris by the words of the Code – a lithographed MS, of seven hundred and thirty-two pages, compiled with extraordinary care. None the less, the pool kept up to an average of four hundred. Marlowe took it all and thrust it into Bressil's hands, begging him to go to Naini Tal for ten days and draw on the pool if the money ran out. Bressil went when the Emmets moved, and Marlowe had said farewell to Miss Emmett, who was hesitating between her two admirers. Bressil was a genius in his ideas of combinations. After four days, he sent Marlowe a huge telegram, giving him the outlines of the action to take; and then began to beg and beseech Miss Emmett for a dance, at the next ball, which he well knew was a running one, given for the season to Marlowe's rival. This sort of petition can be renewed at any time and hour, and unless she be bored to death, the petitioner is always pleased. Bressil renewed his request twice in one day. At dinner, his seat faced the door, he said, *Apropos* of nothing in particular, for the third time: – 'Will you give me number seven. Miss Emmett?' As he spoke, and as Miss Emmett was bridling, a servant put a telegram on her plate. She read it and began to scream, for the telegram was from Marlowe, and it said: – 'No. To me and I'll sit out with you in the spirit.' Miss Emmett did not go to that dance. She was afraid – afraid of everything, but of Marlowe most of all. He followed up the telegram by a letter, many pages long, and was accepted by return of post. Miss Emmett was nervous and hysterical, but she made a good wife; and her parents were very respectful to Marlowe. They quoted a play called *Ingomar and Parthenia*, and also said that there were 'more things in Heaven and Earth than were dreamt of in their philosophy.'

Houligan never had the heart to indulge in another 'presentiment'. He wooed on his own merits after Miss Norris's fever; but was accepted chiefly on account of the presentiment. Miss Norris was a healthy young lady, but she was deeply touched by the idea of a man who watched over her from afar. So were her parents. These two couples married, and Bressil was left to make way with Miss Yaulton, who was a most difficult maiden. She believed in 'missions', and 'spheres', and 'destinies', and held that her destiny was to drift away from Bressil and become a 'woman working for women' at Home. She was different from the average of Anglo-Indian girls. She said Bressel was a 'very dear friend', but she could never marry him; for his work lay in India and hers in England. They met on a high and spiritual platform, which was not what Bressil wanted. Then they parted for no earthly reason, except Miss Yaulton's ideas; and Bressil was miserable. Houligan and Marlowe had taken their wives Home, and were beginning to be loved for themselves and not for their mediumistic attainments. Bressil assumed that the Dreitarbund was dead. He had helped Houligan and Marlowe to their wives, and Fate had not put them in a position to help him. That was all. The pool was empty and the Codes were lost. All that remained to him was Miss Yaulton's address. But the Dreitarbund was only suspended for a while. The Houligans met Miss Yaulton at a big country-house in Wiltshire. She had not found her mission or sphere, nor had she forgotten Bressil. There was a riding-party over the downs, and Miss Yaulton, being, as you will have seen by this time, as obstinate as a mule, insisted on riding a big black horse that was not fit for a lady. In consequence, she was bolted with and nearly thrown.

For this reason she announced her intention of riding the brute next morning, though all the house tried to dissuade her.

Houligan was not a clever man, but he fancied that he recognised in this the finger of Providence. He went away to the nearest town – a small one – and paralysed the local telegraph office by pouring in a Foreign Telegram, the like of which had never been seen by the telegraph officials before. He spilt his words like water that nothing should be misunderstood, and paid for repetitions in a princely style. Altogether he spent £15-10 on the telegram, and alluded to many things beside the horse. No one knows what Bressil thought on receipt of it. He may have struggled with himself against the meanness of the trick, or he may not. He delayed several hours in sending his answer. At breakfast next morning in the Wiltshire country-house. Miss Yaulton, booted and habited, received Bressil's message: – 'For Heaven's sake don't ride *Dandy*.' She did not. She took the telegram into her own room and recast her ideas on all 'missions and destinies' independent of Bressil. She also was awed; but her awe was different from the nervous dread of Miss Emmett, or the frightened bewilderment of Miss Norris. She sent back a three-word telegram to Bressil that drew him to England and then . . . and then the Dreitarbund really died.

Houligan admits the immorality in the abstract of the work of the Bund. But he says that other Bunds have been much worse, and that 'if the Psychical Research Society pops a good notion into your head, why on earth shouldn't you work it out?'

BUBBLING WELL ROAD

Look out on a large scale map the place where the Chenab river falls into the Indus fifteen miles or so above the hamlet of Chachuran. Five miles west of Chachuran lives Bubbling Well Road, and the house of the *gosain* or priest of Arti-goth. It was the priest who showed me the road, but it is no thanks to him that I am able to tell this story.

Five miles west of Chachuran is a patch of the plumed jungle-grass, that turns over in silver when the wind blows, from ten to twenty feet high and from three to four miles square. In the heart of the patch hides the *gosain* of Bubbling Well Road. The villagers stone him when he peers into the daylight, although he is a priest, and he runs back again as a strayed wolf turns into tall crops. He is a one-eyed man and carries, burnt between his brows, the impress of two copper coins. Some say that he was tortured by a native prince in the old days; for he is so old that he must have been capable of mischief in the days of Runjit Singh. His most pressing need at present is a halter, and the care of the British Government.

These things happened when the jungle-grass was tall; and the villagers of Chachuran told me that a sounder of pig had gone into the Arti-goth patch. To enter jungle-grass is always an unwise proceeding, but I went, partly because I knew nothing of pig-hunting, and partly because the villagers said that the big boar of the sounder owned foot long tushes. Therefore I wished to shoot him, in order to produce the tushes in after years, and say that I had ridden him down in fair chase. I took a gun and went into the hot, close patch, believing that it would be an easy thing to unearth one pig in ten square miles of jungle. Mr Wardle, the terrier, went with me because he believed that I was incapable of existing for an hour without his advice and countenance. He managed to slip in and out between the grass clumps, but I had to force my way, and in twenty minutes was as completely lost as though I had been in the heart of Central Africa. I did not notice this at first till I had grown wearied of stumbling and pushing through the grass, and Mr Wardle was beginning to sit down very often and hang out his tongue very far. There was nothing but grass everywhere, and it was impossible to see two yards in any direction. The grass stems held the heat exactly as boiler-tubes do.

In half an hour, when I was devoutly wishing that I had left the big boar alone, I came to a narrow path which seemed to be a compromise between a native foot-path and a pig-run. It was barely six inches wide, but I could sidle along it in comfort. The grass was extremely thick here, and where the path was ill defined it was necessary to crush into the tussocks either with both hands before the face, or to back into it, leaving both hands free to manage the rifle. None the less it was a path, and valuable because it might lead to a place.

At the end of nearly fifty yards of fair way, just when I was preparing to back into an unusually stiff tussock, I missed Mr Wardle, who for his girth is an unusually frivolous dog and never keeps to heel. I called him three times and said aloud, 'Where has the little beast gone to?' Then I stepped backwards several paces, for almost under my feet a deep voice repeated, 'Where has the little beast gone?' To appreciate an unseen voice thoroughly you should hear it when you are lost in stifling jungle grass. I called Mr Wardle again and the underground echo assisted me. At that I ceased calling and listened very attentively, because I thought I heard a man laughing in a peculiarly offensive manner. The heat made me sweat, but the laughter made me shake. There is no earthly need for laughter in high grass. It is indecent, as well as impolite. The chuckling stopped, and I took courage and continued to call till I thought that I had located the echo somewhere behind and below the tussock into which I was preparing to back just before I lost Mr Wardle. I drove my rifle up to the triggers between the grass-stems in a downward and forward direction. Then I waggled it to and fro, but it did not seem to touch ground on the far side of the tussock as it should have done. Every time that I grunted with the exertion of driving a heavy rifle through thick grass, the grunt was faithfully repeated from below, and when I stopped to wipe my face the sound of low laughter was distinct beyond doubting.

I went into the tussock, face first, an inch at a time, my mouth open and my eyes fine, full, and prominent. When I had overcome the resistance of the grass I found that I was looking straight across a black gap in the ground. That I was actually lying on my chest leaning over the mouth of a well so deep I could scarcely see the water in it.

There were things in the water, – black things, – and the water was as black as pitch with blue scum atop. The laughing sound came from the noise of a little spring, spouting halfway down one side of the well. Sometimes as the black things circled round, the trickle from the spring fell upon their tightly-stretched skins, and then the laughter changed into a sputter of mirth. One thing turned over on its back, as I watched, and drifted round and round the circle of the mossy brickwork with a hand and half an arm held clear of the water in a stiff and horrible flourish, as though it were a very wearied guide paid to exhibit the beauties of the place.

I did not spend more than half-an-hour in creeping round that well and finding the path on the other side. The remainder of the journey I accomplished by feeling every foot of ground in front of me, and crawling like a snail through every tussock. I carried Mr Wardle in my arms and he licked my nose. He was not frightened in the least, nor was I, but we wished to reach open ground in order to enjoy the view. My knees were loose, and the apple in my throat refused to slide up and down. The path on the far side of the well was a very good one, though boxed in on all sides by grass, and it led me in time to a priest's hut in the centre of a little clearing. When that priest saw my very white face coming through the grass he howled with terror and embraced my boots; but when I reached the bedstead set outside his door I sat down quickly and Mr Wardle mounted guard over me. I was not in a condition to take care of myself.

When I awoke I told the priest to lead me into the open, out of the Arti-goth patch and to walk slowly in front of me. Mr Wardle hates natives, and the priest was more afraid of Mr Wardle than of me, though we were both angry. He walked very slowly down a narrow little path from his hut. That path crossed three paths, such as the one I had come by in the first instance, and every one of the three headed towards the Bubbling Well. Once when we stopped to draw breath, I heard the Well laughing to itself alone in the thick grass, and only my need for his services prevented my firing both barrels into the priest's back.

When we came to the open the priest crashed back into cover, and I went to the village of Arti-goth for a drink. It was pleasant to be able to see the horizon all round, as well as the ground underfoot.

The villagers told me that the patch of grass was full of devils and ghosts, all in the service of the priest, and that men and women and children had entered it and had never returned. They said the priest used their livers for purposes of witchcraft. When I asked why they had not told me of this at the outset, they said that they were afraid they would lose their reward for bringing news of the pig.

Before I left I did my best to set the patch alight, but the grass was too green. Some fine summer day, however, if the wind is favourable, a file of old newspapers and a box of matches will make clear the mystery of Bubbling Well Road.

THE SENDING OF DANA DA

When the Devil rides on your chest remember the low-caste man.
Native Proverb

Once upon a time, some people in India made a new Heaven
and a new Earth out of broken teacups, a missing brooch or
two, and a hairbrush. These were hidden under bushes, or
stuffed into holes in the hillside, and an entire Civil Service of
subordinate Gods used to find or mend them again; and every
one said: 'There are more things in Heaven and Earth than are
dreamt of in our philosophy.' Several other things happened
also, but the Religion never seemed to get much beyond its
first manifestations; though it added an air-line postal service
and orchestral effects in order to keep abreast of the times and
choke off competition.

This Religion was too elastic for ordinary use. It stretched
itself and embraced pieces of everything that the medicine-
men of all ages have manufactured. It approved of and stole
from Freemasonry; looted the Latter-day Rosicrucians of half
their pet words; took any fragments of Egyptian philosophy
that it found in the *Encyclopaedia Britannica*; annexed as many
of the Vedas as had been translated into French or English,
and talked of all the rest; built in the German versions of what
is left of the Zend Avesta; encouraged White, Grey, and Black
Magic, including spiritualism, palmistry, fortune-telling by
cards, hot chestnuts, double-kernelled nuts, and tallow drop-
pings; would have adopted Voodoo and Obeah had it known
anything about them, and showed itself, in every way, one of
the most accommodating arrangements that had ever been
invented since the birth of the Sea.

When it was in thorough working order, with all the
machinery, down to the subscriptions, complete, Dana Da

came from nowhere, with nothing in his hands, and wrote a chapter in its history which has hitherto been unpublished. He said that his first name was Dana, and his second was Da. Now, setting aside Dana of the *New York Sun*, Dana is a Bhil name, and Da fits no native of India unless you accept the Bengali De as theoriginal spelling. Da is Lap or Finnish; and Dana Da was neither Finn, Chin, Bhil, Bengali, Lap, Nair, Gond, Romany, Magh, Bokhariot, Kurd, Armenian, Levantine, Jew, Persian, Punjabi, Madrasi, Parsee, nor anything else known to ethnologists. He was simply Dana Da, and declined to give further information. For the sake of brevity and as roughly indicating his origin, he was called 'The Native'. He might have been the original Old Man of the Mountains, who is said to be the only authorised Head of the Tea-cup Creed. Some people said that he was; but Dana Da used to smile and deny any connection with the cult, explaining that he was an 'Independent Experimenter'.

As I have said, he came from nowhere, with his hands behind his back, and studied the Creed for three weeks, sitting at the feet of those best competent to explain its mysteries. Then he laughed aloud and went away, but the laugh might have been either of devotion or derision.

When he returned he was without money, but his pride was unabated. He declared that he knew more about the Things in Heaven and Earth than those who taught him, and for this contumacy was abandoned altogether.

His next appearance in public life was at a big cantonment in Upper India, and he was then telling fortunes with the help of three leaden dice, a very dirty old cloth, and a little tin box of opium pills. He told better fortunes when he was allowed half a bottle of whisky; but the things which he invented on the opium were quite worth the money. He was in reduced circumstances. Among other people's he told the fortune of an Englishman who had once been interested in the Simla Creed, but who, later on, had married and forgotten all his old knowledge in the study of babies and things. The Englishman allowed Dana Da to tell a fortune for charity's sake, and gave him five rupees, a dinner, and some old clothes. When he had eaten, Dana Da professed gratitude, and asked if there were anything he could do for his host – in the esoteric line.

'Is there any one that you love?' said Dana Da. The Englishman loved his wife, but had no desire to drag her name into the conversation. He therefore shook his head.

'Is there any one that you hate?' said Dana Da. The Englishman said that there were several men whom he hated deeply.

'Very good,' said Dana Da, upon whom the whisky and the opium were beginning to tell. 'Only give me their names, and I will despatch a Sending to them and kill them.'

Now a Sending is a horrible arrangement, first invented, they say, in Iceland. It is a Thing sent by a wizard, and may take any form, but, most generally, wanders about the land in the shape of a little purple cloud till it finds the Sendee, and him it kills by changing into the form of a horse, or a cat, or a man without a face. It is not strictly a native patent, though *chamars* of the skin and hide castes can, if irritated, despatch a Sending which sits on the breast of their enemy by night and nearly kills him. Very few natives care to irritate *chamars* for this reason.

'Let me despatch a Sending,' said Dana Da. 'I am nearly dead now with want, and drink, and opium; but I should like to kill a man before I die. I can send a Sending anywhere you choose, and in any form except in the shape of a man.'

The Englishman had no friends that he wished to kill, but partly to soothe Dana Da, whose eyes were rolling, and partly to see what would be done, he asked whether a modified Sending could not be arranged for – such a Sending as should make a man's life a burden to him, and yet do him no harm. If this were possible, he notified his willingness to give Dana Da ten rupees for the job.

'I am not what I was once,' said Dana Da, 'and I must take the money because I am poor. To what Englishman shall I send it?'

'Send a Sending to Lone Sahib,' said the Englishman, naming a man who had been most bitter in rebuking him for his apostasy from the Tea-cup Creed. Dana Da laughed and nodded.

'I could have chosen no better man myself,' said he. 'I will see that he finds the Sending about his path and about his bed.'

He lay down on the hearth-rug, turned up the whites of his eyes, shivered all over, and began to snort. This was Magic, or Opium, or the Sending, or all three. When he opened his eyes he vowed that the Sending had started upon the war-path, and was at that moment flying up to the town where Lone Sahib lived.

'Give me my ten rupees,' said Dana Da wearily, 'and write a letter to Lone Sahib, telling him, and all who believe with him, that you and a friend are using a power greater than theirs. They will see that you are speaking the truth.'

He departed unsteadily, with the promise of some more rupees if anything came of the Sending.

The Englishman sent a letter to Lone Sahib, couched in what he remembered of the terminology of the Creed. He wrote: 'I also, in the days of what you held to be my backsliding have obtained Enlightenment, and with Enlightenment has come Power,' Then he grew so deeply mysterious that the recipient of the letter could make neither head nor tail of it, and was proportionately impressed; for he fancied that his friend had become a 'fifth-rounder'. When a man is a 'fifth-rounder' he can do more than Slade and Houdini combined.

Lone Sahib read the letter in five different fashions, and was beginning a sixth intepretation when his bearer dashed in with the news that there was a cat on the bed. Now if there was one thing that Lone Sahib hated more than another, it was a cat. He scolded the bearer for not turning it out of the house. The bearer said that he was afraid. All the doors of the bedroom had been shut throughout the morning, and no *real* cat could possibly have entered the room. He would prefer not to meddle with the creature.

Lone Sahib entered the room gingerly, and there, on the pillow of his bed, sprawled and whimpered a wee white kitten; not a jumpsome, frisky little beast, but a slug-like crawler with its eyes barely opened and its paws lacking strength or direction – a kitten that ought to have been in a basket with its mamma. Lone Sahib caught it by the scruff of its neck, handed it over to the sweeper to be drowned, and fined the bearer four annas.

That evening, as he was reading in his room, he fancied that he saw something moving about on the hearth-rug, outside the circle of light from his reading-lamp. When the thing began to myowl he realized that it was a kitten – a wee white kitten, nearly blind and very miserable. He was seriously angry, and spoke bitterly to his bearer, who said that there was no kitten in the room when he brought in the lamp, and *real* kittens of tender age generally had mother-cats in attendance.

'If the Presence will go out into the veranda and listen,' said the bearer, 'he will hear no cats. How, therefore, can the kitten on the bed and the kitten on the hearth-rug be real kittens?'

Lone Sahib went out to listen, and the bearer followed him, but there was no sound of any one mewing for her children. He returned to his room, having hurled the kitten down the hillside, and wrote out the incidents of the day for the benefit of his co-religionists. Those people were so absolutely free from superstition that they ascribed anything a little out of the common to Agencies. As it was their business to know all about the Agencies, they were on terms of almost indecent familiarity with Manifestations of every kind. Their letters dropped from the ceiling – unstamped – and Spirits used to squatter up and down their staircases all night; but they had never come into contact with kittens. Lone Sahib wrote out the facts, noting the hour and the minute, as every Psychical Observer is bound to do, and appending the Englishman's letter, because it was the most mysterious document and might have had a bearing upon anything in this world or the next. An outsider would have translated all the tangle thus. 'Look out! You laughed at me once, and now I am going to make you sit up.'

Lone Sahib's co-religionists found that meaning in it; but their translation was refined and full of four-syllable words. They held a sederunt, and were filled with tremulous joy, for, in spite of their familiarity with all the other worlds and cycles, they had a very human awe of things sent from Ghostland. They met in Lone Sahib's room in shrouded and sepulchral gloom, and their conclave was broken up by a clinking among the photo-frames on the mantelpiece. A wee white kitten, nearly blind, was looping and writhing itself between the clock and the candlesticks. That stopped all investigations or doublings. Here was the Manifestation in the flesh. It was, so far as could be seen, devoid of purpose, but it was a Manifestation of undoubted authenticity.

They drafted a Round Robin to the Englishman, the back-slider of old days, adjuring him in the interests of the Creed to explain whether there was any connection between the embodiment of some Egyptian God or other (I have forgotten the name) and his communication. They called the kitten Ra, or Thoth, or Tum, or something; and when Lone Sahib confessed that the first one had, at his most misguided instance, been drowned by the sweeper, they said consolingly that in his next life he would be a 'bounder', and not even a 'rounder' of the lowest grade. These words may not be quite correct, but they accurately express the sense of the house.

When the Englishman received the Round Robin – it came by post – he was startled and bewildered. He sent into the bazar for Dana Da, who read the letter and laughed. 'That is my Sending,' said he. 'I told you I would work well. Now give me another ten rupees.'

'But what in the world is this gibberish about Egyptian Gods?' asked the Englishman.

'Cats,' said Dana Da with a hiccough, for he had discovered the Englishman's whisky-bottle. 'Cats, and cats, and cats! Never was such a Sending. A hundred of cats. Now give me ten more rupees and write as I dictate.'

Dana Da's letter was a curiosity. It bore the Englishman's signature, and hinted at cats – at a Sending of Cats. The mere words on paper were creepy and uncanny to behold.

'What have you done, though?' said the Englishman. 'I am as much in the dark as ever. Do you mean to say that you can actually send this absurd Sending you talk about?'

'Judge for yourself,' said Dana Da. 'What does that letter mean? In a little time they will all be at my feet and yours, and I – oh, glory! – will be drugged or drunk all day long.'

Dana Da knew his people.

When a man who hates cats wakes up in the morning and finds a little squirming kitten on his breast, or puts his hand into his ulster-pocket and finds a little half-dead kitten where his gloves should be, or opens his trunk and finds a vile kitten among his dress-shirts, or goes for a long ride with his mackintosh strapped on his saddle-bow and shakes a little squawling kitten from its folds when he opens it, or goes out to dinner and finds a little blind kitten under his chair, or stays at home and finds a writhing kitten under the quilt, or wriggling among his boots, or hanging, head downwards, in his tobacco-jar, or being mangled by his terrier in the veranda – when such a man finds one kitten, neither more nor less, once a day in a place where no kitten rightly could or should be, he is naturally upset. When he dare not murder his daily trove because he believes it to be a Manifestation, an Emissary, an Embodiment, and half-a-dozen other things all out of the regular course of nature, he is more than upset. He is actually distressed. Some of Lone Sahib's co-religionists thought that he was a highly-favoured individual; but many said that if he had treated the first kitten with proper respect – as suited a Thoth-Ra-Tum-Sennacherib Embodiment – all this trouble would have been averted. They compared him to the Ancient Mariner, but none the less they were proud of him and proud of the Englishman who had sent the Manifestation. They did not call it a Sending because Icelandic magic was not in their programme.

After sixteen kittens, that is to say, after one fortnight, for there were three kittens on the first day to impress the fact of the Sending, the whole camp was uplifted by a letter – it came flying through a window – from the Old Man of the Mountains – the Head of all the Creed – explaining the Manifestation in the most beautiful language and soaking up all the credit for himself. The Englishman, said the letter, was not there at all. He was a backslider without Power or Asceticism who could not even raise a table by force of volition, much less project an army of kittens through space. The entire arrangement, said the letter, was strictly orthodox, worked and sanctioned by the highest Authorities within the pale of the Creed. There was great joy at this, for some of the weaker brethren, seeing that an outsider who had been working on independent lines could create kittens, whereas their own rulers had never gone beyond crockery – and broken at best – were showing a desire to break line on their own trail. In fact, there was the promise of a schism. A second Round Robin was drafted to the Englishman, beginning: 'O Scoffer,' and ending with a selection of curses from the Rites of Mizraim and Memphis, and the Commination of Jugana, who was a 'fifth-rounder' upon whose name an upstart 'third-rounder' once traded. A papal excommunication is a *billet-doux* compared with the Commination of Jugana. The Englishman had been proved, under hand and seal of the Old Man of the Mountains, to have appropriated Virtue and pretended to have Power which, in reality, belonged only to the Supreme Head. Naturally the Round Robin did not spare him.

He handed the letter to Dana Da to translate into decent English. The effect on Dana Da was curious. At first he was furiously angry, and then he laughed for five minutes.

'I had thought,' he said, 'that they would have come to me. In another week I would have shown that I sent the Sending, and they would have discrowned the Old Man of the Mountains who has sent this Sending of mine. Do you do nothing. The time has come for me to act. Write as I dictate, and I will put them to shame. But give me ten more rupees.'

At Dana Da's dictation the Englishman wrote nothing less than a formal challenge to the Old Man of the Mountains. It wound up: 'And if this Manifestation be from your hand, then let it go forward; but if it be from my hand, I will that the Sending shall cease in two days' time. On that day there shall be twelve kittens and thenceforward none at all. The people shall judge between us.' This was signed by Dana Da, who added pentacles and pentagrams, and a *crux ansata*, and half-a-dozen *swastikas*, and a Triple Tau to his name, just to show that he was all he laid claim to be.

The challenge was read out to the gentlemen and ladies, and they remembered then that Dana Da had laughed at them some years ago. It was officially announced that the Old Man of the Mountains would treat the matter with contempt; Dana Da being an Independent Investigator without a single 'round' at the back of him. But this did not soothe his people. They wanted to see a fight. They were very human for all their spirituality. Lone Sahib, who was really being worn out with kittens, submitted meekly to his fate. He felt that he was being 'kittened to prove the power of Dana Da', as the poet says.

When the stated day dawned the shower of kittens began. Some were white and some were tabby, and all were about the same loathsome age. Three were on his hearth-rug, three in his bathroom, and the other six turned up at intervals among the visitors who came to see the prophecy break down. Never was a more satisfactory Sending. On the next day there were no kittens, and next day and all the other days were kittenless and quiet. The people murmured and looked to the Old Man of the Mountains for an explanation. A letter, written on a palm-leaf, dropped from the ceiling, but every one except Lone Sahib felt that letters were not what the occasion demanded. There should have been cats, there should have been cats – full-grown ones. The letter proved conclusively that there had been a hitch in the Psychic Current which, colliding with a Dual Identity, had interfered with the Percipient Activity all along the main line. The kittens were still going on, but owing to some failure in the Developing Fluid, they were not materialized. The air was thick with letters for a few days afterwards. Unseen hands played Glück and Beethoven on finger-bowls and clock-shades; but all men felt that Psychic Life was a mockery without materialised kittens. Even Lone Sahib shouted with the majority on this head. Dana Da's letters were very insulting, and if he had then offered to lead a new departure, there is no knowing what might have happened.

But Dana Da was dying of whisky and opium in the Englishman's godown, and had small heart for honours.

'They have been put to shame,' said he. 'Never was such a Sending. It has killed me.'

'Nonsense!' said the Englishman. 'You are going to die,

Dana Da, and that sort of stuff must be left behind. I'll admit that you have made some queer things come about. Tell me honestly, now, how was it done?'

'Give me ten more rupees,' said Dana Da faintly, 'and if I die before I spend them, bury them with me.' The silver was counted out while Dana Da was fighting with Death. His hand closed upon the money and he smiled a grim smile.

'Bend low,' he whispered. The Englishman bent.

'*Bunnia* – Mission-school – expelled – *box-wallah* [pedler] – Ceylon pearl-merchant – all mine English education – out-casted, and made up name Dana Da – England with American thought-reading man and – and – you gave me ten rupees several times – I gave the Sahib's bearer two-eight a month for cats – little, little cats. I wrote – and he put them about – very clever man. Very few kittens now in the bazar. Ask Lone Sahib's sweeper wife.'

So saying, Dana Da gasped and passed away into a land where, if all be true, there are no materialisations and the making of new creeds is discouraged.

But consider the gorgeous simplicity of it all

MY OWN TRUE GHOST STORY

'As I came through the Desert thus it was –
As I came through the Desert.'

The City of Dreadful Night

Somewhere in England where there are books and pictures and plays and shop windows to look at, and thousands of men who spend their lives in building up all four, lives a gentleman who writes real stories about the real insides of people; and his name is Mr Walter Besant. But he will insist upon treating his ghosts – he has published half a workshopful of them – with levity. He makes his ghostseers talk familiarly, and, in some cases, flirt outrageously with the phantoms. You may treat anything, from a Viceroy to a Vernacular Paper, with levity; but you must behave reverently towards a ghost, and particularly an Indian one.

There are, in this land, ghosts who take the form of fat, cold, pobby corpses, and hide in trees near the roadside till a traveller passes. Then they drop upon his neck and remain. There are also terrible ghosts of women who have died in childbed. These wander along the pathways at dusk, or hide in the crops near a village, and call seductively. But to answer their call is death in this world and the next. Their feel are turned backwards that all sober men may recognise them. There are ghosts of little children who have been thrown into wells. These haunt well-kerbs and the fringes of jungles, and wail under the stars, or catch women by the wrist and beg to be taken up and carried. These and the corpse-ghosts, however, are only vernacular articles and do not attack *Sahibs*. No native ghost has yet been authentically reported to have frightened an Englishman; but many English ghosts have scared the life out of both white and black.

Nearly every other station in India owns a ghost. There are

said to be two at Simla, not counting the woman who blows the bellows at Syree dâk-bungalow on the Old Road; Mussoorie has a house haunted of a very lively Thing; a White Lady is supposed to do night-watchman round a house in Lahore; Dalhousie says that one of her houses 'repeats' on autumn evenings all the incidents of a horrible horse-and-precipice accident; Murree has a merry ghost, and now that she has been swept by cholera, will have room for some sorrowful ones; there are Officers' Quarters in Mian Mir whose doors open without reason, and whose furniture is guaranteed to creak, not with the heat of June but with the weight of Invisibles who come to lounge in the chairs; Peshawar possesses houses that none will willingly rent; and there is something – not fever – wrong with a big bungalow in Allahabad. The older Provinces simply bristle with haunted houses, and march phantom armies along their main thoroughfares.

Some of the dâk-bungalows or rest houses on the Grand Trunk Road have handy little cemeteries in their compound – witnesses to the 'changes and chances of this mortal life' in the days when men drove behind horses from Calcutta to the North-West. These bungalows are objectionable places to put up in. They are generally very old, always dirty, while the butler is as ancient as the bungalow. He either chatters senilely, or falls into the long trances of age. In both moods he is useless. If you get angry with him, he refers to some *Sahib* dead and buried these thirty years, and says that when he was in that *Sahib*'s service not a butler in the Province could touch him. Then he jabbers and mows and trembles and fidgets among the dishes, and you repent of your irritation.

In these dâk-bungalows, ghosts are most likely to be found, and when found, they should be made a note of. Not long ago it was my business to live in dâk-bungalows. I never inhabited the same house for three nights running, and grew to be learned in the breed. I lived in Government-built ones with red brick walls and rail ceilings, an inventory of the furniture posted in every room, and an excited snake at the threshold to give welcome. I lived in 'converted' ones – old houses officiating as dâk-bungalows – where nothing was in its proper place and there wasn't even a fowl for dinner. I lived in second-hand palaces where the wind blew through open-work marble tracery just as uncomfortably as through a broken pane. I lived in dâk-bungalows where the last entry in the visitors'-book was fifteen months old and where they slashed off the curry-kid's head with a sword. It was my good luck to meet all sorts of men, from sober-travelling missionaries and deserters flying from British Regiments, to drunken loafers who threw whisky bottles at all who passed; and my still greater good fortune just to escape a maternity case. Seeing that a fair proportion of the tragedy of our lives in India acted itself in dâk-bungalows, I wondered that I had met no ghosts. A ghost that would voluntarily hang about a dâk-bungalow would be mad of course; but so many men have died mad in dâk-bungalows, that there must be a fair percentage of lunatic ghosts.

In due time I found my ghost, or ghosts rather, for there were two of them. Up till that hour I had sympathised with Mr Besant's method of handling them, as shown in *The Strange Case of Mr Lucraft and other Stories*. I am now in the opposition.

We will call the bungalow Katmal dâk-bungalow. But the *Katmals* were the smallest part of the horror. A man with a sensitive hide has no right to sleep in dâk-bungalows. He should marry. Katmal dâk-bungalow was old and rotten and unrepaired. The floor was of worn brick, the walls were filthy, and the windows were nearly black with grime. It stood on a bye-path largely used by native Sub-Deputy Assistants in the Finance and Forest Departments but real *Sahibs* were rare. The butler, who was nearly bent double with old age, said so.

When I arrived, there was a fitful, undecided rain on the face of the land, accompanied by a restless wind, and every gust made a noise like the rattling of dry bones in the stiff toddy-palms out-side. The butler completely lost his head on my arrival. He had served a *Sahib* once. Did I know that *Sahib*? He gave me the name of a well-known man who has been buried for more than a quarter of a century, and showed me an ancient daguerreotype of that man in his prehistoric youth. I had seen a steel engraving of him at the head of a double volume of Memoirs a month before, and I felt ancient beyond telling.

The day shut in and the butler went to get me food. He did not go through the pretence of calling it *khana* – man's victuals. He said *ratub*, and that means, among other things, 'grub' – dog's rations. There was no insult in his choice of the term. He had forgotten the other word I suppose.

While he was cutting up the dead bodies of animals, I settled myself down, after exploring the dâk-bungalow. There were three rooms, besides my own, which was a corner kennel, each giving into the other through dingy white doors fastened with long iron bars. The bungalow was a very solid one, but the partition-walls of the rooms were almost jerry-built in their flimsiness. Every step or bang of a trunk echoed from my room down the other three, and every footfall came back tremulously from the far walls. For this reason I shut the door. There were no lamps – only candles in long glass shades. An oil wick was set in the bathroom.

For bleak, unadulterated misery that dâk-bungalow was the worst of the many that I had ever set foot in. There was no fireplace and the windows would not open; so a brazier of charcoal would have been useless. The rain and the wind splashed and gurgled and moaned round the house, and the toddy-palms rattled and roared. Half-a-dozen jackals went through the compound singing, and a hyæna stood afar off and mocked them. A hyæna would convince a Sadducee of the Resurrection of the Dead – the worst sort of Dead. Then came the *ratub* – a curious meal, half native and half English in composition – with the old man babbling behind my chair about dead and gone masters and the windblown candles playing shadow-bo-peep with the bed and the mosquito-curtains. It was just the sort of dinner and evening to make a man think of every single one of his past sins, and of all the others that he intended to commit if he lived.

Sleep, for several hundred reasons, was not easy. The lamp in the bathroom threw the most absurd shadows into the room, and the wind was beginning to talk nonsense.

Just when the reasons were drowsy with blood-sucking I

heard the regular: 'Let-us-take-and-heave-him-over' grunt of doolie-bearers in the compound. First one doolie came in, then a second, and then a third. I heard the palanquins dumped on the ground, and the shutter in front of my door shook. 'That's some one trying to come in,' I said. But no one spoke, and I persuaded myself that it was the gusty wind. The shadow of the room next to mine was attacked, flung back, and the inner door opened. 'That's some Sub-Deputy Assistant,' I said, 'and he has brought his friends with him. Now they'll talk and spit and smoke for an hour.'

But there were no voices and no footsteps. No one was putting his luggage into the next room. The door shut and I thanked Providence that I was to be left in peace. But I was curious to know where the doolies had gone. I got out of bed and looked into the darkness. There was never a sign of a doolie. Just as I was getting into bed again, I heard in the next room, the sound that no man in his senses can possibly mistake – the whirr of a billiard-ball down the length of the slates when the striker is stringing for break. No other sound is like it. A minute afterwards, there was another whirr and I got into bed. I was not frightened – indeed I was not. I was very curious to know what had become of the doolies, I jumped into bed for that reason.

Next minute, I heard the double click of a cannon and my hair sat up. It is a mistake to say that hair stands up. The skin of the head tightens and you can feel a faint, prickly bristling all over the scalp. That is the hair sitting up.

There was a whirr and a click, and both sounds could only have been made by one thing – a billiard-ball. I argued the matter out at great length with myself; and the more I argued the less probable it seemed that one bed, one table, and two chairs – all the furniture of the room next to mine – could so exactly duplicate the sounds of a game of billiards. After another cannon, a three-cushion one to judge by the whirr, I argued no more. I had found my ghost and would have given worlds to have escaped from that dâk-bungalow. I listened, and with each listen the game grew clearer. There was whirr on whirr and click on click. Sometimes there was a double click and a whirr and another click. Beyond any sort of doubt, people were playing billiards in the next room.

And the next room was not big enough to hold a billiard-table!

Between the pauses of the wind I heard the game go forward – stroke after stroke. I tried to believe that I could not hear voices; but that attempt was a failure.

Do you know what Fear is? Not ordinary fear of insult, injury or death, but abject, quivering dread of something that you cannot see – fear that dries the inside of the mouth and half of the throat – fear that makes you sweat in the palms of the hands, and gulp in order to keep the uvula at work? This is a fine Fear – a great cowardice, and must be fell to be appreciated. The very improbability of billiards in a dâk-bungalow proved the reality of the thing. No man – drunk or sober – could imagine a game of billiards, or invent the spitting crack of a screw-cannon.

A severe course of dâk-bungalows has this disadvantage – it breeds infinite credulity. If a man said to a confirmed dâk-bungalow-haunter: 'There is a corpse in the next room, and there's a mad girl in the next but one, and the woman and man on that camel have just eloped from a place sixty miles away,' the hearer would not disbelieve because he would know that nothing is too wild, grotesque, or horrible to happen in a dâk-bungalow.

This credulity, unfortunately, extends to ghosts. A rational person fresh from his own house would have turned on his side and slept. I did not. So surely as I was given up as a bad carcass by the scores of things in the bed because the bulk of my blood was in my heart, so surely did I hear every stroke of a long game of billiards played in the echoing room behind the iron-barred door. My dominant fear was that the players might want a marker. It was an absurd fear; because creatures who could play in the dark would be above such superfluities. I only know that that was my terror; and it was real.

After a long, long while, the game stopped, and the door banged. I slept because I was dead tired. Otherwise I should have preferred to have kept awake. Not for everything in Asia would I have dropped the door-bar and peered into the dark of the next room.

When the morning came, I considered that I had done well and wisely, and enquired for the means of departure.

'By the way, butler,' I said, 'what were those three doolies doing in my compound in the night?'

'There were no doolies,' said he.

I went into the next room and the daylight streamed through the open door. I was immensely brave. I would, at that hour, have played Black Pool with the owner of the big Black Pool down below.

'Has this place always been a dâk-bungalow?' I asked.

'No,' said the butler. 'Ten or twenty years ago, I have forgotten how long, it was a billiard-room.'

'A how much?'

'A billiard-room for the *Sahibs* who built the Railway. I was servant then in the big house where all the Railway-*Sahibs* lived, and I used to come across with the brandy-wine. These three rooms were all one, and they held a big table on which the *Sahibs* played every evening. But the *Sahibs* are all dead now and the Railway runs, you say, nearly to Kabul.'

'Do you remember anything about the *Sahibs*?'

'It is long ago, but I remember that one *Sahib*, a fat man and always angry, was playing here one night and he said to me: "Mangal Khan, give me a drink," and I filled the glass, and he bent over the table to strike, and his head fell lower and lower till it hit the table, and his spectacles came off, and when we – the *Sahibs* and I myself – ran to lift him, he was dead. I helped to carry him out. Aha, he was a strong *Sahib*! But he is dead and I, old Mangal Khan, am still living, by your favour.'

That was more than enough! I had my ghost – a first-hand, authenticated article. I would write to the Society for Psychical Research – I would paralyse the Empire with the news! But I would, first of all, put eighty miles of sound assessed crop-land between myself and that dâk-bungalow before nightfall. The Society might send their regular agent to investigate later on.

I went into my own room and prepared to pack after noting down the facts of the case. As I smoked I heard the game begin again – with a miss in balk this time, for the whirr was a short one.

The door was open and I could see into the room. *Click – click*! That was a cannon. I entered the room without fear, for there was sunlight within and a fresh breeze without. The unseen game was going on at a tremendous rate. And well it might, when a restless little rat was running to and fro inside the dingy ceiling-cloth, and a piece of loose window-sash was making fifty breaks off the window bolt as it shook in the breeze.

Impossible to mistake the sound of billiard-balls! Impossible to mistake the whirr of a ball over the slate! But I was to be excused. Even when I shut my enlightened eyes the sound was marvellously like that of a fast game.

Entered angrily the faithful partner of my sorrows. Kadir Baksh.

'This bungalow is very bad and low-caste! No wonder the Presence was disturbed and is speckled. Three sets of doolie-bearers came to the bungalow late last night when I was sleeping outside, and said that it was their custom to rest in the rooms set apart for the white men! What honour has the butler? They tried to enter, but I told them to go. No wonder, if these low people have been here, that the Presence is sorely spotted. It is shame, and the work of a dirty man!'

Kadir Baksh did not say that he had taken from each gang two annas for rent in allowance, and then, beyond my ear-shot, had beaten them with the big green umbrella whose use I could never before divine. But Kadir Baksh has no notions of morality.

There was an interview with the butler, but as he promptly lost his head, wrath gave place to pity, and pity led to a long conversation, in the course of which he put the fat Engineer-*Sahib*'s tragic death in three separate stations – two of them fifty miles away. The third shift was to Calcutta, and there the *Sahib* died while driving a dog-cart.

If I had encouraged him the butler would have wandered all through Bengal with his corpse.

I did not go away as soon as I intended. I stayed for the

night, while the wind and the rat and the sash and the window-bolt played a ding-dong 'hundred and fifty up'. Then the wind ran out and the billiards stopped, and I felt that I had ruined my one genuine ghost-story.

Had I only stopped at the proper time, I could have made nearly anything out of it.

That was the bitterest thought of all!

SLEIPNER, LATE THURINDA

There are men, both good and wise, who hold that in a future state
  Dumb creatures we have cherished here below
Will give us joyous welcome as we pass the Golden Gate.
  Is it folly if I hope it may be so?

The Place Where the Old Horse Died

If there were any explanation available here, I should be the first person to offer it. Unfortunately, there is not, and I am compelled to confine myself to the facts of the case as vouched for by Hordene and confirmed by 'Guj,' who is the last man in the world to throw away a valuable horse for nothing.

Jale came up with *Thurinda* to the Shayid Spring meeting; and besides *Thurinda* his string included *Divorce*, *Meg's Diversions* and *Benoni* – ponies of sorts. He won the Officers' Scurry – five furlongs – with *Benoni* on the first day, and that sent up the price of the stable in the evening lotteries; for *Benoni* was the worst-looking of the three, being a pigeon-toed, split-chested *dâk* horse, with a wonderful gift of blundering in on his shoulders – ridden out to the last ounce – but *first*. Next day Jale was riding *Divorce* in the Wattle and Dab Stakes – round the jump course; and she turned over at the on-and-off course when she was leading and managed to break her neck. She never stirred from the place where she dropped, and Jale did not move either till he was carried off the ground to his tent close to the big *shamiana* where the lotteries were held. He had ricked his back, and everything below the hips was as dead as timber. Otherwise he was perfectly well. The doctor said that the stiffness would spread and that he would die before morning. Jale insisted upon knowing the worst, and when he heard it sent a pencil note to the Honorary Secretary, saying that they were not to stop the races or do anything foolish of that kind. If he hung on till the next day the nominations for the third day's racing would not be void, and he would settle up all claims before he threw up his hand. This relieved the Honorary Secretary, because most of the horses had come from a long distance, and, under any circumstance, even had the Judge dropped dead in the box, it would have been impossible to have postponed the racing. There was a great deal of money on the third day, and five or six of the owners were gentlemen who would make even one day's delay an excuse. Well, settling would not be easy. No one knew much about Jale. He was an outsider from down country, but every one hoped that, since he was doomed, he would live through the third day and save trouble.

Jale lay on his charpoy in the tent and asked the doctor and the man who catered to the refreshments – he was the nearest at the time – to witness his will. 'I don't know how long my arms will be workable,' said Jale, 'and we'd better get this business over.' The private arrangements of the will concern nobody but Jale's friends; but there was one clause that was rather curious. 'Who was that man with the brindled hair who put me up for a night until the tent was ready? The man who rode down to pick me up when I was smashed. Nice sort of fellow he seemed.' 'Hordene?' said the doctor. 'Yes, Hordene. Good chap, Hordene. He keeps Bull whisky. Write down that I give this Johnnie Hordene *Thurinda* for his own, if he can sell the other ponies. *Thurinda*'s a good mare. He can enter her – post-entry – for the All Horse Sweep if he likes – on the last day. Have you got that down? I suppose the Stewards'll recognise the gift?' 'No trouble about that,' said the doctor. 'All right. Give him the other two ponies to sell. They're entered for the last day, but I shall be dead then. Tell him to send the money to—' Here he gave an address. 'Now I'll sign and you sign, and that's all. This deadness is coming up between my shoulders.'

Jale lived, dying very slowly, till the third day's racing, and up till the time of the lotteries on the fourth day's racing. The doctor was rather surprised. Hordene came in to thank him for his gift, and to suggest it would be much better to sell *Thurinda* with the others. She was the best of them all, and would have fetched twelve hundred on her looking-over merits only. 'Don't you bother,' said Jale. 'You take her. I rather like you. I've got no people, and that Bull whisky was first-class stuff. I'm pegging out now, I think.'

The lottery-tent outside was beginning to fill, and Jale heard the click of the dice. 'That's all right,' said he. 'I wish I was there, but – I'm – going to the drawer.' Then he died quietly. Hordene went into the lottery-tent, after calling the doctor. 'How's Jale?' said the Honorary Secretary. 'Gone to the drawer,' said Hordene, settling into a chair and reaching out for a lottery paper. 'Poor beggar!' said the Honorary Secretary. ' 'Twasn't the fault of our on-and-off, though. The mare blundered. Gentlemen! gentlemen! Nine hundred and eighty rupees in the lottery, and *River of Years* for sale!' The lottery lasted far into the night, and there was a supplementary lottery on the All Horse Sweep, where *Thurinda* sold for a song, and was not bought by her owner. 'It's not lucky,' said Hordene, and the rest of the men agreed with him. 'I ride her myself, but I don't know anything about her, and I wish to goodness I hadn't taken her,' said he. 'Oh, bosh! Never refuse a horse or a drink, however you come by them. No one objects, do they? Not going to refer this matter to Calcutta, are we? Here, somebody, bid! Eleven hundred and fifty rupees in the lottery, and *Thurinda* – absolutely unknown, acquired under the most dramatic circumstances from about *the* toughest man it has ever been my good fortune to meet – for sale. Hullo, Nurji, is that you? Gentlemen, where a Pagan bids shall enlightened Christians hang back? Ten! Going, going, gone!' 'You want ha-af, sar?' said the battered native trainer to Hordene. 'No, thanks – not a bit of her for me.'

The All Horse Sweep was run, and won by *Thurinda* by about a street and three-quarters, to be very accurate, amid derisive cheers, which Hordene, who flattered himself that he knew something about riding, could not understand. On pulling up he looked over his shoulder and saw that the second horse was only just passing the box. 'Now, how did I make much a fool of myself?' he said as he returned to weigh out. His friends gathered round him and asked tenderly whether this was the first time that he had got up, and whether it was *absolutely* necessary that the winning horse should be ridden out when the field were hopelessly pumped, a quarter of a mile behind, etc, etc. 'I – I – thought *River of Years* was pressing me,' explained Hordene. '*River of Years* was wallowing, absolutely wallowing,' said a man, 'before you turned into the straight. You rode like a – hang it – like a Militia subaltern!'

The Shayid Spring meeting broke up and the sportsmen turned their steps towards the next carcase – the Ghoriah Spring. With them went *Thurinda*'s owner, the happy possessor of an almost perfect animal. 'She's as easy as a Pullman car and about twice as fast,' he was wont to say in moments of confidence to his intimates. 'For all her bulk, she's as handy as a polo-pony; a child might ride her, and when she's at the post she's as cute – she's as cute as the bally starter himself.' Many times had Hordene said this, till at last one unsympathetic friend answered with: 'When a man *bukhs* too much about his wife or his horse, it's a sure sign he's trying to make himself like 'em. I mistrust your *Thurinda*. She's too good, or else—' 'Or else what?' 'You're trying to believe you like her.' 'Like her! I *love* her! I trust that darling as I'm shot if I'd trust you. I'd hack her for tuppence.' 'Hack away, then. I don't want to hurt your feelings. I don't hack my stable myself, but some horses go better for it. Come and peacock at the band-stand this evening.' To the band-stand accordingly Hordene came, and the lovely *Thurinda* comported herself with all the gravity and decorum that might have been expected. Hordene rode home with the scoffer, through the dusk, discoursing on matters indifferent. 'Hold up a minute,' said his friend, 'there's Gagley riding behind us.' Then, raising his voice: 'Come along, Gagley! I want to speak to you about the Race Ball.' But no Gagley came; and the couple went forward at a trot. 'Hang it! There's that man behind us still.' Hordene listened and could clearly hear the sound of a horse trotting, apparently just behind them. 'Come on, Gagley! Don't play bo-peep in that ridiculous way,' shouted the friend. Again no Gagley. Twenty yards farther there was a crash and a stumble as the friend's horse came down over an unseen rathole. 'How much damaged?' asked Hordene. 'Sprained my wrist,' was the dolorous answer, 'and there is something wrong with my knee-cap. There goes my mount to-morrow, and this gee is cut like a cab-horse.'

On the first day of the Ghoriah meeting *Thurinda* was hopelessly ridden out by a native jockey, to whose care Hordene had at the last moment been compelled to confide her. 'You forsaken idiot!' said he, 'what made you begin riding as soon as you were clear? She had everything safe, if you'd only left her alone. You rode her out before the home turn, you hog!' 'What could I do?' said the jockey sullenly. 'I was pressed by another horse.' 'Whose "other horse"? There were twenty yards of daylight between you and the ruck. If you'd kept her there even then 'twouldn't ha' mattered. But you rode her out – you rode her out!' 'There was another horse and he pressed me to the end, and when I looked round he was no longer there.' Let us, in charity, draw a veil over Hordene's language at this point. 'Goodness knows whether she'll be fit to pull out again for the last event. D–n you and your other horses! I wish I'd broken your neck before letting you get up!' *Thurinda* was done to a turn, and it seemed a cruelty to ask her to run again in the last race of the day. Hordene rode this time, and was careful to keep the mare within herself at the outset. Once more *Thurinda* left her field – with one exception – a grey horse that hung upon her flanks and could not be shaken off. The mare was done, and refused to answer the call upon her. She tried hopelessly in the straight and was caught and passed by her old enemy. *River of Years* – the chestnut of Kurnaul. 'You rode well – like a native, Hordene,' was the unflattering comment. 'The mare was ridden out before *River of Years*.' 'But the grey,' began Hordene, and then ceased, for he knew that there was no grey in the race. *Blue Point* and *Diamond Dust*, the only greys at the meeting, were running in the Arab Handicap.

He caught his native jockey. 'What horse, d'you say, pressed you?' 'I don't know. It was a grey with nutmeg tickings behind the saddle.' That evening Hordene sought the great Major Blare-Tyndar, who knew personally the father, mother and ancestors of almost every horse brought from *ekka* or ship, that had ever set foot on an Indian race-course. 'Say, Major, what is a grey horse with nutmeg tickings behind the saddle?' 'A curiosity. *Wendell Holmes* is a grey, with nutmeg on the near shoulder, but there is no horse marked your way, now.' Then, after a pause: 'No, I'm wrong – you ought to know. The pony that got you *Thurinda* was grey and nutmeg.' 'How much?' '*Divorce*, of course. The mare that broke her neck at the Shayid meeting and killed Jale. A big thirteen-three she was. I recollect when she was hacking old Snuffy Beans to office. He bought her from a dealer, who had her left on his hands as a rejection when the Pink Hussars were buying team up country and then—Hullo! The man's gone!' Hordene had departed on receipt of information which he already knew. He only demanded extra confirmation. Then he began to argue with himself, bearing in mind that he himself was a sane man, neither gluttonous nor a wine-bibber, with an unimpaired digestion, and that *Thurinda* was to all appearances a horse of ordinary flesh and exceedingly good blood. Arrived at these satisfactory conclusions, he reargued the whole matter.

Being by nature intensely superstitious, he decided upon scratching *Thurinda* and facing the howl of indignation that would follow. He also decided to leave the Ghoriah meet and change his luck. But it would have been sinful – positively wicked – to have left without waiting for the polo match that was to conclude the festivities. At the last moment before the match, one of the leading players of the Ghoriah team and Hordene's host discovered that, through the kindly foresight of his head *sais*, every single pony had been taken down to the ground. 'Lend me a hack, old man,' he shouted to Hordene as he was changing. 'Take *Thurinda*,' was the reply. 'She'll bring you down in ten minutes.' And *Thurinda* was accordingly saddled for Marish's benefit. 'I'll go down with you,' said Hordene. The two rode off together at a hand canter. 'By Jove! Somebody's *sais* 'll get kicked for this!' said Marish, looking round. 'Look there! He's coming for the mare! Pull out into the middle of the road.' 'What on earth d'you mean?' 'Well, if *you* can take a strayed horse so calmly, I can't. Didn't you see what a lather that grey was in?' 'What grey?' 'The grey that just passed us – saddle and all. He's got away from the ground, I suppose. Now he's turned the corner; but you can hear his hoofs. Listen!' There was a furious gallop of shod horses, gradually dying into silence. 'Come along,' said Hordene. 'We're late as it is. We shall know all about it on the ground.' 'Anybody lost a tat?' asked Marish cheerily as they reached the ground. 'No, we've lost *you*. Double up. You're late enough as it is. Get up and go in. The teams are waiting.' Marish mounted his polo-pony and cantered across. Hordene watched the game idly for a few moments. There was a scrimmage, a cloud of dust, and a cessation of play, and a shouting for *saises*. The umpire clattered forward and returned. 'What has happened?' 'Marish! Neck broken! Nobody's fault. Pony crossed its legs and came down. Game's stopped. Thank God, he hasn't got a wife!' Again Hordene pondered as he sat on his horse's back. 'Under any circumstances it was written that he was to be killed. I had no interest in his death, and he had his warning, I suppose. I can't make out the system that this infernal mare runs under. Why *him*? Anyway, I'll shoot her.' He looked at *Thurinda*, the calm-eyed, the beautiful, and repented. 'No! I'll sell her.'

'What in the world has happened to *Thurinda* that Hordene is so keen on getting rid of her?' was the general question. 'I want money,' said Hordene unblushingly, and the few who knew how his accounts stood saw that this was a varnished lie. But they held their peace because of the great love and trust that exists among the ancient and honourable fraternity of sportsmen.

'There's nothing wrong with her,' explained Hordene. 'Try her as much as you like, but let her stay in my stable until you've made up your mind one way or the other. Nine hundred's my price.'

'I'll take her at that,' quoth a red-haired subaltern, nicknamed Carrots, later Gaja, and then for brevity's sake, Guj. 'Let me have her out this afternoon. I want her more for hacking than anything else.'

Guj tried *Thurinda* exhaustively and had no fault to find

with her. 'She's all right,' he said briefly. 'I'll take her. It's a cash deal.' 'Virtuous Guj!' said Hordene, pocketing the cheque. If you go on like this you'll be loved and respected by all who know you.'

A week later Guj insisted that Hordene should accompany him on a ride. They cantered merrily for a time. Then said the subaltern: 'Listen to the mare's beat a minute, will you? Seems to me that you've sold me two horses.'

Behind the mare was plainly audible the cadence of a swiftly trotting horse. 'D'you hear anything?' said Guj. 'No – nothing but the regular triplet,' said Hordene; and he lied when he answered. Guj looked at him keenly and said nothing. Two or three months passed and Hordene was perplexed to see his old property running, and running well, under the curious title of 'Sleipner – late Thurinda.' He consulted the Great Major, who said: 'I don't know a horse called Sleipner, but I know of one. He was a northern bred, and belonged to Odin.' 'A mythological beast?' 'Exactly. Like Bucephalus and the rest of 'em. He was a great horse. I wish I had some of his get in my stable.' 'Why?' 'Because he had eight legs. When he had used up one set, he let down the other four to come up the straight on. Stewards were lenient in those days. Now it's all you can do to get a crock with three sound legs.'

Hordene cursed the red-haired Guj in his heart for finding out the mare's peculiarity. Then he cursed the dead man Jale for his ridiculous interference with a free gift. 'If it was given – it was given,' said Hordene, 'and he has no right to come messing about after it.' When Guj and he next met, he enquired tenderly after Thurinda. The red-haired subaltern, impassive as usual, answered: 'I've shot her,' 'Well – you know your own affairs best,' said Hordene. 'You've given yourself away,' said Guj. 'What makes you think I shot a sound horse? She might have been bitten by a mad dog, or lamed.' 'You didn't say that.' 'No, I didn't, because I've a notion that you knew what was wrong with her.' 'Wrong with her! She was as sound as a bell—' 'I know that. Don't pretend to misunderstand. You'll believe me, and I'll believe you in this show; but no one else will believe us. That mare was a bally nightmare.'

'Go on,' said Hordene. 'I stuck the noise of the other horse as long as I could, and called her *Sleipner* on the strength of it. *Sleipner* was a stallion, but that's a detail. When it got to interfering with every race I rode it was more than I could stick. I took her off racing, and, on my honour, since that time I've been nearly driven out of my mind by a grey and nutmeg pony. It used to trot round my quarters at night, fool about the Mall, and graze about the compound. You *know* that pony. It isn't a pony to catch or ride or hit, is it?' 'No,' said Hordene; 'I've seen it.' 'So I shot *Thurinda*; that was a thousand rupees out of my pocket. And old Stiffer, who's got his new crematorium in full blast, cremated her. I say, what *was* the matter with the mare? Was she bewitched?'

Hordene told the story of the gift, which Guj heard out to the end. 'Now, that's a nice sort of yarn to tell in a messroom, isn't it? They'd call it jumps or insanity,' said Guj. 'There's no reason in it. It doesn't lead up to anything. It only killed poor Marish and made you stick me with the mare; and yet it's true. Are you mad or drunk, or am I? That's the only explanation.' 'Can't be drunk for nine months on end, and madness would show in that time,' said Hordene.

'All right,' said Guj recklessly, going to the window. 'I'll lay that ghost.' He leaned out into the night and shouted: 'Jale! Jale! Jale! Wherever you are.' There was a pause and then up the compound-drive came the clatter of a horse's feet. The red-haired subaltern blanched under his freckles to the colour of glycerine soap. '*Thurinda*'s dead,' he muttered, 'and – and all bets are off. Go back to your grave again.'

Hordene was watching him open-mouthed.

'Now bring me a strait-jacket or a glass of brandy,' said Guj. 'That's enough to turn a man's hair white. What did the poor wretch mean by knocking about the earth!'

'Don't know,' whispered Hordene hoarsely. 'Let's get over to the Club. I'm feeling a bit shaky.'

THE MAN WHO WOULD BE KING

Brother to a Prince and fellow to a beggar if he be found worthy.

The Law, as quoted, lays down a fair conduct of life and one not easy to follow. I have been fellow to a beggar again and again under circumstances which prevented either of us finding out whether the other was worthy. I have still to be brother to a Prince, though I once came near to kinship with what might have been a veritable King, and was promised the reversion of a Kingdom – army, law-courts, revenue and policy all complete. But, to-day, I greatly fear that my King is dead, and if I want a crown I must go and hunt it for myself.

The beginning of everything was in a railway train upon the road to Mhow from Ajmir. There had been a deficit in the Budget which necessitated travelling, not Second-class, which is only half as dear as First-class, but by Intermediate, which is very awful indeed. There are no cushions in the Intermediate-class, and the population are either Intermediate, which is Eurasian, or native, which for a long night journey is nasty, or Loafer, which is amusing though intoxicated. Intermediates do not patronise refreshment rooms. They carry their food in bundles, and pots, and buy sweets from the native sweetmeat sellers, and drink the roadside water. That is why in the hot weather Intermediates are taken out of the carriages dead, and in all weathers are most properly looked down upon.

My particular Intermediate happened to be empty till I reached Nasirabad, when a huge gentleman in shirt-sleeves entered, and, following the custom of Intermediates, passed the time of day. He was a wanderer and a vagabond like myself, but with an educated taste for whiskey. He told tales of things he had seen and done, of out-of-the-way corners of the Empire into which he had penetrated, and of adventures in which he risked his life for a few days' food. 'If India was filled with men like you and me, not knowing more than the crows where they'd get their next day's rations, it isn't seventy millions of revenue the land would be paying – it's seven hundred millions,' said he; and as I looked at his mouth and chin I was disposed to agree with him. We talked politics – the politics of Loaferdom that sees things from, the underside where the lath and plaster is not smoothed off – and we talked postal arrangements because my friend wanted to send a telegram back from the next station to Ajmir which is the turning-off place from the Bombay to the Mhow line as you travel westward. My friend had no money beyond eight annas which he wanted for dinner, and I had no money at all, owing to the hitch in the Budget before mentioned. Further I was going into a wilderness where, though I should resume touch with the Treasury, there were no telegraph offices. I was, therefore, unable to help him in any way.

'We might threaten a Station-master and make him send a wire on tick,' said my friend, 'but that'd mean enquiries for you and for me, and I've got my hands full these days. Did you say you are travelling back along this line within any days?'

'Within ten,' I said.

'Can't you make it eight?' said he. 'Mine is rather urgent business.'

'I can send your telegram within ten days if that will serve you,' I said.

'I couldn't trust the wire to fetch him now I think of it. It's this way. He leaves Delhi on the 23rd for Bombay. That means he'll be running through Ajmir about the night of the 23rd.'

'But I'm going into the Indian Desert,' I explained.

'Well *and* good,' said he. 'You'll be changing at Marwar Junction to get into Jodhpore territory – you must do that – and he'll be coming through Marwar Junction in the early morning of the 24th by the Bombay Mail. Can you be at Marwar Junction on that time? 'Twon't be inconveniencing you because I know that there's precious few pickings to be got out of these Central India States – even though you pretend to be correspondent of the *Backwoodsman*.'

'Have you ever tried that trick?' I asked.

'Again and again, but the Residents find you out, and then you get escorted to the Border before you've time to get your knife into them. But about my friend here. I *must* give him a word o' mouth to tell him what's come to me or else he won't know where to go. I would take it more than kind of you if you was to come out of Central India in time to catch him at Marwar Junction, and say to him: "He has gone South for the week". He'll know what that means. He's a big man with a red beard, and a great swell he is. You'll find him sleeping like a gentleman with all his luggage round him in a Second-class compartment. But don't you be afraid. Slip down the window and say: "He has gone South for the week," and he'll tumble. It's only cutting your time of stay in those parts by two days. I ask you as a stranger – going to the West,' he said with emphasis.

'Where have *you* come from?' said I.

'From the East,' said he, 'and I am hoping that you will give him the message on the square – for the sake of my mother as well as your own.'

Englishmen are not usually softened by appeals to the memory of their mothers, but for certain reasons, which will be fully apparent, I saw fit to agree.

'It's more than a little matter,' said he, 'and that's why I ask you to do it – and now I know that I can depend on you doing it. A Second-class carriage at Marwar Junction, and a red-haired man asleep in it. You'll be sure to remember. I get out at the next station, and I must hold on there till he comes or sends me what I want.'

'I'll give the message if I catch him,' I said, 'and for the sake of your mother as well as mine I'll give you a word of advice. Don't try to run the Central India States just now as the correspondent of the *Backwoodsman*. There's a real one knocking about here, and it might lead to trouble.'

'Thank you,' said he simply, 'and when will the swine be gone? I can't starve because he's ruining my work. I wanted to get hold of the Degumber Rajah down here about his father's widow, and give him a jump.'

'What did he do to his father's widow, then ?'

'Filled her up with red pepper and slippered her to death as she hung from a beam. I found that out myself, and I'm the only man that would dare going into the State to get hush-money for it. They'll try to poison me, same as they did in Chortumna when I went on the loot there. But you'll give the man at Marwar Junction my message?'

He got out at a little roadside station, and I reflected. I had heard, more than once, of men personating correspondents of newspapers and bleeding small Native States with threats of exposure, but I had never met any of the caste before. They lead a hard life, and generally die with great suddenness. The Native States have a wholesome horror of English newspapers, which may throw light on their peculiar methods of government, and do their best to choke correspondents with champagne, or drive them out of their mind with four-in-hand barouches. They do not understand that nobody cares a straw for the internal administration of Native States so long as oppression and crime are kept within decent limits, and the ruler is not drugged, drunk or diseased from one end of the year to the other. Native States were created by Providence in order to supply picturesque scenery, tigers and tall-writing. They are the dark places of the earth, full of unimaginable cruelty; touching the Railway and the Telegraph on one side, and, on the other, the days of Harun-al-Raschid. When I left the train I did business with divers Kings, and in eight days passed through many changes of life. Sometimes I wore dress-clothes and consorted with Princes and Politicals, drinking from crystal and eating from silver. Sometimes I lay out upon the ground and devoured what I could get, from a plate made of leaves, and drank the running water, and slept under the same rug as my servant. It was all in the day's work.

Then I headed for the Great Indian Desert upon the proper date, as I had promised, and the night Mail set me down at Marwar Junction, where a funny little, happy-go-lucky, native-managed railway runs to Jodhpore. The Bombay Mail from

Delhi makes a short halt at Marwar. She arrived as I got in, and I had just time to hurry to her platform and go down the carriages. There was only one Second-class on the train. I slipped the window and looked down upon a flaming red beard, half covered by a railway rug. That was my man, fast asleep, and I dug him gently in the ribs. He woke with a grunt and I saw his face in the light of the lamps. It was a great and shining face.

'Tickets again ?' said he.

'No,' said I. 'I am to tell you that he is gone South for the week. He is gone South for the week.'

The train had begun to move out. The red man rubbed his eyes. 'He has gone South for the week,' he repeated. 'Now that's just like his impidence. Did he say that I was to give you anything? – 'Cause I won't.'

'He didn't,' I said and dropped away, and watched the red lights die out in the dark. It was horribly cold because the wind was blowing off the sands. I climbed into my own train – not an Intermediate carriage this time – and went to sleep.

If the man with the beard had given me a rupee I should have kept it as a memento of a rather curious affair. But the consciousness of having done my duty was my only reward.

Later on I reflected that two gentlemen like my friends could not do any good if they foregathered and personated correspondents of newspapers, and might, if they 'stuck up' one of the little rat-trap states of Central India or Southern Rajputana, get themselves into serious difficulties. I, therefore, took some trouble to describe them as accurately as I could remember to people who would be interested in deporting them: and succeeded, so I was later informed, in having them headed back from the Degumber borders.

Then I became respectable, and returned to an office where there were no kings and no incidents except the daily manufacture of a newspaper. A newspaper office seems to attract every conceivable sort of person, to the prejudice of discipline. Zenana-mission ladies arrive and beg that the Editor will instantly abandon all his duties to describe a Christian prize-giving in a back-slum of a perfectly inaccessible village; Colonels who have been overpassed for commands sit down and sketch the outline of a series of ten, twelve or twenty-four leading articles on Seniority *versus* Selection; missionaries wish to know why they have not been permitted to escape from their regular vehicles of abuse and swear at a brother missionary under special patronage of the editorial We: stranded theatrical companies troop up to explain that they cannot pay for their advertisements, but on their return from New Zealand or Tahiti will do so with interest; inventors of patent punkah-pulling machines, carriage couplings and unbreakable swords and axle trees call with specifications in their pockets and hours at their disposal; tea-companies enter and elaborate their prospectuses with the office pens; secretaries of ball-committees clamour to have the glories of their last dance more fully expounded; strange ladies rustle in and say: 'I want a hundred ladies' cards printed *at once*, please,' which is manifestly part of an Editor's duty; and every dissolute ruffian that ever tramped the Grand Trunk Road makes it his business to ask for employment as a proof-reader. And, all the time, the telephone bell is ringing madly, and kings are being killed on the Continent, and empires are saying 'You're another,' and Mister Gladstone is calling down brimstone upon the British Dominions, and the little black copy-boys are whining like tired bees for more copy to feed the racing machines, and most of the paper is as blank as Modred's shield.

That is the amusing part of the year. There are other six months wherein none ever come to call, and the thermometer walks inch by inch to the top of the glass, and the office is darkened to just above reading-light, and the press machines are red-hot of touch, and nobody writes anything but accounts of amusements in the Hill-stations or obituary notices. Then the telephone becomes a tinkling terror, because it tells you of the sudden deaths of men and women whom you knew intimately, and the prickly heat covers you as with a garment, and you sit down and write: 'A slight increase of sickness is reported from the Khuda Jhanta Khan District. The outbreak is purely sporadic in its nature, and, thanks to the energetic efforts of the District authorities is now almost at an end. It is, however, with deep regret we record the death, &c.'

Then the sickness really breaks out, and the less recording and reporting the better for the peace of the subscribers. But the Empires and the Kings continue to divert themselves as selfishly as before, and the Foreman thinks that a daily paper really ought to come out once in twenty-four hours, and all the people at the Hill Stations in the middle of their amusements say: 'Good gracious! Why can't the paper be sparkling? I'm sure there's plenty going on up here.'

That is the dark half of the moon, and as the advertisements say 'must be experienced to be appreciated'.

It was in that season, and a remarkably evil season, that the paper began running the last issue of the week on Saturday night, which is to say Sunday morning. This was a great convenience, for immediately after the paper was put to bed, the dawn would lower the thermometer from 96° to almost 84° for half an hour, and in that chill – you have no idea how cold is 84° on the grass until you begin to pray for it – a very tired man could set off to sleep ere the heat roused him.

One Saturday night it was my pleasant duty to put the paper to bed alone. A king or courtier, or a courtezan, or a community was going to die or get a new constitution, or do something that was important on the other side of the world, and the paper was to be held open till the latest possible minute in order to catch the telegram. It was a pitchy black night, as stifling as a June night can be, and the *loo*, the red-hot wind from the westward, was booming among the tinder-dry trees and pretending that the rain was on its heels. Now and again a spot of almost boiling water would fall on the dust with the flop of a frog, but all our weary world knew that was only pretence. It was a shade cooler in the press-room than the office, so I sat there, while the type ticked and clicked, and the night-jars hooted at the windows, and the all but naked compositors wiped the sweat from their foreheads and called for water. The thing that was keeping us back, whatever it was, would not come off, though the *loo* dropped, and the last type was set, and the whole round earth stood still in the choking heat, with its finger on its lip, to wait the event. I drowsed, and wondered, whether the telegraph was a blessing, and whether this dying man or struggling people, was aware of the incon-venience the delay was causing. There was no special reason beyond the heat and worry to make tension, but, as the clock-hands crept up to three o'clock, and the machines spun their fly-wheels two and three times to see that all was in order, before I said the word that would set them off, I could have shrieked aloud.

Then the roar and rattle of the wheels shivered the quiet into little bits. I rose to go away, but two men in white clothes stood in front of me. The first one said: 'It's him!' the second one said: 'So it is!' and they both laughed almost as loudly as the machinery roared, and mopped their foreheads. 'We see there was a light burning across the road and we were sleeping in that ditch there for coolness, and I said to my friend here: "The office is open. Let's come along and speak to him as turned us back from the Degumber State,"' said the smaller of the two. He was the man I had met in Mhow train, and his fellow was the red-bearded man of Marwar Junction. There was no mistaking the eyebrows of the one or the beard of the other.

I was not pleased, because I wished to go to sleep, not to squabble with loafers. 'What do you want?' I asked.

'Half an hour's talk with you, cool and comfortable, in the office?' said the red-bearded man. 'We'd *like* some drink – the Contrack doesn't begin yet, Peachey, so you needn't look – but what we really want is advice. We don't want money. We ask you as a favour, because you did us a bad turn about Degumber.'

I led from the press-room to the stifling office with the maps on the walls, and the red-haired man rubbed his hands. 'That's something like,' said he. 'This was the proper shop to come to. Now, Sir, let me introduce to you Brother Peachey Carnehan, that's him, and Brother Daniel Dravot, that is *me*, and the less said about our professions the better, for we have been most things in our time. Soldier, sailor, compositor, photographer, proof-reader, street-preacher, and correspondents of the *Back-woodsman*, when we thought the paper wanted one. Carnehan is sober, and so am I. Look at us first and see that's sure. It will save you cutting into my talk. We'll take one of your cigars apiece, and you shall see us light it.'

I watched the test. The men were absolutely sober, so I gave them each a tepid peg.

'Well *and* good,' said Carnehan of the eyebrows, wiping the froth from his moustache. 'Let me talk now, Dan. We have been all over India, mostly on foot. We have been boiler fitters, engine drivers, petty contractors and all that, and we have decided that India isn't big enough for such as us.'

They certainly were too big for the office. Dravot's beard seemed to fill half the room and Carnehan's shoulders the other half, as they sat on the big table. Carnehan continued: 'The country isn't half worked out because they that governs it won't let you touch it. They spend all their blessed time in governing it, and you can't lift a spade nor chip a rock, nor look for oil nor anything like that without all the Government saying: "Leave it alone and let us govern". Therefore, such as it is, we will let it alone, and go away some other place where a man isn't crowded and can to his own. We are not little men, and there is nothing that we are afraid of except drink, and we have signed a Contrack on that. *Therefore*, we are going away to be Kings.'

'Kings in our own right,' muttered Dravot.

'Yes, of course,' I said. 'You've been tramping in the sun, and it's a very warm night, and hadn't you better sleep over the notion ? Come to-morrow.'

'Neither drunk nor sunstruck,' said Drayot. 'We have slept over the notion half a year, and require to see Books and Atlases, and we have decided that there is only one place now in the world that two strong men can Sar-a-*whack*. They call it Kafiristan. By my reckoning it's the top right-hand corner of Afghanistan, not more than three hundred miles from Peshawar. They have two-and-thirty heathen idols there, and we'll be the thirty-third. It's a mountaineous country, and the women of those parts are very beautiful.'

'But that is provided against in the Contrack,' said Carnehan. 'Neither Women nor Liqu-or, Daniel.'

'And that's all we know, except that no one has gone there,

and they fight, and in any place where they fight a man who knows how to drill men can always be a King. We shall go to those parts and say to any King we find: "D'you want to vanquish your foes?" and we will show him how to drill men; for that we know better than anything else. Then we will subvert that King and seize his Throne and establish a Dy-nasty.'

'You'll be cut to pieces before you're fifty miles across the Border,' I said. 'You have to travel through Afghanistan to get to that country. It's one mass of mountains and peaks and glaciers, and no Englishman has been through it. The people are utter brutes, and even if you reached them you couldn't do anything.'

'That's more like,' said Carnehan. 'If you could think us a little more mad we would be more pleased. We have come to you to know about this country, to read a book about it, and to be shown maps. We want you to tell us that we are fools and to show us your books.' He turned to the book-cases.

'Are you at all in earnest?' I said.

'A little,' said Dravot sweetly. 'As big a map as you have got, even if it's all blank where Kafiristan is, and any books you've got. We can read, though we aren't very educated.'

I uncased the big thirty-two miles to the inch map of India and two smaller Frontier maps, hauled down volume INF-KAN of the Encyclopædia and the men consulted them.

'See here!' said Dravot, his thumb on the map. 'Up to Jagdallak, Peachey and me know the road. We was there with Robert's Army. We'll have to turn off to the right at Jagdallak through Laghmann territory. Then we get among the hills – fourteen thousand feet – fifteen thousand – it will be cold work there, but it don't look very far on the map.'

I handed him Wood on the *Sources of the Oxus*. Carnehan was deep in the Encyclopædia.

'They're a mixed lot,' said Dravot reflectively; 'and it won't help us to know the names of their tribes. The more tribes the more they'll fight, and the better for us. From Jagdallak to Ashang. H'mm!'

'But all the information about the country is as sketchy and inaccurate as can be,' I protested. 'No one knows anything about it really. Here's the file of the *United Services Institute Journal*. Read what Bellew says.'

'Blow Bellew!' said Carnehan. 'Dan, they're an all-fired lot of heathens, but this book here says they think they're related to us English.'

I smoked while the men pored over Raverty, Wood, the maps and the Encyclopædia.

'There is no use your waiting,' said Dravot politely. 'It's about four o'clock now. We'll go before six o'clock if you want to sleep, and we won't steal any of the papers. Don't you sit up. We're two harmless lunatics, and if you come to-morrow evening, down to the Serai we'll say good-bye to you.'

'You are two fools,' I answered. 'You'll be turned back at the Frontier or cut up the minute you set foot in Afghanistan. Do you want any money or a recommendation down country? I can help you to the chance of work next week.'

'Next week we shall be hard at work ourselves, thank you,' said Dravot. 'It isn't so easy being a King as it looks. When we've got our Kingdom in going order we'll let you know, and you can come up and help us to govern it.'

'Would two lunatics make a Contrack like that?' said Carnehan, with subdued pride, showing me a greasy half-sheet of note paper on which was written the following. I copied it, then and there, as a curiosity:–

This Contrackt between me and you persuing witnesseth in name of God Amen and so forth.

(One). That me and you will settle this matter together:
i.e., to be Kings of Kafiristan.

(Two). That you and me will not while this matter is being settled look at any Liquor nor any Woman black white or brown so as to get mixed up with one or the other harmful.

(Three). That we conduct ourselves with dignity and discretion and if one of us gets into trouble you will stay by him.

Signed by you and me this day.
Peachey Taliaferro Carnehan.
Daniel Dravot.
Both Gentlemen at Large.

'There was no need for the last article,' said Carnehan blushing modestly; 'but it looks regular. Now you know the sort of men that loafers are – we *are* loafers, Dan, until we get out of India – and do you think that we would sign a Contrack like that unless we was in earnest? We have kept away from the two things that make life worth having.'

'You won't enjoy your lives much longer if you are going to try this idiotic adventure. Don't set the office on fire,' I said, 'and go away before nine o'clock.'

I left them still poring over the maps and making notes on the back of the 'Contrack'. 'Be sure to come down to the Serai to-morrow,' were their parting words.

The Kumharsen Serai is the great four-square sink of humanity where the strings of camels and horses from the North load and unload. All the nationalities of Central Asia may be found there, and most of the folk of India proper, Balkh, and Bokhara, there meet Bengal and Bombay, and try to draw eye-teeth. You can buy ponies, turquoises, Persian pussy-cats, saddle-bags, fat-tailed sheep and musk in the Kumharsen Serai, and get many strange things for nothing. In the afternoon I went down there, to see whether my friends intended to keep their word or were lying about drunk.

A Mohammedan priest attired in fragments of ribbons and rags stalked up to me, gravely twisting a child's paper whirligig. Behind him was his servant bending under the load of a crated of mud toys. The two were loading up two camels, and the inhabitants of the Serai watched thcm with laughter.

'The *mullah* is mad,' said a horse-dealer to me. 'He is going up to Kabul to sell toys to the Amir. He will either be raised to honour or have his head cut off. He came in here this morning and has been behaving madly ever since.'

'The witless are under the protection of God,' stammered a flat-cheeked Usbeg in broken Hindi. 'They foretell future events.'

'Would they could have foretold that my caravan would have been cut up by the Shinwaris almost within shadow of the Pass?' grunted the Eusufzai agent of a Rajputana trading-house whose goods had been feloniously diverted into the hands of other robbers just across the Border, and whose misfortunes were the laughing-stock of the *bazar*. Ohé, *mullah*, whence come you and whither do you go?'

'From Roum have I come,' shouted the *mullah*, waving his whirligig; 'from Roum, blown by the breath of a hundred devils across the sea! Oh, thieves, robbers, liars, the blessing of Pir Khan on pigs, dogs and perjurers! Who will take the Protected of God to the North to sell charms that are never still to the Amir? The camels shall not gall, the sons shall not fall sick, and the wives shall remain faithful while they are away, of the men who give me place in their caravan. Who will assist me to slipper the King of the Roos with a golden slipper with a silver heel? The protection of Pir Khan be upon his labours!' He spread out the skirts of his gaberdine and pirouetted between the lines of tethered horses.

'There starts a caravan from Peshawar to Kabul in twenty days, holy father,' said the Eusufzai trader. 'My camels go therewith. Do thou also go and bring us good luck.'

'I will go even now!' shouted the *mullah*. 'I will depart on my winged camels, and be at Peshawar in a day! Ho! Hazar Mir Khan,' he yelled to his servant; 'drive out the camels, but let me first mount my own.'

He leaped on the back of his beast as it knelt, and turning round to me cried: 'Come thou also, *Sahib*, a little along the road, and I will sell thee a charm – an amulet that shall make thee King of Kafiristan.'

Then the light broke upon me, and I followed the two camels out of tbe Serai till we reached open road and the *mullah* halted.

'What d'you think o' that?' said he in English. 'Carnehan can't talk their patter, so I've made him my servant. He makes a handsome servant. 'Tisn't for nothing that I've been knocking about the country for fourteen years. Didn't I do that talk neat? We'll hitch on to a caravan at Peshawar till we get to Jagdallak, and then we'll see if we can get donkeys for our camels, and strike into Kafiristan. Whirligigs for the Amir. O Lor! Put your hand under the camel-bags and tell me what you feel.'

I felt the butt of a Martini, and another and another.

'Twenty of 'em,' said Dravot placidly. 'Twenty of 'em, and ammunition to correspond, under the whirligigs and the mud dolls.'

'Heaven help you if you are caught with those things!' I said. 'A Martini is worth her weight in silver among the Pathans.'

'Fifteen hundred rupees of capital – every rupee we could beg, borrow or steal – are invested on these two camels,' said Dravot. 'We won't get caught. We're going through the Khaiber with a regular caravan. Who'd touch a poor mad *mullah*?'

'Have you got everything you want,' I asked overcome with astonishment.

'Not yet, but we shall soon. Give us a memento of your kindness, Brother. You did me a service yesterday, and that time in Marwar. Half my kingdom shall you have, as the saying is.' I slipped a small charm-compass from my watch-chain and handed it up to the *mullah*.

'Good-bye,' said Dravot, giving me his hand cautiously. 'It's the last time we'll shake hands with an Englishman these many days. Shake hands with him, Carnehan,' he cried, as the second camel passed me.

Carnehan leant down and shook hands. Then the camels passed away along the dusty road and I was left alone to wonder. My eye could detect no failure in the disguises. The scene in the Serai showed that they were complete to the native mind. There was just the chance, therefore, that Carnehan and Dravot would be able to wander through Afghanistan without detection. But, beyond, they would find death, certain and awful death.

Ten days later a native friend of mine, giving me the news of the day from Peshawar, wound up his letter with: 'There has been much laughter here on account of a certain mad *mullah* who is going in his estimation to sell petty gauds and in-significant trinkets, which he ascribes as great charms, to H. H. the Amir of Afghanistan. He passed through Peshawar and associated himself to the second summer caravan that goes to Kabul. The merchants are pleased because through superstition they imagine that such mad fellows bring good fortune.'

The two, then, were beyond the Border. I would have prayed for them, but, that night, a real King died in Europe and demanded an obituary notice.

The wheel of the world swings through the same phases again and again. Summer passed and winter thereafter, and came and passed again. The daily paper continued and I with it, and upon the third summer there fell a hot night, a night-issue, and a strained waiting for something to be telegraphed from the other side of the world, exactly as had happened before. A few great men had died in the past two years, the machines worked with more clatter, and some of the trees in the office garden were a few feet taller. But that was all the difference.

I passed over to the press room, and went through just such a scene as I have already described. The nervous tension was stronger than it had been two years before, and I felt the heat more acutely. At three o'clock I cried, 'print off,' and turned to go, when there crept to my chair what was left of a man. He was bent into a circle, his head was sunk between his shoulders, and he moved his feet one over the other like a bear. I could hardly see whether he walked or crawled – this rag-wrapped, whining cripple who addressed me by name, crying that he was come back. 'Can you give me a drink?' he whimpered: 'For the Lord's sake give me a drink!'

I went back to the office, the man following with groans of pain, and I turned up the lamp.

'Don't you know me?' he gasped, dropping into a chair; and he turned his drawn face, surmounted by a shock of grey hair, to the light.

I looked at him intently. Once before had I seen eyebrows that met over the nose in an inch-broad black band, but for the life of me I could not tell where.

'I don't know you,' I said, handing him the whiskey. 'What can I do for you.'

He took a gulp of the spirit raw, and shivered in spite of the suffocating heat.

'I've come back,' he repeated; 'and I was the King of Kafiristan – me and Dravot – crowned kings we was! In this office we settled it – you setting there and giving us the books. I am Peachey – Peachey Taliaferro Carnehan, and you've been setting here ever since – O Lord!'

I was more than a little astonished and expressed my feelings accordingly.

'It's true,' said Carnehan, with a dry cackle, nursing his feet which were wrapped in rags. 'True as gospel. Kings we were, with crowns upon our heads – me and Dravot – poor Dan – oh, poor, poor Dan that would never take advice, not though I begged of him!'

'Take the whiskey,' I said, 'and take your own time. Tell me all you can recollect of everything from beginning to end. You got across the Border on your camels, Dravot dressed as a mad *mullah*, and you his servant. Do you remember that?'

'I ain't mad – yet, but I shall be that way soon. Of course I remember. Keep looking at me, or maybe my words will go all to pieces. Keep looking at me in my eyes and don't say anything.'

I leaned forward and looked into his face as steadily as I could. He dropped one hand upon the table and I grasped it by the wrist. It was twisted like a bird's claw, and upon the back was a ragged, red, diamond-shaped scar.

'No, don't look there. Look at *me*,' said Carnehan. 'That comes afterwards, but for the Lord's sake don't distrack me. We left with that caravan, me and Dravot playing all sorts of antics to amuse the people we were with. Dravot used to make us laugh in the evenings when all the people was cooking their dinners – cooking their dinners and . . . what did they do then? They lit little fires with sparks that went into Dravot's beard, and we all laughed – fit to die. Little red fires they was, going into Dravot's big red beard – so funny.' His eyes left mine and he smiled foolishly.

'You went as far as Jagdallak with that caravan,' I said at a venture, 'after you had lit those fires. To Jagdallak where you turned off to try to get into Kafiristan.'

'No we didn't neither. What are you talking about? We

turned off before Jagdallak because we heard the roads was good. But they wasn't good enough for our two camels – mine and Dravot's. When we left the caravan, Dravot took off all his clothes and mine too, and said we would be heathen, because the Kafirs didn't allow Mohammedans to talk to them. So we dressed betwixt and between, and such a sight as Daniel Dravot I never saw yet, nor yet expect to see again. He burned half his beard, and slung a sheep-skin over his shoulder, and shaved his head into patterns. He shaved mine, too, and made me wear outrageous things to look like a heathen. That was in a most mountaineous country, and our camels couldn't go along any more because of the mountains. They were tall and black, and coming home I saw them fight like wild goats – there are lots of goats in Kafiristan. And these mountains they never keep still, no more than the goats. Always fighting they are, and don't let you sleep at night.'

'Take some more whiskey,' I said very slowly. 'What did you and Daniel Dravot do when the camels could go no further, because of the rough roads that led into Kafiristan?'

'What did which do? There was a party called Peachey Taliaferro Carnehan that was with Dravot. Shall I tell you about him? He died out there in the cold. Slap from the bridge fell old Peachey, turning and twisting in the air like a penny paper whirligig that you can sell to the Amir – No; they was two for three ha'pence, those whirligigs, or I am much mistaken and woeful sore. And then these camels were no use, and Peachey said to Dravot: "For the Lord's sake let's get out of this before our heads are chopped off," and with that they killed the camels all among the mountains, not having anything in particular to eat, but first they took off the boxes with the guns and the ammunition, till two men came along driving four mules. Dravot up and dances in front of them, singing, "Sell me four mules". Says the first man, "If you are rich enough to buy you are rich enough to rob"; but before ever he could put his hand to his knife, Dravot breaks that man's neck over his knee, and the other party runs away. So Carnehan loaded the mules with the rifles that was taken off the camels, and together we starts forward into those bitter cold mountaineous parts, and never a road broader than the back of your hand.'

He paused for a moment, while I asked him if he could remember the nature of the country through which he had journeyed.

'I am telling you as straight as I can, but my head isn't as good as it might be. They drove nails through it to make me hear better how Dravot died. The country was mountaineous and the mules were most contrary, and the inhabitants was dispersed and solitary. They went up and up, and down and down, and that other party, Carnehan, was imploring of Dravot not to sing and whistle so loud, for fear of bringing down the tremenjus avalanches. But Dravot says that if a King couldn't sing it wasn't worth being King, and whacked the mules over the rump, and never took no heed for ten cold days. We came to a big level valley all among the mountains, and the mules were near dead, so we killed them, not having anything in special for them or us to eat. We sat upon the boxes and played odd and even with the cartridges that was jolted out.

'Then ten men with bows and arrows ran down that valley, chasing twenty men with bows and arrows, and the row was tremenjus. They was fair men – fairer than you or me – with yellow hair and remarkable well built. Says Dravot, unpacking the guns: "This is the beginning of the business. We'll fight for the ten men," and with that he fires two rifles at the twenty men, and drops one of them at two hundred yards from the rock where we was sitting. The other men began to run, but Carnehan and Dravot sits on the boxes picking them off at all ranges, up and down the valley. Then we goes up to the ten men that had run across the snow too, and they fires a footy little arrow at us. Dravot he shoots above their heads and they all falls down flat.

'Then he walks over them and kicks them, and then he lifts them up and shakes hands, all round to make them friendly like. He calls them and gives them the boxes to carry, and waves his hand for all the world as though he was King already. They takes the boxes and him across the valley and up the hill into a pine wood on the top, where there was half a dozen big stone idols. Dravot he goes to the biggest – a fellow they call Imbra – and lays a rifle and a cartridge at his feet, rubbing his nose respectful with his own nose, patting him on the head and saluting in front of it. He turns round to the men and nods his head and says: "That's all right. I'm in the know too, and all these old jim-jams are my friends."

'Then he opens his mouth and points down it, and when the first man brings him food he says "No," and when the second man brings him food he says "No,"; but when one of the old priests and the boss of the village brings him food, he says, "Yes," very haughty, and eats it very slow. That was how we came to our first village, without any trouble, just as though we had tumbled from the skies. But we tumbled from one of those damned rope-bridges, you see, and you couldn't expect a man to laugh much after that.'

'Take some more whiskey and go on,' I said. 'That was the first village you came into. How did you get to be King?'

'I wasn't King,' said Carnehan. 'Dravot he was the King and a handsome man he looked with the gold crown on his head and all. Him and the other party stayed in that village, and every morning Dravot sat by the side of old Imbra, and the people came and bowed down before him. That was Dravot's order. Then a lot of men came into the valley and Carnehan and Dravot picks them off with the rifles before they knew where they was, and runs down into the valley, and up again the other side and finds another village, same as the first one, and the people all falls down flat on their faces, and Dravot says: "Now what is the trouble between you two villages?" and the people points to a woman, as fair as you or me, that was carried off, and Dravot takes her back to the first village and counts up the dead – eight there was. For each dead man Dravot pours a little milk on the ground and waves his arms like a whirligig and "that's all right," says he. Then he and Carnehan takes the big boss of each village by the arm and walks them down into the valley, and shows them how to scratch a line with a spear right down the valley, and gives each a sod of turf from both sides of the line. Then all the people comes down and shouts like the devil and all, and Dravot says: "Go and dig the land, and be fruitful and multiply," which they did, though they didn't understand. Then we asks the names of things in their lingo – bread and water and fire and idols and such, and Dravot leads the priests of each village up to the idol and says he must sit there and judge the people, and if anything goes wrong he is to be shot.

'Next week they was all turning up the land in the valley as quiet as bees and much prettier, and the priests heard all the complaints and told Dravot in dumb show what it was about. "That's just the beginning," says Dravot. "They think we're Gods." He and Carnehan picks out twenty good men and shows them how to click off a rifle, and form fours, and advance in line, and they was very pleased to do so, and – clever to see the hang of it.

'Then he takes out his pipe and his baccy-pouch and leaves one at one village and one at the other, and off we two goes to see what was to be done in the next valley. That was all rock, and there was a little village there, and Carnehan says: "Send 'em to the old valley to plant," and takes 'em there and gives 'em some land that wasn't took before. They were a poor lot, and we blooded 'em with a kid before letting 'em into the new Kingdom. That was to impress the people, and then they settled down quiet, and Carnehan went back to Dravot who had got into another valley, all snow and ice and most mountaineous. There was no people there and the Army got afraid, so Dravot shoots one of 'em, and goes on till he finds some people in a village, and the Army explains that unless the people wants to be killed they had better not shoot their little matchlocks; for they had matchlocks. We makes friends with the priest and I stays there alone with two of the Army, teaching the men how to drill, and a thundering big chief comes across the snow with kettle-drums and horns twanging, because he heard there was a new God kicking about. Carne-han sights for the brown of the men half a mile across the snow and wings one of them. Then he sends a message to the chief that, unless he wished to be killed, he must come and shake hands with me and leave his arms behind. The chief comes alone first, and Carnehan shakes hands with, him and whirls his arms about, same as Dravot used, and very much surprised that chief was and strokes my eyebrows. Then Carnehan goes alone to the chief and asks him in dumb show if he had an enemy he hated. "I have," says the chief. So Carnehan weeds out the pick of his men and sets the two of the Army to show them drill, and at the end of two weeks the men can manœuvre about as well as volunteers. So he marches with the chief to a great big plain on the top of a mountain, and the chief's men rushes into a village and takes it; we three Martinis firing into the brown of the enemy. So we took that village too, and I gives the chief a rag from my coat and says, "occupy till I come": which was scriptural. By way of a reminder, when me and the Army was eighteen hundred yards away, I drops a bullet near him standing on the snow, and all the people falls fiat on their faces. Then I sends a letter to Dravot, wherever he be by land or by sea.'

At the risk of throwing the creature out of train I interrupted: 'How could you write a letter up yonder?'

'The letter – Oh – the letter! Keep looking at me between the eyes, please. It was a string-talk letter, that we'd learned the way of it from a blind beggar in the Punjab.'

I remembered that there had once come to the office a blind man with a knotted twig and a piece of string which he wound round the twig according to some cipher of his own. He could, after the lapse of days or hours, repeat the sentence which he had reeled up. He had reduced the alphabet to eleven primitive sounds; and tried to teach me his method, but failed.

'I sent that letter to Dravot,' said Carnehan, 'and told him to come back because this Kingdom was growing too big for me to handle, and then I struck for the first valley to see how the priests were working. They called the village we took along with the Chief, Bashkai, and the first village we took, Er-Heb. The priests at Er-Heb was doing all right, but they had a lot of pending cases about land to shew me, and some men from another villiage had been firing arrows at night. I went out and looked for that village and fired four rounds at it from a thousand yards. That used all the cartridges I cared to spend, and I waited for Dravot who had been away two or three months, and I kept my people quiet.

'One morning, I heard the devil's own noise of drums and horns, and Dan Dravot marches down the hill with his Army and a tail of hundreds of men, and, which was the most amazing, a great gold crown on his head, "My Gord, Carnehan," says Daniel, "this is a tremenjus business, and we've got the whole country as far as it's worth having. I am the son of Alexander by Queen Semiramis, and you're my younger brother and a God too! It's the biggest thing we've ever seen. I've been marching and fighting for six weeks with the Army, and every footy little village for fifty miles has come in rejoiceful; and more than that, I've got the key of the whole show, as you'll see, and I've got a crown for you! I told 'em to make two of 'em at a place called Shu, where the gold lies in the rock like suet in mutton. Gold I've seen, and turquoise I've kicked out of the cliffs and there's garnets in the sands of the river and here's a chunk of amber that a man brought me. Call up all the priests and, here, take your crown.'

'One of the men opens a black hair bag and I slips the crown on. It was too small and too heavy, but I wore it for the glory. Hammered gold it was – five pound weight like a hoop of a barrel.

' "Peachey," says Dravot, "we don't want to fight no more. The Craft's the trick so help me!" and – he brings forward that same Chief that I left at Bashkai – Billy Fish we called him afterwards, because he was so like Billy Fish that drove the big tank-engine at Mach on the Bolan, in the old days. "Shake hands with him," says Dravot, and I shook hands and nearly dropped, for Billy Fish gave me the Grip. I said nothing but tried him with the Fellow Craft Grip. He answers all right, and I tried the Master's Grip but that was a slip. "A Fellow Craft he is!" I says to Dan. "Does he know the Word?" "He does," says Dan, "and all the priests know. It's a miracle! The Chiefs and the priests can work a Fellow Craft lodge in a way that's very like ours, and they've cut the marks on the rocks, but they don't know the Third Degree, and they've come to find out. It's Gord's truth. I've known these long years that the Afghans knew up to the Fellow Craft Degree, but this is a miracle. A God and a Grand Master of the Craft am I, and a lodge in the Third Degree I will open, and we'll raise the head priests and the Chiefs of the villages."

' "It's against all the law," I says, holding a Lodge without warrant from any one; and we never held office in any Lodge.'

' "It's a master-stroke of policy," says Dravot. "It means running the country as easy as a four-wheeled bogey on a down grade. We can't stop to enquire now, or they'll turn against us. I've forty Chiefs at my heel, and passed and raised according to their merit they shall be. Billet these men on the villages and see that we run up a Lodge of some kind. The temple of Imbra will do for the Lodge-room. The women must make aprons as you show them. I'll hold a levée of Chiefs to-night and Lodge to-morrow."

'I was fair run off my legs, but I wasn't such a fool as not to see what a pull this Craft business gave us. I showed the priests' families how to make aprons of the degrees, but for Dravot's apron, the border and marks was made of turquoise lamps on white hide, not cloth. We took a great square stone in the temple for the Master's chair, and little stones for the officers' chairs, and painted the black pavement with white squares, and did what we could to make things regular.

'At the levée which was held that night on the hill side with big bon-fires, Dravot gives out that him and me were Gods and sons of Alexander, and past Grand Masters in the Craft, and was come to make Kafiristan a country where every man should eat in peace and drink in quiet, and specially obey us. Then the Chiefs come round to shake hands, and they was so hairy and white and fair, it was just shaking hands with old friends. We gave them names according as they was like men we had known in India – Billy Fish, Holly Dilworth, Pikky Kergan that was Bazaar-master when I was at Mhow, and so on and so forth.

'*The* most amazing miracle was at Lodge next night. One of the old priests was watching us continuous, and I felt uneasy, for I knew we'll have to fudge the Ritual, and I didn't know what the men knew. The old priest was a stranger come in from beyond the village of Bashkai. The minute Dravot puts on the Master's apron that the girls had made for him the priest fetches a whoop and a howl and tries to overturn the stone that Dravot was sitting on. "It's all up now," I says. "That's come of meddling with the Craft without warrant!" Dravot never winked an eye, not when ten priests took and tilted over the Grand-Master's chair – which was to say the stone of Imbra. The priest begins rubbing the bottom end of it to clear away the black dirt, and presently he shows all the other priests the Master's Mark, same as was on Dravot's apron, cut into the stone. Not even the priest's of the temple of Imbra knew it was there. The old chap falls flat on his face at Dravot's feet and kisses 'em. "Luck again," says Dravot across the Lodge to me, "They say it's the missing Mark that no one could understand the why of. We're more than safe now." Then he bangs the butt of his gun for a gavel and says: "By virtue of the authority vested in me by my own right hand and the help of Peachey I declare myself Grand Master of all Freemasonry in Kafiristan in this, the Mother Lodge o' the country, and King of Kafiristan equally with Peachey!" At that he puts on his crown and I puts on mine – I was doing Senior Warden – and we opens the Lodge in most ample form. It was an amazing miracle! The priests moved in Lodge through the first two degrees almost without telling, as if the memory was coming back to them.

'After that, Peachey and Dravot raised such as was worthy – high priests and chiefs of far-off villages. Billy Fish was the first, and I can tell you we scared the soul out of him. It was not in any way according to Ritual, but it served our turn. We didn't raise more than ten of the biggest men, because we didn't want to make the degree common. And they was clamouring to be raised.

' "In another six months," says Dravot, "we'll hold another communication and see how you are working." Then he asks them about their villages, and learns that they was always fighting one against the other and were fair sick and tired of it. And when they wasn't doing that they was fighting with the Mohammedans and Afghans. "You can fight those when they came into our country," says Dravot. "Tell off every tenth man of your tribes for a frontier guard, and send two hundred at a time to this valley to be drilled. Nobody is going to be shot or speared anymore so long as he does well, and I know that you won't cheat me because you're white people – sons of Alexander – and not like common black Mohammedans. You are *my* people and by God," says he running off into English at the end – "I'll make a damned fine nation of you, or die in the making!"

'I can't tell all we did for the next six months because Dravot did a lot I couldn't see the lean of, and he learned their lingo in a way I never could. My work, was to help the people plough, and now and again go out with some of the army and see what the other villages were doing, and make 'em throw ropebridges across the ravines which cut up the country horrid. Dravot was very kind to me, but when he walked up and down in the pine wood pulling that bloody red beard of his with both fists I knew he was thinking plans which I could not advise him. regarding, and I just waited for orders.

'But Dravot never showed me disrespect before the people, They were afraid of me and the army, but they loved Dan. He was the best of friends with the priests and the chiefs; but any one could come across the hills with a complaint and Dravot would hear him out fair, and call four priests together and say what was to be done. He used to call in Billy Fish from Bashkai, and Picky Kergan from Shu, and an old chief we called Kafuzelum – it was like enough to his real name – and hold councils with 'em when there was any fighting needful in the small villages. That was his council of war, and the four priests of Bashkai, Shu, Khawak and Madora was his Privy Council. Between the lot of 'em they sent me, with forty men and twenty rifles, and sixty men carrying baskets of turquoises, into the Ghorbaud country to buy those hand-made Martini rifles, that come out of the Amir's workshops at Kabul, from one of the Amir's Herati regiments that would have sold the very teeth out of their mouths for turquoises.

'I stayed in Ghorband a month, and gave the Governor there the pick of my baskets for hush money, and bribed the

Colonel of the regiment some more, and, between the two and the tribespeople, we got more than a hundred hand-made Martinis, a hundred good Kohat Jezails that'll throw to six hundred yards, and forty man-loads of very bad ammunition for the rifles. I came back with what I had and distributed 'em among the men that the chiefs sent in to me to drill. Dravot was too busy to attend to those things, but the old Army that we first made, helped me, and we turned out five hundred men that could drill, and two hundred that knew how to hold arms pretty straight. Even those cork-screwed, hand-made Martinis was a miracle to them. Dravot talked big about powder-shops and factories, walking up and down in the pine wood when the winter was coming on.

' "I won't make a nation," says he. "I'll make an Empire! These men aren't niggers: they're English! Look at their eyes – look at their mouths. Look at the way they stand up. They sit on chairs in their own houses. They're the Lost Tribes or something like it, and they've grown to be English. I'll take a census in the spring if the priests don't get frightened. There must be a fair two million of 'em in these hills. The villages are full o' little children. Two million people – two hundred and fifty thousand fighting men – and all English! They only want rifles and a little drilling. Two hundred and fifty thousand men, ready to cut in on Russia's right flank when she tries for India! Peachey, man," he says, chewing his beard in great hunks, "we shall be Emperors – Emperors of the Earth! Rajah Brooke will be a suckling to us. I'll treat with the Viceroy on equal terms. I'll ask him to send me twelve picked English – twelve that I know of – to help us govern a bit. There's Mackray, Sergeant-pensioner at Segowli – many's the good dinner he's given me, and his wife, a pair of trousers. There's Donkin, the Warder of Tounghoo Jail; there's hundreds that I could lay my hand on if I was in India. The Viceroy shall do it for me. I'll send a man through to India in the spring to ask for those men, and I'll write for a dispensation from the Grand Lodge for what I've done as Grand Master. That and all the Sniders that'll be thrown out when the native troops in India take up the Martini. They'll be wore smooth, but they'll do for fighting in these hills. Twelve English, a hundred thousand Sniders run through the Amir's country in driblets – I'd be content with twenty thousand in one year and we'd be an Empire. When everything was shipshape, I'd hand over the crown – this very crown I'm wearing now – to Queen Victoria on my knees, and she'd say: 'Rise up, Sir Daniel Dravot'. Oh, it's big! It's big I tell you! But's there's so much to be done in every place – Bashkai, Khawak, Shu, and everywhere else."

' "What is it?" I says. "There are no more men coming in to be drilled this autumn. Look at those fat, black clouds. They're bringing the snow."

' "It isn't that," says Daniel putting his hand very hard on my shoulder; "and I don't wish to say anything that's against you, for no other living man would have followed me and made me what I am as you have done. You're a first-class Commander-in-Chief, and the people know you; but – it's a big country, and somehow you can't help me, Peachey, the way I want to be helped."

' "Go to your blasted priests, then!" I said, and I was sorry when I made that remark, but it did hurt me sore to find Daniel talking so superior when I drilled all the men, and done all he told me.

' "Don't let's quarrel, Peachey," says Daniel without cursing. "You're a King too, and the half o' this Kingdom is yours; but can't you see, Peachey, we want cleverer men than us now – three or four of 'em, that we can scatter about for our deputies. It's a hugeous great state, and I can't always tell the right thing to do, and I haven't time for all I want to do, and here's the winter coming on and all." He put half his beard into his mouth, and it was as red as the gold of his crown.

' "I'm sorry, Daniel," says I. "I've done all I could. I've drilled the men and shown the people how to stack their oats better; and I've brought in those tinware rifles from Ghorband – but I know what you're driving at. I take it Kings always feel oppressed that way."

' "There's another thing too," says Dravot, walking up and down. "The winter's coming and these people won't be giving much trouble, and if they do we can't move about. I want a wife."

' "For God's sake leave the women alone!" I says. We've both got all the work we can, though I *am* a fool. Remember our Contrack and keep clear o' women."

' "The Contrack only lasted till such time as we was Kings; and Kings we have been these months past," says Dravot, weighing his crown in his hand. "You go get a wife too, Peachey – a nice, strappin', plump girl that'll keep you warm in the winter. They're prettier than English girls, and we can take the pick of 'em. Boil 'em once or twice in hot water, and they'll come as fair as chicken and ham."

' "Don't tempt me!" I says. "I will not have any dealings with a woman not till we are a dam' side more settled than we are now. I've been doing the work o' two men, and you've been doing the work o' three. Let's lie off a bit, and see if we can get some better tobacco from Afghan country and run in some good liquor; but no women."

' "Who's talking o' *women*?" says Dravot. "I said *wife* – a Queen to breed a King's son for the King. A Queen out of the strongest tribe, that'll make them your blood brothers, and that'll lie by your side and tell you all the people thinks about you and their own affairs. That's what I want."

' "Do you remember that Bengali woman I kept at Mogul Serai when I was a plate-layer?" says I. "A fat lot o' good she was to me. She taught me the lingo and one or two other things; but what happened? She ran away with the Station Master's *khitmatgar* and half my month's pay. Then she turned up at Dadur Junction in tow of a half-caste and had the impidence to say I was her husband – all among the drivers in the running-shed!"

' "We've done with that," says Dravot. "These women are whiter than you or me, and a Queen I will have for the winter months."

' "For the last time o' asking, Dan, do *not*," I says. "It'll only bring us harm. The Bible says that Kings ain't to waste their strength on women, especially when they've got a new raw Kingdom to work over."

' "For the last time of answering I will," said Dravot, and he went away through the pine trees looking like a big red devil. The low sun hit his crown and beard on one side, and the two blazed like hot coals.

'But getting a wife was not as easy as Dan thought. He put it before the Council, and there was no answer till Billy Fish said that he'd better ask the girls. Dravot damned them all round. "What's wrong with me?" he shouts, standing by the idol Imbra. "Am I a dog or am I not enough of a man for your wenches. Haven't I put the shadow of my hand over this country? Who stopped the last Afghan raid?" It was me really, but Dravot was too angry to remember. "Who bought your guns? Who repaired the bridges? Who's the Grand Master of the sign cut in the stone?" and he thumped his hand on the block that he used to sit on in Lodge and at Council which opened like Lodge always. Billy Fish said nothing and no more did the others.

' "Keep your hair on, Dan," said I; "and ask the girls. That's how it's done at home, and these people are quite English."

' "The marriage of the King is a matter of State," says Dan, in a white-hot rage, for he could feel, I hope, that he was going against his better mind. He walked out of the Council-room, and the others sat still, looking at the ground.

' "Billy Fish," says I to the chief of Bashkai, "what's the difficulty here? A straight answer to a true friend."

' "You know," says Billy Fish. "How should a man tell you who know everything? How can daughters of men marry Gods or Devils? It's not proper."

'I remembered something like that in the Bible; but if, after seeing us as long as they had, they still believed we were Gods, it wasn't for me to undeceive them.

' "A God can do anything," says I. "If the King is fond of a girl he'll not let her die." "She'll have to," said Billy Fish. "There are all sorts of Gods and Devils in these mountains, and now and again a girl marries one of them and isn't seen any more. Besides, you two know the Mark cut in the stone. Only the Gods know that. We thought you was men till you showed the sign of the Master."

'I wished then that we had explained about the loss of the genuine secrets of a master mason at the first go-off; but I said nothing. All that night there was a blowing of horns in a little dark temple half way down the hill, and I heard a girl crying fit to die. One of the priests told us that she was being prepared to marry the King.

'"I'll have no nonsense of that kind," says Dan. "I don't want to interfere with your customs, but I'll take my own wife."

'"The girl's a bit afraid," says the priest. "She thinks she's going to die, and they are a-heartening of her up down in the temple."

'"Hearten her very tender, then," says Dravot, "or I'll hearten you with the butt of a gun so that you'll never want to be heartened again." He licked his lips, did Dan, and stayed up walking about more than half the night, thinking of the wife that he was going to get in the morning. I wasn't any means comfortable, for I knew that dealings with a woman in foreign parts, though you was a crowned King twenty times over, could not but be risky. I got up very early in the morning while Dravot was asleep, and I saw the priests talking together in whispers, and the chiefs talking together too, and they looked at me out of the corners of their eyes.

'"What is up, Fish?" I says to the Bashkai man who was wrapped up in his furs and looking splendid to behold.

'"I can't rightly say," says he; "but if you can induce the King to drop all this nonsense about marriage, you'll be doing him and me and yourself a great service."

'"That I do believe," says I. "But sure, you know, Billy, as well as me, having fought against and for us, that the King and me are nothing more than two of the finest men that God Almighty ever made. Nothing more, I do assure you."

'"That may be," says Billy Fish, "and yet I should be sorry if it was." He sinks his head upon his great fur cloak for a minute and thinks. "King," says he. "Be you man or God or Devil, I'll stick by you to-day. I have twenty of my men with me, and they will follow me. We'll go to Bashkai until the storm blows over."

'A little snow had fallen in the night, and everything was white except the greasy fat clouds that blew down and down from the north. Dravot came out with his crown on his head, swinging his arms and stamping his feet, and looking more pleased than Punch.

' "For the last time, drop it, Dan," says I in a whisper. "Billy Fish here says that there will be a row."

' "A row among my people!" says Dravot. "Not much. Peachey you're a fool not to get a wife too. Where's the girl?" says he, with a voice as loud as the braying of a jackass. "Call up all the chiefs and priests, and let the Emperor see if his wife suits him."

'There was no need to call any one. They were all there leaning on their guns and spears round the clearing in the centre of the pine wood. A crowd of priests went down to the little temple to bring up the girl, and the horns blew up fit to wake the dead. Billy Fish saunters round and gets as close to Daniel as he could, and behind him stood his own twenty men with matchlocks. Not a man of them under six feet. I was next to Dravot, and behind me was twenty men of the regular Army. Up comes the girl, and a strapping wench she was, covered with silver and turquoises but white as death, and looking back every minute at the priests.

' "She'll do," said Dan, looking her over. "What's to be afraid of, lass? Come and kiss me." He puts his arm round her. She shuts her eyes, gives a bit of a squeak, and down goes her face in the side of Dan's flaming red beard.

' "The slut's bitten me!" says he, clapping his hand to his neck, and sure enough his hand was red with blood. Billy Fish and two of his matchlock men catches hold of Dan by the shoulders and drags him into the Bashkai lot, while the priests howl in their lingo: "Neither God nor Devil but a man!" I was all taken aback, for a priest cut at me in front, and the Army behind began firing into the Bashkai men.

' "God a-mighty !" says Dan. "What is the meaning o' this?"

' "Come back! Come away!" says Billy Fish. "Ruin and Mutiny is the matter. We'll break for Bashkai if we can."

'I tried to give some sort of orders to my men – the men o'

the regular Army – but it wasn't no use, so I fired into the brown of 'em with an English Martini and drilled three beggars in a line. The valley was full of howling creatures, and every soul was shrieking, "Not a God nor a Devil but only a man!" The Bashkai troops stuck to Billy Fish all they were worth, but their matchlocks wasn't half as good as the Kabul breech-loaders, and four of 'em dropped. Dan was bellowing like a bull, for he was very wrathy; and Billy Fish had a hard job to prevent him running out at the crowd.

' "We can't stand," says Billy Fish. "Make a run for it down the valley! The whole place is against us." The matchlock-men ran, and we went down the valley in spite of Dravot's protestations. He was swearing horribly and crying out that he was a King. The priests rolled great stones on us, and the regular Army fired hard, and there wasn't more than six men, not counting Dan, Billy Fish and me, that came down to the bottom of the valley alive.

'Then they stopped firing and the horns in the temple blew again. "Come away – for Gord's sake come away!" says Billy Fish. "They'll send runners out to all the villages before ever we get to Bashkai. I can protect you there, but I can't do anything now."

'My own notion is that Dan began to go mad in his head from that hour. He stared up and down like a stuck pig. Then he was all for walking back alone and killing the priests with his bare hands; which he could have done. "An Emperor am I," says Daniel, "and next year I shall be a Knight of the Queen."

' "All right, Dan," says I; "but come along now while there's time."

' "It's your fault," says he, "for not looking after your Army better. There was mutiny in the midst, and you didn't know – you damned engine-driving, plate-laying, missionary's-pass-hunting hound!" He sat upon a rock and called me every foul name he could lay tongue to. I was too heart-sick to care, though it was all his foolishness that brought the smash.

' "I'm sorry, Dan," says I, "but there's no accounting for

natives. This business is our Fifty-Seven. Maybe we'll make something out of it yet, when we've got to Bashkai."

' "Let's go to Bashkai, then," says Dan, "and, by God, when I come back here again I'll sweep the valley so there isn't a bug in a blanket left!"

'We walked all that day, and all that night Dan was stumping up and down on the snow chewing his beard and muttering to himself.

' "There's no hope o' getting clear," said Billy Fish. "The priests will have sent runners to the villages to say that you are only men. Why didn't you stick on as Gods till things was more settled? I'm a dead man," says Billy Fish, and he throws himself down on the snow and begins to pray to his Gods.

'Next morning we was in a cruel bad country – all up and down, no level ground at all, and no food either. The six Bashkai men looked at Billy Fish hungry-wise as if they wanted to ask something, but they said never a word. At noon we came to the top of a flat mountain, all covered with snow, and when we climbed up into it, behold there was an army in position waiting in the middle!

' "The runners have been very quick," says Billy Fish, with a little bit of a laugh. "They are waiting for us."

'Three or four men began to fire from the enemy's side, and a chance shot took Daniel in the calf of the leg. That brought him to his senses. He looks across the snow at the Army, and sees the rifles that we had brought into the country.

' "We're done for," says he. "They are Englishmen, these people, and it's my blasted nonsense that has brought you to this. Get back, Billy Fish, and take your men away; you've done what you could, and now cut for it. Carnehan," says he, "shake hands with me and go along with Billy. Maybe they won't kill you. I'll go and meet 'em alone. It's me that did it. Me, the King!"

' "Go!" says I. "Go to Hell, Dan. I'm with you here. Billy Fish you clear out, and we two will meet those folk."

' "I'm a Chief," says Billy Fish, quite quiet. "I stay with you. My men can go."

'The Bashkai fellows didn't wait for a second word but ran

off, and Dan and me and Billy Fish walked across to where the drums were drumming and the horns were horning. It was cold – awful cold. I've got that cold in the back of my head now. There's a lump of it there.'

The punkah-coolies had gone to sleep. Two kerosene lamps were blazing in the office, and the perspiration poured down my face and splashed on the blotter as I leaned forward. Carnehan was shivering, and I feared that his mind might go. I wiped my face, took a fresh grip of the piteously mangled hands, and said: 'What happened after that?'

The momentary shift of my eyes had broken the clear current.

'What was you pleased to say?" whined Carnehan. 'They took them without any sound. Not a little whisper all along the snow, not though the King knocked down the first man that set hand on him – not though old Peachey fired his last cartridge into the brown of 'em. Not a single solitary sound did those swines make. They just closed up tight, and I tell you their furs stunk. There was a man called Billy Fish, a chief and a good friend of us all, and they cut his throat, Sir, then and there like a pig; and the King kicks up the bloody snow and says: "We've had a dashed fine run for our money. What's coming next?" But Peachey, Peachey Taliaferro, I tell you, Sir, in confidence as betwixt two friends, he lost his head, Sir. No, he didn't neither. The King lost his head, so he did, all along o' one of those cunning rope-bridges. Kindly let me have the paper-cutter, Sir. It tilted this way. They marched him a mile across that snow to a rope-bridge over a ravine with a river at the bottom. You may have seen such. They prodded him behind like an ox. "Damn your eyes!" says the King. "D'you suppose I can't die like a gentleman?" He turns to Peachey – Peachey that was crying like a child. "I've brought you to this, Peachey," says he. "Brought you out of your happy life to be killed in Kafiristan, where you was late Commander-in-Chief of the Emperor's forces. Say you forgive me, Peachey." "I do," says Peachey. "Fully and freely do I forgive you, Dan." "Shake hands, Peachey," says he. "I'm going now." Out he goes looking neither right nor left, and when he was plumb in the middle of those dizzy dancing-ropes, "Cut you beggars," he shouts; and they cut, and old Dan fell, turning round and round and round, twenty thousand miles, for he took half an hour to fall till he struck the water, and I could see his body caught on a rock with the gold crown close beside.

'But do you know what they did to Peachey between two pine trees? They crucified him, Sir, as Peachey's hands will show. They used wooden pegs for his hands and his feet; and he didn't die. He hung there and screamed, and they took him down next day, and said that it was a miracle that he wasn't dead. They took him down – poor old Peachey that hadn't done them any harm – that hadn't done them any . . .'

He rocked to and fro and wept bitterly, wiping his eyes with the backs of his scarred hands and moaning like a child for some ten minutes.

'They was cruel enough to feed him up in the temple, because they said he was more of a God than old Daniel that was a man. Then they turned him out on the snow, and told him to go home, and Peachey came home in about a year, begging along the roads quite safe; for Daniel Dravot he walked before and said: "Come along, Peachey. It's a big thing we're doing." The mountains they danced at night, and the mountains they tried to fall on Peachey's head, but Dan he held up his hand, and Peachey came along bent double. He never let go of Dan's hand, and he never let go of Dan's head. They gave it to him as a present in the temple, to remind him not to come again, and though the crown was pure gold, and Peachey was starving, never would Peachey sell the same. You knew Dravot, Sir! You knew Right Worshipful Brother Dravot! Look at him now!'

He fumbled in the mass of rags round his bent waist; brought out a black horse-hair bag embroidered with silver thread; and shook therefrom on to my table – the dried, withered head of Daniel Dravot! The morning sun that had long been paling the lamps struck the red beard and blind sunken eyes; struck, too, a heavy circlet of gold studded with raw turquoises that Carnehan placed tenderly on the battered temples.

'You behold now,' said Carnehan, 'the Emperor in his habit as he lived – the King of Kafiristan with his crown upon his head. Poor old Daniel that was a real monarch once!'

I shuddered, for, in spite of defacements manifold, I recognised the head of the man of Marwar Junction.

Carnehan rose to go. I attempted to stop him. He was not fit to walk abroad. 'Let me take away the whiskey, and give me a little money,' he gasped. 'I was a King once. I'll go to the Deputy Commissioner and ask leave to set in the Poorhouse till I get my health. No, thank you, I can't wait till you get a carriage for me. I've urgent private affairs – in the South – at Marwar. He has gone South for the week, you know.'

He shambled out of the office and departed in the direction of the Deputy Commissioner's house. That day at noon I had occasion to go down the blinding hot Mall, and I saw a crooked man crawling along the white dust of the roadside, his hat in his hand, quavering dolorously after the fashion of street-singers at Home. There was not a soul in sight, and he was out of all possible earshot of the houses. And he sang through his nose, turning his head, tortoise fashion, from right to left: –

'The Son of Man goes forth to war,
　A golden crown to gain;
His blood-red banner streams afar—
　Who follows in his train?'

I waited to hear no more but put the poor wretch into my carriage and drove him off to the nearest missionary for eventual transfer to the Asylum. He repeated the hymn twice while he was with me, whom he did not in the least recognise, and I left him singing it to the missionary.

Two days later I enquired after his welfare of the Superintendent of the Asylum.

'He was admitted suffering from sunstroke. He died early yesterday morning,' said the Superintendent. 'Is it true that he was half an hour bareheaded in the sun at midday?'

'Yes,' said I, 'but do you happen to know if he had anything upon him by any chance when he died?'

'Not to my knowledge,' said the Superintendent.

And there the matter rests.

THE SOLID MULDOON

Did ye see John Malone, wid his shinin' brand-new hat?
Did ye see how he walked like a grand aristocrat?
There was flags an' banners wavin' high, an' dhress and shtyle were
   shown,
But the best av all the company was Misther John Malone.

John Malone

There had been a royal dog-fight in the ravine at the back of
the rifle-butts, between Learoyd's Jock and Ortheris's Blue
Rot – both mongrel Rampur hounds, chiefly ribs and teeth. It
lasted for twenty happy, howling minutes, and then Blue Rot
collapsed and Ortheris paid Learoyd three rupees, and we
were all very thirsty. A dog-fight is a most heating entertainment, quite apart from the shouting, because Rampurs fight
over a couple of acres of ground. Later, when the sound of
belt-badges clicking against the necks of beer-bottles had died
away, conversation drifted from dog- to man-fights of all
kinds. Humans resemble red deer in some respects. Any talk
of fighting seems to wake up a sort of imp in their breasts, and
they bell one to the other, exactly like challenging bucks. This
is noticeable even in men who consider themselves superior to
Privates of the Line. It shows the Refining Influence of
Civilisation and the March of Progress.

Tale provoked tale, and each tale more beer. Even dreamy
Learoyd's eyes began to brighten, and he unburdened himself
of a long history in which a trip to Malham Cove, a girl at
Pateley Brigg, a ganger, himself, and a pair of clogs were
mixed in a drawling tangle.

'An' soa Ah coot's heead oppen from t' chin to t' hair, an' he
was abed for t' matter o' a month,' concluded Learoyd
pensively.

Mulvaney came out of a reverie – he was lying down – and

flourished his heels in the air. 'You're a man, Learoyd,' said he critically, 'but you've only fought wid men, an' that's an ivryday expayrience; but I've stud up to a ghost, an' that was *not* an ivryday experience.'

'No?' said Ortheris, throwing a cork at him. 'You git up an' address the 'ouse – you an' yer expayriences. Is it a bigger one nor usual?'

' 'Twas the livin' truth!' answered Mulvaney, stretching out a huge arm and catching Ortheris by the collar. 'Now where are ye, me son? Will ye take the Wurrud av the Lorrd out av my mouth another time?' He shook him to emphasise the question.

'No, somethin' else, though,' said Ortheris, making a dash at Mulvaney's pipe, capturing it, and holding it at arm's length; 'I'll chuck it acrost the Ditch if you don't let me go!'

'Ye maraudin' haythen! 'tis the only cutty I iver loved. Handle her tinder or I'll chuck *you* acrost the nullah. If that poipe was bruk—Ah! Give her back to me, sorr!'

Ortheris had passed the treasure to my hand. It was an absolutely perfect clay, as shiny as the black ball at Pool. I took it reverently, but I was firm.

'Will you tell us about the ghost-fight if I do?' I said.

'Is ut the shtory that's throublin' you? Av coorse I will. I mint to all along. I was only gettin' at ut my own way, as Popp Doggle said t whin they found him thryin' to ram a cartridge down the muzzle. Orth'ris, fall away!'

He released the little Londoner, took back his pipe, filled it, and his eyes twinkled. He has the most eloquent eyes of anyone that I know.

'Did I iver tell you,' he began, 'that I was wanst the divil av a man?'

'You did,' said Learoyd with a childish gravity that made Ortheris yell with laughter, for Mulvaney was always impressing upon us his great merits in the old days.

'Did I iver tell you,' Mulvaney continued calmly, 'that I was wanst more av a divil than I am now?'

'Mer—ria! You don't mean it?' said Ortheris.

'Whin I was Corp'ril – I was rejuiced aftherwards – but, as I say, *whin* I was Corp'ril, I was the divil av a man.'

He was silent for nearly a minute, while his mind rummaged among old memories and his eye glowed. He bit upon the pipe-stem and charged into his tale.

'Eyah! They was great times. I'm ould now. Me hide's wore off in patches; sinthry-go has disconceited me, an' I'm married tu. But I've had my day – I've had my day, an' nothin' can take away the taste av that! Oh, my time past, whin I put me fut through ivry livin' wan av the Tin Commandmints betune Revelry and Lights Out, blew the froth off a pewter, wiped me moustache wid the back av me hand, an' slept on ut all as quiet as a little child! But ut's over – ut's over – an' 'twill niver come back to me; not though I prayed for a week av Sundays. Was there *any* wan in the Ould Rig'mint to touch Corp'ril Terence Mulvaney whin that same was turned out for sedukshin? I niver met him. Ivry woman that was not a witch was worth the runnin' afther in those days, an' ivry man was my dearest frind or – had stripped to him an' we knew which was the betther av the tu.

'Whin I was Corp'ril I wud not ha' changed wid the Colonel – no, nor yet the Commandher-in-Chief. I wud be a Sargint. There was nothin' I wud not be! Mother av Hivin, look at me! Fwhat am I *now*?

'We was quartered in a big cantonmint – 'tis no manner av use namin' names, for ut might give the barricks disreputation – an' I was the Imperor av the Earth in me own mind, an' wan or tu wimmen thought the same. Small blame to thim. Afther we had lain there a year, Bragin, the Colour-Sargint av E Comp'ny, wint an' took a wife that was lady's maid to some big lady in the station. She's dead now, is Annie Bragin – died in child-bed at Kirpa Tal, or ut may ha' been Almorah – sivin – nine years gone, an' Bragin he married agin. But she was a pretty woman whin Bragin inthrojuced her to cantonmint society. She had eyes like the brown av a butterfly's wing whin the sun catches ut, an' a waist no thicker than me arrum, an' a little sof' button av a mouth I wud ha' gone through all Asia bristlin' wid bay'nits to get the kiss av. An' her hair was as

179

long as the tail av the Colonel's charger – forgive me men-
tionin' that blundherin' baste in the same mouthful wid
Annie Bragin – but 'twas all shpun gowld, an' time was whin a
lock av ut was more than di'monds to me. There was niver
pretty woman yet, an' I've had thruck wid a few, cud open the
door to Annie Bragin.

' 'Twas in the Cath'lic Chapel I saw her first, me eye rollin'
round as usual to see fwhat was to be seen. "You're too good
for Bragin, me love," thinks I to mesilf, "but that's a mistake I
can put straight, or me name is not Terence Mulvaney."

'Now take me wurrud for ut, you Orth'ris there an' Learoyd, an' kape out av the Married Quarters – as I did *not*. No
good iver comes av ut, an' there's always the chance av your
bein' found wid your face in the dirt, a long picket in the back
av your head, an' your hands playin' the fifes on the tread av
another man's doorstep. 'Twas so we found O'Hara, he that
Rafferty killed six years gone, whin he wint to his death wid his
hair oiled, whistlin' *Larry O'Rourke* betune his teeth. Kape out
av the Married Quarters, I say, as I did not. 'Tis onwholesim,
'tis dangerous, an' 'tis ivrything else that's bad, but – O my
sowl, 'tis swate while ut lasts!

'I was always hangin' about there whin I was off jooty an'
Bragin wasn't, but niver a swate word beyon' ordinar' did I get
from Annie Bragin. " 'Tis the pervarsity av the sect," sez I to
mesilf, an' gave me cap another cock on me head an' straightened me back – 'twas the back av a Dhrum-Major in those days
– an' wint off as tho' I did not care, wid all the wimmen in the
Married Quarters laughin'. I was pershuaded – most bhoys *are*,
I'm thinkin' – that no woman born av woman cud stand agin'
me av I hild up me little finger. I had good cause for to think
that way – till I met Annie Bragin.

'Time an' agin whin I was blandandherin' in the dusk a man
wud go past me as quiet as a cat. "That's quare," thinks I, "for
I am, or I shud be, the only man in these parts. Now what
divilmint can Annie be up to?" Thin I called myself a blayguard for thinkin' such things; but I thought thim all the same.
An' that, mark you, is the way av a man.

'Wan evenin' I said: "Mrs Bragin, manin' no disrespect to

you, who *is* that Corp'ril man" – I had seen the shtripes though I cud niver get sight av his face – "*who* is that Corp'ril man that comes in always whin I'm goin' away?"

' "Mother av God!" sez she, turnin' as white as my belt; "have *you* seen him too?"

' "Seen him!" sez I; "av coorse I have. Did ye wish me not to see him, for" – we were standin' talkin' in the dhark, outside the verandah av Bragin's quarters – "you'd betther tell me to shut me eyes. Onless I'm mistaken, he's come now."

'An', sure enough, the Corp'ril man was walkin' to us, hangin' his head down as though he was ashamed av himsilf.

' "Good night, Mrs Bragin," sez I, very cool. " 'Tis not for me to interfere wid your *a-moors*; but you might manage some things wid more dacincy. I'm off to Canteen," I sez.

'I turned on my heel an' wint away, swearin' I wud give that man a dhressin' that wud shtop him messin' about the Married Quarters for a month an' a week. I had not tuk ten paces before Annie Bragin was hangin' on to my arrum, an' I cud feel that she was shakin' all over.

' "Shtay wid me, Mister Mulvaney," sez she. "You're flesh and blood, at the least – are ye not?"

' "I'm *all* that," sez I, an' my anger wint in a flash. "Will I want to be asked twice, Annie?"

'Wid that I slipped my arrum round her waist, for, begad, I fancied she had surrindered at discretion, an' the honours av war were mine.

' "Fwhat nonsinse is this?" sez she, dhrawin' hersilf up on the tips av her dear little toes. "Wid the mother's milk not dhry on your impident mouth! Let go!" she sez.

' "Did ye not say just now that I was flesh and blood?" sez I. "I have not changed since," I sez; and I kep' my arrum where ut was.

' "Your arrums to yoursilf!" sez she, an' her eyes sparkild.

' "Sure, 'tis only human natur'." sez I; an' I kep' my arrum where ut was.

' "Natur' or no natur'," says she, "you take your arrum away or I'll tell Bragin, an' he'll alter the natur' av your head. Fwhat d'you take me for?" she sez.

' "A woman," sez I; "the prettiest in the barricks."

' "A *wife*," sez she. "The straightest in cantonmints!"

'Wid that I dropped my arrum, fell back tu paces, an' saluted, for I saw that she mint fwhat she said.'

'Then you know something that some men would give a good deal to be certain of. How could you tell?' I demanded in the interests of Science.

'Watch the hand,' said Mulvaney. 'Av she shuts her hand tight, thumb down over the knuckle, take up your hat an' go. You'll only make a fool av yoursilf av you shtay. But av the hand lies opin on the lap, or av you see her thryin' to shut ut, an' she can't, – go on! She's not past reasonin' wid.

'Well, as I was sayin', I fell back, saluted, an' was goin' away.

' "Shtay wid me," she sez. "Look! He's comin' agin."

'She pointed to the veranda, an' by the Height av Impart'nince, the Corp'ril man was comin' out av Bragin's quarters.

' "He's done that these five evenin's past," sez Annie Bragin. "Oh, fwhat will I do!"

' "He'll not do ut agin," sez I, for I was fightin' mad.

'Kape away from a man that has been a thrifle crossed in love till the fever's died down. He rages like a brute baste.

'I wint up to the man in the verandah, manin', as sure as I sit, to knock the life out av him. He slipped into the open. "Fwhat are you doin' philadherin' about here, ye scum av the gutter?" sez I polite, to give him his warnin', for I wanted him ready.

'He niver lifted hs head, but sez, all mournful an' melancolious, as if he thought I wud be sorry for him: "I can't find her," sez he.

' "My troth," sez I, "you've lived too long – you an' your seekin's an' findin's in a dacint married woman's quarters! Hould up your head, ye frozen thief av Genesis," sez I, "an' you'll find all you want an' more!"

'But he niver hild up, an' I let go from the shoulther to where the hair is short over the eyebrows.

' "That'll do your business," sez I, but it nearly did mine instid. I put me bodyweight behind the blow, but I hit nothing at all, an' near put me shoulther out. The Corp'ril man was not there, an' Annie Bragin, who had been watchin' from the veranda, throws up her heels, an' carries on like a cock whin his neck's wrung by the dhrummer-bhoy. I wint back to her, for a livin' woman, an' a woman like Annie Bragin, is more than a p'rade-groun' full av ghosts. I'd niver seen a woman faint before, an' I stud like a shtuck calf, askin' her whether she was dead, an' prayin' her for the love av me, an' the love av her husband, an' the love av the Virgin to opin her blessed eyes agin, an' callin' mesilf all the names undher the canopy av Hivin for plaguin' her wid my miserable *a-moors* whin I ought to ha' stud betune her an' this Corp'ril man that had lost the number av his mess.

'I misremimber fwhat nonsince I said, but I was not so far gone that I cud not hear a fut on the dirt outside. 'Twas Bragin comin' in, an' by the same token Annie was comin' to. I jumped to the far end av the verandah an' looked as if butther wudn't melt in my mouth. But Mrs Quinn, the Quartermaster's wife that was, had tould Bragin about my hangin' round Annie.

' "I'm not plazed wid you, Mulvaney," sez Bragin, unbucklin' his sword, for he had been on jooty.

' "That's bad hearin'," I sez, an' I knew that me pickets were dhriven in. "What for, Sargint?" sez I.

' "Come outside," sez he, "an' I'll show you why."

' "I'm willin'," I sez; "but my shtripes are none so ould that I can afford to lose thim. Tell me now, *who* do I go out wid?" sez I.

'He was a quick man an' a just, an' saw fwhat I wud be afther. "Wid Mrs Bragin's husband," sez he. He might ha' known by me askin' that favour that I had done him no wrong.

'We wint to the back av the arsenal an' I stripped to him, an' for ten minut's 'twas all I cud do to prevent him killin' himsilf agin' my fistes. He was mad as a dumb dog – just frothin' wid rage; but he had no chanst wid me in reach, or learnin', or anything else.

' "Will ye hear reason?" sez I, whin his first wind was run out.

' "Not whoile I can see," sez he. Wid that I gave him both,

one afther the other, smash through the low gyard that he'd been taught whin he was a bhoy, an' the eyebrow shut down on the cheek-bone like the wing av a sick crow.

' "Will you hear reason now, brave man?" sez I.

' "Not whoile I can speak," sez he, staggerin' up blind as a stump. I was loath to du ut, but I wint round an' swung into the jaw side-on an' shifted ut a half-pace to the lef'.

' "Will ye hear reason now?" sez I. "I can't keep my timper much longer, an' 'tis like I will hurt you."

' "Not whoile I can stand," he mumbles out av one corner av his mouth. So I closed an' threw him – blind, dumb, an' sick, an' jammed the jaw straight.

' "You're an ould fool, *Mister* Bragin," sez I.

' "You're a young thafe," sez he, "an' you've bruk my heart, you an' Annie betune you!"

'Thin he began cryin' like a child as he lay. I was sorry as I had niver been before. 'Tis an awful thing to see a strong man cry.

' "I'll swear on the Cross!" sez I.

' "I care for none av your oaths," sez he.

' "Come back to your quarters," sez I, "an' if you don't believe the livin', begad, you shall listen to the dead," I sez.

'I hoisted him an' tuk him back to his quarters. "Mrs Bragin," sez I, "here's a man that you can cure quicker than me."

' "You've shamed me before my wife," he whimpers.

' "Have I so?" sez I. "By the look on Mrs Bragin's face I think I'm for a dhressin'-down worse than I gave you."

'An' I was! Annie Bragin was woild wid indignation. There was not a name that a dacint woman cud use that was not given my way. I've had my Colonel walk roun' me like a cooper roun' a cask for fifteen minut's in Ord'ly-Room, bekaze I wint into the Corner Shop an unstrapped lewnatic; but all that I iver tuk from his tongue was ginger-pop to fwhat Annie tould me. An' that, mark you, is the way av a woman.

'Whin ut was done for want av breath, an' Annie was bendin' over her husband, I sez: " 'Tis all thrue, an' I'm a blayguard an' you're an honust woman; but will you tell him av wan service that I did you?"

'As I finished speakin' the Corp'ril man came up to the veranda, and Annie Bragin shquealed. The moon was up, an' we cud see his face.

' "I can't find her," sez the Corp'ril man, an' wint out like the puff av a candle.

' "Saints stand betune us an' evil!" sez Bragin, crossin' himself; "that's Flahy av the Tyrone."

' "Who was he?" I sez, "for he has given me a dale av fightin' this day."

'Bragin tould us that Flahy was a Corp'ril who lost his wife av cholera in those quarters three years gone, an' wint mad, an' *walked* afther they buried him, huntin' for her.

' "Well," sez I to Bragin "he's been hookin' out av Purgathory to kape company wid Mrs Bragin ivry evenin' for the last fortnight. You may tell Mrs Quinn, wid my love, for I know that she's been talkin' to you, an' you've been listenin', that she ought to ondhersthand the differ 'twixt a man an' a ghost. She's had three husbands," sez I, "an' *you've* got a wife too good for you. Instid av which you lave her to be boddered by ghosts an—an' all manner av evil spirruts. I'll niver go talkin' in the way av politeness to a man's wife agin. Good night to you both," sez I; an' wid that I wint away, havin' fought wid woman, man, *an'* Divil all in the heart av an hour. By the same token I gave Father Victor wan rupee to say a mass for Flahy's soul, me havin' dishcommoded him by shtickin' my fist into his systim.'

'Your ideas of politeness seem rather large, Mulvaney,' I said.

'That's as you look at ut,' said Mulvaney calmly. 'Annie Bragin niver cared for me. For all that, I did not want to leave anythin' behin' me that Bragin cud take hould av to be angry wid her about – whin an honust wurrud cud ha' cleared all up. There's nothing like opin-spakin'. Orth'ris, ye scutt, let me put me eye to that bottle, for my throat's as dhry as whin I thought I wud gel a kiss from Annie Bragin. An' that's fourteen years gone!

'Eyah! Cork's own city an' the blue sky above ut – an' the times that was – the times that was!'

BABOO MOOKERJI'S UNDERTAKING

Baboo Mookerji said he knew a something worth knowing. He told me this with a fat, grave smile of self-confidence; and he told this to others. People became anxious to hear what it was about, in what line, and how he knew what he said. They asked him, so that they might value him more than they did. For they valued Baboo Mookerji. Besides being a clerk in a Government office, he always wore a greasy look which betokened prosperity and much consumption of clarified butter, which it is very estimable and popular to do. He wore transparent garments where they should have been opaque, and opaque where clothes could be excused for transparency; and a pair of boots. In short, he was highly respectable; and when Baboo Mookerji, hearing that a man had died from snake-bite, said that he knew something, everybody enquired. 'Only bring me,' said Baboo Mookerji in reply, 'only bring me a man, not who is dying from snake – for that is nothing – but who is dead from snake. There is in snake-bite,' said Baboo Mookerji, smiling with superior knowledge, 'a power to cause semblance of death, but not death. The vital breath is only suspended – not extinct; but I grant,' said Baboo Mookerji, 'that few know it; and still fewer,' said Baboo Mookerji, 'still fewer can work against it,' 'Is that true?' said all the people. Baboo Mookerji put another betel ball into his mouth, and said 'Bring a man dead from snake – as *you* call it – to me. That is all I ask.' It was a reasonable request; but though such a man is often got when there is no experiment on hand, he was scarce when he was wanted. Search was made, and a sharp look-out was kept for a case of snake-bite; and Baboo Mookerji scoffed within my hearing at the English doctors and at

English methods of treatment. Baboo Mookerji detailed to me anecdotes which proved that there *was* a way, but unknown to the ignorant and gross, of getting a man all right after he had apparently expired from snake-venom. He had no objection to say that the recovery could be effected only by the snake, and the snake would not do it but by the power of charms. The charms were the secret; but Baboo Mookerji instructed me in the manner of working. He had only to scatter four shells, fraught with powerful invocation, to the four points of the compass, and the snake would have to re-appear in obedience to the summons, and be compelled to suck out the poison which it had injected. The poison once out, of course the man would be as right as before.

'These things,' said Baboo Mookerji, 'are not generally known.' 'Have you cured any cases, Mr Mookerji?' I asked. 'A few,' said Baboo Mookerji, shoving another betel ball into his cheek with unconcern. 'But', said Baboo Mookerji, 'I never take any remuneration. Should I do so the mercenary character of my motive will destroy the virtue of the charm.'

This naturally excited my curiosity, and I went about the station anxious for somebody to be bitten. In the meantime Baboo Mookerji waxed impatient, and demanded a dead person soon in order to make him alive; and, infected with his impatience, I went to the distant villages, and almost entreated somebody to qualify for it. I argued on the new plan which Baboo Mookerji was so eager to employ only for my satisfaction, and guaranteed that the Baboo would restore the dead man to life. Baboo Mookerji, however, here always made a distinction and a correction stating that man is never really dead, but only comatose. This I repeated to the rustics who were more inclined to suppose this likely, and to regard resuscitation more probable than resurrection. Receiving a promise from them to look out for a case – and even, I fear, to stretch a point – I departed. Rustics take a long time to act on any suggestion, and it was not before a week that a messenger was sent to me with good tidings. I repaired joyously to Baboo Mookerji's office, and departed with him to the scene of the occurrence. There were four other Baboos there, and a large gathering of rustics assembled on the spot. 'I hope you all tried to recover him in the first instance,' said Baboo Mookerji; 'because' said Baboo Mookerji, 'I should like to try my power after all other resources have failed.' My confidence in Baboo Mookerji arose on hearing him, and I was glad to see that I was right in my estimate of him, and safe in my recommendation. The rustics assured Baboo Mookerji that they had tried to bandage the young man's arm, and given him curds to eat, without avail, and had subjected him to their own enchanters; but the music and the water could not arrest his droop and collapse.

Then did I see that Baboo Mookerji prepared to rise to the occasion. He put aside his shawl, and examined the wound. 'Get me', said Baboo Mookerji, 'six bottles of liquor at once for libation to the gods. Don't delay.' 'Sir,' said the weeping father, 'only liquor of this country can be got here.' 'Bring even that,' said Baboo Mookerji with a displeased look.

The liquor was brought, and Baboo Mookerji caused it to be taken inside the hut, which he entered with his coadjutors, and fastened the door. 'How do you think he will proceed, Sahib?' asked a villager of me. I explained the whole process anew, and said that Baboo Mookerji, if successful, would not only introduce a great blessing into the country, but would make a fortune over it. The Government would buy up his charms, and these would thenceforth find a place in the British pharmacopoea.

We retired under a tope of mango trees and talked about the marvels that were daily coming to the knowledge of man. We talked about two hours, till we heard sounds issuing from the hut, and felt that we were summoned to witness the operation. When we reached it. Baboo Mookerji tumbled out of the room with a screech, and, observing us, Baboo Mookerji smiled faintly and staggered at us. 'What is the meaning of this word?' said a villager, 'he has drunk our liquor and is very drunk, and has no intention of curing our brother.' And when the villagers realised this, they fell upon my Baboo Mookerji and beat him sorely; and they drew out the other revellers and put them, protesting, to much discomfort. They they reverted to Baboo Mookerji, who vaguely threatened law, and gave him some more, till he was overcome. And forasmuch as I had been prevailed upon to laud and commend him, I think I kicked Baboo Mookerji as he rolled on the ground, and thereby felt greatly relieved and gratified.

Thus did Baboo Mookerji fail in his undertaking.

This I solemnly declare is not a parable on the National Congress – no allegory whatever on Bengali pretensions but a narrative mainly of fact.

THE JOKER

'And when The Joker turns up, y'know,' said Vennel, explaining the principles of Euchre at the Club, 'you can make your own trumps.'

'Pardon me a moment, gentlemen, I am The Joker and I – ahem – have turned up. May I come in?'

No one had seen the baize door of the card-room swing, but at the table stood a young man, his eyes suspiciously bright and his cheeks flushed, as with wine. He was in evening dress and at his watch-chain dangled a tiny hour-glass charm.

'Oh. No objection I'm sure if these men don't object,' stammered Vennel, and under his breath murmured: 'S'pose it's one of the men from the out-stations. Club's so full these days no one knows t'other from which. He's a dashed cool fish, though.'

The visitor limped slightly as he dropped into his chair: 'Three-handed euchre, was it?' he said gaily. 'Two combining against one when one is too successful? I think I know something about that game.'

'This is dashed lunacy,' muttered Keevin. 'The man's had too much.'

'Not in the least,' said the stranger. 'You have no idea what a hard head mine is. My deal, isn't it?' He dealt the five cards and turned up the seven of Diamonds.

'I pass,' said Vennel, who was the eldest hand. 'Diamonds aren't good enough for me.'

'I play,' said Keevin, looking at the stranger, who by the arrangement of the table should be his partner.

'It's against the game to advise, but I should recommend you to go alone,' said the stranger with supreme disregard of the first conventions of the card-room. No one rebuked him, and Keevin announced his intention of going alone. The stranger threw down his cards. Keevin played both Bowers, the king and ace of Diamonds. His last card was a low Club. Maisey, who was Vennel's partner, took it with a ten, and Keevin's chance of winning all five tricks was gone.

'Four Diamonds and a low Club,' chuckled the stranger – 'a very fair hand indeed, but you were euchred. There's nothing in the world better than Diamonds, is there?'

'Nothing,' said Keevin with an energy that astonished the table. 'Diamonds and dibs – there's nothing better or more desirable under Heaven. I say you queer devil, show me how to make Diamonds trumps and hold a hand of 'em that'll sweep the show.'

'What a holy exhibition Keevin's making of himself,' said Vennel. 'We knew he was always keen about *pice*, but he needn't explain it to a stranger.'

'It's as simple as dying,' said the stranger. 'Discard Hearts, don't deal too much with Clubs and keep away from any place where Spades may turn up trumps. Your deal, Mr Vennel.'

Vennel dealt and turned up Hearts. Keevin grunted and passed.

'I'll go alone,' said Maisey.

'Quite right,' said the stranger calmly. 'Never assist where Hearts are trumps. A partner under those circumstances is a nuisance.'

Maisey led with The Joker and drew low trumps all round.

'Bad play,' said the stranger drily. The Right Bower followed, took the next trick, and then the queen.

'Very bad play,' said the stranger. 'Poor lady. I'm sorry to have to take her, but euchre is euchre,' and he slid out the Left Bower. Miasey took the remaining two tricks, but the sweep which he had counted on was gone.

'If you had kept The Joker back you could have taken my Left Bower. Always look out for the Left Bower when Hearts are trumps. He's generally round the corner, somewhere,' said the stranger.

'See here,' stuttered Maisey flushing. 'You spoilt my hand

with your interference. What's the way to hold Hearts every time? There's nothing in this forsaken land like Hearts – fresh ones every few months. I'll give you anything you please, you rummy *janwar*, if you'll show me how to play Hearts properly – sweeps every time.'

Keevin chuckled. '*In vino veritas*,' said he, sipping his peg. 'Maisey, you needn't wear *your* heart on your sleeve in that disgustingly open fashion. Play euchre if you like, but don't make a show of yourself.'

'No, never make a show of yourself,' said the stranger approvingly. 'Lead another suit ostentatiously, Mr Maisey, and you'll be surprised how the Hearts range themselves in your hand. If that fails and your hand's a poor one, order up Diamonds and the chances are that you hold the Left Bower – as I held just now. Above all don't risk your best cards first.'

'H'mm,' said Vennel. 'That's nonsense. Keevin, it's your deal.'

Keevin turned up Hearts again and all the players passed once, and a second time it came to Vennel's turn to make his trump.

'I make Clubs,' said he. 'And I'll go alone on this hand. Both Bowers, the ace, king and queen. That's good enough. Put down your cards.'

'Not quite,' murmured the stranger. 'You have forgotten The Joker,' and he laid it on the table. 'Never mind playing the tricks out. The Joker has a knack of turning up unexpectedly among the clubs. You're euchred, too, Mr Vennel.'

'How do you hold cards that always get in the way?' grumbled Vennel with far more heat than the game demanded. 'You did Maisey out of his sweep of Hearts and now you've done me. Teach me how to hold Clubs as long as I live – clubs that are always new and always good for something – clubs that you don't get tired of looking at – first-class clubs, *recherche-wallahs* – good liquor, twenty billiard tables – stories that haven't all been told and all that, you know. You've dropped in from deuce knows where, and you pretend to know all about everything. Have a peg and show me how to turn up Clubs.'

'Heigho!' said Maisey behind his cheroot. 'That comes of

mixing old brandy with champagne and pegging all the afternoon. Vennel's a coarse-minded ruffian when he lets himself go,' and he winked at Keevin.

The stranger drank his peg and never did soda-water fizz so fiercely as the liquor that touched his lips. 'Clubs?' said he lazily. 'They are a safe suit so long as you have Diamonds to back 'em and keep clear of Hearts. But then the Spade *will* interfere sometimes. Let's go on, Mr Maisey.'

Maisey turned up Diamonds and all passed twice. The deal was lost and the stranger took the pack. 'I go alone,' and he without looking at the card he turned up, 'and I hope that you are all as well stocked as I am.'

'Hold on. You've turned up The Joker, What are you going to make trumps?' said Vennel.

'Spades,' said the stranger. 'Down with your dust.' The Joker took the left Bower from Vennel and lay-cards from the other two men.

'No trumps. How strange!' said the stranger. 'Glad I drew that Bower. Right, king, queen, ace, and you had all Clubs, Mr Vennel, all Diamonds partner, and all Hearts, Mr Maisey – the suit in fact that each one wanted. I don't think I need to learn how to make Spades. Shall we go on? By the way, when I sat down I entirely forgot to ask what we were playing for: for we must settle that little matter.'

'It was a blessed bear-garden,' said Vennel sulkily. 'You came in and played miracles. Do you suppose that that's going to be reckoned as a serious round?'

'I do very much suppose so,' said the stranger quietly. 'It's one of the most serious games you've ever played, and in return for the instruction I've given you, you will be good enough to pay up.'

'Pay up what? This is frivolling. Here pony and let us get to business. Who in the world are you to tell us how the game goes?'

'I don't quite know,' said the stranger. 'Some people call me one thing and some another. You'd better call me The Joker.'

'Then you'd better not joke here,' said Vennel angrily. He was as causelessly upset as the other two men.

'Oh, but I must though. That's my little way. You're a most ungrateful set of men. I show you how to get your heart's desire and you refuse to pay me. I suppose I must take my reward. Vennel will please to turn reddish-blue and take off his signet-ring.'

'The thing hurts or else I shouldn't,' said Vennel placing it on the table. His fingers were certainly swelling and his face was heavily flushed.

'Maisey, a few of those luxuriant locks from just above the temple. They're very pretty, but you don't want 'em. Drop the eyelid slightly and I think we can make that mouth a little coarser,' said the stranger.

It may have been the heat of the room that caused Maisey to half shut his eyes and drop his lower lip, and it may have been a draught through the door that blew back the hair above the forehead and showed how far the baldness ran up into the scalp.

'One moment, Keevin. A touch of grey on the eyebrows would improve you and we'll take the curve out of that cheek and put a line from the nose to the corner of the mouth. And now I think you're about finished. You'll forgive my flying, but I've got to see a man. There go the bells, gentlemen, and armed with all my knowledge I wish you a Happy New Year.'

The three stared at each other in silence while the bells clashed and hammered without, and in the billiard-room men sang *Auld Lang Syne*.

'Let's get out of this,' said Vennel in a sudden fury. 'Let's hammer the brute!' And he charged into the billiard-room followed by Keevin and Maisey.

'What a group you are! Who's been rubbing billiard-chalk on your eyebrow, Keevin, and painting you with burnt matches? Vennel, I'd advise you to drop oysters. They make you look bloated, old man! Maisey, wake up and open those beautiful blue eyes of yours and don't stand like a codfish,' were some of the sentences that greeted their appearance.

'Have you seen a brute in evening-dress?' began Vennel and a shout of laughter cut him short.

'There was a rummy sort of sun-dried Johnnie in here –

s'pose he's one of the visitors – making us all laugh about nothing, and chalking our coats. Confound the man, he's marked my front with a great ace of spades!' said one pool-player.

'And mine!' said two others. There were thirty-nine men in the room.

'That's the fellow we're looking for,' said Maisey; but on second thoughts he added, 'I don't think we shall find him. I say, you fellows, do you believe in the Devil?'

'At midnight certainly. Khitmatgar, *Devilly huldee sub log Kiwasti* and *bahut pipa* beer *sharab*. That was a happy thought of yours, Maisey.'

THE WANDERING JEW

'If you go once round the world in an easterly direction, you gain one day,' said the men of science to John Hay. In after years John Hay went east, west, north, and south, transacted business, made love, and begat a family, as have done many men, and the scientific information above recorded lay neglected in the deeps of his mind with a thousand other matters of equal importance.

When a rich relative died, he found himself wealthy beyond any reasonable expectation that he had entertained in his previous career, which had been a chequered and evil one. Indeed, long before the legacy came to him, there existed in the brain of John Hay a little cloud – a momentary obscuration of thought that came and went almost before he could realise that there was any solution of continuity. So do the bats flit round the eaves of a house to show that the darkness is falling. He entered upon great possessions in money, land, and houses; but behind his delight stood a ghost that cried out that his enjoyment of these things should not be of long duration. It was the ghost of the rich relative, who had been permitted to return to earth to torture his nephew into the grave. Wherefore, under the spur of this constant reminder, John Hay, always preserving the air of heavy business-like stolidity that hid the shadow on his mind, turned investments, houses, and lands into sovereigns – rich, round, red, English sovereigns, each one worth twenty shillings. Lands may become valueless, and houses fly heavenward on the wings of red flame, but till the Day of Judgment a sovereign will always be a sovereign – that is to say, a king of pleasures.

Possessed of his sovereigns, John Hay would fain have spent

them one by one on such coarse amusements as his soul loved; but he was haunted by the instant fear of Death; for the ghost of his relative stood in the hall of his house close to the hatrack, shouting up the stairway that life was short, that there was no hope of increase of days, and that the undertakers were already roughing out his nephew's coffin. John Hay was generally alone in the house, and even when he had company, his friends could not hear the clamorous uncle. The shadow inside his brain grew larger and blacker. His fear of death was driving John Hay mad.

Then, from the deeps of his mind, where he had stowed away all his discarded information, rose to light the scientific fact of the easterly journey. On the next occasion that his uncle shouted up the stairway urging him to make haste and live, a shriller voice cried, 'Who goes round the world once easterly, gains one day.'

His growing diffidence and distrust of mankind made John Hay unwilling to give this precious message of hope to his friends. They might take it up and analyse it. He was sure it was true, but it would pain him acutely were rough hands to examine it too closely. To him alone of all the toiling generations of mankind had the secret of immortality been vouchsafed. It would be impious – against all the designs of the Creator – to set mankind hurrying eastward. Besides, this would crowd the steamers inconveniently, and John Hay wished of all things to be alone. If he could get round the world in two months – some one of whom he had read, he could not remember the name, had covered the passage in eighty days – he would gain a clear day; and by steadily continuing to do it for thirty years, would gain one hundred and eighty days, or nearly the half of a year. It would not be much, but in course of time, as civilisation advanced, and the Euphrates Valley Railway was opened, he could improve the pace.

Armed with many sovereigns, John Hay, in the thirty-fifth year of his age, set forth on his travels, two voices bearing him company from Dover as he sailed to Calais. Fortune favoured him. The Euphrates Valley Railway was newly opened, and he was the first man who took ticket direct from Calais to Calcutta – thirteen days in the train. Thirteen days in the train are not good for the nerves; but he covered the world and returned to Calais from America in twelve days over the two months, and started afresh with four and twenty hours of precious time to his credit. Three years passed, and John Hay religiously went round this earth seeking for more time wherein to enjoy the remainder of his sovereigns. He became known on many lines as the man who wanted to go on; when people asked him what he was and what he did, he answered –

'I'm the person who intends to live, and I am trying to do it now.'

His days were divided between watching the white wake spinning behind the stern of the swiftest steamers, or the brown earth flashing past the windows of the faster trains; and he noted in a pocket-book every minute that he had railed or screwed out of remorseless eternity.

'This is better than praying for long life,' quoth John Hay as he turned his face eastward for his twentieth trip. The years had done more for him than he dared to hope. By the extension of the Brahmaputra Valley line to meet the newly-developed China Midland, the Calais railway ticket held good *via* Karachi and Calcutta to Hongkong. The round trip could be managed in a fraction over forty-seven days, and, filled with fatal exultation, John Hay told the secret of his longevity to his only friend, the house-keeper of his rooms in London. He spoke and passed; but the woman was one of resource, and immediately took counsel with the lawyers who had first informed John Hay of his golden legacy. Very many sovereigns still remained, and another Hay longed to spend them on things more sensible than railway tickets and steamer accommodation.

The chase was long, for when a man is journeying literally for the dear life, he does not tarry upon the road. Round the world Hay swept anew, and overtook the wearied Doctor, who had been sent out to look for him, in Madras. It was there that he found the reward of his toil and the assurance of a blessed immortality. In half an hour the Doctor, watching always the parched lips, the shaking hands, and the eye that turned eternally to the east, won John Hay to rest in a little house close to the Madras surf. All that Hay need do was to hang by ropes from the roof of the room and let the round earth swing free beneath him. This was better than steamer or train, for he gained a day in a day, and was thus the equal of the undying sun. The other Hay would pay his expenses throughout eternity.

It is true that we cannot yet take tickets from Calais to Hongkong, though that will come about in fifteen years; but men say that if you wander along the southern coast of India you shall find in a neatly whitewashed little bungalow, sitting in a chair swung from the roof, over a sheet of thin steel which he knows so well destroys the attraction of the earth, an old and worn man who for ever faces the rising sun, a stop-watch in his hand, racing against eternity. He cannot drink, he does not smoke, and his living expenses amount to perhaps twenty-five rupees a month, but he is John Hay, the Immortal. Without, he hears the thunder of the wheeling world with which he is careful to explain he has no connection whatever; but if you say that it is only the noise of the surf, he will cry bitterly, for the shadow on his brain is passing away as the brain ceases to work, and he doubts sometimes whether the Doctor spoke the truth.

'Why does not the sun always remain over my head?' asks John Hay.

THE COURTING OF DINAH SHADD

What did the colonel's lady think?
    Nobody never knew,
Somebody asked the sergeant's wife
    An' she told 'em true.
When you git to a man in the case
    They're like a row o' pins,
For the colonel's lady an' Judy O'Grady
    Are sisters under their skins.

Barrack Room Ballad

All day I had followed at the heels of a pursuing army engaged on one of the finest battles that ever camp of exercise beheld. Thirty thousand troops, had, by the wisdom of the Government of India, been turned loose over a few thousand square miles of country to practise in peace what they would never attempt in war. Consequently cavalry charged unshaken infantry at the trot. Infantry captured artillery by frontal attacks delivered in line of quarter columns, and mounted infantry skirmished up to the wheels of an armoured train which carried nothing more deadly than a twenty-five pounder Armstrong, two Nordenfeldts, and a few score volunteers all cased in three-eighths-inch boiler-plate. Yet it was a very lifelike camp. Operations did not cease at sundown; nobody knew the country and nobody spared man or horse. There was unending cavalry scouting and almost unending forced work over broken ground. The Army of the South had finally pierced the centre of the Army of the North, and was pouring through a gap hot-foot to capture a city of strategic importance. Its front extended fanwise, the sticks being represented by regiments strung out along the line of route backwards to the divisional transport columns and all the lumber that trails behind an army on the move. On its right the broken left of the Army of the North was flying in mass, chased by the Southern horse and hammered by the Southern guns till these had been pushed far beyond the limits of their last support. Then the flying sat down to rest, while the elated commandant of the pursuing force telegraphed that he held all in check and observation.

Unluckily he did not observe that three miles to his right flank a flying column of Northern horse with a detachment of Ghoorkhas and British troops had been pushed round as fast as the failing light allowed, to cut across the entire rear of the Southern Army, – to break, as it were, all the ribs of the fan where they converged by striking at the transport, reserve ammunition, and artillery supplies. Their instructions were to go in, avoiding the few scouts who might not have been drawn off by the pursuit, and create sufficient excitement to impress the Southern Army with the wisdom of guarding their own flank and rear before they captured cities. It was a pretty manœuvre neatly carried out.

Speaking for the second division of the Southern Army, our first intimation of the attack was at twilight, when the artillery were labouring in deep sand, most of the escort were trying to help them out, and the main body of the infantry had gone on. A Noah's Ark of elephants, camels, and the mixed menagerie of an Indian transport-train bubbled and squealed behind the guns, when there appeared from nowhere in particular British infantry to the extent of three companies, who sprang to the heads of the gun-horses and brought all to a standstill amid oaths and cheers.

'How's that, umpire?' said the major commanding the attack, and with one voice the drivers and limber gunners answered 'Hout!' while the colonel of artillery sputtered.

'All your scouts are charging our main body,' said the major. 'Your flanks are unprotected for two miles. I think we've broken the back of this division. And listen, – there go the Ghoorkhas!'

A weak fire broke from the rear-guard more than a mile away, and was answered by cheerful howlings. The Ghoorkhas, who should have swung clear of the second division, had stepped on its tail in the dark, but drawing off hastened to reach the next line of attack, which lay almost parallel to us five or six miles away.

Our column swayed and surged irresolutely – three batteries, the divisional ammunition reserve, the baggage, and a section of the hospital and bearer corps. The commandant ruefully promised to report himself 'cut up' to the nearest umpire, and commending his cavalry and all other cavalry to the special care of Eblis, toiled on to resume touch with the rest of the division.

'We'll bivouac here to-night,' said the major, 'I have a notion that the Ghoorkhas will get caught. They may want us to re-form on. Stand easy till the transport gets away.'

A hand caught my beast's bridle and led him out of the choking dust; a larger hand deftly canted me out of the saddle; and two of the hugest hands in the world received me sliding. Pleasant is the lot of the special correspondent who falls into such hands as those of Privates Mulvaney, Ortheris, and Learoyd.

'An' that's all right,' said the Irishman calmly. 'We thought we'd find you somewheres here by. Is there anything av yours in the transport? Orth'ris'll fetch ut out.'

Ortheris did 'fetch ut out', from under the trunk of an elephant, in the shape of a servant and an animal both laden with medical comforts. The little man's eyes sparkled.

'If the brutil an' licentious soldiery av these parts gets sight av the thruck,' said Mulvaney, making practised investigation, 'they'll loot ev'rything. They're bein' fed on iron-filin's an' dog-biscuit these days, but glory's no compensation for a bellyache. Praise be, we're here to protect you, sorr. Beer, sausage, bread (soft an' that's a cur'osity), soup in a tin, whisky by the smell av ut, an' fowls! Mother av Moses, but ye take the field like a confectioner! 'Tis scand'lus.'

'Ere's a orficer,' said Ortheris significantly. 'When the sergent's done lushin' the privit may clean the pot.'

I bundled several things into Mulvaney's haversack before the major's hand fell on my shoulder and he said tenderly,

'Requisitioned for the Queen's service. Wolsey was quite wrong about special correspondents: they are the soldier's best friends. Come and take pot-luck with us to-night.'

And so it happened amid laughter and shoutings that my well-considered commissariat melted away to reappear later at the mess-table, which was a waterproof sheet spread on the ground. The flying column had taken three days' rations with it, and there be few things nastier than Government rations – especially when Government is experimenting with German toys. Erbswurst, tinned beef of surpassing tinniness, compressed vegetables, and meat-biscuits may be nourishing, but what Thomas Atkins needs is bulk in his inside. The major, assisted by his brother officers, purchased goats for the camp, and so made the experiment of no effect. Long before the fatigue-party sent to collect brushwood had returned, the men were settled down by their valises, kettles and pots had appeared from the surrounding country, and were dangling over fires as the kid and the compressed vegetable bubbled together; there rose a cheerful clinking of mess-tins; outrageous demands for 'a little more stuffin' with that there liverwing;' and gust on gust of chaff as pointed as a bayonet and as delicate as a gun-butt.

'The boys are in a good temper,' said the major. 'They'll be singing presently. Well, a night like this is enough to keep them happy.'

Over our heads burned the wonderful Indian stars, which are not all pricked in on one plane, but, preserving an orderly perspective, draw the eye through the velvet of the void up to the barred doors of heaven itself. The earth was a grey shadow more unreal than the sky. We could hear her breathing lightly in the pauses between the howling of the jackals, the movement of the wind in the tamarisks, and the fitful mutter of musketry-fire leagues away to the left. A native woman from some unseen hut began to sing, the mail-train thundered past on its way to Delhi, and a roosting crow cawed drowsily. Then there was a belt-loosening silence about the fires, and the even breathing of the crowded earth took up the story.

The men, full fed, turned to tobacco and song, – their

officers with them. The subaltern is happy who can win the approval of the musical critics in his regiment, and is honoured among the more intricate step-dancers. By him, as by him who plays cricket cleverly, Thomas Atkins will stand in time of need, when he will let a better officer go on alone. The ruined tombs of forgotten Mussulman saints heard the ballad of *Agra Town, The Buffalo Battery, Marching to Kabul, The long, long Indian Day, The Place where the Punkah-coolie died*, and the crashing chorus which announces,

Youth's daring spirit, manhood's fire,
 Firm hand and eagle eye,
Must he acquire, who would aspire
 To see the grey boar die.

To-day, of all those jovial thieves who appropriated my commissariat and lay and laughed round that waterproof sheet, not one remains. They went to camps that were not of exercise and battles without umpires. Burmah, and Soudan, and the frontier, – fever and fight, – took them in their time.

I drifted across to the men's fires in search of Mulvaney, whom I found strategically greasing his feet by the blaze. There is nothing particularly lovely in the sight of a private thus engaged after a long day's march, but when you reflect on the exact proportion of the 'might, majesty, dominion, and power' of the British Empire which stands on those feet you take an interest in the proceedings.

'There's a blister, bad luck to ut, on the heel,' said Mulvaney. 'I can't touch ut. Prick ut out, little man.'

Ortheris took out his house-wife, eased the trouble with a needle, stabbed Mulvaney in the calf with the same weapon, and was swiftly kicked into the fire.

'I've bruk the best av my toes over you, ye grinnin' child av disruption,' said Mulvaney, sitting cross-legged and nursing his feet; then seeing me, 'Oh, ut's you, sorr! Be welkim, an' take that maraudin' scutt's place. Jock, hold him down on the cindhers for a bit.'

But Ortheris escaped and went elsewhere, as I took

possession of the hollow he had scraped for himself and lined with his greatcoat. Learoyd on the other side of the fire grinned affably and in a minute fell fast asleep.

'There's the height av politeness for you,' said Mulvaney, lighting his pipe with a flaming branch. 'But Jock's eaten half a box av your sardines at wan gulp, an' I think the tin too. What's the best wid you, sorr, an' how did you happen to be on the losin' side this day whin we captured you?'

'The Army of the South is winning all along the line,' I said.

'Then that line's the hangman's rope, savin' your presence. You'll learn to-morrow how we rethreated to dhraw thim on before we made thim trouble, an' that's what a woman does. By the same tokin, we'll be attacked before the dawnin' an' ut would be betther not to slip your boots. How do I know that? By the light av pure reason. Here are three companies av us ever so far inside av the enemy's flank an' a crowd av roarin', tarin', squealin' cavalry gone on just to turn out the whole hornet's nest av them. Av course the enemy will pursue, by brigades like as not, an' thin we'll have to run for ut. Mark my words. I am av the opinion av Polonius whin he said, "Don't fight wid ivry scutt for the pure joy av fightin', but if you do, knock the nose av him first an' frequint." We ought to ha' gone on an' helped the Ghoorkhas.'

'But what do you know about Polonius?' I demanded. This was a new side of Mulvaney's character.

'All that Shakespeare iver wrote an' a dale more that the gallery shouted,' said the man of war, carefully lacing his boots. 'Did I not tell you av Silver's theatre in Dublin whin I was younger than I am now an' a patron av the drama? Ould Silver wud never pay actor-man or woman their just dues, an' by consequince his comp'nies was collapsible at the last minut. Thin the bhoys wud clamour to take a part, an' oft as not ould Silver made them pay for the fun. Faith, I've seen Hamlut played wid a new black eye an' the queen as full as a cornucopia. I remimber wanst Hogin that 'listed in the Black Tyrone an' was shot in South Africa, he sejuced ould Silver into givin' him Hamlut's part instid av me that had a fine fancy for rhetoric in those days. Av course I wint into the gallery an' began to fill the pit wid other people's hats, an' I passed the time av day to Hogin walkin' through Denmark like a ham-strung mule wid a pall on his back. "Hamlut," sez I, "there's a hole in your heel. Pull up your shtockin's, Hamlut," sez I. "Hamlut, Hamlut, for the love av decincy dhrop that skull an' pull up your shtockin's." The whole house begun to tell him that. He stopped his soliloquishms mid-between. "My shtock-in's may be comin' down or they may not," sez he, screwin' his eyes into the gallery, for well he knew who I was. "But afther this performince is over me an' the Ghost'll trample the tripes out av you, Terence, wid your ass's bray!" An' that's how I come to know about Hamlut. Eyah! Those days, those days! Did you iver have onendin' devilmint an' nothin' to pay for it in your life, sorr?'

'Never, without having to pay,' I said.

'That's thrue! 'Tis mane whin you considher on ut; but ut's the same wid horse or fut. A headache if you dhrink, an' a belly-ache if you eat too much, an' a heart-ache to kape all down. Faith, the beast only gets the colic, an' he's the lucky man.'

He dropped his head and stared into the fire, fingering his moustache the while. From the far side of the bivouac the voice of Corbet-Nolan, senior subaltern of B company, uplifted itself in an ancient and much appreciated song of sentiment, the men moaning melodiously behind him.

The north wind blew coldly, she drooped from that hour,
My own little Kathleen, my sweet little Kathleen,
Kathleen, my Kathleen, Kathleen O'Moore!

With forty-five O's in the last word: even at that distance you might have cut the soft South Irish accent with a shovel.

'For all we take we must pay, but the price is cruel high,' murmured Mulvaney when the chorus had ceased.

'What's the trouble?' I said gently, for I knew that he was a man of an extinguishable sorrow.

'Hear now,' said he. 'Ye know what I am now. *I* know what I mint to be at the beginnin' av my service. I've tould you time an' again, an' what I have not Dinah Shadd has. An' what am I? Oh, Mary Mother av Hiven, an ould dhrunken, untrustable baste av a privit that has seen the reg'ment change out from colonel to drummer-boy, not wanst or twice, but scores av times! Ay, scores! An' me not so near gettin' promotion as in the first! An' me livin' on an' kapin' clear av clink, not by my own good conduck, but the kindness av some orf'cer-bhoy young enough to be son to me? Do I not know ut? Can I not tell whin I'm passed over at p'rade, tho' I'm rockin' full av liquor an' ready to fall all in wan piece, such as even a suckin' child might see, bekaze, "Oh, 'tis only ould Mulvaney!" An' whin I'm let off in ord'ly-room through some thrick of the tongue an' a ready answer an' the ould man's mercy, is ut smilin' I feel whin I fall away an' go back to Dinah Shadd, thryin' to carry ut all off as a joke? Not I! 'Tis hell to me, dumb hell through ut all; an' next time whin the fit comes I will be as bad again. Good cause the reg'ment has to know me for the best soldier in ut. Better cause have I to know mesilf for the worst man. I'm only fit to tache the new drafts what I'll niver learn myself; an' I am sure, as tho' I heard ut, that the minut wan av these pink-eyed recruities gets away from my "Mind ye now," an "Listen to this, Jim, bhoy," – sure I am that the sergint houlds me up to him for a warnin'. So I tache, as they say at musketry-instruction, by direct and ricochet fire. Lord be good to me, for I have stud some throuble!'

'Lie down and go to sleep,' said I, not being able to comfort or advise. 'You're the best man in the regiment, and, next to Ortheris, the biggest fool. Lie down and wait till we're attacked. What force will they turn out? Guns, think you?'

'Try that wid your lorrds an' ladies, twistin' an' turnin' the talk, tho' you mint ut well. Ye cud say nothin' to help me, an' yet ye niver knew what cause I had to be what I am.'

'Begin at the beginning and go on to the end,' I said royally. 'But rake up the fire a bit first.'

I passed Ortheris's bayonet for a poker.

'That shows how little we know what we do,' said Mulvaney, putting it aside. "Fire takes all the heart out av the steel, an' the next time, may be, that our little man is fighting for his life his bradawl'll break, an' so you'll ha' killed him, manin' no more than to kape yourself warm. 'Tis a recruity's thrick that. Pass the clanin'-rod, sorr.'

I snuggled down abashed; and after an interval the voice of Mulvaney began.

'Did I iver tell you how Dinah Shadd came to be wife av mine?'

I dissembled a burning anxiety that I had felt for some months – ever since Dinah Shadd, the strong, the patient, and the infinitely tender, had of her own good love and free will washed a shirt for me, moving in a barren land where washing was not.

'I can't remember,' I said casually. 'Was it before or after you made love to Annie Bragin, and got no satisfaction?'

The story of Annie Bragin is written in another place. It is one of the many less respectable episodes in Mulvaney's chequered career.

'Before – before – long before, was that business av Annie Bragin an' the corp'ril's ghost. Niver woman was the worse for me whin I had married Dinah. There's a time for all things, an' I know how to kape all things in place – barrin' the dhrink, that kapes me in my place wid no hope av comin' to be aught else.'

'Begin at the beginning,' I insisted. 'Mrs Mulvaney told me that you married her when you were quartered in Krab Bokhar barracks.'

'An' the same is a cess-pit,' said Mulvaney piously. 'She spoke thrue, did Dinah. 'Twas this way. Talkin' av that, have ye iver fallen in love, sorr?'

I preserved the silence of the damned. Mulvaney continued – 'Thin I will assume that ye have not. I did. In the days av my youth, as I have no more than wanst told you, I was a man that filled the eye an' delighted the sowl av women. Niver man was hated as I have bin. Niver man was loved as I – no, not within half a day's march av ut! For the first five years av my service, whin I was what I wud give my sowl to be now, I tuk whatever was within my reach an' digested ut – an' that's more than most men can say. Dhrink I tuk, an' ut did me no harm. By the Hollow av Hiven, I cud play wid four women at wanst, an' kape them from findin' out anythin' about the other three, an' smile like a full-blown marigold through ut all. Dick Coulhan, av the battery we'll have down on us to-night, could drive his team no better than I mine, an' I hild the worser cattle! An' so I lived, an' so I was happy till afther that business wid Annie Bragin – she that turned me off as cool as a meat-safe, an' taught me where I stud in the mind av an honest woman. 'Twas no sweet dose to swallow.

'Afther that I sickened awhile an' tuk thought to my reg'mental work; conceiting mesilf I wud study an' be a sargint, an' a major-gineral twinty minutes afther that. But on top av my ambitiousness there was an empty place in my sowl, an' me own opinion av mesilf cud not fill ut. Sez I to mesilf, "Terence, you're a great man an' the best set-up in the reg'mint. Go on an' get promotion." Sez mesilf to me, "What for?" Sez I to mesilf, "For the glory av ut!" Sez mesilf to me, "Will that fill these two strong arrums av yours, Terence?" – "Go to the devil," sez I to mesilf. "Go to the married lines," sez mesilf to me. " 'Tis the same thing," sez I to mesilf. "Av you're the same man, ut is," said mesilf to me; an' wid that I considhered on ut a long while. Did you iver feel that way, sorr?'

I snored gently, knowing that if Mulvaney were uninter-rupted he would go on. The clamour from the bivouac fires beat up to the stars, as the rival singers of the companies were pitted against each other.

'So I felt that way an' a bad time ut was. Wanst, bein' a fool, I wint into the married lines more for the sake av spakin' to our ould colour-sergint Shadd than for any thruck wid women-folk. I was a corp'ril then – rejuced aftherwards, but a corp'ril then. I've got a photograft av mesilf to prove ut. "You'll take a cup av tay wid us?" sez Shadd. "I will that," I sez, "tho' tay is not my divarsion."

' " 'Twud be better for you if ut were," sez ould Mother Shadd, an' she had ought to know, for Shadd, in the ind av his service, dhrank bungfull each night.

'Wid that I tuk off my gloves – there was pipeclay in thim, so that they stud alone – an' pulled up my chair, lookin' round at the china ornaments an' bits av things in the Shadds' quarters. They were things that belonged to a man, an' no camp-kit, here to-day an' dishipated next. "You're comfortable in this place, sergint," sez I. "Tis the wife that did ut, boy," sez he, pointin' the stem av his pipe to ould Mother Shadd, an' she smacked the top av his bald head apon the compliment. "That manes you want money," sez she.

'An' thin – an' thin whin the kettle was to be filled, Dinah came in – my Dinah – her sleeves rowled up to the elbow an' her hair in a winkin' glory over her forehead, the big blue eyes beneath twinklin' like stars on a frosty night, an' the tread av her two feet lighter than waste-paper from the colonel's basket in ord'ly-room whin ut's emptied. Bein' but a shlip av a girl she went pink at seein' me, an' I twisted me moustache an' looked at a picture forninst the wall. Niver show a woman that ye care the snap av a finger for her, an' begad she'll come bleatin' to your boot-heels!'

'I suppose that's why you followed Annie Bragin till everybody in the married quarters laughed at you,' said I, remembering that unhallowed wooing and casting off the disguise of drowsiness.

'I'm layin' down the gin'ral theory av the attack,' said Mulvaney, driving his boot into the dying fire. 'If you read the *Soldier's Pocket Book*, which niver any soldier reads, you'll see that there are exceptions. Whin Dinah was out av the door (an' 'twas as tho' the sunlight had shut too) – "Mother av Hiven, sergint," sez I, "but is that your daughter?" – "I've believed that way these eighteen years," sez ould Shadd, his eyes twinklin'; "but Mrs Shadd has her own opinion, like iv'ry woman." – " 'Tis wid yours this time, for a mericle," sez Mother Shadd. "Thin why in the name av fortune did I niver see her before?" sez I. "Bekaze you've been thrapesin' round wid the married women these three years past. She was a bit av a child till last year, an' she shot up wid the spring," sez ould Mother Shadd. "I'll thrapese no more," sez I. "D'you mane that?" sez ould Mother Shadd, lookin' at me side-ways like a hen looks at a hawk whin the chickens are runnin' free. "Try me, an' tell," sez I. Wid that I pulled on my gloves, dhrank off the tay, an' went out av the house as stiff as a gin'ral p'rade, for well I knew that Dinah Shadd's eyes were in the small av my back out av the scullery window. Faith! that was the only time I mourned I was not a cav'l'ry man for the pride av the spurs to jingle.

'I want out to think, an' I did a powerful lot av thinkin', but ut all came round to that shlip av a girl in the dotted blue dhress, wid the blue eyes an' the sparkil in them. Thin I kept off canteen, an' I kept to the married quarthers, or near by, on the chanst av meetin' Dinah. Did I meet her? Oh, my time past, did I not; wid a lump in my throat as big as my valise an' my heart goin' like a farrier's forge on a Saturday morning? 'Twas "Good day to ye. Miss Dinah," an' "Good day t'you, corp'ril," for a week or two, and divil a bit further could I get bekaze av the respect I had to that girl that I cud' ha' broken betune finger an' thumb.'

Here I giggled as I recalled the gigantic figure of Dinah Shadd when she handed me my shirt.

'Ye may laugh,' grunted Mulvaney. 'But I'm speakin' the trut,' an' 'tis you that are in fault. Dinah was a girl that wud ha' taken the imperiousness out av the Duchess av Clonmel in those days. Flower hand, foot av shod air, an' the eyes av the livin' mornin' she had that is my wife to-day – ould Dinah, and niver aught else than Dinah Shadd to me.

' 'Twas after three weeks standin' off an' on, an' niver makin' headway excipt through the eyes, that a little drummer-boy grinned in me face whin I had admonished him wid the buckle av my belt for riotin' all over the place. "An' I'm not the only wan that doesn't kape to barricks," sez he. I tuk him by the scruff av his neck, – my heart was hung on a hair-thrigger those days, you will onderstand – an' "Out wid ut," sez I, "or I'll lave no bone av you unbreakable." – "Speak to Dempsey," sez he howlin'. "Dempsey which?" sez I, "ye unwashed limb av Satan." – "Av the Bob-tailed Dhragoons," sez he. "He's seen her home from her aunt's house in the civil lines four times this fortnight." – "Child!" sez I, dhroppin' him, "your tongue's stronger than your body. Go to your quarters. I'm sorry I dhressed you down."

'At that I went four ways to wanst huntin' Dempsey. I was mad to think that wid all my airs among women I shud ha' been chated by a basin-faced fool av a cav'lryman not fit to trust on a trunk. Presintly I found him in our lines – the Bobtails was quartered next us – an' a tallowy, topheavy son av a she-mule he was wid his big brass spurs an' his plastrons on his epigastrons an' all. But he niver flinched a hair.

' "A word wid you, Dempsey," sez I. "You've walked wid Dinah Shadd four times this fortnight gone." '

' "What's that to you?" sez he. "I'll walk forty times more, an' forty on top av that, ye shovel-futted clod-breakin' infantry lance-corp'ril." '

'Before I cud gyard he had his gloved fist home on my cheek an' down I went full-sprawl. "Will that content you?" sez he, blowin' on his knuckles for all the world like a Scots Greys orf'cer. "Content!" sez I. "For your own sake, man, take off your spurs, peel your jackut, an' onglove. 'Tis the beginnin' av the overture; stand up!"

'He stud all he know, but he niver peeled his jacket, an' his shoulders had no fair play. I was fightin' for Dinah Shadd an' that cut on my cheek. What hope had he forninst me? "Stand up," sez I, time an' again whin he was beginnin' to quarter the ground an' gyard high an' go large. "This isn't ridin'-school," I sez. "O man, stand up an' let me get in at ye." But whin I saw he wud be runnin' about, I grup his shtock in my left an' his waist-belt in my right an' swung him clear to my right front, head undher, he hammerin' my nose till the wind was knocked out av him on the bare ground. "Stand up," sez I, "or I'll kick your head into your chest!" and I wud ha' done ut too, so ragin' mad I was.

' "My collar-bone's bruk," sez he. "Help me back to lines. I'll walk wid her no more." So I helped him back.'

'And was his collar-bone broken?' I asked, for I fancied that only Learoyd could neatly accomplish that terrible throw.

'He pitched on his left shoulder-point. Ut was. Next day the news was in both barracks, an' whin I met Dinah Shadd wid a cheek on me like all the reg'mintal tailor's samples there was no "Good mornin', corp'ril," or aught else. "An' what have I done, Miss Shadd," sez I, very bould, plantin' mesilf forninst her, "that ye should not pass the time of day?"

' "Ye've half-killed rough-rider Dempsey," sez she, her dear blue eyes fillin' up.

' "May be," sez I. "Was he a friend av yours that saw ye home four times in the fortnight?"

' "Yes," sez she, but her mouth was down at the corners. "An' – an' what's that to you?" she sez.

' "Ask Dempsey," sez I, purtendin' to go away.

' "Did you fight for me then, ye silly man?" she sez, tho' she knew ut all along.

' "Who else?" sez I, an' I tuk wan pace to the front.

' "I wasn't worth ut," sez she, fingerin' in her apron.

' "That's for me to say," sez I. "Shall I say ut?"

' "Yes," sez she in a saint's whisper, an' at that I explained mesilf; and she tould me what ivry man that is a man, an' many that is a woman, hears wanst in his life.

' "But what made ye cry at startin', Dinah, darlin'?" sez I.

' "Your – your bloody cheek," sez she, duckin' her little head down on my sash (I was on duty for the day) an' whimperin' like a sorrowful angil.

'Now a man cud take that two ways. I tuk ut as pleased me best an' my first kiss wid ut. Mother av Innocence! but I kissed her on the tip av the nose an' undher the eye; an' a girl that lets a kiss come tumbleways like that has never been kissed before. Take note av that, sorr. Thin we wint hand in hand to ould Mother Shadd like two little childher, an' she said 'twas no bad thing, an' ould Shadd nodded behind his pipe, an' Dinah ran way to her own room. That day I throd on rollin' clouds. All earth was too small to hould me. Begad, I cud ha' hiked the sun out av the sky for a live coal to my pipe, so magnificent I was. But I tuk recruities at squad-drill instid, an' began wid general battalion advance whin I shud ha' been balance-steppin' them. Eyah! that day! that day!'

A very long pause. 'Well?' said I.

' 'Twas all wrong,' said Mulvaney, with an enormous sigh. 'An I know that ev'ry bit av ut was my own foolishness. That night I tuk maybe the half av three pints – not enough to turn the hair of a man in his natural senses. But I was more than half drunk wid pure joy, an' that canteen beer was so much whisky to me. I can't tell how it came about, but *bekaze* I had no thought for anywan except Dinah, *bekaze* I hadn't slipped her little white arms from my neck five minuts, *bekaze* the breath of her kiss was not gone from my mouth, I must go through the married lines on my way to quarters, an' I must stay talkin' to a red-headed Mullingar heifer av a girl, Judy Sheehy, that was daughter to Mother Sheehy, the wife of Nick Sheehy, the canteen-sergint – the Black Curse av Shielygh be on the whole brood that are above groun' this day!

' "An' what are ye houldin' your head that high for, corp'ril?" sez Judy. "Come in an' thry a cup av tay," she sez, standin' in the doorway. Bein' an ontrustable fool, an' thinkin' av anything but tay, I wint.

' "Mother's at canteen," sez Judy, smoothin' the hair av hers that was like red snakes, an' lookin' at me corner-ways out av her green cats' eyes. "Ye will not mind, corp'ril?"

' "I can endure," sez I; ould Mother Sheehy bein' no divarsion av mine, nor her daughter too. Judy fetched the tea things an' put thim on the table, leanin' over me very close to get thim square. I dhrew back, thinkin' av Dinah.

' "Is ut afraid you are av a girl alone?" sez Judy.

' "No," sez I. "Why should I be?" '

' "That rests wid the girl," sez Judy, dhrawin' her chair next to mine.

' "Thin there let ut rest," sez I; an' thinkin' I'd been a trifle onpolite, I sez, "The tay's not quite sweet enough for my taste. Put your little finger in the cup, Judy. 'Twill make ut necthar."

' "What's necthar?" sez she.

' "Somethin' very sweet," sez I; an' for the sinful life av me I cud not help lookin' at her out av the corner av my eye, as I was used to look at a woman.

' "Go on wid ye, corp'ril," sez she. "You're a flirrt."

' "On me sowl I'm not," sez I.

' "Then you're a cruel handsome man, an' that's worse,' sez she, heaving big sighs an' lookin' crossways.

' "You know your own mind," sez I.

' "Twud be better for me if I did not," she sez.

' "There's a dale to be said on both sides av that," sez I, unthinkin'.

' "Say your own part av ut, then, Terence, darlin'," sez she; "for begad I'm thinkin' I've said too much or too little for an honest girl," an' wid that she put her arms round my neck an' kissed me.

' "There's no more to be said afther that," sez I, kissin' her back again – Oh the mane scutt that I was, my head ringin' wid Dinah Shadd! How does ut come about, sorr, that when a man has put the comether on wan woman, he's sure bound to put it on another? 'Tis the same thing at musketry. Wan day ivry shot goes wide or into the bank, an' the next, lay high lay low, sight or snap, ye can't get off the bull's-eye for ten shots runnin'.'

'That only happens to a man who has had a good deal of experience. He does it without thinking,' I replied.

'Thankin' you for the complimint, sorr, ut may be so. But I'm doubtful whether you mint ut for a complimint. Hear now; I sat there wid Judy on my knee tellin' me all manner av nonsinse an' only sayin' "yes" an' "no", when I'd much better ha' kept tongue betune teeth. An' that was not an hour afther I had left Dinah! What I was thinkin' av I cannot say. Presintly, quiet as a cat, ould Mother Sheeny came in velvet-dhrunk. She had her daughter's red hair, but 'twas bald in patches, an' I cud see in her wicked ould face, clear as lightnin', what Judy wud be twenty years to come. I was for jumpin' up, but Judy niver moved.

' "Terence has promust, mother," sez she, an' the could sweat bruk out all over me. Ould Mother Sheehy sat down of a heap an' began playin' wid the cups. "Thin you're a well-matched pair," she sez very thick. "For he's the biggest rogue that iver spoiled the Queen's shoe-leather, an—"

' "I'm off, Judy," sez I. "Ye should not talk nonsinse to your mother. Get her to bed, girl."

' "Nonsinse!" sez the ould woman, prickin' up her ears like a cat an' grippin' the table-edge. " 'Twill be the most non-sinsical nonsinse for you, ye grinnin' badger, if nonsinse 'tis. Git clear, you. I'm goin' to bed."

'I ran out into the dhark, my head in a stew an' my heart sick, but I had sinse enough to see that I'd brought ut all on mysilf. "It's this to pass the time av day to a panjandhrum av hellcats," sez I. "What I've said, an' what I've not said do not matther. Judy an' her dam will hould me for a promust man, an' Dinah will give me the go, an' I desarve ut. I will go an' get dhrunk," sez I, "an' forget about ut, for 'tis plain I'm not a marrin' man."

'On my way to canteen I ran against Lascelles, colour-sergeant that was av E Comp'ny, a hard, hard man, wid a torment av a wife. "You've the head av a drowned man on your shoulders," sez he; "an' you're goin' where you'll get a worse wan. Come back," sez he. "Let me go," sez I. "I've thrown my luck over the wall wid my own hand!" – "Then that's not the way to get ut back again," sez he. "Have out wid your throuble, ye fool-bhoy." An' I tould him how the matther was.

'He sucked in his lower lip. "You've been thrapped," sez he. "Ju Sheehy wud be the bether for a man's name to hers as soon as can. An' ye thought ye'd put the comether on her, – that's the natural vanity of the baste. Terence, you're a big born fool, but you're not bad enough to marry into that comp'ny. If you said anythin', an' for all your protestations I'm sure ye did – or did not, which is worse, – eat ut all – lie like the father of all lies, but come out av ut free av Judy. Do I not know what ut is to marry a woman that was the very spit an' image av Judy whin she was young? I'm gettin' old an' I've larnt patience, but you, Terence, you'd raise hand on Judy an' kill her in a year. Never mind if Dinah gives you the go, you've desarved ut; never mind if the whole reg'mint laughs you all day. Get shut av Judy an' her mother. They can't dhrag you to church, but if they do, they'll dhrag you to hell. Go back to your quarters and lie down," sez he. Thin over his shoulder, "You *must* ha' done with thim."

'Next day I wint to see Dinah, but there was no tucker in me as I walked. I knew the throuble wud come soon enough widout any handlin' av mine, an I dreaded ut sore.

'I heard Judy callin' me, but I hild straight on to the Shadd's quarthers, an' Dinah wud ha' kissed me but I put her back.

' "Whin all's said, darlin'," sez I, "you can give ut me if ye will, tho' I misdoubt 'twill be so easy to come by then."

'I had scarce begun to put the explanation into shape before Judy an' her mother came to the door. I think there was a verandah, but I'm forgettin'.

' "Will ye not step in?" sez Dinah, pretty and polite, though the Shadds had no dealin's with the Sheehys. Old Mother Shadd looked up quick, an' she was the fust to see the throuble; for Dinah was her daughter.

' "I'm pressed for time to-day," sez Judy as bould as brass; "an' I've only come for Terence, – my promust man. 'Tis strange to find him here the day afther the day."

'Dinah looked at me as though I had hit her, an' I answered straight.

' "There was some nonsinse last night at the Sheehys' quarthers, an' Judy's carryin' on the joke, darlin'," sez I.

' "At the Sheehys' quarthers?" sez Dinah very slow an' Judy cut in wid: "He was there from nine till ten, Dinah Shadd, an' the betther half av that time I was sittin' on his knee, Dinah Shadd. Ye may look and ye may look an' ye may look me up an' down, but ye won't look away that Terence is my promust man. Terence, darlin', 'tis time for us to be comin' home."

'Dinah Shadd niver said word to Judy. "Ye left me at half-past eight," she sez to me, "an' I niver thought that ye'd leave me for Judy, – promises or no promises. Go back wid her, you that have to be fetched by a girl! I'm done with you," sez she, and she ran into her own room, her mother followin'. So I was alone wid those two women and at liberty to spake my sentiments.'

' "Judy Sheehy," sez I, "if you made a fool av me betune the lights you shall not do ut in the day. I niver promised you words or lines."

' "You lie," sez ould Mother Sheehy, "an' may ut choke you where you stand!" She was far gone in dhrink.

' "An, tho' ut choked me where I stud I'd not change," sez I. "Go home, Judy. I take shame for a decent girl like you dhraggin' your mother out bare-headed on this errand. Hear now, and have ut for an answer. I gave my word to Dinah Shadd yesterday, an', more blame on me, I was wid you last night talkin' nonsinse but nothin' more. You've chosen to thry to hould me on ut. I will not be held thereby for anythin' in the world. Is that enough?"

'Judy wint pink all over. "An' I wish you joy av the perjury," sez she, duckin' a curtsey. "You've lost a woman that would ha' wore her hand to the bone for your pleasure; an' 'deed, Terence, ye were not thrapped. . . ." Lascelles must ha' spoken plain to her. "I am such as Dinah is – deed I am! Ye've lost a fool av a girl that'll niver look at you again, an' ye've lost what ye niver had, – your common honesty. If you manage your men as you manage your love-makin', small wondher they call you the worst corp'ril in the comp'ny. Come away, mother," sez she.

'But divil a fut would the ould woman budge! "D'you hould by that?" sez she, peerin' up under her thick grey eyebrows.

'"Ay, an' wud," sez I, "tho' Dinah gave me the go twinty times. I'll have no thruck with you or yours," sez I. "Take your child away, ye shameless woman."

'"An' am I shameless?" sez she, bringin' her hands up above her head. "'Thin what are you, ye lyin', schamin', weak-kneed, dhirty-souled son av a sutler? An I shameless? Who put the open shame on me an' my child that we shud go beggin' through the lines in the broad daylight for the broken word of a man? Double portion of my shame be on you, Terence Mulvaney, that think yourself so strong! By Mary and the saints, by blood and water an' by ivry sorrow that came into the world since the beginnin', the black blight fall on you and yours, so that you may niver be free from pain for another when ut's not your own! May your heart bleed in your breast drop by drop wid all your friends laughin' at the bleedin'! Strong you think yourself? May your strength be a curse to you to dhrive you into the divil's hands against your own will! Clear-eyed you are? May your eyes see clear evry step av the dark path you take till the hot cindhers av hell put thim out! May the ragin' dry thirst in my own ould bones go to you that you shall niver pass bottle full nor glass empty. God preserve the light av your onderstandin' to you, my jewel av a bhoy, that ye may niver forget what you mint to be an' do, whin you're wallowin' in the muck! May ye see the betther and follow the worse as long as there's breath in your body; an' may ye die quick in a strange land, watchin' your death before ut takes you, an' onable to stir hand or foot!"

'I heard a scufflin' in the room behind, and thin Dinah Shadd's hand dhropped into mine like a rose-leaf into a muddy road.

'"The half av that I'll take," sez she, "an' more too if I can. Go home, ye silly talkin' woman, – go home an' confess."

'"Come away! Come away!" sez Judy, pullin' her mother by the shawl. "'Twas none av Terence's fault. For the love av Mary stop the talkin'!"

'"An' you!" said ould Mother Sheehy, spinnin' round forninst Dinah. "Will ye take the half av that man's load? Stand off from him, Dinah Shadd, before he takes you down too – you that look to be a quarther-master-sergeant's wife in five years. You look too high, child. You shall *wash* for the quarther-master-sergeant, whin he plases to give you the job out av charity; but a privit's wife you shall be to the end, an' evry sorrow of a privit's wife you shall know and niver a joy but wan, that shall go from you like the running tide from a rock. The pain av bearin' you shall know but niver the pleasure av giving the breast; an' you shall put away man-child into the common ground wid niver a priest to say a prayer over him, an' on that man-child ye shall think ivry day av your life. Think long, Dinah Shadd, for you'll niver have another tho' you pray till your knees are bleedin'. The mothers av childer shall mock you behind your back when you're wringing over the wash-tub. You shall know what ut is to help a dhrunken husband home an' see him go to the gyard-room. Will that plase you, Dinah Shadd, that won't be seen talkin' to my daughter? You shall talk to worse than Judy before all's over. The sergints' wives shall look down on you contemptuous, daughter av a sergint, an' you shall cover ut all up wid a smiling face whin your heart's burstin'. Stand off av him, Dinah Shadd, for I've put the Black Curse of Shielygh upon him an' his own mouth shall make ut good."

'She pitched forward on her head an' began foamin' at the mouth. Dinah Shadd ran out wid water, an' Judy dhragged the ould woman into the verandah till she sat up.

' "I'm old an' forlore," she sez, thremblin' an' cryin', "and 'tis like I say a dale more than I mane."

' "When you're able to walk, – go," says ould Mother Shadd. "This house has no place for the likes av you that have cursed my daughter."

' "Eyah!" said the ould woman. "Hard words break no bones, an' Dinah Shadd 'll kape the love av her husband till my bones are green corn. Judy darlin', I misremember what I came here for. Can you lend us the bottom av a taycup av tay, Mrs Shadd?"

'But Judy dhragged her off cryin' as tho' her heart wud break. An' Dinah Shadd an' I, in ten minutes we had forgot ut all.'

'Then why do you remember it now?' said I.

'Is ut like I'd forget? Ivry word that wicked ould woman spoke fell thrue in my life afterwards, an' I cud ha' stud ut all – stud ut all, – excipt when my little Shadd was born. That was on the line av march three months afther the regiment was taken with cholera. We were betune Umballa an' Kalka thin, an' I was on picket. Whin I came off duty the women showed me the child, an' ut turned on uts side an' died as I looked. We buried him by the road, an' Father Victor was a day's march behind wid the heavy baggage, so the comp'ny captain read a prayer. An' since then I've been a childless man, an' all else that ould Mother Sheehy put upon me an' Dinah Shadd. What do you think, sorr?'

I thought a good deal, but it seemed better then to reach out for Mulvaney's hand. The demonstration nearly cost me the use of three fingers. Whatever he knows of his weaknesses, Mulvaney is entirely ignorant of his strength.

'But what do you think?' he repeated, as I was straightening out the crushed fingers.

My reply was drowned in yells and outcries from the next

fire, where ten men were shouting for 'Orth'ris,' 'Privit Orth'ris,' 'Mistah Or-ther-ris!' 'Deah boy,' 'Cap'n Orth'ris,' 'Field-Marshal Orth'ris,' 'Stanley, you pen'north o' pop, come 'ere to your own comp'ny!' And the cockney, who had been delighting another audience with recondite and Rabelaisian yarns, was shot down among his admirers by the major force.

'You've crumpled my dress-shirt 'orrid,' said he, 'an' I shan't sing no more to this 'ere bloomin' drawin'-room.'

Learoyd, roused by the confusion, uncoiled himself, crept behind Ortheris, and slung him aloft on his shoulders.

'Sing, ye bloomin' hummin' bird!' said he, and Ortheris, beating time on Learoyd's skull, delivered himself, in the raucous voice of the Ratcliffe Highway, of this song: –

My girl she give me the go onst,
    When I was a London lad,
An' I went on the drink for a fortnight,
    An' then I went to the bad.
The Queen she give me a shillin'
    To fight for 'er over the seas;
But Guv'ment built me a fever-trap.
    An' Injia give me disease.

Chorus.
Ho! don't you 'eed what a girl says,
    An' don't you go for the beer;
But I was an ass when I was at grass,
    An' that is why I'm here.

I fired a shot at a Afghan,
    The beggar 'e fired again,
An' I lay on my bed with a 'ole in my 'ed.
    An' missed the next campaign!
I up with my gun at a Burman
    Who carried a bloomin' *dah*,
But the cartridge stuck and the bay'nit bruk,
    An' all I got was the scar.

Chorus.
Ho! don't you aim at a Afghan,
    When you stand on the sky-line clear;

An' don't you go for a Burman
   If none o' your friends is near.

I served my time for a corp'ral.
   An' wetted my stripes with pop,
For I went on the bend with a intimate friend,
   An' finished the night in the 'shop.'
I served my time for a sergeant;
   The colonel 'e sez 'No!
The most you'll see is full CB.'[1]
   An' . . . very next night 'twas so.

Chorus.

Ho! don't you go for a corp'ral
   Unless your 'ed is clear;
But I was an ass when I was at grass,
   An' that is why I'm 'ere.

I've tasted the luck o' the army
   In barrack an' camp an' clink,
An' I lost my tip through the bloomin' trip
   Along o' the women an' drink.
I'm down at the heel o' my service,
   An, when I am laid on the shelf,
My very wust friend from beginning to end
   By the blood of a mouse was myself!

Chorus.

Ho! don't you 'eed what a girl says,
   An' don't you go for the beer;
But I was an ass when I was at grass
   An' that is why I'm 'ere.

'Ay, listen to our little man now, singin' an' shoutin' as tho' trouble had niver touched him. D'you remember when he went mad with the home-sickness?' said Mulvaney, recalling a never-to-be-forgotten season when Ortheris waded through the deep waters of affliction and behaved abominably. 'But he's talkin' bitter truth, though. Eyah!

[1] Confined to barracks.

'My very worst frind from beginnin' to ind
    By the blood av a mouse was mesilf!'

'Harkout' he continued, jumping to his feet.
'What did I tell you, sorr?'
Fttl', spttl', whttl' went the rifles of the picket in the
darkness, and we heard their feet rushing towards us as
Ortheris tumbled past me and into his great-coat. It is an
impressive thing, even in peace, to see an armed camp spring
to life with clatter of accoutrements, click of Martini levers,
and blood curdling speculations as to the fate of missing boots.
'Pickets dhriven in', said Mulvaney, staring like a buck at bay
into the soft, clinging gloom. 'Stand by an' kape close to us. If
'tis cav'lry, they may blundher into the fires'.
Tr-ra-ra' -ta-ra-la' sung the thrice blessed bugle, and the
rush to form square began. There is much rest and peace
in the heart of a square if you arrive in time, and are not
trodden upon too frequently. The smell of leather belts,
fatigue uniform and packed humanity is comforting.
A dull grumble, that seemed to come from every point
of the compass, at once, struck our listening ears, and little
thrills of excitement ran down the faces of the square. Those
who write so learnedly about judging distance by sound should
hear cavalry on the move at night. A high-pitched yell on the
left told us that the disturbers were friends, the cavalry of the
attack, who had missed their direction, in the darkness, and
were feeling blindly for some sort of support and camping-
ground. The difficulty explained, they jingled on.
'Double pickets out there; by your arms lie down and sleep
the rest', said the major, and the square melted away as the
men scrambled for their places by the fire.

When I woke I saw Mulvaney, the night-dew gemming his
moustache, leaning on his rifle at picket, lonely as Prometheus
on his rock, with I know not what vultures tearing his liver.

THE MARK OF THE BEAST

Your Gods and my Gods – do you or I know which are the stronger?
Native Proverb

East of Suez, some hold, the direct control of Providence ceases; Man being there handed over to the power of the Gods and Devils of Asia, and the Church of England Providence only exercising an occasional and modified supervision in the case of Englishmen.

This theory accounts for some of the more unnecessary horrors of life in India; it may be stretched to explain my story.

My friend Strickland of the Police, who knows as much of natives of India as is good for any man, can bear witness to the facts of the case. Dumoise, our doctor, also saw what Strickland and I saw. The inference which he drew from the evidence was entirely incorrect. He is dead now; he died in a rather curious manner, which has been elsewhere described.

When Fleete came to India he owned a little money and some land in the Himalayas, near a place called Dharmsala. Both properties had been left him by an uncle, and he came out to finance them. He was a big, heavy, genial, and inoffensive man. His knowledge of natives was, of course, limited, and he complained of the difficulties of the language.

He rode in from his place in the hills to spend New Year in the station, and he stayed with Strickland. On New Year's Eve there was a big dinner at the club, and the night was excusably wet. When men foregather from the uttermost ends of the Empire they have a right to be riotous. The Frontier had sent down a contingent o' Catch-'em-Alive-O's who had not seen twenty white faces for a year, and were used to ride fifteen miles to dinner at the next Fort at the risk of a Khyberee bullet where their drinks should lie. They profited by their new security, for they tried to play pool with a curled-up hedgehog found in the garden, and one of them carried the marker round the room in his teeth. Half a dozen planters had come in from the south and were talking 'horse' to the Biggest Liar in Asia, who was trying to cap all their stories at once. Everybody was there, and there was a general closing up of ranks and taking stock of our losses in dead or disabled that had fallen during the past year. It was a very wet night, and I remember that we sang 'Auld Lang Syne' with our feet in the Polo Championship Cup, and our heads among the stars, and swore that we were all dear friends. Then some of us went away and annexed Burma, and some tried to open up the Soudan and were opened up by Fuzzies in that cruel scrub outside Suakim, and some found stars and medals, and some were married, which was bad, and some did other things which were worse, and the others of us stayed in our chains and strove to make money on insufficient experiences.

Fleete began the night with sherry and bitters, drank champagne steadily up to dessert, then raw, rasping Capri with all the strength of whisky, took Benedictine with his coffee, four or five whiskies and sodas to improve his pool strokes, beer and bones at half-past two, winding up with old brandy. Consequently, when he came out, at half-past three in the morning, into fourteen degrees of frost, he was very angry with his horse for coughing, and tried to leapfrog into the saddle. The horse broke away and went to his stables; so Strickland and I formed a Guard of Dishonour to take Fleete home.

Our road lay through the bazaar, close to a little temple of Hanuman, the Monkey-god, who is a leading divinity worthy of respect. All gods have good points, just as have all priests. Personally, I attach much importance to Hanuman, and am kind to his people – the great grey apes of the hills. One never knows when one may want a friend.

There was a light in the temple, and as we passed we could hear voices of men chanting hymns. In a native temple the priests rise at all hours of the night to do honour to their god. Before we would stop him, Fleete dashed up the steps, patted two priests on the back, and was gravely grinding the ashes of his cigar-butt in to the forehead of the red stone image of Hanuman. Strickland tried to drag him out, but he sat down and said solemnly:

'Shee that? 'Mark of the B-beasht! *I* made it. Ishn't it fine?'

In half a minute the temple was alive and noisy, and Strickland, who knew what came of polluting gods, said that things might occur. He, by virtue of his official position, long residence in the country, and weakness for going among the natives, was known to the priests and he felt unhappy. Fleete sat on the ground and refused to move. He said that 'good old Hanuman' made a very soft pillow.

Then, without any warning, a Silver Man came out of a recess behind the image of the god. He was perfectly naked in that bitter, bitter cold, and his body shone like frosted silver, for he was what the Bible calls 'a leper as white as snow'. Also he had no face, because he was a leper of some years' standing, and his disease was heavy upon him. We two stooped to haul Fleete up, and the temple was filling and filling with folk who seemed to spring from the earth, when the Silver Man ran in under our arms, making a noise exactly like the mewing of an otter, caught Fleete round the body and dropped his head on Fleete's breast before we could wrench him away. Then he retired to a corner and sat mewing while the crowd blocked all the doors.

The priests were very angry until the Silver Man touched Fleete. That nuzzling seemed to sober them.

At the end of a few minutes' silence one of the priests came to Strickland and said, in perfect English, 'Take your friend away. He has done with Hanuman but Hanuman has not done with him.' The crowd gave room and we carried Fleete into the road.

Strickland was very angry. He said that we might all three have been knifed, and that Fleete should thank his stars that he had escaped without injury.

Fleete thanked no one. He said that he wanted to go to bed. He was gorgeously drunk.

We moved on, Strickland silent and wrathful, until Fleete

was taken with violent shivering fits and sweating. He said that the smells of the bazaar were overpowering, and he wondered why slaughter-houses were permitted so near English residences. 'Can't you smell the blood?' said Fleete.

We put him to bed at last, just as the dawn was breaking, and Strickland invited me to have another whisky and soda. While we were drinking he talked of the trouble in the temple, and admitted that it baffled him completely. Strickland hates being mystified by natives, because his business in life is to overmatch them with their own weapons. He has not yet succeeded in doing this, but in fifteen or twenty years he will have made some small progress.

'They should have mauled us,' he said, 'instead of mewing at us. I wonder what they meant. I don't like it one little bit.'

I said that the Managing Committee of the temple would in all probability bring a criminal action against us for insulting their religion. There was a section of the Indian Penal Code which exactly met Fleete's offence. Strickland said he only hoped and prayed that they would do this. Before I left I looked into Fleete's room, and saw him lying on his right side, scratching his left breast. Then I went to bed cold, depressed, and unhappy, at seven o'clock in the morning.

At one o'clock I rode over to Strickland's house to inquire after Fleete's head. I imagined that it would be a sore one. Fleete was breakfasting and seemed unwell. His temper was gone, for he was abusing the cook for not supplying him with an underdone chop. A man who can eat raw meat after a wet night is a curiosity. I told Fleete this and he laughed.

'You breed queer mosquitoes in these parts,' he said. 'I've been bitten to pieces, but only in one place.'

'Let's have a look at the bite,' said Strickland. 'It may have gone down since this morning.'

While the chops were being cooked, Fleete opened his shirt and showed us, just over his left breast, a mark, the perfect double of the black rosettes – the five or six irregular blotches arranged in a circle – on a leopard's hide. Strickland looked and said, 'It was only pink this morning. It's grown black now.'

Fleete ran to a glass.

'By Jove!' he said, 'this is nasty. What is it?'

We could not answer. Here the chops came in, all red and juicy, and Fleete bolted three in a most offensive manner. He ate on his right grinders only, and threw his head over his right shoulder as he snapped the meat. When he had finished, it struck him that he had been behaving strangely, for he said apologetically, 'I don't think I ever felt so hungry in my life. I've bolted like an ostrich.'

After breakfast Strickland said to me, 'Don't go. Stay here, and stay for the night.'

Seeing that my house was not three miles from Strickland's, this request was absurd. But Strickland insisted, and was going to say something, when Fleete interrupted by declaring in a shame-faced way that he felt hungry again. Strickland sent a man to my house to fetch over my bedding and a horse, and we three went down to Strickland's stables to pass the hours until it was time to go out for a ride. The man who has a weakness for horses never wearies of inspecting them; and when two men are killing time in this way they gather knowledge and lies the one from the other.

There were five horses in the stables, and I shall never forget the scene as we tried to look them over. They seemed to have gone mad. They reared and screamed and nearly tore up their pickets; they sweated and shivered and lathered and were distraught with fear. Strickland's horses used to know him as well as his dogs; which made the matter more curious. We left the stable for fear of the brutes throwing themselves in their panic. Then Strickland turned back and called me. The horses were still frightened, but they let us 'gentle' and make much of them, and put their heads in our bosoms.

'They aren't afraid of *us*, said Strickland. 'D'you know, I'd give three months' pay if *Outrage* here could talk.'

But *Outrage* was dumb, and could only cuddle up to his master and blow out his nostrils, as is the custom of horses when they wish to explain things but can't. Fleete came up when we were in the stalls, and as soon as the horses saw him, their fright broke out afresh. It was all that we could do to escape from the place unkicked. Strickland said, 'They don't seem to love you, Fleete.'

'Nonsense,' said Fleete; 'my mare will follow me like a dog.' He went to her; she was in a loose-box; but as he slipped the bars she plunged, knocked him down, and broke away into the garden. I laughed, but Strickland was not amused. He took his moustache in both fists and pulled at it till it nearly came out. Fleete, instead of going off to chase his property, yawned, saying that he felt sleepy. He went to the house to lie down, which was a foolish way of spending New Year's Day.

Strickland sat with me in the stables and asked if I had noticed anything peculiar in Fleete's manner. I said that he ate his food like a beast; but that this might have been the result of living alone in the hills out of the reach of society as refined and elevating as ours for instance. Strickland was not amused. I do not think that he listened to me, for his next sentence referred to the mark on Fleete's breast, and I said that it might have been caused by blister-flies, or that it was possibly a birth-mark newly born and now visible for the first time. We both agreed that it was unpleasant to look at, and Strickland found occasion to say that I was a fool.

'I can't tell you what I think now,' said he, 'because you would call me a madman; but you must stay with me for the next few days, if you can. I want you to watch Fleete, but don't tell me what you think till I have made up my mind.'

'But I am dining out to-night,' I said.

'So am I,' said Strickland, 'and so is Fleete. At least if he doesn't change his mind.'

We walked about the garden smoking, but saying nothing – because we were friends, and talking spoils good tobacco – till our pipes were out. Then we went to wake up Fleete. He was wide awake and fidgeting about his room.

'I say, I want some more chops,' he said. 'Can I get them?'

We laughed and said, 'Go and change. The ponies will be round in a minute.'

'All right,' said Fleete. 'I'll go when I get the chops – underdone ones, mind.'

He seemed to be quite in earnest. It was four o'clock, and we had had breakfast at one; still, for a long time, he demanded those underdone chops. Then he changed into riding clothes and went out into the verandah. His pony – the mare had not been caught – would not let him come near. All three horses were unmanageable – mad with fear – and finally Fleete said that he would stay at home and get something to eat. Strickland and I rode out wondering. As we passed the temple of Hanuman the Silver Man came out and mewed at us.

'He is not one of the regular priests of the temple,' said Strickland. 'I think I should peculiarly like to lay my hands on him.'

There was no spring in our gallop on the racecourse that evening. The horses were stale, and moved as though they had been ridden out.

'The fright after breakfast has been too much for them,' said Strickland.

That was the only remark he made through the remainder of the ride. Once or twice, I think, he swore to himself; but that did not count.

We came back in the dark at seven o'clock, and saw that there was no lights in the bungalow. 'Careless ruffians my servants are!' said Strickland.

My horse reared at something on the carriage drive, and Fleete stood up under its nose.

'What are you doing, grovelling about the garden?' said Strickland.

But both horses bolted and nearly threw us. We dismounted by the stables and returned to Fleete, who was on his hands and knees under the orange-bushes.

'What the devil's wrong with you?' said Strickland.

'Nothing, nothing in the world,' said Fleete, speaking very quickly and thickly. 'I've been gardening – botanising, you know. The smell of the earth is delightful. I think I'm going for a walk – a long walk – all night.'

Then I saw that there was something excessively out of order somewhere, and I said to Strickland, 'I am not dining out.'

'Bless you!' said Strickland. 'Here, Fleete, get up. You'll

catch fever there. Come in to dinner and let's have the lamps lit. We'll dine at home.'

Fleete stood up unwillingly, and said, 'No lamps – no lamps. It's much nicer here. Let's dine outside and have some more chops – lots of 'em and underdone – bloody ones with gristle.'

Now a December evening in Northern India is bitterly cold, and Fleete's suggestion was that of a maniac.

'Come in,' said Strickland sternly. 'Come in at once.'

Fleete came, and when the lamps were brought, we saw that he was literally plastered with dirt from head to foot. He must have been rolling in the garden. He shrank from the light and went to his room. His eyes were horrible to look at. There was a green light behind them, not in them, if you understand, and the man's lower lip hung down.

Strickland said, 'There is going to be trouble – big trouble – to-night. Don't you change your riding-things.'

We waited and waited for Fleete's reappearance, and ordered dinner in the meantime. We could hear him moving about his own room, but there was no light there. Presently from the room came the long-drawn howl of a wolf.

People write and talk lightly of blood running cold and hair standing up, and things of that kind. Both sensations are too horrible to be trifled with. My heart stopped as though a knife had been driven through it, and Strickland turned as white as the tablecloth.

The howl was repeated, and was answered by another howl far across the fields.

That set the gilded roof on the horror. Strickland dashed into Fleete's room. I followed, and we saw Fleete getting out of the window. He made beast-noises in the back of his throat. He could not answer us when we shouted at him. He spat.

I don't quite remember what followed, but I think that Strickland must have stunned him with the long boot-jack, or else I should never have been able to sit on his chest. Fleete could not speak, he could only snarl, and his snarls were those of a wolf, not of a man. The human spirit must have been giving way all day and have died out with the twilight. We were dealing with a beast that had once been Fleete.

The affair was beyond any human and rational experience. I tried to say 'Hydrophobia,' but the word wouldn't come, because I knew that I was lying.

We bound this beast with leather thongs of the punkah-rope, and tied its thumbs and big toes together, and gagged it with a shoe-horn, which makes a very efficient gag if you know how to arrange it. Then we carried it into the dining-room, and sent a man to Dumoise, the doctor, telling him to come over at once. After we had despatched the messenger and were drawing breath, Strickland said, 'It's no good. This isn't any doctor's work.' I, also, knew that he spoke the truth.

The beast's head was free, and it threw it about from side to side. Anyone entering the room would have believed that we were curing a wolf's pelt. That was the most loathsome accessory of all.

Strickland sat with his chin in the heel of his fist, watching the beast as it wriggled on the ground, but saying nothing. The shirt had been torn open in the scuffle and showed the black rosette mark on the left breast. It stood out like a blister.

In the silence of the watching we heard something without mewing like a she-otter. We both rose to our feet, and, I answer for myself, not Strickland, felt sick – actually and physically sick. We told each other, as did the men in *Pinafore*, that it was the cat.

Dumoise arrived, and I never saw a little man so unprofessionally shocked. He said that it was a heart-rending case of hydrophobia, and that nothing could be done. At least any palliative measures would only prolong the agony. The beast was foaming at the mouth. Fleete, as we told Dumoise, had been bitten by dogs once or twice. Any man who keeps half a dozen terriers must expect a nip now and again. Dumoise could offer no help. He could only certify that Fleete was dying of hydrophobia. The beast was then howling, for it had managed to spit out the shoe-horn. Dumoise said that he would be ready to certify to the cause of death, and that the end was certain. He was a good little man, and he offered to remain with us; but Strickland refused the kindness. He did not wish to poison Dumoise's New Year. He would only ask him not to give the real cause of Fleete's death to the public.

So Dumoise left, deeply agitated; and as soon as the noise of the cart-wheels had died away, Strickland told me, in a whisper, his suspicions. They were so wildly improbable that he dared not say them out aloud; and I, who entertained all Strickland's beliefs, was so ashamed of owning to them that I pretended to disbelieve.

'Even if the Silver Man had bewitched Fleete for polluting the image of Hanuman, the punishment could not have fallen so quickly.'

As I was whispering this the cry outside the house rose again, and the beast fell into a fresh paroxysm of struggling till we were afraid that the thongs that held it would give way.

'Watch!' said Strickland. 'If this happens six times I shall take the law into my own hands. I order you to help me.'

He went into his room and came out in a few minutes with the barrels of an old shot-gun, a piece of fishing-line, some thick cord, and his heavy wooden bedstead. I reported that the convulsions had followed the cry by two seconds in each case, and the beast seemed perceptibly weaker.

Strickland muttered, 'But he can't take away the life! He can't take away the life!'

I said, though I knew that I was arguing against myself, 'It may be a cat. It must be a cat. If the Silver Man is responsible, why does he dare to come here?'

Strickland arranged the wood on the hearth, put the gun-barrels into the glow of the fire, spread the twine on the table, and broke a walking stick in two. There was one yard of fishing line, gut lapped with wire, such as is used for *mahseer*-fishing, and he tied the two ends together in a loop.

Then he said, 'How can we catch him? He must be taken alive and unhurt.'

I said that we must trust in Providence, and go out softly with polo-sticks into the shrubbery at the front of the house. The man or animal that made the cry was evidently moving round the house as regularly as a night-watchman. We could wait in the bushes till he came by and knock him over.

Strickland accepted this suggestion, and we slipped out from a bath-room window into the front verandah and then across the carriage drive into the bushes.

In the moonlight we could see the leper coming round the corner of the house. He was perfectly naked, and from time to time he mewed and stopped to dance with his shadow. It was an unattractive sight, and thinking of poor Fleete, brought to such degradation by so foul a creature, I put away all my doubts and resolved to help Strickland from the heated gun-barrels to the loop of twine – from the loins to the head and back again – with all tortures that might be needful.

The leper halted in the front porch for a moment and we jumped out on him with the sticks. He was wonderfully strong, and we were afraid that he might escape or be fatally injured before we caught him. We had an idea that lepers were frail creatures, but this proved to be incorrect. Strickland knocked his legs from under him and I put my foot on his neck. He mewed hideously, and even through my riding-boots I could feel that his flesh was not the flesh of a clean man.

He struck at us with his hand and feet-stumps. We looped the lash of a dog-whip round him, under the arm-pits, and dragged him backwards into the hall and so into the dining-room where the beast lay. There we tied him with trunk-straps. He made no attempt to escape, but mewed.

When we confronted him with the beast the scene was beyond description. The beast doubled backwards into a bow as though he had been poisoned with strychnine, and moaned in the most pitiable fashion. Several other things happened also, but they cannot be put down here.

'I think I was right,' said Strickland. 'Now we will ask him to cure this case.'

But the leper only mewed. Strickland wrapped a towel round his hand and took the gun-barrels out of the fire. I put the half of the broken walking stick through the loop of fishing-line and buckled the leper comfortably to Strickland's bedstead. I understood then how men and women and little children can endure to see a witch burnt alive; for the beast was moaning on the floor, and though the Silver Man had no face, you could see horrible feelings passing through the slab that took its place, exactly as waves of heat play across red-hot iron – gun-barrels for instance.

Strickland shaded his eyes with his hands for a moment and we got to work. This part is not to be printed.

The dawn was beginning to break when the leper spoke. His mewings had not been satisfactory up to that point. The beast had fainted from exhaustion and the house was very still. We unstrapped the leper and told him to take away the evil spirit. He crawled to the beast and laid his hand upon the left breast. That was all. Then he fell face down and whined, drawing in his breath as he did so.

We watched the face of the beast, and saw the soul of Fleete coming back into the eyes. Then a sweat broke out on the forehead and the eyes – they were human eyes – closed. We waited for an hour, but Fleete still slept. We carried him to his room and bade the leper go, giving him the bedstead, and the sheet on the bedstead to cover his nakedness, the gloves and the towels with which we had touched him, and the whip that had been hooked round his body. He put the sheet about him and went out into the early morning without speaking or mewing.

Strickland wiped his face and sat down. A night-gong, far away in the city, made seven o'clock.

'Exactly four-and-twenty hours!' said Strickland. 'And I've done enough to ensure my dismissal from the service, besides permanent quarters in a lunatic asylum. Do you believe that we are awake?'

The red-hot gun-barrel had fallen on the floor and was singeing the carpet. The smell was entirely real.

That morning at eleven we two together went to wake up Fleete. We looked and saw that the black leopard-rosette on his chest had disappeared. He was very drowsy and tired, but as soon as he saw us, he said, 'Oh! Confound you fellows. Happy New Year to you. Never mix your liquors. I'm nearly dead.'

'Thanks for your kindness, but you're over time,' said

Strickland. 'To-day is the morning of the second. You've slept the clock round with a vengeance.'

The door opened, and little Dumoise put his head in. He had come on foot, and fancied that we were laying out Fleete.

'I've brought a nurse,' said Dumoise. 'I suppose that she can come in for . . . what is necessary.'

'By all means,' said Fleete cheerily, sitting up in bed. 'Bring on your nurses.'

Dumoise was dumb. Strickland led him out and explained that there must have been a mistake in the diagnosis. Dumoise remained dumb and left the house hastily. He considered that his professional reputation had been injured, and was inclined to make a personal matter of the recovery. Strickland went out too. When he came back, he said that he had been to call on the Temple of Hanuman to offer redress for the pollution of the god, and had been solemnly assured that no white man had ever touched the idol, and that he was an incarnation of all the virtues labouring under a delusion. 'What do you think?' said Strickland.

I said, ' "There are more things . . ." '

But Strickland hates that quotation. He says that I have worn it threadbare.

One other curious thing happened which frightened me as much as anything in all the night's work. When Fleete was dressed he came into the dining-room and sniffed. He had a quaint trick of moving his nose when he sniffed. 'Horrid doggy smell, here,' said he. 'You should really keep those terriers of yours in better order. Try sulphur, Strick.'

But Strickland did not answer. He caught hold of the back of a chair, and, without warning, went into an amazing fit of hysterics. It is terrible to see a strong man overtaken with hysteria. Then it struck me that we had fought for Fleete's soul with the Silver Man in that room, and had disgraced ourselves as Englishmen for ever, and I laughed and gasped and gurgled just as shamefully as Strickland, while Fleete thought that we had both gone mad. We never told him what we had done.

Some years later, when Strickland had married and was a church-going member of society for his wife's sake, we reviewed the incident dispassionately, and Strickland suggested that I should put it before the public.

I cannot myself see that this step is likely to clear up the mystery; because, in the first place, no one will believe a rather unpleasant story, and, in the second, it is well known to every right-minded man that the gods of the heathen are stone and brass, and any attempt to deal with them otherwise is justly condemned.

AT THE END OF THE PASSAGE

The sky is lead and our faces are red,
  And the gates of Hell are opened and riven,
  And the winds of Hell are loosened and driven,
And the dust flies up in the face of Heaven,
  And the clouds come down in a fiery sheet,
Heavy to raise and hard to be borne.
  And the soul of man is turned from his meat,
Turned from the trifles for which he has striven
  Sick in his body, and heavy hearted,
  And his soul flies up like the dust in the sheet
  Breaks from his flesh and is gone and departed,
As the blasts they blow on the cholera-horn.

Himalayan

Four men, each entitled to 'life, liberty, and the pursuit of happiness', sat at a table playing whist. The thermometer marked – for them – one hundred and one degrees of heat. The room was darkened till it was only just possible to distinguish the pips of the cards and the very white faces of the players. A tattered, rotten punkah of whitewashed calico was puddling the hot air and whining dolefully at each stroke. Outside lay gloom of a November day in London. There was neither sky, sun, nor horizon, – nothing but a brown purple haze of heat. It was as though the earth were dying of apoplexy.

From time to time clouds of tawny dust rose from the ground without wind or warning, flung themselves tablecloth-wise among the tops of the parched trees, and came down again. Then a-whirling dust-devil would scutter across the plain for a couple of miles, break, and fall outward, though there was nothing to check its flight save a long low line of piled rail way-sleepers white with the dust, a cluster of huts made of mud, condemned rails, and canvas, and the one squat four-roomed bungalow that belonged to the assistant engineer in charge of a section of the Gaudhari State line then under construction.

The four, stripped to the thinnest of sleeping-suits, played whist crossly, with wranglings as to leads and returns. It was not the best kind of whist, but they had taken some trouble to arrive at it. Mottram of the Indian Survey had ridden thirty and railed one hundred miles from his lonely post in the desert since the night before; Lowndes of the Civil Service, on special duty in the political department, had come as far to escape for an instant the miserable intrigues of an impoverished native State whose king alternately fawned and blustered for more money from the pitiful revenues contributed by hard-wrung peasants and despairing camel-breeders; Spurstow, the doctor of the line, had left a cholera-stricken camp of coolies to look after itself for forty-eight hours while he associated with white men once more. Hummil, the assistant engineer, was the host. He stood fast and received his friends thus every Sunday if they could come in. When one of them failed to appear, he would send a telegram to his last address, in order that he might know whether the defaulter were dead or alive. There are very many places in the East where it is not good or kind to let your acquaintances drop out of sight even for one short week.

The players were not conscious of any special regard for each other. They squabbled whenever they met; but they ardently desired to meet, as men without water desire to drink. They were lonely folk who understood the dread meaning of loneliness. They were all under thirty years of age, – which is too soon for any man to possess that knowledge.

'Pilsener?' said Spurstow, after the second rubber, mopping his forehead.

'Beer's out, I'm sorry to say, and there's hardly enough soda-water for tonight,' said Hummil.

'What filthy bad management!' Spurstow snarled.

'Can't help it. I've written and wired; but the trains don't come through regularly yet. Last week the ice ran out, – as Lowndes knows.'

'Glad I didn't come. I could ha' sent you some if I had known, though. Phew! it's too hot to go on playing bumble-puppy.' This with a savage scowl at Lowndes, who only laughed. He was a hardened offender.

Mottram rose from the table and looked out of a chink in the shutters.

'What a sweet day!' said he.

The company yawned all together and betook themselves to an aimless investigation of all Hummil's possessions, – guns, tattered novels, saddlery, spurs, and the like. They had fingered them a score of times before, but there was really nothing else to do.

'Got anything fresh?' said Lowndes.

'Last week's *Gazette of India*, and a cutting from a home paper. My father sent it out. It's rather amusing.'

'One of those vestrymen that call 'emselves MPs again, is it?' said Spurstow, who read his newspapers when he could get them.

'Yes. Listen to this. It's to your address, Lowndes. The man was making a speech to his constituents, and he piled it on. Here's a sample. "And I assert unhesitatingly that the Civil Service in India is the preserve – the pet preserve – of the aristocracy of England. What does the democracy – what do the masses – get from that country, which we have step by step fraudulently annexed? I answer, nothing whatever. It is farmed with a single eye to their own interests by the scions of the aristocracy. They take good care to maintain their lavish scale of incomes, to avoid or stifle any inquiries into the nature and conduct of their administration, while they themselves force the unhappy peasant to pay with the sweat of his brow for all the luxuries in which they are lapped."' Hummil waved the cutting above his head. ' 'Ear! 'ear!' said his audience.

Then Lowndes, meditatively, 'I'd give – I'd give three months' pay to have that gentleman spend one month with me and see how the free and independent native prince works things. Old Timbersides' – this was his flippant title for an honoured and decorated feudatory prince – 'has been wearing my life out this week past for money. By Jove, his latest performance was to send me one of his women as a bribe!'

'Good for you! Did you accept it?' said Mottram.

'No. I rather wish I had, now. She was a pretty little person, and she yarned away to me about the horrible destitution among the king's women-folk. The darlings haven't had any new clothes for nearly a month, and the old man wants to buy a new drag from Calcutta, – solid silver railings and silver lamps, and trifles of that kind. I've tried to make him understand that he has played the deuce with the revenues for the last twenty years and must go slow. He can't see it.'

'But he has the ancestral treasure-vaults to draw on. There must be three millions at least in jewels and coin under his palace,' said Hummil.

'Catch a native king disturbing the family treasure! The priests forbid it except as the last resort. Old Timbersides has added something like a quarter of a million to the deposit in his reign.'

'Where the mischief does it all come from?' said Mottram.

'The country. The state of the people is enough to make you sick. I've known the taxmen wait by a milch-camel till the foal was born and then hurry off the mother for arrears. And what can I do? I can't get the court clerks to give me any accounts; I can't raise anything more than a fat smile from the commander-in-chief when I find out the troops are three months in arrears; and old Timbersides begins to weep when I speak to him. He has taken to the King's Peg heavily, – liqueur brandy for whisky, and Heidsieck for soda-water.'

'That's what the Rao of Jubela took to. Even a native can't last long at that,' said Spurstow. 'He'll go out.'

'And a good thing, too. Then I suppose we'll have a council of regency, and a tutor for the young prince, and hand him back his kingdom with ten years' accumulations.'

'Whereupon that young prince, having been taught all the vices of the English, will play ducks and drakes with the money and undo ten years' work in eighteen months. I've seen that business before,' said Spurstow. 'I should tackle the king with a light hand if I were you, Lowndes. They'll hate you quite enough under any circumstances.'

'That's all very well. The man who looks on can talk about the light hand; but you can't clean a pig-stye with a pen dipped in rose-water. I know my risks; but nothing has happened yet. My servant's an old Pathan, and he cooks for me. They are hardly likely to bribe him, and I don't accept food from my true friends, as they call themselves. Oh, but it's weary work! I'd sooner be with you, Spurstow. There's shooting near your camp.'

'Would you? I don't think it. About fifteen deaths a day don't incite a man to shoot anything but himself. And the worst of it is that the poor devils look at you as though you ought to save them. Lord knows, I've tried everything. My last attempt was empirical, but it pulled an old man through. He was brought to me apparently past hope, and I gave him gin and Worcester sauce with cayenne. It cured him; but I don't recommend it.'

'How do the cases run generally?' said Hummil.

'Very simply indeed. Chlorodyne, opium pill, chlorodyne, collapse, nitre, bricks to the feet, and then – the burning-ghaut. The last seems to be the only thing that stops the trouble. It's black cholera, you know. Poor devils! But, I will say, little Bunsee Lai, my apothecary, works like a demon. I've recommended him for promotion if he comes through it all alive.'

'And what are your chances, old man?' said Mottram.

'Don't know; don't care much; but I've sent the letter in. What are you doing with yourself generally?'

'Sitting under a table in the tent and spitting on the sextant to keep it cool,' said the man of the survey. 'Washing my eyes to avoid ophthalmia, which I shall certainly get, and trying to make a sub-surveyor understand that an error of five degrees in an angle isn't quite so small as it looks. I'm altogether alone, y'know, and shall be till the end of the hot weather.'

'Hummil's the lucky man,' said Lowndes, flinging himself into a long chair. 'He has an actual roof – torn as to the ceiling-cloth, but still a roof – over his head. He sees one train daily. He can get beer and soda-water and ice 'em when God is good. He has books, pictures,' – they were torn from the *Graphic*, – 'and the society of the excellent sub-contractor Jevins, besides the pleasure of receiving us weekly.'

Hummil smiled grimly. 'Yes, I'm the lucky man, I suppose. Jevins is luckier.'

'How? Not—'

'Yes. Went out. Last Monday.'

'By his own hand?' said Spurstow quickly, hinting the suspicion that was in everybody's mind. There was no cholera near Hummil's section. Even fever gives a man at least a week's grace, and sudden death generally implied self-slaughter.

'I judge no man this weather,' said Hummil. 'He had a touch of the sun, I fancy; for last week, after you fellows had left, he came into the verandah and told me that he was going home to see his wife, in Market Street, Liverpool, that evening.

'I got the apothecary in to look at him, and we tried to make him lie down. After an hour or two he rubbed his eyes and said he believed he had had a fit, – hoped he hadn't said anything rude. Jevins had a great idea of bettering himself socially. He was very like Chucks in his language.'

'Well?'

'Then he went to his own bungalow and began cleaning a rifle. He told the servant that he was going to shoot buck in the morning. Naturally he fumbled with the trigger, and shot himself through the head – accidentally. The apothecary sent in a report to my chief, and Jevins is buried somewhere out there. I'd have wired to you, Spurstow, if you could have done anything.'

'You're a queer chap,' said Mottram. 'If you'd killed the man yourself you couldn't have been more quiet about the business.'

'Good Lord! what does it matter?' said Hummil calmly, 'I've got to do a lot of his overseeing work in addition to my own. I'm the only person that suffers. Jevins is out of it, – by pure accident, of course, but out of it. The apothecary was going to write a long screed on suicide. Trust a babu to drivel when he gets the chance.'

'Why didn't you let it go in as suicide?' said Lowndes.

'No direct proof. A man hasn't many privileges in this country, but he might at least be allowed to mishandle his own rifle. Besides, some day I may need a man to smother up an accident to myself. Live and let live. Die and let die.'

'You take a pill,' said Spurstow, who had been watching Hummil's white face narrowly. 'Take a pill, and don't be an ass. That sort of talk is skittles. Anyhow, suicide is shirking your work. If I were Job ten times over, I should be so interested in what was going to happen next that I'd stay on and watch.'

'Ah! I've lost that curiosity,' said Hummil.

'Liver out of order?' said Lowndes feelingly.

'No. Can't sleep. That's worse.'

'By Jove, it is!' said Mottram. 'I'm that way every now and then, and the fit has to wear itself out. What do you take for it?'

'Nothing. What's the use? I haven't had ten minutes' sleep since Friday morning.'

'Poor chap! Spurstow, you ought to attend to this,' said Mottram. 'Now you mention it, your eyes are rather gummy and swollen.'

Spurstow, still watching Hummil, laughed lightly. 'I'll patch him up, later on. Is it too hot, do you think, to go for a ride?'

'Where to?' said Lowndes wearily. 'We shall have to go away at eight, and there'll be riding enough for us then. I hate a horse when I have to use him as a necessity. Oh, heavens! what is there to do?'

'Begin whist again, at chick points ["a chick" is supposed to be eight shillings] and a gold mohur on the rub,' said Spurstow promptly.

'Poker. A month's pay all round for the pool, – no limit, – and fifty-rupee raises. Somebody would be broken before we got up,' said Lowndes.

'Can't say that it would give me any pleasure to break any man in this company,' said Mottram. 'There isn't enough excitement in it, and it's foolish.' He crossed over to the worn and battered little camp-piano, – wreckage of a married house-hold that had once held the bungalow, – and opened the case.

'It's used up long ago,' said Hummil. 'The servants have picked it to pieces.'

The piano was indeed hopelessly out of order, but Mottram managed to bring the rebellious notes into a sort of agreement, and there rose from the ragged keyboard something that might once have been the ghost of a popular music-hall song. The men in the long chairs turned with evident interest as Mottram banged the more lustily.

'That's good!' said Lowndes. 'By Jove! the last time I heard that song was in '79, or thereabouts, just before I came out.'

'Ah!' said Spurstow with pride, 'I was home in '80.' And he mentioned a song of the streets popular at that date.

Mottram executed it roughly. Lowndes criticised and volunteered emendations. Mottram dashed into another ditty, not of the music-hall character, and made as if to rise.

'Sit down,' said Hummil. 'I didn't know that you had any music in your composition. Go on playing until you can't think of anything more. I'll have that piano tuned up before you come again. Play something festive.'

Very simple indeed were the tunes to which Mottram's art and the limitations of the piano could give effect, but the men listened with pleasure, and in the pauses talked all together of what they had seen or heard when they were last at home. A dense dustentorm sprung up outside, and swept roaring over the house, enveloping it in the choking darkness of midnight, but Mottram continued unheeding, and the crazy tinkle reached the ears of the listeners above the flapping of the tattered ceiling-cloth.

In the silence after the storm he glided from the more directly personal songs of Scotland, half humming them as he played, into the Evening Hymn.

'Sunday,' said he, nodding his head.

'Go on. Don't apologise for it,' said Spurstow.

Hummil laughed long and riotously. 'Play it, by all means. You're full of surprises to-day. I didn't know you had such a gift of finished sarcasm. How does that thing go?'

Mottram took up the tune.

'Too slow by half. You miss the note of gratitude,' said Hummil. 'It ought to go to the "Grasshopper's Polka", – this way.' And he chanted, *prestissimo*, –

'Glory to thee, my God, this night,
For all the blessings of the light.

'That shows we really feel our blessings. How does it go on? –

'If in the night I sleepless lie,
My soul with sacred thoughts supply;
May no ill dreams disturb my rest, –

'Quicker, Mottram! –

Or powers of darkness me molest!

'Bah! what an old hypocrite you are!'

'Don't be an ass,' said Lowndes. 'You are at full liberty to make fun of anything else you like, but leave that hymn alone. It's associated in my mind with the most sacred recollections—'

'Summer evenings in the country, – stained-glass window, – light going out, and you and she jamming your heads together over one hymnbook,' said Mottram.

'Yes, and a fat old cockchafer hitting you in the eye when you walked home. Smell of hay, and a moon as big as a bandbox sitting on the top of a haycock; bats, – roses, – milk and midges,' said Lowndes.

'Also mothers. I can just recollect my mother singing me to sleep with that when I was a little chap,' said Spurstow.

The darkness had fallen on the room. They could hear Hummil squirming in his chair.

'Consequently,' said he testily, 'you sing it when you are seven fathoms deep in Hell! It's an insult to the intelligence of the Deity to pretend we're anything but tortured rebels.'

'Take *two* pills,' said Spurstow; 'that's tortured liver.'

'The usually placid Hummil is in a vile bad temper. I'm sorry for his coolies to-morrow,' said Lowndes, as the servants brought in the lights and prepared the table for dinner.

As they were settling into their places about the miserable goat-chops, and the smoked tapioca pudding, Spurstow took occasion to whisper to Mottram, 'Well done, David!'

'Look after Saul, then,' was the reply.

'What are you two whispering about?' said Hummil suspiciously.

'Only saying that you are a damned poor host. This fowl can't be cut,' returned Spurstow with a sweet smile. 'Call this a dinner?'

'I can't help it. You don't expect a banquet, do you?'

Throughout that meal Hummil contrived laboriously to insult directly and pointedly all his guests in succession, and at each insult Spurstow kicked the aggrieved persons under the table; but he dared not exchange a glance of intelligence with either of them. Hummil's face was white and pinched, while his eyes were unnaturally large. No man dreamed for a moment of resenting his savage personalities, but as soon as the meal was over they made haste to get away.

'Don't go. You're just getting amusing, you fellows. I hope I haven't said anything that annoyed you. You're such touchy devils.' Then, changing the note into one of almost abject entreaty, Hummil added, 'I say, you surely aren't going?'

'In the language of the blessed Jorrocks, where I dines I sleeps,' said Spurstow. 'I want to have a look at your coolies to-morrow, if you don't mind. You can give me a place to lie down in, I suppose?'

The others pleaded the urgency of their several duties next day, and, saddling up, departed together, Hummil begging them to come next Sunday. As they jogged off, Lowndes unbosomed himself to Mottram –

' . . . And I never felt so like kicking a man at his own table in my life. He said I cheated at whist, and reminded me I was in debt! Told you you were as good as a liar to your face! You aren't half indignant enough over it.'

'Not I,' said Mottram. 'Poor devil! Did you ever know old

Hummy behave like that before or within a hundred miles of it?'

'That's no excuse. Spurstow was hacking my shin all the time, so I kept a hand on myself. Else I should have—'

'No, you wouldn't. You'd have done as Hummy did about Jevins; judge no man this weather. By Jove! the buckle of my bridle is hot in my hand! Trot out a bit, and 'ware ratholes.'

Ten minutes' trotting jerked out of Lowndes one very sage remark when he pulled up, sweating from every pore –

'Good thing Spurstow's with him to-night.'

'Ye-es. Good man, Spursiow. Our roads turn here. See you again next Sunday, if the sun doesn't bowl me over.'

'S'pose so, unless old Timbersides' finance minister manages to dress some of my food. Good-night, and – God bless you!'

'What's wrong now?'

'Oh, nothing,' Lowndes gathered up his whip, and, as he flicked Mottram's mare on the flank, added, 'You're not a bad little chap, – that's all.' And the mare bolted half a mile across the sand, on the word.

In the assistant engineer's bungalow Spurstow and Hummil smoked the pipe of silence together, each narrowly watching the other. The capacity of a bachelor's establishment is as elastic as its arrangements are simple. A servant cleared away the dining-room table, brought in a couple of rude native bedsteads made of tape strung on a light wood frame, flung a square of cool Calcutta matting over each, set them side by side, pinned two towels to the punkah so that their fringes should just sweep clear of the sleeper's nose and mouth, and announced that the couches were ready.

The men flung themselves down, ordering the punkah-coolies by all the power of Hell to pull. Every door and window was shut, for the outside air was that of an oven. The atmosphere within was only 104°, as the thermometer bore witness, and heavy with the foul smell of badly-trimmed kerosene lamps; and this stench, combined with that of native tobacco, baked brick, and dried earth, sends the heart of many a strong man down to his boots, for it is the smell of the Great Indian Empire when she turns herself for six months into a house of torment. Spurstow packed his pillows craftily so that he reclined rather than lay, his head at a safe elevation above his feet. It is not good to sleep on a low pillow in the hot weather if you happen to be of thick-necked build, for you may pass with lively snores and gugglings from natural sleep into the deep slumber of heat-apoplexy.

'Pack your pillows,' said the doctor sharply, as he saw Hummil preparing to lie down at full length.

The night-light was trimmed; the shadow of the punkah wavered across the room, and the '*flick*' of the punkah-towel and the soft whine of the rope through the wall-hole followed it. Then the punkah flagged, almost ceased. The sweat poured from Spurstow's brow. Should he go out and harangue the coolie? It started forward again with a savage jerk, and a pin came out of the towels. When this was replaced, a tomtom in the coolie-lines began to beat with the steady throb of a swollen artery inside some brain-fevered skull. Spurstow turned on his side and swore gently. There was no movement on Hummil's part. The man had composed himself as rigidly as a corpse, his hands clinched at his sides. The respiration was too hurried for any suspicion of sleep. Spurstow looked at the set face. The jaws were clinched, and there was a pucker round the quivering eyelids.

'He's holding himself as tightly as ever he can,' thought Spurstow. 'What in the world is the matter with him? – Hummil!'

'Yes,' in a thick constrained voice.

'Can't you get to sleep?'

'No.'

'Head hot? Throat feeling bulgy? or how?'

'Neither, thanks. I don't sleep much, you know.'

'Feel pretty bad?'

'Pretty bad, thanks. There is a tomtom outside, isn't there? I thought it was my head at first . . . Oh, Spurstow, for pity's sake give me something that will put me asleep, – sound asleep, – if it's only for six hours!' He sprang up, trembling from head to foot. 'I haven't been able to sleep naturally for days, and I can't stand it! – I can't stand it!'

'Poor old chap!'

'That's no use. Give me something to make me sleep. I tell you I'm nearly mad. I don't know what I say half my time. For three weeks I've had to think and spell out every word that has come through my lips before I dared say it. Isn't that enough to drive a man mad? I can't see things correctly now, and I've lost my sense of touch. My skin aches – my skin aches! Make me sleep. Oh, Spurstow, for the love of God make me sleep sound. It isn't enough merely to let me dream. Let me sleep!'

'All right, old man, all right. Go slow; you aren't half as bad as you think.'

The flood-gates of reserve once broken, Hummil was clinging to him like a frightened child. 'You're pinching my arm to pieces.'

'I'll break your neck if you don't do something for me. No, I didn't mean that. Don't be angry, old fellow.' He wiped the sweat off himself as he fought to regain composure. 'I'm a bit restless and off my oats, and perhaps you could recommend some sort of sleeping mixture, – bromide of potassium.'

'Bromide of skittles! Why didn't you tell me this before? Let go of my arm, and I'll see if there's anything in my cigarette-case to suit your complaint.' Spurstow hunted among his day-clothes, turned up the lamp, opened a little silver cigarette-case, and advanced on the expectant Hummil with the daintiest of fairy squirts.

'The last appeal of civilisation,' said he, 'and a thing I hate to use. Hold out your arm. Well, your sleeplessness hasn't ruined your muscle; and what a thick hide it is! Might as well inject a buffalo subcutaneously. Now in a few minutes the morphia will begin working. Lie down and wait.'

A smile of unalloyed and idiotic delight began to creep over Hummil's face. 'I think,' he whispered, – 'I think I'm going off now. Gad! it's positively heavenly! Spurstow, you must give me that case to keep; you—' The voice ceased as the head fell back.

'Not for a good deal,' said Spurstow to the unconscious

form. 'And now, my friend, sleeplessness of your kind being very apt to relax the moral fibre in little matters of life and death, I'll just take the liberty of spiking your guns.'

He paddled into Hummil's saddle-room in his bare feet and uncased a twelve-bore rifle, an express, and a revolver. Of the first he unscrewed the nipples and hid them in the bottom of a saddlery-case; of the second he abstracted the lever, kicking it behind a big wardrobe. The third he merely opened, and knocked the doll-head bolt of the grip up with the heel of a riding-boot.

'That's settled,' he said, as he shook the sweat off his hands. These little precautions will at least give you time to turn. You have too much sympathy with gun-room accidents.'

And as he rose from his knees, the thick muffled voice of Hummil cried in the doorway, 'You fool!'

Such tones they use who speak in the lucid intervals of delirium to their friends a little before they die.

Spurstow started, dropping the pistol. Hummil stood in the doorway, rocking with helpless laughter.

'That was awf'ly good of you, I'm sure,' he said, very slowly, feeling for his words. 'I don't intend to go out by my own hand at present. I say, Spurstow, that stuff won't work. What shall I do? What shall I do?' And panic terror stood in his eyes.

'Lie down and give it a chance. Lie down at once.'

'I daren't. It will only take me halfway again, and I shan't be able to get away this time. Do you know it was all I could do to come out just now? Generally I am as quick as lightning; but you had clogged my feet. I was nearly caught.'

'Oh yes, I understand. Go and lie down.'

'No, it isn't delirium; but it was an awfully mean trick to play on me. Do you know I might have died?'

As a sponge rubs a slate clean, so some power unknown to Spurstow had wiped out of Hummil's face all that stamped it for the face of a man, and he stood at the doorway in the expression of his lost innocence. He had slept back into terrified childhood.

'Is he going to die on the spot?' thought Spurstow. Then, aloud, 'All right, my son. Come back to bed, and tell me all about it. You couldn't sleep; but what was all the rest of the nonsense?'

'A place, – a place down there,' said Hummil, with simple sincerity. The drug was acting on him by waves, and he was flung from the fear of a strong man to the fright of a child as his nerves gathered sense or were dulled.

'Good God! I've been afraid of it for months past, Spurstow. It has made every night hell to me; and yet I'm not conscious of having done anything wrong.'

'Be still, and I'll give you another dose. We'll stop your nightmares, you unutterable idiot!'

'Yes, but you must give me so much that I can't get away. You must make me quite sleepy, – not just a little sleepy. It's so hard to run then.'

'I know it; I know it. I've felt it myself. The symptoms are exactly as you describe.'

'Oh, don't laugh at me, confound you! Before this awful sleeplessness came to me I've tried to rest on my elbow and put a spur in the bed to sting me when I fell back. Look!'

'By Jove! the man has been rowelled like a horse! Ridden by the nightmare with a vengeance! And we all thought him sensible enough. Heaven send us understanding! You like to talk, don't you?'

'Yes, sometimes. Not when I'm frightened. *Then* I want to run. Don't you?'

'Always. Before I give you your second dose try to tell me exactly what your trouble is.'

Hummil spoke in broken whispers for nearly ten minutes, while Spurstow looked into the pupils of his eyes and passed his hand before them once or twice.

At the end of the narrative the silver cigarette-case was produced, and the last words that Hummil said as he fell back for the second time were, 'Put me quite to sleep; for if I'm caught I die, – I die!'

'Yes, yes; we all do that sooner or later, – thank Heaven who has set a term to our miseries,' said Spurstow, settling the cushions under the head. 'It occurs to me that unless I drink something I shall go out before my time. I've stopped sweating, and – I wear a seventeen-inch collar.' He brewed himself scalding hot tea, which is an excellent remedy against heat-apoplexy if you take three or four cups of it in time. Then he watched the sleeper.

'A blind face that cries and can't wipe its eyes, a blind face that chases him down corridors! H'm! Decidedly, Hummil ought to go on leave as soon as possible; and, sane or otherwise, he undoubtedly did rowel himself most cruelly. Well, Heaven send us understanding!'

At mid-day Hummil rose, with an evil taste in his mouth, but an unclouded eye and a joyful heart.

'I was pretty bad last night, wasn't I?' said he.

'I have seen healthier men. You must have had a touch of the sun. Look here: if I write you a swingeing medical certificate, will you apply for leave on the spot?'

'No.'

'Why not? You want it.'

'Yes, but I can hold on till the weather's a little cooler.'

'Why should you, if you can get relieved on the spot?'

'Burkett is the only man who could be sent; and he's a born fool.'

'Oh, never mind about the line. You aren't so important as all that. Wire for leave, if necessary.'

Hummil looked very uncomfortable.

'I can hold on till the Rains,' he said evasively.

'You can't. Wire to headquarters for Burkett.'

'I won't. If you want to know why, particularly, Burkett is married, and his wife's just had a kid, and she's up at Simla, in the cool, and Burkett has a very nice billet that takes him into Simla from Saturday to Monday. That little woman isn't at all well. If Burkett was transferred she'd try to follow him. If she left the baby behind she'd fret herself to death. If she came, – and Burkett's one of those selfish little beasts who are always talking about a wife's place being with her husband, – she'd die. It's murder to bring a woman here just now. Burkett hasn't the physique of a rat. If he came here he'd go out; and I know she hasn't any money, and I'm pretty sure she'd go out too. I'm salted in a sort of way, and I'm not married. Wait till the Rains, and then Burkett can get thin down here. It'll do him heaps of good.'

'Do you mean to say that you intend to face – what you have faced, till the Rains break?'

'Oh, it won't be so bad, now you've shown me a way out of it. I can always wire to you. Besides, now I've once got into the way of sleeping, it'll be all right. Anyhow, I shan't put in for leave. That's the long and the short of it.'

'My great Scott! I thought all that sort of thing was dead and done with.'

'Bosh! You'd do the same yourself. I feel a new man, thanks to that cigarette-case. You're going over to camp now, aren't you?'

'Yes; but I'll try to look you up every other day, if I can.'

'I'm not bad enough for that. I don't want you to bother. Give the coolies gin and ketchup.'

'Then you feel all right?'

'Fit to fight for my life, but not to stand out in the sun talking to you. Go along, old man, and bless you!'

Hummil turned on his heel to face the echoing desolation of his bungalow, and the first thing he saw standing in the verandah was the figure of himself. He had met a similar apparition once before, when he was suffering from overwork and the strain of the hot weather.

'This is bad, – already,' he said, rubbing his eyes. 'If the thing slides away from me all in one piece, like a ghost, I shall know it is only my eyes and stomach that are out of order. If it walks – my head is going.'

He approached the figure, which naturally kept at an unvarying distance from him, as is the use of all spectres that are born of overwork. It slid through the house and dissolved into swimming specks within the eyeball as soon as it reached the burning light of the garden. Hummil went about his business till even. When he came in to dinner he found himself sitting at the table. The vision rose and walked out hastily. Except that it cast no shadow it was in all respects real.

No living man knows what that week held for Hummil. An increase of the epidemic kept Spurstow in camp among the coolies, and all he could do was to telegraph to Mottram, bidding him to go to the bungalow and sleep there. But Mottram was forty miles away from the nearest telegraph, and knew nothing of anything save the needs of the survey till he met, early on Sunday morning, Lowndes and Spurstow heading towards Hummil's for the weekly gathering.

'Hope the poor chap's in a better temper,' said the former, swinging himself off his horse at the door. 'I suppose he isn't up yet.'

'I'll just have a look at him,' said the doctor. 'If he's asleep there's no need to wake him.'

And an instant later, by the tone of Spurstow's voice calling upon them to enter, the men knew what had happened. There was no need to wake him.

The punkah was still being pulled over the bed, but Hummil had departed this life at least three hours.

The body lay on its back, hands clinched by the side, as Spurstow had seen it lying seven nights previously. In the staring eyes was written terror beyond the expression of any pen.

Mottram, who had entered behind Lowndes, bent over the dead and touched the forehead lightly with his lips. 'Oh, you lucky, lucky devil!' he whispered.

But Lowndes had seen the eyes, and withdrew shuddering to the other side of the room.

'Poor chap! poor old chap! And the last time I met him I was – angry. Spurstow, we should have watched him. Has he—?'

Deftly Spurstow continued his investigations, ending by a search round the room.

'No, he hasn't,' he snapped. 'There's no trace of anything. Call the servants.'

They came, eight or ten of them, whispering and peering over each other's shoulders.

'When did your Sahib go to bed?' said Spurstow.

'At eleven or ten, we think,' said Hummil's personal servant.

'He was well then? But how should you know?'

'He was not ill, as far as our comprehension extended. But

he had slept very little for three nights. This I know, because I saw him walking much, and specially in the heart of the night.'

As Spurstow was arranging the sheet, a big straight-necked hunting-spur tumbled on the ground. The doctor groaned. The personal servant peeped at the body.

'What do you think Chuma?' said Spurstow, catching the look on the dark face.

'Heaven-born, in my poor opinion, this that was my master has descended into the Dark Places, and there has been caught because he was not able to escape with sufficient speed. We have the spur for evidence that he fought with Fear. Thus have I seen men of my race do with thorns when a spell was laid upon them to overtake them in their sleeping hours and they dared not sleep.'

'Chuma, you're a mud-head. Go out and prepare seals to be set on the Sahib's property.'

'God has made the Heaven-born. God has made me. Who are we, to inquire into the dispensations of God? I will bid the other servants hold aloof while you are reckoning the tale of the Sahib's property. They are all thieves, and would steal.'

'As far as I can make out, he died from – oh, anything; stoppage of the heart's action, heat-apoplexy, or some other visitation,' said Spurstow to his companions. 'We must make an inventory of his effects, and so on.'

'He was scared to death,' insisted Lowndes. 'Look at those eyes! For pity's sake don't let him be buried with them open!'

'Whatever it was, he's clear of all the trouble now,' said Mottram softly.

Spurstow was peering into the open eyes.

'Come here,' said he. 'Can you see anything there?'

'I can't face it!' whimpered Lowndes. 'Cover up the face! Is there any fear on earth that can turn a man into that likeness? It's ghastly. Oh, Spurstow, cover it up!'

'No fear – on earth,' said Spurstow. Mottram leaned over his shoulder and looked intently.

'I see nothing except some grey blurs in the pupil. There can be nothing there, you know.'

'Even so. Well, let's think. It'll take half a day to knock

up any sort of coffin; and he must have died at midnight. Lowndes, old man, go out and tell the coolies to break ground next to Jevins's grave. Mottram, go round the house with Chuma and see that the seals are put on things. Send a couple of men to me here, and I'll arrange.'

The strong-armed servants when they returned to their own kind told a strange story of the doctor Sahib vainly trying to call their master back to life by magic arts, – to wit, the holding of a little green box that clicked to each of the dead man's eyes, and of a bewildered muttering on the part of the doctor Sahib, who took the little green box away with him.

The resonant hammering of a coffin-lid is no pleasant thing to hear, but those who have experience maintain that much more terrible is the soft swish of the bed-linen, the reeving and unreeving of the bed-tapes, when he who has fallen by the roadside is apparelled for burial, sinking gradually as the tapes are tied over, till the swaddled shape touches the floor and there is no protest against the indignity of hasty disposal.

At the last moment Lowndes was seized with scruples of conscience. 'Ought you to read the service, – from beginning to end?' said he to Spurstow.

'I intend to. You're my senior as a civilian. You can take it if you like.'

'I didn't mean that for a moment. I only thought if we could get a chaplain from somewhere, – I'm willing to ride anywhere, – and give poor Hummil a better chance. That's all.'

'Bosh!' said Spurstow, as he framed his lips to the tremendous words that stand at the head of the burial service.

After breakfast they smoked a pipe in silence to the memory of the dead. Then Spurstow said absently –

' 'Tisn't in medical science.'

'What?'

'Things in a dead man's eye.'

'For goodness' sake leave that horror alone!' said Lowndes. 'I've seen a native die of pure fright when a tiger chivied him. I know what killed Hummil.'

'The deuce you do! I'm going to try to see.' And the doctor retreated into the bath-room with a Kodak camera. After a few minutes there was the sound of something being hammered to pieces, and he emerged, very white indeed.

'Have you got a picture?' said Mottram. 'What does the thing look like?'

'It was impossible, of course. You needn't look, Mottram. I've torn up the films. There was nothing there. It was impossible.'

'That,' said Lowndes, very distinctly, watching the shaking hand striving to relight the pipe, 'is a damned lie.'

Mottram laughed uneasily. 'Spurstow's right,' he said. 'We're all in such a state now that we'd believe anything. For pity's sake let's try to be rational.'

There was no further speech for a long time. The hot wind whistled without, and the dry trees sobbed. Presently the daily train, winking brass, burnished steel, and spouting steam, pulled up panting in the intense glare. 'We'd better go on on that,' said Spurstow. 'Go back to work. I've written my certificate. We can't do any more good here, and work'll keep our wits together. Come on.'

No one moved. It is not pleasant to face railway journeys at mid-day in June. Spurstow gathered up his hat and whip, and, turning in the doorway, said –

'There may be Heaven, – there must be Hell,
Meantime, there is our life here. We-ell?'

Neither Mottram nor Lowndes had any answer to the question.

THE RECRUDESCENCE OF IMRAY

The doors were wide, the story saith,
Out of the night came the patient wraith,
He might not speak, and he could not stir
A hair of the Baron's minniver –
Speechless and strengthless, a shadow thin,
He roved the castle to seek his kin.
And oh, 'twas a piteous thing to see
The dumb ghost follow his enemy!

The Baron

Imray achieved the impossible. Without warning, for no conceivable motive, in his youth, at the threshold of his career he chose to disappear from the world – which is to say, the little Indian station where he lived.

Upon a day he was alive, well, happy, and in great evidence among the billiard-tables at his Club. Upon a morning he was not, and no manner of search could make sure where he might be. He had stepped out of his place; he had not appeared at his office at the proper time, and his dogcart was not upon the public roads. For these reasons, and because he was hampering, in a microscopical degree, the administration of the Indian Empire, that Empire paused for one microscopical moment to make inquiry into the fate of Imray. Ponds were dragged, wells were plumbed, telegrams were despatched down the lines of railways and to the nearest seaport town – twelve hundred miles away; but Imray was not at the end of the drag-ropes nor the telegraph wires, He was gone, and his place knew him no more. Then the work of the great Indian Empire swept forward, because it could not be delayed, and Imray from being a man became a mystery – such a thing as men talk over at their tables in the Club for a month, and then forget utterly. His guns, horses, and carts were sold to the highest bidder. His superior officer wrote an altogether absurd letter to his mother, saying that Imray had unaccountably disappeared, and his bungalow stood empty.

After three or four months of the scorching hot weather had gone by, my friend Strickland, of the Police, saw fit to rent the bungalow from the native landlord. This was before he was engaged to Miss Youghal – an affair which has been described in another place – and while he was pursuing his investigations into native life. His own life was sufficiently peculiar, and men complained of his manners and customs. There was always food in his house, but there were no regular times for meals. He ate, standing up and walking about, whatever he might find at the sideboard, and this is not good for human beings. His domestic equipment was limited to six rifles, three shot-guns, five saddles, and a collection of stiff-jointed *mahseer*-rods, bigger and stronger than the largest salmon-rods. These occupied one-half of his bungalow, and the other half was given up to Strickland and his dog Tietjens – an enormous Rampur slut who devoured daily the rations of two men. She spoke to Strickland in a language of her own; and whenever, walking abroad, she saw things calculated to destroy the peace of Her Majesty the Queen-Empress, she returned to her master and laid information. Strickland would take steps at once, and at the end of his labours was trouble and fine and imprisonment for other people. The natives believed that Tietjens was a familiar spirit, and treated her with the great reverence that is born of hate and fear. One room in the bungalow was set apart for her special use. She owned a bedstead, a blanket, and a drinking-trough, and if anyone came into Strickland's room at night her custom was to knock down the invader and give tongue till someone came with a light. Strickland owed his life to her when he was on the Frontier, in search of a local murderer, who came in the grey dawn to send Strickland much farther than the Andaman islands. Tietjens caught the man as he was crawling into Strickland's tent with a dagger between his teeth; and after his record of iniquity was established in the eyes of the law he was hanged. From that date

Tietjens wore a collar of rough silver, and employed a monogram on her night-blanket; and the blanket was of double woven Kashmir cloth, for she was a delicate dog.

Under no circumstances would she be separated from Strickland; and once, when he was ill with fever, made great trouble for the doctors, because she did not know how to help her master and would not allow another creature to attempt aid. Macarnaght, of the Indian Medical Service, beat her over her head with a gun-butt before she could understand that she must give room for those who could give quinine.

A short time after Strickland had taken Imray's bungalow, my business took me through that Station, and naturally, the Club quarters being full, I quartered myself upon Strickland. It was a desirable bungalow, eight-roomed and heavily thatched against any chance of leakage from rain. Under the pitch of the roof ran a ceiling-cloth which looked just as neat as a white-washed ceiling. The landlord had repainted it when Strickland took the bungalow. Unless you knew how Indian bungalows were built you would never have suspected that above the cloth lay the dark three-cornered cavern of the roof, where the beams and the underside of the thatch harboured all manner of rats, bats, ants and foul things.

Tietjens met me in the verandah with a bay like the boom of the bell of St Paul's, putting her paws on my shoulder to show she was glad to see me. Strickland had contrived to claw together a sort of meal which he called lunch, and immediately after it was finished went out about his business. I was left alone with Tietjens and my own affairs. The heat of the summer had broken up and turned to the warm damp of the rains. There was no motion in the heated air, but the rain fell like ramrods on the earth, and flung up a blue mist when it splashed back. The bamboos, and the custard-apples, the poinsettias, and the mango-trees in the garden stood still while the warm water lashed through them, and the frogs began to sing among the aloe hedges. A little before the light failed, and when the rain was at its worst, I sat in the back verandah and heard the water roar from the eaves, and scratched myself because I was covered with the thing called prickly-heat. Tietjens came out with me and put her head in my lap and was very sorrowful; so I gave her biscuits when tea was ready, and I took tea in the back verandah on account of the little coolness found there. The rooms of the nouse were dark behind me. I could smell Strickland's saddlery and the oil on his guns, and I had no desire to sit among these things. My own servant came to me in the twilight, the muslin of his clothes clinging tightly to his drenched body, and told me that a gentleman had called and wished to see someone. Very much against my will, but only because of the darkness of the rooms, I went into the naked drawing-room, telling my man to bring the lights. There might or might not have been a caller waiting – it seemed to me that I saw a figure by one of the windows – but when the lights came there was nothing save the spikes of the rain without, and the smell of the drinking earth in my nostrils. I explained to my servant that he was no wiser than he ought to be, and went back to the verandah to talk to Tietjens. She had gone out into the wet, and I could hardly coax her back to me, even with biscuits with sugar tops. Strickland came home, dripping wet, just before dinner, and the first thing he said was:

'Has anyone called?'

I explained, with apologies, that my servant had summoned me into the drawing-room on a false alarm; or that some loafer had tried to call on Strickland, and thinking better of it had fled after giving his name. Strickland ordered dinner, without comment, and since it was a real dinner with a white tablecloth attached, we sat down.

At nine o'clock Strickland wanted to go to bed, and I was tired too. Tietjens, who had been lying underneath the table, rose up, and swung into the least exposed verandah as soon as her master moved to his own room, which was next to the stately chamber set apart for Tietjens. If a mere wife had wished to sleep out of doors in that pelting rain it would not have mattered; but Tietjens was a dog, and therefore the better animal. I looked at Strickland, expecting to see him flay her with a whip. He smiled queerly, as a man would smile after telling some unpleasant domestic tragedy. 'She has done this ever since I moved in here,' said he. 'Let her go.'

The dog was Strickland's dog, so I said nothing, but I felt all that Strickland felt in being thus made light of. Tietjens encamped outside my bedroom window, and storm after storm came up, thundered on the thatch, and died away. The lightning spattered the sky as a thrown egg spatters a barn-door, but the light was pale blue, not yellow; and, looking through my split bamboo blinds, I could see the great dog standing, not sleeping, in the verandah, the hackles alift on her back, and her feet anchored as tensely as the drawn wire-rope of a suspension bridge. In the very short pauses of the thunder I tried to sleep, but it seemed that someone wanted me very urgently. He, whoever he was, was trying to call me by name, but his voice was no more than a husky whisper. The thunder ceased, and Tietjens went into the garden and howled at the low moon. Somebody tried to open my door, walked about and about through the house, and stood breathing heavily in the verandahs, and just when I was falling asleep I fancied that I heard a wild hammering and clamouring above my head or on the door.

I ran into Strickland's room and asked him whether he was ill, and had been calling for me. He was lying on his bed half dressed, a pipe in his mouth. 'I thought you'd come,' he said. 'Have I been walking round the house recently?'

I explained that he had been tramping in the dining-room and the smoking-room and two or three other places; and he laughed and told me to go back to bed. I went back to bed and slept till the morning, but through all my mixed dreams I was sure I was doing someone an injustice in not attending to his wants. What those wants were I could not tell; but a fluttering, whispering, bolt-fumbling, lurking, loitering Someone was reproaching me for my slackness, and, half awake, I heard the howling of Tietjens in the garden and the threshing of the rain.

I lived in that house for two days. Strickland went to his office daily, leaving me alone for eight or ten hours with Tietjens for my only companion. As long as the full light lasted I was comfortable, and so was Tietjens; but in the twilight she and I moved into the back verandah and cuddled each other for company. We were alone in the house, but none the less it was much too fully occupied by a tenant with whom I did not wish to interfere. I never saw him, but I could see the curtains between the rooms quivering where he had just passed through; I could hear the chairs creaking as the bamboos sprung under a weight that had just quitted them; and I could feel when I went to get a book from the dining-room that somebody was waiting in the shadows of the front verandah till I should have gone away. Tietjens made the twilight more interesting by glaring into the darkened rooms with every hair erect, and following the motions of something that I could not see. She never entered the rooms, but her eyes moved interestedly: that was quite sufficient. Only when my servant came to trim the lamps and make all light and habitable she would come in with me and spend her time sitting on her haunches, watching an invisible extra man as he moved about behind my shoulder. Dogs are cheerful companions.

I explained to Strickland, gently as might be, that I would go over to the Club and find for myself quarters there. I admired his hospitality, was pleased with his guns and rods, but I did not much care for his house and its atmosphere. He heard me out to the end, and then smiled very wearily, but without contempt, for he is a man who understands things. 'Stay on,' he said, 'and see what this thing means. All you have talked about I have known since I took the bungalow. Stay on and wait. Tietjens has left me. Are you going too?'

I had seen him through one little affair, connected with a heathen idol, that had brought me to the doors of a lunatic asylum, and I had no desire to help him through further experiences. He was a man to whom unpleasantnesses arrived as do dinners to ordinary people.

Therefore I explained more clearly than ever that I liked him immensely, and would be happy to see him in the daytime; but that I did not care to sleep under his roof. This was after dinner, when Tietjens had gone out to lie in the verandah.

''Pon my soul, I don't wonder,' said Strickland, with his eyes on the ceiling-cloth. 'Look at that!'

The tails of two brown snakes were hanging between the cloth and the cornice of the wall. They threw long shadows in the lamplight.

'If you are afraid of snakes of course—' said Strickland.

I hate and fear snakes, because if you look into the eyes of any snake you will see that it knows all and more of the mystery of man's fall, and that it feels all the contempt that the Devil felt when Adam was evicted from Eden. Besides which its bite is generally fatal, and it twists up trouser legs.

'You ought to get your thatch overhauled,' I said. 'Give me a *mahseer*-rod, and we'll poke 'em down.'

'They'll hide among the roof-beams,' said Strickland. 'I can't stand snakes overhead. I'm going up into the roof. If I shake 'em down, stand by with a cleaning-rod and break their backs.'

I was not anxious to assist Strickland in his work, but I took the cleaning-rod and waited in the dining-room, while Strickland brought a gardener's ladder from the verandah, and set it against the side of the room. The snake-tails drew themselves up and disappeared. We could hear the dry rushing scuttle of long bodies running over the baggy ceiling cloth. Strickland took a lamp with him, while I tried to make clear to him the danger of hunting roof-snakes between a ceiling-cloth and a thatch, apart from the deterioration of property caused by ripping out ceiling-cloths.

'Nonsense!' said Strickland. 'They're sure to hide near the walls by the cloth. The bricks are too cold for 'em, and the heat of the room is just what they like.' He put his hand to the corner of the stuff and ripped it from the cornice. It gave with a great sound of tearing, and Strickland put his head through the opening into the dark of the angle of the roof-beams. I set my teeth and lifted the rod, for I had not the least knowledge of what might descend.

'H'm!' said Strickland, and his voice rolled and rumbled in the roof. 'There's room for another set of rooms up here, and, by Jove, someone is occupying 'em!'

'Snakes?' I said from below.

'No. It's a buffalo. Hand me up the two last joints of a *mahseer*-rod, and I'll prod it. It's lying on the main roof-beam.'

I handed up the rod.

'What a nest for owls and serpents! No wonder the snakes live here,' said Strickland, climbing farther into the roof. I could see his elbow thrusting with the rod. 'Come out of that, whoever you are! Heads below there! It's falling.'

I saw the ceiling cloth nearly in the centre of the room bag with a shape that was pressing it downwards and downwards towards the lighted lamp on the table. I snatched the lamp out of danger and stood back. Then the cloth ripped out from the walls, lore, split, swayed, and shot down upon the table something that I dared not look at, till Strickland had slid down the ladder and was standing by my side.

He did not say much, being a man of few words; but he picked up the loose end of the tablecloth and threw it over the remnants on the table.

'It strikes me,' said he, putting down the lamp, 'our friend Imray has come back. Oh! you would, would you?'

There was a movement under the cloth, and a little snake wriggled out, to be back-broken by the butt of the *mahseer*-rod. I was sufficiently sick to make no remarks worth recording.

Strickland meditated, and helped himself to drinks. The arrangements under the cloth made no more signs of life.

'Is it Imray?' I said.

Strickland turned back the cloth for a moment, and looked.

'It is Imray,' he said; 'and his throat is cut from ear to ear.'

Then we spoke, both together and to ourselves: 'That's why he whispered about the house.'

Tietjens, in the garden, began to bay furiously. A little later her great nose heaved open the dining-room door.

She snuffed and was still. The tattered ceiling-cloth hung down almost to the level of the table, and there was hardly room to move away from the discovery.

Tietjens came in and sat down; her teeth bared under her lip and her forepaws planted. She looked at Strickland.

'It's a bad business, old lady,' said he. 'Men don't climb up into the roofs of their bungalows to die, and they don't fasten up the ceiling cloth behind 'em. Let's think it out.'

'Let's think it out somewhere else,' I said.

'Excellent idea! Turn the lamps out. We'll get into my room.'

I did not turn the lamps out. I went into Strickland's room first, and allowed him to make the darkness. Then he followed me, and we lit tobacco and thought. Strickland thought. I smoked furiously, because I was afraid.

'Imray is back,' said Strickland. 'The question is – who killed Imray? Don't talk, I've a notion of my own. When I took this bungalow I took over most of Imray's servants. Imray was guileless and inoffensive, wasn't he?'

I agreed; though the heap under the cloth had looked neither one thing nor the other.

'If I call in all the servants they will stand fast in a crowd and lie like Aryans. What do you suggest?'

'Call 'em in one by one,' I said.

'They'll run away and give the news to all their fellows,' said Strickland. 'We must segregate 'em. Do you suppose your servant knows anything about it?'

'He may, for aught I know; but I don't think it's likely. He has only been here for two or three days,' I answered. 'What's your notion?'

'I can't quite tell. How the dickens did the man get the wrong side of the ceiling-cloth?'

There was a heavy coughing outside Strickland's bedroom door. This showed that Bahadur Khan, his body-servant, had waked from sleep and wished to put Strickland to bed.

'Come in,' said Strickland. 'It's a very warm night, isn't it?'

Bahadur Khan, a great, green-turbaned, six-foot Mahomedan, said that it was a very warm night; but that there was more rain pending, which, by his Honour's favour, would bring relief to the country.

'It will be so, if God pleases,' said Strickland, tugging off his boots. 'It is in my mind, Bahadur Khan, that I have worked thee remorselessly for many days – ever since that time when thou first earnest into my service. What time was that?'

'Has the Heaven-born forgotten? It was when Imray Sahib

went secretly to Europe without warning given; and I – even I – came into the honoured service of the protector of the poor.'

'And Imray Sahib went to Europe?'

'It is so said among those who were his servants.'

'And thou wilt take service with him when he returns?'

'Assuredly, Sahib. He was a good master, and cherished his dependants.'

'That is true. I am very tired, but I go buck-shooting tomorrow. Give me the little sharp rifle that I use for black-buck; it is in the case yonder.'

The man stooped over the case; handed barrels, stock, and fore-end to Strickland, who fitted all together, yawning dolefully. Then he reached down to the gun-case, took a solid-drawn cartridge, and slipped it into the breech of the .360 Express.

'And Imray Sahib has gone to Europe secretly! That is very strange, Bahadur Khan, is it not?'

'What do I know of the ways of the white man. Heaven-born?'

'Very little, truly. But thou shall know more anon. It has reached me that Imray Sahib has returned from his so long journeyings, and that even now he lies in the next room, waiting his servant.'

'Sahib!'

The lamplight slid along the barrels of the rifle as they levelled themselves at Bahadur Khan's broad breast.

'Go and look!' said Strickland. 'Take a lamp. Thy master is tired, and he waits thee. Go!'

The man picked up a lamp, and went into the dining-room, Strickland following, and almost pushing him with the muzzle of the rifle. He looked for a moment at the black depths behind the ceiling-cloth; at the writhing snake under foot; and last, a grey glaze settling on his face, at the thing under the tablecloth.

'Hast thou seen?' said Strickland after a pause.

'I have seen. I am clay in the white man's hands. What does the Presence do?'

'Hang thee within the month. What else?'

'For killing him? Nay, Sahib, consider. Walking among us, his servants, he cast his eyes upon my child, who was four years old. Him he bewitched, and in ten days he dies of the fever – my child!'

'What said Imray Sahib?'

'He said he was a handsome child, and patted him on the head; wherefore my child died. Wherefore I killed Imray Sahib in the twilight, when he had come back from office, and was sleeping. Wherefore I dragged him up into the roof-beams and made all fast behind him. The Heaven-born knows all things. I am the servant of the Heaven-born.'

Strickland looked at me above the rifle, and said, in the vernacular, 'Thou are witness to this saying? He has killed.'

Bahadur Khan stood ashen grey in the light of the one lamp. The need for justification came upon him very swiftly. 'I am trapped,' he said, 'but the offence was that man's. He cast an evil eye upon my child, and I killed and hid him. Only such as are served by devils,' he glared at Tietjens, couched stolidly before him, 'only such could know what I did.'

'It was clever. But thou shouldst have lashed him to the beam with a rope. Now, thou thyself wilt hang by a rope. Orderly!'

A drowsy policeman answered Strickland's call. He was followed by another, and Tietjens sat wondrous still.

'Take him to the police station,' said Strickland. 'There is a case toward.'

'Do I hang, then?' said Bahadur Khan, making no attempt to escape, and keeping his eyes on the ground.

'If the sun shines or the water runs – yes!' said Strickland.

Bahadur Khan stepped back one long pace, quivered, and stood still. The two policemen waited further orders.

'Go!' said Strickland.

'Nay; but I go very swiftly,' said Bahadur Khan. 'Look! I am even now a dead man.'

He lifted his foot, and to the little toe there clung the head of the half-killed snake, firm fixed in the agony of death.

'I come of land-holding stock,' said Bahadur Khan, rocking where he stood. 'It were a disgrace to me to go to the public scaffold: therefore I take this way. Be it remembered that the Sahib's shirts are correctly enumerated, and that there is an extra piece of soap in his wash-basin. My child was bewitched and I slew the wizard. Why should you seek to slay me with the rope? My honour is saved, and – and – I die.'

At the end of an hour he died, as they die who are bitten by the little brown *karait*, and the policemen bore him and the thing under the tablecloth to their appointed places. All were needed to make clear the disappearance of Imray.

'This,' said Strickland, very calmly, as he climbed into bed, 'is called the nineteenth century. Did you hear what that man said?' 'I heard,' I answered. 'Imray made a mistake.'

'Simply and solely through not knowing the nature of the Oriental, and the coincidence of a little seasonal fever. Bahadur Khan had been with him for four years.'

I shuddered. My own servant had been with me for exactly that length of time. When I went over to my own room I found my man waiting, impassive as the copper head on a penny, to pull off my boots.

'What has befallen Bahadur Khan?' said I.

'He was bitten by a snake and died. The rest the Sahib knows,' was the answer.

'And how much of this matter has thou known?'

'As much as might be gathered from One coming in the twilight to seek satisfaction. Gently, Sahib. Let me pull off those boots.'

I had just settled to the sleep of exhaustion when I heard Strickland shouting from his side of the house –

'Tietjens has come back to her place!'

And so she had. The great deerhound was couched statelily on her own bedstead on her own blanket, while, in the next room, the idle, empty, ceiling-cloth waggled as it trailed on the table.

THE FINANCES OF THE GODS

The evening meal was ended in Dhunni Bhagat's Chubara and the old priests were smoking or counting their beads. A little naked child pattered in, with its mouth wide open, a handful of marigold flowers in one hand, and a lump of conserved tobacco in the other. It tried to kneel and make obeisance to Gobind, but it was so fat that it fell forward on its shaven head, and rolled on its side, kicking and gasping, while the marigolds tumbled one way and the tobacco the other. Gobind laughed, set it up again, and blessed the marigold flowers as he received the tobacco.

'From my father,' said the child. 'He has the fever, and cannot come. Wilt thou pray for him, father?'

'Surely, littlest; but the smoke is on the ground, and the night-chill is in the airs, and it is not good to go abroad naked in the autumn.'

'I have no clothes,' said the child, 'and all to-day I have been carrying cow-dung cakes to the bazar. It was very hot, and I am very tired.' It shivered a little, for the twilight was cool.

Gobind lifted an arm under his vast tattered quilt of many colours, and made an inviting little nest by his side. The child crept in, and Gobind filled his brass-studded leather waterpipe with the new tobacco. When I came to the Chubara the shaven head with the tuft atop, and the beady black eyes looked out of the folds of the quilt as a squirrel looks out from his nest, and Gobind was smiling while the child played with his beard.

I would have said something friendly, but remembered in time that if the child fell ill afterwards I should be credited with the Evil Eye, and that is a horrible possession.

'Sit thou still, Thumbling,' I said as it made to get up and run away. 'Where is thy slate, and why has the teacher let such an evil character loose on the streets when there are no police to protect us weaklings? In which ward dost thou try to break thy neck with flying kites from the house-tops?'

'Nay, Sahib, nay,' said the child, burrowing its face into Gobind's beard, and twisting uneasily. There was a holiday to-day among the schools, and I do not always fly kites. I play ker-li-kit like the rest.'

Cricket is the national game among the schoolboys of the Punjab, from the naked hedge-school children, who use an old kerosene-tin for wicket, to the BAs of the University, who compete for the Championship belt.

'Thou play kerlikit! Thou art half the height of the bat!' I said.

The child nodded resolutely. 'Yea, I *do* play, *Perlayball Ow-at! Ran, ran, ran!* I know it all.'

'But thou must not forget with all this to pray to the Gods according to custom,' said Gobind, who did not altogether approve of cricket and western innovations.

'I do not forget,' said the child in a hushed voice.

'Also to give reverence to thy teacher, and' – Gobind's voice softened – 'to abstain from pulling holy men by the beard, little badling. Eh, eh, eh?'

The child's face was altogether hidden in the great white beard, and it began to whimper till Gobind soothed it as children are soothed all the world over, with the promise of a story.

'I did not think to frighten thee, senseless little one. Look up! Am I angry? Aré, aré, aré! Shall I weep too, and of our tears make a great pond and drown us both, and then thy father will never get well, lacking thee to pull his beard? Peace, peace, and I will tell thee of the Gods. Thou hast heard many tales?'

'Very many, father.'

'Now, this is a new one which thou hast not heard. Long and long ago when the Gods walked with men as they do to-day, but that we have not faith to see, Shiv, the greatest of Gods, and Parbati his wife, were walking in the garden of a temple.'

'Which temple? That in the Nandgaon ward?' said the child. 'Nay, very far away. Maybe at Trimbak or Hurdwar, whither thou must make pilgrimage when thou art a man. Now, there was sitting in the garden under the jujube trees, a mendicant that had worshipped Shiv for forty years, and he lived on the offerings of the pious, and meditated holiness night and day.'

'Oh father, was it thou?' said the child, looking up with large eyes.

'Nay, I have said it was long ago, and, moreover, this mendicant was married.'

'Did they put him on a horse with flowers on his head, and forbid him to go to sleep all night long? Thus they did to me when they made my wedding,' said the child, who had been married a few months before.

'And what didst thou do?' said I.

'I wept, and they called me evil names, and then I smote her, and we wept together.' 'Thus did not the mendicant,' said Gobind; 'for he was a holy man, and very poor. Parbati perceived him sitting naked by the temple steps where all went up and down, and she said to Shiv, "What shall men think of the Gods when the Gods thus scorn their worshippers? For forty years yonder man has prayed to us, and yet there be only a few grains of rice and some broken cowries before him after all. Men's hearts will be hardened by this thing." And Shiv said, "It shall be looked to," and so he called to the temple which was the temple of his son, Ganesh of the elephant head, saying, "Son, there is a mendicant without who is very poor. What wilt thou do for him?" Then that great elephant-headed One awoke in the dark and answered, "In three days, if it be thy will, he shall have one lakh of rupees." Then Shiv and Parbati went away.

'But there was a money-lender in the garden hidden among the marigolds' – the child looked at the ball of crumpled blossoms in its hands – 'ay, among the yellow marigolds, and he heard the Gods talking. He was a covetous man, and of a black heart, and he desired that lakh of rupees for himself. So he went to the mendicant and said, "O brother, how much do the pious give thee daily?" The mendicant said, "I cannot tell. Sometimes a little rice, sometimes a little pulse, and a few cowries and, it has been, pickled mangoes, and dried fish." '

'That is good,' said the child, smacking its lips.

'Then said the money-lender, "Because I have long watched thee, and learned to love thee and thy patience, I will give thee now five rupees for all thy earnings of the three days to come. There is only a bond to sign on the matter." But the mendicant said, "Thou art mad. In two months I do not receive the worth of five rupees," and he told the thing to his wife that evening. She, being a woman, said, "When did money-lender ever make a bad bargain? The wolf runs through the corn for the sake of the fat deer. Our fate is in the hands of the Gods. Pledge it not even for three days."

'So the mendicant returned to the money-lender, and would not sell. Then that wicked man sat all day before him offering more and more for those three days' earnings. First, ten, fifty, and a hundred rupees; and then, for he did not know when the Gods would pour down their gifts, rupees by the thousand, till he had offered half a lakh of rupees. Upon this sum the mendicant's wife shifted her counsel, and the mendicant signed the bond, and the money was paid in silver; great white bullocks bringing it by the cartload. But saving only all that money, the mendicant received nothing from the Gods at all, and the heart of the money-lender was uneasy on account of expectation. Therefore at noon of the third day the money-lender went into the temple to spy upon the councils of the Gods, and to learn in what manner that gift might arrive. Even as he was making his prayers, a crack between the stones of the floor gaped, and, closing, caught him by the heel. Then he heard the Gods walking in the temple in the darkness of the columns, and Shiv called to his son Ganesh, saying, "Son, what hast thou done in regard to the lakh of rupees for the mendicant?" And Ganesh woke, for the money-lender heard the dry rustle of his trunk uncoiling, and he answered, "Father, one half of the money has been paid, and the debtor for the other half I hold here fast by the heel." '

The child bubbled with laughter. 'And the moneylender paid the mendicant?' it said.

'Surely, for he whom the Gods hold by the heel must pay to the uttermost. The money was paid at evening, all silver, in great carts, and thus Ganesh did his work.'

'Nathu! Ohé Nathu!'

A woman was calling in the dusk by the door of the courtyard.

The child began to wriggle. 'That is my mother,' it said.

'Go then, littlest,' answered Gobind; 'but stay a moment.'

He ripped a generous yard from his patchwork-quilt, put it over the child's shoulders, and the child ran away.

THE FINEST STORY IN THE WORLD

'Or ever the knightly years were gone
　With the old world to the grave,
I was a king in Babylon
　And you were a Christian slave.'

W. E. Henley

His name was Charlie Mears; he was the only son of his
mother, who was a widow, and he lived in the north of
London, coming into the City every day to work in a bank.
He was twenty years old and was full of aspirations. I met him
in a public billiard-saloon where the markers called him by his
first name, and he called the marker 'Bullseye.' Charlie
explained, a little nervously, that he had only come to the
place to look on, and since looking on at games of skill is not a
cheap amusement for the young, I suggested that Charlie
should go back to his mother.

That was our first step towards better acquaintance. He
would call on me sometimes in the evenings instead of running
about London with his fellow-clerks; and before long, speaking of himself as a young man must, he told me of his
aspirations, which were all literary. He desired to make himself
an undying name chiefly through verse, though he was not
above sending stories of love and death to the penny-in-the-
slot journals. It was my fate to sit while Charlie read me poems
of many hundred lines, and bulky fragments of plays that
would surely shake the world. My reward was his unreserved
confidence, and the self-revelations and troubles of a young
man are almost as holy as those of a maiden. Charlie had never
fallen in love, but was anxious to do so on the first opportunity; he believed in all things good and all things honourable,
but at the same time, was curiously careful to let me see that he

knew his way about the world as befitted a bank-clerk on twenty-five shillings a week. He rhymed 'dove' with 'love' and 'moon' with 'June,' and devoutly believed that they had never so been rhymed before. The long lame gaps in his plays he filled up with hasty words of apology and description, and swept on, seeing all that he intended to do so clearly that he esteemed it already done, and turned to me for applause.

I fancy that his mother did not encourage his aspirations; and I know that his writing-table at home was the edge of his washstand. This he told me almost at the outset of our acquaintance – when he was ravaging my bookshelves, and a little before I was implored to speak the truth as to his chances of 'writing something really great, you know.' Maybe I encouraged him too much, for, one night, he called on me, his eyes flaming with excitement, and said breathlessly:

'Do you mind – can you let me stay here and write all this evening? I won't interrupt you, I won't really. There's no place for me to write in at my mother's.'

'What's the trouble?' I said, knowing well what that trouble was.

'I've a notion in my head that would make the most splendid story that was ever written. Do let me write it out here. It's *such* a notion!'

There was no resisting the appeal. I set him a table; he hardly thanked me, but plunged into his work at once. For half an hour the pen scratched without stopping. Then Charlie sighed and tugged his hair. The scratching grew slower, there were more erasures, and at last ceased. The finest story in the world would not come forth.

'It looks such awful rot now,' he said mournfully. 'And yet it seemed so good when I was thinking about it. What's wrong?'

I could not dishearten him by saying the truth. So I answered: 'Perhaps you don't feel in the mood for writing.'

'Yes, I do – except when I look at this stuff. Ugh!'

'Read me what you've done,' I said.

He read, and it was wondrous bad, and he paused at all the specially turgid sentences, expecting a little approval; for he was proud of those sentences, as I knew he would be.

'It needs compression,' I suggested cautiously.

'I hate cutting my things down. I don't think you could alter a word here without spoiling the sense. It reads better aloud than when I was writing it.'

'Charlie, you're suffering from an alarming disease afflicting a numerous class. Put the thing by, and tackle it again in a week.'

'I want to do it at once. What do you think of it?'

'How can I judge from a half-written tale? Tell me the story as it lies in your head.'

Charlie told, and in the telling there was everything that his ignorance had so carefully prevented from escaping into the written word. I looked at him, wondering whether it were possible that he did not know the originality, the power of the notion that had come in his way? It was distinctly a Notion among notions. Men had been puffed up with pride by ideas not a tithe as excellent and practicable. But Charlie babbled on serenely, interrupting the current of pure fancy with samples of horrible sentences that he purposed to use. I heard him out to the end. It would be folly to allow his thought to remain in his own inept hands, when I could do so much with it. Not all that could be done indeed; but, oh so much!

'What do you think?' he said at last. 'I fancy I shall call it "The Story of a Ship."'

'I think the idea's pretty good; but you won't be able to handle it for ever so long. Now I—'

'Would it be of any use to you? Would you care to take it? I should be proud,' said Charlie promptly.

There are a few things sweeter in this world than the guileless, hot-headed, intemperate, open admiration of a junior. Even a woman in her blindest devotion does not fall into the gait of the man she adores, tilt her bonnet to the angle at which he wears his hat, or interlard her speech with his pet oaths. And Charlie did all these things. Still it was necessary to salve my conscience before I possessed myself of Charlie's thoughts.

'Let's make a bargain. I'll give you a fiver for the notion,' I said.

Charlie became a bank-clerk at once.

'Oh, that's impossible. Between two pals, you know, if I may call you so, and speaking as a man of the world, I couldn't. Take the notion if it's any use to you. I've heaps more.'

He had – none knew this better than I – but they were the notions of other men.

'Look at it is a matter of business – between men of the world,' I returned. 'Five pounds will buy any number of poetry-books. Business is business, and you may be sure I shouldn't give that price unless—'

'Oh, if you put it *that* way,' said Charlie, visibly moved by the thought of the books. The bargain was clinched with an agreement that he should at unstated intervals come to me with all the notions that he possessed, should have a table of his own to write at, and unquestioned right to inflict upon me all his poems and fragments of poems. Then I said, 'Now tell me how you came by this idea.'

'It came by itself.' Charlie's eyes opened a little.

'Yes, but you told me a great deal about the hero that you must have read before somewhere.'

'I haven't any time for reading, except when you let me sit here, and on Sundays I'm on my bicycle or down the river all day. There's nothing wrong about the hero, is there?'

'Tell me again and I shall understand clearly. You say that your hero went pirating. How did he live?'

'He was on the lower deck of this ship-thing that I was telling you about.'

'What sort of ship?'

'It was the kind rowed with oars, and the sea spurts through the oar-holes, and the men row sitting up to their knees in water. Then, there's a bench running down between the two lines of oars, and an overseer with a whip walks up and down the bench to make the men work.'

'How do you know that?'

'It's in the tale. There's a rope running overhead, looped to the upper-deck, for the overseer to catch hold of when the ship rolls. When the overseer misses the rope once and falls among the rowers, remember the hero laughs at him and gets licked for it. He's chained to his oar, of course – the hero.'

'How is he chained?'

'With an iron band round his waist fixed to the bench he sits on, and a sort of handcuff on his left wrist chaining him to the oar. He's on the lower deck where the worst men are sent, and the only light comes from the hatchways and through the oar-holes. Can't you imagine the sunlight just squeezing through between the handle and the hole and wobbling about as the ship moves?'

'I can, but I can't imagine your imagining it.'

'How could it be any other way? Now you listen to me. The long oars on the upper deck are managed by four men to each bench, the lower ones by three, and the lowest of all by two. Remember its quite dark on the lowest deck and all the men there go mad. When a man dies at his oar on that deck he isn't thrown overboard, but cut up in his chains and stuffed through the oar-hole in little pieces.'

'Why?' I demanded amazed, not so much at the information as the tone of command in which it was flung out.

'To save trouble and to frighten the others. It needs two overseers to drag a man's body up to the top deck; and if the men at the lower deck oars were left alone, of course they'd stop rowing and try to pull up the benches by all standing up together in their chains.'

'You've a most provident imagination. Where have you been reading about galleys and galley-slaves?'

'Nowhere that I remember. I row a little when I get the chance. But, perhaps, if you say so, I may have read something.'

He went away shortly afterwards to deal with booksellers, and I wondered how a bank-clerk aged twenty could put into my hands with a profligate abundance of detail, all given with absolute assurance, the story of extravagant and bloodthirsty adventure, riot, piracy, and death in unnamed seas. He had led his hero a desperate dance through revolt against the overseers, to command of a ship of his own, and at last to the establishment of a kingdom on an island 'somewhere in the sea, you know;' and, delighted with my paltry five pounds, had gone out to buy the notions of other men, that these might teach him how to write. I had the consolation of knowing that this notion was mine by right of purchase, and I thought that I could make something of it.

When next he came to me he was drunk – royally drunk on many poets for the first time revealed to him. His pupils were dilated, his words tumbled over each other, and he wrapped himself in quotations – as a beggar would enfold himself in the purple of emperors. Most of all was he drunk with Longfellow.

'Isn't it splendid? Isn't it superb?' he cried, after hasty greetings. 'Listen to this –

' "Wouldst thou," – so the helmsman answered,
   "Learn the secret of the sea?
Only those who brave its dangers
   Comprehend its mystery." '

By gum!

' "Only those who brave its dangers
Comprehend its mystery," '

he repeated twenty times, walking up and down the room and forgetting me. 'But *I* can understand it too,' he said to himself. 'I don't know how to thank you for that fiver. And this; listen –

' "I remember the black wharves and the slips
   And the sea-tides tossing free;
And Spanish sailors with bearded lips,
And the beauty and mystery of the ships,
   And the magic of the sea."

I haven't braved any dangers, but I feel as if I knew all about it.'

'You certainly seem to have a grip of the sea. Have you ever seen it?'

'When I was a little chap I went to Brighton once; we used

to live in Coventry, though, before we came to London. I never saw it,

' "When descends on the Atlantic
    The gigantic
Storm-wind of the Equinox." '

He shook me by the shoulder to make me understand the passion that was shaking himself.

'When that storm comes,' he continued, 'I think that all the oars in the ship that I was talking about get broken, and the rowers have their chests smashed in by the oar-heads bucking. By the way, have done anything with that notion of mine yet?'

'No. I was waiting to hear more of it from you. Tell me how in the world you're so certain about the fittings of the ship. You know nothing of ships.'

'I don't know. It's as real as anything to me until I try to write it down. I was thinking about it only last night in bed, after you had lent me *Treasure Island*; and I made up a whole lot of new things to go into the story.'

'What sort of things?'

'About the food the men ate; rotten figs and black beans and wine in a skin bag, passed from bench to bench.'

'Was the ship built so long ago as *that*?'

'As what? I don't know whether it was long ago or not. It's only a notion, but sometimes it seems just as real as if it was true. Do I bother you with talking about it?'

'Not in the least. Did you make up anything else?'

'Yes, but it's nonsense,' Charlie flushed a little.

'Never mind; let's hear about it.'

'Well, I was thinking over the story, and after awhile I got out of bed and wrote down on a piece of paper the sort of stuff the men might be supposed to scratch on their oars with the edges of their handcuffs. It seemed to make the thing more life-like. It *is* so real to me, y'know.'

'Have you the paper on you?'

'Ye-es, but what's the use of showing it? It's only a lot of scratches. All the same, we might have 'em reproduced in the book on the front page.'

'I'll attend to those details. Show me what your men wrote.'

He pulled out of his pocket a sheet of notepaper, with a single line of scratches upon it, and I put this carefully away.

'What is it supposed to mean in English?' I said.

'Oh I don't know. I mean it to mean "I'm beastly tired." It's great nonsense,' he repeated, 'but all those men in the ship seem as real as real people to me. Do do something to the notion soon; I should like to see it written and printed.'

'But all you've told me would make a long book.'

'Make it then. You've only to sit down and write it out.'

'Give me a little time. Have you any more notions?'

'Not just now. I'm reading all the books I've bought. They're splendid.'

When he had left I looked at the sheet of notepaper with the inscription upon it. Then I took my head tenderly between both hands, to make certain that it was not coming off or turning round. Then . . . but there seemed to be no interval between quitting my rooms and finding myself arguing with a policeman outside a door marked *Private* in a corridor of the British Museum. All I demanded, as politely as possible, was 'the Greek antiquities man.' The policeman knew nothing except the rules of the Museum, and it became necessary to forage through all the houses and offices inside the gates. An elderly gentleman called away from his lunch put an end to my search by holding the notepaper between finger and thumb and sniffing at it scornfully.

'What does this mean? H'mm,' said he. 'So far as I can ascertain it is an attempt to write extremely corrupt Greek on the part' – here he glared at me with intention – 'of an extremely illiterate – ah – person.' He read slowly from the paper, '*Pollock, Erckmann, Tauchnitz, Henniker*' – four names familiar to me.

'Can you tell me what the corruption is supposed to mean – the gist of the thing?' I asked.

' "I have been – many times – overcome with weariness in this particular employment." That is the meaning,' He returned me the paper, and I fled without a word of thanks, explanation, or apology.

I might have been excused for forgetting much. To me of all men had been given the chance to write the most marvellous tale in the world, nothing less than the story of a Greek galley-slave, as told by himself. Small wonder that his dreaming had seemed real to Charlie. The Fates that are so careful to shut the doors of each successive life behind us had, in this case, been neglectful, and Charlie was looking, though that he did not know, where never man had been permitted to look with full knowledge since Time began. Above all, he was absolutely ignorant of the knowledge sold to me for five pounds; and he would retain that ignorance, for bank-clerks do not understand metempsychosis, and a sound commercial education does not include Greek. He would supply me – here I capered among the dumb gods of Egypt and laughed in their battered faces – with material to make my tale sure – so sure that the world would hail it as an impudent and vamped fiction. And I – I alone would know that it was absolutely literally true. I – I alone held this jewel to my hand for the cutting and polishing! Therefore I danced again among the gods of the Egyptian Court till a policeman saw me and took steps in my direction.

It remained now only to encourage Charlie to talk, and here there was no difficulty. But I had forgotten those accursed books of poetry. He came to me time after time, as useless as a surcharged phonograph – drunk on Byron, Shelley, or Keats. Knowing now what the boy had been in his past lives, and desperately anxious not to lose one word of his babble, I could not hide from him my respect and interest. He misconstrued both into respect for the present soul of Charlie Mears, to whom life was as new as it was to Adam, and interest in his readings; and stretched my patience to breaking-point by reciting poetry – not his own now, but that of others. I wished every English poet blotted out of the memory of mankind. I blasphemed the mightiest names of song because they had drawn Charlie from the path of direct narrative, and would, later, spur him to imitate them; but I choked down my impatience until the first flood of enthusiasm should have spent itself and the boy returned to his dreams.

'What's the use of my telling you what *I* think, when these chaps wrote things for the angels to read?' he growled, one evening. 'Why don't you write something like theirs?'

'I don't think you're treating me quite fairly,' I said, speaking under strong restraint.

'I've given you the story,' he said shortly, replunging into 'Lara.'

'But I want the details.'

'The things I make up about that damned ship that you call a galley? They're quite easy. You can just make 'em up for yourself. Turn up the gas a little, I want to go on reading.'

I could have broken the gas-globe over his head for his amazing stupidity. I could indeed make up things for myself did I only know what Charlie did not know that he knew. But since the doors were shut behind me I could only wait his youthful pleasure and strive to keep him in good temper. One minute's want of guard might spoil a priceless revelation: now and again he would toss his books aside – he kept them in my rooms, for his mother would have been shocked at the waste of good money had she seen them – and launched into his sea-dreams. Again I cursed all the poets of England. The plastic mind of the bank-clerk had been overlaid, coloured, and distorted by that which he had read, and the result as delivered was a confused tangle of other voices most like the mutter and hum through a City telephone in the busiest part of the day.

He talked of the galley – his own galley had he but known it – with illustrations borrowed from 'The Bride of Abydos.' .He pointed the experiences of his hero with quotations from 'The Corsair,' and threw in deep and desperate moral reflections from 'Cain' and 'Manfred,' expecting me to use them all. Only when the talk turned on Longfellow were the jarring cross-currents dumb, and I knew that Charlie was speaking the truth as he remembered it.

'What do you think of this?' I said one evening, as soon as I understood the medium in which his memory worked best, and, before he could expostulate, read him nearly the whole of 'The Saga of King Olaf'!

He listened open-mouthed, flushed, his hands drumming on the back of the sofa where he lay, till I came to the Song of Einar Tamberskelver and the verse: –

'Einar then, the arrow taking
  From the loosened string,
Answered, "That was Norway breaking
  From thy hand, O King!"'

He gasped with pure delight of sound.

'That's better than Byron, a little?' I ventured.

'Better! Why it's *true*! How could he have known?'

I went back and repeated: –

'"What was that?" said Olaf, standing
  On the quarter-deck.
"Something heard I like the stranding
  Of a shattered wreck."'

'How could he have known how the ships crash and the oars rip out and go *z-zzp* all along the line? Why, only the other night . . . But go back, please, and read "The Skerry of Shrieks" again.'

'No, I'm tired. Let's talk. What happened the other night?'

'I had an awful dream about that galley of ours. I dreamed I was drowned in a fight. You see, we ran alongside another ship in harbour. The water was dead still except where our oars whipped it up. You know where I always sit in the galley?' He spoke haltingly at first, under a fine English fear of being laughed at.

'No. That's news to me.' I answered meekly, my heart beginning to beat.

'On the fourth oar from the bow on the right side on the upper deck. There were four of us at that oar, all chained. I remember watching the water and trying to get my handcuffs off before the row began. Then we closed up on the other ship, and all their fighting men jumped over our bulwarks, and my bench broke and I was pinned down with the three other fellows on top of me, and the big oar jammed across our backs.'

'Well?' Charlie's eyes were alive and alight. He was looking at the wall behind my chair.

'I don't know how we fought. The men were trampling all over my back, and I lay low. Then our rowers on the left side – tied to their oars, you know – began to yell and back water. I could hear the water sizzle, and we spun round like a cock-chafer, and I knew, lying where I was, that there was a galley coming up bow-on to ram us on the left side. I could just lift up my head and see her sail over the bulwarks. We wanted to meet her bow to bow, but it was too late. We could only turn a little bit because the galley on our right had hooked herself on to us and stopped our moving. Then, by gum! there was a crash! Our left oars began to break as the other galley, the moving one y'know, stuck her nose into them. Then the lower-deck oars shot up through the deck planking, butt first, and one of them jumped clear up into the air and came down again close at my head.'

'How was that managed?'

'The moving galleys' bow was plunking them back through their own oar-holes, and I could hear no end of a shindy on the decks below. Then her nose caught us nearly in the middle, and we tilted sideways, and the fellows in the right-hand galley unhitched their hooks and ropes and threw things on to our upper deck – arrows, and hot pitch or something that stung, and we went up and up and up on the left side, and the right side dipped, and I twisted my head round and saw the water stand still as it topped the right bulwarks, and then it curled over and crashed down on the whole lot of us on the right side, and I felt it hit my back, and I woke.'

'One minute, Charlie. When the sea topped the bulwarks, what did it look like?' I had my reasons for asking. A man of my acquaintance had once gone down with a leaking ship in a still sea, and had seen the water-level pause for an instant ere it fell on the deck.

'It looked just like a banjo-string drawn tight, and it seemed to stay there for years,' said Charlie.

Exactly! The other man had said: 'It looked like a silver wire laid down along the bulwarks, and I thought it was never going to break.' He had paid everything except the bare life for this little valueless piece of knowledge, and I had travelled ten thousand weary miles to meet him and take his knowledge at second hand. But Charlie, the bank-clerk on twenty-five shillings a week, who had never been out of sight of a made road, knew it all. It was no consolation to me that once in his lives he had been forced to die for his gains. I also must have died scores of times, but behind me, because I could have used my knowledge, the doors were shut.

'And then?' I said, trying to put away the devil of envy.

'The funny thing was, though, in all the row I didn't feel a bit astonished or frightened. It seemed as if I'd been in a good many fights, because I told my next man so when the row began. But that cad of an overseer on my deck wouldn't unloose our chains and give us a chance. He always said that we'd all be set free after a battle, but we never were; we never were.' Charlie shook his head mournfully.

'What a scoundrel!'

'I should say he was. He never gave us enough to eat, and sometimes we were so thirsty that we used to drink salt-water. I can taste that salt-water still.'

'Now tell me something about the harbour where the fight was fought.'

'I didn't dream about that. I know it was a harbour, though; because we were tied up to a ring on a white wall and all the face of the stone under water was covered with wood to prevent our ram getting chipped when the tide made us rock.'

'That's curious. Our hero commanded the galley, didn't he?'

'Didn't he just! He stood by the bows and shouted like a good 'un. He was the man who killed the overseer.'

'But you were all drowned together, Charlie, weren't you?'

'I can't make that fit quite,' he said, with a puzzled look. 'The galley must have gone down with all hands, and yet I fancy that the hero went on living afterwards. Perhaps he climbed into the attacking ship. I wouldn't see that, of course, I was dead, you know.'

He shivered slightly and protested that he could remember no more. I did not press him further, but to satisfy myself that he lay in ignorance of the workings of his own mind, deliberately introduced him to Mortimer Collins's *Transmigration*, and gave him a sketch of the plot before he opened the pages.

'What rot it all is!' he said frankly, at the end of an hour. 'I don't understand his nonsense about the Red Planet Mars and the King, and the rest of it. Chuck me the Longfellow again.'

I handed him the book and wrote out as much as I could remember of his description of the sea-fight, appealing to him from time to time for confirmation of fact or detail. He would answer without raising his eyes from the book as assuredly as though all his knowledge lay before him on the printed page. I spoke under the normal key of my voice that the current might not be broken, and I knew that he was not aware of what he was saying, for his thoughts were out on the sea with Longfellow.

'Charlie,' I asked, 'when the rowers on the galleys mutinied how did they kill their overseers?'

'Tore up the benches and brained 'em. That happened when a heavy sea was running. An overseer on the lower deck slipped from the centre plank and fell among the rowers. They choked him to death against the side of the ship with their chained hands quite quietly, and it was too dark for the other overseer to see what had happened. When he asked, he was pulled down too and choked, and the lower deck fought their way up deck by deck, with pieces of the broken benches banging behind 'em. How they howled!'

'And what happened after that?'

'I don't know. The hero went away – red hair and red beard and all. That was after he had captured our galley, I think.'

The sound of my voice irritated him, and he motioned slightly with his left hand as a man does when interruption jars.

'You never told me he was red-headed before, or that he captured your galley,' I said, after a discreet interval.

Charlie did not raise his eyes.

'He was as red as a red bear,' said he abstractedly. 'He came from the north; they said so in the galley when he looked for rowers – not slaves, but free men. Afterwards – years and years afterwards – news came from another ship, or else he came back—'

His lips moved in silence. He was rapturously retasting some poem before him.

'Where had he been, then?' I was almost whispering that the sentence might come gently to whichever section of Charlie's brain was working on my behalf.

'To the Beaches – the Long and Wonderful Beaches!' was the reply after a minute of silence.

'To Furdurstrandi?' I asked, tingling from head to foot.

'Yes, to Furdurstrandi.' He pronounced the word in a new fashion.' 'And I too saw—' The voice failed.

'Do you know what you have said?' I shouted incautiously.

He lifted his eyes, fully roused now. 'No!' he snapped. 'I wish you'd let a chap go on reading. Hark to this:–

' "But Othere, the old sea-captain,
He neither paused nor stirred
    Till the King listened, and then
    Once more took up his pen
And wrote down every word.

' "And to the King of the Saxons,
In witness to the truth,
    Raising his noble head,
    He stretched his brown hand and said,
'Behold this walrus-tooth!" '

By Jove, what chaps those must have been, to go sailing all over the shop never knowing where they'd fetch the land! Hah!'

'Charlie,' I pleaded, 'if you'll only be sensible for a minute or two I'll make our hero in our tale every inch as good as Othere.'

'Umph! Longfellow wrote that poem. I don't care about writing things any more. I want to read.' He was thoroughly out of tune now, and raging over my own ill-luck, I left him.

Conceive yourself at the door of the world's treasure-house guarded by a child – an idle, irresponsible child playing knuckle-bones – on whose favour depends the gift of the key, and you will imagine one-half my torment. Till that evening Charlie had spoken nothing that might not lie within the experiences of a Greek galley-slave. But now, or there was no virtue in books, he had talked of some desperate adventure of the Vikings, of Thorfin Karlsefne's sailing to Wineland, which is America, in the ninth or tenth century. The battle in the harbour he had seen; and his own death he had described. But this was a much more startling plunge into the past. Was it possible that he had skipped half a dozen lives, and was then dimly remembering some episode of a thousand years later? It was a maddening jumble, and the worst of it was that Charlie Mcars in his normal condition was the last person in the world to clear it up. I could only wail and watch, but I went to bed that night full of the wildest imaginings. There was nothing that was not possible if Charlie's detestable memory only held good.

I might rewrite the Saga of Thorlin Karlsefne as it had never been written before, might tell the story of the first discovery of America, myself the discoverer. But I was entirely at Charlie's mercy, and so long as there was a three-and-sixpenny Bohn volume within his reach Charlie would not tell. I dared not curse him openly; I hardly dared jog his memory, for I was dealing with the experiences of a thousand years ago, told through the mouth of a boy of today; and a boy of today is affected by every change of tone and gust of opinion, so that he must lie even when he most desires to speak the truth.

I saw no more of Charlie for nearly a week. When next I met him it was in Gracechurch Street with a bill-book chained to his waist. Business took him over London Bridge, and I accompanied him. He was very full of the importance of that book and magnified it. As we passed over the Thames we paused to look at a steamer unloading great slabs of white and brown marble. A barge drifted under the steamer's stern and a lonely ship's cow in that barge bellowed. Charlie's face changed from the face of the bank-clerk to that of an unknown and – though he would not have believed this – a much shrewder man. He flung out his arm across the parapet of the bridge and, laughing very loudly, said: –

'When they heard *our* bulls bellow the Skroelings ran away!'

I waited only for an instant, but the barge and the cow had disappeared under the bows of the steamer before I answered.

'Charlie, what do you suppose are Skroelings?'

'Never heard of 'em before. They sound like a new kind of seagull. What a chap you are for asking questions!' he replied. 'I have to go to the cashier of the Omnibus Company yonder. Will you wait for me and we can lunch somewhere together? I've a notion for a poem.'

'No, thanks. I'm off. You're sure you know nothing about Skroelings?'

'Not unless he's been entered for the Liverpool Handicap.' He nodded and disappeared in the crowd.

Now it is written in the Saga of Eric the Red or that of Thorfin Karlsefne, that nine hundred years ago, when Karlsefne's galleys came to Leif's booths, which Leif had erected in the unknown land called Markland, which may or may not have been Rhode Island, the Skroelings – and the Lord He knows who these may or may not have been – came to trade with the Vikings, and ran away because they were frightened at the bellowing of the cattle which Thorfin had brought with him in the ships. But what in the world could a Greek slave know of that affair? I wandered up and down among the streets trying to unravel the mystery, and the more I considered it the more baffling it grew. One thing only seemed certain, and that certainty took away my breath for the moment. If I came to full knowledge of anything at all, it would not be one life of the soul in Charlie Mears's body, but half a dozen – half a dozen several and separate existences spent on blue water in the morning of the world!

Then I reviewed the situation.

Obviously if I used my knowledge I should stand alone and unapproachable until all men were as wise as myself. That would be something, but, manlike, I was ungrateful. It seemed bitterly unfair that Charlie's memory should fail me when I needed it most. Great Powers Above – I looked up at them through the fog-smoke – did the Lords of Life and Death know what this meant to me? Nothing less than eternal fame of the best kind, that comes from One, and is shared by one alone. I would be content – remembering Clive, I stood astounded at my own moderation – with the mere right to tell one story, to work out one little contribution to the light literature of the day. If Charlie were permitted full recollection of one hour – for sixty short minutes – of existences that had extended over a thousand years – I would forego all profit and honour from all that I should make of his speech. I would take no share in the commotion that would follow throughout the particular corner of the earth that calls itself 'the world.' The thing should be put forth anonymously. Nay, I would make other men believe that they had written it. They would hire bull-hided, self-advertising Englishmen to bellow it abroad. Preachers would found a fresh conduct of life upon it, swearing, that it was new and that they had lifted the fear of death from all mankind. Every Orientalist in Europe would patronise it discursively with Sanskrit and Pali texts. Terrible women would invent unclean variants of the men's belief for the elevation of their sisters. Churches and religions would war over it. Between the hailing and restarting of an omnibus I foresaw the scuffles that would arise among half a dozen denominations all professing 'the doctrine of the True Metempsychosis as applied to the world and the New Era'; and saw, too, the respectable English newspapers shying, like frightened kine, over the beautiful simplicity of the tale. The mind leaped forward a hundred – two hundred – a thousand years. I saw with sorrow that men would mutilate and garble the story; that rival creeds would turn it upside down till, at last, the western world which clings to the dread of death more closely than the hope of life, would set it aside as an interesting superstition and stampede after some faith so long forgotten that it seemed altogether new. Upon this I changed the terms of the bargain that I would make with the Lords of Life and Death. Only let me know, let me write, the story with sure knowledge that I wrote the truth, and I would burn the manuscript as a solemn sacrifice. Five minutes after the last line was written I would destroy it all. But I must be allowed to write it with absolute certainty.

There was no answer. The flaming colours of an Aquarium poster caught my eye, and I wondered whether it would be wise or prudent to lure Charlie into the hands of the professional mesmerist there, and whether, if he were under his power, he would speak of his past lives. If he did, and if people believed him . . . but Charlie would be frightened and flustered, or made conceited by the interviews. In either case he would begin to lie through fear or vanity. He was safest in my own hands.

'They are very funny fools, your English,' said a voice at my elbow, and turning round I recognised a casual acquaintance, a young Bengali law student, called Grish Chunder, whose father had sent him to England to become civilised. The old man was a retired native official, and on an income of five pounds a month contrived to allow his son two hundred pounds a year, and the run of his teeth in a city where he could pretend to be the cadet of a royal house, and tell stories of the brutal Indian bureaucrats who ground the faces of the poor.

Grish Chunder was a young, fat, full-bodied Bengali, dressed with scrupulous care in frock coat, tall hat, light trousers, and tan gloves. But I had known him in the days when the brutal Indian Government paid for his university education, and he contributed cheap sedition to the *Sachi Durpan*, and intrigued with the wives of his fourteen-year-old schoolmates.

'That is very funny and very foolish,' he said, nodding at the poster. 'I am going down to the Northbrook Club. Will you come too?'

I walked with him for some time. 'You are not well,' he said. 'What is there on your mind? You do not talk.'

'Grish Chunder, you've been too well educated to believe in a God, haven't you?'

'Oah, yes, *here*! But when I go home I must conciliate popular superstition, and make ceremonies of purification, and my – women will anoint idols.'

'And hang up *tulsi* and feast the *purohit*, and take you back into the caste again, and make a good *khuttri* of you again, you advanced Freethinker. And you'll eat *desi* food, and like it all, from the smell in the courtyard to the mustard oil over you.'

'I shall very much like it,' said Grish Chunder unguardedly. 'Once a Hindu – always a Hindu. But I like to know what the English think they know.'

'I'll tell you something that one Englishman knows. It's an old tale to you.'

I began to tell the story of Charlie in English, but Grish Chunder put a question in the vernacular, and the history went forward naturally in the tongue best suited for its telling. After all, it could never have been told in English. Grish Chunder heard me, nodding from time to time, and then came up to my rooms where I finished the tale.

'*Beshak*,' he said philosophically. '*Lekin darwaza band hai*. (Without doubt; but the door is shut.) I have heard of this remembering of previous existences among my people. It is of course an old tale with us, but, to happen to an Englishman – a cow-fed *Mlechh* – an outcaste. By Jove, that is *most* peculiar!'

'Outcaste yourself, Grish Chunder! You eat cow-beef every day. Let's think the thing over. The boy remembers his incarnations.'

'Does he know that?' said Grish Chunder quietly, swinging his legs as he sat on my table. He was speaking in his English now.

'He does not know anything. Would I speak to you if he did? Go on!'

'There is no going on at all. If you tell that to your friends they will say you are mad and put it in the papers. Suppose, now, you prosecute for libel.'

'Let's leave that out of the question entirely. Is there any chance of his being made to speak?'

'There is a chance. Oah, yess! But *if* he spoke it would mean that all this world would end now – *instanto* – fall down on your head. These things are not allowed, you know. As I said, the door is shut.'

'Not a ghost of a chance?'

'How can there be? You are a Christi-an, and it is forbidden to eat, in your books, of the Tree of Life, or else you would never die. How shall you all fear death if you all know what your friend does not know that he knows? I am afraid to be kicked, but I am not afraid to die, because I know what I know. You are not afraid to be kicked, but you are afraid to die. If you were not, by God! you English would be all over the shop in an hour, upsetting the balances of power, and making commotions. It would not be good. But no fear. He will remember a little and a little less, and he will call it dreams. Then he will forget altogether. When I passed my First Arts Examination in Calcutta that was all in the cram-book on Wordsworth. "Trailing clouds of glory," you know.'

'This seems to be an exception to the rule.'

'There are no exceptions to rules. Some are not so hard-looking as others, but they are all the same when you touch. If this friend of yours said so-and-so and so-and-so, indicating that he remembered all his lost lives, or one piece of a lost life, he would not be in the bank another hour. He would be what you call sacked because he was mad, and they would send him to an asylum for lunatics. You can see that, my friend.'

'Of course I can, but I wasn't thinking of him. His name need never appear in the story.'

'Ah! I see. That story will never be written. You can try.'

'I am going to.'

'For your own credit and for the sake of money, *of course*?'

'No. For the sake of writing the story. On my honour that will be all.'

'Even then there is no chance. You cannot play with the gods. It is a very pretty story now. As they say. Let it go on that – I mean at that. Be quick; he will not last long.'

'How do you mean?'

'What I say. He has never, so far, thought about a woman.'

'Hasn't he, though!' I remembered some of Charlie's confidences.

'I mean no woman has thought about him. When that comes; *bus* – *hogya* all up! I know. There are millions of women here. Housemaids, for instance. They kiss you behind doors.'

I winced at the thought of my story being ruined by a housemaid. And yet nothing was more probable.

Grish Chunder grinned.

'Yes – also pretty girls – cousins of his house, and perhaps *not* of his house. One kiss that he gives back again and remembers will cure all this nonsense, or else—'

'Or else what? Remember he does not know that he knows.'

'I know that. Or else, if nothing happens he will become immersed in the trade and the financial speculation like the rest. It must be so. You can see that it must be so. But the woman will come first, *I* think.'

There was a rap at the door, and Charlie charged in impetuously. He had been released from the office, and by the look in his eyes I could see that he had come over for a long talk; most probably with poems in his pockets. Charlie's poems were very wearying, but sometimes they led him to speak about the galley.

Grish Chunder looked at him keenly for a minute.

'I beg your pardon,' Charlie said uneasily; 'I didn't know you had any one with you.'

'I am going,' said Grish Chunder.

He drew me into the lobby as he departed.

'That is your man,' he said Quickly. 'I tell you he will never speak all you wish. That is rot – bosh. But he would be most good to make to see things. Suppose now we pretend that it was only play' – had never seen Grish Chunder so excited – 'and pour the ink-pool into his hand. Eh, what do you think? I tell you that he could see *anything* that a man could see. Let me get the ink and the camphor. He is a seer and he will tell us very many things.'

'He may be all you say, but I'm not going to trust him to your gods and devils.'

'It will not hurt him. He will only feel a little stupid and dull when he wakes up. You have seen boys look into the ink-pool before.'

'That is the reason why I am not going to see it any more. You'd better go, Grish Chunder.'

He went, insisting far down the staircase that it was throwing away my only chance of looking into the future.

This left me unmoved, for I was concerned for the past, and no peering of hypnotised boys into mirrors and ink-pools would help me to that. But I recognised Grish Chunder's point of view and sympathised with it.

'What a big black brute that was!' said Charlie, when I returned to him. 'Well, look here, I've just done a poem; did it instead of playing dominoes after lunch. May I read it?'

'Let me read it to myself.'

'Then you miss the proper expression. Besides, you always make my things sound as if the rhymes were all wrong.'

'Read it aloud, then. You're like the rest of 'em.'

Charlie mouthed me his poem, and it was not much worse than the average of his verses. He had been reading his books faithfully, but he was not pleased when I told him that I preferred my Longfellow undiluted with Charlie.

Then we began to go through the MS line by line, Charlie parrying every objection and correction with:

'Yes, that may be better, but you don't catch what I'm driving at.'

Charlie was, in one way at least, very like one kind of poet.

There was a pencil scrawl at the back of the paper, and 'What's that?' I said.

'Oh, that's not poetry at all. It's some rot I wrote last night before I went to bed, and it was too much bother to hunt for rhymes; so I made it a sort of blank verse instead.'

Here is Charlie's 'blank verse': –

'We pulled for you when the wind was against us and the sails were low.
     Will you never let us go?
We ate bread and onions when you took towns, or ran abroad

quickly when you were beaten back by the foe,

The captains walked up and down the deck in fair weather
singing songs, but we were below.

We fainted with our chins on the oars and you did not see that
we were idle, for we still swung to and fro.

Will you never let us go?

The salt made the oar-handles like shark-skin; our knees were
cut to the bone with salt cracks; our hair was stuck to our foreheads;
and our lips were cut to our gums, and you whipped us because we
could not row.

Will you never let us go?

But in a little time we shall run out of the portholes as the water
runs along the oar-blade, and though you tell the others to row
after us you will never catch us till you catch the oar-thresh and tie
up the winds in the belly of the sail. Aho!'

Will you never let us go?

'H'm. What's oar-thresh, Charlie?'

'The water washed up by the oars. That's the sort of song
they might sing in the galley y' know. Aren't you ever going to
finish that story and give me some of the profits?'

'It depends on yourself. If you had only told me more about
your hero in the first instance it might have been finished by
now. You're so hazy in your notions.'

'I only want to give you the general notion of it – the
knocking about from place to place and the fighting and all
that. Can't you fill in the rest yourself? Make the hero save a
girl on a pirate-galley and marry her or do something.'

'You're a really helpful collaborator. I suppose the hero
went through some few adventures before he married.'

'Well, then, make him a very artful card – a low sort of man
– a sort of political man who went about making treaties and
breaking them – a black-haired chap who hid behind the mast
when the fighting began.'

'But you said the other day that he was red-haired.'

'I couldn't have. Make him black-haired of course. You've
no imagination.'

Seeing that I had just discovered the entire principles upon which the half-memory falsely called imagination is based, I felt entitled to laugh, but forbore for the sake of the tale.

'You're right. *You're* the man with imagination. A black-haired chap in a decked ship,' I said.

'No, an open ship – like a big boat.'

This was maddening.

'Your ship has been built and designed, closed and decked in; you said so yourself,' I protested.

'No, no, not that ship. That was open or half-decked because – By Jove, you're right. You made me think of the hero as a red-haired chap. Of course if he were red, the ship would be an open one with painted sails.'

Surely, I thought, he would remember now that he had served in two galleys at least – in a three-decked Greek one under the black-haired 'political man,' and again in a Viking's open sea-serpent under the man 'red as a red bear' who went to Markland. The Devil prompted me to speak.

'Why "of course," Charlie?' said I.

'I don't know. Are you making fun of me?'

The current was broken for the time being. I took up a note-book and pretended to make rnany entries in it.

'It's a pleasure to work with an imaginative chap like your-self,' I said, after a pause. 'The way that you've brought out the character of the hero is simply wonderful.'

'Do you think so?' he answered, with a pleased flush. 'I often tell myself that there's more in me than my mo— than people think.'

'There's an enormous amount in you.'

'Then, won't you let me send an essay on The Ways of Bank-Clerks to *Tit-Bits*, and get the guinea prize?'

'That wasn't exactly what I meant, old fellow: perhaps it would be better to wait a little and go ahead with the galley-story.'

'Ah, but I shan't get the credit of that. *Tit-Bits* would publish my name and address if I win. What are you grinning at? They *would.*'

'I know it. Suppose you go for a walk. I want to look through my notes about our story.'

Now this reprehensible youth who left me, a little hurt and put aback, might for aught he or I knew have been one of the crew of the Argo – had been certain slave or comrade to Thorfin Karlsefne. Therefore he was deeply interested in guinea competitions. Remembering what Grish Chunder had said I laughed aloud. The Lords of Life and Death would never allow Charlie Mears to speak with full knowledge of his pasts, and I must even piece out what he had told me with ray own poor inventions while Charlie wrote of the ways of bank-clerks.

I got together and placed on one file all my notes; and the net result was not cheering. I read them a second time. There was nothing that might not have been compiled at second hand from other people's books – except, perhaps, the story of the fight in the harbour. The adventures of a Viking had been written many times before; the history of a Greek galley-slave was no new thing, and though I wrote both, who could challenge or confirm the accuracy of my details? I might as well tell a tale of two thousand years hence. The Lords of Life and Death were as cunning as Grish Chunder had hinted. They would allow nothing to escape that might trouble or make easy the minds of men. Though I was convinced of this, yet I could not leave the tale alone. Exaltation followed re-action not once, but twenty times in the next few weeks. My moods varied with the March sunlight and flying clouds. By night or in the beauty of a spring morning I perceived that I could write that tale and shift continents thereby. In the wet windy afternoons, I saw that the tale might indeed be written, but would be nothing more than a faked, false-varnished, sham-rusted piece of Wardour Street work in the end. Then I blessed Charlie in many ways -though it was no fault of his. He seemed to be busy with prize competitions, and I saw less and less of him as the weeks went by and the earth cracked and grew ripe to spring, and the buds swelled in their sheaths. He did not care to read or talk of what he had read, and there was a new ring of self-assertion in his voice. I hardly cared to remind him of the galley when we met; but Charlie alluded it on every occasion, always as a story from which money was to be made.

'I think I deserve twenty-five per cent, don't I, at least?' he said, with beautiful frankness. 'I supplied all the ideas, didn't I?'

This greediness for silver was a new side in his nature. I assumed that it had been developed in the City, where Charlie was picking up the curious nasal drawl of the underbred City man.

'When the thing's done we'll talk about it. I can't make anything of it at present. Red-haired or black-haired heroes are equally difficult.'

He was sitting by the fire staring at the red coals. '*I* can't understand what you find so difficult. It's all as clear as mud to me,' he replied. A jet of gas puffed out between the bars, took light, and whistled softly. 'Suppose we take the red-haired hero's adventures first, from the time that he came south to my galley and captured it and sailed to the Beaches.'

I knew better now than to interrupt Charlie. I was out of reach of pen and paper, and dared not move to get them lest I should break the current. The gas-jet puffed and whinnied, Charlie's voice dropped almost to a whisper, and he told a tale of the sailing of an open galley to Furdurstrandi, of sunsets on the open sea, seen under the curve of the one sail evening after evening when the galley's beak was notched into the centre of the sinking disc, and 'we sailed by that, for we had no other guide,' quoth Charlie. He spoke of a landing on an island and explorations in its woods, where the crew killed three men whom they found asleep under the pines. Their ghosts, Charlie said, followed the galley, swimming and choking in the water, and the crew cast lots and threw one of their number overboard as a sacrifice to the strange gods whom they had offended. Then they ate sea-weed when their provisions failed, and their legs swelled, and their leader, the red-haired man, killed two rowers who mutinied, and after a year spent among the woods they set sail for their own country, and a wind that never failed carried them back so safely that they all slept at night. This and much more Charlie told. Sometimes the voice fell so low that I could not catch the words, though every nerve was on the strain. He spoke of their leader, the red-haired man, as a pagan speaks of his God; for it was he who cheered them and slew them impartially as he thought best for their needs; and it was he who steered them for three days among floating ice, each floe crowded with strange beasts that 'tried to sail with us,' said Charlie, 'and we beat them back with the handles of the oars.'

The gas-jet went out, a burnt coal gave way, and the fire settled with a tiny crash to the bottom of the grate. Charlie ceased speaking, and I said no word.

'By Jove!' he said at last, shaking his head. 'I've been staring at the fire till I'm dizzy. What was I going to say?'

'Something about the galley book.'

'I remember now. It's twenty-five per cent of the profits, isn't it?'

'It's anything you like when I've done the tale.'

'I wanted to be sure of that. I must go now. I've – I've an appointment.' And he left me.

Had not my eyes been held I might have known that that broken muttering over the fire was the swan-song of Charlie Mears. But I thought it the prelude to fuller revelation. At last and at last I should cheat the Lords of Life and Death!

When next Charlie came to me I received him with rapture. He was nervous and embarrassed, but his eyes were very full of light, and his lips a little parted.

'I've done a poem,' he said; and then, quickly: 'It's the best I've ever done. Read it.' He thrust it into my hand and retreated to the window.

I groaned inwardly. It would be the work of half an hour to criticise – that is to say, praise – the poem sufficiently to please Charlie. Then I had good reason to groan, for Charlie, discarding his favourite centipede metres, had launched into shorter and choppier verse, and verse with a motive at the back of it. This is what I read: –

'The day is most fair, the cheery wind
　Halloos behind the hill,
Where he bends the wood as seemeth good.
　And the sapling to his will!

Riot, O wind; there is that in my blood
   That would not have thee still!

'She gave me herself, O Earth, O Sky;
   Gray sea, she is mine alone!
Let the sullen boulders hear my cry,
   And rejoice tho' they be but stone!

'Mine! I have won her, O good brown earth,
   Make merry! 'Tis hard on Spring;
Make merry; my love is doubly worth
   All worship your fields can bring!
Let the hind that tills you feel my mirth
   At the early harrowing!'

'Yes, it's the early harrowing, past a doubt,' I said, with a dread at my heart. Charlie smiled, but did not answer.

'Red cloud of the sunset, tell it abroad;
   I am victor. Greet me, O Sun,
Dominant master and absolute lord
   Over the soul of one!'

'Well?' said Charlie, looking over my shoulder.

I thought it far from well, and very evil indeed, when he silently laid a photograph on the paper – the photograph of a girl with a curly head and a foolish slack mouth.

'Isn't it – isn't it wonderful?' he whispered, pink to the tips of his ears, wrapped in the rosy mystery of first love. 'I didn't know; I didn't think – it came like a thunderclap.'

'Yes. It comes like a thunderclap. Are you very happy, Charlie?'

'My God – she – she loves me!' He sat down repeating the last words to himself. I looked at the hairless face, the narrow shoulders already bowed by desk-work, and wondered when, where, and how he had loved in his past lives.

'What will your mother say?' I asked cheerfully.

'I don't care a damn what she says!'

At twenty the things for which one does not care a damn

should, properly, be many, but one must not include mothers in the list. I told him this gently; and he described Her, even as Adam must have described to the newly-named beasts the glory and tenderness and beauty of Eve. Incidentally I learned that She was a tobacconist's assistant with a weakness for pretty dress, and had told him four or five times already that She had never been kissed by a man before.

Charlie spoke on and on, and on; while I, separated from him by thousands of years, was considering the beginnings of things. Now I understood why the Lords of Life and Death shut the doors so carefully behind us. It is that we may not remember our first and most beautiful wooings. Were this not so, our world would be without inhabitants in a hundred years.

'Now, about the galley-story,' I said still more cheerfully, in a pause in the rush of the speech.

Charlie looked up as though he had been hit. 'The galley – what galley? Good heavens, don't joke, man! This is serious! You don't know how serious it is!'

Grish Chunder was right. Charlie had tasted the love of woman that kills remembrance, and the finest story in the world would never be written.

THE CHILDREN OF THE ZODIAC

Though thou love her as thyself,
As a self of purer clay,
Though her parting dim the day,
Stealing grace from all alive,
   Heartily know
   When half Gods go
The Gods arrive.

Emerson

Thousands of years ago, when men were greater than they are
to-day, the Children of the Zodiac lived in the world. There
were six Children of the Zodiac – the Ram, the Bull, Leo,
the Twins, and the Girl; and they were afraid of the Six
Houses which belonged to the Scorpion, the Balance, the
Crab, the Fishes, the Archer, and the Waterman. Even when
they first stepped down upon the earth and knew that they
were immortal Gods, they carried this fear with them; and the
fear grew as they became better acquainted with mankind and
heard stories of the Six Houses. Men treated the Children as
Gods and came to them with prayers and long stories of
wrong, while the Children of the Zodiac listened and could
not understand.

A mother would fling herself before the feet of the Twins, or
the Bull, crying: 'My husband was at work in the fields and the
Archer shot him and he died; and my son will also be killed by
the Archer. Help me!' The Bull would lower his huge head
and answer: 'What is that to me?' Or the Twins would smile
and continue their play, for they could not understand why the
water ran out of people's eyes. At other times a man and a
woman would come to Leo or the Girl crying: 'We two are
newly married and we are very happy. Take these flowers.' As
they threw the flowers they would make mysterious sounds to

show that they were happy, and Leo and the Girl wondered even more than the Twins why people shouted 'Ha! ha! ha!' for no cause.

This continued for thousands of years by human reckoning, till on a day, Leo met the Girl walking across the hills and saw that she had changed entirely since he had last seen her. The Girl, looking at Leo, saw that he too had changed altogether. Then they decided that it would be well never to separate again, in case even more startling changes should occur when the one was not at hand to help the other. Leo kissed the Girl and all Earth felt that kiss, and the Girl sat down on a hill and the water ran out of her eyes; and this had never happened before in the memory of the Children of the Zodiac.

As they sat together a man and a woman came by, and the man said to the woman:

'What is the use of wasting flowers on those dull Gods? They will never understand, darling.'

The Girl jumped up and put her arms round the woman, crying, 'I understand. Give me the flowers and I will give you a kiss.'

Leo said beneath his breath to the man 'What was the new name that I heard you give to your woman just now?'

The man answered, 'Darling, of course.'

'Why "of course"?' said Leo; 'and if of course, what does it mean?'

'It means "very dear," and you have only to look at your wife to see why.'

'I see,' said Leo; 'you are quite right'; and when the man and the woman had gone on he called the Girl 'darling wife'; and the Girl wept again from sheer happiness.

'I think,' she said at last, wiping her eyes, 'I think that we two have neglected men and women too much. What did you do with the sacrifices they made to you, Leo?'

'I let them burn,' said Leo; 'I could not eat them. What did you do with the flowers?'

'I let them wither. I could not wear them, I had so many of my own,' said the Girl, 'and now I am sorry.'

'There is nothing to grieve for,' said Leo; 'we belong to each other.'

As they were talking the years of men's life slipped by unnoticed, and presently the man and the woman came back, both white-headed, the man carrying the woman.

'We have come to the end of things,' said the man quietly. 'This that was my wife—'

'As I am Leo's wife,' said the Girl quickly, her eyes staring.

'—was my wife, has been killed by one of your Houses.' The man set down his burden, and laughed.

'Which House?' said Leo angrily, for he hated all the Houses equally.

'You are Gods, you should know,' said the man. 'We have lived together and loved one another, and I have left a good farm for my son. What have I to complain of except that I still live?'

As he was bending over his wife's body there came a whistling through the air, and he started and tried to run away, crying, 'It is the arrow of the Archer. Let me live a little longer – only a little longer!' The arrow struck him and he died. Leo looked at the Girl and she looked at him, and both were puzzled.

'He wished to die,' said Leo. 'He said that he wished to die, and when Death came he tried to run away. He is a coward.'

'No, he is not,' said the Girl; 'I think I feel what he felt. Leo, we must learn more about this for their sakes.'

'For *their* sakes,' said Leo, very loudly.

'Because *we* are never going to die,' said the Girl and Leo together, still more loudly.

'Now sit you still here, darling wife,' said Leo, 'while I go to the Houses whom we hate, and learn how to make these men and women live as we do.'

'And love as we do,' said the Girl.

'I do not think they need to be taught that,' said Leo, and he strode away very angry, with his lion-skin swinging from his shoulder, till he came to the House where the Scorpion lives in the darkness, brandishing his tail over his back.

'Why do you trouble the children of men?' said Leo, with his heart between his teeth.

'Are you so sure that I trouble the children of men alone?' said the Scorpion. 'Speak to your brother the Bull, and see what he says.'

'I come on behalf of the children of men,' said Leo. 'I have learned to love as they do, and I wish them to live as I – as we do.'

'Your wish was granted long ago. Speak to the Bull. He is under my special care,' said the Scorpion.

Leo dropped back to the earth again, and saw the great star Aldebaran, that is set in the forehead of the Bull, blazing very near to the earth. When he came up to it he saw that his brother the Bull, yoked to a countryman's plough, was toiling through a wet rice-field with his head bent down, and the sweat streaming from his flanks. The countryman was urging him forward with a goad.

'Gore that insolent to death,' cried Leo, 'and for the sake of our honour come out of the mire.'

'I cannot,' said the Bull, 'the Scorpion has told me that some day, of which I cannot be sure, he will sting me where my neck is set on my shoulders, and that I shall die bellowing.'

'What has that to do with this disgraceful work?' said Leo, standing on the dyke that bounded the wet field.

'Everything. This man could not plough without my help. He thinks that I am a stray beast.'

'But he is a mud-crusted cottar with matted hair,' insisted Leo. 'We are not meant for his use.'

'You may not be; I am. I cannot tell when the Scorpion may choose to sting me to death – perhaps before I have turned this furrow.' The Bull flung his bulk into the yoke, and the plough tore through the wet ground behind him, and the countryman goaded him till his flanks were red.

'Do you like this?' Leo called down the dripping furrows.

'No,' said the Bull over his shoulder as he lifted his hind legs from the clinging mud and cleared his nostrils.

Leo left him scornfully and passed to another country, where he found his brother the Ram in the centre of a crowd of country people who were hanging wreaths round his neck and feeding him on freshly-plucked green corn.

'This is terrible,' said Leo. 'Break up that crowd and come away, my brother. Their hands are spoiling your fleece.'

'I cannot,' said the Ram. 'The Archer told me that on some day of which I had no knowledge, he would send a dart through me, and that I should die in very great pain.'

'What has that to do with this disgraceful show?' said Leo, but he did not speak as confidently as before.

'Everything in the world,' said the Ram. 'These people never saw a perfect sheep before. They think that I am a stray, and they will carry me from place to place as a model to all their flocks.'

'But they are greasy shepherds; we are not intended to amuse them,' said Leo.

'You may not be, I am,' said the Ram. 'I cannot tell when the Archer may choose to send his arrow at me – perhaps before the people a mile down the road have seen me.' The Ram lowered his head that a yokel newly arrived might throw a wreath of wild garlic-leaves over it, and waited patiently while the farmers tugged his fleece.

'Do you like this?' cried Leo over the shoulders of the crowd.

'No,' said the Ram, as the dust of the trampling feet made him sneeze, and he snuffed at the fodder piled before him.

Leo turned back intending to retrace his steps to the Houses, but as he was passing down a street he saw two small children, very dusty, rolling outside a cottage door, and playing with a cat. They were the Twins.

'What are you doing here?' said Leo, indignant.

'Playing,' said the Twins calmly.

'Cannot you play on the banks of the Milky Way?' said Leo.

'We did,' said they, 'till the Fishes swam down and told us that some day they would come for us and not hurt us at all and carry us away. So now we are playing at being babies down here. The people like it.'

'Do you like it?' said Leo.

'No,' said the Twins, 'but there are no cats in the Milky

Way,' and they pulled the cat's tail thoughtfully. A woman came out of the doorway and stood behind them, and Leo saw in her face a look that he had sometimes seen in the Girl's.

'She thinks that we are foundlings,' said the Twins, and they trotted indoors to the evening meal.

Then Leo hurried as swiftly as possible to all the Houses one after another; for he could not understand the new trouble that had come to his brethren. He spoke to the Archer, and the Archer assured him that so far as that House was concerned Leo had nothing to fear. The Waterman, the Fishes, and the Scorpion gave the same answer. They knew nothing of Leo, and cared less. They were the Houses, and they were busied in killing men.

At last he came to that very dark House where Cancer the Crab lies so still that you might think he was asleep if you did not see the ceaseless play and winnowing motion of the feathery branches round his mouth. That movement never ceases. It is like the eating of a smothered fire into rotten timber in that it is noiseless and without haste.

Leo stood in front of the Crab, and the half darkness allowed him a glimpse of that vast blue-black back and the motionless eyes. Now and again he thought that he heard some one sobbing, but the noise was very faint.

'Why do you trouble the children of men?' said Leo. There was no answer, and against his will Leo cried, 'Why do you trouble us? What have we done that you should trouble us?'

This time Cancer replied, 'What do I know or care? You were born into my House, and at the appointed time I shall come for you.'

'When is the appointed time?' said Leo, stepping back from the restless movement of the mouth.

'When the full moon fails to call the full tide,' said the Crab, 'I shall come for the one. When the other has taken the earth by the shoulders, I shall take that other by the throat.'

Leo lifted his hand to the apple of his throat, moistened his lips, and recovering himself, said:

'Must I be afraid for two, then?'

'For two,' said the Crab, 'and as many more as may come after.'

'My brother, the Bull, had a better fate,' said Leo, sullenly; 'he is alone.'

A hand covered his mouth before he could finish the sentence, and he found the Girl in his arms. Womanlike, she had not stayed where Leo had left her, but had hastened off at once to know the worst, and passing all the other Houses, had come straight to Cancer.

'That is foolish,' said the Girl, whispering. 'I have been waiting in the dark for long and long before you came. *Then* I was afraid. But now—' She put her head down on his shoulder and sighed a sigh of contentment.

'I am afraid now,' said Leo.

'That is on my account,' said the Girl, 'I know it is, because I am afraid for your sake. Let us go, husband.'

They went out of the darkness together and came back to, the Earth, Leo very silent, and the Girl striving to cheer him. 'My brother's fate is the better one,' Leo would repeat from time to time, and at last he said: 'Let us each go our own way and live alone till we die. We were born into the House of Cancer, and he will come for us.'

'I know; I know. But where shall I go? And where will you sleep in the evening? But let us try. I will stay here. Do you go on?'

Leo took six steps forward very slowly, and three long steps backward very quickly, and the third step set him again at the Girl's side. This time it was she who was begging him to go away and leave her, and he was forced to comfort her all through the night. That night decided them both never to leave each other for an instant, and when they had come to this decision they looked back at the darkness of the House of Cancer high above their heads, and with their arms round each other's necks laughed, 'Ha! ha! ha!' exactly as the children of men laughed. And that was the first time in their lives that they had ever laughed.

Next morning they returned to their proper home, and saw

the flowers and the sacrifices that had been laid before their doors by the villagers of the hills. Leo stamped down the fire with his heel, and the Girl flung the flower-wreaths out of sight, shuddering as she did so. When the villagers returned, as of custom, to see what had become of their offerings, they found neither roses nor burned flesh on the altars, but only a man and a woman, with frightened white faces, sitting hand in hand on the altar-steps.

'Are you not Virgo?' said a woman to the Girl. 'I sent you flowers yesterday.'

'Little sister,' said the Girl, flushing to her forehead, 'do not send any more flowers, for I am only a woman like yourself.' The man and the woman went away doubtfully.

'Now, what shall we do?' said Leo.

'We must try to be cheerful, I think,' said the Girl. 'We know the very worst that can happen to us, but we do not know the best that love can bring us. We have a great deal to be glad of.'

'The certainty of death,' said Leo.

'All the children of men have that certainty also; yet they laughed long before we ever knew how to laugh. We must learn to laugh, Leo. We have laughed once already.'

People who consider themselves Gods, as the Children of the Zodiac did, find it hard to laugh, because the Immortals know nothing worth laughter or tears. Leo rose up with a very heavy heart, and he and the Girl together went to and fro among men; their new fear of death behind them. First they laughed at a naked baby attempting to thrust its fat toes into its foolish pink mouth; next they laughed at a kitten chasing her own tail; and then they laughed at a boy trying to steal a kiss from a girl, and getting his ears boxed. Lastly, they laughed because the wind blew in their faces as they ran down a hill-side together, and broke panting and breathless into a knot of villagers at the bottom. The villagers laughed too at their flying clothes and wind-reddened faces; and in the evening gave them food and invited them to a dance on the grass, where everybody laughed through the mere joy of being able to dance.

That night Leo jumped up from the Girl's side crying: 'Every one of those people we met just now will die—'

'So shall we,' said the Girl sleepily. 'Lie down again, dear.' Leo could not see that her face was wet with tears.

But Leo was up and far across the fields, driven forward by the fear of death for himself and for the Girl, who was dearer to him than himself. Presently he came across the Bull drowsing in the moonlight after a hard day's work, and looking through half-shut eyes at the beautiful straight furrows that he had made.

'Ho!' said the Bull, 'so you have been told these things too. Which of the Houses holds your death?'

Leo pointed upwards to the dark House of the Crab and groaned: 'And he will come for the Girl too,' he said.

'Well,' said the Bull, 'what will you do?'

Leo sat down on the dyke and said that he did not know.

'You cannot pull a plough,' said the Bull, with a little touch of contempt. 'I can, and that prevents me from thinking of the Scorpion.'

Leo was angry and said nothing till the dawn broke, and the cultivator came to yoke the Bull to his work.

'Sing,' said the Bull, as the stiff muddy ox-bow creaked and strained. 'My shoulder is galled. Sing one of the songs that we sang when we thought we were all Gods together.'

Leo stepped back into the cane-brake and lifted up his voice in a song of the Children of the Zodiac – the war-whoop of the young Gods who are afraid of nothing. At first he dragged the song along unwillingly, and then the song dragged him, and his voice rolled across the fields, and the Bull stepped to the tune, and the cultivator banged his flanks out of sheer light-heartedness, and the furrows rolled away behind the plough more and more swiftly. Then the Girl came across the fields looking for Leo and found him singing in the cane. She joined her voice to his, and the cultivator's wife brought her spinning into the open and listened with all her children round her. When it was time for the nooning, Leo and the Girl had sung themselves both thirsty and hungry, but the cultivator and his wife gave them rye-bread and milk, and many thanks, and the

Bull found occasion to say: 'You have helped me to do a full half-field more than I should have done. But the hardest part of the day is to come, brother.'

Leo wished to lie down and brood over the words of the Crab. The Girl went away to talk to the cultivator's wife and baby, and the afternoon ploughing began.

'Help us now,' said the Bull. 'The tides of the day are running down. My legs are very stiff. Sing if you never sang before.'

'To a mud-spattered villager?' said Leo.

'He is under the same doom as ourselves. Are you a coward?' said the Bull. Leo flushed and began again with a sore throat and a bad temper. Little by little he dropped away from the songs of the Children and made up a song as he went along; and this was a thing he could never have done had he not met the Crab face to face. He remembered facts concerning cultivators, and bullocks, and rice-fields, that he had not particularly noticed before the interview, and he strung them all together, growing more interested as he sang, and he told the cultivator much more about himself and his work than the cultivator knew. The Bull grunted approval as he toiled down the furrows for the last time that day, and the song ended, leaving the cultivator with a very good opinion of himself in his aching bones. The Girl came out of the hut where she had been keeping the children quiet, and talking woman-talk to the wife, and they all ate the evening meal together.

'Now yours must be a very pleasant life,' said the cultivator, 'sitting as you do on a dyke all day and singing just what comes into your head. Have you been at it long, you two – gipsies?'

'Ah!' lowed the Bull from his byre. 'That's all the thanks you will ever get from men, brother.'

'No. We have only just begun it,' said the Girl; 'but we are going to keep to it as long as we live. Are we not, Leo?'

'Yes,' said he, and they went away hand-in-hand.

'You can sing beautifully, Leo,' said she, as a wife will to her husband.

'What were you doing?' said he.

'I was talking to the mother and the babies,' she said. 'You would not understand the little things that make us women laugh.'

'And – and I am to go on with this – this gipsy-work?' said Leo.

'Yes, dear, and I will help you.'

There is no written record of the life of Leo and of the Girl, so we cannot tell how Leo took to his new employment which he detested. We are only sure that the Girl loved him when and wherever he sang; even when, after the song was done, she went round with the equivalent of a tambourine, and collected the pence for the daily bread. There were times too when it was Leo's very hard task to console the Girl for the indignity of horrible praise that people gave him and her – for the silly wagging peacock feathers that they stuck in his cap, and the buttons and pieces of cloth that they sewed on his coat. Woman-like, she could advise and help to the end, but the meanness of the means revolted.

'What does it matter,' Leo would say, 'so long as the songs make them a little happier?' And they would go down the road and begin again on the old old refrain: that whatever came or did not come the children of men must not be afraid. It was heavy teaching at first, but in process of years Leo discovered that he could make men laugh and hold them listening to him even when the rain fell. Yet there were people who would sit down and cry softly, though the crowd was yelling with delight, and there were people who maintained that Leo made them do this; and the Girl would talk to them in the pauses of the performance and do her best to comfort them. People would die too, while Leo was talking, and singing, and laughing, for the Archer, and the Scorpion, and the Crab, and the other Houses were as busy as ever. Sometimes the crowd broke, and were frightened, and Leo strove to keep them steady by telling them that this was cowardly; and sometimes they mocked at the Houses that were killing them, and Leo explained that this was even more cowardly than running away.

In their wanderings they came across the Bull, or the Ram,

or the Twins, but all were too busy to do more than nod to each other across the crowd, and go on with their work. As the years rolled on even that recognition ceased, for the Children of the Zodiac had forgotten that they had ever been Gods working for the sake of men. The Star Aldebaran was crusted with caked dirt on the Bull's forehead, the Ram's fleece was dusty and torn, and the Twins were only babies fighting over the cat on the doorstep. It was then that Leo said: 'Let us stop singing and making jokes.' And it was then that the Girl said 'No—' but she did not know why she said 'No' so energetically. Leo maintained that it was perversity, till she herself, at the end of a dusty day, made the same suggestion to him, and he said 'most certainly not,' and they quarrelled miserably between the hedgerows, forgetting the meaning of the stars above them. Other singers and other talkers sprang up in the course of the years, and Leo, forgetting that there could never be too many of these, hated them for dividing the applause of the children of men, which he thought should be all his own. The Girl would grow angry too, and then the songs would be broken, and the jests fall flat for weeks to come, and the children of men would shout: 'Go home, you two gipsies. Go home and learn something worth singing!'

After one of these sorrowful shameful days, the Girl, walking by Leo's side through the fields, saw the full moon coming up over the trees, and she clutched Leo's arm, crying: 'The time has come now. Oh, Leo, forgive me!'

'What is it?' said Leo. He was thinking of the other singers.

'My husband!' she answered, and she laid his hand upon her breast, and the breast that he knew so well was hard as stone. Leo groaned, remembering what the Crab had said.

'Surely we were Gods once,' he cried.

'Surely we are Gods still,' said the Girl. 'Do you not remember when you and I went to the House of the Crab and – were not very much afraid? And since then . . . we have forgotten what we were singing for – we sang for the pence, and, oh, we fought for them! – We, who are the Children of the Zodiac.'

'It was my fault,' said Leo.

'How can there be any fault of yours that is not mine too?' said the Girl. 'My time has come, but you will live longer, and . . .' The look in her eyes said all she could not say.

'Yes, I will remember that we are Gods,' said Leo.

It is very hard, even for a Child of the Zodiac, who has forgotten his Godhead, to see his wife dying slowly and to know that he cannot help her. The Girl told Leo in those last months of all that she had said and done among the wives and the babies at the back of the roadside performances, and Leo was astonished that he knew so little of her who had been so much to him. When she was dying she told him never to fight for pence or quarrel with the other singers; and, above all, to go on with his singing immediately after she was dead.

Then she died, and after he had buried her he went down the road to a village that he knew, and the people hoped that he would begin quarrelling with a new singer that had sprung up while he had been away. But Leo called him 'my brother.' The new singer was newly married – and Leo knew it – and when he had finished singing, Leo straightened himself and sang the 'Song of the Girl,' which he had made coming down the road. Every man who was married or hoped to be married, whatever his rank or colour, understood that song – even the bride leaning on the new husband's arm understood it too – and presently when the song ended, and Leo's heart was bursting in him, the men sobbed. 'That was a sad tale,' they said at last, 'now make us laugh.' Because Leo had known all the sorrow that a man could know, including the full knowledge of his own fall who had once been a God – he, changing his song quickly, made the people laugh till they could laugh no more. They went away feeling ready for any trouble in reason, and they gave Leo more peacock feathers and pence than he could count. Knowing that pence led to quarrels and that peacock feathers were hateful to the Girl, he put them aside and went away to look for his brothers, to remind them that they too were Gods.

He found the Bull goring the undergrowth in a ditch, for the Scorpion had stung him, and he was dying, not slowly, as the Girl had died, but quickly.

'I know all,' the Bull groaned, as Leo came up. 'I had forgotten too, but I remember now. Go and look at the fields I ploughed. The furrows are straight. I forgot that I was a God, but I drew the plough perfectly straight, for all that. And you, brother?'

'I am not at the end of the ploughing,' said Leo. 'Does Death hurt?'

'No, but dying does,' said the Bull, and he died. The cultivator who then owned him was much annoyed, for there was a field still unploughed.

It was after this that Leo made the Song of the Bull who had been a God and forgotten the fact, and he sang it in such a manner that half the young men in the world conceived that they too might be Gods without knowing it. A half of that half grew impossibly conceited, and died early. A half of the remainder strove to be Gods and failed, but the other half accomplished four times more work than they would have done under any other delusion.

Later, years later, always wandering up and down and making the children of men laugh, he found the Twins sitting on the bank of a stream waiting for the Fishes to come and carry them away. They were not in the least afraid, and they told Leo that the woman of the House had a real baby of her own, and that when that baby grew old enough to be mischievous he would find a well-educated cat waiting to have its tail pulled. Then the Fishes came for them, but all that the people saw was two children drowned in a brook; and though their foster-mother was very sorry, she hugged her own real baby to her breast and was grateful that it was only the foundlings.

Then Leo made the Song of the Twins, who had forgotten that they were Gods and had played in the dust to amuse a foster-mother. That song was sung far and wide among the women. It caused them to laugh and cry and hug their babies closer to their hearts all in one breath; and some of the women who remembered the Girl said 'Surely that is the voice of Virgo. Only she could know so much about ourselves.'

After those three songs were made, Leo sang them over and

over again till he was in danger of looking upon them as so many mere words, and the people who listened grew tired, and there came back to Leo the old temptation to stop singing once and for all. But he remembered the Girl's dying words and persisted.

One of his listeners interrupted him as he was singing. 'Leo,' said he, 'I have heard you telling us not to be afraid for the past forty years. Can you not sing something new now?'

'No,' said Leo, 'it is the only song that I am allowed to sing. You must not be afraid of the Houses, even when they kill you.' The man turned to go, wearily, but there came a whistling through the air, and the arrow of the Archer was seen skimming low above the earth, pointing to the man's heart. He drew himself up, and stood still waiting till the arrow struck home.

'I die,' he said quietly. 'It is well for me, Leo, that you sang for forty years.'

'Are you afraid?' said Leo, bending over him.

'I am a man, not a God,' said the man. 'I should have run away but for your songs. My work is done, and I die without making a show of my fear.'

'I am very well paid,' said Leo to himself. 'Now that I see what my songs are doing, I will sing better ones.'

He went down the road, collected his little knot of listeners, and began the Song of the Girl. In the middle of his singing he felt the cold touch of the Crab's claw on the apple of his throat. He lifted his hand, choked, and stopped for an instant.

'Sing on, Leo,' said the crowd. 'The old song runs as well as ever it did.'

Leo went on steadily till the end with the cold fear at his heart. When his song was ended, he felt the grip on his throat tighten. He was old, he had lost the Girl, he knew that he was losing more than half his power to sing, he could scarcely walk to the diminishing crowds that waited for him, and could not see their faces when they stood about him. None the less, he cried angrily to the Crab:

'Why have you come for me *now*?'

'You were born under my care. How can I help coming for

you?' said the Crab wearily. Every human being whom the Crab killed had asked that same question.

'But I was just beginning to know what my songs were doing,' said Leo.

'Perhaps that is why,' said the Crab, and the grip tightened.

'You said you would not come till I had taken the world by the shoulders,' gasped Leo, falling back.

'I always keep my word. You have done that three times with three songs. What more do you desire?'

'Let me live to see the world know it,' pleaded Leo. 'Let me be sure that my songs—'

'Make men brave?' said the Crab. 'Even then there would be one man who was afraid. The Girl was braver than you are. Come.'

Leo was standing close to the restless, insatiable mouth.

'I forgot,' said he simply. 'The Girl was braver. But I am a God too, and I am not afraid.'

'What is that to me?' said the Crab.

Then Leo's speech was taken from him and he lay still and dumb, watching Death till he died.

Leo was the last of the Children of the Zodiac. After his death there sprang up a breed of little mean men, whimpering and flinching and howling because the Houses killed them and theirs, who wished to live for ever without any pain. They did not increase their lives, but they increased their own torments miserably, and there were no Children of the Zodiac to guide them; and the greater part of Leo's songs were lost.

Only he had carved on the Girl's tombstone the last verse of the Song of the Girl, which stands at the head of this story.

One of the children of men, coming thousands of years later, rubbed away the lichen, read the lines, and applied them to a trouble other than the one Leo meant. Being a man, men believed that he had made the verses himself; but they belong to Leo, the Child of the Zodiac, and teach, as he taught, that whatever comes or does not come we men must not be afraid.

THE LOST LEGION

When the Indian Mutiny broke out, and a little time before the siege of Delhi, a regiment of Native Irregular Horse was stationed at Peshawur on the frontier of India. That regiment caught what John Lawrence called at the time 'the prevalent mania' and would have thrown in its lot with the mutineers, had it been allowed to do so. The chance never came, for, as the regiment swept off down south, it was headed off by a remnant of an English corps into the hills of Afghanistan, and there the tribesmen, newly conquered by the English, turned against it as wolves turn against buck. It was hunted for the sake of its arms and accoutrements from hill to hill, from ravine to ravine, up and down the dried beds of rivers and round the shoulders of bluffs, till it disappeared as water sinks in the sand – this officerless, rebel regiment. The only trace left of its existence today is a nominal roll drawn up in neat round-hand and countersigned by an officer who called himself 'Adjutant, late – Irregular Cavalry.' The paper is yellow with years and dirt, but on the back of it you can still read a pencil note by John Lawrence, to this effect: 'See that the two native officers who remained loyal are not deprived of their estates. – J. L.' Of six hundred and fifty sabres only two stood the strain, and John Lawrence in the midst of all the agony of the first months of the Mutiny found time to think about their merits.

That was more than thirty years ago, and the tribesmen across the Afghan border who helped to annihilate the regiment are now old men. Sometimes a greybeard speaks of his share in the massacre. 'They came,' he will say, 'across the Border, very proud, calling upon us to rise and kill the English, and go down to the sack of Delhi. But we who had just been conquered by the same English knew that they were over-bold, and that the Government could account easily for those down-country dogs. This Hindustani regiment, therefore, we treated with fair words, and kept standing in one place till the redcoats came after them very hot and angry. Then this regiment ran forward a little more into our hills to avoid the wrath of the English, and we lay upon their flanks watching from the sides of the hills till we were well assured that their path was lost behind them. Then we came down, for we desired their clothes, and their bridles, and their rifles, and their boots – more expecially their boots. That was a great killing – done slowly.' Here the old man will rub his nose, and shake his snaky locks, and lick his bearded lips, grinning till the yellow tooth-slumps show. 'Yea, we killed them because we needed their gear, and we knew that their lives had been forfeited to God on account of their sin – the sin of treachery to the salt which they had eaten. They rode up and down the valleys, stumbling and rocking in their saddles, and howling for mercy. We drove them slowly like cattle till they were all assembled in one place, the flat, wide valley of Sheor Kôt. Many had died from want of water, but there still were many left, and they could not make any stand. We went among them pulling them down with our hands two at a time, and our boys killed them who were new to the sword. My share of the plunder was such and such – so many guns, and so many saddles. The guns were good in those days. Now we steal the Government rifles, and despise smooth barrels. Yes, beyond doubt we wiped that regiment from off the face of the earth, and even the memory of the deed is now dying. But men say—'

At this point the tale would stop abruptly, and it was impossible to find out what men said across the Border. The Afghans were always a secretive race, and vastly preferred doing something wicked to saying anything at all. They would for months be quiet and well-behaved, till one night, without word or warning, they would rush a police-post, cut the throats of a constable or two, dash through a village, carry away three or four women, and withdraw, in the red glare of burning thatch, driving the cattle and goats before them to their desolate hills. The Indian Government would become almost tearful on these occasions. First it would say, 'Please be good, and we'll forgive you.' The tribe concerned in the latest depredation would collectively put its thumb to its nose and answer rudely. Then the Government would say: 'Hadn't you better pay up a little money for those few corpses you left behind you the other night?' Here the tribe would temporise, and lie and bully, and some of the younger men, merely to show contempt of authority, would raid another police-post and fire into some frontier mud fort, and, if lucky, kill a real English officer. Then the Government would say: – 'Observe; if you persist in this line of conduct, you will be hurt.' If the tribe knew exactly what was going on in India, it would apologise or be rude, according as it learned whether the Government was busy with other things or able to devote its full attention to their performances. Some of the tribes knew to one corpse how far to go. Others became excited, lost their heads, and told the Government to 'come on.' With sorrow and tears, and one eye on the British taxpayer at home, who insisted on regarding these exercises as brutal wars of annexation, the Government would prepare an expensive little field-brigade and some guns, and send all up into the hills to chase the wicked tribe out of the valleys, where the corn grew into the hill-tops, where there was nothing to eat. The tribe would turn out in full strength and enjoy the campaign, for they knew that their women would never be touched, that their wounded would be nursed, not mutilated, and that as soon as each man's bag of corn was spent they could surrender and palaver with the English General as though they had been a real enemy. Afterwards, years afterwards, they would pay the blood-money, driblet by driblet, to the Government, and tell their children how they had slain the redcoats by thousands. The only drawback to this kind of picnic-war was the weakness of the redcoats for solemnly blowing up with powder the Afghan fotified towers and keeps. This the tribes always considered mean.

Chief among the leaders of the smaller tribes – the mean

little clans who knew to one penny the expense of moving white troops against them – was a priestly bandit-chief whom we will call the Gulla Kutta Mullah. His enthusiasm for Border murder as an art was almost dignified. He would cut down a mail-runner in pure wantonness, or bombard a mud fort with rifle fire when he knew that our men needed sleep. In his leisure moments he would go on circuit among his neighbours, and try to incite other tribes to devilry. Also, he kept a kind of hotel for fellow-outlaws in his village, which lay in a valley called Bersund. Any respectable murderer of that section of the frontier was sure to lie up at Bersund for it was reckoned an exceedingly safe place. The sole entry to it ran through a narrow gorge which could be converted into a death-trap in five minutes. It was surrounded by high hills, reckoned inaccessible to all save born mountaineers, and here the Gulla Kutta Mullah lived in great state, the head of a colony of mud and stone huts, and in each mud hut hung some portion of a red uniform and the plunder of dead men. The Government particularly wished for his capture, and once invited him formally to come out and be hanged on account of seventeen murders in which he had taken a direct part. He replied:–

'I am only twenty miles, as the crow flies, from your border. Come and fetch me.'

'Some day we will come,' said the Government, 'and hanged will you be.'

The Gulla Kutta Mullah let the matter from his mind. He knew that the patience of the Government was as long as a summer day; but he did not realise that its arm was as long as a winter night.

Months afterwards, when there was peace on the Border, and all India was quiet, the Indian Government turned in its sleep and remembered the Gulla Kutta Mullah at Bersund, with his thirteen outlaws. The movement against him of one single regiment – which the telegrams would have translated as brutal war – would have been highly impolitic. This was a time for silence and speed, and above all, absence of bloodshed.

You must know that all along the north-west frontier of

India is spread a force of some thirty thousand foot and horse, whose duty it is to quietly and unostentatiously shepherd the tribes in front of them. They move up and down, and down and up, from one desolate little post to another; they are ready to take the field at ten minutes' notice; they are always half in and half out of a difficulty somewhere along the monotonous line; their lives are as hard as their own muscles, and the papers never say anything about them. It was from this force that the Government picked its men.

One night at a station where the mounted night patrol fire as they challenge, and the wheat rolls in great blue-green waves under our cold northern moon, the officers were playing billiards in the mud-walled clubhouse, when orders came to them that they were to go on parade at once for a night drill. They grumbled, and went to turn out their men – a hundred English troops, let us say, two hundred Goorkhas, and about a hundred of the finest native cavalry in the world.

When they were on the parade ground, it was explained to them in whispers that they must set off at once across the hills to Bersund. The English troops were to post themselves round the hills at the side of the valley; the Goorkhas would command the gorge and the death-trap, and the cavalry would fetch a long march round and get to the back of the circle of hills, whence, if there were any difficulty, they could charge down on the Mullah's men. But the orders were very strict that there should be no fighting and no noise. They were to return in the morning with every round of ammunition intact, and the Mullah and the thirteen outlaws bound in their midst. If they were successful, no one would know or care anything about their work; but failure meant probably a small border war, in which the Gulla Kutta Mullah would be posed in the English newspapers as a popular leader against a big, bullying Power, instead of a common Border murderer.

Then there was silence, broken only by the clicking of the compass needles and snapping of watch-cases, as the heads of columns compared bearings and made appointments for the rendezvous. Five minutes later the parade-ground was empty; the green coats of the Goorkhas and the overcoats of the

English troops had faded into the darkness, and the cavalry were cantering away in the face of a blinding drizzle.

What the Goorkhas and the English did will be seen later on. The heavy work lay with the horse, for it had to go far and pick its way clear of habitations. Many of the troopers were natives of that part of the world, ready and anxious to fight against their kin, and some of the officers had made private and unofficial excursions into those hills before. They crossed the Border, found a dried river-bed, cantered up that, walked through a stony gorge, risked crossing a low hill under cover of the darkness, skirted another hill, leaving their hoof-marks deep in some ploughed ground, felt their way along another watercourse, ran over the neck of a spur praying that no one would hear their horses grunting, and so worked on in the rain and the darkness, till they had left Bersund and its crater of hills a little behind them, and to the left, and it was time to swing round. The ascent commanding the back of Bersund was steep, and they halted to draw breath in a broad level valley below the height. That is to say, the men reined up, but the horses blown as they were, refused to halt. There was unchristian language, the worse for being delivered in a whisper, and you heard the saddles squeaking in the darkness as the horses plunged.

The subaltern at the rear of one troop turned in his saddle and said very softly:

'Carter, what the Blessed Heavens are you doing at the rear? Bring your men up, man.'

There was no answer, till a trooper replied:

'Carter Sahib is forward – not there. There is nothing behind us.'

'There is,' said the subaltern. 'The squadron's walking on its own tail.'

Then the Major in command moved down to the rear, swearing softly and asking for the blood of Lieutenant Halley – the subaltern who had just spoken.

'Look after your rearguard,' said the Major. 'Some of your infernal thieves have got lost. They're at the head of the squadron, and you're a several kinds of idiot.'

'Shall I tell off my men, sir?' said the subaltern sulkily, for he was feeling wet and cold.

'Tell 'em off!' said the Major. '*Whip* 'em off, by Gad! You're squandering them all over the place. There's a troop behind you *now*!'

'So I was thinking,' said the subaltern calmly. 'I have all my men here, sir. Better speak to Carter.'

'Carter Sahib sends salaam and wants to know why the squadron is stopping,' said a trooper to Lieutenant Halley.

'Where under heaven *is* Carter?' said the Major.

'Forward, with his troop,' was the answer.

'Are we walking in a ring, then, or are we the centre of a blessed brigade?' said the Major.

By this time there was silence all along the column. The horses were still; but, through the drive of the fine rain, men could hear the feet of many horses moving over stony ground.

'We're being stalked,' said Lieutenant Halley.

'They've no horses here. Besides they'd have fired before this,' said the Major. 'It's – it's villagers' ponies.'

'Then our horses would have neighed and spoilt the attack long ago. They must have been near us for half an hour,' said the subaltern.

'Queer that we can't smell the horses,' said the Major, damping his finger and rubbing it on his nose as he sniffed up-wind.

'Well, it's a bad start,' said the subaltern, shaking the wet from his overcoat. 'What shall we do, sir?'

'Get on,' said the Major; 'we shall catch it to-night.'

The column moved forward very gingerly for a few paces. Then there was an oath, a shower of blue sparks as shod hoofs crashed on small stones, and a man rolled over with a jangle of accoutrements that would have waked the dead.

'Now we've gone and done it,' said Lieutenant Halley. 'All the hillside awake, and all the hillside to climb in the face of musketry fire. This comes of trying to do night-hawk work.'

The trembling trooper picked himself up and tried to explain that his horse had fallen over one of the little cairns that are built of loose stones on the spot where a man has been murdered. There was no need to go on. The Major's big Australian charger blundered next, and the men came to a halt in what seemed to be a very graveyard of little cairns all about two feet high. The manoeuvres of the squadron are not reported. Men said that it felt like mounted quadrilles without the training and without the music; but at last the horses, breaking rank and choosing their own way, walked clear of the cairns, till every man of the squadron re-formed and drew rein a few yards up the slope of the hill. Then, according to Lieutenant Halley, there began another scene very like the one which has been described. The Major and Carter insisted that all the men had not joined ranks, and that there were more of them in the rear clicking and blundering among the dead men's cairns. Lieutenant Halley told off his own troopers for the second or third time, and resigned himself to wait. Later on he said to me:–

'I didn't much know, and I didn't much care, what was going on. The row of that trooper falling ought to have scared half the country, and I would take my oath that we were being stalked by a full regiment in the rear, and *they* were making row enough to rouse all Afghanistan. I sat tight, but nothing happened.'

The mysterious part of the night's work was the silence on the hillside. Everybody knew that the Gulla Kutta Mullah had his outpost huts on the reverse side of the hill, and everybody expected, by the time that the Major had sworn himself into a state of quiet, that the watchmen there would open fire. When nothing occurred, they thought that the gusts of the rain had deadened the sound of the horses, and thanked Providence. At last the Major satisfied himself (*a*) that he had left no one behind among the cairns, and (*b*) that he was not being taken in the rear by a large and powerful body of cavalry. The men's tempers were thoroughly spoiled, the horses were lathered and unquiet and one and all prayed for the daylight.

They set themselves to climb up the hill, each man leading his mount carefully. Before they had covered the lower slopes or the breast-plates had begun to tighten, a thunderstorm came up behind, rolling across the low hills and drowning any noise less than that of cannon. The first flash of the lightning showed the bare ribs of the ascent, the hill-crest standing steely blue against the black sky, the little falling lines of the rain, and, a few yards of their left flank, an Afghan watchtower, two-storied, built of stone, and entered by a ladder from the upper story. The ladder was up, and a man with a rifle was leaning from the window. The darkness and the thunder rolled down in an instant, and, when the lull followed, a voice from the watchtower cried, 'Who goes there?'

The cavalry were very quiet, but each man gripped his carbine and stood to his horse. Again the voice called, 'Who goes there?' and in a louder key, 'O brothers, give the alarm!' Now, every man in the cavalry would have died in his long boots sooner than have asked for quarter; but it is a fact that the answer to the second call was a long wail of 'Marf karo! Marf karo!' which means, 'Have mercy! Have mercy!' It came from the climbing regiment.

The cavalry stood dumbfoundered, till the big troopers had time to whisper one to another: 'Mir Khan, was that thy voice? Abdullah, didst *thou* call?' Lieutenant Halley stood beside his charger and waited. So long as no firing was going on he was content. Another flash of lightning showed the horses with heaving flanks and nodding heads, the men, white eyeballed, glaring beside them, and the stone watchtower to the left. This time there was no head at the window, and the rude iron-clamped shutter that could turn a rifle-bullet was closed.

'Go on, men,' said the Major. 'Get up to the top at any rate.'

The squadron toiled forward the horses wagging their tails and the men pulling at the bridles, the stones rolling down the hillside and the sparks flying. Lieutenant Halley declares that he never heard a squadron make so much noise in his life. They scrambled up, he said, as though each horse had eight legs and a spare horse to follow him. Even then there was no sound from the watchtower, and the men stopped exhausted on the ridge that overlooked the pit of darkness in which the village of Bersund lay. Girths were loosed, curb-chains shifted, and saddles adjusted, and the men dropped down among the stones. Whatever might happen now, they held the upper ground of any attack.

The thunder ceased, and with it the rain, and the soft, thick darkness of a winter night before the dawn covered them all. Except for the sound of running water among the ravines, everything was still. They heard the shutter of the watchtower below them thrown back with a clang, and the voice of the watcher calling: 'Oh, Hafiz Ullah!'

The echoes took up the call – 'La-la-la!' – and an answer came from a watchtower hidden round the curve of the hill, 'What is it, Shahbaz Khan?'

Shahbaz Khan replied, in the high-pitched voice of the mountaineer: 'Hast thou seen?'

The answer came back: 'Yes. God deliver us from all evil spirits!'

There was a pause, and then: 'Hafiz Ullah, I am alone! Come to me!'

'Shahbaz Khan, I am alone also; but I dare not leave my post!'

'That is a lie; thou art afraid.'

A longer pause followed, and then: 'I am afraid. Be silent! They are below us still. Pray to God and sleep.'

The troopers listened and wondered, for they could not understand what save earth and stone could lie below the watchtowers.

Shahbaz Khan began to call again: 'They are below us. I can see them. For the pity of God come over to me, Hafiz Ullah! My father slew ten of them. Come over!'

Hafiz Ullah answered to the darkness in a very loud voice, 'Mine was guiltless. Hear, ye Men of the Night, neither my father nor my blood had any part in that sin. Bear thou thine own punishment, Shahbaz Khan.'

'Oh, someone ought to stop those two chaps crowing away like cocks there,' said Lieutenant Halley, shivering under his rock.

He had hardly turned round to expose a new side of him to the rain before a long-locked, evil-smelling Afghan rushed up the hill, and tumbled into his arms. Halley sat upon him, and thrust as much of a sword-hilt as could be spared down the man's gullet. 'If you cry out, I kill you,' he said cheerfully.

The man was beyond, any expression of terror: he lay and quaked, gasping. When Halley took the sword-hilt from between his teeth, he was still inarticulate, but clung to Halley's arm, feeling it from elbow to wrist.

'The Rissala! the dead Rissala!' he gulped at last. 'It is down there!'

'No; the Rissala, the very much alive Rissala. It is up here,' said Halley, unshipping his watering-bridle, and fastening the man's hands. 'Why were you in the towers so foolish as to let us pass?'

'The valley is full of the dead,' said the Afghan. 'It is better to fall into the hands of the English than the hands of the dead. They march to and fro below there. I saw them in the lightning.'

He recovered his composure after a little, and whispering, because Halley's pistol was at his stomach, said: 'What is this? There is no war between us now, but the Mullah will kill me for not seeing you pass!'

'Rest easy,' said Halley; 'we are coming to kill the Mullah, if God please. His teeth have grown too long. No harm will come to thee unless the daylight shows thine as a face which is desired by the gallows for crime done. But what of the dead regiment?'

'I only kill within my own border,' said the man, immensely relieved. 'The Dead Regiment is below. The men must have passed through it on their journey – four hundred dead on horses, stumbling among their own graves, among the little heaps – dead men all, whom we slew.'

'Whew!' said Halley. 'That accounts for my cursing Carter and the Major cursing me. Four hundred sabres, eh? No wonder we thought there were a few extra men in the troop. Kurruk Shah,' he whispered to a grizzled native officer that lay within a few feet of him, 'hast thou heard anything of the dead Rissala in these hills?'

'Assuredly,' said Kurruk Shah with a chuckle. 'When I was a young man I saw the killing in the valley of Sheor-Kôt there at our feet, and I know the tale that grew up therefrom. But how can the ghosts of unbelievers prevail against us who are of the Faith? Strap that dog's hands a little tighter. Sahib. An Afghan is like an eel.'

'But a dead Rissala,' said Halley, jerking his captive's wrist. 'That is foolish talk, Kurruk Shah. The dead are dead. Hold still, *sag*.' The Afghan wriggled.

'The dead are dead, and for that reason they walk at night. What need to talk? We be men, we have our eyes and ears. Thou canst both see and hear them, down the hillside,' said Kurruk Shah.

Halley stared and listened long and intently. The valley was full of stifled noises, as every valley must be at night; but whether he saw or heard more than was natural Halley alone knows, and he does not choose to speak on the subject.

At last, and just before the dawn, a green rocket shot up from the far side of the valley of Bersund, at the head of the gorge, to show that the Goorkhas were in position. A red light from the infantry at left and right answered it, and the cavalry burnt a white flare. Afghans in winter are late sleepers, and it was not till full day that the Gulla Kutta Mullah's men began to straggle from their huts, rubbing their eyes. They saw men in green, and red, and brown uniforms, leaning on their arms, neatly arranged all round the crater of the village of Bersund, in a cordon that not a wolf could have broken. They rubbed their eyes the more when a pink-faced young man, who was not even in the Army, but represented the Political Department, tripped down the hillside with two orderlies, rapped at the door of the Gulla Kutta Mullah's hut, and told him quietly to step out and be tied up for safe transport. That same young man passed on through the huts, tapping here one cateran, and there another lightly with his cane; and as each was pointed out, so he was tied up, staring hopelessly at the crowned heights around where the English soldiers looked down with incurious eyes. Only the Mullah tried to carry it off by curses and high words, till a soldier who was tying his hands, said –

'None o' your lip! Why didn't you come out when you was ordered, instead o' keepin' us awake all night? You're no better than my own barrick-sweeper, you white-'eaded old polyanthus! Kim up!'

Half an hour later the troops had gone away with the Mullah and his thirteen friends; the dazed villagers were looking ruefully at a pile of broken muskets and snapped swords, and wondering how in the world they had come so to miscalculate the forebearance of the Indian Government.

It was a very neat little affair, neatly carried out, and the men concerned were unofficially thanked for their services.

Yet it seems to me that much credit is also due to another regiment whose name did not appear in the Brigade Orders, and whose very existence is in danger of being forgotten.

A MATTER OF FACT

And if ye doubt the tale I tell,
Steer through the South Pacific swell;
Go where the branching coral hives
Unending strife of endless lives,
Where, leagued about the 'wildered boat,
The rainbow jellies fill and float;
And, lilting where the laver lingers,
The starfish trips on all her fingers;
Where, 'neath his myriad spines ashock,
The sea-egg ripples down the rock;
An orange wonder dimly guessed,
From darkness where the cuttles rest,
Moored o'er the darker deeps that hide
The blind white Sea-snake and his bride
Who, drowsing, nose the long-lost ships
Let down through darkness to their lips.

The Palms

Once a priest, always a priest; once a mason, always a mason; but once a journalist, always and for ever a journalist.

There were three of us, all newspaper men, the only passengers on a little tramp steamer that ran where her owners told her to go. She had once been in the Bilbao iron ore business, had been lent to the Spanish Government for service at Manilla; and was ending her days in the Cape Town coolie-trade, with occasional trips to Madagascar and even as far as England. We found her going to Southampton in ballast, and shipped in her because the fares were nominal. There was Keller, of an American paper, on his way back to the States from palace executions in Madagascar; there was a burly half-Dutchman, called Zuyland, who owned and edited a paper up country near Johannesburg; and there was myself, who had solemnly put away all journalism, vowing to forget

335

that I had ever known the difference between an imprint and a stereo advertisment.

Ten minutes after Keller spoke to me, as the *Rathmines* cleared Cape Town, I had forgotten the aloofness I desired to feign, and was in heated discussion on the immorality of expanding telegrams beyond a certain fixed point. Then Zuyland came out of his cabin, and we were all at home instantly, because we were men of the same profession needing no introduction. We annexed the boat formally, broke open the passengers' bath-room door – on the Manilla lines the Dons do not wash – cleaned out the orange-peel and cigar ends at the bottom of the bath, hired a Lascar to shave us throughout the voyage, and then asked each other's names.

Three ordinary men would have quarrelled through sheer boredom before they reached Southampton. We, by virtue of our craft, were anything but ordinary men. A large percentage of the tales of the world, the thirty-nine that cannot be told to ladies and the one that can, are common properly coming of a common stock. We told them all, as a matter of form, with all their local and specific variants which are surprising. Then came, in the intervals of steady card-play, more personal histories of adventure and things seen and suffered: panics among white folk, when the blind terror ran from man to man on the Brooklyn Bridge, and the people crushed each other to death they knew not why; fires, and faces that opened and shut their mouths horribly at red-hot window frames; wrecks in frost and snow, reported from the sleet-sheathed rescue-tug at the risk of frost-bite; long rides after diamond thieves; skirmishes on the veldt and in municipal committees with the Boers; glimpses of lazy tangled Cape politics and the mule-rule in the Transvaal; card-tales, horse-tales, woman-tales, by the score and half hundred; till the first mate, who had seen more than us all put together, but lacked words to clothe his tales with, sat open-mouthed far into the dawn.

When the tales were done we picked up cards till a curious hand or a chance remark made one or other of us say, 'That reminds me of a man who— or a business which—' and the anecdotes would continue while the *Rathmines* kicked her way northward through the warm winter.

In the morning of one specially warm night we three were sitting immediately in front of the wheel-house, where an old Swedish boatswain whom we called 'Frithiof the Dane' was at the wheel, pretending that he could not hear our stories. Once or twice Frithiof spun the spokes curiously, and Keller lifted his head from a long chair to ask, 'What is it? Can't you get any steerage-way on her?'

'There is a feel in the water,' said Frithiof, 'that I cannot understand. I think that we run downhills or somethings. She steers bad this morning.'

Nobody seems to know the laws that govern the pulse of the big waters. Sometimes even a landsman can tell that the solid ocean is atilt, and that the ship is working herself up a long unseen slope; and sometimes the captain says, when neither full steam nor fair wind justifies the length of a day's run, that the ship is sagging downhill; but how these ups and downs come about had not yet been settled authoritatively.

'No, it is a following sea,' said Frithiof; 'and with a following sea you shall not get good steerage-way.'

The sea was as smooth as a duck-pond, except for a regular oily swell. As I looked over the side to see where it might be following us from, the sun rose in a perfectly clear sky and struck the water with its light so sharply that it seemed as though the sea should clang like a burnished gong. The wake of the screw and the little white streak cut by the log-line hanging over the stern were the only marks on the water as far as eye could reach.

Keller rolled out of his chair and went aft to get a pine-apple from the ripening stock that was hung inside the after awning.

'Frithiof, the log-line has got tired of swimming. It's coming home,' he drawled.

'What?' said Frithiof, his voice jumping several octaves.

'Coming home,' Keller repeated, leaning over the stern. I ran to his side and saw the log-line, which till then had been drawn tense over the stern railing, slacken, loop, and come up off the port quarter. Frithiof called up the speaking-tube to the bridge, and the bridge answered, 'Yes, nine knots.' Then Frithiof spoke again, and the answer was, 'What do you want of the skipper?' and Frithiof bellowed, 'Call him up.'

By this time Zuyland, Keller, and myself had caught something of Frithiof's excitement, for any emotion on shipboard is most contagious. The captain ran out of his cabin, spoke to Frithiof, looked at the log-line, jumped on the bridge, and in a minute we felt the steamer swing round as Frithiof turned her.

'Going back to Cape Town?' said Keller.

Frithiof did not answer, but tore away at the wheel. Then he beckoned us three to help, and we held the wheel down till the *Rathmines* answered it, and we found ourselves looking into the white of our own wake, with the still oily sea tearing past our bows, though we were not going more than half steam ahead.

The captain stretched out his arm from the bridge and shouted. A minute later I would have given a great deal to have shouted too, for one-half of the sea seemed to shoulder itself above the other half, and came on in the shape of a hill. There was neither crest, comb, nor curl-over to it; nothing but black water with little waves chasing each other about the flanks. I saw it stream past and on a level with the *Rathmines'* bow-plates before the steamer hove up her bulk to rise, and I argued that this would be the last of all earthly voyages for me. Then we lifted for ever and ever and ever, till I heard Keller saying in my ear, 'The bowels of the deep, good Lord!' and the *Rathmines* stood poised, her screw racing and drumming on the slope of a hollow that stretched downwards for a good half-mile.

We went down that hollow, nose under for the most part, and the air smelt wet and muddy, like that of an emptied aquarium. There was a second hill to climb; I saw that much: but the water came aboard and carried me aft till it jammed me against the wheel-house door, and before I could catch breath or clear my eyes again we were rolling to and fro in torn water, with the scuppers pouring like eaves in a thunderstorm.

'There were three waves,' said Keller; 'and the stoke-hold's flooded.'

The firemen were on deck waiting, apparently, to be drowned. The engineer came and dragged them below, and the crew, gasping, began to work the clumsy Board of Trade pump. That showed nothing serious, and when I understood that the *Rathmines* was really on the water, and not beneath it, I asked what had happened.

'The captain says it was a blow-up under the sea – a volcano,' said Keller.

'It hasn't warmed anything,' I said. I was feeling bitterly cold, and cold was almost unknown in those waters. I went below to change my clothes, and when I came up everything was wiped out in clinging white fog.

'Are there going to be any more surprises?' said Keller to the Captain.

'I don't know. Be thankful you're alive, gentlemen. That's a tidal wave thrown up by a volcano. Probably the bottom of the sea has been lifted a few feet somewhere or other. I can't quite understand this cold spell. Our sea-thermometer says the surface water is 44°, and it should be 68° at least.'

'It's abominable,' said Keller, shivering. 'But hadn't you better attend to the fog-horn? It seems to me that I heard something.'

'Heard! Good heavens!' said the captain from the bridge, 'I should think you did.' He pulled the string of our fog-horn, which was a weak one. It sputtered and choked, because the stoke-hold was full of water and the fires were half-drowned, and at last gave out a moan. It was answered from the fog by one of the most appalling steam-sirens I have ever heard. Keller turned as white as I did, for the fog, the cold fog, was upon us, and any man may be forgiven for fearing a death he cannot see.

'Give her steam there!' said the captain to the engine-room. 'Steam for the whistle, if we have to go dead slow.'

We bellowed again, and the damp dripped off the awnings on to the deck as we listened for the reply. It seemed to be astern this time, but much nearer than before.

'The *Pembroke Castle* on us!' said Keller; and then, viciously, 'Well, thank God, we shall sink her too.'

'It's a side-wheel steamer,' I whispered. 'Can't you hear the paddles?'

This time we whistled and roared till the steam gave out, and the answer nearly deafened us. There was a sound of frantic threshing in the water, apparently about fifty yards away, and something shot past in the whiteness that looked as though it were grey and red.

'The *Pembroke Castle* bottom up,' said Keller, who, being a journalist, always sought for explanations. 'That's the colours of a Castle liner. We're in for a big thing.'

'The sea is bewitched,' said Frithiof from the wheel-house. 'There are *two* steamers!'

Another siren sounded on our bow, and the little steamer rolled in the wash of something that had passed unseen.

'We're evidently in the middle of a fleet,' said Keller quietly. 'If one doesn't run us down, the other will. Phew! What in creation is that?'

I sniffed, for there was a poisonous rank smell in the cold air – a smell that I had smelt before.

'If I was on land I should say that it was an alligator. It smells like musk,' I answered.

'Not ten thousand alligators could make that smell,' said Zuyland; 'I have smelt them.'

'Bewitched! Bewitched!' said Frithiof. 'The sea she is turned upside down, and we are walking along the bottom.'

Again the *Rathmines* rolled in the wash of some unseen ship, and a silver-grey wave broke over the bow, leaving on the deck a sheet of sediment – the grey broth that has its place in the fathomless deeps of the sea. A sprinkling of the wave fell on my face, and it was so cold that it stung as boiling water stings. The dead and most untouched deep water of the sea had been heaved to the top by the submarine volcano – the chill still water that kills all life and smells of desolation and emptiness. We did not need either the blinding fog or that indescribable smell of musk to make us unhappy – we were shivering with cold and wretchedness where we stood.

'The hot air on the cold water makes this fog,' said the captain; 'it ought to clear in a little time.'

'Whistle, oh! whistle, and let's get out of it,' said Keller.

The captain whistled again, and far and far astern the invisible twin steam-sirens answered us. Their blasting shriek grew louder, till at last it seemed to tear out of the fog just above our quarter, and I cowered while the *Rathmines* plunged bows under on a double swell that crossed.

'No more,' said Frithiof, 'it is not good any more. Let us get away, in the name of God.'

'Now if a torpedo-boat with a *City of Paris* siren went mad and broke her moorings and hired a friend to help her, it's just conceivable that we might be carried as we are now. Otherwise this thing is—'

The last words died on Keller's lips, his eyes began to start from his head, and his jaw fell. Some six or seven feet above the port bulwarks, framed in fog, and as utterly unsupported as the full moon, hung a Face. It was not human, and it certainly was not animal, for it did not belong to this earth as known to man. The mouth was open, revealing a ridiculously tiny tongue – as absurd as the tongue of an elephant; there were tense wrinkles of white skin at the angles of the drawn lips, white feelers like those of a barbel sprung from the lower jaw, and there was no sign of teeth within the mouth. But the horror of the face lay in the eyes, for those were sightless – white, in sockets as white as scraped bone, and blind. Yet for all this the face, wrinkled as the mask of a lion is drawn in Assyrian sculpture, was alive with rage and terror. One long white feeler touched our bulwarks. Then the face disappeared with the swiftness of a blindworm popping into its burrow, and the next thing that I remember is my own voice in my own ears, saying gravely to the mainmast, 'But the air-bladder ought to have been forced out of its mouth, you know.'

Keller came up to me, ashy white. He put his hand into his pocket, took a cigar, bit it, dropped it, thrust his shaking thumb into his mouth and mumbled, 'The giant gooseberry and the raining frogs! Gimme a light – gimme a light! Say, gimme a light.' A little bead of blood dropped from his thumb-joint.

I respected the motive, though the manifestation was

absurd. 'Stop, you'll bite your thumb off,' I said, and Keller laughed brokenly as he picked up his cigar. Only Zuyland, leaning over the port bulwarks, seemed self-possessed. He declared later that he was very sick.

'We've seen it,' he said, turning round. 'That is it.'

'What?' said Keller, chewing the unlighted cigar.

As he spoke the fog was blown into shreds, and we saw the sea, grey with mud, rolling on every side of us and empty of all life. Then in one spot it bubbled and became like the pot of ointment that the Bible speaks of. From that wide-ringed trouble a Thing came up – a grey and red Thing with a neck – a Thing that bellowed and writhed in pain. Frithiof drew in his breath and held it till the red letters of the ship's name, woven across his jersey, straggled and opened out as though they had been type badly set. Then he said with a little cluck in his throat, 'Ah me! It is blind. *Hur illa!* That thing is blind,' and a murmur of pity went through us all, for we could see that the thing on the water was blind and in pain. Something had gashed and cut the great sides cruelly and the blood was spurting out. The grey ooze of the undermost sea lay in the monstrous wrinkles of the back, and poured away in sluices. The blind white head flung back and battered the wounds, and the body in its torment rose clear of the red and grey waves till we saw a pair of quivering shoulders streaked with weed and rough with shells, but as white in the clear spaces as the hairless, maneless, blind, toothless head. Afterwards, came a dot on the horizon and the sound of a shrill scream, and it was as though a shuttle shot all across the sea in one breath, and a second head and neck tore through the levels, driving a whispering wall of water to right and left. The two Things met – the one untouched and the other in its death-throe – male and female, we said, the female coming to the male. She circled round him bellowing, and laid her neck across the curve of his great turtle-back, and he disappeared under water for an instant, but flung up again, grunting in agony while the blood ran. Once the entire head and neck shot clear of the water and stiffened, and I heard Keller saying, as though he was watching a street accident, 'Give him air. For God's sake, give him air.' Then the death-struggle began, with crampings and twistings and jerkings of the white bulk to and fro, till our little steamer rolled again, and each grey wave coated her plates with the grey slime. The sun was clear, there was no wind, and we watched, the whole crew, stokers and all, in wonder and pity, but chiefly pity. The Thing was so helpless, and, save for his mate, so alone. No human eye should have beheld him; it was monstrous and indecent to exhibit him there in trade waters between atlas degrees of latitude. He had been spewed up, mangled and dying from his rest on the sea-floor, where he might have lived till the Judgment Day, and we saw the tides of his life go from him as an angry tide goes out across rocks in the teeth of a landward gale. His mate lay rocking on the water a little distance off, bellowing continually, and the smell of musk came down upon the ship making us cough.

At last the battle for life ended, in a batter of coloured seas. We saw the writhing neck fall like a flail, the carcase turn sideways showing the glint of a white belly and the inset of a gigantic hind leg or flipper. Then all sank, and sea boiled over it, while the mate swam round and round, darting her head in every direction. Though we might have feared that she would attack the steamer, no power on earth could have drawn any one of us from our places that hour. We watched, holding our breaths. The mate paused in her search; we could hear the wash beating along her sides; reared her neck as high as she could reach, blind and lonely in all that loneliness of the sea, and sent one desperate bellow booming across the swells as an oyster-shell skips across a pond. Then she made off to the westward, the sun shining on the white head and the wake behind it, till nothing was left to see but a little pin point of silver on the horizon. We stood on our course again; and the *Rathmines*, coated with the sea-sediment, from bow to stern, looked like a ship made grey with terror.

'We must pool our notes,' was the first coherent remark from Keller. 'We're three trained journalists – we hold absolutely the biggest scoop on record. Start fair.'

I objected to this. Nothing is gained by collaboration in journalism when all deal with the same facts, so we went to work each according to his own lights. Keller triple-headed his account, talked about our 'gallant captain', and wound up with an allusion to American enterprise in that it was a citizen of Dayton, Ohio, that had seen the sea-serpent. This sort of thing would have discredited the Creation, much more a mere sea tale, but as a specimen of the picture-writing of a half-civilized people it was very interesting. Zuyland took a heavy column and a half, giving approximate lengths and breadths and the whole list of the crew whom he had sworn on oath to testify to his facts. There was nothing fantastic or flamboyant in Zuyland. I wrote three-quarters of a leaded bourgeois column, roughly speaking, and refrained from putting any journalese into it for reasons that had begun to appear to me.

Keller was insolent with joy. He was going to cable from Southampton to the New York *World*, mail his account to America on the same day, paralyse London with his three columns of loosely knitted headlines, and generally efface the earth. 'You'll see how I work a big scoop when I get it,' he said.

'Is this your first visit to England?' I asked.

'Yes,' said he. 'You don't seem to appreciate the beauty of our scoop. It's pyramidal – the death of the sea-serpent! Good heavens alive, man, it's the biggest thing ever vouchsafed to a paper!'

'Curious to think that it will never appear in any paper, isn't it?' I said.

Zuyland was near me, and he nodded quickly.

'What do you mean?' said Keller. 'If you're enough of a Britisher to throw this thing away, I shan't. I thought you were a newspaper-man.'

'I am. That's why I know. Don't be an ass, Keller. Remember, I'm seven hundred years your senior, and what your grandchildren may learn five hundred years hence, I learned from my grandfathers about five hundred years ago. You won't do it, because you can't.'

This conversation was held in open sea, where everything

seems possible, some hundred miles from Southampton. We passed the Needles Light at dawn, and the lifting day showed the stucco villas on the green and the awful orderliness of England – line upon line, wall upon wall, solid dock and monolithic pier. We waited an hour in the Customs shed, and there was ample time for the effect to soak in.

'Now, Keller, you face the music. The *Havel* goes out today. Mail by her, and I'll take you to the telegraph-office,' I said.

I heard Keller gasp as the influence of the land closed about him, cowing him as they say Newmarket Heath cows a young horse unused to open courses.

'I want to retouch my stuff. Suppose we wait till we get to London?' he said.

Zuyland, by the way, had torn up his account and thrown it overboard that morning early. His reasons were my reasons.

In the train Keller began to revise his copy, and every time that he looked at the trim little fields, the red villas, and the embankments of the line, the blue pencil plunged remorselessly through the slips. He appeared to have dredged the dictionary for adjectives. I could think of none that he had not used. Yet he was a perfectly sound poker-player and never showed more cards than were sufficient to take the pool.

'Aren't you going to leave him a single bellow?' I asked sympathetically. 'Remember, everything goes in the States, from a trouser-button to a double-eagle.'

'That's just the curse of it,' said Keller below his breath. 'We've played 'em for suckers so often that when it comes to the golden truth – I'd like to try this on a London paper. You have first call there, though.'

'Not in the least. I'm not touching the thing in our papers. I shall be happy to leave 'em all to you; but surely you'll cable it home?'

'No. Not if I can make the scoop here and see the Britishers sit up.'

'You won't do it with three columns of slushy headline, believe me. They don't sit up as quickly as some people.'

'I'm beginning to think that too. Does *nothing* make any

difference in this country?' he said, looking out of the window. 'How old is that farmhouse?'

'New. It can't be more than two hundred years at the most.'

'Um. Fields, too?'

'That hedge there must have been clipped for about eighty years.'

'Labour cheap – eh?'

'Pretty much. Well, I suppose you'd like to try the *Times*, wouldn't you?'

'No,' said Keller, looking at Winchester Cathedral. 'Might as well try to electrify a haystack. And to think that the *World* would take three columns and ask for more – with illustrations too! It's sickening.'

'But the *Times* might,' I began.

Keller flung his paper across the carriage, and it opened in its austere majesty of solid type – opened with the crackle of an encyclopædia.

'Might! You *might* work your way through the bow-plates of a cruiser. Look at that first page!'

'It strikes you that way, does it?' I said. 'Then I'd recommend you to try a light and frivolous journal.'

'With a thing like this of mine – of ours? It's sacred history!'

I showed him a paper which I conceived would be after his own heart, in that it was modelled on American lines.

'That's homey,' he said, 'but it's not the real thing. Now, I should like one of these fat old *Times* columns. Probably there'd be a bishop in the office, though.'

When we reached London Keller disappeared in the direction of the Strand. What his experiences may have been I cannot tell, but it seems that he invaded the office of an evening paper at 11.45 a.m. (I told him English editors were most idle at that hour), and mentioned my name as that of a witness to the truth of his story.

'I was nearly fired out,' he said furiously at lunch. 'As soon as I mentioned you, the old man said that I was to tell you that they didn't want any more of your practical jokes, and that you knew the hours to call if you had anything to sell, and that they'd see you condemned before they helped to puff one of your infernal yarns in advance. Say, what record do you hold for truth in this country, anyway?'

'A beauty. You ran up against it, that's all. Why don't you leave the English papers alone and cable to New York? Everything goes over there.'

'Can't you see that's just why?' he repeated.

'I saw it a long time ago. You don't intend to cable, then?'

'Yes I do,' he answered, in the over-emphatic voice of one who does not know his own mind.

That afternoon I walked him abroad and about, over the streets that run between the pavements like channels of grooved and tongued lava, over the bridges that are made of enduring stone, through subways floored and sided with yard-thick concrete, between houses that are never rebuilt, and by river-steps hewn, to the eye, from the living rock. A black fog chased us into Westminster Abbey, and, standing there in the darkness, I could hear the wings of the dead centuries circling around the head of Litchfield A. Keller, journalist, of Dayton, Ohio, USA, whose mission it was to make the Britishers sit up.

He stumbled gasping into the thick gloom, and the roar of the traffic came to his bewildered ears.

'Let's go to the telegraph-office and cable,' I said. 'Can't you hear the New York *World* crying for news of the great sea-serpent, blind, white, and smelling of musk, stricken to death by a submarine volcano, and assisted by his loving wife to die in mid-ocean, as visualized by an American citizen, the breezy, newsy, brainy newspaper man of Dayton, Ohio? 'Rah for the Buckeye State. Step lively! Both gates! Szz! Boom! Aah!' Keller was a Princeton man, and he seemed to need encouragement.

'You've got me on your own ground,' said he, tugging at his overcoat pocket. He pulled out his copy, with the cable forms – for he had written out his telegram – and put them all into my hand, groaning, 'I pass. If I hadn't come to your cursed country— If I'd sent it off at Southampton— If I ever get you west of the Alleghennies, if—'

'Never mind, Keller. It isn't your fault. It's the fault of your country. If you had been seven hundred years older you'd have done what I am going to do.'

'What are you going to do?'

'Tell it as a lie.'

'Fiction?' This with the full-blooded disgust of a journalist for the illegitimate branch of the profession.

'You can call it that if you like. I shall call it a lie.'

And a lie it has become; for Truth is a naked lady, and if by accident she is drawn up from the bottom of the sea, it behoves a gentleman either to give her a print petticoat or to turn his face to the wall and vow that he did not see.

THE BRIDGE-BUILDERS

The least that Findlayson, of the Public Works Department, expected was a CIE; he dreamed of a CSI: indeed his friends told him that he deserved more. For three years he had endured heat and cold, disappointment, discomfort, danger, and disease, with responsibility almost too heavy for one pair of shoulders; and day by day, through that time, the great Kashi Bridge over the ranges had grown under his charge. Now, in less than three months, if all went well, His Excellency the Viceroy would open the bridge in state, an archbishop would bless it, the first train-load of soldiers would come over it, and there would be speeches.

Findlayson, CE, sat in his trolley on a construction-line that ran along one of the main revetments – the huge stone-faced banks that flared away north and south for three miles on either side of the river – and permitted himself to think of the end. With its approaches, his work was one mile and three-quarters in length; a lattice-girder bridge, trussed with the Findlayson truss, standing on seven-and-twenty brick piers. Each one of those piers was twenty-four feet in diameter, capped with red Agra stone and sunk eighty feet below the shifting sand of the Ganges' bed. Above them ran the railway-line fifteen feet broad; above that, again, a cart-road of eighteen feet, flanked with footpaths. At either end rose towers of red brick, loopholed for musketry and pierced for big guns, and the ramp of the road was being pushed forward to their haunches. The raw earth-ends were crawling and alive with hundreds upon hundreds of tiny asses climbing out of the yawning borrow-pit below with sackfuls of stuff; and the hot afternoon air was filled with the noise of hooves, the rattle of the drivers' sticks, and the swish had roll-down of the dirt. The river was very low, and on the dazzling white sand between the three centre piers stood squat cribs of railway-sleepers, filled within and daubed without with mud, to support the last of the girders as those were riveted up. In the little deep water left by the drought, an overhead-crane travelled to and fro along its spile-pier, jerking sections of iron into place, snorting and backing and grunting as an elephant grunts in the timber-yard. Riveters by the hundred swarmed about the lattice side-work and the iron roof of the railway-line, hung from invisible staging under the bellies of the girders, clustered round the throats of the piers, and rode on the overhang of the footpath-stanchions; their fire-pots and the spurn of flame that answered each hammer-stroke showing no more than pale yellow in the sun's glare. East and west and north and south the construction-trains rattled and shrieked up and down the embankments, the piled trucks of brown and white stone banging behind them till the side-boards were unpinned, and with a roar and a grumble a few thousand tons more material were thrown out to hold the river in place.

Findlayson, CE, turned on his trolley and looked over the face of the country that he had changed for seven miles around. Looked back on the humming village of five thousand workmen; upstream and down, along the vista of spurs and sand; across the river to the far piers, lessening in the haze; overhead to the guard-towers – and only he knew how strong those were – and with a sigh of contentment saw that his work was good. There stood his bridge before him in the sunlight, lacking only a few weeks' work on the girders of the three middle piers – his bridge, raw and ugly as original sin, but *pukka* – permanent – to endure when all memory of the builder, yea, even of the splendid Findlayson truss, had perished. Practically, the thing was done.

Hitchcock, his assistant, cantered along the line on a little switch-tailed Kabuli pony, who, through long practice, could have trotted securely over a trestle, and nodded to his chief.

'All but,' said he, with a smile.

'I've been thinking about it,' the senior answered. 'Not half a bad job for two men, is it?'

'One – and a half. 'Gad, what a Cooper's Hill cub I was when I came on the works!' Hitchcock felt very old in the crowded experiences of the past three years, that had taught him power and responsibility.

'You *were* rather a colt,' said Findlayson. 'I wonder how you'll like going back to office work when this job's over.'

'I shall hate it!' said the young man, and as he went on his eye followed Findlayson's, and he muttered, 'Isn't it damned good?'

'I think we'll go up the service together,' Findlayson said to himself. 'You're too good a youngster to waste on another man. Cub thou wast; assistant thou art. Personal assistant, and at Simla, thou shalt be, if any credit comes to me out of the business!'

Indeed, the burden of the work had fallen altogether on Findlayson and his assistant, the young man whom he had chosen because of his rawness to break to his own needs. There were labour-contractors by the half-hundred – fitters and riveters, European, borrowed from the railway workshops, with perhaps twenty white and half-caste subordinates to direct, under direction, the bevies of workmen – but none knew better than these two, who trusted each other, how the underlings were not to be trusted. They had been tried many times in sudden crises – by slipping of booms, by breaking of tackle, failure of cranes, and the wrath of the river – but no stress had brought to light any man among them whom Findlayson and Hitchcock would have honoured by working as remorselessly as they worked themselves. Findlayson thought it over from the beginning: the months of office work destroyed at a blow when the Government of India, at the last moment, added two feet to the width of the bridge, under the impression that bridges were cut out of paper, and so brought to ruin at least half an acre of calculations – and Hitchcock, new to disappointment, buried his head in his arms and wept; the heart-breaking delays over the filling of the contracts in England; the futile correspondences hinting at great wealth of commission if one, only one, rather doubtful consignment were passed; the war that followed the refusal; the careful, polite obstruction at the other end that followed the war, till young Hitchcock, putting one month's leave to another month, and borrowing ten days from Findlayson, spent his poor little savings of a year in a wild dash to London, and there, as his own tongue asserted and the later consignments proved, put the Fear of God into a man so great that he feared only Parliament, and said so till Hitchcock wrought with him across his own dinner-table, and – he feared the Kashi Bridge and all who spoke in its name. Then there was the cholera that came in the night to the village by the bridge-works; and after the cholera smote the small-pox. The fever they had always with them. Hitchcock had been appointed a magistrate of the third class with whipping powers, for the better government of the community, and Findlayson watched him wield his powers temperately, learning what to overlook and what to look after. It was a long, long reverie, and it covered storm, sudden freshets, death in every manner and shape, violent and awful rage against red tape half frenzying a mind that knows it should be busy on other things; drought, sanitation, finance; birth, wedding, burial, and riot in the village of twenty warring castes; argument, expostulation, persuasion, and the blank despair that a man goes to bed upon, thankful that his rifle is all in pieces in the gun-case. Behind everything rose the black frame of the Kashi Bridge – plate by plate, girder by girder, span by span – and each pier of it recalled Hitchcock, the all-round man, who had stood by his chief without failing from the very first to this last.

So the bridge was two men's work – unless one counted Peroo, as Peroo certainly counted himself. He was a Lascar, a Kharva from Bulsar, familiar with every port between Rockhampton and London, who had risen to the rank of serang on the British India boats, but wearying of routine musters and clean clothes had thrown up the service and gone inland, where men of his calibre were sure of employment. For his knowledge of tackle and the handling of heavy weights, Peroo was worth almost any price he might have chosen to put upon his services; but custom decreed the wage of the overhead-men, and Peroo was not within many silver pieces of his proper value. Neither running water nor extreme heights made him afraid; and, as an ex-serang, he knew how to hold authority. No piece of iron was so big or so badly placed that Peroo could not devise a tackle to lift it – a loose-ended, sagging arrangement, rigged with a scandalous amount of talking, but perfectly equal to the work in hand. It was Peroo who had saved the girder of Number Seven Pier from destruction when the new wire rope jammed in the eye of the crane, and the huge plate tilted in its slings, threatening to slide out sideways. Then the native workmen lost their heads with great shoutings, and Hitchcock's right arm was broken by a falling T-plate, and he buttoned it up in his coat and swooned, and came to and directed for four hours till Peroo, from the top of the crane, reported, 'All's well,' and the plate swung home. There was no one like Peroo, serang, to lash and guy and hold, to control the donkey-engines, to hoist a fallen locomotive craftily out of the borrow-pit into which it had tumbled; to strip and dive, if need be, to see how the concrete blocks round the piers stood the scouring of Mother Gunga, or to adventure upstream on a monsoon night and report on the state of the embankment-facings. He would interrupt the field-councils of Findlayson and Hitchcock without fear, till his wonderful English, or his still more wonderful *lingua franca*, half Portuguese and half Malay, ran out and he was forced to take string and show the knots that he would recommend. He controlled his own gang of tacklemen – mysterious relatives from Kutch Mandvi gathered month by month and tried to the uttermost. No consideration of family or kin allowed Peroo to keep weak hands or a giddy head on the pay-roll. 'My honour is the honour of this bridge,' he would say to the about-to-be-dismissed. 'What do I care for your honour? Go and work on a steamer. That is all you are fit for.'

The little cluster of huts where he and his gang lived centred round the tattered dwelling of a sea-priest – one who had never set foot on Black Water, but had been chosen as ghostly counsellor by two generations of sea-rovers, all unaffected by port missions or those creeds which are thrust upon sailors by agencies along Thames' bank. The priest of the Lascars had nothing to do with their caste, or indeed with anything at all. He ate the offerings of his church, and slept and smoked, and slept again, 'for', said Peroo, who had haled him a thousand miles inland, 'he is a very holy man. He never cares what you eat so long as you do not eat beef, and that is good, because on land we worship Shiva, we Kharvas; but at sea on the Kumpani's boats we attend strictly to the orders of the Burra Malum (the first mate), and on this bridge we observe what Finlinson Sahib says.'

Findlayson Sahib had that day given orders to clear the scaffolding from the guard-tower on the right bank, and Peroo with his mates was casting loose and lowering down the bamboo poles and planks as swiftly as ever they had whipped the cargo out of a coaster.

From his trolley he could hear the whistle of the serang's silver pipe and the creak and clatter of the pulleys. Peroo was standing on the topmost coping of the tower, clad in the blue dungaree of his abandoned service, and as Findlayson motioned to him to be careful, for his was no life to throw away, he gripped the last pole, and, shading his eyes shipfashion, answered with the long-drawn wail of the fo'c'sle look-out: '*Ham dekhta hai*' ['I am looking out']. Findlayson laughed, and then sighed. It was years since he had seen a steamer, and he was sick for home. As his trolley passed under the tower, Peroo descended by a rope, ape-fashion, and cried: 'It looks well now, Sahib. Our bridge is all but done. What think you Mother Gunga will say when the rail runs over?'

'She has said little so far. It was never Mother Gunga that delayed us.'

'There is always time for her; and none the less there has been delay. Has the Sahib forgotten last autumn's flood, when the stone-boats were sunk without warning – or only a halfday's warning?'

'Yes, but nothing save a big flood could hurt us now. The spurs are holding well on the west bank.'

'Mother Gunga eats great allowances. There is always room

354

for more stone on the revetments. I tell this to the Chota Sahib' – he meant Hitchcock – 'and he laughs.'

'No matter, Peroo. Another year thou wilt be able to build a bridge in thine own fashion.'

The Lascar grinned. 'Then it will not be in this way – with stonework sunk under water, as the *Quetta* was sunk. I like sus-sus-pen-sheen bridges that fly from bank to bank, with one big step, like a gang-plank. Then no water can hurt. When does the Lord Sahib come to open the bridge?'

'In three months, when the weather is cooler.'

'Ho! ho! He is like the Burra Malum. He sleeps below while the work is being done. Then he comes upon the quarter-deck and touches with his finger, and says: "This is not clean! Dam jiboonwallah!"'

'But the Lord Sahib does not call me a dam jiboonwallah, Peroo.'

'No, Sahib; but he does not come on deck till the work is all finished. Even the Burra Malum of the *Nerbudda* said once at Tuticorin—'

'Bah! Go! I am busy.'

'I, also!' said Peroo, with an unshaken countenance. 'May I take the light dinghy now and row along the spurs?'

'To hold them with thy hands? They are, I think, sufficiently heavy.'

'Nay, Sahib. It is thus. At sea, on the Black Water, we have room to be blown up and down without care. Here we have no room at all. Look you, we have put the river into a dock, and run her between stone sills.'

Findlayson smiled at the 'we'.

'We have bitted and bridled her. She is not like the sea, that can beat against a soft beach. She is Mother Gunga – in irons.' His voice fell a little.

'Peroo, thou hast been up and down the world more even than I. Speak true talk, now. How much dost thou in thy heart believe of Mother Gunga?'

'All that our priest says, London is London, Sahib. Sydney is Sydney, and Port Darwin is Port Darwin. Also Mother Gunga is Mother Gunga, and when I come back to her banks I know this and worship. In London I did poojah to the big temple by the river for the sake of the God within . . . Yes, I will not take the cushions in the dinghy.'

Findlayson mounted his horse and trotted to the shed of a bungalow that he shared with his assistant. The place had become home to him in the last three years. He had grilled in the heat, sweated in the rains, and shivered with fever under the rude thatch roof; the limewash beside the door was covered with rough drawings and formulæ, and the sentry-path trodden in the matting of the verandah showed where he had walked alone. There is no eight-hour limit to an engineer's work, and the evening meal with Hitchcock was eaten booted and spurred: over their cigars they listened to the hum of the village as the gangs came up from the river-bed and the lights began to twinkle.

'Peroo has gone up the spurs in your dinghy. He's taken a couple of nephews with him, and he's lolling in the stern like a commodore,' said Hitchcock.

'That's all right. He's got something on his mind. You'd think that ten years in the British India boats would have knocked most of his religion out of him.'

'So it has,' said Hitchcock, chuckling. 'I overheard him the other day in the middle of a most atheistical talk with that fat old *guru* of theirs. Peroo denied the efficacy of prayer; and wanted the *guru* to go to sea and watch a gale out with him, and see if he could stop a monsoon.'

'All the same, if you carried off his *guru* he'd leave us like a shot. He was yarning away to me about praying to the dome of St Paul's when he was in London.'

'He told me that the first time he went into the engine-room of a steamer, when he was a boy, he prayed to the low-pressure cylinder.'

'Not half a bad thing to pray to, either. He's propitiating his own Gods now, and he wants to know what Mother Gunga will think of a bridge being run across her. Who's there?' A shadow darkened the doorway, and a telegram was put into Hitchcock's hand.

'She ought to be pretty well used to it by this time. Only a *tar.* It ought to be Ralli's answer about the new rivets . . . Great Heavens!' Hitchcock jumped to his feet.

'What is it?' said the senior, and took the form. '*That's* what Mother Gunga thinks, is it,' he said, reading. 'Keep cool, young 'un. We've got all our work cut for us. Let's see. Muir wires, half an hour ago: "*Floods on the Ramgunga, Look out.*" Well, that gives us – one, two – nine and a half for the flood to reach Melipur Ghaut and seven's sixteen and a half to Latodi – say fifteen hours before it comes down to us.'

'Curse that hill-fed sewer of a Ramgunga! Findlayson, this is two months before anything could have been expected, and the left bank is littered up with stuff still. Two full months before the time!'

'That's why it happens. I've only known Indian rivers for five and twenty years, and I don't pretend to understand. Here comes another *tar.*' Findlayson opened the telegram. 'Cockran, this time, from the Ganges Canal: "*Heavy rains here. Bad.*" He might have saved the last word. Well, we don't want to know any more. We've got to work the gangs all night and clean up the river-bed. You'll take the east bank and work out to meet me in the middle. Get everything that floats below the bridge: we shall have quite enough river-craft coming down adrift anyhow, without letting the stone-boats ram the piers. What have you got on the east bank that needs looking after?'

'Pontoon, one big pontoon with the overhead crane on it. T'other overhead crane on the mended pontoon, with the cart-road rivets from Twenty to Twenty-three piers – two construction lines, and a turning-spur. The pile-work must take its chance,' said Hitchcock.

'All right. Roll up everything you can lay hands on. We'll give the gang fifteen minutes more to eat their grub.'

Close to the verandah stood a big night-gong, never used except for flood, or fire in the village. Hitchcock had called for a fresh horse, and was off to his side of the bridge when Findlayson took the cloth-bound stick and smote with the rubbing stroke that brings out the full thunder of the metal.

Long before the last rumble ceased every night-gong in the village had taken up the warning. To these were added the hoarse screaming of conchs in the little temples; the throbbing of drums and tomtoms; and from the European quarters, where the riveters lived, M'Cartney's bugle, a weapon of offence on Sundays and festivals, brayed desperately, calling to 'Stables'. Engine after engine toiling home along the spurs after her day's work whistled in answer till the whistles were answered from the far bank. Then the big gong thundered thrice for a sign that it was flood and not fire; conch, drum, and whistle echoed the call, and the village quivered to the sound of bare feet running upon soft earth. The order in all cases was to stand by the day's work and wait instructions. The gangs poured by in the dusk; men stopping to knot a loin-cloth or fasten a sandal; gang-foremen shouting to their subordinates as they ran or paused by the tool-issue sheds for bars and mattocks; locomotives creeping down their tracks wheel-deep in the crowd, till the brown torrent disappeared into the dusk of the river-bed, raced over the pilework, swarmed along the lattices, clustered by the cranes, and stood still, each man in his place.

Then the troubled beating of the gong carried the order to take up everything and bear it beyond high-water mark, and the flare-lamps broke out by the hundred between the webs of dull iron as the riveters began a night's work racing against the flood that was to come. The girders of the three centre piers – those that stood on the cribs – were all but in position. They needed just as many rivets as could be driven into them, for the flood would assuredly wash out the supports, and the ironwork would settle down on the caps of stone if they were not blocked at the ends. A hundred crowbars strained at the sleepers of the temporary line that fed the unfinished piers. It was heaved up in lengths, loaded into trucks, and backed up the bank beyond flood-level by the groaning locomotives. The tool-sheds on the sands melted away before the attack of shouting armies, and with them went the stacked ranks of Government stores, iron-bound boxes of rivets, pliers, cutters, duplicate parts of the riveting-machines, spare pumps and chains. The big crane would be the last to be shifted, for she was hoisting all the heavy stuff up to the main structure of the bridge. The concrete blocks on the fleet of stone-boats were dropped overside, where there was any depth of water, to guard the piers, and the empty boats themselves were poled under the bridge downstream. It was here that Peroo's pipe shrilled loudest, for the first stroke of the big gong had brought back the dinghy at racing speed, and Peroo and his people were stripped to the waist, working for the honour and credit which are better than life.

'I knew she would speak,' he cried. '*I* knew, but the telegraph gave us good warning. O sons of unthinkable begetting – children of unspeakable shame – are we here for the look of the thing?' It was two feet of wire rope frayed at the ends, and it did wonders as Peroo leaped from gunnel to gunnel, shouting the language of the sea.

Findlayson was more troubled for the stone-boats than anything else. M'Cartney, with his gangs, was blocking up the ends of the three doubtful spans, but boats adrift, if the flood chanced to be a high one, might endanger the girders; and there was a very fleet in the shrunken channels.

'Get them behind the swell of the guard-tower,' he shouted to Peroo. 'It will be dead-water there; get them below the bridge.'

'*Accha!* [Very good.] *I* know. We are mooring them with wire rope,' was the answer. 'Heh! Listen to the Chota Sahib. He is working hard.'

From across the river came an almost continuous whistling of locomotives, backed by the rumble of stone. Hitchcock at the last minute was spending a few hundred more trucks of Tarakee stone in reinforcing his spurs and embankments.

'The bridge challenges Mother Gunga,' said Peroo, with a laugh. 'But when *she* talks I know whose voice will be the loudest.'

For hours the naked men worked, screaming and shouting under the lights. It was a hot, moonless night; the end of it was darkened by clouds and a sudden squall that made Findlayson very grave.

'She moves!' said Peroo, just before the dawn. 'Mother Gunga is awake! Hear!' He dipped his hand over the side of a boat and the current mumbled on it. A little wave hit the side of a pier with a crisp slap.

'Six hours before her time,' said Findlayson, mopping his forehead savagely. 'Now we can't depend on anything. We'd better clear all hands out of the river-bed.'

Again the big gong beat, and a second time there was the rushing of naked feet on earth and ringing iron; the clatter of tools ceased. In the silence, men heard the dry yawn of water crawling over thirsty sand.

Foreman after foreman shouted to Findlayson, who had posted himself by the guard-tower, that his section of the river-bed had been cleaned out, and when the last voice dropped Findlayson hurried over the bridge till the iron plating of the permanent way gave place to the temporary plank-walk over the three centre piers, and there he met Hitchcock.

'All clear your side?' said Findlayson. The whisper rang in the box of latticework.

'Yes, and the east channel's filling now. We're utterly out of our reckoning. When is this thing down on us?'

'There's no saying. She's filling as fast as she can. Look!' Findlayson pointed to the planks below his feet, where the sand, burned and defiled by months of work, was beginning to whisper and fizz.

'What orders?' said Hitchcock.

'Call the roll – count stores – sit on your hunkers – and pray for the bridge. That's all I can think of. Good-night. Don't risk your life trying to fish out anything that may go downstream.'

'Oh, I'll be as prudent as you are! 'Night. Heavens, how she's filling! Here's the rain in earnest!' Findlayson picked his way back to his bank, sweeping the last of M'Cartney's riveters before him. The gangs had spread themselves along the embankments, regardless of the cold rain of the dawn, and there they waited for the flood. Only Peroo kept his men together behind the swell of the guard-tower, where the stone-boats lay tied fore and aft with hawsers, wire-rope, and chains.

A shrill wail ran along the line, growing to a yell, half fear and half wonder: the face of the river whitened from bank to bank between the stone facings, and the far-away spurs went out in spouts of foam. Mother Gunga had come bank-high in haste, and a wall of chocolate-coloured water was her messenger. There was a shriek above the roar of the water, the complaint of the spans coming down on their blocks as the cribs were whirled out from under their bellies. The stone-boats groaned and ground each other in the eddy that swung round the abutment, and their clumsy masts rose higher and higher against the dim sky-line.

'Before she was shut between these walls we knew what she would do. Now she is thus cramped God only knows what she will do!' said Peroo, watching the furious turmoil round the guard-tower. 'Ohé! Fight, then! Fight hard, for it is thus that a woman wears herself out.'

But Mother Gunga would not fight as Peroo desired. After the first downstream plunge there came no more walls of water, but the river lifted herself bodily, as a snake when she drinks in midsummer, plucking and fingering along the revetments, and banking up behind the piers till even Findlayson began to recalculate the strength of his work.

When day came the village gasped. 'Only last night,' men said, turning to each other, 'it was as a town in the river-bed! Look now!'

And they looked and wondered afresh at the deep water, the racing water that licked the throat of the piers. The farther bank was veiled by rain, into which the bridge ran out and vanished; the spurs upstream were marked by no more than eddies and spoutings, and downstream the pent river, once freed of her guide-lines, had spread like a sea to the horizon. Then hurried by, rolling in the water, dead men and oxen together, with here and there a patch of thatched roof that melted when it touched a pier.

'Big flood,' said Peroo, and Findlayson nodded. It was as big a flood as he had any wish to watch. His bridge would stand what was upon her now, but not very much more; and if by any of a thousand chances there happened to be a weakness in the embankments, Mother Gunga would carry his honour to the sea with the other raffle. Worst of all, there was nothing to do except to sit still; and Findlayson sat still under his macintosh till his helmet became pulp on his head, and his boots were over-ankle in mire. He took no count of time, for the river was marking the hours, inch by inch and foot by foot, along the embankment, and he listened, numb and hungry, to the straining of the stone-boats, the hollow thunder under the piers, and the hundred noises that make the full note of a flood. Once a dripping servant brought him food, but he could not eat; and once he thought that he heard a faint toot from a locomotive across the river, and then he smiled. The bridge's failure would hurt his assistant not a little, but Hitchcock was a young man with his big work yet to do. For himself the crash meant everything – everything that made a hard life worth the living. They would say, the men of his own profession— he remembered the half-pitying things that he himself had said when Lockhart's big water-works burst and broke down in brick heaps and sludge, and Lockhart's spirit broke in him and he died. He remembered what he himself had said when the Sumao Bridge went out in the big cyclone by the sea; and most he remembered poor Hartopp's face three weeks later, when the shame had marked it. His bridge was twice the size of Hartopp's, and it carried the Findlayson truss as well as the new pier-shoe – the Findlayson bolted shoe. There were no excuses in his service. Government might listen, perhaps, but his own kind would judge him by his bridge, as that stood or fell. He went over it in his head, plate by plate, span by span, brick by brick, pier by pier, remembering, comparing, estimating, and recalculating, lest there should be any mistake; and through the long hours and through the flights of formulas that danced and wheeled before him a cold fear would come to pinch his heart. His side of the sum was beyond question; but what man knew Mother Gunga's arithmetic? Even as he was making all sure by the multiplication-table, the river might be scooping pot-holes to the very bottom of any one of those eighty-foot piers that carried his reputation. Again a servant came to him with food, but his mouth was dry, and he could only drink and return to the decimals in his brain. And the river was still rising. Peroo, in a mat shelter-coat, crouched at his feet, watching now his face and now the face of the river, but saying nothing.

At last the Lascar rose and floundered through the mud towards the village, but he was careful to leave an ally to watch the boats.

Presently he returned, most irreverently driving before him the priest of his creed – a fat old man, with a grey beard that whipped the wind with the wet cloth that blew over his shoulder. Never was seen so lamentable a *guru*.

'What good are offerings and little kerosene lamps and dry grain,' shouted Peroo, 'if squatting in the mud is all that thou canst do? Thou hast dealt long with the Gods when they were contented and well-wishing. Now they are angry. Speak to them!'

'What is a man against the wrath of Gods?' whined the priest, cowering as the wind took him. 'Let me go to the temple, and I will pray there.'

'Son of a pig, pray *here*! Is there no return for salt fish and curry powder and dried onions? Call aloud! Tell Mother Gunga we have had enough. Bid her be still for the night. I cannot pray, but I have served in the Kumpani's boats, and when men did not obey my orders I—' A flourish of the wire-rope colt rounded the sentence, and the priest, breaking from his disciple, fled to the village.

'Fat pig!' said Peroo. 'After all that we have done for him! When the flood is down I will see to it that we get a new *guru*. Finlinson Sahib, it darkens for night now, and since yesterday nothing has been eaten. Be wise, Sahib. No man can endure watching and great thinking on an empty belly. Lie down, Sahib. The river will do what the river will do.'

'The bridge is mine; I cannot leave it.'

'Wilt thou hold it up with thy hands, then?' said Peroo, laughing. 'I was troubled for my boats and sheers *before* the flood came. Now we are in the hands of the Gods. The Sahib will not eat and lie down? Take these, then. They are meat and good toddy together, and they kill all weariness, besides the fever that follows the rain. I have eaten nothing else today at all.'

He took a small tin tobacco-box from his sodden waist-belt and thrust it into Findlayson's hand, saying, 'Nay, do not be afraid. It is no more than opium – clean Malwa opium!'

Findlayson shook two or three of the dark-brown pellets into his hand, and hardly knowing what he did, swallowed them. The stuff was at least a good guard against fever – the fever that was creeping upon him out of the wet mud – and he had seen what Peroo could do in the stewing mists of autumn on the strength of a dose from the tin box.

Peroo nodded with bright eyes. 'In a little – in a little the Sahib will find that he thinks well again. I too will—' He dived into his treasure-box, resettled the rain-coat over his head, and squatted down to watch the boats. It was too dark now to see beyond the first pier, and the night seemed to have given the river new strength. Findlayson stood with his chin on his chest, thinking. There was one point about one of the piers – the Seventh – that he had not fully settled in his mind. The figures would not shape themselves to the eye except one by one and at enormous intervals of time. There was a sound, rich and mellow in his ears, like the deepest note of a double-bass – an entrancing sound upon which he pondered for several hours, as it seemed. Then Peroo was at his elbow, shouting that a wire hawser had snapped and the stone-boats were loose. Findlayson saw the fleet open and swing out fanwise to a long-drawn shriek of wire straining across gunnels.

'A tree hit them. They will all go,' cried Peroo. 'The main hawser has parted. What does the Sahib do?'

An immensely complex plan had suddenly flashed into Findlayson's mind. He saw the ropes running from boat to boat in straight lines and angles – each rope a line of white fire. But there was one rope which was the master-rope. He could see that rope. If he could pull it once, it was absolutely and mathematically certain that the disordered fleet would reassemble itself in the backwater behind the guard-tower. But why, he wondered, was Peroo clinging so desperately to his waist as he hastened down the bank? It was necessary to put the Lascar aside, gently and slowly, because it was necessary to save the boats, and, further, to demonstrate the extreme ease of the problem that looked so difficult. And then – but it was of no conceivable importance – a wire rope raced through his hand, burning it, the high bank disappeared, and with it all the slowly dispersing factors of the problem. He was silting in the rainy darkness – sitting in a boat that spun like a top, and Peroo was standing over him.

'I had forgotten,' said the Lascar slowly, 'that to those fasting and unused the opium is worse than any wine. Those who die in Gunga go to the Gods. Still, I have no desire to present myself before such great ones. Can the Sahib swim?'

'What need? He can fly – fly as swiftly as the wind,' was the thick answer.

'He is mad!' muttered Peroo under his breath. 'And He threw me aside like a bundle of dung-cakes. Well, he will not know his death. The boat cannot live an hour here even if she strike nothing. It is not good to look at death with a clear eye.'

He refreshed himself again from the tin box, squatted down in the bows of the reeling, pegged, and stitched craft, staring through the mist at the nothing that was there. A warm drowsiness crept over Findlayson, the Chief Engineer, whose duty was with his bridge. The heavy raindrops struck him with a thousand tingling little thrills, and the weight of all time since time was made hung heavy on his eyelids. He thought and perceived that he was perfectly secure, for the water was so solid that a man could surely step out upon it, and, standing still with his legs apart to keep his balance – this was the most important point – would be borne with great and easy speed to the shore. But yet a better plan came to him. It needed only an exertion of will for the soul to hurl the body ashore as wind drives paper; to waft it kite-fashion to the bank. Thereafter – the boat spun dizzily – suppose the high wind got under the freed body? Would it tower up like a kite and pitch headlong on the faraway sands, or would it duck about beyond control through all eternity? Findlayson gripped the gunnel to anchor himself, for it seemed that he was on the edge of taking the flight before he had settled all his plans. Opium has more effect on the white man than the black. Peroo was only comfortably indifferent to accidents. 'She cannot live,' he grunted. 'Her seams open already. If she were even a dinghy with oars we could have ridden it out; but a box with holes is no good. Finlinson Sahib, she fills.'

'*Accha!* I am going away. Come thou also.'

In his mind Findlayson had already escaped from the boat, and was circling high in air to find a rest for the sole of his foot. His body – he was really sorry for its gross helplessness – lay in the stern, the water rushing about its knees.

'How very ridiculous!' he said to himself, from his eyrie; 'that – is Findlayson – chief of the Kashi Bridge. The poor beast is going to be drowned, too. Drowned when it's close to shore. I'm – I'm on shore already. Why doesn't it come along?'

To his intense disgust, he found his soul back in his body again, and that body spluttering and choking in deep water. The pain of the reunion was atrocious, but it was necessary, also, to fight for the body. He was conscious of grasping wildly at wet sand, and striding prodigiously, as one strides in a dream, to keep foot-hold in the swirling water, till at last he hauled himself clear of the hold of the river, and dropped, panting, on wet earth.

'Not this night,' said Peroo in his ear. 'The Gods have protected us.' The Lascar moved his feet cautiously, and they rustled among dried stumps. 'This is some island of last year's indigo crop,' he went on. 'We shall find no men here; but have great care, Sahib; all the snakes of a hundred miles have been flooded out. Here comes the lightning, on the heels of the wind. Now we shall be able to look; but walk carefully.'

Findlayson was far and far beyond any fear of snakes, or indeed any merely human emotion. He saw, after he had rubbed the water from his eyes, with an immense clearness, and trod, so it seemed to himself, with world-encompassing strides. Somewhere in the night of time he had built a bridge – a bridge that spanned illimitable levels of shining seas; but the Deluge had swept it away, leaving this one island under heaven for Findlayson and his companion, sole survivors of the breed of man.

An incessant lightning, forked and blue, showed all that there was to be seen on the little patch in the flood – a clump of thorn, a clump of swaying creaking bamboos, and a grey gnarled peepul overshadowing a Hindoo shrine, from whose dome floated a tattered red flag. The holy man whose summer resting-place it was had long since abandoned it, and the weather had broken the red-daubed image of his God. The two men stumbled, heavy-limbed and heavy-eyed, over the ashes of a brick-set cooking-place, and dropped down under the shelter of the branches, while the rain and river roared together.

The stumps of the indigo crackled, and there was a smell of cattle, as a huge and dripping Brahminee Bull shouldered his way under the tree. The flashes revealed the trident mark of Shiva on his flank, the insolence of head and hump, the luminous stag-like eyes, the brow crowned with a wreath of sodden marigold blooms, and the silky dewlap that nigh swept the ground. There was a noise behind him of other beasts coming up from the flood-line through the thicket, a sound of heavy feet and deep breathing.

'Here be more beside ourselves,' said Findlayson, his head against the tree-pole, looking through half-shut eyes, wholly at ease.

'Truly,' said Peroo thickly, 'and no small ones.'

'What are they, then? I do not see clearly.'

'The Gods. Who else? Look!'

'Ah, truc! The Gods surely – the Gods.' Findlayson smiled as his head fell forward on his chest. Peroo was eminently right. After the Flood, who should be alive in the land except the Gods that made it – the Gods to whom his village prayed nightly – the Gods who were in all men's mouths and about all men's ways? He could not raise his head or stir a finger for the trance that held him, and Peroo was smiling vacantly at the lightning.

The Bull paused by the shrine, his head lowered to the damp earth. A green Parrot in the branches preened his wet wings and screamed against the thunder as the circle under the tree filled with the shifting shadows of beasts. There was a

Black-buck at the Bull's heels – such a buck as Findlayson in his far-away life upon earth might have seen in dreams – a buck with a royal head, ebon back, silver belly, and gleaming straight horns. Beside him, her head bowed to the ground, the green eyes burning under the heavy brows, with restless tail switching the dead grass, paced a Tigress, full-bellied and deep-jowled.

The Bull crouched beside the shrine, and there leaped from the darkness a monstrous grey Ape, who seated himself man-wise in the place of the fallen image, and the rain spilled like jewels from the hair of his neck and shoulders.

Other shadows came and went behind the circle, among them a drunken Man flourishing staff and drinking-bottle. Then a hoarse bellow broke out from near the ground. 'The flood lessens even now,' it cried. 'Hour by hour the water falls, and their bridge still stands!'

'My bridge,' said Findlayson to himself. 'That must be very old work now. What have the Gods to do with my bridge?'

His eyes rolled in the darkness following the roar. A Crocodile – the blunt-nosed, ford-haunting Mugger of the Ganges – dragged herself before the beasts, lashing furiously to right and left with her tail.

'They have made it too strong for me. In all this night I have only torn away a handful of planks. The walls stand! The towers stand! They have chained my flood, and my river is not free any more. Heavenly Ones, take this yoke away! Give me clear water between bank and bank! It is I, Mother Gunga, that speak. The Justice of the Gods! Deal me the Justice of the Gods!'

'What said I?' whispered Peroo. 'This is in truth a Punch-ayet of the Gods. Now we know that all the world is dead, save you and I, Sahib.'

The Parrot screamed and fluttered again, and the Tigress, her ears flat to her head, snarled wickedly.

Somewhere in the shadow a great trunk and gleaming tusks swayed to and fro, and a low gurgle broke the silence that followed on the snarl.

'We be here,' said a deep voice, 'the Great Ones. One only

and very many. Shiv, my father, is here, with Indra. Kali has spoken already. Hanuman listens also.'

'Kashi is without her Kotwal tonight,' shouted the Man with the drinking-bottle, flinging his staff to the ground, while the island rang to the baying of hounds. 'Give her the Justice of the Gods.'

'Ye were still when they polluted my waters,' the great Crocodile bellowed. 'Ye made no sign when my river was trapped, between the walls. I had no help save my own strength, and that failed – the strength of Mother Gunga failed – before their guard-towers. What could I do? I have done everything. Finish now, Heavenly Ones!'

'I brought the death; I rode the spotted sickness from hut to hut of their workmen, and yet they would not cease.' A nose-slitten, hide-worn Ass, lame, scissor-legged, and galled, limped forward. 'I cast the death at them out of my nostrils, but they would not cease.'

Peroo would have moved, but the opium lay heavy upon him.

'Bah!' he said, spitting. 'Here is Sitala herself; Mata – the small-pox. Has the Sahib a handkerchief to put over his face?'

'Small help! They fed me the corpses for a month, and I flung them out on my sand-bars, but their work went forward. Demons they are, and sons of demons! And ye left Mother Gunga alone for their fire-carriage to make a mock of. The Justice of the Gods on the bridge-builders!'

The Bull turned the cud in his mouth and answered slowly, 'If the Justice of the Gods caught all who made a mock of holy things, there would be many dark altars in the land, mother.'

'But this goes beyond a mock,' said the Tigress, darting forward a griping paw. 'Thou knowest, Shiv, and ye too, Heavenly Ones; ye know that they have defiled Gunga. Surely they must come to the Destroyer. Let Indra judge.'

The Buck made no movement as he answered, 'How long has this evil been?'

'Three years, as men count years,' said the Mugger, close pressed to the earth.

'Does Mother Gunga die, then, in a year, that she is so anxious to see vengeance now? The deep sea was where she runs but yesterday, and tomorrow the sea shall cover her again as the Gods count that which men call time. Can any say that this their bridge endures till tomorrow?' said the Buck.

There was a long hush, and in the clearing of the storm the full moon stood up above the dripping trees.

'Judge ye, then,' said the River sullenly. 'I have spoken my shame. The flood falls still. I can do no more.'

'For my own part' – it was the voice of the great Ape seated – within the shrine – 'it pleases me well to watch these men, remembering that I also builded no small bridge in the world's youth.'

'They say, too,' snarled the Tiger, 'that these men came of the wreck of thy armies, Hanuman, and therefore thou hast aided—'

'They toil as my armies toiled in Lanka, and they believe that their toil endures, Indra is too high, but Shiv, thou knowest how the land is threaded with their fire-carriages.'

'Yea, I know,' said the Bull. 'Their Gods instructed them in the matter.'

A laugh ran round the circle.

'Their Gods! What should their Gods know? They were born yesterday, and those that made them are scarcely yet cold,' said the Mugger. 'Tomorrow their Gods will die.'

'Ho!' said Peroo. 'Mother Gunga talks good talk. I told that to the padre-sahib who preached on the *Mombassa*, and he asked the Burra Malum to put me in irons for a great rudeness.'

'Surely they make these things to please their Gods,' said the Bull again.

'Not altogether,' the Elephant rolled forth. 'It is for the profit of my mahajuns – my fat money-lenders that worship me at each new year, when they draw my image at the head of the account-books. I, looking over their shoulders by lamp-light, see that the names in the books are those of men in far places – for all the towns are drawn together by the fire-carriage, and the money comes and goes swiftly, and the account-books grow as fat as – myself. And I, who am Ganesh of Good Luck, I bless my peoples.'

'They have changed the face of the land – which is my land. They have killed and made new towns on my banks,' said the Mugger.

'It is but the shirting of a little dirt. Let the dirt dig in the dirt if it pleases the dirt,' answered the Elephant.

'But afterwards?' said the Tiger. 'Afterwards they will see that Mother Gunga can avenge no insult, and they fall away from her first, and later from us all, one by one. In the end, Ganesh, we are left with naked altars.'

The drunken Man staggered to his feet, and hiccupped vehemently in the face of the assembled Gods.

'Kali lies. My sister lies. Also this my stick is the Kotwal of Kashi, and he keeps tally of my pilgrims. When the time comes to worship Bhairon – and it is always time – the fire-carriages move one by one, and each bears a thousand pilgrims. They do not come afoot any more, but rolling upon wheels, and my honour is increased.'

'Gunga, I have seen thy bed at Pryag black with the pilgrims,' said the Ape, leaning forward, 'and but for the fire-carriage they would have come slowly and in fewer numbers. Remember.'

'They come to me always,' Bhairon went on thickly. 'By day and night they pray to me, all the Common People in the fields and the roads. Who is like Bhairon today? What talk is this of changing faiths? Is my staff Kotwal of Kashi for nothing? He keeps the tally, and he says that never were so many altars as today, and the fire-carriage serves them well. Bhairon am I – Bhairon of the Common People, and the chiefest of the Heavenly. Ones today. Also my staff says—'

'Peace, thou!' lowed the Bull. 'The worship of the schools is mine, and they talk very wisely, asking whether I be one or many, as is the delight of my people, and ye know what I am. Kali, my wife, thou knowest also.'

'Yea, I know,' said the Tigress, with lowered head.

'Greater am I than Gunga also. For ye know who moved the minds of men that they should count Gunga holy among the rivers. Who die in that water – ye know how men say – come to us without punishment, and Gunga knows that the fire-carriage has borne to her scores upon scores of such anxious ones; and Kali knows that she has held her chiefest festivals among the pilgrimages that are fed by the fire-carriage. Who smote at Pooree, under the Image there, her thousands in a day and a night, and bound the sickness to the wheels of the fire-carriages, so that it ran from one end of the land to the other? Who but Kali? Before the fire-carriage came it was a heavy toil. The fire-carriages have served thee well, Mother of Death. But I speak for mine own altars, who am not Bhairon of the Common Folk, but Shiv. Men go to and fro, making words and telling talk of strange Gods, and I listen. Faith follows faith among my people in the schools, and I have no anger; for when the words are said, and the new talk is ended, to Shiv men return at the last.'

'True. It is true,' murmured Hanuman. 'To Shiv and to the others, mother, they return. I creep from temple to temple in the North, where they worship one God and His Prophet; and presently my image is alone within their shrines.'

'Small thanks,' said the Buck, turning his head slowly. 'I am that One and His Prophet also.'

'Even so, father,' said Hanuman. 'And to the South I go who am the oldest of the Gods as men know the Gods, and presently I touch the shrines of the new faith and the Woman whom we know is hewn twelve-armed, and still they call her Mary.'

'Small thanks, brother,' said the Tigress. 'I am that Woman.'

'Even so, sister; and I go West among the fire-carriages, and stand before the bridge-builders in many shapes, and because of me they change their faiths and are very wise. Ho! ho! I am the builder of bridges indeed – bridges between this and that, and each bridge leads surely to Us in the end. Be content, Gunga. Neither these men nor those that follow them mock thee at all.'

'Am I alone, then, Heavenly Ones? Shall I smooth out my flood lest unhappily I bear away their walls? Will Indra dry my springs in the hills and make me crawl humbly between their wharfs? Shall I bury me in the sand ere I offend?'

'And all for the sake of a little iron bar with the fire-carriage atop. Truly, Mother Gunga is always young!' said Ganesh the Elephant. 'A child had not spoken more foolishly. Let the dirt dig in the dirt ere it return to the dirt. I know only that my people grow rich and praise me. Shiv has said that the men of the schools do not forget; Bhairon is content for his crowd of the Common People: and Hanuman laughs.'

'Surely I laugh,' said the Ape. 'My altars are few beside those of Ganesh or Bhairon, but the fire-carriages bring me new worshippers from beyond the Black Water – the men who believe that their God is toil. I run before them beckoning, and they follow Hanuman.'

'Give them the toil that they desire, then,' said the River. 'Make a bar across my flood and throw the water back upon the bridge. Once thou wast strong in Lanka, Hanuman. Stoop and lift my bed.'

'Who gives life can take life.' The Ape scratched in the mud with a long forefinger. 'And yet, who would profit by the killing? Very many would die.'

There came up from the water a snatch of a love-song such as the boys sing when they watch their cattle in the noon heats of late spring. The Parrot screamed joyously, sidling along his branch with lowered head as the song grew louder, and in a patch of clear moonlight stood revealed the young herd, the darling of the Gopis, the idol of dreaming maids and of mothers ere their children are born – Krishna the Well-beloved. He stooped to knot up his long wet hair, and the Parrot fluttered to his shoulder.

'Fleeting and singing, and singing and fleeting,' hiccupped Bhairon. 'Those make thee late for the council, brother.'

'And then?' said Krishna, with a laugh, throwing back his head. 'Ye can do little without me or Karma here. He fondled the Parrot's plumage and laughed again. 'What is this sitting and talking together? I heard Mother Gunga roaring in the dark, and so came quickly from a hut where I lay warm. And what have ye done to Karma, that he is so wet and silent? And what does Mother Gunga here? Are the heavens full that ye must come paddling in the mud beast-wise? Karma, what do they do?'

'Gunga has prayed for a vengeance on the bridge-builders,, and Kali is with her. Now she bids Hanuman whelm the bridge, that her honour may be made great,' cried the Parrot. 'I waited here, knowing that thou wouldst come, O my master!'

'And the Heavenly Ones said nothing? Did Gunga and the Mother of Sorrows out-talk them? Did none speak for my people?'

'Nay,' said Ganesh, moving uneasily from foot to foot; 'I said it was but dirt at play, and why should we stamp it flat?'

'I was content to let them toil – well content,' said Hanuman.

'What had I to do with Gunga's anger?' said the Bull.

'I am Bhairon of the Common Folk, and this my staff is Kotwal of all Kashi. I spoke for the Common People.'

'Thou?' The young God's eyes sparkled.

'Am I not the first of the Gods in their mouths today?' returned Bhairon, unabashed. 'For the sake of the Common People I said – very many wise things which I have now forgotten – but this my staff—'

Krishna turned impatiently, saw the Mugger at his feet, and kneeling, slipped an arm round the cold neck. 'Mother,' he said gently, 'get thee to thy flood again. The matter is not for thee. What harm shall thy honour take of this live dirt? Thou hast given them their fields new year after year, and by thy flood they are made strong. They come all to thee at the last. What need to slay them now? Have pity, mother, for a little – and it is only for a little.'

'If it be only for a little—' the slow beast began.

'Are they Gods, then?' Krishna returned with a laugh, his eyes looking into the dull eyes of the River. 'Be certain that it is only for a little. The Heavenly Ones have heard thee, and presently justice will be done. Go now, mother, to the flood again. Men and cattle are thick on the waters – the banks fall – the villages melt because of thee.'

'But the bridge – the bridge stands.' The Mugger turned grunting into the undergrowth as Krishna rose.

'It is ended,' said the Tigress, viciously. 'There is no more justice from the Heavenly Ones. Ye have made shame and sport of Gunga, who asked no more than a few score lives.'

'Of *my* people – who lie under the leaf-roofs of the village yonder – of the young girls, and the young men who sing to them in the dark – of the child that will be born next morn – of that which was begotten tonight,' said Krishna. 'And when all is done, what profit? Tomorrow sees them at work. Ay, if ye swept the bridge out from end to end they would begin anew. Hear me! Bhairon is drunk always. Hanuman mocks his people with new riddles.'

'Nay, but they are very old ones,' the Ape said, laughing.

'Shiv hears the talk of the schools and the dreams of the holy men; Ganesh thinks only of his fat traders; but I – I live with these my people, asking for no gifts, and so receiving them hourly.'

'And very tender art thou of thy people,' said the Tigress.

'They are my own. The old women dream of me, turning in their sleep; the maids look and listen for me when they go to fill their lotahs by the river. I walk by the young men waiting without the gates at dusk, and I call over my shoulder to the white-beards. Ye know, Heavenly Ones, that I alone of us all walk upon the earth continually, and have no pleasure in our heavens so long as a green blade springs here, or there are two voices at twilight in the standing crops. Wise are ye, but ye live far off, forgetting whence ye came. So do I not forget. And the fire-carriage feeds your shrines, ye say? And the fire-carriages bring a thousand pilgrimages where but ten came in the old years? True. That is true today.'

'But tomorrow they are dead, brother,' said Ganesh.

'Peace!' said the Bull, as Hanuman leaned forward again. 'And tomorrow, beloved – what of tomorrow?'

'This only. A new word creeping from mouth to mouth among the Common Folk – a word that neither man nor God can lay hold of – an evil word – a little lazy word among the

Common Folk, saying (and none know who set that word afoot) that they weary of ye, Heavenly Ones.'

The Gods laughed together softly. 'And then, beloved?' they said.

'And to cover that weariness they, my people, will bring to thee, Shiv, and to thee, Ganesh, at first greater offerings and a louder noise of worship. But the word has gone abroad, and, after, they will pay fewer dues to your fat Brahmins. Next they will forget your altars, but so slowly that no man can say how his forgetfulness began.'

'I knew – I knew! I spoke this also, but they would not hear,' said the Tigress. 'We should have slain – we should have slain!'

'It is too late now. Ye should have slain at the beginning, when the men from across the water had taught our folk nothing. Now my people see their work, and go away thinking. They do not think of the Heavenly Ones altogether. They think of the fire-carriage and the other things that the bridge-builders have done, and when your priests thrust forward hands asking alms, they give unwillingly a little. That is the beginning, among one or two, or five or ten – for I, moving among my people, know what is in their hearts.'

'And the end, Jester of the Gods? What shall the end be?' said Ganesh.

'The end shall be as it was in the beginning, O slothful son of Shiv! The flame shall die upon the altars and the prayer upon the tongue till ye become little Gods again – Gods of the jungle – names that the hunters of rats and noosers of dogs whisper in the thicket and among the caves – rag-Gods, pot Godlings of the tree, and the village-mark, as ye were at the beginning. That is the end, Ganesh, for thee, and for Bhairon – Bhairon of the Common People.'

'It is very far away,' grunted Bhairon. 'Also, it is a lie.'

'Many women have kissed Krishna. They told him this to cheer their own hearts when the grey hairs came, and he has told us the tale,' said the Bull, below his breath.

'Their Gods came, and we changed them. I took the Woman and made her twelve-armed. So shall we twist all their Gods,' said Hanuman.

'Their Gods! This is no question of their Gods – one or three – man or woman. The matter is with the people. *They* move, and not the Gods of the bridge-builders,' said Krishna.

'So be it. I have made a man worship the fire-carriage as it stood still breathing smoke, and he knew not that he worshipped me,' said Hanuman the Ape. 'They will only change a little the names of their Gods. I shall lead the builders of the bridges as of old; Shiv shall be worshipped in the schools by such as doubt and despise their fellows; Ganesh shall have his mahajuns, and Bhairon the donkey-drivers, the pilgrims, and the sellers of toys. Beloved, they will do no more than change the names, and that we have seen a thousand times.'

'Surely they will do no more than change the names,' echoed Ganesh: but there was an uneasy movement among the Gods.

'They will change more than the names. Me alone they cannot kill, so long as maiden and man meet together or the spring follows the winter rains. Heavenly Ones, not for nothing have I walked upon the earth. My people know not now what they know; but I, who live with them, I read their hearts. Great Kings, the beginning of the end is born already. The fire-carriages shout the names of new Gods that are *not* the old under new names. Drink now and eat greatly! Bathe your faces in the smoke of the altars before they grow cold! Take dues and listen to the cymbals and the drums, Heavenly Ones, while yet there are flowers and songs. As men count time the end is far off; but as we who know reckon it is today. I have spoken.'

The young God ceased, and his brethren looked at each other long in silence.

'This I have not heard before,' Peroo whispered in his companion's ear. 'And yet sometimes, when I oiled the brasses in the engine-room of the *Goorkha*, I have wondered if our priests were so wise – so wise. The day is coming, Sahib. They will be gone by the morning.'

A yellow light broadened in the sky, and the tone of the river changed as the darkness withdrew.

Suddenly the Elephant trumpeted aloud as though man had goaded him.

'Let Indra judge. Father of all, speak thou! What of the things we have heard? Has Krishna lied indeed? Or—'

'Ye know,' said the Buck, rising to his feet. 'Ye know the Riddle of the Gods. When Brahm ceases to dream the Heavens and the Hells and Earth disappear. Be content. Brahm dreams still. The dreams come and go, and the nature of the dreams changes, but still Brahm dreams. Krishna has walked too long upon earth, and yet I love him the more for the tale he has told. The Gods change, beloved – all save One!'

'Ay, all save one that makes love in the hearts of men,' said Krishna, knotting his girdle. 'It is but a little time to wait, and ye shall know if I lie.'

'Truly it is but a little time, as thou sayest, and we shall know. Get thee to thy huts again, beloved, and make sport for the young things, for still Brahm dreams. Go, my children! Brahm dreams – and till He wakes the Gods die not.'

'Whither went they?' said the Lascar, awe-struck, shivering a little with the cold.

'God knows!' said Findlayson. The river and the island lay in full daylight now, and there was never mark of hoof or pug on the wet earth under the peepul. Only a parrot screamed in the branches, bringing down showers of water-drops as he fluttered his wings.

'Up! We are cramped with cold! Has the opium died out? Canst thou move, Sahib?'

Findlayson staggered to his feet and shook himself. His head swam and ached, but the work of the opium was over, and, as he sluiced his forehead in a pool, the Chief Engineer of the Kashi Bridge was wondering how he had managed to fall upon the island, what chances the day offered of return, and, above all, how his work stood.

'Peroo, I have forgotten much. I was under the guard-tower watching the river; and then— Did the flood sweep us away?'

'No. The boats broke loose, Sahib, and' (if the Sahib had forgotten about the opium, decidedly Peroo would not remind him) 'in striving to retie them, so it seemed to me – but it was dark – a rope caught the Sahib and threw him upon a boat.

Considering that we two, with Hitchcock Sahib, built, as it were, that bridge, I came also upon the boat, which came riding on horseback, as it were, on the nose of this island, and so, splitting, cast us ashore. I made a great cry when the boat left the wharf, and without doubt Hitchcock Sahib will come for us. As for the bridge, so many have died in the building that it cannot fall.'

A fierce sun, that drew out all the smell of the sodden land, had followed the storm, and in that clear light there was no room for a man to think of dreams of the dark. Findlayson stared upstream, across the blaze of moving water, till his eyes ached. There was no sign of any bank to the Ganges, much less of a bridge-line.

'We came down far,' he said. 'It was wonderful that we were not drowned a hundred times.'

'That was the least of the wonder, for no man dies before his time. I have seen Sydney, I have seen London, and twenty great ports, but' – Peroo looked at the damp, discoloured shrine under the peepul – 'never man has seen that we saw here.'

'What?'

'Has the Sahib forgotten; or do we black men only see the Gods?'

'There was a fever upon me.' Findlayson was still looking uneasily across the water. 'It seemed that the island was full of beasts and men talking, but I do not remember. A boat could live in this water now, I think.'

'Oho! Then it *is* true. "When Brahm ceases to dream, the Gods die." Now I know, indeed, what he meant. Once, too, the *guru* said as much to me; but then I did not understand. Now I am wise.'

'What?' said Findlayson over his shoulder.

Peroo went on as if he were talking to himself. 'Six – seven – ten monsoons since, I was watch on the fo'c'sle of the *Rewah* – the Kumpani's big boat – and there was a big *tufan*, green and black water beating; and I held fast to the life-lines, choking under the waters. Then I thought of the Gods – of Those whom we saw tonight' – he stared curiously at Findlayson's back, but the white man was looking across the flood. 'Yes, I say of Those whom we saw this night past, and I called upon Them to protect me. And while I prayed, still keeping my look-out, a big wave came and threw me forward upon the ring of the great black bow-anchor, and the *Rewah* rose high and high, leaning towards the left-hand side, and the water drew away from beneath her nose, and I lay upon my belly, holding the ring, and looking down into those great deeps. Then I thought, even in the face of death, if I lose hold I die, and for me neither the *Rewah* nor my place by the galley where the rice is cooked, nor Bombay, nor Calcutta, nor even London, will be any more for me. "How shall I be sure," I said, "that the Gods to whom I pray will abide at all?" This I thought, and the *Rewah* dropped her nose as a hammer falls, and all the sea came in and slid me backwards along the fo'c'sle and over the break of the fo'c'sle, and I very badly bruised my shin against the donkey-engine: but I did not die, and I have seen the Gods. They are good for live men, but for the dead— They have spoken Themselves. Therefore, when I come to the village I will beat the *guru* for talking riddles which are no riddles. When Brahm ceases to dream, the Gods go.'

'Look upstream. The light blinds. Is there smoke yonder?'

Peroo shaded his eyes with his hands. 'He is a wise man and quick. Hitchcock Sahib would not trust a rowboat. He has borrowed the Rao Sahib's steam-launch, and comes to look for us. I have always said that there should have been a steam-launch on the bridge-works for us.'

The territory of the Rao of Baraon lay within ten miles of the bridge; and Findlayson and Hitchcock had spent a fair portion of their scanty leisure in playing billiards and shooting Black-buck with the young man. He had been bear-led by an English tutor of sporting tastes for some five or six years, and was now royally wasting the revenues accumulated during his minority by the Indian Government. His steam-launch, with its silver-plated rails, striped silk awning, and mahogany decks, was a new toy which Findlayson had found horribly in the way when the Rao came to look at the bridge-works.

'It's great luck,' murmured Findlayson, but he was none the less afraid, wondering what news might be of the bridge.

The gaudy blue-and-white funnel came downstream swiftly. They could see Hitchcock in the bows, with a pair of opera-glasses, and his face was unusually white. Then Peroo hailed, and the launch made for the tail of the island. The Rao Sahib, in tweed shooting-suit and a seven-hued turban, waved his royal hand, and Hitchcock shouted. But he need have asked no questions, for Findlayson's first demand was for his bridge.

'All serene! 'Gad, I never expected to see you again, Findlayson. You're seven koss downstream. Yes, there's not a stone shifted anywhere; but how are you? I borrowed the Rao Sahib's launch, and he was good enough to come along. Jump in.'

'Ah, Finlinson, you are very well, eh? That was most unprecedented calamity last night, eh? My royal palace, too, it leaks like the devil, and the crops will also be short all about my country. Now you shall back her out, Hitchcock. I – I do not understand steam-engines. You are wet? You are cold, Finlinson? I have some things to eat here, and you will take a good drink.'

'I'm immensely grateful, Rao Sahib. I believe you've saved my life. How did Hitchcock—'

'Oho! His hair was upon end. He rode to me in the middle of the night and woke me up in the arms of Morpheus. I was most truly concerned, Finlinson, so I came too. My head-priest he is very angry just now. We will go quick, Mister Hitchcock. I am due to attend at twelve forty-five in the state temple, where we sanctify some new idol. If not so I would have asked you to spend the day with me. They are dam-bore, these religious ceremonies, Finlinson, eh?'

Peroo, well known to the crew, had possessed himself of the wheel, and was taking the launch craftily upstream. But while he steered he was, in his mind, handling two feet of partially untwisted wire-rope; and the back upon which he beat was the back of his *guru*.

THE BRUSHWOOD BOY

Girls and boys, come out to play:
The moon is shining as bright as day!
Leave your supper and leave your sleep.
And come with your playfellows out in the street!
Up the ladder and down the wall –

A child of three sat up in his crib and screamed at the top of his voice, his fists clenched and his eyes full of terror. At first no one heard, for his nursery was in the west wing, and the nurse was talking to a gardener among the laurels. Then the housekeeper passed that way, and hurried to soothe him. He was her special pet, and she disapproved of the nurse.

'What was it, then? What was it, then? There's nothing to frighten him, Georgie dear.'

'It was – it was a policeman! He was on the Down – I saw him! He came in. Jane *said* he would.'

'Policemen don't come into houses, dearie. Turn over, and take my hand.'

'I saw him – on the Down. He came here. Where is your hand, Harper?'

The housekeeper waited till the sobs changed to the regular breathing of sleep before she stole out.

'Jane, what nonsense have you been telling Master Georgie about policemen?'

'I haven't told him anything.'

'You have. He's been dreaming about them.'

'We met Tisdall on Dowhead when we were in the donkey-cart this morning. P'r'aps that's what put it into his head.'

'Oh! Now you aren't going to frighten the child into fits with your silly tales, and the master know nothing about it. If ever I catch you again,' etc.

*

A child of six was telling himself stories as he lay in bed. It was a new power, and he kept it a secret. A month before it had occurred to him to carry on a nursery tale left unfinished by his mother, and he was delighted to find that the tale as it came out of his own head was just as new and surprising as though he were listening to it 'all new from the beginning.' There was a prince in that tale, and he killed dragons, but only for one night. Ever afterward Georgie dubbed himself prince, pasha, giant-killer, and all the rest (you see, he could not tell any one, for fear of being laughed at), and his tales faded gradually into dreamland, where adventures were so many that he could not recall the half of them. They all began in the same way, or, as Georgie explained to the shadows of the night-light, there was 'the same starting-off place' – a pile of brushwood stacked somewhere near a beach; and round this pile Georgie found himself running races with little boys and girls. These ended, things began to happen, such as ships that ran high up the dry land and turned into cardboard boxes; or gilt-and-green iron railings that surrounded beautiful gardens, but were all soft and could be walked through and overthrown so long as he remembered it was only a dream. He could never hold that knowledge more than a few seconds before things became real, and instead of pushing down houses full of grown-up people (a just revenge), he sat miserably upon gigantic door-steps trying to sing the multiplication-table up to four times six. It was most amusing at the very beginning, before the races round the pile, when he could shout to the others, 'It's only make-believe, and I'll smack you!'

The princess of his tales was a person of wonderful beauty (she came from the old illustrated edition of Grimm, now out of print), and as she invariably looked on at Georgie's valor among the dragons and buffaloes and so forth, he gave her the two finest names he had ever heard in his life – Annie and Louise, pronounced 'Annie*an*louise.' When the dreams swamped the stories, she would change into one of the little girls round the brushwood pile, still keeping her title and crown. She saw Georgie drown once in a dream-sea by the beach (it was the day after he had been taken to bathe in a real

383

sea by his nurse); and he said as he sank: 'Poor Annie*an*louise! She'll be sorry for me now!' But 'Annie*an*louise,' walking slowly on the beach, called, ' "Ha! ha!" said the duck, laughing,' which to a waking mind might not seem to bear on the situation. It consoled Georgie at once, and must have been some kind of spell, for it raised the bottom of the deep, and he waded out with a twelve-inch flower-pot on each foot. As he was strictly forbidden to meddle with flower-pots in real life, he felt triumphantly wicked.

The movements of the grown-ups, whom Georgie tolerated, but did not pretend to understand, removed his world, when he was seven years old, to a place called 'Oxford-on-a-visit.' Here were huge buildings surrounded by vast prairies, with streets of infinite length, and, above all, something called the 'buttery,' which Georgie was dying to see, because he knew it must be greasy, and therefore delightful. He perceived how correct were his judgments when his nurse led him through a stone arch into the presence of an enormously fat man, who asked him if he would like some bread and cheese. Georgie was used to eat all round the clock, so he took what 'buttery' gave him, and would have taken some brown liquid called 'auditale' but that his nurse led him away to an afternoon performance of a thing called 'Pepper's Ghost,' This was intensely thrilling. People's heads came off and flew all over the stage, and skeletons danced bone by bone, while Mr Pepper himself, beyond question a man of the worst, waved his arms and flapped a long gown, and in a deep bass voice (Georgie had never heard a man sing before) told of his sorrows unspeakable. Some grown-up or other tried to explain that the illusion was made with mirrors, and that there was no need to be frightened. Georgie did not know what illusions were, but he did know that a mirror was the looking-glass with the ivory handle on his mother's dressing-table. Therefore the 'grown-up' was 'just saying things' after the distressing custom of 'grown-ups,' and Georgie cast about for amusement between scenes. Next to him sat a little girl dressed all in black, her hair combed off her forehead exactly like the girl in the book called 'Alice in Wonderland,' which had been given him on his last birthday. The little girl looked at Georgie, and Georgie looked at her. There seemed to be no need of any further introduction.

'I've got a cut on my thumb,' said he. It was the first work of his first real knife, a savage triangular hack, and he esteemed it a most valuable possession.

'I'm tho thorry!' she lisped. 'Let me look – pleathe.'

'There's a di-ack-lum plaster on, but it's all raw under.' Georgie answered, complying.

'Dothent it hurt?' – her gray eyes were full of pity and interest.

'Awf'ly. Perhaps it will give me lockjaw.'

'It lookth very horrid. I'm *tho* thorry!' She put a forefinger to his hand, and held her head sidewise for a better view.

Here the nurse turned, and shook him severely. 'You mustn't talk to strange little girls, Master Georgie.'

'She isn't strange. She's very nice. I like her, an' I've showed her my new cut.'

'The idea! You change places with me.'

She moved him over, and shut out the little girl from his view, while the grown-up behind renewed the futile explanations.

'I am *not* afraid, truly,' said the boy, wriggling in despair; 'But why don't you go to sleep in the afternoons, same as the Provost of Oriel?'

Georgie had been introduced to a grown-up of that name, who slept in his presence without apology. Georgie understood that he was the most important grown-up in Oxford; hence he strove to gild his rebuke with flatteries. This grown-up did not seem to like it, but he collapsed, and Georgie lay back in his seat, silent and enraptured. Mr Pepper was singing again, and the deep, ringing voice, the red fire, and the misty, waving gown all seemed to be mixed up with the little girl Who had been so kind about his cut. When the performance was ended she nodded to Georgie, and Georgie nodded in return. He spoke no more than was necessary till bedtime, but meditated on new colours and sounds and lights and music and things as far as he understood them, the deep-mouthed agony of Mr Pepper mingling with the little girl's lisp. That night he made a new tale, from which he shamelessly removed the Rapunzel-Rapunzel-let-down-your-hair princess, gold crown, Grimm edition, and all, and put a new Annie*an*louise in her place. So it was perfectly right and natural that when he came to the brushwood pile he should find her waiting for him, her hair combed off her forehead more like Alice in Wonderland than ever, and the races and adventures began.

Ten years at an English public school do not encourage dreaming. Georgie got his growth and chest measurement, and a few other things which did not appear in the bills, under a system of compulsory cricket, football, and paper-chases, from four to five days a week, which provided for three lawful cuts of a ground-ash if any boy absented himself from these entertainments without medical certificate or master's written excuse. From the child of eight, timid and shrinking, consoled by the sick-house matron as he wept for his mother, Georgie shot up into a hard-muscled, pugnacious little ten-year-old bully of the preparatory school, and was transplanted to the world of three hundred boys in the big dormitories below the hill, where the cheek so brazen and effective among juniors had to be turned to the smiter many times a day. There he became a rumple-collared, dusty-hatted fag of the Lower Third, and a little half-back at Little Side foot-ball; was pushed and prodded through the slack back-waters of the Lower Fourth, where all the raffle of a school generally accumulates; won his 'second-fifteen' cap at football, enjoyed the dignity of a study with two companions in it, and began to look forward to office as a sub-prefect. At this crisis he was exhorted to work by the head-master, who saw in him the makings of a good man. So he worked slowly and sys-tematically, and in due course sat at the prefects' table with the right to carry a cane, and, under restrictions, to use it. At last he blossomed into full glory as head of the school, ex-officio captain of the games; head of his house, where he and his lieutenants preserved discipline and decency among seventy boys from twelve to seventeen; general arbiter in the quarrels that spring up among the touchy Sixth – quarrels which on no account the vulgar must hear discussed; and intimate friend and ally of the head himself. He had a study of his own, where the black-and-gold 'first-fifteen' cap hung on a bracket above the line of hurdle, long-jump, and half-mile cups that he had picked up year after year at the yearly sports; he used real razors, which the fags stropped with reverence; and outside his door were laid the black-and-yellow match goal-posts carried down in state to the field when the school tried conclusions with other teams. When he stepped forth in the black jersey, white knickers, and black stockings of the first fifteen, the new match-ball under his arm, and his old and frayed cap at the back of his head, the small fry of the lower forms stood apart and worshipped, and the 'new caps' of the team talked to him ostentatiously, that the world might see. And so, in summer, when he came back to the pavilion after a slow but eminently safe game, it mattered not whether he had made nothing in, as once happened, a hundred and three, the school shouted just the same, and women-folk who had come to look at the match looked at Cottar – Cottar *major*; 'that's Cottar!' – and the day-boys felt that though home and mother were pleasant, it were better to live life joyously and whole, a full-blooded boarder in Cottar's house. Above all, he was responsible for that thing called the tone of the school, and few realise with what passionate devotion a certain type of boy throws himself into this work. Home was a far-away country, full of ponies and fishing and shooting, and men-visitors who interfered with one's plans; but school was the real world, where things of vital importance happened, and crises arose that must be dealt with promptly and quietly. Not for nothing was it written, 'Let the consuls look to it that the republic takes no harm,' and Georgie was glad to be back in authority when the holidays ended. Behind him, but not too near, was the wise and temperate head, now suggesting the wisdom of the serpent, now counseling the mildness of the dove; leading him on to see, more by half-hints than by any direct word, how boys and men are all of a piece, and how he who can handle the one will assuredly in time control the other. On the other side

– Georgie did not realise this till later – was the wiry drill-sergeant, contemptuously aware of all the tricks of ten generations of boys, who ruled the gymnasium through the long winter evenings when the squads were at work. There, among the rattle of the single-sticks, the click of the foils, the jar of the spring-bayonet sent home on the plastron, and the incessant 'bat-bat' of the gloves, little Schofield would cool off on the vaulting-horse, and explain to the head of the school by what mysterious ways the worth of a boy could be gauged between half-shut eyelids.

For the rest, the school was not encouraged to dwell on its emotions, but rather to keep in hard condition, to avoid false quantities, and to enter the army direct, without the help of the expensive London crammer, under whose roof young blood learns too much. Cottar *major* went the way of hundreds before him. The head gave him six months' final polish, taught him what kind of answers best please a certain kind of examiners and win marks, and handed him over to the properly constituted authorities, who passed him into Sandhurst fairly high up the list. Here he had sense enough to see that he was in the Lower Third once more, and behaved with respect toward his seniors, till they in turn respected him, and he was promoted to the rank of corporal, and sat in authority over mixed peoples with all the vices of men and boys combined. For the first of many occasions school experience served him well. His reward was another string of athletic cups, a good-conduct sword, and, at last. Her Majesty's commission as a subaltern in a first-class line regiment. He did not know that he bore with him from school and college a character worth much fine gold, but was pleased to find his mess so kindly and companionable. He had plenty of money of his own; his training had set the public-school mask upon his face, and had taught him how many were the 'things no fellow can do.' By virtue of the same training he kept his pores open and his mouth shut; and he looked very well with his company on parade.

The regular working of the empire shifted his world to India, where he tasted utter loneliness in subaltern's quarters,

– one room and one bullock-trunk, – and, with his mess, learned the new life from the beginning. But there were horses in the land – ponies at reasonable price; there was polo for such as could afford it; there were the disreputable remnants of a pack of hounds; and there were cricket, and musketry instruction, and the fitting up of the new gymnasium; and Cottar worried his way along without too much despair. It dawned on him that a regiment in India was nearer the chance of active service than he had conceived, and that a man might as well study his profession. A major of the new school backed this idea with enthusiasm (he was a black little man, full of notions), and he and Cottar accumulated a good library of military works, and read and argued and disputed far into the nights. But the adjutant said the old thing: 'Get to know your men, young un, and they'll follow you anywhere. That's all you want – know your men.' Cottar thought he knew them fairly well at cricket and the regimental sports, but he never realised the true inwardness of them till he was sent off with a detachment of twenty to sit down in a mud fort near a rushing river which was spanned by a bridge of boats. When the floods came they went out and hunted stray pontoons down the banks. Otherwise there was nothing to do, and the men got drunk, gambled, and quarrelled. They were a sickly crew, for a junior subaltern is by custom saddled with the worst men. Cottar endured their rioting as long as he could, and then sent down-country for a dozen pairs of boxing-gloves. (Nothing in the regulations forbids an officer taking part in healthy sports.)

'I wouldn't blame you for fightin',' said he, 'if you only knew how to use your hands; but you don't. Take these things, and I'll show you.' It was great sport, for he could pay back an insubordinate young thief, and teach him something at the same time; and the men appreciated his efforts. Now, instead of blaspheming and swearing at a comrade, and threatening to shoot him, they could take him apart, and soothe themselves to exhaustion. As one man explained whom Cottar found with a shut eye and a diamond-shaped mouth spitting teeth through an embrasure: 'We tried it with the gloves, sir, for twenty minutes, and *that* done us no good, sir. Then we took off the gloves and tried it that way for another twenty minutes, same as you showed us, sir, an' that done us a world o' good. 'Twasn't fightin', sir; there was a bet on.'

Cottar dared not laugh, but he invited his men to other sports, such as racing across country in shirt and trousers after a trail of torn paper, and to single-stick in the evenings, till the native population, who had a lust for sport in every form, wished to know whether the white men understood wrestling. They sent in an ambassador, who took the soldiers by the neck and threw them about the dust; and the entire command were all for this new game. They spent money on learning new falls and holds, which was better than buying beer and other doubtful commodities; and the big-limbed peasantry grinned five deep round the tournaments.

That detachment, who had gone up in bullock-carts, returned to headquarters at an average rate of thirty miles a day, fair heel and toe; no sick, no prisoners, and no court-martials pending. They scattered themselves among their friends, singing the praises of their lieutenant and looking for causes of offence.

'How did you do it, young un?' the adjutant asked.

'Oh, I sweated the beef off 'em, and then I sweated some muscle on to 'em. It was rather a lark.'

'If that's your way of lookin' at it, we can give you all the larks you want. Young Davies isn't feelin' quite fit, and he's next for detachment duty. Care to go with him?'

'Sure he wouldn't mind? I don't want to shove myself forward in any way.'

'You needn't bother on Davies's account. We'll give you the sweepin's of the corps, and you can see what you can make of 'em.'

'All right,' said Cottar. 'It's better fun than loafin' about cantonments.'

'Rummy thing,' said the adjutant, after Cottar had returned to his wilderness with twenty other devils worse than the first. 'If Cottar only knew it, half the women in the station would give their eyes – confound 'em! – to have the young un in tow.'

'That accounts for Mrs Elery sayin' I was workin' my nice new boy too hard,' said a wing commander.

'Oh, yes; and "Why doesn't he come to the band-stand in the evenings?" and "Can't I get him to make up a four at tennis with the Hammon girls?"' the adjutant snorted. 'Look at young Davies makin' an ass of himself over mutton-dressed-as-lamb old enough to be his mother!'

'No one can accuse young Cottar of runnin' after women, white *or* black,' the major replied thoughtfully. 'But, then, that's the kind that generally goes the worst mucker in the end.'

'Not Cottar. I've only run across one of his muster before – a fellow called Ingles, in South Africa. He was just the same hard-trained, athetic-sports build of animal. Always kept himself in the pink of condition. Didn't do him much good, though. Shot at Wesselstroom the week before Majuba. Wonder how the young un will lick his detachment into shape.'

Cottar turned up six weeks later, on foot, with his pupils; and if they did not carry so fine a gloss as the others, it was because they were the baser metal. He never told his experiences, but the men spoke enthusiastically, and fragments of it leaked back to the colonel through sergeants, batmen, and the like.

There was great jealousy between the first and second detachments, but the men united in adoring Cottar, and their way of showing it was by sparing him all the trouble that men know how to make for an unloved officer. He sought popularity as little as he had sought it at school, and therefore it came to him. He favoured no one – not even when the company sloven pulled the company cricket match out of the fire with an unexpected forty-three at the last moment. There was very little getting round him, for he seemed to know by instinct exactly when and where to head off for a trickster or malingerer; but if one were in trouble of mind or body, he headed straight to Cottar, who knew that the difference between a dazed and sulky junior of the upper school and a bewildered, browbeaten lump of a private fresh from the depot was very small indeed. The sergeants, seeing these things, told him secrets generally hid from the young officers, and the regimental sergeant-major gave him the sifted wisdom of twenty years of service to remember against the time when he should be adjutant. His words were quoted as barrack authority on bets in canteen and at tea; his batman treated his belongings as reverently as the fags of old had treated his razors; and the veriest shrew of the corps, bursting with charges against other women who had stolen her fuel or used the cooking-ranges out of turn, forbore to speak when Cottar, as the regulations ordained, asked of a morning if there were 'any complaints.'

'I'm full o' complaints,' said Mrs Corporal Morrison, 'an' I'd kill O'Halloran's fat cow of a wife any day, but ye know how it is. 'E puts 'is head just inside the door, an' looks down 'is blessed nose so bashful, an' 'e whispers, "Any complaints?" Ye can't complain after that. *I* want to kiss him. Some day I think I will. Heigho! she'll be a lucky woman that gets Young Innocence. See 'im now, girls! Do yer blame me?'

Cottar was cantering across to polo, and he looked a very satisfactory figure of a man as he gave easily to the first excited bucks of his pony, and slipped over a low mud wall to the dusty practice-ground. There were more than Mrs Corporal Morrison who felt as she did. But Cottar was busy for eleven hours of the day in one way or another. He did not care to have his tennis spoiled by petticoats giggling about the court, and after one long afternoon at a garden-party he explained to his major that this sort of thing was 'futile piffle,' and the major laughed. Theirs was not a married mess, except for the colonel's wife, and Cottar stood rather in awe of the good lady. She said 'my regiment,' and the world knows what that means. None the less, when they wanted her to give away the prizes after a regimental shooting-match, and she flatly refused because one of the prize-winners was married to a girl who, she believed, had made a jest of her behind her broad back, the mess ordered Cottar to 'tackle her' in his best calling-kit, and he did, simply and laboriously, and she gave way altogether.

'She only wanted to know the facts of the case,' he explained. 'I just told her, and she saw at once.'

'Ye-es,' said the adjutant. 'I expect that's what she did. Comin' to the Fusiliers' dance to-night?'

'No, thanks. I've got a fight on with the major.' The virtuous apprentice sat up till midnight in the major's quarters, with a stop-watch and a pair of compasses, shifting little painted lead blocks about a map of four inches to the mile. Then he turned in and slept the sleep of innocence, which is full of healthy dreams. One peculiarity about his dreams he noticed at the beginning of his second hot weather. Two and three times a month they duplicated or ran in series. He would find himself sliding into dreamland by the same road – a road that ran along a beach near a pile of brushwood. To the right lay the sea, sometimes at full tide, sometimes withdrawn to the very horizon; but he knew it for the same sea. By that road he would travel over a swell of rising ground covered with short, withered grass, into valleys of wonder and unreason. Beyond the ridge, which was crowned with some son of street-lamp, anything was possible; but up to the lamp it seemed to him that he knew the road as well as he knew the parade-ground. He learned to look forward to the place; for, once there, he was sure of a good night's rest, and the hot weather can be rather trying. First, shadowy under closing eyelids, would come the outline of the brushwood pile; next the white sand of the beach road, almost overhanging the black, changeful sea; then the turn inland uphill to the single light. When he was unrestful for any reason, he would tell himself how he was sure to get there – sure to get there – if he shut his eyes and surrendered to the drift of things. But one night after a foolishly hard hour's polo (the thermometer was 94° in his quarters at ten o'clock), sleep stood away from him altogether, though he did his best to find the well-known road, the point where true sleep began. At last he saw the brushwood, and hurried along to the ridge, for behind him he felt was the wide-awake, sultry world. He reached the lamp in safety, tingling with drowsiness, when a policeman – a common country policeman – sprang up before him and touched him on the shoulder before he could dive into the dim valley below. He was filled with terror – the hopeless terror of dreams – for the policeman said, in the awful, distinct voice of dream-people, 'I am Policeman Day coming back from the City of Sleep. You come with me.' Georgie knew it was true – that just beyond him in the valley lay the lights of the City of Sleep, where he would have been sheltered, and that this Policeman Thing had full power and authority to head him back to miserable wakefulness. He found himself looking at the moon-light on the wall, dripping with fright; and he never overcame that horror, though he met the policeman several times that hot weather, and his coming was the forerunner of a bad night.

But other dreams – perfectly absurd ones – filled him with an incommunicable delight. All those that he remembered began by the brushwood pile. For instance, he found a small clockwork steamer (he had noticed it many nights before) lying by the sea-road, and stepped into it, whereupon it moved with surpassing swiftness over an absolutely level sea. This was glorious, for he felt he was exploring great matters; and it stopped by a lily carved in stone, which, most naturally, floated on the water. Seeing the lily was labelled 'Hong-Kong,' Georgie said: 'Of course. This is precisely what I expected Hong-Kong would be like. How magnificent!' Thousands of miles farther on (passengers were arriving and departing all the while) it halted at yet another stone lily, labelled 'Java'; and this again delighted him hugely, because he knew that now he was at the world's end. But the little boat ran on and on till it lay in a deep fresh-water lock the sides of which were carven marble, green with moss. Lily-pads grew in the water, and reeds arched above. Some one moved among the reeds – some one whom Georgie knew he had travelled to this world's end to reach. Therefore everything was entirely well with him. He was unspeakably happy, and vaulted over the ship's side to find this person. When his feet touched that still water, it changed with the rustle of unrolling maps to nothing less than a sixth quarter of the globe, beyond the most remote imagining of man – a place where islands were colored yellow and blue, their lettering strung across their faces. They gave on unknown seas, and Georgie's urgent desire was to return swiftly across this floating atlas to known bearings. He told himself repeatedly that it was no good to hurry, but still he hurried desperately, and the islands slipped and slid under his feet, the straits yawned and widened, till he found himself utterly lost in the world's fourth dimension, with no hope of return. Yet only a little distance away he could see the old world with the rivers and mountain-chains marked according to the Sandhurst rules of map-making. Then that person for whom he had come to the Lily Lock (that was its name) ran up across unexplored territories, and showed him a way. They fled hand in hand till they reached a road that spanned ravines, and ran along the edge of precipices, and was tunnelled through mountains. 'This goes to our brushwood pile,' said his companion, and all his trouble was at an end. He took a pony, because he understood that this was the Thirty-Mile Ride and he must ride swiftly, and raced through the clattering tunnels and round the curves, always downhill, till he heard the sea to his left, and saw it raging under a full moon, against sandy cliffs. It was heavy going, but he recognized the nature of the country, the dark-purple downs inland, and the bents that whistled in the wind. The road was eaten away in places, and the sea lashed at him – black, foamless tongues of smooth and glossy rollers; but he was sure that there was less danger from the sea than from 'Them,' whoever 'They' were, inland to his right. He knew, too, that he would be safe if he could reach the down with the lamp on it. This came as he expected: he saw the one light a mile ahead along the beach, dismounted, turned to the right, walked quietly over to the brushwood pile, found the little steamer had returned to the beach whence he had unmoored it, and – must have fallen asleep, for he could remember no more. 'I'm gettin' the hang of the geography of that place,' he said to himself as he shaved next morning. 'I must have made some sort of circle. Let's see. The Thirty-Mile Ride (now how the deuce did I know it was called the Thirty-Mile Ride?) joins the sea-road beyond the first down where the lamp is. And that atlas country lies at the back of the Thirty-Mile Ride, somewhere out to the right beyond the hills and tunnels. Rummy thing, dreams. Wonder what makes mine fit into each other so?'

He continued on his solid way through the recurring duties of the seasons. The regiment was shifted to another station, and he enjoyed road-marching for two months, with a good deal of mixed shooting thrown in; and when they reached their new cantonments he became a member of the local Tent Club, and chased the mighty boar on horseback with a short stabbing-spear. There he met the *mahseer* of the Poonch, beside whom the tarpon is as a herring, and he who lands him can say that he is a fisherman. This was as new and as fascinating as the big-game shooting that fell to his portion, when he had himself photographed for the mother's benefit, sitting on the flank of his first tiger.

Then the adjutant was promoted, and Cottar rejoiced with him, for he admired the adjutant greatly, and marvelled who might be big enough to fill his place; so that he nearly collapsed when the mantle fell on his own shoulders, and the colonel said a few sweet things that made him blush. An adjutant's position does not differ materially from that of head of the school, and Cottar stood in the same relation to the colonel as he had to his old head in England, Only, tempers wear out in hot weather, and things were said and done that tried him sorely, and he made glorious blunders, from which the regimental sergeant-major pulled him with a loyal soul and a shut mouth. Slovens and incompetents raged against him; the weak-minded strove to lure him from the ways of justice; the small-minded – yea, men whom Cottar believed would never do 'things no fellow can do' – imputed motives mean and circuitous to actions that he had not spent a thought upon; and he tasted injustice, and it made him very sick. But his consolation came on parade, when he looked down the full companies and reflected how few were in hospital or cells, and wondered when the time would come to try the machine of his love and labour. They had risen ten or twelve places in the annual musketry returns; they had a smaller percentage of bad characters and a higher average of chest measurement than half a hundred other corps; and he believed that their tone, which is, after all, what makes a regiment or a school, was good. But they needed and expected the whole of a man's working-day, and maybe three or four hours of the night. Curiously enough, he never dreamed about the regiment as he was popularly supposed to. The mind, set free from the day's doings, generally ceased working altogether, or, if it moved at all, carried him along the old beach road to the downs, the lamp-post, and once in a while to terrible Policeman Day. The second time that he returned to the world's lost continent (this was a dream that repeated itself again and again, with variations, on the same ground) he knew that if he only sat still the person from the Lily Lock would help him, and he was not disappointed. Sometimes he was trapped in mines of vast depth hollowed out of the heart of the world, where men in torment chanted echoing songs; and he heard this person coming along through the galleries, and everything was made safe and delightful. They met again in low-roofed Indian railway-carriages that halted in a garden surrounded by gilt-and-green railings, where a mob of white people, all unfriendly, sat at breakfast-tables covered with roses, and separated Georgie from his companion, while underground voices sang deep-voiced songs. Georgie was filled with enormous despair till they two met again. They foregathered in the middle of an endless, hot tropic night, and crept into a huge house that stood, he knew, somewhere north of the railway-station where the people ate among the roses. It was surrounded with gardens, all moist and dripping; and in one room, reached through leagues of white-washed passages, a Sick Thing lay in bed. Now the least noise, Georgie knew, would unchain some waiting horror, and his companion knew it; but when their eyes met across the bed, Georgie was disgusted to see that she was a child – a little girl in strapped shoes, with her black hair combed back from her forehead.

'What disgraceful folly!' he thought. 'Now she could do nothing whatever if Its head came off.'

Then the Thing coughed, and the ceiling shattered down in plaster on the mosquito-netting, and 'They' rushed in from all quarters. He dragged the child through the stifling garden, voices chanting behind them, and they rode the Thirty-Mile Ride under whip and spur along the sandy beach by the booming sea, till they came to the downs, the lamp-post, and the brushwood pile, which, Georgie shouted, was 'in bounds.' Very often dreams would break up about them in this fashion, and they would be separated, to endure awful adventures alone. But the most amusing times were when he and she had a clear understanding that it was all make-believe, and walked through mile-wide roaring rivers without even taking off their shoes, or set light to populous cities to see how they would burn, and were rude as any children to the vague shadows met in their rambles. Later in the night they were sure to suffer for this, either at the hands of the Railway People eating among the roses, or in the tropic uplands at the far end of the Thirty-Mile Ride. Together, this did not much affright them; but often Georgie would hear her shrill cry of 'Boy! Boy!' half a world away, and hurry to her rescue before 'They' maltreated her.

He and she explored the dark-purple downs as far inland from the brushwood pile as they dared, but that was always a dangerous matter. The interior was filled with 'Them,' and 'They' went about singing in the hollows, and Georgie and she felt safer on or near the seaboard. So thoroughly had he come to know the place of his dreams that even waking he accepted it as a real country, and made a rough sketch of it. A still rougher copy of the sketch is given in this place for the better understanding of geography. He kept his own counsel, of course; but the permanence of the land puzzled him. His ordinary dreams were as formless and as fleeting as any healthy dreams could be, but once at the brushwood pile he moved within known limits and could see where he was going. There were months at a time when nothing that he could remember crossed his sleep. Then the dreams would come in a batch of five or six, and next morning the map that he kept in his writing-case would be written up to date, for Georgie was a most methodical person. There was, indeed, a danger – his seniors said so – of his developing into a regular 'Auntie Fuss' of an adjutant, and when an officer once takes to old-maidism there is more hope for the virgin of seventy than for him.

But fate sent the change that was needed, in the shape of a little winter campaign on the border, which, after the manner of little campaigns, flashed out into a very ugly war; and Cottar's regiment was chosen among the first.

'Now,' said a major, 'this'll shake the cobwebs out of us all – especially you, young Huron; and we can see what your hen-one-chick attitude has done for the regiment.'

There were four months in which to try the men, and Cottar nearly wept with joy as the campaign went forward. They were fit – physically fit beyond the other troops; they were good children in camp, wet or dry, fed or unfed; and they followed their officers with the quick suppleness and trained obedience of a first-class foot-ball fifteen. Once satisfied of this, their officers used them unsparingly, exactly as a man takes liberties with a tried horse. They were cut off from their apology for a base, and cheerfully cut their way back to it again; they crowned and cleaned out hills full of the enemy with the precision of well-broken dogs of chase; and in the hour of retreat, when, hampered with the sick and wounded of the column, they were persecuted down eleven miles of water-less valley, they, serving as rear-guard, covered themselves with a great glory in the eyes of fellow-professionals. Any regiment can advance, but few know how to retreat with a sting in the tail. Then they turned to and made roads, most often under fire, and dismantled some inconvenient mud redoubts. They were the last corps to be withdrawn when the rubbish of the campaign was all swept up; and after a month in standing camp, which tries morals severely, they departed to their own place in column of fours, singing:

'E's goin' to do without 'em –
    Don't want 'em any more;
'E's going to do without 'em,
    As 'e's often done before.
'E's goin' to be a martyr
On a 'ighly novel plan,
An' all the boys and girls will say,
'Ow! what a nice young man – man – man!
Ow! what a nice young man!'

There came out a 'Gazette' in which Cottar found that he had been behaving with 'courage and coolness and discretion' in all his capacities; that he had assisted the wounded under fire, and blown in a gate, also under fire. Net result, his captaincy and a brevet majority, coupled with the Distinguished Service Order, which is vulgarly called the 'Don't Stay On,' inasmuch as it is supposed to block the way permanently to the Victoria Cross.

As to his wounded, he explained that they were both heavy men, whom he could lift more easily than any one else. 'Otherwise, of course, I should have sent out one of my men; and, of course, about that gate business, we were safe the minute we were well under the walls.' But this did not prevent his men from cheering him furiously whenever they saw him, or the mess from giving him a dinner on the eve of his departure to England. (A year's leave was among the things he had 'snaffled out of the campaign,' to use his own words.) The doctor, who had taken quite as much as was good for him, quoted poetry about 'a good blade carving the casques of men,' and so on, and everybody told Cottar that he was an excellent person; but when he rose to make his maiden speech they shouted so that he was understood to say, 'It isn't any use tryin' to speak with you chaps rottin' me like this.' Let's have some pool.'

It is not unpleasant to spend eight and twenty days in an easy-going steamer on warm waters, in the company of a woman who lets you see that you are head and shoulders superior to the rest of the world, even though that woman may be, and most often is, ten counted years your senior. P.O. boats are not lighted with the disgustful particularity of Atlantic liners. There is more phosphorescence at the bows, and greater silence and darkness by the hand-steering-gear aft.

Awful things might have happened to Georgie but for the little fact that he had never studied the first principles of the game he was expected to play. So when Mrs Zuleika, at Aden, told him how motherly an interest she felt in his welfare, medals, brevet, and all, Georgie took her at the foot of the letter, and promptly talked of his own mother, three hundred miles nearer each day her dearness and general sweetness, of his home, and so forth, all the way up the Red Sea. It was much easier than he had supposed to converse with a woman for an hour at a time. Then Mrs Zuleika, turning from parental affection, spoke of love in the abstract as a thing not unworthy of study, and in a discreet twilight after dinner demanded confidences. Georgie would have been delighted to supply them, but he had none, and did not know it was his duty to manufacture them. Mrs Zuleika expressed surprise and unbelief, and asked those questions which deep asks of deep. She learned all that was necessary to conviction, and, being very much a woman, resumed (Georgie never knew that she had abandoned) the motherly attitude.

'Do you know,' she said, somewhere in the Mediterranean, 'I think you're the very dearest boy I have ever met in my life, and I'd like you to remember me a little. You will when you are older, but I want you to remember me now. You'll make some girl very happy.'

'Oh! Hope so,' said Georgie, gravely; 'but there's heaps of time for marryin' an' all that sort of thing, ain't there?'

'That depends. Here are your bean-bags for the Ladies' Competition. I think I'm growing too old to care for these *tamashas*.'

They were getting up sports, and Georgie was on the committee. He never noticed how perfectly the bags were sewn, but another woman did, and smiled once. He liked Mrs Zuleika greatly. She was a bit old, of course, but uncommonly nice. There was no nonsense about her.

A few nights after they passed Gibraltar his dream returned to him. She who waited by the brushwood pile was no longer a little girl, but a woman with black hair that grew into a 'widow's peak,' combed back from her forehead. He knew her for the child in black, the companion of the last six years, and, as it had been in the time of the meetings on the Lost Continent, he was filled with delight unspeakable. 'They,' for some dreamland reason, were friendly or had gone away that night, and the two flitted together over all their country, from the brushwood pile up the Thirty-Mile Ride, till they saw the House of the Sick Thing, a pin-point in the distance to the left; stamped through the Railway Waiting-room where the roses lay on the spread breakfast-tables; and returned, by the ford and the city they had once burned for sport, to the great swells of the downs under the lamp-post. Wherever they moved a strong singing followed them underground, but this night there was no panic. All the land was empty except for themselves, and at the last (they were sitting by the lamp hand in hand) she turned and kissed him. He woke with a start, staring at waving curtain of the cabin door; and he could have sworn that the kiss was real.

Next morning the ship was rolling in a Biscay sea, and people were not happy; but as Georgie came out to breakfast, shaven, tubbed, and smelling of soap, several turned to look at him because of the light in his eyes and the splendour of his countenance.

'Well, you look beastly fit,' snapped a neighbour. 'Any one left you a legacy in the middle of the Bay?'

Georgie reached for the curry, with a seraphic grin. 'I suppose it's the gettin' so near home, and all that. I do feel rather festive this mornin'. Rolls a bit, doesn't she?'

Mrs Zuleika stayed in her cabin till the end of the voyage, when she left without bidding him farewell, and wept passionately on the dock-head for pure joy of meeting her children, who, she had often said, were so like their father.

Georgie headed for his own country, wild with delight of the first long furlough after the lean seasons. Nothing was changed in that orderly life, from the coachman who met him at the station to the white peacock that stormed at the carriage from the stone wall above the shaven lawns. The house took toll of him with due regard to precedence – first the mother; then the father; then the house-keeper, who wept and praised God; then the butler; and so on down to the under-keeper, who had been dog-boy in Georgie's youth, and called him 'Master Georgie,' and was reproved by the groom who had taught Georgie to ride.

'Not a thing changed,' he sighed contentedly, when the

three of them sat down to dinner in the late sunlight, while the rabbits crept out upon the lawn below the cedars, and the big trout in the ponds by the home paddock rose for their evening meal.

'*Our* changes are all over, dear,' cooed the mother; 'and now I am getting used to your size and your tan (you're very brown; Georgie), I see you haven't changed in the least. You're exactly like the pater.'

The father beamed on this man after his own heart, – 'youngest major in the army, and should have had the VC, sir,' – and the butler listened with his professional mask off when Master Georgie spoke of war as it is waged to-day, and his father cross-questioned. The pater had retired when the Martini-Henry was a new thing and the Maxim unborn.

They went out on the terrace to smoke among the roses, and the shadow of the old house lay long across the wonderful English foliage, which is the only living green in the world.

'Perfect! By Jove, it's perfect!' Georgie was looking at the round-bosomed woods beyond the home paddock, where the white pheasant-boxes were ranged; and the golden air was full of a hundred sacred scents and sounds. Georgie felt his father's arm tighten in his.

'It's not half bad – but *hodie mihi, cras tibi*, isn't it? I suppose you'll be turning up some fine day with a girl under your arm, if you haven't one now, eh?'

'You can make your mind easy, sir. I haven't one.'

'Not in all these years?' said the mother.

'I hadn't time, mummy. They keep a man pretty busy, these days, in the service, and most of our mess are unmarried, too.'

'But you must have met hundreds in society – at balls, and so on?'

'I'm like the Tenth, mummy: I don't dance.'

'Don't dance! What have you been doing with yourself, then – backing other men's bills?' said the father.

'Oh, yes; I've done a little of that too; but you see, as things are now, a man has all his work cut out for him to keep abreast of his profession, and my days were always too full to let me lark about half the night.'

'Hmm!' – suspiciously.

'It's never too late to learn. We ought to give some kind of housewarming for the people about, now you've come back. Unless you want to go straight up to town, dear?'

'No. I don't want anything better than this. Let's sit still and enjoy ourselves. I suppose there will be something for me to ride if I look for it?'

'Seeing I've been kept down to the old brown pair for the last six weeks because all the others were being got ready for Master Georgie, I should say there might be,' the father chuckled. 'They're reminding me in a hundred ways that I must take the second place now.'

'Brutes!'

'The pater doesn't mean it, dear; but every one has been trying to make your home-coming a success; and you *do* like it, don't you?'

'Perfect! Perfect! There's no place like England – when you've done your work.'

'That's the proper way to look at it, my son.'

And so up and down the flagged walk till their shadows grew long in the moonlight, and the mother went indoors and played such songs as a small boy once clamoured for, and the squat silver candlesticks were brought in, and Georgie climbed to the two rooms in the west wing that had been his day and night nursery and his playroom in the beginning. Then who should come to tuck him up for the night but the mother? And she sat down on the bed, and they talked for a long hour, as mother and son should, if there is to be any future for the empire. With a simple woman's deep guile she asked questions and suggested answers that should have waked some sign in the face on the pillow, and there was neither quiver of eyelid nor quickening of breath, neither evasion nor delay in reply. So she blessed him and kissed him on the mouth, which is not always a mother's property, and said something to her husband later, at which he laughed profane and incredulous laughs.

All the establishment waited on Georgie next morning, from the tallest, six-year-old, 'with a mouth like a kid glove,

Master Georgie,' to the under-keeper strolling carelessly along the horizon, Georgie's pet rod in his hand, and 'There's a four-pounder risin' below the lasher. You don't 'ave 'em in Injia, Mast— Major Georgie.' It was all beautiful beyond telling, even though the mother insisted on taking him out in the landau (the leather had the hot Sunday smell of his youth) and showing him off to her friends at all the houses for six miles round; and the pater bore him up to town and a lunch at the club, where he introduced him, quite carelessly, to not less than thirty ancient warriors whose sons were not the youngest majors in the army and had not been mentioned in recent gazettes. After that it was Georgie's turn; and remembering his friends, he filled up the house with that kind of officer who lives in cheap lodgings at Southsea or Montpelier Square, Brompton – good men all, but not well off. The mother perceived that they needed girls to play with; and as there was no scarcity of girls, the house hummed like a dovecote in spring. They tore up the place for amateur theatricals; they disappeared into the gardens when they ought to have been rehearsing; they swept off every available horse and vehicle, especially the governess-cart and the fat pony (Georgie could not see where the fun came in here); they fell into the trout-ponds; they picnicked and they tennised; and they sat on gates in the twilight, two by two, and Georgie found that he was not in the least necessary to their entertainment.

'My word!' said he, when he saw the last of their dear backs. 'They told me they've enjoyed 'emselves, but they haven't done half the things they said they would.'

'I know they've enjoyed themselves – immensely,' said the mother. 'You're a public benefactor, dear.'

'Now we can be quiet again, can't we?'

'Oh, quite. I've a very dear friend of mine that I want you to know. She couldn't come with the house so full, because she's an invalid, and she was away when you first came. She's a Mrs Lacy.'

'Lacy! I don't remember the name about here.'

'No; they came after you went to India – from Oxford. Her husband died there, and she lost some money, I believe. They bought The Firs on the Bassett Road. She's a very sweet woman, and we're very fond of them both.'

'She's a widow, didn't you say?'

'She has a daughter. Surely I said so, dear?'

'Does she fall into trout-ponds, and gas and giggle, and "Oh, Major Cottar!" and all that?'

'No, indeed. She's a very quiet girl, and very musical. She always came over here with her music-books – composing, you know; and she generally works all day, so you won't—'

'Talking about Miriam?' said the pater, coming up. The mother edged toward him within elbow-reach. There was no finesse about Georgie's father. 'Oh, Miriam's a dear girl. Plays beautifully. Rides beautifully, too. She's a regular pet of the household. Used to call me—' The elbow went home, and, ignorant but obedient always, the pater shut himself off.

'What used she to call you, sir?'

'All sorts of pet names. I'm very fond of Miriam.'

'Sounds Jewish – Miriam.'

'Jew! You'll be calling yourself a Jew next. She's one of the Herefordshire Lacys. When her aunt dies—' Again the elbow.

'Oh, you won't see anything of her, Georgie, She's busy with her music or her mother all day. Besides, you're going up to town tomorrow, aren't you? I thought you said something about an Institute meeting?' The mother spoke.

'Go up to town *now!* What nonsense!' Once more the pater was shut off.

'I had some idea of it, but I'm not quite sure,' said the son of the house. Why did the mother try to get him away because a musical girl and her invalid parent were expected? He did not approve of unknown females calling his father pet names. He would observe these pushing persons who had been only seven years in the county.

All of which the delighted mother read in his countenance, herself keeping an air of sweet disinterestedness.

'They'll be here this evening for dinner. I'm sending the carriage over for them, and they won't stay more than a week.'

'Perhaps I shall go up to town. I don't quite know yet.' Georgie moved away irresolutely. There was a lecture at the

Institute on the supply of ammunition in the field, and the one man whose theories most irritated Major Cottar would deliver it. A heated discussion was sure to follow, and perhaps he might find himself moved to speak. He took his rod that afternoon and went down to thresh it out among the trout.

'Good sport, dear!' said the mother from the terrace.

' 'Fraid it won't be, mummy. All those men from town, and the girls particularly, have put every trout off his feed for weeks. There isn't one of 'em that cares for fishin' – really. Fancy stampin' and shoutin' on the bank, and tellin' every fish for half a mile exactly what you're goin' to do, and then chuckin' a brute of a fly at him! By Jove, it would scare *me* if I was a trout!'

But things were not as bad as he had expected. The black gnat was on the water, and the water was strictly preserved. A three-quarter-pounder at the second cast set him for the campaign, and he worked downstream, crouching behind the reed and meadow-sweet; creeping between a hornbeam hedge and a foot-wide strip of bank, where he could see the trout, but where they could not distinguish him from the background; lying almost on his stomach to switch the blue-upright (black gnat tail-fly) sidewise through the checkered shadows of a gravelly ripple fenced on three sides by overarching trees; or throat-deep in the rank hemlocks. But he had known every inch of the water since he was four feet high. The aged and astute between the sunk roots of trees, with the large and fat that lay in the frothy scum below some strong rush of water, sucking as lazily as carp, came to trouble in their turn, at the hand that duplicated so delicately the flicker and wimple of an egg-dropping fly. That was so consoling an afternoon that Georgie found himself five miles from home when he ought to have been dressing for dinner. The housekeeper had taken good care that her boy should not go empty, and before he changed to the white moth he sat down to excellent claret with sandwiches of potted egg and things that adoring women make and men never notice. Then back, the pipe between his teeth, to surprise the otter grubbing for fresh-water mussels, the rabbits on the edge of the beechwoods foraging m the clover, and the policeman-like white owl stooping to the little field-mice, till the moon was strong, and he took his rod apart, and went home through well-remembered gaps in the hedges. He fetched a compass round the house, for though he might have broken every law of the establishment every hour, the law of his boyhood was unbreakable: after fishing you went in by the garden back door, cleaned up in the outer scullery, and did not present yourself to your elders and your betters till you had washed and changed.

'Half-past ten, by Jove! Well, we'll make the sport an excuse. They wouldn't want to see me the first evening, at any rate. Gone to bed, probably.' He skirted by the open French windows of the drawing-room. 'No, they haven't. They look very comfy in there.'

He could see his father in his own particular chair, the mother in hers, and the back of a girl at the piano by the big potpourri jar. The gardens looked half divine in the moonlight, and he turned down through the roses to finish out his pipe.

A prelude ended, and there floated out a voice of the kind that in his childhood he used to call 'creamy' – a full, true contralto; and this is the song that he heard, every syllable of it:

Over the edge of the purple down,
    Where the single lamp-light gleams,
Know ye the road to the Merciful Town
    That is hard by the Sea of Dreams –
Where the poor may lay their wrongs away,
    And the sick may forget to weep?
But we – pity us! Oh, pity us!
    We wakeful; ah, pity us! –
We must go back with Policeman Day –
    Back from the City of Sleep!

Weary they turn from the scroll and crown,
    Fetter and prayer and plough –
They that go up to the Merciful Town,
    For her gates are closing now.

It is their right in the baths of Night
    Body and soul to steep:
But we – pity us! ah, pity us!
    We wakeful; oh, pity us! –
We must go back with Policeman Day –
    Back from the City of Sleep!

Over the edge of the purple down,
    Ere the tender dreams begin,
Look – we may look – at the Merciful Town,
    But we may not enter in.
Outcasts all, from her guarded wall
    Back to our watch we creep:
We – pity us! ah, pity us!
    We wakeful; oh, pity us! –
We that go back with Policeman Day –
    Back from the City of Sleep!

At the last echo he was aware that his mouth was dry and
unknown pulses were beating in the roof of it. The house-
keeper, who would have it that he must have fallen in and
caught a chill, was waiting to catch him on the stairs, and,
since he neither saw nor answered her, carried a wild tale
abroad that brought his mother knocking at the door.

'Anything happened, dear? Harper said she thought you
weren't—'

'No; it's nothing. I'm all right, mummy. *Please* don't
bother.'

He did not recognise his own voice, but that was a small
matter beside what he was considering. Obviously, most obviously, the whole coincidence was crazy lunacy – 'blind rot.'
He proved it to the satisfaction of Major George Cottar, who
was going up to town to-morrow to hear a lecture on the
supply of ammunition in the field; and having so proved it, the
soul and brain and heart and body of Georgie cried joyously:
'That's the Lily Lock girl – the Lost Continent girl – the
Thirty-Mile Ride girl – the Brushwood girl! *I* know her!'

He waked, stiff and cramped in his chair, to reconsider the
situation by sunlight, when it did not appear normal. But a

man must eat, and he went to breakfast, his heart between his teeth, holding himself severely in hand.

'Late, as usual,' said the mother. 'This is my son, Miss Lacy.'

A tall girl in black raised her eyes to his, and Georgie's life training deserted him – just as soon as he realised that she did not know. He stared coolly and critically. There was the abundant black hair, growing in a widow's peak, turned back from the forehead, with that peculiar ripple over the right ear; there were the grey eyes set a little close together; the short upper lip, resolute chin, and the known poise of the head. There was also the small, well-cut mouth that had kissed him.

'Georgie – *dear!*' said the mother, amazedly, for Miriam was flushing under the stare.

'I – I beg your pardon!' he gulped. 'I don't know whether the mother has told you, but I'm rather an idiot at times, specially before I've had my breakfast. It's – it's a family failing.' He turned to explore among the hot-water dishes on the sideboard, rejoicing that she did not know – she did not know.

His conversation for the rest of the meal was mildly insane, though the mother thought she had never seen her boy look half so handsome. How could any girl, least of all one of Miriam's discernment, forbear to fall down and worship? But deeply Miriam was displeased. She had never been stared at in that fashion before, and promptly retired into her shell when Georgie announced that he had changed his mind about going to town, and would stay to play with Miss Lacy if she had nothing better to do.

'Oh, but don't let me throw you out. I'm at work. I've things to do all the morning.'

'What possessed Georgie to behave so oddly?' the mother sighed to herself. 'Miriam's a bundle of feelings – like her mother.'

'You compose, don't you? Must be a fine thing to be able to do that. ['Pig – oh, pig!' thought Miriam.] I think I heard you singin' when I came in last night after fishin'. All about a Sea of Dreams, wasn't it? [Miriam shuddered to the core of the soul that afflicted her.] Awfully pretty song. How d'you think of such things?'

'You only composed the music, dear, didn't you?'

'The words too. I'm sure of it,' said Georgie, with a sparkling eye. No; she did not know.

'Yes; I wrote the words too.' Miriam spoke slowly, for she knew she lisped when she was nervous or unhappy.

'Now how *could* you tell, Georgie?' said the mother, as delighted as though the youngest major in the army were ten years old, showing off before company.

'I was sure of it, somehow. Oh, there are heaps of things about me, mummy, that you don't understand. Looks as if it were goin' to be a hot day – for England. Would you care for a ride this afternoon, Miss Lacy? We can start out after tea, if you'd like it.'

Miriam could not in decency refuse, but any woman might see she was not filled with delight.

'That will be very nice, if you take the Bassett Road. It will save me sending Martin down to the village,' said the mother, filling in gaps.

Like all good managers, the mother had her one weakness – a mania for little strategies that should economise horses and vehicles. Her men-folk complained that she turned them into common carriers, and there was a legend in the family that she had once said to the pater on the morning of a meet, 'If you *should* kill near Bassett, dear, and if it isn't too late, would you mind just popping over and matching me this?'

'I knew that was coming. You'd never miss a chance, mother. If it's fish or a trunk, I won't.' Georgie laughed.

'It's only a duck. They can do it up very neatly at Mallett's,' said the mother, simply. 'You won't mind, will you? We'll have a scratch dinner at nine, because it's so hot.'

The long summer day dragged itself out for centuries; but at last there was tea on the lawn, and Miriam appeared.

She was in the saddle before he could offer to help, with the clean spring of the child who mounted the pony for the Thirty-Mile Ride. The day held mercilessly, though Georgie got down thrice to look for imaginary stones in Rufus's foot.

One cannot say even simple things in broad light, and this that Georgie meditated was not simple. So he spoke seldom, and Miriam was divided between relief and scorn. It annoyed her that the great hulking thing should know she had written the words of the song overnight; for though a maiden may sing her most secret fancies aloud, she does not care to have them trampled over by the male Philistine. They rode into the little red-brick street of Bassett, and Georgie made untold fuss over the disposition of that duck. It must go in just such a package, and be fastened to the saddle in just such a manner, though eight o'clock had struck and they were miles from dinner.

'We must be quick!' said Miriam, bored and angry.

'There's no great hurry; but we can cut over Dowhead Down, and let 'em out on the grass. That will save us half an hour.'

The horses capered on the short, sweet-smelling turf, and the delaying shadows gathered in the valley as they cantered over the great dun down that overhangs Bassett and the Western coaching-road. Insensibly the pace quickened without thought of mole-hills; Rufus, gentleman that he was, waiting on Miriam's Dandy till they should have cleared the rise. Then down the two-mile slope they raced together, the wind whistling in their ears, to the steady throb of eight hoofs and the light click-click of the shifting bits.

'Oh, that was glorious!' Miriam cried, reining in. 'Dandy and I are old friends, but I don't think we've ever gone better together.'

'No; but you've gone quicker, once or twice.'

'Really? When?'

'Georgie moistened his lips. 'Don't you remember the Thirty-Mile Ride – with me – when "They" were after us – on the beach road, with the sea to the left – going toward the lamp-post on the downs?'

The girl gasped. 'What – what do you mean?' she said hysterically.

'The Thirty-Mile Ride, and – and all the rest of it.'

'You mean—? I didn't sing anything about the Thirty-Mile Ride. I know I didn't. I have never told a living soul.'

'You told about Policeman Day, and the lamp at the top of the downs, and the City of Sleep. It all joins on, you know – it's the same country – and it was easy enough to see where you had been.'

'Good God! – It joins on – of course it does; but – I have been – you have been – Oh, let's walk, please, or I shall fall off!'

Georgie ranged alongside, and laid a hand that shook below her bridle-hand, pulling Dandy into a walk. Miriam was sobbing as he had seen a man sob under the touch of the bullet.

'It's all right – it's all right,' he whispered feebly. 'Only – only it's true, you know.'

'True! Am I mad?'

'Not unless I'm mad as well. *Do* try to think a minute quietly. How could any one conceivably know anything about the Thirty-Mile Ride having anything to do with you, unless he had been there?'

'But where? But *where?* Tell me!'

'There – wherever it may be – in our country, I suppose. Do you remember the first time you rode it – the Thirty-Mile Ride, I mean? You must.'

'It was all dreams – all dreams!'

'Yes, but tell, please; because I know.'

'Let me think. I – we were on no account to make any noise – on no account to make any noise.' She was staring between Dandy's ears, with eyes that did not see, and a suffocating heart.

'Because "It" was dying in the big house?' Georgie went on, reining in again.

'There was a garden with green-and-gilt railings – all hot. Do *you* remember?'

'I ought to. I was sitting on the other side of the bed before "It" coughed and "They" came in.'

'You!' – the deep voice was unnaturally full and strong, and the girl's wide-opened eyes burned in the dusk as she stared him through and through. 'Then you're the Boy – my Brush-wood Boy, and I've known you all my life!'

She fell forward on Dandy's neck. Georgie forced himself out of the weakness that was overmastering his limbs, and slid an arm round her waist. The head dropped on his shoulder, and he found himself with parched lips kissing the low, white forehead and babbling things that up till then he believed existed only in printed works of fiction. Mercifully the horses were quiet. She made no attempt to draw herself away when she recovered, but lay still, whispering, 'Of course you're the Boy, and I didn't know – I didn't know.'

'I knew last night; and when I saw you at breakfast—'

'Oh, *that* was why! I wondered at the time. You would, of course.'

'I couldn't speak before this. Keep your head where it is, dear. It's all right now – all right now, isn't it?'

'But how was it *I* didn't know – after all these years and years? I remember – oh, what lots of things I remember!'

'Tell me some. I'll look after the horses.'

'I remember waiting for you when the steamer came in. Do you?'

'At the Lily Lock, beyond Hong-Kong and Java?'

'Do *you* call it that too?'

'You told me it was when I was lost in the continent. That was you that showed me the way through the mountains?'

'When the islands slid? It must have been, because you're the only one I remember. All the others were "Them."'

'Awful brutes they were, too.'

'I remember showing you the Thirty-Mile Ride the first time. You ride just as you used to – then. You *are* you!'

'That's odd. I thought that of you this afternoon. Isn't it wonderful?'

'What does it all mean? Why should you and I of the millions of people in the world have this – this thing between us? What does it mean? I'm frightened.'

'This!' said Georgie. The horses quickened their pace. They thought they had heard an order. 'Perhaps when we die we may find out more, but it means this now.'

There was no answer. What could she say? As the world went, they had known each other rather less than eight and a half hours, but the matter was one that did not concern the world. There was a very long silence, while the breath in their nostrils drew cold and sharp as it might have been a fume of ether.

'That's the second,' Georgie whispered. 'You remember, don't you?'

'It's not!' – furiously. 'It's not!'

'On the downs the other night – months ago? You were just as you are now, and we went over the country for miles and miles.'

'It was all empty, too. They had gone away. Nobody frightened us. I wonder why, Boy?'

'Oh, if you remember *that*, you must remember the rest. Confess!'

'I remember lots of things, but I *know* I didn't. I never have – till just now.'

'You *did*, dear.'

'I know I didn't, because – oh, it's no use keeping anything back! – because I truthfully meant to.'

'And truthfully did.'

'No; meant to; but some one else came by.'

'There wasn't any one else. There never has been.'

'There was – there always is. It was another woman – out there on the sea. I saw her. It was the 26th of May. I've got it written down somewhere.'

'Oh, *you*'ve kept a record of your dreams, too? That's odd about the other woman, because I was on the sea just then.'

'I was right. How do I know what you've done when you were awake – and I thought it was only *you!*'

'You never were more wrong in your life. What a little temper you've got! Listen to me a minute, dear.' And Georgie, though he knew it not, committed black perjury. 'It – it isn't the kind of thing one says to any one, because they'd laugh; but on my word and honour, darling, I've never been kissed by a living soul outside my own people in all my life. Don't laugh, dear. I wouldn't tell any one but you, but it's the solemn truth.'

'I knew! You are you. Oh, I *knew* you'd come some day; but I didn't know you were you in the least till you spoke.'

'Then give me another.'

'And you never cared or looked anywhere? Why, all the

round world must have loved you from the very minute they saw you, Boy.'

'They kept it to themselves if they did. No; I never cared.'

'And we shall be late for dinner – horribly late. Oh, how can I look at you in the light before your mother – and mine!'

'We'll play you're Miss Lacy till the proper time comes. What's the shortest limit for people to get engaged? S'pose we have got to go through all the fuss of an engagement, haven't we?'

'Oh, I don't want to talk about that. It's so commonplace. I've thought of something that you don't know. I'm sure of it. What's my name?'

'Miri – no, it isn't, by Jove! Wait half a second, and it'll come back to me. You aren't – you can't? Why, *those* old tales' – before I went to school! I've never thought of 'em from that day to this. Are you the original, only Annie*an*louise?'

'It was what you always called me ever since the beginning. Oh! We've turned into the avenue, and we must be an hour late.'

'What does it matter? The chain goes as far back as those days? It must, of course – of course it must. I've got to ride round with this pestilent old bird – confound him!'

'"Ha! ha! said the duck, laughing" – do you remember *that?*'

'Yes, I do – flower-pots on my feet, and all. We've been together all this while, and I've got to say good-bye to you till dinner. *Sure* I'll see you at dinner-time? *Sure* you won't sneak up to your room, darling, and leave me all the evening? Good-bye, dear, – good-bye.'

'Good-bye, Boy, good-bye. Don't let Rufus bolt into his stables. Good-bye. Yes, I'll come down to dinner; but – what shall I do when I see you in the light!'

THE TOMB OF HIS ANCESTORS

Some people will tell you that if there were but a single loaf of bread in all India it would be divided equally between the Plowdens, the Trevors, the Beadons, and the Rivett-Carnacs. That is only one way of saying that certain families serve India generation after generation as dolphins follow in line across the open sea.

Let us take a small and obscure case. There has been at least one representative of the Devonshire Chinns in or near Central India since the days of Lieutenant-Fireworker Humphrey Chinn, of the Bombay European Regiment, who assisted at the capture of Seringapatam in 1799. Alfred Ellis Chinn, Humphrey's younger brother, commanded a regiment of Bombay Grenadiers from 1804 to 1813, when he saw some mixed fighting; and in 1834 John Chinn of the same family – we will call him John Chinn the First – came to light as a level-headed administrator in time of trouble at a place called Mundesur. He died young, but left his mark on the new country, and the Honourable Board of Directors of the Honourable the East India Company embodied his virtues in a stately resolution, and paid for the expenses of his tomb among the Satpura hills.

He was succeeded by his son, Lionel Chinn, who left the little old Devonshire home just in time to be severely wounded in the Mutiny. He spent his working life within a hundred and fifty miles of John Chinn's grave, and rose to the command of a regiment of small, wild hill-men, most of whom had known his father. His son John was born in the small thatched-roofed, mud-walled cantonment, which is even to-day eighty miles from the nearest railway, in the heart of a scrubby, tigerish country. Colonel Lionel Chinn served thirty years and retired. In the Canal his steamer passed the outward-bound troopship, carrying his son eastward to the family duties.

The Chinns are luckier than most folk, because they know exactly what they must do. A clever Chinn passes for the Bombay Civil Service, and gets away to Central India, where everybody is glad to see him. A dull Chinn enters the Police Department of the Woods and Forests, and sooner or later, he, too, appears in Central India, and that is what gave rise to the saying 'Central India is inhabited by Bhils, Mairs, and Chinns, all very much alike.' The breed is small-boned, dark, and silent, and the stupidest of them are good shots. John Chinn the Second was rather clever, but as the eldest son he entered the army, according to Chinn tradition. His duty was to abide in his father's regiment, for the term of his natural life, though the corps was one which most men would have paid heavily to avoid. They were irregulars, small, dark, and blackish, clothed in rifle-green with black-leather trimmings; and friends called them the 'Wuddars', which means a race of low-caste people who dig up rats to eat. But the Wuddars did not resent it. They were the only Wuddars, and their points of pride were these:

Firstly, they had fewer English officers than any native regiment. Secondly, their subalterns were not mounted on parade, as the general rule, but walked at the head of their men. A man who can hold his own with the Wuddars at their quickstep must be sound in wind and limb. Thirdly, they were the most *pukka shikarries* (out-and-out hunters) in all India. Fourthly – up to one hundredthly – they were the Wuddars – Chinn's Irregular Bhil Levies of the old days, but now, henceforward and for ever, the Wuddars.

No Englishman entered their mess except for love or through family usage. The officers talked to their soldiers in a tongue not two hundred white folk in India understood; and the men were their children, all drawn from the Bhils, who are, perhaps, the strangest of the many strange races in India. They were, and at heart are, wild men, furtive, shy, full of untold superstitions. The races whom we call natives of the country found the Bhil in possession of the land when they first broke into that part of the world thousands of years ago. The books call them Pre-Aryan, Aboriginal, Dravidian, and so forth; and, in other words, that is what the Bhils call themselves. When a Rajput chief, whose bards can sing his pedigree backwards for twelve hundred years, is set on the throne, his investiture is not complete till he has been marked on the forehead with blood from the veins of a Bhil. The Rajputs say the ceremony has no meaning, but the Bhil knows that it is the last, last shadow of his old rights as the long-ago owner of the soil.

Centuries of oppression and massacre made the Bhil a cruel and half-crazy thief and cattle-stealer, and when the English came he seemed to be almost as open to civilisation as the tigers of his own jungles. But John Chinn the First, father of Lionel, grandfather of our John, went into his country, lived with him, learned his language, shot the deer that stole his poor crops, and won his confidence, so that some Bhils learned to plough and sow, while others were coaxed into the Company's service to police their friends.

When they understood that standing in line did not mean instant execution, they accepted soldiering as a cumbrous but amusing kind of sport, and were zealous to keep the wild Bhils under control. That was the thin edge of the wedge. John Chinn the First gave them written promises that, if they were good from a certain date, the Government would overlook previous offences: and since John Chinn was never known to break his word – he promised once to hang a Bhil locally esteemed invulnerable, and hanged him in front of his tribe for seven proved murders – the Bhils settled down as steadily as they knew how. It was slow, unseen work, of the son that is being done all over India to-day; and though John Chinn's only reward came, as I have said, in the shape of a grave at Government expense, the little people of the hills never forgot him.

Colonel Lionel Chinn knew and loved them too, and they were very fairly civilised, for Bhils, before his service ended. Many of them could hardly be distinguished from low-caste Hindoo farmers; but in the south, where John Chinn the First was buried, the wildest still clung to the Satpura ranges, cherishing a legend that some day Jan Chinn, as they called him, would return to his own. In the meantime they mistrusted the white man and his ways. The least excitement would stampede them, plundering at random, and now and then killing; but if they were handled discreetly they grieved like children, and promised never to do it again.

The Bhils of the regiment – the uniformed men – were virtuous in many ways, but they needed humouring. They felt bored and homesick unless taken after tigers as beaters; and their cold-blooded daring – all Wuddars shoot tigers on foot: it is their caste-mark – made even the officers wonder. They would follow up a wounded tiger as unconcernedly as though it were a sparrow with a broken wing; and this through a country full of caves and rifts and pits, where a wild beast could hold a dozen men at his mercy. Now and then some little man was brought to barracks with his head smashed in or his ribs torn away; but his companions never learned caution; they contented themselves with settling the tiger.

Young John Chinn was decanted at the verandah of the Wuddars' lonely mess-house from the back seat of a two-wheeled cart, his gun-cases cascading all round him. The slender, little, hooky-nosed boy looked forlorn as a strayed goat when he slapped the white dust off his knees, and the cart jolted down the glaring road. But in his heart he was contented. After all, this was the place where he had been born, and things were not much changed since he had been sent to England, a child, fifteen years ago.

There were a few new buildings, but the air and the smell and the sunshine were the same; and the little green men who crossed the parade-ground looked very familiar. Three weeks ago John Chinn would have said he did not remember a word of the Bhil tongue, but at the mess-door he found his lips moving in sentences that he did not understand – bits of old nursery rhymes, and tail-ends of such orders as his father used to give the men.

The Colonel watched him come up the steps, and laughed. 'Look!' he said to the Major. 'No need to ask the young un's breed. He's a *pukka* Chinn. Might be his father in the Fifties over again.'

'Hope he'll shoot as straight,' said the Major. 'He's brought enough ironmongery with him.'

'Wouldn't be a Chinn if he didn't. Watch him blowin' his nose. Regular Chinn beak. Flourishes his handkerchief like his father. It's the second edition – line for line.'

'Fairy tale, by Jove!' said the Major, peering through the slats of the jalousies. 'If he's the lawful heir, he'll . . . Now old Chinn could no more pass that chick without fiddling with it than . . .'

'His son!' said the Colonel, jumping up.

'Well, I be blowed!' said the Major. The boy's eye had been caught by a split reed screen that hung on a slew between the verandah pillars, and mechanically he had tweaked the edge to set it level. Old Chinn had sworn three times a day at that screen for many years; he could never get it to his satisfaction. His son entered the anteroom in the middle of a five-fold silence. They made him welcome for his father's sake and, as they took stock of him, for his own. He was ridiculously like the portrait of the Colonel on the wall, and when he had washed a little of the dust from his throat he went to his quarters with the old man's short, noiseless jungle-step.

'So much for heredity,' said the Major. 'That comes of three generations among the Bhils.'

'And the men know it,' said a Wing-officer. 'They've been waiting for this youth with their tongues hanging out. I am persuaded that, unless he absolutely beats 'em over the head, they'll lie down by companies and worship him.'

'Nothin' like havin' a father before you,' said the Major. 'I'm a parvenu with my chaps. I've only been twenty years in the regiment, and my revered parent he was a simple squire. There's no getting at the bottom of a Bhil's mind. Now, *why* is the superior bearer that young Chinn brought with him fleeing across country with his bundle?' He stepped into the verandah, and shouted after the man – a typical new-joined subaltern's servant who speaks English and cheats his master.

'What is it?' he called.

'Plenty bad men here. I going, sar,' was the reply. 'Have taken Sahib's keys, and say will shoot.'

'Doocid lucid – doocid convincin'. How those up-country thieves can leg it! He has been badly frightened by someone.' The Major strolled to his quarters to dress for mess.

Young Chinn, walking like a man in a dream, had fetched a compass round the entire cantonment before going to his own tiny cottage. The captain's quarters, in which he had been born, delayed him for a little; then he looked at the well on the parade-ground, where he had sat of evenings with his nurse, and at the ten-by-fourteen church, where the officers went to service if a chaplain of any official creed happened to come along. It seemed very small as compared with the gigantic building he used to stare up at, but it was the same place.

From time to time he passed a knot of silent soldiers, who saluted. They might have been the very men who had carried him on their backs when he was in his first knickerbockers. A faint light burned in his room, and, as he entered, hands clasped his feet, and a voice murmured from the floor.

'Who is it?' said young Chinn, not knowing he spoke in the Bhil tongue.

'I bore you in my arms, Sahib, when I was a strong man and you were a small one – crying, crying, crying! I am your servant, as I was your father's before you. We are all your servants.'

Young Chinn could not trust himself to reply, and the voice went on:

'I have taken your keys from that fat foreigner, and sent him away; and the studs are in the shirt for mess. Who should know, if I do not know? And so the baby has become a man, and forgets his nurse; but my nephew shall make a good servant, or I will beat him twice a day.'

Then there rose up, with a rattle, as straight as a Bhil arrow, a little white-haired wizened ape of a man, with medals and orders on his tunic, stammering, saluting, and trembling. Behind him a young and wiry Bhil, in uniform, was taking the trees out of Chinn's mess-boots.

Chinn's eyes were full of tears. The old man held out his keys.

'Foreigners are bad people. He will never come back again. We are all servants of your father's son. Has the Sahib forgotten who took him to see the trapped tiger in the village across the river, when his mother was so frightened and he was so brave?'

The scene came back to Chinn in great magic-lantern flashes. 'Bukta!' he cried; and all in a breath: 'You promised nothing should hurt me. *Is* it Bukta?'

The man was at his feet a second time. 'He has not forgotten. He remembers his own people as his father remembered. Now can I die. But first I will live and show the Sahib how to kill tigers. That *that* yonder is my nephew. If he is not a good servant, beat him and send him to me, and I will surely kill him, for now the Sahib is with his own people. Ai, Jan *baba* – Jan *baba*! My Jan *baba*! I will stay here and see that this does his work well. Take off his boots, fool. Sit down upon the bed. Sahib, and let me look. It *is* Jan *baba*!'

He pushed forward the hilt of his sword as a sign of service, which is an honour paid only to viceroys, governors, generals, or to little children whom one loves dearly. Chinn touched the hilt mechanically with three fingers, muttering he knew not what. It happened to be the old answer of his childhood, when Bukta in jest called him the little General Sahib.

The Major's quarters were opposite Chinn's, and when he heard his servant gasp with surprise he looked across the room. Then the Major sat on the bed and whistled; for the spectacle of the senior native commissioned officer of the regiment, an 'unmixed' Bhil, a Companion of the Order of British India, with thirty-five years' spotless service in the army, and a rank among his own people superior to that of many Bengal princelings, valeting the last-joined subaltern, was a little too much for his nerves.

The throaty bugles blew the Mess-call that has a long legend behind it. First a few piercing notes like the shrieks of beaters in a far-away cover, and next, large, full, and smooth, the refrain of the wild song: 'And oh, and oh, the green pulse of Mundore – Mundore!'

'All little children were in bed when the Sahib heard that call last,' said Bukta, passing Chinn a clean handkerchief. The call brought back memories of his cot under the mosquito-netting, his mother's kiss, and the sound of footsteps growing fainter as he dropped asleep among his men. So he hooked the dark collar of his new mess-jacket, and went to dinner like a prince who has newly inherited his father's crown.

Old Bukta swaggered forth curling his whiskers. He knew his own value, and no money and no rank within the gift of the Government would have induced him to put studs in young officers' shirts, or to hand them clean ties. Yet, when he took off his uniform that night, and squatted among his fellows for a quiet smoke, he told them what he had done, and they said that he was entirely right. Thereat Bukta propounded a theory which to a white mind would have seemed raving insanity; but the whispering, level-headed little men of war considered it from every point of view, and thought that there might be a great deal in it.

At mess under the oil-lamps the talk turned as usual to the unfailing subject of *shikar* – big game-shooting of every kind and under all sorts of conditions. Young Chinn opened his eyes when he understood that each one of his companions had shot several tigers in the Wuddar style – on foot, that is – making no more of the business than if the brute had been a dog.

'In nine cases out of ten,' said the Major, 'a tiger is almost as dangerous as a porcupine. But the tenth time you come home feet first.'

That set all talking, and long before midnight Chinn's brain was in a whirl with stories of tigers – man-eaters and cattle-killers each pursuing his own business as methodically as clerks in an office; new tigers that had lately come into such-and-such a district; and old, friendly beasts of great cunning, known by nicknames in the mess – such as 'Puggy', who was lazy, with huge paws, and 'Mrs Malaprop', who turned up when you never expected her, and made female noises. Then they spoke of Bhil superstitions, a wide and picturesque field, till young Chinn hinted that they must be pulling his leg.

' 'Deed we aren't,' said a man on his left. 'We know all about you. You're a Chinn and all that, and you've a son of vested right here; but if you don't believe what we're telling you, what will you do when old Bukta begins his stories? He knows about ghost-tigers, and tigers that go to a hell of their own; and tigers that walk on their hind feet; and your grandpa's riding-tiger, as well. Odd he hasn't spoken of that yet.'

'You know you've an ancestor buried down Satpura way, don't you?' said the Major, as Chinn smiled irresolutely.

'Of course I do,' said Chinn, who had the chronicle of the Book of Chinn by heart. It lies in a worn old ledger on the Chinese lacquer table behind the piano in the Devonshire home, and the children are allowed to look at it on Sundays.

'Well, I wasn't sure. Your revered ancestor, my boy, according to the Bhils, has a tiger of his own – a saddle-tiger that he rides round the country whenever he feels inclined. *I* don't call it decent in an ex-Collector's ghost; but that is what the Southern Bhils believe. Even our men, who might be called moderately cool, don't care to beat that country if they hear that Jan Chinn is running about on his tiger. It is supposed to be a clouded animal – not stripy, but blotchy, like a tortoise-shell tom-cat. No end of a brute, it is, and a sure sign of war or pestilence or – or something. There's a nice family legend for you.'

'What's the origin of it, d'you suppose?' said Chinn.

'Ask the Satpura Bhils. Old Jan Chinn was a mighty hunter before the Lord. Perhaps it was the tiger's revenge, or perhaps he's huntin' 'em still. You must go to his tomb one of these days and inquire. Bukta will probably attend to that. He was asking me before you came whether by any ill-luck you had already bagged your tiger. If not, he is going to enter you under his own wing. Of course, for you of all men it's imperative. You'll have a first-class time with Bukta.'

The Major was not wrong. Bukta kept an anxious eye on young Chinn at drill, and it was noticeable that the first time the new officer lifted up his voice in an order the whole line quivered. Even the Colonel was taken aback, for it might have been Lionel Chinn returned from Devonshire with a new lease of life. Bukta had continued to develop his peculiar theory among his intimates, and it was accepted as a matter of faith in the lines, since every word and gesture on young Chinn's part so confirmed it.

The old man arranged early that his darling should wipe out the reproach of not having shot a tiger; but he was not content to take the first or any beast that happened to arrive. In his own villages he dispensed the high, low, and middle justice, and when his people – naked and fluttered – came to him with word of a beast marked down, he bade them send spies to the kills and the watering-places, that he might be sure the quarry was such an one as suited the dignity of such a man.

Three or four times the reckless trackers returned, most truthfully saying that the beast was mangy, undersized – a tigress worn with nursing, or a broken-toothed old male – and Bukta would curb young Chinn's impatience.

At last, a noble animal was marked down – a ten-foot cattle-killer with a huge roll of loose skin along the belly, glossy-hided, full-frilled about the neck, whiskered, frisky, and young. He had slain a man in pure sport, they said.

'Let him be fed,' quoth Bukta, and the villagers dutifully drove out cows to amuse him, that he might lie up near by.

Princes and potentates have taken ship to India and spent great moneys for the mere glimpse of beasts one-half as fine as this of Bukta's.

'It is not good,' said he to the Colonel, when he asked for shooting-leave, 'that my Colonel's son who may be – that my Colonel's son should lose his maidenhead on any small jungle beast. That may come after. I have waited long for this which is a tiger. He has come in from the Mair country. In seven days we will return with the skin.'

The mess gnashed their teeth enviously. Bukta, had he chosen, might have invited them all. But he went out alone with Chinn, two days in a shooting-cart and a day on foot, till they came to a rocky, glary valley with a pool of good water in it. It was a parching day, and the boy very naturally stripped and went in for a bathe, leaving Bukta by the clothes. A white skin shows far against brown jungle, and what Bukta beheld on

Chinn's back and right shoulder dragged him forward step by step with staring eyeballs.

'I'd forgotten it isn't decent to strip before a man of his position,' thought Chinn, flouncing in the water. 'How the little devil stares! What is it, Bukta?'

'The Mark!' was the whispered answer.

'It is nothing. You know how it is with my people!' Chinn was annoyed. The dull-red birth-mark on his shoulder, something like a conventionalised Tartar cloud, had slipped his memory, or he would not have bathed. It occurred, so they said at home, in alternate generations, appearing, curiously enough, eight or nine years after birth, and, save that it was part of the Chinn inheritance, would not be considered pretty. He hurried ashore, dressed again, and went on till they met two or three Bhils, who promptly fell on their faces. 'My people,' grunted Bukta, not condescending to notice them. 'And so your people. Sahib. When I was a young man we were fewer, but not so weak. Now we are many, but poor stock. As may be remembered. How will you shoot him, Sahib? From a tree; from a shelter which my people shall build; by day or by night?'

'On foot and in the daytime,' said young Chinn.

'That was your custom, as I have heard,' said Bukta to himself. 'I will get news of him. Then you and I will go to him. I will carry one gun. You have yours. There is no need of more. What tiger shall stand against *thee*?'

He was marked down by a little water-hole at the head of a ravine, full-gorged and half asleep in the May sunlight. He was walked up like a partridge, and he turned to do battle for his life. Bukta made no motion to raise his rifle, but kept his eyes on Chinn, who met the shattering roar of the charge with a single shot – it seemed to him hours as he sighted – which tore through his throat, smashing the backbone below the neck and between the shoulders. The brute crouched, choked, and fell, and before Chinn knew well what had happened Bukta bade him stay still while he paced the distance between his feet and the ringing jaws.

'Fifteen,' said Bukta. 'Short paces. No need for a second

shot. Sahib. He bleeds cleanly where he lies, and we need not spoil the skin. I said there would be no need of these, but they came – in case.'

Suddenly the sides of the ravine were crowned with the heads of Bukta's people – a force that should have blown the ribs out of the beast had Chinn's shot failed; but their guns were hidden, and they appeared as interested beaters, some five or six, waiting the word to skin. Bukta watched the life fade from the wild eyes, lifted one hand, and turned on his heel.

'No need to show that *we* care,' said he. 'Now, after this, we can kill what we choose. Put out your hand, Sahib.'

Chinn obeyed. It was entirely steady, and Bukta nodded. 'That also was your custom. My men skin quickly. They will carry the skin to cantonments. Will the Sahib come to my poor village for the night and, perhaps, forget that I am his officer?'

'But those men – the beaters. They have worked hard, and perhaps—'

'Oh, if they skin clumsily, we will skin them. They are my people. In the Lines I am one thing. Here I am another.'

This was very true. When Bukta doffed uniform and reverted to the fragmentary dress of his own people, he left his civilisation of drill in the next world. That night, after a little talk with his subjects, he devoted to an orgy; and a Bhil orgy is a thing not to be safely written about. Chinn, flushed with triumph, was in the thick of it, but the meaning of the mysteries was hidden. Wild folk came and pressed about his knees with offerings. He gave his flask to the elders of the village. They grew eloquent, and wreathed him about with flowers. Gifts and loans, not all seemly, were thrust upon him, and infernal music rolled and maddened round red fires, while singers sang songs of the ancient times, and danced peculiar dances. The aboriginal liquors are very potent, and Chinn was compelled to taste them often, but, unless the stuff had been drugged, how came he to fall asleep suddenly, and to waken late the next day – half a march from the village?

'The Sahib was very tired. A little before dawn he went to

sleep,' Bukta explained. 'My people carried him here, and now it is time we should go back to cantonments.'

The voice, smooth and deferential, the step, steady and silent, made it hard to believe that only a few hours before Bukta was yelling and capering with naked fellow-devils of the scrub.

'My people were very pleased to see the Sahib. They will never forget. When next the Sahib goes out recruiting, he will go to my people, and they will give him as many men as we need.'

Chinn kept his own counsel, except as to the shooting of the tiger, and Bukta embroidered that tale with a shameless tongue. The skin was certainly one of the finest ever hung up in the mess, and the first of many. When Bukta could not accompany his boy on shooting-trips, he took care to put him in good hands, and Chinn learned more of the mind and desire of the wild Bhil in his marches and campings, by talks at twilight or at wayside pools, than an uninstructed man would have come at in a lifetime.

Presently his men in the regiment grew bold to speak of their relatives – mostly in trouble – and to lay cases of tribal custom before him. They would say, squatting in his verandah at twilight, after the easy, confidential style of the Wuddars, that such-and-such a bachelor had run away with such-and-such a wife at a far-off village. Now, how many cows would Chinn Sahib consider a just fine? Or, again, if written order came from the Government that a Bhil was to repair to a walled city of the plains to give evidence in a law-court, would it be wise to disregard that order? On the other hand, if it were obeyed, would the rash voyager return alive?

'But what have I to do with these things?' Chinn demanded of Bukta, impatiently. 'I am a soldier. I do not know the Law.'

'Hoo! Law is for fools and white men. Give them a large and loud order and they will abide by it. Thou art their Law.'

'But wherefore?'

Every trace of expression left Bukta's countenance. The idea might have smitten him for the last time. 'How can I say?' he replied. 'Perhaps it is on account of the name. A Bhil does not love strange things. Give them orders, Sahib – two, three, four words at a time such as they can carry away in their heads. That is enough.'

Chinn gave orders then, valiantly, not realising that a word spoken in haste before mess became the dread unappealable law of villages beyond the smoky hills – was, in truth, no less than the Law of Jan Chinn the First, who, so the whispered legend ran, had come back to earth to oversee the third generation in the body and bones of his grandson.

There could be no sort of doubt in this matter. All the Bhils knew that Jan Chinn reincarnated had honoured Bukta's village with his presence after slaying his first – in this life – tiger; that he had eaten and drunk with the people, as he was used; and – Bukta must have drugged Chinn's liquor very deeply – upon his back and right shoulder all men had seen the same angry red Flying Cloud that the high Gods had set on the flesh of Jan Chinn the First when first he came to the Bhil. As concerned the foolish white world which has no eyes, he was a slim and young officer in the Wuddars; but his own people knew he was Jan Chinn, who had made the Bhil a man; and believing, they hastened to carry his words, careful never to alter them on the way.

Because the savage and the child who plays lonely games have one horror of being laughed at or questioned, the little folk kept their convictions to themselves; and the Colonel, who thought he knew his regiment, never guessed that each one of the six hundred quick-footed, beady-eyed rank-and-file, at attention beside their rifles, believed serenely and unshakenly that the subaltern on the left flank of the line was a demigod twice born – tutelary deity of their land and people. The Earth-gods themselves had stamped the incarnation, and who would dare to doubt the handiwork of the Earth-gods?

Chinn, being practical above all things, saw that his family name served him well in the lines and in camp. His men gave no trouble – one does not commit regimental offences with a god in the chair of justice – and he was sure of the best beaters in the district when he needed them. They believed that the protection of Jan Chinn the First cloaked them, and were bold in that belief beyond the utmost daring of excited Bhils.

His quarters began to look like an amateur natural-history museum, in spite of duplicate heads and horns and skulls that he sent home to Devonshire. The people, very humanly, learned the weak side of their god. It is true he was unbribable, but bird-skins, butterflies, beetles, and, above all, news of big game pleased him. In other respects, too, he lived up to the Chinn tradition. He was fever-proof. A night's sitting out over a tethered goat in a damp valley, that would have filled the Major with a month's malaria, had no effect on him. He was, as they said, 'salted before he was born'.

Now, in the autumn of his second year's service an uneasy rumour crept out of the earth and ran about among the Bhils. Chinn heard nothing of it till a brother-officer said across the mess-table: 'Your revered ancestor's on the rampage in the Satpura country. You'd better look him up.'

'I don't want to be disrespectful, but I'm a little sick of my revered ancestor. Bukta talks of nothing else. What's the old boy supposed to be doing now?'

'Riding cross-country by moonlight on his processional tiger. That's the story. He's been seen by about two thousand Bhils, skipping along the tops of the Satpuras, and scaring people to death. They believe it devoutly, and all the Satpura chaps are worshipping away at his shrine – tomb, I mean – like good 'uns. You really ought to go down there. Must be a queer thing to see your grandfather treated as a god.'

'What makes you think there's any truth in the tale?' said Chinn.

'Because all our men deny it. They say they've never heard of Chinn's tiger. Now that's a manifest lie, because every Bhil *has*.'

'There's only one thing you've overlooked,' said the Colonel, thoughtfully. 'When a local god reappears on earth it's always an excuse for trouble of some kind; and those Satpura Bhils are about as wild as your grandfather left them, young 'un. It means something.'

'Meanin' they may go on the war-path?' said Chinn.

'Can't say – as yet. Shouldn't be surprised a little bit.'

'I haven't been told a syllable.'

'Proves it all the more. They are keeping something back.'

'Bukta tells me everything, too, as a rule. Now, why didn't he tell me that?'

Chinn put the question directly to the old man that night, and the answer surprised him.

'Why should I tell what is well known? Yes, the Clouded Tiger is out in the Satpura country.'

'What do the wild Bhils think that it means?'

'They do not know. They wait. Sahib, what *is* coming? Say only one little word, and we will be content.'

'We? What have tales from the south, where the jungly Bhils live, to do with drilled men?'

'When Jan Chinn wakes is no time for any Bhil to be quiet.'

'But he has not waked, Bukta.'

'Sahib' – the old man's eyes were full of tender reproof – 'if he does not wish to be seen, why does he go abroad in the moonlight? We know he is awake, but we do not know what he desires. Is it a sign for all the Bhils, or one that concerns the Satpura folk alone? Say one little word, Sahib, that I may carry it to the lines, and send on to our villages. Why does Jan Chinn ride out? Who had done wrong? Is it pestilence? Is it murrain? Will our children die? Is it a sword? Remember, Sahib, we are thy people and thy servants, and in this life I bore thee in my arms – not knowing.'

'Bukta has evidently looked on the cup this evening,' Chinn thought; 'but if I can do anything to soothe the old chap I must. It's like the Mutiny rumours on a small scale.'

He dropped into a deep wicker chair, over which was thrown his first tiger-skin, and his weight on the cushion flapped the clawed paws over his shoulders. He laid hold of them mechanically as he spoke, drawing the painted hide, cloak-fashion, about him.

'Now will I tell the truth, Bukta,' he said, leaning forward, the dried muzzle on his shoulder, to invent a specious lie.

'I see that it is the truth,' was the answer, in a shaking voice.

'Jan Chinn goes abroad among the Satpuras, riding on the

Clouded Tiger, ye say? Be it so. Therefore the sign of the wonder is for the Satpura Bhils only, and does not touch the Bhils who plough in the north and east, the Bhils of the Khandesh, or any others, except the Satpura Bhils, who, as we know, are wild and foolish.'

'It is, then, a sign for *them*. Good or bad?'

'Beyond doubt, good. For why should Jan Chinn make evil to those whom he has made men? The nights over yonder are hot; it is ill to lie in one bed over long without turning, and Jan Chinn would look again upon his people. So he rises, whistles his Clouded Tiger, and goes abroad a little to breathe the cool air. If the Satpura Bhils kept to their villages, and did not wander after dark, they would not see him. Indeed, Bukta, it is no more than that he would see the light again in his own country. Send this news south, and say that it is my word.'

Bukta bowed to the floor. 'Good Heavens!' thought Chinn, 'and this blinking pagan is a first-class officer, and as straight as a die! I may as well round it off neatly.' He went on:

'If the Satpura Bhils ask the meaning of the sign, tell them that Jan Chinn would see how they kept their old promises of good living. Perhaps they have plundered; perhaps they mean to disobey the orders of the Government; perhaps there is a dead man in the jungle; and so Jan Chinn has come to see.'

'Is he, then, angry?'

'Bah! Am *I* ever angry with my Bhils? I say angry words, and threaten many things. *Thou* knowest, Bukta. I have seen thee smile behind thy hand. I know, and thou knowest. The Bhils are my children. I have said it many times.'

'Ay. We be thy children,' said Bukta.

'And no otherwise is it with Jan Chinn, my father's father. He would see the land he loved and the people once again. It is a good ghost, Bukta. I say it. Go and tell them. And I do hope devoutly,' he added, 'that it will calm 'em down.' Flinging back the tiger-skin, he rose with a long, unguarded yawn that showed his well-kept teeth.

Bukta fled, to be received in the lines by a knot of panting inquirers.

'It is true,' said Bukta. 'He wrapped himself in the skin and spoke from it. He would see his own country again. The sign is not for us; and, indeed, he is a young man. How should he lie idle of nights? He says his bed is too hot and the air is bad. He goes to and fro for the love of night-running. He has said it.'

The grey-whiskered assembly shuddered.

'He says the Bhils are his children. Ye know he does not lie. He has said it to me.'

'But what of the Satpura Bhils? What means the sign for them?'

'Nothing. It is only night-running, as I have said. He rides to see if they obey the Government, as he taught them to do in his first life.'

'And what if they do not?'

'He did not say.'

The light went out in Chinn's quarters.

'Look,' said Bukta. 'Now he goes away. None the less it is a good ghost, as he has said. How shall we fear Jan Chinn, who made the Bhil a man? His protection is on us; and ye know Jan Chinn never broke a protection spoken or written on paper. When he is older and has found him a wife he will lie in his bed till morning.'

A commanding officer is generally aware of the regimental state of mind a little before the men; and this is why the Colonel said a few days later that some one had been putting the fear of God into the Wuddars. As he was the only person officially entitled to do this, it distressed him to see such unanimous virtue. 'It's too good to last,' he said. 'I only wish I could find out what the little chaps mean.'

The explanation, as it seemed to him, came at the change of the moon, when he received orders to hold himself in readiness to 'allay any possible excitement' among the Satpura Bhils, who were, to put it mildly, uneasy because a paternal Government had sent up against them a Mahratta State-educated vaccinator, with lancets, lymph, and an officially registered calf. In the language of State, they had 'manifested a strong objection to all prophylactic measures', had 'forcibly detained the vaccinator', and 'were on the point of neglecting or evading their tribal obligations'.

434

'That means they are in a blue funk – same as they were at census-time,' said the Colonel; 'and if we stampede them into the hills we'll never catch 'em, in the first place, and, in the second, they'll whoop off plundering till further orders. Wonder who the God-forsaken idiot is who is trying to vaccinate a Bhil? I knew trouble was coming. One good thing is that they'll only use local corps, and we can knock up something we'll call a campaign, and let them down easy. Fancy us potting our best beaters because they don't want to be vaccinated! They're only crazy with fear.'

'Don't you think, sir,' said Chinn the next day, 'that perhaps you could give me a fortnight's shooting-leave?'

'Desertion in the face of the enemy, by Jove!' The Colonel laughed. 'I might, but I'd have to antedate it a little, because we're warned for service, as you might say. However, we'll assume that you applied for leave three days ago, and are now well on your way south.'

'I'd like to take Bukta with me.'

'Of course, yes. I think that will be the best plan. You've some kind of hereditary influence with the little chaps, and they may listen to you when a glimpse of our uniforms would drive them wild. You've never been in that part of the world before, have you? Take care they don't send you to your family vault in your youth and innocence. I believe you'll be all right if you can get 'em to listen to you.'

'I think so, sir; but if – if they should accidentally put an – make asses of 'emselves – they might, you know – I hope you'll represent that they were only frightened. There isn't an ounce of real vice in 'em, and I should never forgive myself if any one of – of my name got them into trouble.'

The Colonel nodded, but said nothing.

Chinn and Bukta departed at once. Bukta did not say that, ever since the official vaccinator had been dragged into the hills by indignant Bhils, runner after runner had skulked up to the lines, entreating, with forehead in the dust, that Jan Chinn should come and explain this unknown horror that hung over his people.

The portent of the Clouded Tiger was now too clear. Let

Jan Chinn comfort his own, for vain was the help of mortal man. Bukta toned down these beseechings to a simple request for Chinn's presence. Nothing would have pleased the old man better than a rough-and-tumble campaign against the Satpuras, whom he, as an 'unmixed' Bhil, despised; but he had a duty to all his nation as Jan Chinn's interpreter, and he devoutly believed that forty plagues would fall on his village if he tampered with that obligation. Besides, Jan Chinn knew all things, and he rode the Clouded Tiger.

They covered thirty miles a day on foot and pony, raising the blue wall-like line of the Satpuras as swiftly as might be. Bukta was very silent.

They began the steep climb a little after noon, but it was near sunset ere they reached the stone platform clinging to the side of a rifted, jungle-covered hill, where Jan Chinn the First was laid, as he had desired, that he might overlook his people. All India is full of neglected graves that date from the beginning of the eighteenth century – tombs of forgotten colonels of corps long since disbanded; mates of East Indiamen who went on shooting expeditions and never came back; factors, agents, writers, and ensigns of the Honourable the East India Company by hundreds and thousands and tens of thousands. English folk forget quickly, but natives have long memories, and if a man has done good in his life it is remembered after his death. The weathered marble four-square tomb of Jan Chinn was hung about with wild flowers and nuts, packets of wax and honey, bottles of native spirits, and infamous cigars, with buffalo horns and plumes of dried grass. At one end was a rude clay image of a white man, in the old-fashioned top-hat, riding on a bloated tiger.

Bukta salaamed reverently as they approached. Chinn bared his head and began to pick out the blurred inscription. So far as he could read it ran thus – word for word, and letter for letter: –

To the Memory of JOHN CHINN, Esq.
   Late Collector of . . . .
 . . . . ithout Bloodshed or . . . error of Authority
Employ . only . . eans of Conciliat . . . and Confiden .

accomplished the . . . tire Subjection . . .
a Lawless and Predatory Peop . . .
. . . . taching them to . . . . ish Government
by a Conque . . over . . . . Minds
The most perma . . . and rational Mode of Domini . .
. . . Governor-General and Counc . . . engal
have ordered thi . . . . erected
. . . arted this Life Aug. 19, 184 . Ag . . .

On the other side of the grave were ancient verses, also very worn. As much as Chinn could decipher said:

```
                         . . . . the savage band
Forsook their Haunts and b . . . . is Command
. . . . mended . . rals check a . . . st for spoil
And . s . ing Hamlets prove his gene . . . . toil
Humanit . . . survey . . . . . . ights restore . .
A nation . . . ield . . subdued without a Sword.
```

For some little time he leaned on the tomb thinking of this dead man of his own blood, and of the house in Devonshire; then, nodding to the plains; 'Yes; it's a big work – all of it – even my little share. He must have been worth knowing . . . Bukta, where are my people?'

'Not here. Sahib. No man comes here except in full sun. They wait above. Let us climb and see.'

But Chinn, remembering the first law of Oriental diplomacy, in an even voice answered: 'I have come this far only because the Satpura folk are foolish, and dared not visit our lines. Now bid them wait on me *here*. I am not a servant, but the master of Bhils.'

'I go – I go,' clucked the old man. Night was falling, and at any moment Jan Chinn might whistle up his dreaded steed from the darkening scrub.

Now for the first time in a long life Bukta disobeyed a lawful command and deserted his leader; for he did not come back, but pressed to the flat table-top of the hill, and called softly. Men stirred all about him – little trembling men with bows and arrows who had watched the two since noon.

'Where is he?' whispered one.

'At his own place. He bids you come,' said Bukta.

'Now?'

'Now.'

'Rather let him loose the Clouded Tiger upon us. We do not go.'

'Nor I, though I bore him in my arms when he was a child in this his life. Wait here till the day.'

'But surely he will be angry.'

'He will be very angry, for he has nothing to eat. But he has said to me many times that the Bhils are his children. By sunlight I believe this, but – by moonlight I am not so sure. What folly have ye Satpura pigs compassed that ye should need him at all?'

'One came to us in the name of the Government with little ghost-knives and a magic calf, meaning to turn us into cattle by the cutting off of our arms. We were greatly afraid, but we did not kill the man. He is here, bound – a black man; and we think he comes from the West. He said it was an order to cut us all with knives – especially the women and the children. We did not hear that it was an order, so we were afraid, and kept to our hills. Some of our men have taken ponies and bullocks from the plains, and others pots and cloths and earrings.'

'Are any slain?'

'By our men? Not yet. But the young men are blown to and fro by many rumours like flames upon a hill. I sent runners asking for Jan Chinn lest worse should come to us. It was this fear that he foretold by the sign of the Clouded Tiger.'

'He says it is otherwise,' said Bukta; and he repeated, with amplifications, all that young Chinn had told him at the conference of the wicker chair.

'Think you,' said the questioner, at last, 'that the Government will lay hands on us?'

'Not I,' Bukta rejoined. 'Jan Chinn will give an order, and ye will obey. The rest is between the Government and Jan Chinn. I myself know something of the ghost-knives and the scratching. It is a charm against the Smallpox. But how it is done I cannot tell. Nor need that concern you.'

'If he stand by us and before the anger of the Government we will most strictly obey Jan Chinn, except – except we do not go down to that place to-night.'

They could hear young Chinn below them shouting for Bukta; but they cowered and sat still, expecting the Clouded Tiger. The tomb had been holy ground for nearly half a century. If Jan Chinn chose to sleep there, who had better right? But they would not come within eyeshot of the place till broad day.

At first Chinn was exceedingly angry, till it occurred to him that Bukta most probably had a reason (which, indeed, he had), and his own dignity might suffer if he yelled without answer. He propped himself against the foot of the grave, and, alternately dozing and smoking, came through the warm night proud that he was a lawful, legitimate, fever-proof Chinn.

He prepared his plan of action much as his grandfather would have done; and when Bukta appeared in the morning with a most liberal supply of food, said nothing of the overnight desertion. Bukta would have been relieved by an outburst of human anger; but Chinn finished his victual leisurely, and a cheroot, ere he made any sign.

'They were very much afraid,' said Bukta, who was not too bold himself. 'It remains only to give orders. They say they will obey if thou wilt only stand between them and the Government.'

'That I know,' said Chinn, strolling slowly to the table-land. A few of the older men stood in an irregular semicircle in an open glade; but the ruck of people – women and children – were hidden in the thicket. They had no desire to face the first anger of Jan Chinn the First.

Seating himself on a fragment of split rock, he smoked his cheroot to the butt, hearing men breathe hard all about him. Then he cried, so suddenly that they jumped:

'Bring the man that was bound!'

A scuffle and a cry were followed by the appearance of a Hindoo vaccinator, quaking with fear, bound hand and foot, as the Bhils of old were accustomed to bind their human sacrifices. He was pushed cautiously before the presence; but young Chinn did not look at him.

'I said – the man that *was* bound. Is it a jest to bring me one tied like a buffalo? Since when could the Bhil bind folk at his pleasure? Cut!'

Half a dozen hasty knives cut away the thongs, and the man crawled to Chinn, who pocketed his case of lancets and tubes of lymph. Then sweeping the semicircle with one comprehensive forefinger, and in the voice of compliment, he said, clearly and distinctly: 'Pigs!'

'Ai!' whispered Bukta. 'Now he speaks. Woe to foolish people!'

'I have come on foot from my house' (the assembly shuddered) 'to make clear a matter which any other than a Satpura Bhil would have seen with both eyes from a distance. Ye know the Smallpox, who pits and scars your children so that they look like wasp-combs. It is an order of the Government that whoso is scratched on the arm with these little knives which I hold up is charmed against Her. All Sahibs are thus charmed, and very many Hindoos. This is the mark of the charm. Look!'

He rolled back his sleeve to the armpit and showed the white scars of the vaccination-mark on the white skin. 'Come, all, and look.'

A few daring spirits came up, and nodded their heads wisely. There was certainly a mark, and they knew well what other dread marks were hidden by the shirt. Merciful was Jan Chinn, that he had not then and there proclaimed his godhead.

'Now all these things the man whom ye bound told you.'

'I did – a hundred times; but they answered with blows,' groaned the operator, chafing his wrists and ankles.

'But, being pigs, ye did not believe; and so came I here to save you, first from Smallpox, next from a great folly of fear, and lastly, it may be, from the rope and the jail. It is no gain to me; it is no pleasure to me; but for the sake of that one who is yonder, who made the Bhil a man' – he pointed down the hill – 'I, who am of his blood, the son of his son, come to turn your people. And I speak the truth, as did Jan Chinn.'

The crowd murmured reverently, and men stole out of the thicket by twos and threes to join it. There was no anger in their god's face.

'These are my orders (Heaven send they'll take 'em, but I seem to have impressed them so far!) I myself will stay among you while this man scratches your arms with knives, after the order of the Government. In three, or it may be five or seven days, your arms will swell and itch and burn. That is the power of Smallpox fighting in your base blood against the orders of the Government. I will therefore stay among you till I see that Smallpox is conquered, and I will not go away till the men and the women and the little children show me upon their arms such marks as I have even now showed you. I bring with me two very good guns, and a man whose name is known among beasts and men. We will hunt together, I and he, and your young men and the others shall eat and lie still. This is my order.'

There was a long pause while victory hung in the balance. A white-haired old sinner, standing on one uneasy leg, piped up:

'There are ponies and some few bullocks and other things for which we need a *kowl* [protection]. They were *not* taken in the way of trade.'

The battle was won, and John Chinn drew a breath of relief. The young Bhils had been raiding, but if taken swiftly all could be put straight.

'I will write a *kowl* as soon as the ponies, the bullocks, and the other things are counted before me and sent back whence they came. But first we will put the Government mark on such as have not been visited by Smallpox.' In an undertone, to the vaccinator: 'If you show you are afraid you'll never see Poona again, my friend.'

'There is not sufficient ample supply of vaccine for all this population,' said the man. 'They have destroyed the offeecial calf.'

'They won't know the difference. Scrape 'em all round, and give me a couple of lancets; I'll attend to the elders.'

The aged diplomat who had demanded protection was the first victim. He fell to Chinn's hand, and dared not cry out. As soon as he was freed he dragged up a companion, and held him fast, and the crisis became, as it were, a child's sport; for the vaccinated chased the unvaccinated to treatment, vowing that all the tribe must suffer equally. The women shrieked, and the children ran howling; but Chinn laughed, and waved the pink-tipped lancet.

'It is an honour,' he cried. 'Tell them, Bukta, how great an honour it is that I myself should mark them. Nay, I cannot mark every one – the Hindoo must also do his work – but I will touch all marks that he makes, so there will be an equal virtue in them. Thus do the Rajputs stick pigs. Ho, brother with one eye! Catch that girl and bring her to me. She need not run away yet, for she is not married, and I do not seek her in marriage. She will not come? Then she shall be shamed by her little brother, a fat boy, a bold boy. He puts out his arm like a soldier. Look! *He* does not flinch at the blood. Some day he shall be in my regiment. And now, mother of many, we will lightly touch thee, for Smallpox has been before us here. It is a true thing, indeed, that this charm breaks the power of Mata. There will be no more pitted faces among the Satpuras, and so ye can ask many cows for each maid to be wed.'

And so on and so on – quick-poured showman's patter, sauced in the Bhil hunting proverbs and tales of their own brand of coarse humour – till the lancets were blunted and both operators worn out.

But, nature being the same the world over, the unvaccinated grew jealous of their marked comrades, and came near to blows about it. Then Chinn declared himself a court of justice, no longer a medical board, and made formal inquiry into the late robberies.

'We are the thieves of Mahadeo,' said the Bhils, simply. 'It is our fate, and we were frightened. When we are frightened we always steal.'

Simply and directly as children, they gave in the tale of the plunder, all but two bullocks and some spirits that had gone a-missing (these Chinn promised to make good out of his own pocket), and ten ringleaders were despatched to the lowlands with a wonderful document, written on the leaf of a note-book, and addressed to an assistant district superintendent of police. There was warm calamity in that note, as Jan Chinn warned them, but anything was better than loss of liberty.

Armed with this protection, the repentant raiders went downhill. They had no desire whatever to meet Mr Dundas Fawne of the Police, aged twenty-two, and of a cheerful countenance, nor did they wish to revisit the scene of their robberies. Steering a middle course, they ran into the camp of the one Government chaplain allowed to the various irregular corps through a district of some fifteen thousand square miles, and stood before him in a cloud of dust. He was by way of being a priest they knew, and what was more to the point, a good sportsman who paid his beaters generously.

When he read Chinn's note he laughed, which they deemed a luck omen, till he called up policemen, who tethered the ponies and the bullocks by the piled house-gear, and laid stern hands upon three of that smiling band of the thieves of Mahadeo. The chaplain himself addressed them magisterially with a riding-whip. That was painful, but Jan Chinn had prophesied it. They submitted, but would not give up the written protection, fearing the jail. On their way back they met Mr D. Fawne, who had heard about the robberies, and was not pleased.

'Certainly,' said the eldest of the gang, when the second interview was at an end, 'certainly Jan Chinn's protection has saved us our liberty, but it is as though there were many beatings in one small piece of paper. Put it away.'

One climbed into a tree, and stuck the letter into a cleft forty feet from the ground, where it could do no harm. Warmed, sore, but happy, the ten returned to Jan Chinn next day, where he sat among uneasy Bhils, all looking at their right arms, and all bound under terror of their god's disfavour not to scratch.

'It was a good *kowl*,' said the leader. 'First the chaplain, who laughed, took away our plunder, and beat three of us, as was promised. Next, we met Fawne Sahib, who frowned, and asked for the plunder. We spoke the truth, and so he beat us all, one after another, and called us chosen names. He then gave us these two bundles' – they set down a bottle of whisky and a box of cheroots – 'and we came away. The *kowl* is left in a tree, because its virtue is that so soon as we show to a Sahib we are beaten.'

'But for that *kowl*,' said Jan Chinn, sternly, 'ye would all have been marching to jail with a policeman on either side. Ye come now to serve as beaters for me. These people are unhappy, and we will go hunting till they are well. To-night we will make a feast.'

It is written in the chronicles of the Satpura Bhils, together with many other matters not fit for print, that through five days, after the day that he had put his mark upon them, Jan Chinn the First hunted for his people; and on the five nights of those days the tribe was gloriously and entirely drunk, Jan Chinn bought country spirits of an awful strength, and slew wild pig and deer beyond counting, so that if any fell sick they might have two good reasons.

Between head- and stomach-aches they found no time to think of their arms, but followed Jan Chinn obediently through the jungles, and with each day's returning confidence men, women, and children stole away to their villages as the little army passed by. They carried news that it was good and right to be scratched with ghost-knives; that Jan Chinn was indeed reincarnated as a god of free food and drink, and that of all nations the Satpura Bhils stood first in his favour, if they would only refrain from scratching. Henceforward that kindly demi-god would be connected in their minds with great gorgings and the vaccine and lancets of a paternal Government.

'And to-morrow I go back to my home,' said Jan Chinn to his faithful few, whom neither spirits, over-eating, nor swollen glands could conquer. It is hard for children and savages to behave reverently at all times to the idols of their make-belief, and they had frolicked excessively with Jan Chinn. But the reference to his home cast a gloom on the people.

'And the Sahib will not come again?' said he who had been vaccinated first.

'That is to be seen,' answered Chinn, warily.

'Nay, but come as a white man – come as a young man whom we know and love; for, as thou alone knowest, we are a weak people. If we again saw why – thy horse—' They were picking up their courage.

'I have no horse. I came on foot – with Bukta, yonder. What is this?'

'Thou knowest – the Thing that thou has chosen for a night-horse.' The little men squirmed in fear and awe.

'Night-horse? Bukta, what is this last tale of children?'

Bukta had been a silent leader in Chinn's presence since the night of his desertion, and was grateful for a chance-flung question.

'They know, Sahib,' he whispered. 'It is the Clouded Tiger. That that comes from the place where thou didst once sleep. It is thy horse – as it has been these three generations.'

'My horse! That was a dream of the Bhils!'

'It is no dream. Do dreams leave the tracks of broad pugs on earth? Why make two faces before thy people? They know of the night-ridings, and they – and they—'

'Are afraid, and would have them cease.'

Bukta nodded. 'If thou hast no further need of him. He is thy horse.'

'The thing leaves a trail, then?' said Chinn.

'We have seen it. It is like a village road under the tomb.'

'Can ye find and follow it for me?'

'By daylight – if one comes with us, and, above all, stands near by.'

'I will stand close, and we will see to it that Jan Chinn does not ride any more.'

The Bhils shouted the last words again and again.

From Chinn's point of view the stalk was nothing more than an ordinary one – down hill, through split and crannied rocks, unsafe, perhaps, if a man did not keep his wits by him, but no worse than twenty others he had undertaken. Yet his men – they refused absolutely to beat, and would only trail – dripped sweat at every move. They showed the marks of enormous pugs that ran, always down hill, to a few hundred feet below Jan Chinn's tomb, and disappeared in a narrow-mouthed cave. It was an insolently open road, a domestic highway, beaten without thought of concealment.

'The beggar might be paying rent and taxes,' Chinn muttered ere he asked whether his friend's taste ran to cattle or man.

'Cattle,' was the answer. 'Two heifers a week. We drive them for him at the foot of the hill. It is his custom. If we did not, he might seek us.'

'Blackmail and piracy,' said Chinn. 'I can't say I fancy going into the cave after him. What's to be done?'

The Bhils fell back as Chinn lodged himself behind a rock with his rifle ready. Tigers, he knew, were shy beasts, but one who had been long cattle-fed in this sumptuous style might prove overbold.

'He speaks!' someone whispered from the rear. 'He knows, too.'

'Well, of *all* the infernal cheek!' said Chinn. There was an angry growl from the cave – a direct challenge.

'Come out then,' Chinn shouted. 'Come out of that! Let's have a look at you.'

The brute knew well enough that there was some connection between brown nude Bhils and his weekly allowance; but the white helmet in the sunlight annoyed him, and he did not approve of the voice that broke his rest. Lazily as a gorged snake he dragged himself out of the cave, and stood yawning and blinking at the entrance. The sunlight fell upon his flat right side, and Chinn wondered. Never had he seen a tiger marked after this fashion. Except for his head, which was staringly barred, he was dappled – not striped, but dappled like a child's rocking-horse in rich shades of smoky black on red gold. That portion of his belly and throat which should have been white was orange, and his tail and paws were black.

He looked leisurely for some ten seconds, and then deliberately lowered his head, his chin dropped and drawn in, staring intently at the man. The effect of this was to throw forward the round arch of his skull, with two broad bands across it, while below the bands glared the unwinking eyes; so that, head on, as he stood, he showed something like a diabolically scowling pantomime-mask. It was a piece of natural mesmerism that he had practised many times on his quarry, and though Chinn was by no means a terrified heifer, he stood for a while, held by the extraordinary oddity of the attack. The head – the body seemed to have been packed away behind it – the ferocious, skull-like head, crept nearer, to the switching of an angry tail-tip in the grass. Left and right the Bhils had scattered to let Jan Chinn subdue his own horse.

'My word!' he thought. 'He's trying to frighten me!' and fired between the saucer-like eyes, leaping aside upon the shot.

A big coughing mass, reeking of carrion, bounded past him up the hill, and he followed discreetly. The tiger made no attempt to turn into the jungle: he was hunting for sight and breath – nose up, mouth open, the tremendous fore-legs scattering the gravel in spurts.

'Scuppered!' said John Chinn, watching the flight. 'Now if he was a partridge he'd tower. Lungs must be full of blood.'

The brute had jerked himself over a boulder and fallen out of sight the other side. John Chinn looked over with a ready barrel. But the red trail led straight as an arrow even to his grandfather's tomb, and there, among the smashed spirit bottles and the fragments of the mud image, the life left with a flurry and a grunt.

'If my worthy ancestor could see that,' said John Chinn, 'he'd have been proud of me. Eyes, lower jaw, and lungs. A very nice shot.' He whistled for Bukta as he drew the tape over the stiffening bulk.

'Ten – six – eight – by Jove! It's nearly eleven – call it eleven. Fore-arm, twenty-four – five – seven and a half. A short tail, too; three feet one. But *what* a skin! Oh, Bukta! Bukta! The men with the knives swiftly.'

'Is he beyond question dead?' said an awe-stricken voice behind a rock.

'That was not the way I killed my first tiger,' said Chinn. 'I did not think that Bukta would run. I had no second gun.'

'It – it is the Clouded Tiger,' said Bukta, unheeding the taunt. 'He is dead.'

Whether all the Bhils, vaccinated and unvaccinated, of the Satpuras had lain by to see the kill, Chinn could not say; but the whole hill's flank rustled with little men, shouting, singing, and stampeding. And yet, till he had made the first cut in the splendid skin, not a man would take a knife; and, when the shadows fell, they ran from the red-stained tomb, and no persuasion would bring them back till dawn. So Chinn spent a second night in the open, guarding the carcass from jackals, and thinking about his ancestor.

He returned to the lowlands to the triumphal chant of an escorting army three hundred strong, the Mahratta vaccinator close at his elbow, and the rudely dried skin a trophy before him. When that army suddenly and noiselessly disappeared, as quail in high corn, he argued he was near civilisation, and a turn in the road brought him upon the camp of a wing of his own corps. He left the skin on a cart-tail for the world to see, and sought the Colonel.

'They're perfectly right,' he explained earnestly. 'There isn't an ounce of vice in 'em. They were only frightened. I've vaccinated the whole boiling, and they like it awfully. What are – what are we doing here, sir?'

'That's what I'm trying to find out,' said the Colonel. 'I don't know yet whether we're a piece of a brigade or a police force. However, I think we'll call ourselves a police force. How did you manage to get a Bhil vaccinated?'

'Well, sir,' said Chinn, 'I've been thinking it over, and, as far as I can make out, I've got a sort of hereditary influence over 'em.'

'So I know, or I wouldn't have sent you; but *what*, exactly?'

'It's rather rummy. It seems, from what I can make out, that I'm my own grandfather reincarnated, and I've been disturbing the peace of the country by riding a pad-tiger of nights. If I hadn't done that, I don't think they'd have objected to the vaccination; but the two together were more than they could stand. And so, sir, I've vaccinated 'em, and shot my tiger-horse as a sort o' proof of good faith. You never saw such a skin in your life.'

The Colonel tugged his moustache thoughtfully. 'Now, how the deuce,' said he, 'am I to include that in my report?'

Indeed, the official version of the Bhils' anti-vaccination stampede said nothing about Lieutenant John Chinn, his godship. But Bukta knew, and the corps knew, and every Bhil in the Satpura hills knew.

And now Bukta is zealous that John Chinn shall swiftly be

wedded and impart his powers to a son; for if the Chinn succession fails, and the little Bhils are left to their own imaginings, there will be fresh trouble in the Satpuras.

WIRELESS

'It's a funny thing, this Marconi business, isn't it?' said Mr Shaynor, coughing heavily. 'Nothing seems to make any difference, by what they tell me – storms, hills, or anything; but if that's true we shall know before morning.'

'Of course it's true,' I answered, stepping behind the counter. 'Where's old Mr Cashell?'

'He's had to go to bed on account of his influenza. He said you'd very likely drop in.'

'Where's his nephew?'

'Inside, getting the things ready. He told me that the last time they experimented they put the pole on the roof of one of the big hotels here and the batteries electrified all the water-supply and' – he giggled – 'the ladies got shocked when they took their baths.'

'I never heard of that.'

'The hotel wouldn't exactly advertise it, would it? Just now, by what young Mr Cashell tells me, they're trying to signal from here to Poole, and they're using stronger batteries than ever. But, you see, he being the guvnor's nephew and all that (and it will be in the papers, too), it doesn't matter how they electrify things in this house. Are you going to watch?'

'Very much. I've never seen this game. Aren't you going to bed?'

'We don't close till ten on Saturdays. There's a good deal of influenza in town, too, and there'll be a dozen prescriptions coming in before morning. I generally sleep in the chair here. It's warmer than jumping out of bed every time. Bitter cold, isn't it?'

'Freezing hard. I'm sorry your cough's worse.'

'Thank you. I don't mind cold so much. It's this wind that fair cuts me to pieces.' He coughed again, hard and hackingly, as an old lady came in for ammoniated quinine. 'We've just run out of it in bottles, madam,' said Mr Shaynor, returning to the professional tone, 'but if you will wait two minutes, I'll make it up for you, madam.'

I had used the shop for some time, and my acquaintance with the proprietor had ripened into friendship. It was Mr Cashell who revealed to me the purpose and power of Apothecaries' Hall that time a fellow-chemist had made an error in a prescription of mine, had lied to cover his sloth, and when error and lie were brought home to him had written vain letters.

'A disgrace to our profession,' said the thin mild-eyed man, hotly, after studying the evidence. 'You couldn't do a better service to the profession than report him to Apothecaries' Hall.'

I did so, not knowing what djinns I should evoke; and the result was such an apology as one might make who had spent a night on the rack. I conceived great respect for Apothecaries' Hall and esteem for Mr Cashell, a zealous craftsman who magnified his calling. Until Mr Shaynor came down from the North his assistants had by no means agreed with Mr Cashell. 'They forget,' said he, 'that first and foremost the compounder is a medicine-man. On him depends the physician's reputation. He holds it literally in the hollow of his hand, sir.'

Mr Shaynor's manners had not, perhaps, the polish of the grocery and Italian warehouse next door, but he knew and loved his dispensary work in every detail. For relaxation he seemed to go no farther afield than the romance of drugs – their discovery, preparation, packing, and export – but it led him to the ends of the earth, and on this subject, and the Pharmaceutical Formulary, and Nicholas Culpepper, most confident of physicians, we met.

Little by little I grew to know something of his beginnings and his hopes – of his mother, who had been a school-teacher in one of the northern counties, and of his red-headed father, a small jobbing master at Kirby Moors, who died when he was a child; of the examinations he had passed (Apothecaries' Hall is a hard master in this respect); of his dreams of a shop in London; of his hate for the price-cutting co-operative stores; and, most interesting, of his mental attitude toward customers.

'There's a way you get into,' he told me, 'of serving them quite carefully, and, I hope, politely, without stopping your own thinking. I've been reading Christie's "New Commercial Plants" all this autumn, and that needs keeping your mind on it, I can tell you. So long as it isn't a prescription, of course, I can carry as much as half a page of Christie in my head, and at the same time I could sell out all that window twice over, and not a penny wrong at the end. As to prescriptions, I think I could make up the general run of 'em in my sleep, almost.'

For reasons of my own, I was deeply interested in Marconi experiments at their outset in England; and it was of a piece with Mr Cashell's unvarying thoughtfulness that, when his nephew the electrician appropriated the house for a long-range installation, he should, as I have said, invite me to see the result.

The old lady went away with her medicine, and Mr Shaynor and I stamped on the tiled floor behind the counter to keep ourselves warm. The shop, by the light of the many electrics, looked like a Paris-diamond mine, for Mr Cashell believed in all the ritual of his craft. Three superb glass jars – red, green, and blue – of the sort that led Rosamond to parting with her shoes, blazed in the broad plate-glass windows, and there was a confused smell of orris, Kodak films, vulcanite, tooth-powder, sachets, and almond-cream in the air. Mr Shaynor fed the dispensary stove, and we sucked cayenne-pepper jujubes for our stomach's sake. The brutal east wind had cleared the streets, and the few passers-by were muffled to their puckered eyes. In the Italian warehouse next door some gay feathered birds and game, hung upon hooks, sagged to the wind across the left edge of our window-frame.

'They ought to take these poultry in – all knocked about like that,' said Mr Shaynor. 'Doesn't it make you feel perishing? See that old hare! The wind's nearly blowing the fur off him.'

I saw the belly-fur of the dead beast blown apart in ridges

and streaks as the wind caught it, showing bluish skin under-neath. 'Bitter cold,' said Mr Shaynor, shuddering. 'Fancy going out on a night like this! Oh, here's young Mr Cashell.'

The door of the inner office behind the dispensary opened, and an energetic, spade-bearded man stepped forth, rubbing his hands.

'I want a bit of tin-foil, Shaynor,' he said. 'Good-evening. My uncle told me you might be coming.' This to me, as I began the first of a hundred questions.

'I've everything in order,' he replied. 'We're only waiting until Poole calls us up. Excuse me a minute. You can come in whenever you like – but I'd better be with the instruments. Give me that tin-foil. Thanks.'

While we were talking, a girl – evidently no customer – had come into the shop, and the face and bearing of Mr Shaynor changed. She leaned confidently across the counter.

'But I can't,' I heard him whisper uneasily – the flush on his cheek was dull red, and his eyes shone like a drugged moth's. 'I can't. I tell you I'm alone in the place.'

'No, you aren't. Who's *that*? Let him look after it for half an hour. A brisk walk will do you good. Ah, come now, John.'

'But he isn't—'

'I don't care. I want you to; we'll only go round by the church. If you don't—'

He crossed to where I stood in the shadow of the dispensary counter, and began some sort of broken apology about a lady-friend.

'Yes,' she interrupted. 'You take the shop for half an hour – to oblige *me*, won't you?'

She had a singularly rich and promising voice that well matched her outline.

'All right,' I said. 'I'll do it – but you'd better wrap yourself up Mr Shaynor.'

'Oh, a brisk walk ought to help me. We're only going round by St Agnes Church.' I heard him cough grievously as they went out together.

I refilled the stove, and, after profligate expenditure of Mr Cashell's coal, drove much warmth into the shop. I explored many of the glass-knobbed drawers that lined the walls, tasted some disconcerting drugs, and, by the aid of a few cardamoms, ground ginger, chloric-ether, and dilute alcohol, manufactured a new and wildish drink, of which I bore a glassful to young Mr Cashell, busy in the back office. He laughed shortly when I told him that Mr Shaynor had stepped out – but a frail coil of wire held all his attention, and he had no word for me bewildered among the batteries and rods. The noise of the sea on the beach began to make itself heard as the traffic in the street ceased. Then briefly, but very lucidly, he gave me the names and uses of the mechanism that crowded the tables and the floor.

'When do you expect to get the messages from Poole?' I demanded, sipping my liquor out of a graduated glass.

'About midnight, if everything is in order. We've got our installation-pole fixed to the roof of the house. I shouldn't advise you to turn on a tap or anything tonight. We've connected up with the plumbing, and all the water will be electrified.' He repeated to me the history of the agitated ladies at the hotel at the time of the first installation.

'But what *is* it?' I asked. 'Electricity is out of my beat altogether.'

'Ah, if you knew *that* you'd know something nobody knows. It's just It – what we call Electricity, but the magic – the manifestations – the Hertzian waves – are all revealed by *this*. The coherer, we call it.'

He picked up a glass tube not much thicker than a thermometer, in which, almost touching, were two tiny silver plugs and between them an infinitesimal pinch of metallic dust. 'That's all,' he said, proudly, as though himself responsible for the wonder. 'That is the thing that will reveal to us the powers – whatever the powers may be – at work – through space – a long distance away.'

Just then Mr Shaynor returned alone and stood coughing his heart out on the mat.

'Serves you right for being such a fool,' said young Mr Cashell, as annoyed as myself at the interruption. 'Never mind – we've all the night before us to see wonders.'

Shaynor clutched the counter, his handkerchief to his lips. When he brought it away I saw two bright red stains.

'I – I've got a bit of a rasped throat from smoking cigarettes,' he panted. 'I think I'll try a cubeb.'

'Better take some of this. I've been compounding while you've been away.' I handed him the brew.

' 'Twon't make me drunk, will it? I'm almost a teetotaller. My word! That's grateful and comforting.'

He set down the empty glass to cough afresh.

'Brr! But it was cold out there! I shouldn't care to be lying in my grave a night like this. Don't *you* ever have a sore throat from smoking?' He pocketed his handkerchief after a furtive peep.

'Oh, yes, sometimes,' I replied, wondering, while I spoke, into what agonies of terror I should fall if ever I saw those bright-red danger-signals under my nose. Young Mr Cashell among the batteries coughed slightly to show that he was quite ready to continue his scientific explanations, but I was thinking still of the girl with the rich voice and the significantly cut mouth, at whose command I had taken charge of the shop. It flashed across me that she distantly resembled the seductive shape on a gold-framed toilet-water advertisement whose charms were unholily heightened by the glare from the red bottle in the window. Turning to make sure, I saw Mr Shaynor's eyes bent in the same direction, and by instinct recognized that the flamboyant thing was to him a shrine. 'What do you take for your – cough?' I asked.

'Well, I'm the wrong side of the counter to believe much in patent medicines. But there are asthma cigarettes and there are pastilles. To tell you the truth, if you don't object to the smell, which is very like incense, I believe, though I'm not a Roman Catholic, Blaudet's Cathedral Pastilles relieve me as much as anything.'

'Let's try.' My chances of raiding chemists' shops are few, and I make the most of them. We unearthed the pastilles – brown, gummy cones of benzoin – and set them alight under the toilet-water advertisement, where they fumed in thin blue spirals.

'Of course,' said Mr Shaynor, to my question, 'what one uses in the shop for one's self comes out of one's own pocket. Why, stock-taking in our business is nearly the same as with jewellers – and I can't say more than that. But one gets them' – he pointed to the pastille-box – 'at trade prices.' Evidently this censing of the gay, seven-tinted wench was an established ritual which cost something.

'And when do we shut up shop?'

'We stay like this all night. The guv – old Mr Cashell – doesn't believe in locks and shutters as compared with electric light. Besides it brings trade. I'll just sit here in the chair by the stove and doze off, if you don't mind. Electricity isn't my prescription.'

The energetic young Mr Cashell snorted within and Shaynor settled himself up in his chair over which he had thrown a staring red, black, and yellow Austrian jute blanket, rather like a tablet-cover. I cast about, amid patent-medicine pamphlets, for something to read, but finding little, returned to the manufacture of the new drink. The Italian warehouse took down its game and went to bed. Across the street blank shutters flung back the gas-light in cold smears; the dried pavement seemed to rough up in goose-flesh under the scouring of the savage wind, and we could hear, long ere he passed, the policeman flapping his arms to keep himself warm. Within, the flavours of cardamoms and chloric-ether disputed those of the pastilles and a score of drug and perfume and soap scents. Our electric lights, set low down in the windows before the tun-bellied Rosamond jars, flung inward three monstrous daubs of red, blue, and green, that broke into kaleidoscopic lights on the faceted knobs of the drug-drawers, the cut-glass scent flagons, and the bulbs of the sparklet bottles. They flushed the white tiled floor in gorgeous patches; splashed along the nickel-silver counter-rails and turned the polished mahogany counter-panels to the likeness of intricate grained marbles – slabs of porphyry and malachite. Mr Shaynor unlocked a drawer and took out a meagre bundle of letters. From my place by the stove, I could see the scalloped edges of the paper with a flaring monogram in the corner and could even smell the reek of chypre. At each page he turned toward the toilet-water lady of the advertisement and devoured her with luminous eyes. He had drawn the Austrian blanket over his shoulders and among those warring lights he looked more than ever the incarnation of a drugged moth – a tiger moth as I thought.

He put his letter into an envelope, stamped it with stiff mechanical movements, and dropped it in the drawer. Then I became aware of the silence of a great city asleep – the silence that underlaid the even voice of the breakers along the sea-front – a thick, tingling quiet of warm life stilled down for its appointed time, and unconsciously I moved about the glittering shop as one moves in a sick-room. Young Mr Cashell was adjusting some wire that crackled from time to time with the tense, knuckle-stretching sound of the electric spark. Upstairs, where a door shut and opened swiftly, I could hear his uncle coughing abed.

'Here,' I said, when the drink was properly warmed, 'take some of this, Mr Shaynor.'

He jerked in his chair with a start and a wrench, and held out his hand for the glass. The mixture, of a rich port-wine colour, frothed at the top.

'It looks,' he said, suddenly, 'it looks – those bubbles – like a string of pearls winking at you – rather like the pearls round that young lady's neck.' He turned again to the advertisement where the female in the dove-coloured corset had seen fit to put on all her pearls before she cleaned her teeth.

'Not bad, is it?' I said.

'Eh?'

He rolled his eyes heavily full on me, and, as I stared, I beheld all meaning and consciousness die out of the swiftly dilating pupils. His figure lost its stark rigidity, softened into the chair, and, chin on chest, hands dropped before him, he rested open-eyed, absolutely still.

'I'm afraid I've rather cooked Shaynor's goose,' I said, bearing, the fresh drink to young Mr Cashell. 'Perhaps it was the chloric-ether.'

'Oh, he's all right.' The spade-bearded man glanced at him

pityingly. 'Consumptives go off in those sort of dozes very often. 'It's exhaustion . . . I don't wonder. I daresay the liquor will do him good. It's grand stuff,' he finished his share appreciatively. 'Well, as I was saying – before he interrupted – about this little coherer. The pinch of dust, you see, is nickel-filings. The Hertzian waves, you see, come out of space from the station that despatches 'em and all these little particles are attracted together – cohere, we call it – for just so long as the current passes through them. Now, it's important to remember that the current is an induced current. There are a good many kinds of induction—'

'Yes, but what *is* induction?'

'That's rather hard to explain untechnically. But the long and the short of it is that when a current of electricity passes through a wire there's a lot of magnetism present round that wire; and if you put another wire parallel to, and within what we call its magnetic field – why then, the second wire will also become charged with electricity.'

'On its own account?'

'On its own account.'

'Then let's see if I've got it correctly. Miles off, at Poole, or wherever it is—'

'It will be anywhere in ten years.'

'You've got a charged wire—'

'Charged with Hertzian waves which vibrate, say, two hundred and thirty million times a second.' Mr Cashell snaked his fore-finger rapidly through the air.

'All right – a charged wire at Poole, giving out these waves into space. Then this wire of yours sticking out into space – on the roof of the house – in some mysterious way gets charged with those waves from Poole—'

'Or anywhere – it only happens to be Poole to-night.'

'And those waves set the coherer at work, just like an ordinary telegraph-office ticker?'

'No! That's where so many people make the mistake. The Herzian waves wouldn't be strong enough to work a great heavy Morse instrument like ours. They can only just make that dust cohere, and while it coheres (a little while for a dot and a longer time for a dash) the current from this battery – the 'home battery' – he laid his hand on the thing – 'can get through to the Morse printing-machine to record the dot or dash. Let me make it clearer. Do you know anything about steam?'

'Very little. But go on.'

'Well, the coherer's like a steam-valve. Any child can open a valve and start a steamer's engines, because a turn of the hand lets in the main steam, doesn't it? Now, this home battery here is the main steam, ready to print. The coherer is the valve, always ready to be turned on. The Hertzian wave is the child's hand that turns it.'

'I see. That's marvellous.'

'Marvellous, isn't it? And, remember, we're only at the beginning. There's nothing we shan't be able to do in ten years. I want to live – my God, how I want to live, and see things happen!' He looked through the door at Shaynor breathing lightly in his chair. 'Poor beast! And he wants to keep company with Fanny Brand.'

'Fanny *who*?' I said, for the name struck an obscurely familiar chord in my brain – something connected with a stained handkerchief, and the word 'arterial.'

'Fanny Brand – the girl you kept shop for!' He laughed. 'That's all I know about her, and for the life of me I can't see what Shaynor sees in her, or she in him.'

'*Can't* you see what he sees in her?' I insisted.

'Oh, yes, if *that's* what you mean. She's a great big fat lump of a girl and so on – I suppose that's why he's so crazy after her. She isn't his sort. Well, it doesn't matter. My uncle says he's bound to die before the year's out. Your drink's given him a good sleep, at any rate.' Young Mr Cashell could not catch Mr Shaynor's face, which was half turned to the advertisement.

I stoked the stove anew, for the room was growing cold, and lightened another pastille. Mr Shaynor in his chair, never moving, looked through and over me with eyes as wide and lustreless as those of a dead hare.

'Poole's late,' said young Mr Cashell, when I stepped back. 'I'll just send them a call.'

He pressed a key in the semi-darkness and with a rending crackle there leaped between two brass knobs a spark, streams of sparks, and sparks again.

'Grand, isn't it? *That's* the Power – our unknown Power – kicking and fighting to be let loose,' said young Mr Cashell. 'There she goes – kick – kick – kick into space. I never get over the strangeness of it when I work a sending-machine – waves going into space, you know. T. R. is our call. Poole ought to answer with L. L. L.'

We waited two, three, five minutes. In that silence, of which the boom of the tide was an orderly part, I caught the clear '*kiss – kiss – kiss*' of the halliards on the roof, as they were blown against the installation-pole.

'Poole is not ready. I'll stay here and call you when he is.'

I returned to the shop, and set down my glass on a marble slab with a careless clink. As I did so, Shaynor rose to his feet, his eyes fixed once more on the advertisement, where the young woman bathed in the light from the red jar simpered pinkly over her pearls. His lips moved without cessation. I stepped nearer to listen. 'And threw – and threw – and threw,' he repeated, his face all sharp with some inexplicable agony.

I moved forward astonished. But it was then he found words – delivered roundly and clearly. These:

And threw warm gules on Madeleine's young breast.

The trouble passed off his countenance, and he returned lightly to his place, rubbing his hands.

It had never occurred to me, though we had many times discussed reading and prize-competitions as a diversion, that Mr Shaynor ever read Keats, or could quote him at all appositely. There was, after all, a certain stained-glass effect of light on the high bosom of the highly polished picture which might, by stretch of fancy, suggest, as a vile chromo recalls some incomparable canvas, the line he had spoken. Night, my drink, and solitude were evidently turning Mr Shaynor into a poet. He sat down again and wrote swiftly on his villanous note-paper, his lips quivering.

I shut the door into the inner office and moved up behind him. He made no sign that he saw or heard; I looked over his shoulder and read, amid half-formed words, sentences, and wild scratches:

– very cold it was. Very cold
The hare – the hare – the hare –
The birds –

He raised his head sharply, and frowned toward the blank shutters of the poulterer's shop where they jutted out against our window. Then one clear line came:

The hare, in spite of fur, was very cold –

The head, moving machine-like, turned right to the advertisement where the Blaudet's Cathedral pastille reeked abominably. He grunted and went on:

Incense in a censer –
Before her darling picture framed in gold –
Maiden's picture – angel's portrait –

'Hsh,' said Mr Cashell, guardedly, from the inner office as though in the presence of spirits. 'There's something coming through from somewhere; but it isn't Poole.' I heard the crackle of sparks as he depressed the keys of the transmitter. In my own brain, too, something crackled, or it might have been the hair on my head. Then I heard my own voice in a harsh whisper: 'Mr Cashell, there is something coming through here, too. Leave me alone till I tell you.'

'But I thought you'd come to see this wonderful thing – sir,' indignantly at the end.

'Leave me alone till I tell you. Be quiet.'

I watched – I waited. Under the blue-veined hand – the dry hand of the consumptive – came away clear, without erasure:

> And my weak spirit fails
> To think how the dead must freeze [he shivered as he wrote]
>   Beneath the churchyard mould.

Then he stopped, laid the pen down, and leaned back.

For an instant, that was half an eternity, the shop spun before me in a rainbow-tinted whirl, in and through which my own soul most dispassionately considered my own soul as that fought with an overmastering fear. Then I smelt the strong smell of cigarettes from Mr Shaynor's clothing and heard, as though it had been the rending of trumpets, the rattle of his breathing. I was still in my place of observation, much as one would watch a rifle-shot at the butts, half bent, hands on my knees and head within a few inches of the black, red, and yellow blanket of his shoulder. I was whispering encouragingly, evidently to my other self, sounding sentences, such as men pronounce in dreams.

'If he has read Keats, it proves nothing. If he hasn't – like causes *must* beget like effects. There is no escape from this law. *You* ought to be grateful that you know "St Agnes' Eve" without the book; because, given the circumstances, such as Fanny Brand, who is the key of the enigma and approximately represents the latitude and longitude of Fanny Brawne; allowing also for the bright red color of the arterial blood upon the handkerchief, which was what you were puzzling over in the shop just now; and counting the effect of the professional environment, here almost perfectly duplicated – the result is logical and inevitable. As inevitable as induction.'

Still the other half of my soul refused to be comforted. It was cowering in some minute and inadequate corner – at an immense distance.

Hereafter, I found myself one person again, my hands still gripping my knees and my eyes glued on the page before Mr Shaynor. As dreamers accept and explain the upheaval of landscapes and the resurrection of the dead with excerpts from the evening hymn or the multiplication-table, so I had accepted the facts, whatever they might be, that I should witness, and had devised a theory, sane and plausible to my mind, that explained them all. Nay, I was even in advance of my facts, walking hurriedly before them, assured that they would fit my theory. And all that I now recall of that epoch-making theory are the lofty words: 'If he has read Keats it's the chloric-ether. If he hasn't, it's the identical bacillus, or Hertzian wave of tuberculosis, *plus* Fanny Brand and the professional status which in conjunction with the main stream of subconscious thought, common to all mankind, has produced, temporarily, the induced Keats.'

Mr Shaynor returned to his work, erasing and rewriting as before, with incredible swiftness. Two or three blank pages he tossed aside. Then wrote, muttering:

'The little smoke of a candle that goes out.'

'No,' he muttered. 'Little smoke – little smoke – little smoke. What else?' He thrust his chin forward toward the advertisement, whereunder the last of the Blaudet's Cathedral pastilles fumed in its holder. 'Ah!' Then with relief:

The little smoke that dies in moonlight cold.

Evidently he was snared by the rhymes of his first verse, for he wrote and rewrote 'gold – cold – mould' many times. Again he sought inspiration from the advertisement and set down, without erasure, the line I had overheard:

And threw warm gules on Madeleine's young breast.

As I remembered the original, it is 'fair' – a trite word – instead of 'young,' and I found myself nodding approval, though I admitted spaciously that the attempt to reproduce 'its little smoke in pallid moonlight died' was a failure.

Followed without a break, ten or fifteen lines of bald prose – the naked soul's confession of its physical yearning for its beloved – unclean as we count uncleanliness; unwholesome, but human exceedingly – the raw material, so it seemed to me in that hour and in that place, whence Keats wove the twenty-sixth, seventh, and eighth stanzas of his poem. Shame I had none in overseeing this revelation; and my fear had gone like the smoke of the pastille.

'That's it,' I murmured. 'That's how it's blocked out. Go on! Ink it in, man. Ink it in.'

Mr Shaynor returned to broken verse wherein 'loveliness' was made to rhyme with a desire to look upon 'her empty dress.' He picked up a fold of the gay, soft blanket, spread it over one hand, caressed it with infinite tenderness, thought, muttered, traced some snatches which I could not decipher, shut his eyes drowsily, shook his head, and dropped the stuff. Here I found myself at fault, for I could not then see (as I do now) in what manner a red, black, and yellow Austrian blanket bore upon his dreams.

In a few minutes he laid aside his pen; and, chin on hand, considered the shop with intelligent and thoughtful eyes. He threw down the blanket, rose, passed along a line of drug-drawers, and read the names on the labels aloud. Returning, he took from his desk Christie's 'New Commercial Plants' and the old Culpepper that I had given him; opened and laid them side by side with a clerkly air, all trace of passion gone from his face; read first in one and then in the other and paused with the pen behind his ear.

'What wonder of Heaven's coming now?' I thought.

'Manna – manna – manna,' he said at last, under wrinkled brows. 'That's what I wanted. Good! Now then! Now then! Good! Good! Oh, by God, that's good!' His voice rose and he spoke richly and fully without a falter:

Candied apple, quince and plum and gourd,
And jellies smoother than the creamy curd,
And lucent sirups tinct with cinnamon,
Manna and dates in Argosy transferred
From Fez; and spiced dainties everyone
From silken Samarcand to cedared Lebanon.

He repeated it once more, using 'blander' for 'smoother' in the second line: then wrote it down without erasure, but this time (my set eyes missed no hairstroke of any word) he substituted 'smoother' for his atrocious second-thought, so that it came away under his hand as it is written in the book – as it is written in the book.

A wind went shouting down the street, and on the heels of the wind followed a spun and rattle of rain.

After a smiling pause – and good right had he to smile – he began anew, always tossing the last sheet over his shoulder:

The sharp rain falling on the window-pane,
Rattling sleet – the windblown sleet.

Then prose: 'It is very cold of mornings when the wind brings rain and sleet with it. I heard the sleet on the window-pane outside and thought of you, my darling. I am always thinking of you. I wish we could both run away like two lovers into the storm and get that little cottage by the sea which we were always thinking about, my own dear darling. We could sit and watch the sea beneath our windows. It would be a fairyland all of our own – a fairy sea – a fairy sea . . .'

He stopped, raised his head and listened. The steady drone of the Channel along the sea-front that had borne us company so long, leaped up a note to the sudden fuller surge that signals the change from ebb to flood. It beat in like the change of step throughout an army – this renewed pulse of the sea – and filled our ears till they, accepting it, marked it no longer.

A fairyland for you and me
Across the foam – beyond . . .
A magic foam, a perilous sea.

He grunted again with effort and bit his underlip. My throat dried, but I dared not gulp to moisten it lest I should break the spell that was drawing him nearer and nearer to the high-water mark but two of the sons of Adam have reached. Remember that in all the millions permitted there are no more than five – five little lines – of which one can say: 'These are the Magic. These are the Vision. The rest is only poetry.' And Mr Shaynor was playing hot and cold with two of them!

I vowed no unconscious thought of mine should influence the blindfold soul and pinned myself desperately to the other three, repeating and re-repeating:

A savage spot as holy and enchanted
As e'er beneath a waning moon was haunted
By woman wailing for her demon lover.

But though I believed my brain thus occupied, my every sense hung upon the writing under the dry, bony hand, all brown-fingered with chemicals and cigarette smoke.

Our windows fronting on the dangerous foam.

(he wrote, after long, irresolute snatches); and then

Our open casements facing desolate seas
Forlorn – forlorn –

Here again his face grew peaked and anxious with that sense of loss I had first seen when the power snatched him. But this time the agony was tenfold keener. As I watched, it mounted like mercury in the tube. It lighted his face from within till I thought the visibly scourged soul must leap forth naked between his jaws, unable to endure. A drop of sweat trickled from my forehead down my nose and splashed on the back of my hand.

Our windows facing on the desolate seas
And perilous foam of magic fairyland –

'Not yet – not yet,' he muttered, 'wait a minute. *Please*, wait a minute. I shall get it then.

Our magic windows fronting on the sea
The dangerous foam of desolate seas . . . for aye.

Ouh, my God!'

466

From head to heel he shook – shook from the marrow of his bones outward – then leaped to his feet with raised arms, and slid the chair screeching across the tiled floor where it struck the drawers behind and fell with a jar. Mechanically, I stooped to recover it.

As I rose, Mr Shaynor was stretching and yawning at leisure.

'I've had a bit of a doze,' he said. 'How did I come to knock the chair over? You look rather—'

'The chair startled me,' I answered. 'It was so sudden in this quiet.'

Young Mr Cashell behind his shut door was offendedly silent.

'I suppose I must have been dreaming,' said Mr Shaynor.

'I suppose you must,' I said. 'Talking of dreams – I – I noticed you writing – before—

He flushed consciously.

'I meant to ask you if you've ever read anything written by a man called Keats.'

'Oh! I haven't much time to read poetry and I can't say that I remember the name exactly. Is he a popular writer?'

'Middling. I thought you might know him because he's the only poet who ever was a druggist. And he's rather what's called the lover's poet.'

'Indeed? I must look into him. What did he write about?'

'A lot of things. Here's a sample that may interest you.'

Then and there, carefully, I repeated the verse he had twice spoken and once written not ten minutes ago.

'Ah. Anybody could see he was a druggist from that line about the tinctures and sirups. It's a fine tribute to our profession.'

'I don't know,' said young Mr Cashell, with icy politeness, opening the door one-half inch, 'if you still happen to be interested in our trifling experiments. But, should such be the case—'

I drew him aside, whispering, 'Shaynor seemed going off into some sort of fit when I spoke to you just now. I thought, even at the risk of being rude, it wouldn't do to take you off your instruments just as the call was coming through. Don't you see?'

'Granted – granted as soon as asked,' he said, unbending. 'I *did* think it a shade odd at the time. So that was why he knocked the chair down?'

'I hope I haven't missed anything,' I said.

'I'm afraid I can't say that but you're just in time for a rather curious performance. You can come in, too, Mr Shaynor. Listen, while I read it off.'

The Morse instrument was ticking furiously. Mr Cashell interpreted: ' "*K.K.V. Can make nothing of your signals.*" ' A pause. ' "*M.M.V. M.M.V. Signals unintelligible. Purpose anchor Sandown Bay. Examine instruments to-morrow.*" Do you know what that means? It's a couple of men-o'-war working Marconi signals off the Isle of Wight. They are trying to talk to each other. Neither can read the other's messages, but all their messages are being taken in by our receiver here. They've been going on for ever so long, I wish you could have heard it.'

'Good heavens!' I said. 'Do you mean we're overhearing Portsmouth ships trying to talk to each other – that we're eavesdropping across half South England?'

'Just that. Their transmitters are all right, but their receivers are out of order, so they only get a dot here and a dash there. Nothing clear.'

'Why is that?'

'God knows – and Science will know to-morrow. Perhaps the induction is faulty; perhaps the receivers aren't tuned to receive just the number of vibrations per second that the transmitter sends. Only a word here and there. Just enough to tantalise.'

Again the Morse sprang to life.

'That's one of 'em complaining now. Listen: "*Disheartening – most disheartening.*" It's quite pathetic. Have you ever seen a spiritualistic seance? It reminds me of that sometimes – odds and ends of messages coming out of nowhere – a word here and there. No good at all.'

'But mediums are all impostors,' said Mr Shaynor, in the

doorway, lighting an asthma-cigarette. 'They only do it for the money they can make. I've seen 'em.'

'Here's Poole, at last – clear as a bell. L. L. L. *Now* we sha'n't be long.' Mr Cashell rattled the keys merrily. 'Anything you'd like to tell 'em?'

'No, I don't think so,' I said. 'I'll go home and get to bed. I'm feeling a little tired.'

'THEY'

One view called me to another; one hill top to its fellow, half across the county, and since I could answer to no more trouble than the snapping forward of a lever, I let the county flow under my wheels. The orchid-studded flats of the East gave way to the thyme, ilex, and grey grass of the Downs; these again to the rich cornland and fig-trees of the lower coast, where you carry the beat of the tide on your left hand for fifteen level miles; and when ; at last I turned inland through a huddle of rounded hills and woods I had run myself clean out of my known marks. Beyond that precise hamlet which stands godmother to the capital of the United States, I found hidden villages where bees, the only things awake, boomed in eighty-foot lindens that overhung grey Norman churches; miraculous brooks diving under stone bridges built for heavier traffic than would ever vex them again; tithe-barns larger than their churches, and an old smithy that cried out aloud how it had once been a hall of the Knights of the Temple. Gipsies I found on a common where the gorse, bracken, and heath fought it out together up a mile of Roman road; and a little farther on I disturbed a red fox rolling dog-fashion in the naked sunlight.

As the wooded hills closed about me I stood up in the car to take the bearings of that great Down whose ringed head is a landmark for fifty miles across the low countries. I judged that the lie of the country would bring me across some westward-running road that went to his feet, but I did not allow for the confusing veils of the woods. A quick turn plunged me first into a green cutting brim-full of liquid sunshine, next into a gloomy tunnel where last year's dead leaves whispered and scuffled about my tyres. The strong hazel stuff meeting overhead had not been cut for a couple of generations at least, nor had any axe helped the moss-cankered oak and beech to spring above them. Here the road changed frankly into a carpeted ride on whose brown velvet spent primrose-clumps showed like jade, and a few sickly, white-stalked blue-bells nodded together. As the slope favoured I shut off the power and slid over the whirled leaves, expecting every moment to meet a keeper; but I only heard a jay, far off, arguing against the silence under the twilight of the trees.

Still the track descended. I was on the point of reversing and working my way back on the second speed ere I ended in some swamp, when I saw sunshine through the tangle ahead and lifted the brake.

It was down again at once. As the light beat across my face my fore-wheels took the turf of a great still lawn from which sprang horsemen ten feet high with levelled lances, monstrous peacocks, and sleek round-headed maids of honour – blue, black, and glistening – all of clipped yew. Across the lawn – the marshalled woods besieged it on three sides – stood an ancient house of lichened and weather-worn stone, with mullioned windows and roofs of rose-red tile. It was flanked by semi-circular walls, also rose-red, that closed the lawn on the fourth side, and at their feet a box hedge grew man-high. There were doves on the roof about the slim brick chimneys, and I caught a glimpse of an octagonal dove-house behind the screening wall.

Here, then, I stayed; a horseman's green spear laid at my breast; held by the exceeding beauty of that jewel in that setting.

'If I am not packed off for a trespasser, or if this knight does not ride a wallop at me,' thought I, 'Shakespeare and Queen Elizabeth at least must come out of that half-open garden door and ask me to tea.'

A child appeared at an upper window, and I thought the little thing waved a friendly hand. But it was to call a companion, for presently another bright head showed. Then I heard a laugh among the yew-peacocks, and turning to make sure (till then I had been watching the house only) I saw the silver of a fountain behind a hedge thrown up against the sun. The doves on the roof cooed to the cooing water; but between the two notes I caught the utterly happy chuckle of a child absorbed in some light mischief.

The garden door – heavy oak sunk deep in the thickness of the wall – opened further: a woman in a big garden hat set her foot slowly on the time-hollowed stone step and as slowly walked across the turf. I was forming some apology when she lifted up her head and I saw that she was blind.

'I heard you,' she said. 'Isn't that a motor car?'

'I'm afraid I've made a mistake in my road. I should have turned off up above – I never dreamed—' I began.

'But I'm very glad. Fancy a motor car coming into the garden! It will be such a treat—' She turned and made as though looking about her. 'You – you haven't seen any one, have you – perhaps?'

'No one to speak to, but the children seemed interested at a distance.'

'Which?'

'I saw a couple up at the window just now, and I think I heard a little chap in the grounds.'

'Oh, lucky you!' she cried, and her face brightened. 'I hear them, of course, but that's all. You've seen them and heard them?'

'Yes,' I answered. 'And if I know anything of children, one of them's having a beautiful time by the fountain yonder. Escaped, I should imagine.'

'You're fond of children?'

I gave her one of two reasons why I did not altogether hate them.

'Of course, of course,' she said. 'Then you understand. Then you won't think it foolish if I asked you to take your car through the gardens, once or twice – quite slowly. I'm sure they'd like to see it. They see so little, poor things. One tries to make their life pleasant, but—' she threw out her hands towards the woods. 'We're so out of the world here.'

'That will be splendid,' I said. 'But I can't cut up your grass.'

She faced to the right. 'Wait a minute,' she said. 'We're at the South gate, aren't we? Behind those peacocks there's a flagged path. We call it the Peacocks' Walk. You can't see it from here, they tell me, but if you squeeze along by the edge of the wood you can turn at the first peacock and get on to the flags.

It was sacrilege to wake that dreaming housefront with the clatter of machinery, but I swung the car to clear the turf, brushed along the edge of the wood and turned in on the broad stone path where the fountain-basin lay like one star-sapphire.

'May I come too?' she cried. 'No, please don't help me. They'll like it better if they see me.'

She felt her way lightly to the front of the car, and with one foot on the step she called: 'Children, oh children! Look and see what's going to happen!'

The voice would have drawn lost souls from the Pit, for the yearning that underlay its sweetness, and I was not surprised to hear an answering shout behind the yews. It must have been the child by the fountain, but he fled at our approach, leaving a little toy boat in the water. I saw the glint of his blue blouse among the still horsemen.

Very disposedly we paraded the length of the walk and at her request backed again. This time the child had got the better of his panic, but stood far off and doubting.

'The little fellow's watching us,' I said. 'I wonder if he'd like a ride.'

'They're very shy still. Very shy. But, oh, lucky you to be able to see them! Let's listen.'

I stopped the machine at once, and the humid stillness, heavy with the scent of box, cloaked us deep. Shears I could hear where some gardener was clipping; a mumble of bees and broken voices that might have been the doves.

'Oh, unkind!' she said weariedly.

'Perhaps they're only shy of the motor. The little maid at the window looks tremendously interested.'

'Yes?' She raised her head. 'It was wrong of me to say that. They are really fond of me. It's the only thing that makes life worth living – when they're fond of you, isn't it? I daren't think what the place would be without them. By the way, is it beautiful?'

'I think it is the most beautiful place I have ever seen.'

'So they all tell me. I can feel it, of course, but that isn't quite the same thing.'

'Then have you never—?' I began, but stopped abashed.

'Not since I can remember. It happened when I was only a few months old, they tell me. And yet I must remember something, else how could I dream about colours. I see light in my dreams, and colours, but I never see *them*. I only hear them just as I do when I'm awake.'

'It's difficult to see faces in dreams. Some people can, but most of us haven't the gift.' I went on, looking up at the window where the child stood all but hidden.

'I've heard that too,' she said. 'And they tell me that one never sees a dead person's face in a dream. Is that true?'

'I believe it is – now I come to think of it.'

'But how is it with yourself – yourself?' The blind eyes turned towards me.

'I have never seen the faces of my dead in any dream,' I answered.

'Then it must be as bad as being blind.'

The sun had dipped behind the woods and the long shades were possessing the insolent horsemen one by one. I saw the light die from off the top of a glossy-leaved lance and all the brave hard green turn to soft black. The house, accepting another day at end, as it had accepted an hundred thousand gone, seemed to settle deeper into its rest among the shadows.

'Have you ever wanted to?' she said after the silence.

'Very much sometimes,' I replied. The child had left the window as the shadows closed upon it.

'Ah! So've I, but I don't suppose it's allowed . . . Where d'you live?'

'Quite the other side of the county – sixty miles and more, and I must be going back. I've come without my big lamp.'

'But it's not dark yet. I can feel it.'

'I'm afraid it will be by the time I get home. Could you lend me someone to set me on my road at first? I've utterly lost myself.'

'I'll send Madden with you to the cross-roads. We are so out of the world, I don't wonder you were lost! I'll guide you round to the front of the house; but you will go slowly, won't you, till you're out of the grounds? It isn't foolish, do you think?'

'I promise you I'll go like this,' I said, and let the car start herself down the flagged path.

We skirted the left wing of the house, whose elaborately cast lead guttering alone was worth a day's journey; passed under a great rose-grown gate in the red wall, and so round to the high front of the house which in beauty and stateliness as much excelled the back as that all others I had seen.

'Is it so very beautiful?' she said wistfully when she heard my raptures. 'And you like the lead-figures too? There's the old azalea garden behind. They say that this place must have been made for children. Will you help me out, please? I should like to come with you as far as the cross-roads, but I mustn't leave them. Is that you, Madden? I want you to show this gentleman the way to the cross-roads. He has lost his way but – he has seen them.'

A butler appeared noiselessly at the miracle of old oak that must be called the front door, and slipped aside to put on his hat. She stood looking at me with open blue eyes in which no sight lay, and I saw for the first time that she was beautiful.

'Remember,' she said quietly, 'if you are fond of them you will come again,' and disappeared within the house.

The butler in the car said nothing till we were nearly at the lodge gates, where catching a glimpse of a blue blouse in a shrubbery I swerved amply lest the devil that leads little boys to play should drag me into child-murder.

'Excuse me,' he asked of a sudden, 'but why did you do that, Sir?'

'The child yonder.'

'Our young gentleman in blue?'

'Of course.'

'He runs about a good deal. Did you see him by the fountain, Sir?'

'Oh, yes, several times. Do we turn here?'

'Yes, Sir. And did you 'appen to see them upstairs too?'

'At the upper window? Yes.'

'Was that before the mistress come out to speak to you. Sir?'

'A little before that. Why d'you want to know?'

He paused a little. 'Only to make sure that – that they had seen the car, Sir, because with children running about, though I'm sure you're driving particularly careful, there might be an accident. That was all, Sir. Here are the cross-roads. You can't miss your way from now on. Thank you, Sir, but that isn't *our* custom, not with—'

'I beg your pardon,' I said, and thrust away the British silver.

'Oh, it's quite right with the rest of 'em as a rule. Good-bye, Sir.'

He retired into the armour-plated conning tower of his caste and walked away. Evidently a butler solicitous for the honour of his house, and interested, probably through a maid, in the nursery.

Once beyond the signposts at the cross-roads I looked back, but the crumpled hills interlaced so jealously that I could not see where the house had lain. When I asked its name at a cottage along the road, the fat woman who sold sweetmeats there gave me to understand that people with motor cars had small right to live – much less to 'go about talking like carriage folk.' They were not a pleasant-mannered community.

When I retraced my route on the map that evening I was little wiser. Hawkin's Old Farm appeared to be the Survey title of the place, and the old County Gazetteer, generally so ample, did not allude to it. The big house of those parts was Hodnington Hall, Georgian with early Victorian embellishments, as an atrocious steel engraving attested. I carried my difficulty to a neighbour – a deep-rooted tree of that soil – and he gave me a name of a family which conveyed no meaning.

A month or so later – I went again, or it may have been that my car took the road of her own volition. She over-ran the fruitless Downs, threaded every turn of the maze of lanes below the hills, drew through the high-walled woods, impenetrable in their full leaf, came out at the cross-roads where the butler had left me, and a little farther on developed an internal trouble which forced me to turn her in on a grass way-waste that cut into a summer-silent hazel wood. So far as I could make sure by the sun and a six-inch Ordnance map, this should be the road flank of that wood which I had first explored from the heights above. I made a mighty serious business of my repairs and a glittering shop of my repair kit, spanners, pump, and the like, which I spread out orderly upon a rug. It was a trap to catch all childhood, for on such a day, I argued, the children would not be far off. When I paused in my work I listened, but the wood was so full of the noises of summer (though the birds had mated) that I could not at first distinguish these from the tread of small cautious feet stealing across the dead leaves. I rang my bell in an alluring manner, but the feet fled, and I repented, for to a child a sudden noise is very real terror. I must have been at work half an hour when I heard in the wood the voice of the blind woman crying: 'Children, oh, children! Where are you?' and the stillness made slow to close on the perfection of that cry. She came towards me, half feeling her way between the tree boles, and though a child it seemed clung to her skirt, it swerved into the leafage like a rabbit as she drew nearer.

'Is that you?' she said, 'from the other side of the county?'

'Yes, it's me from the other side of the county.'

'Then why didn't you come through the upper woods? They were there just now.'

'They were here a few minutes ago. I expect they knew my car had broken down, and came to see the fun.'

'Nothing serious, I hope? How do cars break down?'

'In fifty different ways. Only mine has chosen the fifty-first.'

She laughed merrily at the tiny joke, cooed with delicious laughter, and pushed her hat back.

'Let me hear,' she said.

'Wait a moment,' I cried, 'and I'll get you a cushion.'

She set her foot on the rug all covered with spare parts, and stooped above it eagerly. 'What delightful things!' The hands through which she saw glanced in the chequered sunlight. 'A box here – another box! Why you've arranged them like playing shop!'

'I confess now that I put it out to attract them. I don't need half those things really.'

'How nice of you! I heard your bell in the upper wood. You say they were here before that?'

'I'm sure of it. Why are they so shy? That little fellow in blue who was with you just now ought to have got over his fright. He's been watching me like a Red Indian.'

'It must have been your bell,' she said. 'I heard one of them go past me in trouble when I was coming down. They're shy – so shy even with me.' She turned her face over her shoulder and cried again: 'Children, oh, children! Look and see!'

'They must have gone off together on their own affairs,' I suggested, for there was a murmur behind us of lowered voices broken by the sudden squeaking giggles of childhood. I returned to my tinkerings and she leaned forward, her chin on her hand, listening interestedly.

'How many are they?' I said at last. The work was finished, but I saw no reason to go.

Her forehead puckered a little in thought. 'I don't quite know,' she said simply. 'Sometimes more – sometimes less. They come and stay with me because I love them, you see.'

'That must be very jolly,' I said, replacing a drawer, and as I spoke I heard the inanity of my answer.

'You – you aren't laughing at me,' she cried. 'I – I haven't any of my own. I never married. People laugh at me sometimes about them because – because—'

'Because they're savages,' I returned. 'It's nothing to fret for. That sort laugh at everything that isn't in their own fat lives.'

'I don't know. How should I? I only don't like being laughed at about *them*. It hurts; and when one can't see . . . I don't want to seem silly,' her chin quivered like a child's as she spoke, 'but we blindies have only one skin, I think. Every-thing outside hits straight at our souls. It's different with you. You've such good defences in your eyes – looking out – before

478

anyone can really pain you in your soul. People forget that with us.'

I was silent reviewing that inexhaustible matter – the more than inherited (since it is also carefully taught) brutality of the Christian peoples, beside which the mere heathendom of the West Coast nigger is clean and restrained. It led me a long distance into myself.

'Don't do that!' she said of a sudden, putting her hands before her eyes.

'What?'

She made a gesture with her hand.

'That! It's – it's all purple and black. Don't! That colour hurts.'

'But, how in the world do you know about colours?' I exclaimed, for here was a revelation indeed.

'Colours as colours?' she asked.

'No. *Those* Colours which you saw just now.'

'You know as well as I do,' she laughed, 'else you wouldn't have asked that question. They aren't in the world at all. They're in *you* – when you went so angry.'

'D'you mean a dull purplish patch, like port wine mixed with ink?' I said.

'I've never seen ink or port wine, but the colours aren't mixed. They are separate – all separate.'

'Do you mean black streaks and jags across the purple?'

She nodded. 'Yes – if they are like this,' and zig-zagged her finger again, 'but it's more red than purple – that bad colour.'

'And what are the colours at the top of the – whatever you see?'

Slowly she leaned forward and traced on the rug the figure of the Egg itself.

'I see them so,' she said, pointing with a grass stem, 'white, green, yellow, red, purple, and when people are angry or bad, black across the red – as you were just now.'

'Who told you anything about it – in the beginning?' I demanded.

'About the colours? No one. I used to ask what colours were

when I was little – in table-covers and curtains and carpets, you see – because some colours hurt me and some made me happy. People told me; and when I got older that was how I saw people.' Again she traced the outline of the Egg which it is given to very few of us to see.

'All by yourself?' I repeated.

'All by myself. There wasn't anyone else. I only found out afterwards that other people did not see the Colours.'

She leaned against the tree-bole plaiting and unplaiting chance-plucked grass stems. The children in the wood had drawn nearer. I could see them with the tail of my eye frolicking like squirrels.

'Now I am sure you will never laugh at me,' she went on after a long silence. 'Nor at *them*.'

'Goodness! No!' I cried, jolted out of my train of thought. 'A man who laughs at a child – unless the child is laughing too – is a heathen!'

'I didn't mean that, of course. You'd never laugh *at* children, but I thought – I used to think – that perhaps you might laugh about *them*. So now I beg your pardon . . . What are you going to laugh at?'

I made no sound, but she knew.

'At the notion of your begging my pardon. If you had done your duty as a pillar of the State and a landed proprietress you ought to have summoned me for trespass when I barged through your woods the other day. It was disgraceful of me – inexcusable.'

She looked at me, her head against the tree trunk – long and steadfastly – this woman who could see the naked soul.

'How curious,' she half whispered. 'How very curious.'

'Why, what have I done?'

'You don't understand . . . and yet you understood about the Colours. Don't you understand?'

She spoke with a passion that nothing had justified, and I faced her bewilderedly as she rose. The children had gathered themselves in a roundel behind a bramble bush. One sleek head bent over something smaller, and the set of the little shoulders told me that fingers were on lips. They, too, had some child's tremendous secret. I alone was hopelessly astray there in the broad sunlight.

'No,' I said, and shook my head as though the dead eyes could note. 'Whatever it is, I don't understand yet. Perhaps I shall later – if you'll let me come again.'

'You will come again,' she answered. 'You will surely come again and walk in the wood.'

'Perhaps the children will know me well enough by that time to let me play with them – as a favour. You know what children are like.'

'It isn't a matter of favour but of right,' she replied, and while I wondered what she meant, a dishevelled woman plunged round the bend of the road, loose-haired, purple, almost lowing with agony as she ran. It was my rude, fat friend of the sweetmeat shop. The blind woman heard and stepped forward. 'What is it, Mrs Madehurst?' she asked.

The woman flung her apron over her head and literally grovelled in the dust, crying that her grandchild was sick to death, that the local doctor was away fishing, that Jenny the mother was at her wits' end, and so forth, with repetitions and bellowings.

'Where's the next nearest doctor?' I asked between paroxysms.

'Madden will tell you. Go round to the house and take him with you. I'll attend to this. Be quick!' She half-supported the fat woman into the shade. In two minutes I was blowing all the horns of Jericho under the front of the House Beautiful, and Madden, in the pantry, rose to the crisis like a butler and a man.

A quarter of an hour at illegal speeds caught us a doctor five miles away. Within the half-hour we had decanted him, much interested in motors, at the door of the sweetmeat shop, and drew up the road to await the verdict.

'Useful things cars,' said Madden, all man and no butler. 'If I'd had one when mine took sick she wouldn't have died.'

'How was it?' I asked.

'Croup. Mrs Madden was away. No one knew what to do. I drove eight miles in a tax cart for the doctor. She was choked when we came back. This car 'd ha' saved her. She'd have been close on ten now.'

'I'm sorry,' I said. 'I thought you were rather fond of children from what you told me going to the cross-roads the other day.'

'Have you seen 'em again. Sir – this mornin'?'

'Yes, but they're well broke to cars. I couldn't get any of them within twenty yards of it.'

He looked at me carefully as a scout considers a stranger – not as a menial should lift his eyes to his divinely appointed superior.

'I wonder why,' he said just above the breath that he drew.

We waited on. A light wind from the sea wandered up and down the long lines of the woods, and the wayside grasses, whitened already with summer dust, rose and bowed in sallow waves.

A woman, wiping the suds off her arms, came out of the cottage next the sweetmeat shop.

'I've be'n listenin' in de back-yard,' she said cheerily. 'He says Arthur's unaccountable bad. Did ye hear him shruck just now? Unaccountable bad. I reckon t'will come Jenny's turn to walk in de wood nex' week along, Mr Madden.'

'Excuse me, Sir, but your lap-robe is slipping, said Madden deferentially. The woman started, dropped a curtsey, and hurried away.

'What does she mean by "walking in the wood"?' I asked.

'It must be some saying they use hereabouts. I'm from Norfolk myself,' said Madden. 'They're an independent lot in this country. She took you for a chauffeur, Sir.'

I saw the Doctor come out of the cottage followed by a draggle-tailed wench who clung to his arm as though he could make treaty for her with Death. 'Dat sort,' she wailed – 'dey're just as much to us dat has 'em as if dey was lawful born. Just as much – just as much! An' God he'd be just as pleased if you saved 'un, Doctor. Don't take it from me. Miss Florence will tell ye de very same. Don't leave 'im. Doctor!'

'I know, I know,' said the man; 'but he'll be quiet for a while now. We'll get the nurse and the medicine as fast as we can.'

He signalled me to come forward with the car, and I strove not to be privy to what followed; but I saw the girl's face, blotched and frozen with grief, and I felt the hand without a ring clutching at my knees when we moved away.

The Doctor was a man of some humour, for I remember he claimed my car under the Oath of Æsculapius, and used it and me without mercy. First we convoyed Mrs Madehurst and the blind woman to wait by the sick bed till the nurse should come. Next we invaded a neat county town for prescriptions (the Doctor said the trouble was cerebro-spinal meningitis), and when the County Institute, banked and flanked with scared market cattle, reported itself out of nurses for the moment we literally flung ourselves loose upon the county. We conferred with the owners of great houses – magnates at the ends of overarching avenues whose big-boned womenfolk strode away from their tea-tables to listen to the imperious Doctor. At last a white-haired lady sitting under a cedar of Lebanon and surrounded by a court of magnificent Borzois – all hostile to motors – gave the Doctor, who received them as from a princess, written orders which we bore many miles at top speed, through a park, to a French nunnery, where we took over in exchange a pallid-faced and trembling Sister. She knelt at the bottom of the tonneau telling her beads without pause till, by short cuts of the Doctor's invention, we had her to the sweetmeat shop once more. It was a long afternoon crowded with mad episodes that rose and dissolved like the dust of our wheels; cross-sections of remote and incomprehensible lives through which we raced at right angles; and I went home in the dusk, wearied out, to dream of the clashing horns of cattle; round-eyed nuns walking in a garden of graves; pleasant tea-parties beneath shaded trees; the carbolic-scented, grey-painted corridors of the County Institute; the steps of shy children in the wood, and the hands that clung to my knees as the motor began to move.

I had intended to return in a day or two, but it pleased Fate to hold me from that side of the county, on many pretexts, till the elder and the wild rose had fruited. There came at last a brilliant day, swept clear from the south-west, that brought the hills within hand's reach – a day of unstable airs and high filmy clouds. Through no merit of my own I was free, and set the car for the third time on that known road. As I reached the crest of the Downs I felt the soft air change, saw it glaze under the sun; and, looking down at the sea, in that instant beheld the blue of the Channel turn through polished silver and dulled steel to dingy pewter. A laden collier hugging the coast steered outward for deeper water, and, across copper-coloured haze, I saw sails rise one by one on the anchored fishing-fleet. In a deep dene behind me an eddy of sudden wind drummed through sheltered oaks, and spun left aloft the first dry sample of autumn leaves. When I reached the beach road the sea-fog fumed over the brickfields, and the tide was telling all the groins of the gale beyond Ushant. In less than an hour summer England vanished in chill grey. We were again the shut island of the North, all the ships of the world bellowing at our perilous gates; and between their outcries ran the piping of bewildered gulls. My cap dripped moisture, the folds of the rug held it in pools or sluiced it away in runnels, and the salt-rime stuck to my lips.

Inland the smell of autumn loaded the thickened fog among the trees, and the drip became a continuous shower. Yet the late flowers – mallow of the wayside, scabious of the field, and dahlia of the garden – showed gay in the mist, and beyond the sea's breath there was little sign of decay in the leaf. Yet in the villages the house doors were all open, and bare-legged, bare-headed children sat at ease on the damp doorsteps to shout 'pip-pip' at the stranger.

I made bold to call at the sweetmeat shop, where Mrs Madehurst met me with a fat woman's hospitable tears. Jenny's child, she said, had died two days after the nun had come. It was, she felt, best out of the way, even though insurance offices, for reasons which she did not pretend to follow, would not willingly insure such stray lives. 'Not but what Jenny didn't tend to Arthur as though he'd come all proper at de end of de first year – like Jenny herself.' Thanks to Miss Florence, the child had been buried with a pomp which, in Mrs Madehurst's opinion, more than covered the small irregularity of its birth. She described the coffin, within and without, the glass hearse, and the evergreen lining of the grave.

'But how's the mother?' I asked.

'Jenny? Oh, she'll get over it. I've felt dat way with one or two o' my own. She'll get over. She's walkin' in de wood now.'

'In this weather?'

Mrs Madehurst looked at me with narrowed eyes across the counter.

'I dunno but it opens de 'eart like. Yes, it opens de 'eart. Dat's where losin' and bearin' comes so alike in de long run, we do say.'

Now the wisdom of the old wives is greater than that of all the Fathers, and this last oracle sent me thinking so extendedly as I went up the road, that I nearly ran over a woman and a child at the wooded corner by the lodge gates of the House Beautiful.

'Awful weather!' I cried, as I slowed dead for the turn.

'Not so bad,' she answered placidly out of the fog. 'Mine's used to 'un. You'll find yours indoors, I reckon.'

Indoors, Madden received me with professional courtesy, and kind inquiries for the health of the motor, which he would put under cover.

I waited in a still, nut-brown hall, pleasant with late flowers and warmed with a delicious wood fire – a place of good influence and great peace. (Men and women may sometimes, after great effort, achieve a creditable lie; but the house, which is their temple, cannot say anything save the truth of those who have lived in it.) A child's cart and a doll lay on the black-and-white floor, where a rug had been kicked back. I felt that the children had only just hurried away – to hide themselves, most like – in the many turns of the great adzed staircase that climbed statelily out of the hall, or to crouch at gaze behind the lions and roses of the carven gallery above. Then I heard her voice above me, singing as the blind sing – from the soul:

In the pleasant orchard-closes.

And all my early summer came back at the call.

In the pleasant orchard-closes,
   God bless all our gains say we –
But may God bless all our losses,
   Better suits with our degree.

She dropped the marring fifth line, and repeated –

Better suits with our degree!

I saw her lean over the gallery, her linked hands white as pearl against the oak.

'Is that you – from the other side of the county?' she called.

'Yes, me – from the other side of the county,' I answered, laughing.

'What a long time before you had to come here again.' She ran down the stairs, one hand lightly touching the broad rail. 'It's two months and four days. Summer's gone!'

'I meant to come before, but Fate prevented.'

'I knew it. Please do something to that fire. They won't let me play with it, but I can feel it's behaving badly. Hit it!'

I looked on either side of the deep fireplace, and found but a half-charred hedge-stake with which I punched a black log into flame.

'It never goes out, day or night,' she said, as though explaining. 'In case any one comes in with cold toes, you see.'

'It's even lovelier inside than it was out,' I murmured. The red light poured itself along the age-polished dusky panels till the Tudor roses and lions of the gallery took colour and motion. An old eagle-topped convex mirror gathered the picture into its mysterious heart, distorting afresh the distorted shadows, and curving the gallery lines into the curves of a ship. The day was shutting down in half a gale as the fog turned to stringy scud. Through the uncurtained mullions of the broad window I could see valiant horsemen of the lawn rear and recover against the wind that taunted them with legions of dead leaves.

'Yes, it must be beautiful,' she said. 'Would you like to go over it? There's still light enough upstairs.'

I followed her up the unflinching, wagon-wide staircase to the gallery whence opened the thin fluted Elizabethan doors.

'Feel how they put the latch low down for the sake of the children.' She swung a light door inward.

'By the way, where are they?' I asked. 'I haven't even heard them to-day.'

She did not answer at once. Then, 'I can only hear them,' she replied softly. 'This is one of their rooms – everything ready, you see.'

She pointed into a heavily-timbered room. There were little low gate tables and children's chairs. A doll's house, its hooked front half open, faced a great dappled rocking-horse, from whose padded saddle it was but a child's scramble to the broad window-seat overlooking the lawn. A toy gun lay in a corner beside a gilt wooden cannon.

'Surely they've only just gone,' I whispered. In the failing light a door creaked cautiously. I heard the rustle of a frock and the patter of feet – quick feet through a room beyond.

'I heard that,' she cried triumphantly. 'Did you? Children, oh, children! Where are you?'

The voice filled the walls that held it lovingly to the last perfect note, but there came no answering shout such as I had heard in the garden. We hurried on from room to oak-floored room; up a step here, down three steps there; among a maze of passages; always mocked by our quarry. One might as well have tried to work an unstopped warren with a single ferret. There were bolt-holes innumerable – recesses in walls, embrasures of deep slitten windows now darkened, whence they could start up behind us; and abandoned fireplaces, six feet deep in the masonry, as well as the tangle of communicating doors. Above all, they had the twilight for their helper in our game. I had caught one or two joyous chuckles of evasion, and once or twice had seen the silhouette of a child's frock against some darkening window at the end of a passage; but we returned empty-handed to the gallery, just as a middle-aged woman was setting a lamp in its niche.

'No, I haven't seen her either this evening. Miss Florence,' I heard her say, 'but that Turpin he says he wants to see you about his shed.'

'Oh, Mr Turpin must want to see me very badly. Tell him to come to the hall, Mrs Madden.'

I looked down into the hall whose only light was the dulled fire, and deep in the shadow I saw them at last. They must have slipped down while we were in the passages, and now thought them-selves perfectly hidden behind an old gilt leather screen. By child's law, my fruitless chase was as good as an introduction, but since I had taken so much trouble I resolved to force them to come forward later by the simple trick, which children detest, of pretending not to notice them. They lay close, in a little huddle, no more than shadows except when a quick flame betrayed an outline.

'And now we'll have some tea,' she said. 'I believe I ought to have offered it you at first, but one doesn't arrive at manners somehow when one lives alone and is considered – h'm – peculiar.' Then with very pretty scorn, 'Would you like a lamp to see to eat by?'

'The firelight's much pleasanter, I think.' We descended into that delicious gloom and Madden brought tea.

I took my chair in the direction of the screen ready to surprise or be surprised as the game should go, and at her permission, since a hearth is always sacred, bent forward to play with the fire.

'Where do you get these beautiful short faggots from?' I asked idly. 'Why, they are tallies!'

'Of course,' she said. 'As I can't read or write I'm driven back on the early English tally for my accounts. Give me one and I'll tell you what it meant.'

I passed her an unburned hazel-tally, about a foot long, and she ran her thumb down the nicks.

'This is the milk-record for the home farm for the month of April last year, in gallons,' said she. 'I don't know what I should have done without tallies. An old forester of mine taught me the system. It's out of date now for every one else; but my tenants respect it. One of them's coming now to see me. Oh, it doesn't matter. He has no business here out of office hours. He's a greedy, ignorant man – very greedy or – he wouldn't come here after dark.'

'Have you much land then?'

'Only a couple of hundred acres in hand, thank goodness. The other six hundred are nearly all let to folk who knew my folk before me, but this Turpin is quite a new man – and a highway robber.'

'But are you sure I shan't be—?'

'Certainly not. You have the right. He hasn't any children.'

'Ah, the children!' I said and slid my low chair back till it nearly touched the screen that hid them. 'I wonder whether they'll come out for me.'

There was a murmur of voices – Madden's and a deeper note – at the low, dark side door, and a ginger-headed, canvas-gaitered giant of the unmistakable tenant-farmer type stumbled or was pushed in.

'Come to the fire, Mr Turpin,' she said.

'If – if you please. Miss, I'll – I'll be quite as well by the door.' He clung to the latch as he spoke like a frightened child. Of a sudden I realised that he was in the grip of some almost overpowering fear.

'Well?'

'About the new shed for the young stock – that was all. These first autumn storms settin' in . . . but I'll come again, Miss.' His teeth did not chatter much more than the door latch.

'I think not,' she answered levelly. 'The new shed – m'm. What did my agent write you on the 15th?'

'I – fancied p'raps that if I came to see you – ma-man to man like, Miss. But—'

His eyes rolled into every corner of the room wide with horror. He half opened the door through which he had entered, but I noticed it shut again – from without and firmly.

'He wrote what I told him,' she went on. 'You are over-stocked already. Dunnett's Farm never carried more than fifty bullocks – even in Mr Wright's time. And *he* used cake. You've sixty-seven and you don't cake. You've broken the lease in that respect. You're dragging the heart out of the farm.'

'I'm – I'm getting some minerals – superphosphates – next week. I've as good as ordered a truck-load already. I'll go down to the station to-morrow about 'em. Then I can come and see you man to man like, Miss, in the daylight . . . That gentleman's not going away, is he?' He almost shrieked.

I had only slid the chair a little farther back, reaching behind me to tap on the leather of the screen, but he jumped like a rat.

'No. Please attend to me, Mr Turpin.' She turned in her chair and faced him with his back to the door. It was an old and sordid little piece of scheming that she forced from him – his plea for the new cow-shed at his landlady's expense, that he might with the covered manure pay his next year's rent out of the valuation after, as she made clear, he had bled the enriched pastures to the bone. I could not but admire the intensity of his greed, when I saw him out – facing for its sake whatever terror it was that ran wet on his forehead.

I ceased to tap the leather – was, indeed, calculating the cost of the shed – when I felt my relaxed hand taken and turned softly between the soft hands of a child. So at last I had triumphed. In a moment I would turn and acquaint myself with these quick-footed wanderers . . .

The little brushing kiss fell in the centre of my palm – as a gift on which the fingers were, once, expected to close: as the all-faithful half-reproachful signal of a waiting child not used to neglect even when grown-ups were busiest – a fragment of the mute code devised very long ago.

Then I knew. And it was as though I had known from the first day when I looked across the lawn at the high window.

I heard the door shut. The woman turned to me in silence, and I felt that she knew.

What time passed after this I cannot say. I was roused by the fail of a log, and mechanically rose to put it back. Then I returned to my place in the chair very close to the screen.

'Now you understand,' she whispered, across the packed shadows.

'Yes, I understand – now. Thank you.'

'I – I only hear them.' She bowed her head in her hands. 'I

have no right, you know – no other right. I have neither borne nor lost – neither borne nor lost!'

'Be very glad then,' said I, for my soul was torn open within me.

'Forgive me!'

She was still, and I went back to my sorrow and my joy.

'It was because I loved them so,' she said at last, brokenly. '*That* was why it was, even from the first – even before I knew that they – they were all I should ever have. And I loved them so!'

She stretched out her arms to the shadows and the shadows within the shadow.

'They came because I loved them – because I needed them. I – I must have made them come. Was that wrong, think you?'

'No – no.'

'I – I grant you that the toys and – and all that sort of thing were nonsense, but – but I used to so hate empty rooms myself when I was little.' She pointed to the gallery. 'And the passages all empty . . . And how could I ever bear the garden door shut? Suppose—'

'Don't! For pity's sake, don't!' I cried. The twilight had brought a cold rain with gusty squalls that plucked at the leaded windows.

'And the same thing with keeping the fire in all night. *I* don't think it so foolish – do you?'

I looked at the broad brick hearth, saw, through tears I believe, that there was no unpassable iron on or near it, and bowed my head.

'I did all that and lots of other things – just to make believe. Then they came. I heard them, but I didn't know that they were not mine by right till Mrs Madden told me—'

'The butler's wife? What?'

'One of them – I heard – she saw. And knew. Hers! *Not* for me. I didn't knew at first. Perhaps I was jealous. Afterwards, I began to understand that it was only because I loved them, not because— . . . Oh, you *must* bear or lose,' she said piteously. 'There is no other way – and yet they love me. They must! Don't they?'

There was no sound in the room except the lapping voices of the fire, but we two listened intently, and she at least took comfort from what she heard. She recovered herself and half rose. I sat still in my chair by the screen.

'Don't think me a wretch to whine about myself like this, but – but I'm all in the dark, you know, and *you* can see.'

In truth I could see, and my vision confirmed me in my resolve, though that was like the very parting of spirit and flesh. Yet a little longer I would stay since it was the last time.

'You think it is wrong, then?' she cried sharply, though I had said nothing.

'Not for you. A thousand times no. For you it is right . . . I am grateful to you beyond words. For me it would be wrong. For me only . . .'

'Why?' she said, but passed her hand before her face as she had done at our second meeting in the wood. 'Oh, I see,' she went on simply as a child. 'For you it would be wrong.' Then with a little indrawn laugh, 'and d'you remember, I called you lucky – once – at first. You must never come here again!'

She left me to sit a little longer by the screen, and I heard the sound of her feet die out along the gallery above.

WITH THE NIGHT MAIL:
A STORY OF 2000 AD

From 'The Windsor Magazine,' October, AD 2147

AT 9.30 p.m. of a windy winter's night I stood the lower stages of the GPO Outward Mail Tower. My purpose was a run to Quebec in 'postal packet 162, or such other as may be appointed'; and the Postmaster-General himself countersigned the order. This talisman opened all doors, even those in the Despatching-caisson at the foot of the Tower, where they were delivering the sorted Continental mail. The bags were packed close as herrings in the long grey underbodies which our GPO stilt calls 'coaches.' Five such coaches were filled as I watched, and were shot up the guides, to be locked on to their waiting packets three hundred feet nearer the stars.

From the Despatching-caisson I was conducted by a courteous and wonderfully learned official – Mr L. L. Geary, Second Despatcher of the Western Route – to the Captain's Room (this wakes an echo of old romance), where the Mail captains come on for their turn of duty. He introduces me to the captain of 162 – Captain Purnall, and his relief, Captain Hodgson. The one is small and dark, the other large and red, but each has the brooding, sheathed glance characteristic of eagles and aeronauts. You can see it in the pictures of our racing professionals, from L. V. Rautsch to little Ada Warleigh – the fathomless abstraction of eyes habitually turned through naked space.

On the notice-board in the Captain's Room the pulsing arrows of some twenty indicators register degree by geographical degree the progress of as many homeward-bound packets. The word 'Cape' rises across the face of a dial; a gong strikes: that is all. The South African mid-weekly mail is in at the

Highgate Receiving-Towers. It reminds one comically of the traitorous little bell which in pigeon-fanciers' lofts notifies the return of a homer.

'Time for us to be on the move,' says Captain Purnall, and we are shot up by the passenger-lift to the top of the Despatch-towers. Our 'coach' will lock on when it is filled, and the clerks are aboard . . .

Number 162 waits for us in Slip E of the topmost stage. The great curve of her back shines frostily under the lights, and some minute alteration of trim makes her rack a little in her holding-down clips.

Captain Purnall frowns and dives inside. Hissing softly, 162 comes to rest level as a rule. From her North Atlantic Winter nose-cap (worn bright as diamond with boring through uncounted leagues of hail, snow, and ice) to the inset of her three built-out propeller-shafts is some two hundred and fifty feet. Her extreme diameter, carried well forward, is thirty-seven. Contrast this with the nine hundred by ninety-four of any crack liner, and you will realise the power that must drive this hull through all weathers at more than twice the emergency speed of the *Cyclonic*.

The eye detects no joint in her skin-plating, save the sweeping hair-crack of the bow rudder – Magniac's rudder, that assured us the dominion of the unstable air, and left its inventor penniless and half-blind. It is calculated to Castelli's 'gull-wing' curve. Raise a few feet of that all but invisible plate three-eighths of an inch, and 162 will yaw five miles to port or starboard ere she is under control again. Give her full helm, and she returns on her track like a whiplash. Cant the whole forward – a touch on the wheel will suffice – and she sweeps at your good direction up or down. Open the full circle, and she presents to the air a mushroom head that will bring her up all standing within half the mile.

'Yes,' says Captain Hodgson, answering my thought. 'Castelli thought that he'd discovered the secret of controlling aeroplanes, when he'd only found out how to steer dirigible balloons. Magniac invented his rudder to help war-boats ram each other; and war went out of fashion, and Magniac he went out of his mind because he said he couldn't serve his country any more. I wonder if any of us ever know what we're really doing.'

'If you want to see the coach locked, you'd better go aboard. It's due now,' says Mr Geary. I enter through the door amidships. There is nothing here for display. The inner skin of the gas-tanks comes down to within a foot or two of my head and turns over just short of the turn of the bilges. Liners and yachts disguise their tanks with decoration, but the GPO serves them raw under a lick of grey official paint. The inner skin shuts off fifty feet of the bow and as much of the stern, but the bow-bulkhead is recessed for the lift-shunting apparatus as the stern is pierced for the shaft-tunnels. The engine-room lies almost amidships. Forward of it, extending to the turn of the bow tanks, is an aperture – bottomless hatch at present – into which our coach will be locked. One looks down over the coamings three hundred feet to the despatching-caisson whence voices boom upward. The light below is obscured to a sound of thunder, as our coach rises on its guides. It enlarges rapidly from a postage-stamp to a playing-card; to a punt and last a pontoon. The two clerks, its crew, do not even look up as it comes into place. The Quebec letters fly under their fingers and leap into the docketed racks, while both captains and Mr Geary satisfy themselves that the coach is locked home. A clerk passes the way-bill over the hatch coaming. Captain Purnall thumb-marks and passes it to Mr Geary. Receipt has been given and taken. 'Pleasant run,' says Mr Geary, and disappears through the door which a foot high pneumatic compressor locks after him.

'A-ah!' sighs the compressor released. Our holding-down clips part with a tang. We are clear.

Captain Hodgson opens the great colloid underbody port-hole through which I watch over-lighted London slide eastward as the gale gets hold of us. The first of the low winter clouds cuts off the well-known view and darkens Middlesex. On the south edge of it I can see a postal packet's light ploughing through the white fleece. For an instant she gleams like a star ere she drops toward the Highgate Receiving

Towers. 'The Bombay Mail,' says Captain Hodgson, and looks at his watch. 'She's forty minutes late.'

'What's our level?' I ask.

'Four thousand. Aren't you coming up on the bridge?'

The bridge (let us ever praise the GPO as a repository of ancientest tradition!) is represented by a view of Captain Hodgson's legs where he stands on the Control Platform that runs thwart-ships overhead. The bow colloid is unshuttered and Captain Purnall, one hand on the wheel, is feeling for a fair slant. The dial shows 4300 feet. 'It's steep to-night,' he mutters, as tier on tier of cloud drops under. 'We generally pick up an easterly draught below three thousand at this time o' the year. I hate slathering through fluff.'

'So does Van Cutsem. Look at him huntin' for a slant!' says Captain Hodgson. A foglight breaks cloud a hundred fathoms below. The Antwerp Night Mail makes her signal and rises between two racing clouds far to port, her flanks blood-red in the glare of Sheerness Double Light. The gale will have us over the North Sea in half-an-hour, but Captain Purnall lets her go composedly – nosing to every point of the compass as she rises.

'Five thousand-six, six thousand eight hundred' – the dip-dial reads ere we find the easterly drift, heralded by a flurry of snow at the thousand fathom level. Captain Purnall rings up the engines and keys down the governor on the switch before him. There is no sense in urging machinery when Eolus himself gives you good knots for nothing. We are away in earnest now – our nose notched home on our chosen star. At this level the lower clouds are laid out, all neatly combed by the dry fingers of the East. Below that again is the strong westerly blow through which we rose. Overhead, a film of southerly drifting mist draws a theatrical gauze across the firmament. The moonlight turns the lower strata to silver without a stain except where our shadow underruns us. Bristol and Cardiff Double Lights (those statelily inclined beams over Severnmouth) are dead ahead of us; for we keep the Southern Winter Route. Coventry Central, the pivot of the English system, stabs upward once in ten seconds its spear of diamond

496

light to the north; and a point or two off our starboard bow The Leek, the great cloud-breaker of Saint David's Head, swings its unmistakable green beam twenty-five degrees each way. There must be half a mile of fluff over it in this weather, but it does not affect The Leek.

'Our planet's over-lighted if anything,' says Captain Purnall at the wheel, as Cardiff-Bristol slides under. 'I remember the old days of common white verticals that 'ud show two or three thousand feet up in a mist if you knew where to look for 'em. In really fluffy weather they might as well have been under your hat. One could get lost coming home then and have some fun. *Now* it's like driving down Piccadilly.'

He points to the pillars of light where the cloud-breakers bore through the cloud-floor. We see nothing of England's outlines – only a white pavement pierced in all directions by these manholes of variously coloured fire – Holy Island's white and red – St Bees' interrupted white, and so on as far as the eye can reach. Blessed be Sargent, Ahrens, and the Dubois Brothers who invented the cloud-breakers of the world whereby we travel in security!

'Are you going to lift for The Shamrock?' asks Captain Hodgson. Cork light (green fixed) enlarges as we rush to it. Captain Purnall nods. There is heavy traffic hereabouts – the bank beneath us is streaked with running fissures of flame, where the Atlantic boats are hurrying Londonwards just clear of the fluff. Mail-packets are supposed to have the five-thousand foot lanes and above to themselves, but the foreigner in a hurry is apt to take liberties with English air. 162 lifts to a long-drawn wail of the air in the fore-flange of the rudder, and we make Valencia (white-green-white) at a safe 7,000 feet, dipping our beam to an incoming Washington packet.

There is no cloud on the Atlantic, and faint streaks of cream round Dingle Bay show where the east-driven seas hammer the coast. A big SATA liner (*Société Anonyme des Transports Aériens*) is diving and lifting half a mile below us in search of some break in the solid west wind. Lower still lies a Dane in trouble: she is telling the liner all about it in International. Our General Communication dial has caught her talk, and begins to eavesdrop. Captain Hodgson makes a motion to cut it off, but checks himself. 'Perhaps you'd like to listen,' he says to me.

'*Argol* of St Thomas,' the GC whispers. 'Report owners three starboard shaft collar-bearings fused. Can make Flores as we are, but impossible further. Shall we buy spares at Fayal?'

The liner acknowledges, and recommends inverting the bearings. The *Argol* answers that she has already done so without effect, and begins to relieve her mind about cheap German enamels for collar-bearings. The Frenchman assents cordially, cries: '*Courage, mon ami!*' and switches off.

Their lights sink under the curve of the world.

'That's one of Lundt and Bleamer's boats,' says Captain Hodgson. 'Serves 'em right for putting German compos in their thrust-blocks. *She* won't be in Fayal to-night! By the way, wouldn't you like to look round the engine-room?'

I have been waiting eagerly for this invitation, and I follow Captain Hodgson from the control-platform, stooping low to avoid the bulge of the tanks. We know that Fleury's gas can lift anything, as the world-famous trials of '78 showed, but its almost indefinite powers of expansion necessitate vast tank room. Even in this thin air the lift-shunts are busy taking out one-third of its normal lift, and still 162 must be checked by an occasional downdraw of the rudder, or our flight would become a climb to the stars. Captain Purnall prefers an over-lifted to an underlifted ship, but no two captains trim ship alike. 'When I take the bridge,' says Captain Hodgson, 'you'll see me shunt forty per cent of the lift out of the gas and run her on the upper rudder. With a swoop upwards instead of a swoop downwards, *as* you say. Either way will do. It's only habit. Watch our dip-dial. Tim fetches her down once every thirty knots as regularly as breathing.'

So it is shown on the dip-dial. For five or six minutes the arrow creeps from 6,700 to 7,300. There is the faint 'szgee' of the rudder, and back slides the arrow to 6,500 on a falling slant of ten or fifteen knots.

'In heavy weather you jockey her with the screws as well,'

says Captain Hodgson, and unclipping the jointed bar which divides the engine-room from the bare deck, he leads me on the floor.

Here we find Fleury's Paradox of the Bulkheaded Vacuum – which we accept now without thought – literally in full blast. The three engines are assisted-vacuo Fleury turbines running from 3,000 to the Limit; that is to say, up to the point when the blades make the air bell – cut out a vacuum for themselves precisely as do overdriven marine propellers. 162's Limit is low on account of the small size of her nine screws, which, though handier than the old colloid Thelussons, bell sooner. The 'midships engine generally used as a reinforce is not running; so the port and starboard turbine vacuum-chambers draw direct into the return-mains.

The turbines whistle reflectively. From the low-arched expansion-tanks on either side the valves descend pillar-wise to the turbine-chests, and thence the obedient gas whirls through the spirals of set blades with a force that would whip the teeth out of a power-saw. Behind, is its own pressure, held in leash or spurred on by the lift-shunts; before it, the vacuum where Fleury's Ray dances in violet-green bands and whirled tourbillons of flame. The jointed U-tubes of the vacuum-chamber are pressure-tempered colloid (no glass would endure the strain for an instant), and a junior engineer with tinted spectacles watches the Ray intently. It is the very heart of the machine – a mystery to this day. Even Fleury, who begat it and, unlike Magniac, died a multi-millionaire, could not explain how that restless little imp pirouetting in the U-tube can, in the fractional fraction of a second, strike down the furious blast of gas into a chill greyish-green liquid that drains (you can hear it trickle) from the far end of the vacuum through the eduction-pipes and the mains back to the bilges. Here it returns to its gaseous – one had almost written sagacious – state and climbs to work afresh. Bilge-tank, upper-tank, dorsal-tank, expansion-chamber, vacuum, main-return (as a liquid) and bilge-tank once more is the ordained cycle. Fleury's Ray sees to that; and the engineer with the tinted spectacles sees to Fleury's Ray. If a speck of oil – if even the natural grease of the human finger touch the hooded terminals,

Fleury's Ray will wink and disappear and must be laboriously built up again. This means half-a-day's work for all hands, and an expense of one hundred and seventy odd pounds to the GPO for radium-salts and such trifles.

'Now look at our thrust-collars. You won't find much German compo there. Full-jewelled, you see,' says Captain Hodgson, as the engineer shunts open the top of a cap. Our shaft-bearings are CDC (Commercial Diamond Company) stones, ground with as much care as the lenses of a telescope. They cost thirty-seven pounds apiece. So far we have not arrived at their term of life. These bearings are over fifty years old. They came from *No. 97*, which took them over from the old *Dominion of Light*, which had them out of the wreck of the *Perseus* aeroplane in the years when men still flew tin kites over Thorium engines.

They are a shining reproof to all low-grade German 'ruby' enamels, so-called 'boort' facings, and the dangerous and unsatisfactory aluminia compounds which please dividend-hunting owners and turn skippers crazy.

The rudder-gear and the gas lift-shunt, seated side by side under the engine-room dials, are the only machines in visible motion. The former sighs from time to time as the oil-plunger rises and falls half an inch. The latter, cased and guarded like the U-tube aft, exhibits another Fleury Ray, but inverted and more green than violet. Its function is to shunt the lift out of the gas, and this it will do without watching. That is all! One tiny pump-rod wheezing and whining to itself beside a sputtering green lamp. A hundred and fifty feet aft, down the flat-topped tunnel of the tanks, a violet light restless and irresolute. Between the two, three white-painted turbine-trunks, like eel-baskets laid on their side, accentuate the empty perspectives. You can hear the trickle of the liquefied gas flowing from the vacuum into the bilge-tanks, and the soft *gluck-glock* of gas-locks closing as Captain Purnall brings 162 down by the head. The hum of the turbines and the boom of the air on our skin is no more than a cotton-wool wrapping to the universal stillness. And we are running an eighteen-second mile.

I peer from the fore-end of the engine-room over the hatch-coamings into the coach. The mail-clerks are sorting the Winnipeg Calgary and Medicine Hat bags: but there is a pack of cards ready on the table.

Suddenly a bell thrills; the engineers at the turbine-valves stand by; but the spectacled slave of the Ray in the U-tube never lifts his head. He must watch where he is. We are hard-braked and going astern; and there is high language from the control-platform.

'Tim's temper has fused on something,' says the unruffled Captain Hodgson. 'Let's look.'

Captain Purnall is not the man we left half an hour ago, but the embodied authority of the GPO. Ahead of us floats an ancient aluminium-patched, twin-screw tramp of the dingiest, with no more right to the 5,000-foot lanes than has a horse-cart to London. She carries an obsolete 'barbette' conning-tower – a six-foot affair with railed platform forward, and our warning beam plays on the top of it as a policeman's lantern flashes on the area-sneak. Like a sneak-thief, too, emerges a shock-headed navigator in his shirt-sleeves. Captain Purnall wrenches open the colloid to talk with him man to man. There are times when science does not satisfy.

'What under the stars are you doing here, you sky-scraping chimney-sweep?' he shouts as we two drift side by side. 'Do you know this is a Mail lane? You call yourself a skipper, sir? You ain't fit to paddle toy aeroplanes in the Strand. Your name and number! Report and get down!'

'I've been blown up once,' the shock-headed man cries hoarsely as a dog barking under the stars. 'I don't care two flips of a contact for anything *you* can do, Postey.'

'Don't you, sir? But I'll make you care. I'll have your stinking gasogene towed stern first to Disko and broke up. You can't recover insurance if you're broke for obstruction. Do you understand *that*?'

Then the stranger bellows: 'Look at my propellers! There's been a wullie-wa down under that has blown me into umbrella-frames! We're leakin'! 'We're all one conjurer's watch inside! My mate's arm's broke; my engineer's head's cut open; my Ray went out when the engines smashed; and – and – for pity's sake give me my height, Captain! We doubt we're dropping.'

'Six thousand eight hundred. Can you hold it?' Captain Purnall overlooks all insults, and leans half out of the colloid, staring and sniffing. The stranger leaks pungently. He calls –

'We thought to blow hack to St John's with luck. We're trying to plug the fore-tank now, but she's simply whistlin' it away.'

'She's sinkin' like a log,' says Captain Purnall in an undertone. 'Call up the Mark Boat, George.' Our dip-dial shows that we keeping abreast the tramp, have dropped five hundred feet the last few minutes. Captain Purnall presses a switch, and our signal-beam swings through the night, twizzling spokes of light across infinity.

'That'll fetch something,' he says, while Captain Hodgson watches the General Communicator. He has called up the Banks Mark Boat a few hundred miles west, and is reporting.

'I'll stand by you!' Captain Purnall roars to the lone figure on the conning-tower.

'Is it as bad as that?' comes the answer. 'She isn't insured.'

'Might have guessed as much,' mutters Hodgson. 'Owner's risk is the worst risk of all!'

'Can't I fetch St John's – not even with this breeze?' the voice quavers.

'Stand by to abandon ship! Haven't you *any* lift in you, fore or aft?'

'Nothing but the 'midships tanks, and they're none too tight. Yon see, my Ray gave out and—' he coughs in the reek of the escaping gas.

'You poor devil!' This does not reach our friend. 'What does the Mark Boat say, George?'

'Wants to know if there's any danger to traffic. Says she's in a bit of weather herself and can't quit station. I've turned in a General Call, so even if they don't see our beam, someone's bound to – or else we must. Shall I clear our slings? Hold on! Here we are! A Planet liner, too! She'll be up in a tick!'

'Tell her to get her slings ready,' cries his brother Captain.

'There won't be much time to spare . . . Tie up your mate!' he roars to the tramp.

'My mate's all right. It's my engineer. He's gone crazy.'

'Shunt the lift out of him with a spanner. Hurry!'

'But I can make land – if I've half a chance.'

'You'll make the deep Atlantic in twenty minutes. You're less than fifty-four hundred now. Get your log and papers.'

A Planet liner – east bound – heaves up in a superb spiral and takes the air of us humming. Her underbody colloid is open, and her transporter-slings hang down like tentacles. We shut off our beam as she adjusts herself – steering to a hair – over the tramp's conning-tower. The mate emerges, his arm strapped to his side, and stumbles into the cradle. A man with a ghastly scarlet head follows, shouting that he must go back and build up his Ray. The mate assures him that he will find a nice new Ray all ready in the liner's engine-room. The bandaged head goes up wagging excitedly. A youth and a woman follow. The liner cheers hollowly above us, and we see the passengers' faces at the saloon colloid.

'That's a good girl. What's the fool waiting for now?' says Captain Purnall.

The skipper comes up still appealing to us to stand by and see him fetch St John's. He dives below and returns – at which we little human beings in the void cheer louder than ever – with the ship's kitten. Up fly the liner's hissing slings; her underbody crashes home and she hurtles away again. Our dial shows less than 3,000 feet.

The Mark Boat signals that we must attend to the derelict, now whistling her death-song as she falls beneath us in long, sick zigzags.

'Keep our beam on her and send out a general warning,' says Captain Purnall, following her down.

There is no need. Not a liner in air but knows the meaning of that vertical beam, and gives us and our quarry a wide berth.

'But she'll drown in the water, won't she?' I asked of Tim.

'I've known a derelict up-end and sift her engines out of herself, and flicker round the Lower Lanes for three weeks on her forward tanks only. We'll run no risks. Pith her, George, and look sharp. There's weather ahead.'

Captain Hodgson opens the underbody colloid, swings the heavy pithing-iron out of its rack which, in liners, is generally cased as a settee, and at two hundred feet releases they catch. We hear the whirr of the crescent-shaped arms opening as they descend. The derelict's forehead is punched in, starred across, and rent diagonally. She falls stern-first, our beam upon her; slides like a lost soul down that pitiless ladder of light, and the Atlantic takes her.

'A filthy business,' says Hodgson. 'I wonder what it must have been like in the old days.'

The thought had crossed my mind too. What if that wavering carcass had been filled with international-speaking men of all the Internationalities, each of them taught (*that* is the horror of it) that after death he would very possibly go for ever to unspeakable torment? And not a century since we (one knows now that we are only our fathers re-enlarged upon the earth) – *we*, I say, ripped and rammed and pithed to admiration.

Here Tim, from the control-platform, shouts that we are to get into our inflators and to bring him his at once.

We hurry into the heavy rubber suits – the engineers are already half-dressed – and inflate at the air-pump taps. GPO inflators are thrice as thick as a racing man's 'heavies,' and chafe abominably under the arm-pits. George takes the wheel until Tim has blown himself up to the extreme of rotundity. If you kicked him off the c.p. to the deck, he would bounce back. But it is 162 that will do the kicking to-night.

'The Mark Boat's mad – stark ravin' crazy,' Tim snorts, returning to command. 'She says there's a bad blow-out ahead, and wants me to pull over to Greenland. I'll see her pithed first! We've wasted an hour and a quarter over that dead bird down under, and now I'm expected to go rabbin' my back all the Pole round! What does she think a postal packet's made of. Gummed silk? Tell her we're comin' on straight.'

George buckles him into the Frame and switches on the Direct Control. Now, under Tim's left toe, lies the port-engine accelerator; under his left heel the reverse, and so with the other foot. The lift-shunt stops stand out on the rim of the steering-wheel, where the fingers of his left hand can play on them. At his right hand is the 'midships engine-lever, ready to be thrown into gear at a moment's notice. He leans forward in his belt, eyes glued to the bow-colloid, and one ear cocked toward the General Communicator. Henceforth he is the strength and direction of 162, through whatever may befall.

The Banks Mark Boat is reeling out pages of Aerial Route Directions to the traffic at large. We are to 'secure all loose objects,' hood up our Fleury Rays; and on no account to attempt to clear snow from our conning-towers till the weather abates. Under-powered craft can ascend to the limit of their lift, mail-packets to look out for them accordingly: the traffic lanes are pitting very badly with frequent blow-outs, vortices, and laterals. In other words, we are in for a storm with electric trimmings.

Still the clear dark holds up unblemished. The only warning is the electric skin-tension (I feel as though I were a lace-maker's pillow), and an intense irritability which the gibbering of the General Communicator increases almost to hysteria.

We have risen eight thousand feet since we pithed the tramp, and our turbines are giving us an honest two hundred an hour.

Very far to the west an elongated blur of light low down shows us the Banks Mark Boat, There are specks of fire round her rising and falling – bewildered planets about an unstable sun – helpless shipping hanging on to her light for company's sake. No wonder she could not quit station.

She warns us to look out for the backwash of the bad vortex in which (her beam shows it) she is even now reeling.

The pits of gloom about us being to fill with very faintly luminous films – wreathing and uneasy shapes. One forms itself into a globe of pale flame that waits shivering with eagerness as we sweep by. It leaps monstrously across the blackness, alights on the precise tip of our nose, grimaces there an instant, and swings off. Our roaring bow sinks as though that light were lead – sinks and recovers to lurch and stumble again beneath the next blow-out. Tim's fingers on the lift-shunt strike chords of numbers: 1.4.7; 2.4.6; 7.5.3; and so on; for he is running by his tanks only, lifting and dropping her by instinct. All three engines are at work; the sooner we have skated over this thin ice, the better. Higher we dare not go. The whole upper vault is charged with pale Krypton vapours, which our skin-friction may excite to unholy manifestations. Between the upper and the lower levels – 5,000 and 7,000 hints the Mark Boat – we may perhaps bolt through if . . .

Our bow clothes itself in blue flame and falls like a sword. No human skill can keep pace with the changing tensions. A vortex has us by the beak, and we dive down a two-thousand foot slant at an angle (the dip-dial and my bouncing body record it) of thirty-five. Our turbines scream shrilly; the propellers cannot bite on the wild air; Tim shunts the lift out of five tanks at once, and by sheer weight drives her bulletwise through the maelstrom till she cushions with a jar of the brake three thousand feet below.

'*Now* we've done it,' says George in my ear. 'Our skin-friction that last slide has played Old Harry with the tensions! Look out for laterals, Tim.'

'I've got her,' is the answer. 'Come *up*, you crazy old kite!'

She comes up nobly, but the laterals buffet her left and right like the pinions of angry angels. She is jolted off her chosen star twenty degrees port or starboard, and cuffed into place again, only to be swung away and dropped into a new blow-out. We are never without a corposant grinning on our bows or rolling head over heels from nose to 'midships; and to the crackle of electricity round and within us is added once or twice the rattle of hail – hail that will never fall on any sea. Slow we must, or we shall break out back, pitch-poling.

'Air's a perfectly elastic fluid!' roars George above the tumult. 'Elastic as a head sea off the Fastnet!'

He is less than just to the good element. If one intrudes on the heavens when they are balancing their volt-accounts; if one disturbs the High Gods' market-rates by hurling steel hulls at ninety knots across tremblingly adjusted tensions, one must not complain of any rudeness in the reception. Tim met it with an unmoved countenance, a corner of his under-lip caught up on a tooth, his eyes fleeting into the blackness twenty miles ahead, and the fierce sparks flying from his knuckles at every play of the hand. Now and again he shook his head to clear the sweat trickling through his eyebrows, and it was then that George, watching his chance, would slide down the life-rail and swab his face quickly with a big red handkerchief. I never imagined that a human being could so continuously labour and so collectedly think, as did Tim through that Hell's half-hour when the flurry was at its worst. We were dragged hither and yon by warm or frozen suctions, belched up on the tops of wullie-was, spun down by vortices, and clubbed aside by laterals under a dizzying rush of stars, in the company of a drunken moon. I heard the swishing click of the 'midships engine-lever sliding in and out, the low growl of the lift-shunts, and, louder than the yelling winds without, the scream of the bow-rudder gouging into any lull that promised hold even for an instant. At last we began to claw up on a cant, bow-rudder and port-propeller together; only the nicest balancing of our lift saved us from spinning like the rifle-bullet of the old days.

'We've got to hitch to windward of the Mark Boat some-how,' George cried.

'There's no windward,' I protested feebly where I swung shackled to a stanchion. 'How can there be?'

He laughed – as we pitched into a thousand-foot blow-out – that red man laughed under his inflated hood.

'Look!' he said. 'We must clear those refugees, anyhow.'

The Mark Boat was below, and a little to the sou'-west of us, fluctuating in the centre of her distraught galaxy. The air was thick with moving lights at every level. I take it most of them were lying head to wind, but, not being hydras, they failed. An under-tanked Moghrabi boat had risen to the limit of her lift, and finding no improvement, had dropped a couple of thou-sand. There she met a superb wullie-wa and was blown up spinning like a dead leaf. Instead of shutting off, she braked hard, and naturally rebounded as from a wall almost into the Mark Boat, whose language (our GC took it all in) was humanly simple.

'If they'd only ride it out quietly, it 'ud be better,' said George in a calm, as we climbed like a bat above them all. 'But some skippers *will* navigate without power. What does that Tad-boat think she is doing, Tim?'

'Playin' kiss in the ring,' was Tim's unmoved reply. A Trans-Asiatic Direct Liner had found a smooth, and butted into it full power. But there was a vortex at the tail of that smooth, and the TAD was flipped out like a paper boomerang, braking madly as she fled down, and all but over-ending.

'Now I hope she's satisfied,' said Tim, 'If she'd met a lateral, she'd have poked up under us or thereabouts. I'm glad I'm not a Mark Boat . . . Do I want help?' The whispering GC dial had caught his ear. 'George, you may tell that gentleman, with my love – love, remember, George – that I do not want help. Who *is* the officious sardine-tin?'

'Rimonski drogher on the look-out for a tow.'

'Very kind of the Rimonski drogher – but this postal packet isn't being towed at present.'

'Those droghers will go anywhere on a chance of salvage,' George explained. 'We call 'em kittiwakes.'

A long-beaked, bright steel ninety-footer floated at ease, for one instant within hail of us, her slings coiled ready for rescues, and a single hand in her open tower. He was smoking. Surrendered to the insurrection of the airs through which we tore our way, he lay in absolute peace. I saw the smoke of his pipe ascend untroubled ere his boat dropped under like a stone in a well.

We had just cleared the Mark Boat and her disorderly chickens, when the storm ended as suddenly as it had begun. A shooting star to northward filled the sky with the green blink of a meteorite dissipating itself in our atmosphere.

Said George: 'This may iron out all the tensions.' Even as he spoke, the conflicting winds came to rest; the levels filled; the laterals died out in long, easy sighs; the airways were smoothed before us. In less than three minutes the covey round the Mark Boat had shipped their power-lights and whirred away upon their businesses.

'What's happened?' I gasped. The nerve-storm within and

the volt-tingle without had passed; my inflators weighed like lead.

'God He knows,' said Captain George soberly. 'That old shooting-star's friction has discharged the different levels. I've seen it happen before. Phew! What a relief!'

We dropped from twelve to six thousand, and got rid of our clammy suits. Tim shut off and stepped out of the Frame. The Mark Boat was coming up behind us. He opened the colloid in that heavenly stillness and mopped his face.

'Hello, Williams!' he cried. 'A degree or two out o' station, ain't you?'

'Maybe,' was the slow answer. 'I've had some company this evening.'

'So I noticed. Wasn't that quite a little flurry?'

'I warned you. Why didn't you pull out round by Disko? The East-bound packets have.'

'Me? Not till I'm running a Polar Consumptives Sanatorium Boat! I was squinting out of a colloid before you were out of your cradle, my son.'

'I'd be the last man to deny it,' the captain of the Mark Boat replied softly. 'The way you handled her just now – I'm a pretty fair judge of traffic in a volt-flurry – it was a thousand revolutions beyond anything even I've ever seen.'

Tim's back supples visibly under this oiling. Captain George on the c.p. winks and points to the portrait of a singularly attractive maiden pinned up on Tim's telescope-bracket above the steering-wheel. She is Tim's daughter.

I see. Wholly and entirely do I see.

There is some talk overhead of 'coming round to tea on Friday,' a brief report of the derelict's fate, and Tim volunteers, as he descends: 'For an ABC man, young Williams is less of a high-tension fool than some . . . Were you thinking of taking her, George? Then I'll just have a look round that port thrust – seems to me it's a trifle warm – and we'll fan along.'

The Mark Boat hums off joyously and hangs herself up in her appointed place in the skies. Here she will stay, a shutterless observatory; a lifeboat station; a salvage tug; a court of ultimate appeal-cum-meteorological bureau for a thousand miles round in all directions till Wednesday next, when her relief slides across the stars to take her buffeted place. Her black hull, double conning-tower, and ever-ready slings represent all that remains to this planet of effective authority. She is responsible only to the Aerial Board of Control – the ABC of which Tim speaks so flippantly. But that semi-elected, semi-nominated body of a few score persons of both sexes governs this planet. 'Transportation is civilisation,' our motto runs. Theoretically we do what we please so long as we do not interfere with the traffic *and all it implies*. Practically, the ABC confirms or annuls most international arrangements, and, to judge by its last report, finds our tolerant, humorous, lazy little planet only too ready to lay the whole burden of private administration on its shoulder.

I discuss this with Tim sipping *maté* on the c.p., while George fans her along over the white blur of the Newfoundland Banks in beautiful upward curves of fifty miles each. The dip-dial translates them on the tape in flowing freehand.

Tim gathers up a skein of it and surveys the last few feet which record 162's path through the volt-flurry.

'I haven't had a fever-chart like this to show up in five years,' he says ruefully.

A postal-packet's dip-dial records every yard of every run. The tapes then go to the ABC, which collates them and makes composite photographs of them for the instruction of skippers. Tim studies his irrevocable past shaking his head.

'Hullo! Here's a fifteen-hundred-foot drop at eighty-five degrees! We must have been standing on our head then, George.'

'You don't say so,' George answers. 'I fancied I noticed a bit of a duck.'

George may not have Captain Purnall's catlike swiftness, but he is an artist to the tips of the broad fingers that play on the shunt-stops. The delicious flight-curves come away on the tape with never a waver. The Mark Boat's vertical spindle of light lies down to eastward setting in the face of the following stars. Westward, where no planet should rise, the triple white verticals of Trinity Bay (we keep still to the Southern route) makes a low-lifting haze. We seem the only things at rest under all the heavens; floating at ease till earth's revolution shall turn up our landing-towers.

And minute by minute our silent clock shows us a sixteen-second mile.

'Some fine night,' says Tim, 'we'll be even with that clock's master.'

'He's coming now,' says George. 'I'm chasing the night already.'

The stars ahead dim no more than if a film of mist had been drawn under unobserved, but the deep air-boom on our skin changes to a joyful shout.

'The dawn-gust,' says Tim. 'It'll go on to meet the sun. Look! Look! There's the night being crammed back over our bow! Come to the after-colloid. I'll show you something pretty.'

The engine-room is hot and stuffy; the clerks in the coach are asleep, and the Slave of the Ray is near to follow them. Tim slides open the after-colloid and reveals the curve of the world – the ocean's deepest purple – edged with fuming and intolerable gold. Then the sun rises and, through the colloid, strikes out our lamps. Tim scowls in his face.

'Squirrels in a cage,' he mutters. 'That's all we are. Squirrels in a cage! He's running twice as fast as us . . . Just you wait a few years, my shining friend, and we'll take steps that will amaze you. We'll Joshua you!'

Yes; that is our dream – to turn all earth to the Vale of Ajalon at our pleasure. So far we can drag out the dawn to twice its normal length in these latitudes. But some days – even on the Equator – we shall hold the sun level in his full stride!

Now we look down on a sea thronged with heavy traffic. A big submersible breaks water suddenly. Another and another follows with a swash and a suck and a savage bubbling of relieved pressures. The deep-sea freighters are rising to lung up after the long night, and the leisurely ocean is all patterned with peacock's eyes of foam.

'We'll lung up, too,' says Tim, and when we return to the c.p., George shuts off, the colloids are opened, and the fresh air sweeps her out. There is no hurry. The old contracts (they will be revised at the end of this year) allow twelve hours for a run which any packet can put behind her in ten. We breakfast in the arms of an easterly slant which pushes us along at a languid twenty.

To enjoy life, and tobacco, begin both on a sunny morning half a mile or so above the dappled Atlantic cloud-belts, and after a volt-flurry which has cleared and tempered your nerves. While we discussed the thickening traffic with the superiority that comes of having a high level to ourselves, we heard (and I for the first time) morning service on a Hospital boat.

She was cloaked by a skein of ravelled fluff beneath us, and we caught her chant before she rose into the sunlight: '*O ye Winds of God*,' sang the unseen voices, '*bless ye the Lord! Praise Him, and magnify Him for ever!*'

We slid off our caps and joined in. When our shadow fell across her great open platforms, they looked up and stretched out their hands neighbourly while they sang. We could see the doctors and the nurses and the white-button-like faces of the cot-patients. She passed slowly beneath us, heading north-ward, her hull, wet with the dews of night, all ablaze in the sunshine. So took she the shadow of a cloud and vanished; her song continuing –

'*O ye holy and humble men of heart, bless ye the Lord! Praise Him, and magnify Him for ever!*'

'She's a lunger, or she wouldn't have been singing the *Benedicite*; and she's a Greenlander, or she wouldn't have snow-blinds over her colloids,' said George at last. 'She'll be bound for Frederikshavn or one of the Glacier sanatoriums for a month. If she was an accident ward, she'd be hung up at the ten-thousand-foot level. Yes – consumptives.'

'Funny how the new things are the old things. I've read in books,' Tim answered, 'that savages used to haul their sick and wounded to the tops of the hills because microbes were fewer there. We hoist 'em into sterilised air for a while. Same thing, isn't it?'

'Did you ever read about the epidemics we used to have in the old days – right *on* the ground?' said George, knocking out his pipe. 'It must have been bad. And we talked about Fresh Air, too! Fresh air – in a city – with horses and cows and pigs an' rats and people in direct contact! I wonder we didn't all die twice a week. We must have been an enamel-faced community.'

'Dunno – we died at seventy or thereabouts (I've read), and a centenarian was a curio in those days. How much do the doctors say we've added to the average life of a man?'

'Thirty years,' says George, with a twinkle in his eye. 'Are you going to spend 'em all up here, Tim? Our letters'll be a trifle discharged.'

'Flap along, then. Flap along. Who's hindering?' The senior captain laughed, as we went in.

We held a good lift to clear the coast and Continental shipping, and we had need of it. Though our route is in no sense a populated one, there is a steady trickle of traffic this way about. We met Hudson Bay furriers out of the Great Preserve hurrying to make their departures from Bonavista with sable and black fox for the insatiable markets; we overcrossed Keewahdin liners small and cramped; but their captains, who see no land between Trepassy and Blanco, know what gold they bring back from West Africa. Trans-Asiatic Directs we met soberly ringing the world round the Fiftieth Meridian, at an honest seventy knots; and white-painted Ackroyd and Hunt fruiters out of the South fled beneath us, their ventilated hulls whistling like Chinese kites. Their market is in the North, among the northern sanatoria, where you can smell their grape-fruit and bananas across the cold snows. Brazilian beef-boats we sighted of enormous capacity and Teutonic outline. They too feed the Northern health-stations in ice-bound ports where submersibles dare not rise. Yellow-bellied ore-flats and Ungava petrol-tanks punted down leisurely out of the North like strings of unfrightened wild-duck. It does not pay to 'fly' minerals and oil a mile further than is necessary; but the risks of transhipping to submersibles in the ice-pack off Nain or Hebron are so great that these heavy freighters fly down to Halifax direct, and scent the air as they go. They are the biggest tramps aloft, except the

Athabasca grain-tubs. But these, now that the wheat is moved, are busy over the planet's left shoulder, timber-lifting in Siberia.

We held to the St Lawrence (it is astonishing how the old waterways still pull us children of the air!) and followed his broad line of black between its drifting ice-blocks, all down the Park that the wisdom of our fathers has saved to the world.

But everyone knows the Quebec run.

We dropped to the Heights Receiving-Towers twenty minutes ahead of time, and there hung at ease till the Yokohama Intermediate Packet could pull out and give us our proper slip. It was curious to watch the action of the holding-down-clips all along the frosty river front as boats cleared or came to rest. A big Hamburger was leaving Pont Levis, and her crew, unshipping the platform railings, began to sing 'Elsinore' – the oldest of our chanteys. You know it, of course?

Mother Rugen's tea-house on the Baltic –
  Forty couple waltzing on the floor!
And you can mind my Ray,
For I must go away
  And dance with Ella Sweyn at Elsinore!

Then, while they sweated home the covering-plate:

Nor – Nor – Nor – Nor –
West from Sourabaya to the Baltic –
  Ninety knot an hour to the Skaw!
Mother Rugen's tea-house on the Baltic,
  And a dance with Ella Sweyn at Elsinore!

The clips parted with a gesture of indignant dismissal, as though Quebec, glittering under her snows, were casting out these light and unworthy lovers. Our signal came from the Heights. Tim turned and floated up, but surely it was with passionate appeal that the great arms flung open from our tower – or did I think so because on the upper staging a little hooded figure also stretched arms wide towards her father?

*

In ten seconds the coach with its clerks clashed down to the Receiving-caissons; the hostlers displaced the engineers at the cold turbines, and Tim, prouder of this than all, introduced me to the maiden of the photograph on the shelf. 'And by the way,' said he, stepping forth in the sunshine under the hat of civil life, 'I saw young Williams in the Mark Boat. I've asked him to tea on Friday.'

THE HOUSE SURGEON

On an evening after Easter Day, I sat at a table in a homeward
bound steamer's smoking-room, where half a dozen of us told
ghost stories. As our party broke up, a man, playing Patience
in the next alcove, said to me: 'I didn't quite catch the end of
that last story about the Curse on the family's first-born.'

'It turned out to be drains,' I explained. 'As soon as new ones
were put into the house the Curse was lifted, I believe. I never
knew the people myself.'

'Ah! I've had *my* drains up twice; I'm on gravel too.'

'You don't mean to say you've a ghost in your house? Why
didn't you join our party?'

'Any more orders, gentlemen, before the bar closes?' the
steward interrupted.

'Sit down again and have one with me,' said the Patience
player. 'No, it isn't a ghost. Our trouble is more depression
than anything else.'

'How interesting! Then it's nothing any one can see?'

'It's – it's nothing worse than a little depression. And the
odd part is that there hasn't been a death in the house since it
was built – in 1863. The lawyer said so. That decided me – my
good lady, rather – and he made me pay an extra thousand for
it.'

'How curious. Unusual, too!' I said.

'Yes, ain't it? It was built for three sisters – Moultrie was the
name – three old maids. They all lived together; the eldest
owned it. I bought it from her lawyer a few years ago, and
if I've spent a pound on the place first and last, I must have
spent five thousand. Electric light, new servants' wing, garden
– all that sort of thing. A man and his family ought to be happy

after so much expense, ain't it?' He looked at me through the bottom of his glass.

'Does it affect your family much?'

'My good lady – she's a Greek by the way – and myself are middle-aged. We can bear up against depression; but it's hard on my little girl. I say little; but she's twenty. We send her visiting to escape it. She almost lived at hotels and hydros last year, but that isn't pleasant for her. She used to be a canary – a perfect canary – always singing. You ought to hear her. She doesn't sing now. That sort of thing's unwholesome for the young, ain't it?'

'Can't you get rid of the place?' I suggested.

'Not except at a sacrifice, and we are fond of it. Just suits us three. We'd love it if we were allowed.'

'What do you mean by not being allowed?'

'I mean because of the depression. It spoils everything.'

'What's it like exactly?'

'I couldn't very well explain. It must be seen to be appreciated, as the auctioneers say. Now, I was much impressed by the story you were telling just now.'

'It wasn't true,' I said.

'My tale is true. If you would do me the pleasure to come down and spend a night at my little place, you'd learn more than you would if I talked till morning. Very likely 'twouldn't touch your good self at all. You might be – immune, ain't it? On the other hand, if this influenza-influence *does* happen to affect you, why, I think it will be an experience.'

While he talked he gave me his card, and I read his name was L. Maxwell M'Leod, Esq., of Holmescroft. A City address was tucked away in a corner.

'My business,' he added, 'used to be furs. If you are interested in furs – I've given thirty years of my life to 'em.'

'You're very kind,' I murmured.

'Far from it, I assure you. I can meet you next Saturday afternoon anywhere in London you choose to name, and I'll be only too happy to motor you down. It ought to be a delightful run at this time of year – the rhododendrons will be out. I mean it. You don't know how truly I mean it. Very probably – it won't affect you at all. And – I think I may say I have the finest collection of narwhal tusks in the world. All the best skins and horns have to go through London, and L. Maxwell M'Leod, he knows where they come from, and where they go to. That's his business.'

For the rest of the voyage up-channel Mr M'Leod talked to me of the assembling, preparation, and sale of the rarer furs; and told me things about the manufacture of fur-lined coats which quite shocked me. Somehow or other, when we landed on Wednesday, I found myself pledged to spend that week-end with him at Holmescroft.

On Saturday he met me with a well-groomed motor, and ran me out in an hour-and-a-half to an exclusive residential district of dustless roads and elegantly designed country villas, each standing in from three to five acres of perfectly appointed land. He told me land was selling at eight hundred pounds the acre, and the new golf links, whose Queen Anne pavilion we passed, had cost nearly twenty-four thousand pounds to create.

Holmescroft was a large, two-storied, low, creeper-covered residence. A verandah at the south side gave on to a garden and two tennis courts, separated by a tasteful iron fence from a most park-like meadow of five or six acres, where two Jersey cows grazed. Tea was ready in the shade of a promising copper beech, and I could see groups on the lawn of young men and maidens appropriately clothed, playing lawn tennis in the sunshine.

'A pretty scene, ain't it?' said Mr M'Leod. 'My good lady's sitting under the tree, and that's my little girl in pink on the far court. But I'll take you to your room, and you can see 'em all later.'

He led me through a wide parquet-floored hall furnished in pale lemon, with huge cloisonné vases, an ebonised and gold grand piano, and banks of pot flowers in Benares brass bowls, up a pale oak staircase to a spacious landing, where there was a green velvet settee trimmed with silver. The blinds were down, and the light lay in parallel lines on the floors.

He showed me my room, saying cheerfully: 'You may be a little tired. One often is without knowing it after a run through traffic. Don't come down till you feel quite restored. We shall all be in the garden.'

My room was rather close, and smelt of perfumed soap. I threw up the window at once, but it opened so close to the floor and worked so clumsily that I came within an ace of pitching out, where I should certainly have ruined a rather lop-sided laburnum below. As I set about washing off the journey's dust, I began to feel a little tired. But, I reflected, I had not come down here in this weather and among these new surroundings to be depressed, so I began to whistle.

And it was just then that I was aware of a little grey shadow, as it might have been a snowflake seen against the light, floating at an immense distance in the background of my brain. It annoyed me, and I shook my head to get rid of it. Then my brain telegraphed that it was the forerunner of a swift-striding gloom which there was yet time to escape if I would force my thoughts away from it, as a man leaping for life forces his body forward and away from the fall of a wall. But the gloom overtook me before I could take in the meaning of the message. I moved toward the bed, every nerve already aching with the foreknowledge of the pain that was to be dealt it, and sat down, while my amazed and angry soul dropped, gulf by gulf, into that horror of great darkness which is spoken of in the Bible, and which, as auctioneers say, must be experienced to be appreciated.

Despair upon despair, misery upon misery, fear after fear, each causing their distinct and separate woe, packed in upon me for an unrecorded length of time, until at last they blurred together, and I heard a click in my brain like the click in the ear when one descends in a diving bell, and I knew that the pressures were equalised within and without, and that, for the moment, the worst was at an end. But I knew also that at any moment the darkness might come down anew; and while I dwelt on this speculation precisely as a man torments a raging tooth with his tongue, it ebbed away into the little grey shadow on the brain of its first coming, and once more I heard my brain, which knew what would recur, telegraph to every quarter for help, release, or diversion.

The door opened, and M'Leod reappeared. I thanked him politely, saying I was charmed with my room, anxious to meet Mrs M'Leod, much refreshed with my wash, and so on and so forth. Beyond a little stickiness at the corners of my mouth, it seemed to me that I was managing my words admirably, the while that I myself cowered at the bottom of unclimbable pits. M'Leod laid his hand on my shoulder, and said: 'You've got it now already, ain't it?'

'Yes,' I answered, 'it's making me sick!'

'It will pass off when you come outside. I give you my word it will then pass off. Come!'

I shambled out behind him, and wiped my forehead in the hall.

'You mustn't mind,' he said. 'I expect the run tired you. My good lady is sitting there under the copper beech.'

She was a fat woman in an apricot-coloured gown, with a heavily powdered face, against which her black long-lashed eyes showed like currants in dough. I was introduced to many fine ladies and gentlemen of those parts. Magnificently appointed landaus and covered motors swept in and out of the drive, and the air was gay with the merry outcries of the tennis players.

As twilight drew on they all went away, and I was left alone with Mr and Mrs M'Leod, while tall men-servants and maid-servants took away the tennis and tea things. Miss M'Leod had walked a little down the drive with a light-haired young man, who apparently knew everything about every South American railway stock. He had told me at tea that these were the days of financial specialisation.

'I think it went off beautifully, my dear,' said Mr M'Leod to his wife; and to me: 'You feel all right now, ain't it? Of course you do.'

Mrs M'Leod surged across the gravel. Her husband skipped nimbly before her into the south verandah, turned a switch, and all Holmescroft was flooded with light.

'You can do that from your room also,' he said as they went in. 'There is something in money, ain't it?'

Miss M'Leod came up behind me in the dusk. 'We have not

yet been introduced,' she said, 'but I suppose you are staying the night?'

'Your father was kind enough to ask me,' I replied.

She nodded. 'Yes, *I* know; and you know too, don't you? I saw your face when you came to shake hands with mamma. You felt the depression very soon. It is simply frightful in that bedroom sometimes. What do you think it is – bewitchment? In Greece, where I was a little girl, it might have been; but not in England, do you think? Or *do* you?'

'I don't know what to think,' I replied. 'I never felt anything like it. Does it happen often?'

'Yes, sometimes. It comes and goes.'

'Pleasant!' I said, as we walked up and down the gravel at the lawn edge. 'What has been your experience of it?'

'That is difficult to say, but – sometimes that – that depression is like as it were' – she gesticulated in most un-English fashion – 'a light. Yes, like a light turned into a room – only a light of blackness, do you understand? – into a happy room. For sometimes we are so happy, all we three, – so very happy. Then this blackness, it is turned on us just like – ah, I know what I mean now – like the head-lamp of a motor, and we are eclipsed. And there is another thing –'

The dressing gong roared, and we entered the over-lighted hall. My dressing was a brisk athletic performance, varied with outbursts of song – careful attention paid to articulation and expression. But nothing happened. As I hurried downstairs, I thanked Heaven that nothing had happened.

Dinner was served breakfast fashion; the dishes were placed on the sideboard over heaters, and we helped ourselves.

'We always do this when we are alone, so we talk better,' said Mr M'Leod.

'And we are always alone,' said the daughter.

'Cheer up, Thea. It will all come right,' he insisted.

'No, papa,' She shook her dark head. 'Nothing is right while *it* comes.'

'It is nothing that we ourselves have ever done in our lives – that I will swear to you,' said Mrs M'Leod suddenly. 'And we have changed our servants several times. So we know it is not *them.*'

'Never mind. Let us enjoy ourselves while we can,' said Mr M'Leod, opening the champagne.

But we did not enjoy ourselves. The talk failed. There were long silences.

'I beg your pardon,' I said, for I thought some one at my elbow was about to speak.

'Ah! That is the other thing!' said Miss M'Leod. Her mother groaned.

We were silent again, and, in a few seconds it must have been, a live grief beyond words – not ghostly dread or horror, but aching, helpless grief – overwhelmed us, each, I felt, according to his or her nature, and held steady like the beam of a burning-glass. Behind that pain I was conscious there was a desire on somebody's part to explain something on which some tremendously important issue hung.

Meantime I rolled bread pills and remembered my sins; M'Leod considered his own reflection in a spoon; his wife seemed to be praying, and the girl fidgeted desperately with hands and feet, till the darkness passed on – as though the malignant rays of a burning glass had been shifted from us.

'There,' said Miss M'Leod, half rising. 'Now you see what makes a happy home. Oh, sell it – sell it, father mine, and let us go away!'

'But I've spent thousands on it. You shall go to Harrogate next week, Thea dear.'

'I'm only just back from hotels. I am *so* tired of packing.'

'Cheer up, Thea. It is over. You know it does not often come here twice in the same night. I think we shall dare now to be comfortable.'

He lifted a dish-cover, and helped his wife and daughter. His face was lined and fallen like an old man's after debauch, but his hand did not shake, and his voice was clear. As he worked to restore us by speech and action, he reminded me of a grey-muzzled collie herding demoralised sheep.

After dinner we sat round the dining-room fire – the drawing-room might have been under the Shadow for aught we knew –

talking with the intimacy of gipsies by the wayside, or of wounded comparing notes after a skirmish. By eleven o'clock the three between them had given me every name and detail they could recall that in any way bore on the house, and what they knew of its history.

We went to bed in a fortifying blaze of electric light. My one fear was that the blasting gust of depression would return – the surest way, of course, to bring it. I lay awake till dawn, breathing quickly and sweating lightly, beneath what De Quincey inadequately describes as 'the oppression of inexpiable guilt.' Now as soon as the lovely day was broken, I fell into the most terrible of all dreams – that joyous one in which all past evil has not only been wiped out of our lives, but has never been committed; and in the very bliss of our assured innocence, before our loves shriek and change countenance, we wake to the day we have earned.

It was a coolish morning, but we preferred to breakfast in the south verandah. The forenoon we spent in the garden, pretending to play games that come out of boxes, such as croquet and clock golf. But most of the time we drew together and talked. The young man who knew all about South American railways took Miss M'Leod for a walk in the afternoon, and at five M'Leod thoughtfully whirled us all up to dine in town.

'Now, don't say you will tell the Psychological Society, and that you will come again,' said Miss M'Leod, as we parted. 'Because I know you will not.'

'You should not say that,' said her mother. 'You should say, "Good-bye, Mr Perseus. Come again."'

'Not him!' the girl cried. 'He has seen the Medusa's head!'

Looking at myself in the restaurant's mirrors, it seemed to me that I had not much benefited by my week-end. Next morning I wrote out all my Holmescroft notes at fullest length, in the hope that by so doing I could put it all behind me. But the experience worked on my mind, as they say certain imperfectly understood rays work on the body.

I am less calculated to make a Sherlock Holmes than any

man I know, for I lack both method and patience, yet the idea of following up the trouble to its source fascinated me. I had no theory to go on, except a vague idea that I had come between two poles of a discharge, and had taken a shock meant for some one else. This was followed by a feeling of intense irritation. I waited cautiously on myself, expecting to be overtaken by horror of the supernatural, but my self persisted in being humanly indignant, exactly as though it had been the victim of a practical joke. It was in great pains and upheavals – that I felt in every fibre – but its dominant idea, to put it coarsely, was to get back a bit of its own. By this I knew that I might go forward if I could find the way.

After a few days it occurred to me to go to the office of Mr J. M. M. Baxter – the solicitor who had sold Holmescroft to M'Leod. I explained I had some notion of buying the place. Would he act for me in the matter?

Mr Baxter, a large, greyish, throaty-voiced man, showed no enthusiasm. 'I sold it to Mr M'Leod,' he said. 'It 'ud scarcely do for me to start on the running-down tack now. But I can recommend—'

'I know he's asking an awful price,' I interrupted, 'and atop of it he wants an extra thousand for what he calls your clean bill of health.'

Mr Baxter sat up in his chair. I had all his attention.

'Your guarantee with the house. Don't you remember it?'

'Yes, yes. That no death had taken place in the house since it was built. I remember perfectly.'

He did not gulp as untrained men do when they lie, but his jaws moved stickily, and his eyes, turning towards the deed boxes on the wall, dulled. I counted seconds, one, two, three – one, two, three – up to ten. A man, I knew, can live through ages of mental depression in that time.

'I remember perfectly.' His mouth opened a little as though it had tasted old bitterness.

'Of course *that* sort of thing doesn't appeal to me.' I went on. '*I* don't expect to buy a house free from death.'

'Certainly not. No one does. But it was Mr M'Leod's fancy – his wife's rather, I believe; and since we could meet it – it was my duty to my clients – at whatever cost to my own feelings – to make him pay.'

'That's really why I came to you. I understood from him you knew the place well.'

'Oh yes. Always did. It originally belonged to some connections of mine.'

'The Misses Moultrie, I suppose. How interesting! They must have loved the place before the country round about was built up.'

'They were very fond of it indeed.'

'I don't wonder. So restful and sunny. I don't see how they could have brought themselves to part with it.'

Now it is one of the most constant peculiarities of the English that in polite conversation – and I had striven to be polite – no one ever does or sells anything for mere money's sake.

'Miss Agnes – the youngest – fell ill' (he spaced his words a little), 'and, as they were very much attached to each other, that broke up the home.'

'Naturally. I fancied it must have been something of that kind. One doesn't associate the Staffordshire Moultries' (my Demon of Irresponsibility at that instant created 'em), 'with – with being hard up.'

'I don't know whether we're related to them,' he answered importantly. 'We may be, for our branch of the family comes from the Midlands.'

I give this talk at length, because I am so proud of my first attempt at detective work. When I left him, twenty minutes later, with instructions to move against the owner of Holmescroft with a view to purchase, I was more bewildered than any Doctor Watson at the opening of a story.

Why should a middle-aged solicitor turn plover's egg colour and drop his jaw when reminded of so innocent and festal a matter as that no death had ever occurred in a house that he had sold? If I knew my English vocabulary at all, the tone in which he said the youngest sister 'fell ill' meant that she had gone out of her mind. That might explain his change of countenance, and it was just possible that her demented influence still hung about Holmescroft; but the rest was beyond me.

I was relieved when I reached M'Leod's City office, and could tell him what I had done – not what I thought.

M'Leod was quite willing to enter into the game of the pretended purchase, but did not see how it would help if I knew Baxter.

'He's the only living soul I can get at who was connected with Holmescroft,' I said.

'Ah! Living soul is good,' said M'Leod. 'At any rate our little girl will be pleased that you are still interested in us. Won't you come down some day this week?'

'How is it there now?' I asked.

He screwed up his face. 'Simply frightful!' he said. 'Thea is at Droitwich.'

'I should like it immensely, but I must cultivate Baxter for the present. You'll be sure and keep him busy your end, won't you?'

He looked at me with quiet contempt. 'Do not be afraid. I shall be a good Jew. I shall be my own solicitor.'

Before a fortnight was over, Baxter admitted ruefully that M'Leod was better than most firms in the business. We buyers were coy, argumentative, shocked at the price of Holmescroft, inquisitive, and cold by turns, but Mr M'Leod the seller easily met and surpassed us; and Mr Baxter entered every letter, telegram, and consultation at the proper rates in a cinematograph-film of a bill. At the end of a month he said it looked as though M'Leod, thanks to him, were really going to listen to reason. I was many pounds out of pocket, but I had learned something of Mr Baxter on the human side. I deserved it. Never in my life have I worked to conciliate, amuse, and flatter a human being as I worked over my solicitor.

It appeared that he golfed. Therefore, I was an enthusiastic beginner, anxious to learn. Twice I invaded his office with a bag (M'Leod lent it) full of the specilicans needed in this detestable game, and a vocabulary to match. The third time the ice broke, and Mr Baxter took me to his links, quite ten miles off, where in a maze of tramway lines, railroads, and nursery-maids, we skelped our divoted way round nine holes like barges plunging through head seas. He played vilely and had never expected to meet any one worse; but as he realised my form, I think he began to like me, for he took me in hand by the two hours together. After a fortnight he could give me no more than a stroke a hole, and when, with this allowance, I once managed to beat him by one, he was honestly glad, and assured me that I should be a golfer if I stuck to it. I was sticking to it for my own ends, but now and again my conscience pricked me; for the man was a nice man. Between games he supplied me with odd pieces of evidence, such as that he had known the Moultries all his life, being their cousin, and that Miss Mary, the eldest, was an unforgiving woman who would never let bygones be. I naturally wondered what she might have against him; and somehow connected him unfavourably with mad Agnes.

'People ought to forgive and forget,' he volunteered one day between rounds. 'Specially where, in the nature of things, they can't be sure of their deductions. Don't you think so?'

'It all depends on the nature of the evidence on which one forms one's judgment,' I answered.

'Nonsense!' he cried. 'I'm lawyer enough to know that there's nothing in the world so misleading as circumstantial evidence. Never was.'

'Why? Have you ever seen men hanged on it?'

'Hanged? People have been supposed to be eternally lost on it,' his face turned grey again. 'I don't know how it is with you, but my consolation is that God must know. He *must*! Things that seem on the face of 'em like murder, or say suicide, may appear different to God. Heh?'

'That's what the murderer and the suicide can always hope – I suppose.'

'I have expressed myself clumsily as usual. The facts as God knows 'em – may *be* indifferent – even after the most clinching evidence. I've always said that – both as a lawyer and a man, but some people won't – I don't want to judge 'em – we'll say they can't – believe it; whereas *I* say there's always a working chance – a certainty – that the worst hasn't happened.' He stopped and cleared his throat. 'Now, let's come on! This time next week I shall be taking my holiday.'

'What links?' I asked carelessly, while twins in a perambulator got out of our line of fire.

'A potty little nine-hole affair at a Hydro in the Midlands. My cousins stay there. Always will. Not but what the fourth and the seventh holes take some doing. You could manage it, though,' he said encouragingly. 'You're doing much better. It's only your approach shots that are weak.'

'You're right, I can't approach for nuts! I shall go to pieces while you're away – with no one to coach me,' I said mournfully.

'I haven't taught you anything,' he said, delighted with the compliment.

'I owe all I've learned to you, anyhow. When will you come back?'

'Look here,' he began. 'I don't know your engagements, but I've no one to play with at Burry Mills. Never have. Why couldn't you take a few days off and join me there? I warn you it will be rather dull. It's a throat and gout place – baths, massage, electricity, and so forth. But the fourth and the seventh holes really take some doing.'

'I'm for the game,' I answered valiantly. Heaven well knowing that I hated every stroke and word of it.

'That's the proper spirit. As their lawyer I must ask you not to say anything to my cousins about Holmescroft. It upsets 'em. Always did. But speaking as man to man, it would be very pleasant for me if you could see your way to—'

I saw it as soon as decency permitted, and thanked him sincerely. According to my now well-developed theory he had certainly misappropriated his aged cousins' monies under power of attorney, and had probably driven poor Agnes Moultrie out of her wits, but I wished that he was not so gentle, and good-tempered, and innocent-eyed.

Before I joined him at Burry Mills Hydro, I spent a night at Holmescroft. Miss M'Leod had returned from her Hydro, and first we made very merry on the open lawn in the sunshine over the manners and customs of the English resorting to such places. She knew dozens of hydros, and warned me how to behave in them, while Mr and Mrs M'Leod stood aside and adored her.

'Ah! That's the way she always comes back to us,' he said. 'Pity it wears off so soon, ain't it? You ought to hear her sing "With mirth, thou pretty bird."'

We had the house to face through the evening, and there we neither laughed nor sang. The gloom fell on us as we entered, and did not shift till ten o'clock, when we crawled out, as it were, from beneath it.

'It has been bad this summer,' said Mrs M'Leod in a whisper after we realised that we were freed. 'Sometimes I think the house will get up and cry out – it is so bad.'

'How?'

'Have you forgotten what comes after the depression?'

So then we waited about the small fire, and the dead air in the room presently filled and pressed down upon us with the sensation (but words are useless here) as though some dumb and bound power were striving against gag and bond to deliver its soul of an articulate word. It passed in a few minutes, and I fell to thinking about Mr Baxter's conscience and Agnes Moultrie, gone mad in the well-lit bedroom that waited me. These reflections secured me a night during which I rediscovered how, from purely mental causes, a man can be physically sick; but the sickness was bliss compared to my dreams when the birds waked. On my departure, M'Leod gave me a beautiful narwhal's horn, much as a nurse gives a child sweets for being brave at a dentist's.

'There's no duplicate of it in the world,' he said, 'else it would have come to old Max M'Leod,' and he tucked it into the motor. Miss M'Leod on the far side of the car whispered, 'Have you found out anything, Mr Perseus?'

I shook my head.

'Then I shall be chained to my rock all my life,' she went on. 'Only don't tell papa.'

I supposed she was thinking of the young gentleman who specialised in South American rails, for I noticed a ring on the third finger of her left hand.

I went straight from that house to Burry Mills Hydro, keen for the first time in my life on playing golf, which is guaranteed to occupy the mind. Baxter had taken me a room communicating with his own, and after lunch introduced me to a tall, horse-headed elderly lady of decided manners, whom a white-haired maid pushed along in a bath-chair through the park-like grounds of the Hydro. She was Miss Mary Moultrie, and she coughed and cleared her throat just like Baxter. She suffered – she told me it was the Moultrie castemark – from some obscure form of chronic bronchitis, complicated with spasm of the glottis; and, in a dead flat voice, with a sunken eye that looked and saw not, told me what washes, gargles, pastilles, and inhalations she had proved most beneficial. From her I was passed on to her younger sister, Miss Elizabeth, a small and withered thing with twitching lips victim, she told me, to very much the same sort of throat, but secretly devoted to another set of medicines. When she went away with Baxter and the bath-chair, I fell across a major of the Indian army with gout in his glassy eyes, and a stomach which he had taken all round the Continent. He laid everything before me; and him I escaped only to be confided in by a matron with a tendency to follicular tonsilitis and eczema. Baxter waited hand and foot on his cousins till five o'clock, trying, as I saw, to atone for his treatment of the dead sister. Miss Mary ordered him about like a dog.

'I warned you it would be dull,' he said when we met in the smoking-room.

'It's tremendously interesting,' I said. 'But how about a look round the links?'

'Unluckily damp always affects my eldest cousin. I've got to buy her a new bronchitis-kettle. Arthurs broke her old one yesterday.'

We slipped out to the chemist's shop in the town, and he bought a large glittering tin thing whose workings he explained.

'I'm used to this sort of work. I come up here pretty often,' he said. 'I've the family throat too.'

'You're a good man,' I said. 'A very good man.'

He turned towards me in the evening light among the beeches, and his face was changed to what it might have been a generation before.

'You see,' he said huskily, 'There was the youngest – Agnes. Before she fell ill, you know. But she didn't like leaving her sisters. Never would.' He hurried on with his odd-shaped load and left me among the ruins of my black theories. The man with that face had done Agnes Moultrie no wrong.

We never played our game. I was waked between two and three in the morning from my hygienic bed by Baxter in an ulster over orange and white pyjamas, which I should never have suspected from his character.

'My cousin has had some sort of a seizure,' he said. 'Will you come? I don't want to wake the doctor. Don't want to make a scandal. Quick!'

So I came quickly, and led by the white-haired Arthurs in a jacket and petticoat, entered a double-bedded room reeking with steam and Friar's Balsam. The electrics were all on. Miss Mary – I knew her by her height – was at the open window, wrestling with Miss Elizabeth, who gripped her round the knees. Her hand was at her throat, which was streaked with blood.

'She's done it. She's done it too!' Miss Elizabeth panted. 'Hold her! Help me!'

'Oh, I say! Woman don't cut their throats,' Baxter whispered.

'My God! Has she cut her throat?' the maid cried, and with no warning rolled over in a faint. Baxter pushed her under the washbasins, and leaped to hold the gaunt woman who crowed and whistled as she struggled towards the window. He took her by the shoulder, and she struck out wildly.

'All right! She's only cut her hand,' he said. 'Wet towel – quick!'

While I got that he pushed her backward. Her strength seemed almost as great as his. I swabbed at her throat when I could, and found no mark; then helped him to control her a little. Miss Elizabeth leaped back to bed, wailing like a child.

'Tie up her hand somehow,' said Baxter. 'Don't let it drip about the place. She' – he stepped on broken glass in his slippers, 'She must have smashed a pane.'

Miss Mary lurched towards the open window again, dropped on her knees, her head on the sill, and lay quiet, surrendering the cut hand to me.

'What did she do?' Baxter turned towards Miss Elizabeth in the far bed.

'She was going to throw herself out of the window,' was the answer. 'I stopped her, and sent Arthurs for you. Oh, we can never hold up our heads again!'

Miss Mary writhed and fought for breath. Baxter found a shawl which he threw over her shoulders.

'Nonsense!' said he. That isn't like Mary'; but his face worked when he said it.

'You wouldn't believe about Aggie, John. Perhaps you will now!' said Miss Elizabeth. 'I *saw* her do it, and she's cut her throat too!'

'She hasn't,' I said. 'It's only her hand.'

Miss Mary suddenly broke from us with an indescribable grunt, flew, rather than ran, to her sister's bed, and there shook her as one furious schoolgirl would shake another.

'No such thing,' she croaked. 'How dare you think so, you wicked little fool?'

'Get into bed, Mary,' said Baxter. 'You'll catch a chill.'

She obeyed, but sat up with the grey shawl round her lean shoulders, glaring at her sister. 'I'm better now,' she crowed. 'Arthurs let me sit out too long. Where's Arthurs? The kettle.'

'Never mind Arthurs,' said Baxter. '*You* get the kettle.' I hastened to bring it from the side table. 'Now Mary, as God sees you, tell me what you've done.'

His lips were dry, and he could not moisten them with his tongue.

Miss Mary applied herself to the mouth of the kettle, and between indraws of steam said: 'The spasm came on just now, while I was asleep. I was nearly choking to death. So I went to the window. I've done it often before, without waking any one. Bessie's such an old maid about draughts. I tell you I was choking to death. I couldn't manage the catch, and I nearly fell out. That window opens too low. I cut my hand trying to save myself. Who has tied it up in this filthy handkerchief? I wish you had had my throat, Bessie. I never was nearer dying!' She scowled on us all impartially, while her sister sobbed.

From the bottom of the bed we heard a quivering voice: 'Is she dead? Have they took her away? Oh, I never could bear the sight o' blood!'

'Arthurs,' said Miss Mary, 'you are an hireling. Go away!'

It is my belief that Arthurs crawled out on all fours, but I was busy picking up broken glass from the carpet.

Then Baxter, seated by the side of the bed, began to cross-examine in a voice I scarcely recognised. No one could for an instant have doubted the genuine rage of Miss Mary against her sister, her cousin, or her maid; and that the doctor should have been called in – for she did me the honour of calling me doctor – was the last drop. She was choking with her throat; had rushed to the window for air; had near pitched out, and in catching at the window bars had cut her hand. Over and over she made this clear to the intent Baxter. Then she turned on her sister and tongue-lashed her savagely.

'You mustn't blame me,' Miss Bessie faltered at last. 'You know what we think of night and day.'

'I'm coming to that,' said Baxter. 'Listen to me. What *you* did, Mary, misled four people into thinking you – you meant to do away with yourself.'

'Isn't one suicide in the family enough? Oh God, help and pity us! You *couldn't* have believed that!' she cried.

'The evidence was complete. Now, don't you think,' Baxter's finger wagged under her nose – '*can't* you think that poor Aggie did the same thing at Holmescroft when she fell out of the window?'

'She had the same throat,' said Miss Elizabeth. 'Exactly the same symptoms. Don't you remember, Mary?'

'Which was her bedroom?' I asked of Baxter in an undertone.

'Over the south verandah, looking on to the tennis lawn.'

'I nearly fell out of that very window when I was at

Holmescroft – opening it to get some air. The sill doesn't come much above your knees,' I said.

'You hear that, Mary? Mary, do you hear what this gentleman says? Won't you believe that what nearly happened to you must have happened to poor Aggie that night? For God's sake – for her sake – Mary, *won't* you believe?'

There was a long silence while the steam kettle puffed.

'If I could have proof – if I could have proof,' said she, and broke into most horrible tears.

Baxter motioned to me, and I crept away to my room, and lay awake till morning, thinking more specially of the dumb Thing at Holmescroft which wished to explain itself. I hated Miss Mary as perfectly as though I had known her for twenty years, but I felt that, alive or dead, I should not like her to condemn me.

Yet at mid-day, when I saw Miss Mary in her bath-chair, Arthurs behind and Baxter and Miss Elizabeth on either side, in the park-like grounds of the Hydro, I found it difficult to arrange my words.

'Now that you know all about it,' said Baxter aside, after the first strangeness of our meeting was over, 'it's only fair to tell you that my poor cousin did not die in Holmescroft at all. She was dead when they found her under the window in the morning. Just dead.'

'Under that laburnum outside the window?' I asked, for I suddenly remembered the crooked evil thing.

'Exactly. She broke the tree in falling. But no death has ever taken place *in* the house, so far as we were concerned. You can make yourself quite easy on that point. Mr M'Leod's extra thousand for what you called the "clean bill of health" was something towards my cousins' estate when we sold. It was my duty as their lawyer to get it for them – at any cost to my own feelings.'

I know better than to argue when the English talk about their duty. So I agreed with my solicitor.

'Their sister's death must have been a great blow to your cousins,' I went on. The bath-chair was behind me.

'Unspeakable,' Baxter whispered. 'They brooded on it day

and night. No wonder. If their theory of poor Aggie making away with herself was correct, she was eternally lost!'

'Do you believe that she made away with herself?'

'No, thank God! Never have! And after what happened to Mary last night, I see perfectly what happened to poor Aggie. She had the family throat too. By the way, Mary thinks you are a doctor. Otherwise she wouldn't like your having been in her room.'

'Very good. Is she convinced now about her sister's death?'

'She'd give anything to be able to believe it, but she's a hard woman, and brooding along certain lines makes one groovy. I have sometimes been afraid for her reason – on the religious side, don't you know. Elizabeth doesn't matter. Brain of a hen. Always had.'

Here Arthurs summoned me to the bath-chair and the ravaged face, beneath its knitted Shetland wool hood, of Miss Mary Moultrie.

'I need not remind you, I hope, of the seal of secrecy – absolute secrecy – in your profession,' she began. 'Thanks to my cousin's and my sister's stupidity, you have found out—' she blew her nose.

'Please don't excite her, sir,' said Arthurs at the back.

'But, my dear Miss Moultrie, I only know what I've seen, of course, but it seems to me that what you thought was a tragedy in your sister's case, turns out, on your own evidence, so to speak, to have been an accident – a dreadfully sad one – but absolutely an accident.'

'Do you believe that too?' she cried. 'Or are you only saying it to comfort me?'

'I believe it from the bottom of my heart. Come down to Holmescroft for an hour – for half an hour – and satisfy yourself.'

'Of what? You don't understand. I see the house every day – every night. I am always there in spirit – waking or sleeping. I couldn't face it in reality.'

'But you must,' I said. 'If you go there in the spirit the greater need for you to go there in the flesh. Go to your sister's room once more, and see the window – I nearly fell out of it myself. It's – it's awfully low and dangerous. That would convince you,' I pleaded.

'Yet Aggie had slept in that room for years,' she interrupted.

'You've slept in your room here for a long time, haven't you? But you nearly fell out of the window when you were choking.'

'That is true. That is one thing true,' she nodded. 'And I might have been killed as – perhaps – Aggie was killed.'

'In that case your own sister and cousin and maid would have said you had committed suicide, Miss Moultrie. Come down to Holmescroft, and go over the place just once.'

'You are lying,' she said quite quietly. 'You don't want me to come down to see a window. It is something else. I warn you we are Evangelicals. We don't believe in prayers for the dead. "As the tree falls—"'

'Yes. I daresay. But you persist in thinking that your sister committed suicide—'

'No! No! I have always prayed that I might have misjudged her.'

Arthurs at the bath-chair spoke up: 'Oh, Miss Mary! you *would* 'ave it from the first that poor Miss Aggie 'ad made away with herself; an', of course, Miss Bessie took the notion from you. Only Master – Mister John stood out, and – and I'd 'ave taken my Bible oath *you* was making away with yourself last night.'

Miss Mary leaned towards me, one finger on my sleeve.

'If going to Holmescroft kills me,' she said, 'you will have the murder of a fellow-creature on your conscience for all eternity.'

'I'll risk it,' I answered. Remembering what torment the mere reflection of her torments had cast on Holmescroft, and remembering, above all, the dumb Thing that filled the house with its desire to speak, I felt that there might be worse things.

Baxter was amazed at the proposed visit, but at a nod from that terrible woman went off to make arrangements. Then I sent a telegram to M'Leod bidding him and his vacate Holmescroft for that afternoon. Miss Mary should be alone with her dead, as I had been alone.

I expected untold trouble in transporting her, but to do her justice, the promise given for the journey, she underwent it without murmur, spasm, or unnecessary word. Miss Bessie, pressed in a corner by the window, wept behind her veil, and from time to time tried to take hold of her sister's hand. Baxter wrapped himself in his newly-found happiness as selfishly as a bridegroom, for he sat still and smiled.

'So long as I know that Aggie didn't make away with herself,' he explained, 'I tell you frankly I don't care what happened. She's as hard as a rock – Mary. Always was. *She* won't die.'

We led her out on to the platform like a blind woman, and so got her into the fly. The half-hour crawl to Holmescroft was the most racking experience of the day. M'Leod had obeyed my instructions. There was no one visible in the house or the gardens; and the front door stood open.

Miss Mary rose from beside her sister, stepped forth first, and entered the hall.

'Come, Bessie,' she cried.

'I daren't. Oh, I daren't.'

'Come!' Her voice had altered. I felt Baxter start. 'There's nothing to be afraid of.'

'Good heavens!' said Baxter. 'She's running up the stairs. We'd better follow.'

'Let's wait below. She's going to the room.'

We heard the door of the bedroom I knew open and shut, and we waited in the lemon-coloured hall, heavy with the scent of flowers.

'I've never been into it since it was sold,' Baxter sighed. 'What a lovely restful place it is! Poor Aggie used to arrange the flowers.'

'Restful?' I began, but stopped of a sudden, for I felt all over my bruised soul that Baxter was speaking truth. It was a light, spacious, airy house, full of the sense of well-being and peace – above all things, of peace. I ventured into the dining-room where the thoughtful M'Leods had left a small fire. There was no terror there, present or lurking; and in the drawing-room, which for good reasons we had never cared to enter, the sun and the peace and the scent of the flowers worked together as is fit in an inhabited house. When I returned to the hall, Baxter was sweetly asleep on a couch, looking most unlike a middle-aged solicitor who had spent a broken night with an exacting cousin.

There was ample time for me to review it all – to felicitate myself upon my magnificent acumen (barring some errors about Baxter as a thief and possibly a murderer), before the door above opened, and Baxter, evidently a light sleeper, sprang awake.

'I've had a heavenly little nap,' he said, rubbing his eyes with the backs of his hands like a child. 'Good Lord! That's not *their* step!'

But it was. I had never before been privileged to see the Shadow turned backward on the dial – the years ripped bodily off poor human shoulders – old sunken eyes filled and alight – harsh lips moistened and human.

'John,' Miss Mary called, 'I know now. Aggie didn't do it!' and 'She didn't do it!' echoed Miss Bessie and giggled.

'I did not think it wrong to say a prayer,' Miss Mary continued. 'Not for her soul, but for our peace. Then I was convinced.'

'Then we got conviction,' the younger sister piped.

'We've misjudged poor Aggie, John. But I feel she knows now. Wherever she is, she knows that we know she is guiltless.'

'Yes, she knows. I felt it too,' said Miss Elizabeth.

'I never doubted,' said John Baxter, whose face was beautiful at that hour. 'Not from the first. Never have!'

'You never offered me proof, John. Now, thank God, it will not be the same any more. I can think henceforward of Aggie without sorrow,' She tripped, absolutely tripped, across the hall, 'What ideas these Jews have of arranging furniture!' She spied me behind a big cloisonné vase.

'I've seen the window,' she said remotely. 'You took a great risk in advising me to undertake such a journey. However, as it turns out . . . I forgive you, and I pray you may never know what mental anguish means! Bessie! Look at this peculiar piano! Do you suppose, Doctor, these people would offer one tea? I miss mine.'

'I will go and see,' I said, and explored M'Leod's new-built servants' wing. It was in the servants' hall that I unearthed the M'Leod family, bursting with anxiety.

'Tea for three, quick,' I said. 'If you ask me any questions now, I shall have a fit!' So Mrs M'Leod got it, and I was butler, amid murmured apologies from Baxter, still smiling and self-absorbed, and the cold disapproval of Miss Mary, who thought the pattern of the china vulgar. However, she ate well, and even asked me whether I would not like a cup of tea for myself.

They went away in the twilight – the twilight that I had once feared. They were going to an hotel in London to rest after the fatigues of the day, and as their fly turned down the drive, I capered on the doorstep, with the all-darkened house behind me.

Then I heard the uncertain feet of the M'Leods, and bade them not to turn on the lights, but to feel – to feel what I had done; for the Shadow was gone, with the dumb desire in the air. They drew short, but afterwards deeper, breaths, like bathers entering chill water, separated one from the other, moved about the hall, tiptoed upstairs, raced down, and then Miss M'Leod, and I believe her mother, though she denies this, embraced me. I know M'Leod did.

It was a disgraceful evening. To say we rioted through the house is to put it mildly. We played a sort of Blind Man's Buff along the darkest passages, in the unlighted drawing-room, and little dining-room, calling cheerily to each other after each exploration that here, and here, and here, the trouble had removed itself. We came up to *the* bedroom – mine for the night again – and sat, the women on the bed, and we men on chairs, drinking in blessed draughts of peace and comfort and cleanliness of soul, while I told them my tale in full, and received fresh praise, thanks, and blessings.

When the servants, returned from their day's outing, gave us a supper of cold fried fish, M'Leod had sense enough to open no wine. We had been practically drunk since nightfall, and grew incoherent on water and milk.

'I like that Baxter,' said M'Leod. 'He's a sharp man. The death wasn't in the house, but he ran it pretty close, ain't it?'

'And the joke of it is that he supposes I want to buy the place from you,' I said. 'Are you selling?'

'Not for twice what I paid for it – now,' said M'Leod. 'I'll keep you in furs all your life, but not our Holmescroft.'

'No – never our Holmescroft,' said Miss M'Leod. 'We'll ask *him* here on Tuesday, mamma.' They squeezed each other's hands.

'Now tell me,' said Mrs M'Leod – 'that tall one I saw out of the scullery window – did *she* tell you she was always here in the spirit? I hate her. She made all this trouble. It was not her house after she had sold it. What do you think?'

'I suppose,' I answered, 'she brooded over what she believed was her sister's suicide night and day – she confessed she did – and her thoughts being concentrated on this place, they felt like a – like a burning-glass.'

'Burning-glass is good,' said M'Leod.

'I said it was like a light of blackness turned on us,' cried the girl, twiddling her ring. 'That must have been when the tall one thought worst about her sister and the house.'

'Ah, the poor Aggie!' said Mrs M'Leod. 'The poor Aggie, trying to tell every one it was not so! No wonder we felt Something wished to say Something. Thea, Max, do you remember that night—'

'We need not remember any more,' M'Leod interrupted. 'It is not our trouble. They have told each other now.'

'Do you think, then,' said Miss M'Leod, 'that those two, the living ones, were actually told something – upstairs – in your – in the room?'

'I can't say. At any rate they were made happy, and they ate a big tea afterwards. As your father says, it is not our trouble any longer – thank God!'

'Amen!' said M'Leod. 'Now, Thea, let us have some music after all these months. "With mirth, thou pretty bird," ain't it? You ought to hear that.'

And in the half-lighted hall, Thea sang an old English song that I had never heard before.

With mirth, thou pretty bird, rejoice
　　Thy Maker's praise enhanced;
Lift up thy shrill and pleasant voice,
　　Thy God is high advanced!
Thy food before He did provide,
And gives it in a fitting side,
　　Wherewith be thou sufficed!
Why shouldst thou now unpleasant be,
　　Thy wrath against God venting,
That He a little bird made thee,
　　Thy silly head tormenting,
Because He made thee not a man?
Oh, Peace! He hath well thought thereon,
　　Therewith be thou sufficed!

THE KNIFE AND THE NAKED CHALK

The children went to the seaside for a month, and lived in a flint village on the bare windy chalk Downs, quite thirty miles away from home. They made friends with an old shepherd, called Mr Dudeney, who had known their Father when their Father was little. He did not talk like their own people in the Weald of Sussex, and he used different names for farm things, but he understood how they felt, and let them go with him. He had a tiny cottage about half a mile from the village, where his wife made mead from thyme honey, and nursed sick lambs in front of a coal fire, while Old Jim, who was Mr Dudeney's sheep-dog's father, lay at the door. They brought up beef bones for Old Jim (you must never give a sheep-dog mutton bones), and if Mr Dudeney happened to be far in the Downs, Mrs Dudeney would tell the dog to take them to him, and he did.

One August afternoon when the village water-cart had made the street smell specially townified, they went to look for their shepherd as usual, and, as usual, Old Jim crawled over the door-step and took them in charge. The sun was hot, the dry grass was very slippery, and the distances were very distant.

'It's just like the sea,' said Una, when Old Jim halted in the shade of a lonely flint barn on a bare rise. 'You see where you're going, and – you go there, and there's nothing between.'

Dan slipped off his shoes. 'When we get home I shall sit in the woods all day,' he said.

'Whuff!' said Old Jim, to show he was ready, and struck across a long rolling stretch of turf. Presently he asked for his beef bone.

'Not yet,' said Dan. 'Where's Mr Dudeney? Where's Master?'

Old Jim looked as if he thought they were mad, and asked again.

'Don't you give it him,' Una cried. 'I'm not going to be left howling in a desert.'

'Show, boy! Show!' said Dan, for the Downs seemed as bare as the palm of your hand.

Old Jim sighed, and trotted forward. Soon they spied the blob of Mr Dudeney's hat against the sky a long way off.

'Right! All right!' said Dan. Old Jim wheeled round, took his bone carefully between his blunted teeth, and returned to the shadow of the old barn, looking just like a wolf. The children went on. Two kestrels hung bivvering and squealing above them. A gull flapped lazily along the white edge of the cliffs. The curves of the Downs shook a little in the heat, and so did Mr Dudeney's distant head.

They walked toward it very slowly and found themselves staring into a horseshoe-shaped hollow a hundred feet deep, whose steep sides were laced with tangled sheep-tracks. The flock grazed on the flat at the bottom, under charge of Young Jim. Mr Dudeney sat comfortably knitting on the edge of the slope, his crook between his knees. They told him what Old Jim had done.

'Ah, he thought you could see my head as soon as he did. The closeter you be to the turf the more you see things. You look warm-like,' said Mr Dudeney.

'We be,' said Una, flopping down. '*And* tired.'

'Set beside o' me here. The shadow'll begin to stretch out in a little while, and a heat-shake o' wind will come up with it that'll overlay your eyes like so much wool.'

'We don't want to sleep,' said Una indignantly; but she settled herself as she spoke, in the first strip of early afternoon shade.

'O' course not. You come to talk with me same as your father used. *He* didn't need no dog to guide him to Norton Pit.'

'Well, he belonged here,' said Dan, and laid himself down at length on the turf.

'He did. And what beats me is why he went off to live among them messy trees in the Weald, when he might ha' stayed here and looked all about him. There's no profit to trees. They draw the lightning, and sheep shelter under 'em, and *so*, like as not, you'll lose a half-score ewes struck dead in one storm. Tck! Your father knew that.'

'Trees aren't messy,' Una rose on her elbow. 'And what about firewood? I don't like coal.'

'Eh? You lie a piece more uphill and you'll lie more natural,' said Mr Dudeney, with his provoking deaf smile. 'Now press your face down and smell to the turf. That's Southdown thyme which makes our Southdown mutton beyond compare, and, my mother told me, 'twill cure anything except broken necks, or hearts. I forget which.'

They sniffed, and somehow forgot to lift their cheeks from the soft thymy cushions.

'You don't get nothing like that in the Weald. Watercress, maybe?' said Mr Dudeney.

'But we've water – brooks full of it – where you paddle in hot weather,' Una replied, watching a yellow-and-violet-banded snail-shell close to her eye.

'Brooks flood. Then you must shift your sheep – let alone foot-rot afterward. I put more dependence on a dew-pond any day.'

'How's a dew-pond made?' said Dan, and tilted his hat over his eyes. Mr Dudeney explained.

The air trembled a little as though it could not make up its mind whether to slide into the Pit or move across the open. But it seemed easiest to go downhill, and the children felt one soft puff after another slip and sidle down the slope in fragrant breaths that baffed on their eyelids. The little whisper of the sea by the cliffs joined with the whisper of the wind over the grass, the hum of insects in the thyme, the ruffle and rustle of the flock below, and a thickish mutter deep in the very chalk beneath them. Mr Dudeney stopped explaining, and went on with his knitting.

They were roused by voices. The shadow had crept half-way down the steep side of Norton Pit, and on the edge of it, his back to them, Puck sat beside a half-naked man who seemed busy at some work. The wind had dropped, and in that funnel of ground every least noise and movement reached them like whispers up a water-pipe.

'That is clever,' said Puck, leaning over. 'How truly you shape it!'

'Yes, but what does The Beast care for a brittle flint tip? Bah! The man flicked something contemptuously over his shoulder. It fell between Dan and Una – a beautiful dark-blue flint arrow-head still hot from the maker's hand.

The man reached for another stone, and worked away like a thrush with a snail-shell.

'Flint work is fool's work,' he said at last. 'One does it because one always did it; but when it comes to dealing with The Beast – no good!' He shook his shaggy head.

'The Beast was dealt with long ago. He has gone,' said Puck.

'He'll be back at lambing-time. *I* know him.' He chipped very carefully, and the flints squeaked.

'Not he. Children can lie out on the Chalk now all day through and go home safe.'

'Can they? Well, call The Beast by his True Name, and I'll believe it,' the man replied.

'Surely!' Puck leaped to his feet, curved his hands round his mouth and shouted: 'Wolf! Wolf!'

Norton Pit threw back the echo from its dry sides – 'Wuff! Wuff!' like Young Jim's bark.

'You see? You hear?' said Puck. 'Nobody answers. Grey Shepherd is gone. Feet-in-the-Night has run off. There are no more wolves.'

'Wonderful!' The man wiped his forehead as though he were hot. 'Who drove him away? You?'

'Many men through many years, each working in his own country. Were you one of them?' Puck answered.

The man slid his sheepskin cloak to his waist, and without a word pointed to his side, which was all seamed and blotched with scars. His arms, too, were dimpled from shoulder to elbow with horrible white dimples.

'I see,' said Puck. 'It is The Beast's mark. What did you use against him?'

'Hand, hammer, and spear, as our fathers did before us.'

'So? Then how' – Puck twitched aside the man's dark-brown cloak – 'how did a Flint-worker come by *that*? Show, man, show!' He held out his little hand.

The man slipped a long dark iron knife, almost a short sword, from his belt, and after breathing on it, handed it hilt-first to Puck, who took it with his head on one side, as you should when you look at the works of a watch, squinted down the dark blade, and very delicately rubbed his forefinger from the point to the hilt.

'Good!' said he, in a surprised tone.

'It should be. The Children of the Night made it,' the man answered.

'So I see by the iron. What might it have cost you?'

'This!' The man raised his hand to his cheek. Puck whistled like a Weald starling.

'By the Great Rings of the Chalk!' he cried. 'Was *that* your price? Turn sunward that I may see better, and shut your eye.'

He slipped his hand beneath the man's chin and swung him till he faced the children up the slope. They saw that his right eye was gone, and the eyelid lay shrunk. Quickly Puck turned him round again, and the two sat down.

'It was for the sheep. The sheep are the people,' said the man, in an ashamed voice. 'What else could I have done? *You* know, Old One.'

Puck sighed a little fluttering sigh. 'Take the knife. I listen.'

The man bowed his head, drove the knife into the turf, and while it still quivered said: 'This is witness between us that I speak the thing that has been. Before my Knife and the Naked Chalk I speak. Touch!'

Puck laid a hand on the hilt. It stopped shaking. The children wriggled a little nearer.

'I am of the People of the Worked Flint. I am the one son of the Priestess who sells the Winds to the Men of the Sea. I am the Buyer of the Knife – the Keeper of the People,' the man began, in a sort of singing shout. 'These are my names in this country of the Naked Chalk, between the Trees and the Sea.'

'Yours was a great country. Your names are great too,' said Puck.

'One cannot feed some things on names and songs.' The man hit himself on the chest. 'It is better – always better – to count one's children safe round the fire, their Mother among them.'

'Ahai!' said Puck. 'I think this will be a very old tale.'

'I warm myself and eat at any fire that I choose, but there is no *one* to light me a fire or cook my meat. I sold all that when I bought the Magic Knife for my people. It was not right that The Beast should master man. What else could I have done?'

'I hear. I know. I listen,' said Puck.

'When I was old enough to take my place in the Sheep-guard, The Beast gnawed all our country like a bone between his teeth. He came in behind the flocks at watering-time, and watched them round the Dew-ponds; he leaped into the folds between our knees at the shearing; he walked out alongside the grazing flocks, and chose his meat on the hoof while our boys threw flints at him; he crept by night into the huts, and licked the babe from between the mother's hands; he called his companions and pulled down men in broad daylight on the Naked Chalk. No – not always did he do so! *This* was his cunning! He would go away for a while to let us forget him. A year – two years perhaps – we neither smelt, nor heard, nor saw him. When our flocks had increased; when our men did not always look behind them; when children strayed from the fenced places; when our women walked alone to draw water – back, back, back came the Curse of the Chalk, Grey Shepherd, Feet-in-the-Night – The Beast, The Beast, The Beast!

'He laughed at our little brittle arrows and our poor blunt spears. He learned to run in under the stroke of the hammer. I think he knew when there was a flaw in the flint. Often it does not show till you bring it down on his snout. Then – *Pouf!* – the false flint falls all to flinders, and you are left with the hammer-handle in your fist, and his teeth in your flank! I have

547

felt them. At evening, too, in the dew, or when it has misted and rained, your spear-head lashings slack off, though you have kept them beneath your cloak all day. You are alone – but so close to the home ponds that you stop to tighten the sinews with hands, teeth, and a piece of driftwood. You bend over and pull – so! That is the minute for which he has followed you since the stars went out. "Aarh!" he says. "Wurr-aarh!" he says.' (Norton Pit gave back the growl like a pack of real wolves.) 'Then he is on your right shoulder feeling for the vein in your neck, and – perhaps your sheep run on without you. To fight The Beast is nothing, but to be despised by The Beast when he fights you – that is like his teeth in the heart! Old One, why is it that men desire so greatly, and can do so little?'

'I do not know. Did you desire so much?' said Puck.

'I desired to master The Beast. It is not right that The Beast should master man. But my people were afraid. Even my Mother, the Priestess, was afraid when I told her what I desired. We were accustomed to be afraid of The Beast. When I was made a man, and a maiden – she was a Priestess – waited for me at the Dew-ponds, The Beast flitted from off the Chalk. Perhaps it was a sickness; perhaps he had gone to his Gods to learn how to do us new harm. But he went, and we breathed more freely. The women sang again; the children were not so much guarded; our flocks grazed far out. I took mine yonder' – he pointed inland to the hazy line of the Weald – 'where the new grass was best. They grazed north. I followed till we were close to the Trees' – he lowered his voice – 'close *there* where the Children of the Night live.' He pointed north again.

'Ah, now I remember a thing,' said Puck. 'Tell me, why did your people fear the Trees so extremely?'

'Because the Gods hate the Trees and strike them with lightning. We can see them burning for days all along the Chalk's edge. Besides, all the Chalk knows that the Children of the Night, though they worship our Gods, are magicians. When a man goes into their country, they change his spirit; they put words into his mouth; they make him like talking water. But a voice in my heart told me to go toward the north. While I watched my sheep there I saw three Beasts chasing a man, who ran toward the Trees. By this I knew he was a Child of the Night. We Flint-workers fear the Trees more than we fear The Beast. He had no hammer. He carried a knife like this one. A Beast leaped at him. He stretched out his knife. The Beast fell dead. The other Beasts ran away howling, which they would never have done from a Flint-worker. The man went in among the Trees. I looked for the dead Beast. He had been killed in a new way – by a single deep, clean cut, without bruise or tear, which had split his bad heart. Wonderful! So I saw that the man's knife was magic, and I thought how to get it, – thought strongly how to get it.

'When I brought the flocks to the shearing, my Mother the Priestess asked me, "What is the new thing which you have seen and I see in your face?" I said, "It is a sorrow to me"; and she answered, "All new things are sorrow. Sit in my place, and eat sorrow." I sat down in her place by the fire, where she talks to the ghosts in winter, and two voices spoke in my heart. One voice said, "Ask the Children of the Night for the Magic Knife. It is not fit that The Beast should master man." I listened to that voice.

'One voice said, "If you go among the Trees, the Children of the Night will change your spirit. Eat and sleep here." The other voice said, "Ask for the Knife." I listened to that voice.

'I said to my Mother in the morning, "I go away to find a thing for the people, but I do not know whether I shall return in my own shape." She answered, "Whether you live or die, or are made different, I am your Mother."'

'True,' said Puck. 'The Old Ones themselves cannot change men's mothers even if they would.'

'Let us thank the Old Ones! I spoke to my Maiden, the Priestess who waited for me at the Dew-ponds. She promised fine things too.' The man laughed. 'I went away to that place where I had seen the magician with the knife. I lay out two days on the short grass before I ventured among the Trees. I felt my way before me with a stick. I was afraid of the terrible talking Trees. I was afraid of the ghosts in the branches; of the soft ground underfoot; of the red and black waters. I was afraid, above all, of the Change. It came!'

They saw him wipe his forehead once again, and his strong back-muscles quivered till he laid his hand on the knife-hilt.

'A fire without a flame burned in my head; an evil taste grew in my mouth; my eyelids shut hot over my eyes; my breath was hot between my teeth, and my hands were like the hands of a stranger. I was made to sing songs and to mock the Trees, though I was afraid of them. At the same time I saw myself laughing, and I was very sad for this fine young man, who was myself. Ah! The Children of the Night know magic.'

'I think that is done by the Spirits of the Mist. They change a man if he sleeps among them,' said Puck. 'Had you slept in any mists?'

'Yes – but *I* know it was the Children of the Night. After three days I saw a red light behind the Trees, and I heard a heavy noise. I saw the Children of the Night dig red stones from a hole, and lay them in fires. The stones melted like tallow, and the men beat the soft stuff with hammers. I wished to speak to these men, but the words were changed in my mouth, and all I could say was, "Do not make that noise. It hurts my head." By this I knew that I was bewitched, and I clung to the Trees, and prayed the Children of the Night to take off their spells. They were cruel. They asked me many questions which they would never allow me to answer. They changed my words between my teeth till I wept. Then they led me into a hut and covered the floor with hot stones and dashed water on the stones, and sang charms till the sweat poured off me like water. I slept. When I waked, my own spirit — not the strange, shouting thing – was back in my body, and I was like a cool bright stone on the shingle between the sea and the sunshine. The magicians came to hear me – women and men – each wearing a Magic Knife. Their Priestess was their Ears and their Mouth.

'I spoke. I spoke many words that went smoothly along like sheep in order when their shepherd, standing on a mound, can count those coming, and those far off getting ready to come. I asked for Magic Knives for my people. I said that my people would bring meat, and milk, and wool, and lay them in the short grass outside the Trees, if the Children of the Night would leave Magic Knives for our people to take away. They were pleased. Their Priestess said, "For whose sake have you come?" I answered, "The sheep are the people. If The Beast kills our sheep, our people die. So I come for a Magic Knife to kill The Beast."

'She said, "We do not know if our God will let us trade with the people of the Naked Chalk. Wait till we have asked."

'When they came back from the Question-place (their Gods are our Gods), their Priestess said, "The God needs a proof that your words are true." I said, "What is the proof?" She said, "The God says that if you have come for the sake of your people you will give him your right eye to be put out; but if you have come for any other reason you will not give it. This proof is between you and the God. We ourselves are sorry."

'I said, "This is a hard proof. Is there no other road?"

'She said, "Yes. You can go back to your people with your two eyes in your head if you choose. But then you will not get any Magic Knives for your people."

'I said, "It would be easier if I knew that I were to be killed."

'She said, "Perhaps the God knew this too. See! I have made my knife hot."

'I said, "Be quick, then !" With her knife heated in the flame she put out my right eye. She herself did it. I am the son of a Priestess. She was a Priestess. It was not work for any common man.'

'True! Most true,' said Puck. 'No common man's work, that. And, afterwards?'

'Afterwards I did not see out of that eye any more. I found also that a one eye does not tell you truly where things are. Try it!'

At this Dan put his hand over one eye, and reached for the flint arrow-head on the grass. He missed it by inches. 'It's true,' he whispered to Una. 'You can't judge distances a bit with only one eye.'

Puck was evidently making the same experiment, for the man laughed at him.

'I know it is so,' said he. 'Even now I am not always sure of my blow. I stayed with the Children of the Night till my eye healed. They said I was the son of Tyr, the God who put his right hand in a Beast's mouth. They showed me how they melted their red stone and made the Magic Knives of it. They told me the charms they sang over the fires and at the beatings. I can sing many charms.' Then he began to laugh like a boy.

'I was thinking of my journey home,' he said, 'and of the surprised Beast. He had come back to the Chalk. I saw him – I smelt his lairs as soon as ever I left the Trees. He did not know I had the Magic Knife – I hid it under my cloak – the Knife that the Priestess gave me. Ho! Ho! That happy day was too short! See! A Beast would wind me. "Wow!" he would say. "Here is my Flint-worker!" He would come leaping, tail in air; he would roll; he would lay his head between his paws out of merriness of heart at his warm, waiting meal. He would leap – and, oh, his eye in mid-leap when he saw – when he saw the knife held ready for him! It pierced his hide as a rush pierces curdled milk. Often he had no time to howl. I did not trouble to flay any beasts I killed. Sometimes I missed my blow. Then I took my little flint hammer and beat out his brains as he cowered. He made no fight. He knew the Knife! But The Beast is very cunning. Before evening all The Beasts had smelt the blood on my knife, and were running from me like hares. *They* knew! Then I walked as a man should – the Master of The Beast!

'So came I back to my Mother's house. There was a lamb to be killed. I cut it in two halves with my knife, and I told her all my tale. She said, "This is the work of a God." I kissed her and laughed. I went to my Maiden who waited for me at the Dew-ponds. There was a lamb to be killed. I cut it in two halves with my knife, and told her all my tale. She said, "It is the work of a God." I laughed, but she pushed me away, and being on my blind side, ran off before I could kiss her. I went to the Men of the Sheepguard at watering-time. There was a sheep to be killed for their meat. I cut it in two halves with my knife, and told them all my tale. They said, "It is the work of a God."'

I said, "We talk too much about Gods. Let us eat and be happy, and tomorrow I will take you to the Children of the Night, and each man will find a Magic Knife."

'I was glad to smell our sheep again; to see the broad sky from edge to edge, and to hear the sea. I slept beneath the stars in my cloak. The men talked among themselves.

'I led them, the next day, to the Trees, taking with me meat, wool, and curdled milk, as I had promised. We found the Magic Knives laid out on the grass, as the Children of the Night had promised. They watched us from among the Trees. Their Priestess called to me and said, "How is it with your people?" I said, "Their hearts are changed. I cannot see their hearts as I used to." She said, "That is because you have only one eye. Come to me and I will be both your eyes." But I said, "I must show my people how to use their knives against The Beast, as you showed me how to use my knife." I said this because the Magic Knife does not balance like the flint. She said, "What you have done, you have done for the sake of a woman, and not for the sake of your people." I asked of her, "Then why did the God accept my right eye, and why are you so angry?" She answered, "Because any man can lie to a God, but no man can lie to a woman. And I am not angry with you. I am only very sorrowful for you. Wait a little, and you will see out of your one eye why I am sorry." So she hid herself.

'I went back with my people, each one carrying his Knife, and making it sing in the air – *tssee-sssse*. The Flint never sings. It mutters – *ump-ump*. The Beast heard. The Beast saw. *He* knew! Everywhere he ran away from us. We all laughed. As we walked over the grass my Mother's brother – the Chief on the Men's Side – he took off his Chief's necklace of yellow sea-stones.'

'How? Eh? Oh, I remember! Amber,' said Puck.

'And would have put them on my neck. I said, "No, I am content. What does my one eye matter if my other eye sees fat sheep and fat children running about safely?' My Mother's brother said to them, "I told you he would never take such things." Then they began to sing a song in the Old Tongue – *The Song of Tyr*. I sang with them, but my Mother's brother

553

said, "This is *your* song, O Buyer of the Knife. Let *us* sing it, Tyr."

'Even then I did not understand, till I saw that – that no man stepped on my shadow; and I knew that they thought me to be a God, like the God Tyr, who gave his right hand to conquer a Great Beast.'

'By the Fire in the Belly of the Flint was that so?' Puck rapped out.

'By my Knife and the Naked Chalk, so it was! They made way for my shadow as though it had been a Priestess walking to the Barrows of the Dead. I was afraid. I said to myself, "My Mother and my Maiden will know I am not Tyr." But *still* I was afraid, with the fear of a man who falls into a steep flint-pit while he runs, and feels that it will be hard to climb out.

'When we came to the Dew-ponds all our people were there. The men showed their knives and told their tale. The sheepguards also had seen The Beast flying from us. The Beast went west across the river in packs – howling! He knew the Knife had come to the Naked Chalk at last – at last! *He* knew! So my work was done. I looked for my Maiden among the Priestesses. She looked at me, but she did not smile. She made the sign to me that our Priestesses must make when they sacrifice to the Old Dead in the Barrows. I would have spoken, but my Mother's brother made himself my Mouth, as though I had been one of the Old Dead in the Barrows for whom our Priests speak to the people on Midsummer Mornings.'

'I remember. Well I remember those Midsummer Mornings!' said Puck.

'Then I went away angrily to my Mother's house. She would have knelt before me. Then I was more angry, but she said, "Only a God would have spoken to me thus, a Priestess. A man would have feared the punishment of the Gods." I looked at her and I laughed. I could not stop my unhappy laughing. They called me from the door by the name of Tyr himself. A young man with whom I had watched my first flocks, and chipped my first arrow, and fought my first Beast, called me by that name in the Old Tongue. He asked my leave to take my

Maiden. His eyes were lowered, his hands were on his fore-head. He was full of the fear of a God, but of *me*, a man, he had no fear when he asked. I did not kill him. I said, "Call the maiden." She came also without fear – this very one that had waited for me, that had talked with me, by our Dew-ponds. Being a Priestess, she lifted her eyes to me. As I look on a hill or a cloud, so she looked at me. She spoke in the Old Tongue which Priestesses use when they make prayers to the Old Dead in the Barrows. She asked leave that she might light the fire in my companion's house – and that I should bless their children. I did not kill her. I heard my own voice, little and cold, say, "Let it be as you desire," and they went away hand in hand. My heart grew little and cold; a wind shouted in my ears; my eye darkened. I said to my Mother, "Can a God die?" I heard her say, "What is it? What is it, my son?" and I fell into darkness full of hammer-noise. I was not.'

'Oh, poor – poor God!' said Puck. 'And your wise Mother?'

'*She* knew. As soon as I dropped she knew. When my spirit came back I heard her whisper in my ear, "Whether you live or die, or are made different, I am your Mother." That was good – better even than the water she gave me and the going away of the sickness. Though I was ashamed to have fallen down, yet I was very glad. She was glad too. Neither of us wished to lose the other. There is only the one Mother for the one son. I heaped the fire for her, and barred the doors, and sat at her feet as before I went away, and she combed my hair, and sang.

'I said at last, "What is to be done to the people who say that I am Tyr?"

'She said, "He who has done a God-like thing must bear himself like a God. I see no way out of it. The people are now your sheep till you die. You cannot drive them off."

'I said, "This is a heavier sheep than I can lift." She said, "In time it will grow easy. In time perhaps you will not lay it down for any maiden anywhere. Be wise – be very wise, my son, for nothing is left you except the words, and the songs, and the worship of a God."'

'Oh, poor God!' said Puck. 'But those are not altogether bad things.'

'I know they are not; but I would sell them all – all – all for one small child of my own, smearing himself with the ashes of our own house-fire.'

He wrenched his knife from the turf, thrust it into his belt and stood up.

'And yet, what else could I have done?' he said. 'The sheep are the people.'

'It is a very old tale,' Puck answered. 'I have heard the like of it not only on the Naked Chalk, but also among the Trees – under Oak, and Ash, and Thorn.'

The afternoon shadows filled all the quiet emptiness of Norton Pit. The children heard the sheep-bells and Young Jim's busy bark above them, and they scrambled up the slope to the level.

'We let you have your sleep out,' said Mr Dudeney, as the flock scattered before them. 'It's making for tea-time now.'

'Look what I've found,' said Dan, and held up a little blue flint arrow-head as fresh as though it had been chipped that very day.

'Oh,' said Mr Dudeney, 'the closeter you be to the turf the more you're apt to see things. I've found 'em often. Some says the fairies made 'em, but I says they was made by folks like ourselves – only a goodish time back. They're lucky to keep. Now, you couldn't ever have slept – not to any profit – among your father's trees same as you've laid out on Naked Chalk – could you?'

'One doesn't want to sleep in the woods,' said Una.

'Then what's the good of 'em?' said Mr Dudeney. 'Might as well set in the barn all day. Fetch 'em 'long, Jim boy!'

The Downs, that looked so bare and hot when they came, were full of delicious little shadow-dimples; the smell of the thyme and the salt mixed together on the south-west drift from the still sea; their eyes dazzled with the low sun, and the long grass under it looked golden. The sheep knew where their fold was, so Young Jim came back to his master, and they all four strolled home, the scabious-heads swishing about their ankles, and their shadows streaking behind them like the shadows of giants.

IN THE SAME BOAT

'A throbbing vein,' said Dr Gilbert soothingly, 'is the mother of delusion.'

'Then how do you account for my knowing when the thing is due?' Conroy's voice rose almost to a break.

'Of course, but you should have consulted a doctor before using – palliatives.'

'It was driving me mad. And now I can't give them up.'

'Not so bad as that! One doesn't form fatal habits at twenty-five. Think again. Were you ever frightened as a child?'

'I don't remember. It began when I was a boy.'

'With or without the spasm? By the way, do you mind describing the spasm again?'

'Well,' said Conroy, twisting in the chair, 'I'm no musician, but suppose you were a violin-string – vibrating – and some one put his finger on you? As if a finger were put on the naked soul! Awful!'

'So's indigestion – so's nightmare – while it lasts.'

'But the horror afterwards knocks me out for days. And the waiting for it . . . and then this drug habit! It can't go on!' He shook as he spoke, and the chair creaked.

'My dear fellow,' said the doctor, 'when you're older you'll know what burdens the best of us carry. A fox to every Spartan.'

'That doesn't help *me*. I can't! I can't!' cried Conroy, and burst into tears.

'Don't apologise,' said Gilbert, when the paroxysm ended. 'I'm used to people coming a little – unstuck in this room.'

'It's those tabloids!' Conroy stamped his foot feebly as he

blew his nose. 'They've knocked me out. I used to be fit once. Oh, I've tried exercise and everything. But – if one sits down for a minute when it's due – even at four in the morning it runs up behind one.'

'Ye-es. Many things come in the quiet of the morning. You always know when the visitation is due?'

'What would I give not to be sure!' he sobbed.

'We'll put that aside for the moment. I'm thinking of a case where what we'll call anæmia of the brain was masked (I don't say cured) by vibration. He couldn't sleep, or thought he couldn't, but a steamer voyage and the thump of the screw—'

'A steamer? After what I've told you!' Conroy almost shrieked. 'I'd sooner . . .'

'Of course *not* a steamer in your case, but a long railway journey the next time you think it will trouble you. It sounds absurd, but—'

'I'd try anything. I nearly have,' Conroy sighed.

'Nonsense! I've given you a tonic that will clear *that* notion from your head. Give the train a chance, and don't begin the journey by bucking yourself up with tabloids. Take them along, but hold them in reserve – in reserve.'

'D'you think I've self-control enough, after what you've heard?' said Conroy.

Dr Gilbert smiled. 'Yes. After what I've seen,' he glanced round the room, 'I have no hesitation in saying you have quite as much self-control as many other people. I'll write you later about your journey. Meantime, the tonic,' and he gave some general directions before Conroy left.

An hour later Dr Gilbert hurried to the links, where the others of his regular week-end game awaited him. It was a rigid round, played as usual at the trot, for the tension of the week lay as heavy on the two King's Counsels and Sir John Chartres as on Gilbert. The lawyers were old enemies of the Admiralty Court, and Sir John of the frosty eyebrows and Abernethy manner was bracketed with, but before, Rutherford Gilbert among nerve-specialists.

At the Club-house afterwards the lawyers renewed their

squabble over a tangled collision case, and the doctors as naturally compared professional matters.

'Lies – all lies,' said Sir John, when Gilbert had told him Conroy's trouble. '*Post hoc, propter hoc.* The man or woman who drugs is *ipso facto* a liar. You've no imagination.'

'' 'Pity you haven't a little – occasionally.

'I have believed a certain type of patient in my time. It's always the same. For reasons not given in the consulting-room they take to the drug. Certain symptoms follow. They will swear to you, and believe it, that they took the drug to mask the symptoms. What does your man use? Najdolene? I thought so. I had practically the duplicate of your case last Thursday. Same old Najdolene – same old lie.'

'Tell me the symptoms, and I'll draw my own inferences, Johnnie.'

'Symptoms! The girl was rank poisoned with Najdolene. Ramping, stamping possession. Gad, I thought she'd have the chandelier down.'

'Mine came unstuck too, and he has the physique of a bull,' said Gilbert. 'What delusions had yours?'

'Faces – faces with mildew on them. In any other walk of life we'd call it the Horrors. She told me, of course, she took the drugs to mask the faces. *Post hoc, propter hoc* again. All liars!'

'What's that?' said the senior KC quickly. 'Sounds professional.'

'Go away! Not for you, Sandy.' Sir John turned a shoulder against him and walked with Gilbert in the chill evening.

'To Conroy in his chambers came, one week later, this letter:

'Dear Mr Conroy – If your plan of a night's trip on the 17th still holds good, and you have no particular destination in view, you could do me a kindness. A Miss Henschil, in whom I am interested, goes down to the West by the 10.8 from Waterloo (Number 3 platform) on that night. She is not exactly an invalid, but, like so many of us, a little shaken in her nerves. Her maid, of course, accompanies her, but if I knew you were in the same train it would be an additional source of strength. Will you please write and let me know whether the 10.8 from Waterloo, Number 3 platform, on the 17th, suits you, and I will meet you there? Don't forget my caution, and keep up the tonic. – Yours sincerely,

L. Rutherford Gilbert

'He knows I'm scarcely fit to look after myself,' was Conroy's thought. 'And he wants me to look after a woman!'

Yet, at the end of half an hour's irresolution, he accepted.

Now Conroy's trouble, which had lasted for years, was this:

On a certain night, while he lay between sleep and wake, he would be overtaken by a long shuddering sigh, which he learned to know was the sign that his brain had once more conceived its horror, and in time – in due time – would bring it forth.

Drugs could so well veil that horror that it shuffled along no worse than as a freezing dream in a procession of disorderly dreams; but over the return of the event drugs had no control. Once that sigh had passed his lips the thing was inevitable, and through the days granted before its rebirth he walked in torment. For the first two years he had striven to fend it off by distractions, but neither exercise nor drink availed. Then he had come to the tabloids of the excellent M. Najdol. These guarantee, on the label, 'Refreshing and absolutely natural sleep to the soul-weary.' They are carried in a case with a spring which presses one scented tabloid to the end of the tube, whence it can be lipped off in stroking the moustache or adjusting the veil.

Three years of M. Najdol's preparations do not fit a man for many careers. His friends, who knew he did not drink, assumed that Conroy had strained his heart through valiant outdoor exercises, and Conroy had with some care invented an imaginary doctor, symptoms, and regimen, which he discussed with them and with his mother in Hereford. She maintained that he would grow out of it, and recommended nux vomica.

When at last Conroy faced a real doctor, it was, he hoped, to be saved from suicide by a strait-waistcoat. Yet Dr Gilbert had but given him more drugs – a tonic, for instance, that would couple railway carriages – and had advised a night in the train. Not alone the horrors of a railway journey (for which a man who dare keep no servant must e'en pack, label, and address his own bag), but the necessity for holding himself in hand before a stranger 'a little shaken in her nerves.'

He spent a long forenoon packing, because when he assembled and counted things his mind slid off to the hours that remained of the day before his night, and he found himself counting minutes aloud. At such times the injustice of his fate would drive him to revolts which no servant should witness, but on this evening Dr Gilbert's tonic held him fairly calm while he put up his patent razors.

Waterloo Station shook him into real life. The change for his ticket needed concentration, if only to prevent shillings and pence turning into minutes at the booking-office; and he spoke quickly to a porter about the disposition of his bag. The old 10.8 from Waterloo to the West was an all-night caravan that halted, in the interests of the milk traffic, at almost every station.

Dr Gilbert stood by the door of the one composite corridor coach; an older and stouter man behind him. 'So glad you're here!' he cried. 'Let me get your ticket.'

'Certainly not,' Conroy answered. 'I got it myself – long ago. My bag's in too,' he added proudly.

'I beg your pardon. Miss Henschil's here. I'll introduce you.'

'But – but,' he stammered – 'think of the state I'm in. If anything happens I shall collapse.'

'Not you. You'd rise to the occasion like a bird. And as for the self-control you were talking of the other day' – Gilbert swung him round – 'look!'

A young man in an ulster over a silk-faced frock-coat stood by the carriage window, weeping shamelessly.

'Oh, but that's only drink,' Conroy said. 'I haven't had one of my – my things since lunch.'

'Excellent!' said Gilbert. 'I knew I could depend on you. Come along. Wait for a minute, Chartres.'

A tall woman, veiled, sat by the far window. She bowed her

head as the doctor murmured Conroy knew not what. Then he disappeared and the inspector came for tickets.

'My maid – next compartment,' she said slowly.

Conroy showed his ticket, but in returning it to the sleeve-pocket of his ulster the little silver Najdolene case slipped from his glove and fell to the floor. He snatched it up as the moving train flung him into his seat.

'How nice!' said the woman. She leisurely lifted her veil, unbuttoned the first button of her left glove, and pressed out from its palm a Najdolene case.

'Don't!' said Conroy, not realising he had spoken.

'I beg your pardon.' The deep voice was measured, even, and low. Conroy knew what made it so.

'I said "don't"! He wouldn't like you to do it!'

'No, he would not.' She held the tube with its ever-presented tabloid between finger and thumb. 'But aren't you one of the – ah – "soul-weary" too?'

'That's why. Oh, please don't! Not at first. I – I haven't had one since morning. You – you'll set me off!'

'You? Are you so far gone as that?'

He nodded, pressing his palms together. The train jolted through Vauxhall points, and was welcomed with the clang of empty milk-cans for the West.

After long silence she lifted her great eyes, and, with an innocence that would have deceived any sound man, asked Conroy to call her maid to bring her a forgotten book.

Conroy shook his head. 'No. Our sort can't read. Don't!'

'Were you sent to watch me?' The voice never changed.

'Me? I need a keeper myself much more – *this* night of all!'

'This night? Have you a night, then? They disbelieved *me* when I told them of mine.' She leaned back and laughed, always slowly. 'Aren't doctors stu-upid? They don't know.'

She leaned her elbow on her knee, lifted her veil that had fallen, and, chin in hand, stared at him. He looked at her – till his eyes were blurred with tears.

'Have *I* been there, think you?' she said.

'Surely – surely,' Conroy answered, for he had well seen the fear and the horror that lived behind the heavy-lidded eyes, the fine tracing on the broad forehead, and the guard set about the desirable mouth.

'Then – suppose we have one – just one apiece? I've gone without since this afternoon.'

He put up his hand, and would have shouted, but his voice broke.

'Don't! Can't you see that it helps me to help you to keep it off? Don't let's both go down together.'

'But I want one. It's a poor heart that never rejoices. Just one. It's my night.'

'It's mine – too. My sixty-fourth, fifth, sixth, seventh.' He shut his lips firmly against the tide of visualised numbers that threatened to carry him along.

'Ah, it's only my thirty-ninth.' She paused as he had done. 'I wonder if I shall last into the sixties . . . Talk to me or I shall go crazy. You're a man. You're the stronger vessel. Tell me when you went to pieces.'

'One, two, three, four, five, six, seven – eight – I beg your pardon.'

'Not in the least. I always pretend I've dropped a stitch of my knitting. I count the days till the last day, then the hours, then the minutes. Do you?'

'I don't think I've done very much else for the last—' said Conroy, shivering, for the night was cold, with a chill he recognised.

'Oh, how comforting to find some one who can talk sense! It's not always the same date, is it?'

'What difference would that make?' He unbuttoned his ulster with a jerk. 'You're a sane woman. Can't you see the wicked – wicked – wicked' (dust flew from the padded arm-rest as he struck it) 'unfairness of it? What have I done?'

She laid her large hand on his shoulder very firmly.

'If you begin to think over that,' she said, 'you'll go to pieces and be ashamed. Tell me yours, and I'll tell you mine. Only be quiet – be quiet, lad, or you'll set me off!' She made shift to soothe him, though her chin trembled.

'Well,' said he at last, picking at the arm-rest between them, 'mine's nothing much, of course.'

'Don't be a fool! That's for doctors – and mothers.'

'It's Hell,' Conroy muttered. 'It begins on a steamer – on a stifling hot night. I come out of my cabin. I pass through the saloon where the stewards have rolled up the carpets, and the boards are bare and hot and soapy.'

'I've travelled too,' she said.

'Ah! I come on deck. I walk down a covered alleyway. Butcher's meat, bananas, oil, that sort of smell.'

Again she nodded.

'It's a lead-coloured steamer, and the sea's lead-coloured. Perfectly smooth sea – perfectly still ship, except for the engines running, and her waves going off in lines and lines and lines – dull grey. All this time I know something's going to happen.'

'*I* know. Something going to happen,' she whispered.

'Then I hear a thud in the engine-room. Then the noise of machinery falling down – like fire-irons – and then two most awful yells. They're more like hoots, and I know – I know while I listen – that it means that two men have died as they hooted. It was their last breath hooting out of them – in most awful pain. Do you understand?'

'I ought to. Go on.'

'That's the first part. Then I hear bare feet running along the alleyway. One of the scalded men comes up behind me and says quite distinctly, "My friend! All is lost!" Then he taps me on the shoulder and I hear him drop down dead.' He panted and wiped his forehead.

'So that is your night?' she said.

'That is my night. It comes every few weeks – so many days after I get what I call sentence. Then I begin to count.'

'Get sentence? D'you mean *this*? 'She half closed her eyes, drew a deep breath, and shuddered. "Notice" I call it. Sir John thought it was all lies.'

She had unpinned her hat and thrown it on the seat opposite, showing the immense mass of her black hair, rolled low in the nape of the columnar neck and looped over the left ear. But Conroy had no eyes except for her grave eyes.

'Listen now!' said she. 'I walk down a road, a white sandy

road near the sea. There are broken fences on either side, and Men come and look at me over them.'

'Just men? Do they speak?'

'They try to. Their faces are all mildewy – eaten away,' and she hid her face for an instant with her left hand. 'It's the Faces – the Faces!'

'Yes, like my two hoots. *I* know.'

'Ah! But the place itself – the bareness – and the glitter and the salt smells, and the wind blowing the sand! The Men run after me and I run . . . I know what's coming too. One of them touches me.'

'Yes! What comes then? We've both shirked that.'

'One awful shock – not palpitation, but shock, shock, shock!'

'As though your soul were being stopped – as you'd stop a finger-bowl humming?' he said.

'Just that,' she answered. 'One's very soul – the soul that one lives by – stopped. So!'

She drove her thumb deep into the arm-rest. 'And now,' she whined to him, 'now that we've stirred each other up this way, mightn't we have just one?'

'No,' said Conroy, shaking. 'Let's hold on. We're past'– he peered out of the black windows – 'Woking. There's the Necropolis. How long till dawn?'

'Oh, cruel long yet. If one dozes for a minute, it catches one.'

'And how d'you find that this' – he tapped the palm of his glove – 'helps you?'

'It covers up the thing from being too real – if one takes enough – you know. Only – only – one loses everything else. I've been no more than a bogie-girl for two years. What would you give to be real again? This lying's such a nuisance.'

'One must protect oneself – and there's one's mother to think of,' he answered.

'True. I hope allowances are made for us somewhere. Our burden – can you hear? – our burden is heavy enough.'

She rose, towering into the roof of the carriage. Conroy's ungentle grip pulled her back.

'Now *you* are foolish. Sit down,' said he.

'But the cruelty of it! Can't you see it? Don't you feel it? Let's take one now – Before I—'

'Sit down!' cried Conroy, and the sweat stood again on his forehead. He had fought through a few nights, and had been defeated on more, and he knew the rebellion that flares beyond control to exhaustion.

She smoothed her hair and dropped back, but for a while her head and throat moved with the sickening motion of a captured wry-neck.

'Once,' she said, spreading out her hands, 'I ripped my counterpane from end to end. That takes strength. I had it then. I've little now. "All dorn," as my little niece says. And you, lad?'

'"All dorn"! Let me keep your case for you till the morning.'

'But the cold feeling is beginning.'

'Lend it me, then.'

'And the drag down my right side. I shan't be able to move in a minute.'

'I can scarcely lift my arm myself,' said Conroy. 'We're in for it.'

'Then why are you so foolish? You know it'll be easier if we have only one – only one apiece.'

She was lifting the case to her mouth. With tremendous effort Conroy caught it. The two moved like jointed dolls, and when their hands met it was as wood on wood.

'You must – not!' said Conroy. His jaws stiffened, and the cold climbed from his feet up.

'Why – must – I – not?' She repeated the words idiotically.

Conroy could only shake his head, while he bore down on the hand and the case in it.

Her speech went from her altogether. The wonderful lips rested half over the even teeth, the breath was in the nostrils only, the eyes dulled, the face set grey, and through the glove the hand struck like ice.

Presently her soul came back and stood behind her eyes – only thing that had life in all that place – stood and looked for

Conroy's soul. He too was fettered in every limb, but somewhere at an immense distance he heard his heart going about its work as the engine-room carries on through and beneath the all but overwhelming wave. His one hope, he knew, was not to lose the eyes that clung to his, because there was an Evil abroad which would possess him if he looked aside by a hairbreadth.

The rest was darkness through which some distant planet spun while cymbals clashed. (Beyond Farnborough the 10.8 rolls out many empty milk-cans at every halt.) Then a body came to life with intolerable pricklings. Limb by limb, after agonies of terror, that body returned to him, steeped in most perfect physical weariness such as follows a long day's rowing. He saw the heavy lids droop over her eyes – the watcher behind them departed – and, his soul sinking into assured peace, Conroy slept.

Light on his eyes and a salt breath roused him without shock. Her hand still held his. She slept, forehead down upon it, but the movement of his waking waked her too, and she sneezed like a child.

'I – I think it's morning,' said Conroy.

'And nothing has happened! Did you see your Men? I didn't see my Faces. Does it mean we've escaped? Did – did you take any after I went to sleep? I'll swear *I* didn't,' she stammered.

'No, there wasn't any need. We've slept through it.'

'No need! Thank God! There was no need! Oh, look!'

The train was running under red cliffs along a sea-wall washed by waves that were colourless in the early light. Southward the sun rose mistily upon the Channel.

She leaned out of the window and breathed to the bottom of her lungs, while the wind wrenched down her dishevelled hair and blew it below her waist.

'Well!' she said with splendid eyes. 'Aren't you still waiting for something to happen?'

'No. Not till next time. We've been let off,' Conroy answered, breathing as deeply as she.

'Then we ought to say our prayers.'

'What nonsense! Some one will see us.'

'We needn't kneel. Stand up and say "Our Father." We *must*!'

It was the first time since childhood that Conroy had prayed. They laughed hysterically when a curve threw them against an arm-rest.

'Now for breakfast!' she cried. 'My maid – Nurse Blaber – has the basket and things. It'll be ready in twenty minutes. Oh! Look at my hair!' and she went out laughing.

Conroy's first discovery, made without fumbling or counting letters on taps, was that the London and South Western's allowance of washing-water is inadequate. He used every drop, rioting in the cold tingle on neck and arms. To shave in a moving train balked him, but the next halt gave him a chance, which, to his own surprise, he took. As he stared at himself in the mirror he smiled and nodded. There were points about this person with the clear, if sunken, eye and the almost uncompressed mouth. But when he bore his bag back to his compartment, the weight of it on a limp arm humbled that new pride.

'My friend,' he said, half aloud, 'you go into training. You're putty.'

She met him in the spare compartment, where her maid had laid breakfast.

'By Jove,' he said, halting at the doorway, 'I hadn't realised how beautiful you were!'

'The same to you, lad. Sit down. I could eat a horse.'

'I shouldn't,' said the maid quietly. 'The less you eat the better.' She was a small, freckled woman, with light fluffy hair and pale-blue eyes that looked through all veils.

'This is Miss Blaber,' said Miss Henschil. 'He's one of the soul-weary too, Nursey.'

'I know it. But when one has just given it up a full meal doesn't agree. That's why I've only brought you bread and butter.'

She went out quietly, and Conroy reddened.

'We're still children, you see,' said Miss Henschil. 'But I'm well enough to feel some shame of it. D'you take sugar?'

They starved together heroically, and Nurse Blaber was good enough to signify approval when she came to clear away.

'Nursey?' Miss Henschil insinuated, and flushed.

'Do you smoke?' said the nurse coolly to Conroy.

'I haven't in years, Now you mention it, I think I'd like a cigarette – or something.'

'I used to. D'you think it would keep me quiet?' Miss Henschil said.

'Perhaps. Try these.' The nurse handed them her cigarette-case.

'Don't take anything else,' she commanded, and went away with the tea-basket.

'Good!' grunted Conroy, between mouthfuls of tobacco.

'Better than nothing,' said Miss Henschil; but for a while they felt ashamed, yet with the comfort of children punished together.

'Now,' she whispered, 'who were you when you were a man?'

Conroy told her, and in return she gave him her history. It delighted them both to deal once more in worldly concerns – families, names, places, and dates – with a person of understanding.

She came, she said, of Lancashire folk – wealthy cotton-spinners, who still kept the broadened *a* and slurred aspirate of the old stock. She lived with an old masterful mother in an opulent world north of Lancaster Gate, where people in Society gave parties at a Mecca called the Langham Hotel.

She herself had been launched into Society there, and the flowers at the ball had cost eighty-seven pounds; but, being reckoned peculiar, she had made few friends among her own sex. She had attracted many men, for she was a beauty – *the* beauty, in fact, of Society, she said.

She spoke utterly without shame or reticence, as a life-prisoner tells his past to a fellow-prisoner; and Conroy nodded across the smoke-rings.

'Do you remember when you got into the carriage?' she asked. '(Oh, I wish I had some knitting!) Did you notice aught, lad?'

Conroy thought back. It was ages since. 'Wasn't there some one outside the door – crying?' he asked.

'He's – he's the little man I was engaged to,' she said. 'But I made him break it off. I told him 'twas no good. But he won't, yo' see.'

'*That* fellow? Why, he doesn't come up to your shoulder.'

'That's naught to do with it. I think all the world of him. I'm a foolish wench' – her speech wandered as she settled herself cosily, one elbow on the arm-rest 'We'd been engaged – I couldn't help that – and he worships the ground I tread on. But it's no use. I'm not responsible, you see. His two sisters are against it, though I've the money. They're right, but they think it's the dri-ink,' she drawled. 'They're Methody – the Skinners. You see, their grandfather that started the Patton Mills, he died o' the dri-ink.'

'I see,' said Conroy. The grave face before him under the lifted veil was troubled.

'George Skinner.' She breathed it softly. 'I'd make him a good wife, by God's gra-ace – if I could. But it's no use. I'm not responsible. But he'll not take "No" for an answer. I used to call him "Toots." He's of no consequence, yo' see.'

'That's in Dickens,' said Conroy, quite quickly, 'I haven't thought of Toots for years. He was at Doctor Blimber's.'

'And so – that's my trouble,' she concluded, ever so slightly wringing her hands. 'But I – don't you think – there's hope now?'

'Eh?' said Conroy. 'Oh yes! This is the first time I've turned my corner without help. With your help, I should say.'

'It'll come back, though.'

'Then shall we meet it in the same way? Here's my card. Write me your train, and we'll go together.'

'Yes. We must do that. But between times – when we want—' She looked at her palm, the four fingers working on it. 'It's hard to give 'em up.'

'But think what we have gained already, and let me have the case to keep.'

She shook her head, and threw her cigarette out of the window. 'Not yet.'

'Then let's lend our cases to Nurse, and we'll get through to-day on cigarettes. I'll call her while we feel strong.'

She hesitated, but yielded at last, and Nurse accepted the offerings with a smile.

'*You'll* be all right,' she said to Miss Henschil. 'But if I were you' – to Conroy –, 'I'd take strong exercise.'

When they reached their destination Conroy set himself to obey Nurse Blaber. He had no remembrance of that day, except one streak of blue sea to his left, gorse-bushes to his right, and, before him, a coast-guard's track marked with white-washed stones that he counted up to the far thousands. As he returned to the little town he saw Miss Henschil on the beach below the cliffs. She kneeled at Nurse Blaber's feet, weeping and pleading.

Twenty-five days later a telegram came to Conroy's rooms: '*Notice given. Waterloo again. Twenty-fourth.*' That same evening he was wakened by the shudder and the sigh that told him his sentence had gone forth. Yet he reflected on his pillow that he had, in spite of lapses, snatched something like three weeks of life, which included several rides on a horse before breakfast – the hour one most craves Najdolene; five consecutive evenings on the river at Hammersmith in a tub where he had well stretched the white arms that passing crews mocked at; a game of rackets at his club; three dinners, one small dance, and one human flirtation with a human woman. More notable still, he had settled his month's accounts, only once confusing petty cash with the days of grace allowed him. Next morning he rode his hired beast in the park victoriously. He saw Miss Henschil on horseback near Lancaster Gate, talking to a young man at the railings.

She wheeled and cantered toward him.

'By Jove! How well you look!' he cried, without salutation. 'I didn't know you rode.'

'I used to once,' she replied. 'I'm all soft now.'

They swept off together down the ride.

'Your beast pulls,' he said.

'Wa-ant him to. Gi-gives me something to think of. How've

you been?' she panted. 'I wish chemists' shops hadn't red lights.'

'Have you slipped out and bought some, then?'

'You don't know Nursey. Eh, but it's good to be on a horse again! This chap cost me two hundred.'

'Then you've been swindled,' said Conroy.

'I know it, but it's no odds. I must go back to Toots and send him away. He's neglecting his work for me.'

She swung her heavy-topped animal on his none too sound hocks. ' 'Sentence come, lad?'

'Yes. But I'm not minding it so much this time.'

'Waterloo, then – and God help us!' She thundered back to the little frock-coated figure that waited faithfully near the gate.

Conroy felt the spring sun on his shoulders and trotted home. That evening he went out with a man in a pair oar, and was rowed to a standstill. But the other man owned he could not have kept the pace five minutes longer.

He carried his bag all down Number 3 platform at Waterloo, and hove it with one hand into the rack.

'Well done!' said Nurse Blaber, in the corridor. 'We've improved too.'

Dr Gilbert and an older man came out of the next compartment.

'Hallo!' said Gilbert. 'Why haven't you been to see me, Mr Conroy? Come under the lamp. Take off your hat. No – no. Sit, you young giant. Ve-ry good. Look here a minute, Johnnie.'

A little, round-bellied, hawk-faced person glared at him.

'Gilbert was right about the beauty of the beast,' he muttered. 'D'you keep it in your glove now?' he went on, and punched Conroy in the short ribs.

'No,' said Conroy meekly, but without coughing. 'Nowhere – on my honour! I've chucked it for good.'

'Wait till you are a sound man before you say *that*, Mr Conroy.' Sir John Chartres stumped out, saying to Gilbert in the corridor, 'It's all very fine, but the question is shall I or we

"Sir Pandarus of Troy become," eh? We're bound to think of the children.'

'Have you been vetted?' said Miss Henschil, a few minutes after the train started. 'May I sit with you? I – I don't trust myself yet. I can't give up as easily as you can, seemingly.'

'Can't you? I never saw any one so improved in a month.'

'Look here!' She reached across to the rack, single-handed lifted Conroy's bag, and held it at arm's length. 'I counted ten slowly. And I didn't think of hours or minutes,' she boasted.

'Don't remind me,' he cried.

'Ah! Now I've reminded myself. I wish I hadn't. Do you think it'll be easier for us to-night?'

'Oh, don't.' The smell of the carriage had brought back all his last trip to him, and Conroy moved uneasily.

'I'm sorry. I've brought some games,' she went on. 'Draughts and cards – but they all mean counting. I wish I'd brought chess, but I can't play chess. What can we do? Talk about something.'

'Well, how's Toots, to begin with?' said Conroy.

'Why? Did you see him on the platform?'

'No. Was he there? I didn't notice.'

'Oh yes. He doesn't understand. He's desperately jealous. I told him it doesn't matter. Will you please let me hold your hand? I believe I'm beginning to get the chill.'

'Toots ought to envy me,' said Conroy.

'He does. He paid you a high compliment the other night. He's taken to calling again – in spite of all they say.'

Conroy inclined his head. He felt cold, and knew surely he would be colder.

'He said,' she yawned. '(Beg your pardon.) He said he couldn't see how I could help falling in love with a man like you; and he called himself a damned little rat, and he beat his head on the piano last night.'

'The piano? You play, then?'

'Only to him. He thinks the world of my accomplishments. Then I told him I wouldn't have you if you were the last man on earth instead of only the best-looking – not with a million in each stocking.'

'No, not with a million in each stocking,' said Conroy vehemently. 'Isn't that odd?'

'I suppose so – to any one who doesn't know. Well, where was I? Oh, George as good as told me I was deceiving him, and he wanted to go away without saying good-night. He hates standing a-tiptoe, but he must if I won't sit down.'

Conroy would have smiled, but the chill that foreran the coming of the Lier-in-Wait was upon him, and his hand closed warningly on hers.

'And – and so—' she was trying to say, when her hour also overtook her, leaving alive only the fear-dilated eyes that turned to Conroy. Hand froze on hand and the body with it as they waited for the horror in the blackness that heralded it. Yet through the worst Conroy saw, at an uncountable distance, one minute glint of light in his night. Thither would he go and escape his fear; and behold, that light was the light in the watchtower of her eyes, where her locked soul signalled to his soul; 'Look at me!'

In time, from him and from her, the Thing sheered aside, that each soul might step down and resume its own concerns. He thought confusedly of people on the skirts of a thunderstorm, withdrawing from windows where the torn night is, to their known and furnished beds. Then he dozed, till in some drowsy turn his hand fell from her warmed hand.

'That's all. The Faces haven't come,' he heard her say. 'All – thank God! I don't feel even I need what Nursey promised me. Do you?'

'No.' He rubbed his eyes. 'But don't make too sure.'

'Certainly not. We shall have to try again next month. I'm afraid it will be an awful nuisance for you.'

'Not to me, I assure you,' said Conroy, and they leaned back and laughed at the flatness of the words, after the hells through which they had just risen.

'And now,' she said, strict eyes on Conroy, '*why* wouldn't you take me – not with a million in each stocking?'

'I don't know. That's what I've been puzzling over.'

'So have I. We're as handsome a couple as I've ever seen. Are you well off, lad?'

'They call me so,' said Conroy, smiling.

'That's North country.' She laughed again. 'Setting aside my good looks and yours, I've four thousand a year of my own, and the rents should make it six. That's a match some old cats would lap tea all night to fettle up.'

'It is. Lucky Toots!' said Conroy.

'Ay,' she answered, 'he'll be the luckiest lad in London if I win through. Who's yours?'

'No – no one, dear. I've been in Hell for years. I only want to get out and be alive and – so on. Isn't that reason enough?'

'Maybe, for a man. But I never minded things much till George came. I was all stu-upid like.'

'So was I, but now I think I can live. It ought to be less next month, oughtn't it?' he said.

'I hope so. Ye-es. There's nothing much for a maid except to be married, and – ask no more. Whoever yours is, when you've found her, she shall have a wedding present from Mrs George Skinner that—'

'But she wouldn't understand it any more than Toots.'

'He doesn't matter – except to me. I can't keep my eyes open, thank God! Good-night, lad.'

Conroy followed her with his eyes. Beauty there was, grace there was, strength, and enough of the rest to drive better men than George Skinner to beat their heads on piano-tops – but for the new-found life of him Conroy could not feel one flutter of instinct or emotion that turned to herward. He put up his feet and fell asleep, dreaming of a joyous, normal world recovered – with interest on arrears. There were many things in it, but no one face of any one woman.

Thrice afterward they took the same train, and each time their trouble shrank and weakened. Miss Henschil talked of Toots, his multiplied calls, the things he had said to his sisters, the much worse things his sisters had replied; of the late (he seemed very dead to them) M. Najdol's gifts for the soul-weary; of shopping, of house rents, and the cost of really artistic furniture and linen.

Conroy explained the exercises in which he delighted –

mighty labours of play undertaken against other mighty men, till he sweated and; having bathed, slept. He had visited his mother, too, in Hereford, and he talked something of her and of the home-life, which his body, cut out of all clean life for five years, innocently and deeply enjoyed. Nurse Blaber was a little interested in Conroy's mother, but, as a rule, she smoked her cigarette and read her paper-backed novels in her own compartment.

On their last trip she volunteered to sit with them, and buried herself in *The Cloister and the Hearth* while they whispered together. On that occasion (it was near Salisbury) at two in the morning, when the Lier-in-Wait brushed them with his wing, it meant no more than that they should cease talk for the instant, and for the instant hold hands, as even utter strangers on the deep may do when their ship rolls underfoot.

'But still,' said Nurse Blaber, not looking up, 'I think your Mr Skinner might feel jealous of all this.'

'It would be difficult to explain,' said Conroy.

'Then you'd better not be at my wedding,' Miss Henschil laughed.

'After all we've gone through, too. But I suppose you ought to leave me out. Is the day fixed?' he cried.

'Twenty-second of September – in spite of both his sisters. I can risk it now.' Her face was glorious as she flushed.

'My dear chap!' He shook hands unreservedly, and she gave back his grip without flinching. 'I can't tell you how pleased I am!'

'Gracious Heavens!' said Nurse Blaber, in a new voice. 'Oh, I beg your pardon. I forgot I wasn't paid to be surprised.'

'What at? Oh, I see!' Miss Henschil explained to Conroy. 'She expected you were going to kiss me, or I was going to kiss you, or something.'

'After all you've gone through, as Mr Conroy said.'

'But I couldn't, could you?' said Miss Henschil, with a disgust as frank as that on Conroy's face.

'It would be horrible – horrible. And yet, of course, you're wonderfully handsome. How d'you account for it, Nursey?'

Nurse Blaber shook her head. 'I was hired to cure you of a habit, dear. When you're cured I shall go on to the next case – that senile-decay one at Bournemouth I told you about.'

'And I shall be left alone with George! But suppose it isn't cured,' said Miss Henschil of a sudden. 'Suppose it comes back again. What can I do? I can't send for *him* in this way when I'm a married woman!' She pointed like an infant.

'I'd come, of course,' Conroy answered. 'But, seriously, that is a consideration.'

They looked at each other, alarmed and anxious, and then toward Nurse Blaber, who closed her book, marked the place, and turned to face them.

'Have you ever talked to your mother as you have to me?' she said.

'No. I might have spoken to dad – but mother's different. What d'you mean?'

'And you've never talked to your mother either, Mr Conroy?'

'Not till I took Najdolene. Then I told her it was my heart. There's no need to say anything, now that I'm practically over it, is there?'

'Not if it doesn't come back, but—' She beckoned with a stumpy, triumphant finger that drew their heads close together. 'You know I always go in and read a chapter to mother at tea, child.'

'I know you do. You're an angel.' Miss Henschil patted the blue shoulder next her. 'Mother's Church of England now,' she explained. 'But she'll have her Bible with her pikelets at tea every night like the Skinners.'

'It was Naaman and Gehazi last Tuesday that gave me a clue. I said I'd never seen a case of leprosy, and your mother said she'd seen too many.'

'Where? She never told me,' Miss Henschil began.

'A few months before you were born – on her trip to Australia – at Mola or Molo something or other. It took me three evenings to get it all out.'

'Ay – mother's suspicious of questions,' said Miss Henschil to Conroy. 'She'll lock the door of every room she's in, if it's but for five minutes. She was a Tackberry from Jarrow way, yo' see.'

'She described your men to the life – men with faces all eaten away, staring at her over the fence of a lepers' hospital in this Molo Island. They begged from her, and she ran, she told me, all down the street, back to the pier. One touched her and she nearly fainted. She's ashamed of that still.'

'My men? The sand and the fences?' Miss Henschil muttered.

'Yes. You know how tidy she is and how she hates wind. She remembered that the fences were broken – she remembered the wind blowing. Sand – sun – salt wind – fences – faces – I got it all out of her, bit by bit. You don't know what I know! And it all happened three or four months before you were born. There!' Nurse Blaber slapped her knee with her little hand triumphantly.

'Would that account for it?' Miss Henschil shook from head to foot.

'Absolutely. I don't care who you ask! You never imagined the thing. It was *laid* on you. It happened on earth to *you*! Quick, Mr Conroy, she's too heavy for me! I'll get the flask.'

Miss Henschil leaned forward and collapsed, as Conroy told her afterwards, like a factory chimney. She came out of her swoon with teeth that chattered on the cup.

'No – no,' she said, gulping. 'It's not hysterics. Yo' see I've no call to hev 'em any more. No call – no reason whatever. God be praised! Can't yo' *feel* I'm a right woman now?'

'Stop hugging me!' said Nurse Blaber. 'You don't know your strength. Finish the brandy and water. It's perfectly reasonable, and I'll lay long odds Mr Conroy's case is something of the same. I've been thinking—'

'I wonder—' said Conroy, and pushed the girl back as she swayed again.

Nurse Blaber smoothed her pale hair. 'Yes. Your trouble, or something like it, happened somewhere on earth or sea to the mother who bore you. Ask her, child. Ask her and be done with it once for all.'

'I will,' said Conroy . . . 'There ought to be—' He opened his bag and hunted breathlessly.

'Bless you! Oh, God bless you, Nursey!' Miss Henschil was sobbing. 'You don't know what this means to me. It takes it all off – from the beginning.'

'But doesn't it make any difference to you now?' the nurse asked curiously. 'Now that you're rightfully a woman?'

Conroy, busy with his bag, had not heard. Miss Henschil stared across, and her beauty, freed from the shadow of any fear, blazed up within her. 'I see what you mean,' she said. 'But it hasn't changed anything. I want Toots. *He* has never been out of his mind in his life – except over silly me.'

'It's all right,' said Conroy, stooping under the lamp, Bradshaw in hand. 'If I change at Templecombe – for Bristol (Bristol – Hereford – yes) – I can be with mother for breakfast in her room and find out.'

'Quick, then,' said Nurse Blaber. 'We've passed Gillingham quite a while. You'd better take some of our sandwiches.' She went out to get them. Conroy and Miss Henschil would have danced, but there is no room for giants in a South-Western compartment.

'Good-bye, good luck, lad. Eh, but you've changed already – like me. Send a wire to our hotel as soon as you're sure,' said Miss Henschil. 'What should I have done without you?'

'Or I?' said Conroy. 'But it's Nurse that's saving us really.'

'Then thank her,' said Miss Henschil, looking straight at him. 'Yes, I would. She'd like it.'

When Nurse Blaber came back after the parting at Templecombe her nose and her eyelids were red, but, for all that, her face reflected a great light even while she sniffed over *The Cloister and the Hearth*.

Miss Henschil, deep in a house furnisher's catalogue, did not speak for twenty minutes. Then she said, between adding totals of best, guest, and servants' sheets, 'But why should our times have been the same, Nursey?'

'Because a child is born somewhere every second of the clock,' Nurse Blaber answered.

'And besides that, you probably set each other off by talking and thinking about it. You shouldn't, you know.'

'Ay, but you've never been in Hell,' said Miss Henschil.

The telegram handed in at Hereford at 12.46 and delivered to Miss Henschil on the beach of a certain village at 2.7 ran thus:

' "*Absolutely confirmed. She says she remembers hearing noise of accident in engine-room returning from India eighty-five.*" '

'He means the year, not the thermometer,' said Nurse Blaber, throwing pebbles at the cold sea.

' "*And two men scalded thus explaining my hoots.*" (The idea of telling me that!) "*Subsequently silly clergyman passenger ran up behind her calling for joke, 'Friend, all is lost,' thus accounting very words.*"

Nurse Blaber purred audibly.

' "*She says only remembers being upset minute or two. Unspeakable relief. Best love Nursey, who is jewel. Get out of her what she would like best.*" Oh, I oughtn't to have read that,' said Miss Henschil.

'It doesn't matter. I don't want anything,' said Nurse Blaber, 'and if I did I shouldn't get it.'

AS EASY AS A. B. C.
A TALE OF 2150 AD

The ABC, that semi-elected semi-nominated body of a few score persons, controls the Planet. Transformation is Civilisation, our motto runs. Theoretically we do what we please, so long as we do not interfere with the traffic and all it implies. Practically the ABC confirms or annuls all international arrangements, and, to judge from its last report, finds our tolerant, humorous, lazy little Planet only too ready to shift the whole burden of public administration on its shoulders.

With the Night Mail, 2000 AD

Isn't it almost time our Planet took some interest in the proceedings of the Aerial Board of Control? One knows that easy communications nowadays, and lack of privacy in the past, have killed all curiosity among mankind, but as the Board's Official Reporter I am bound to tell my tale.

At 9.30 a.m. on the 26th, the Board, sitting in London, was informed by De Forest (US) that the District of Northern Illinois had riotously cut itself out of all systems and would remain disconnected till the Board should take over and administer it direct.

Every Northern Illinois freight and passenger tower was, he reported, out of action; all District main, local and guiding lights had been extinguished; all General Communicators were dumb, and through traffic had been diverted. No reason had been given, but he gathered unofficially from the Mayor of Chicago that the District complained of 'crowd-making and invasion of privacy.'

As a matter of fact, it is of no importance whether Northern Illinois stays in or out of planetary circuit; as a matter of policy any complaint of invasion of privacy needs immediate investigation, lest worse should follow.

By 9.45 a.m., De Forest, Dragomiroff (Russia), Takahira

(Japan), and Pirolo (Italy) were empowered to visit Illinois and 'to take such steps as might be necessary for the resumption of traffic and *all that that implies*.' By 10 a.m. the Hall was empty, and the four Members and I were aboard what Pirolo insisted on calling 'My leetle godchild' – that is to say, the new *Victor Pirolo*. Our Planet prefers to know Victor Pirolo as a gentle, grey-haired enthusiast who spends his time near Foggia, inventing or creating new breeds of Spanish-Italian olive-trees; but there is another side to his nature – the manufacture of quaint inventions, of which the *Victor Pirolo* is perhaps not the least surprising. She and a few score sister-craft of the same type embody his latest ideas. But she is not comfortable. An ABC boat does not take the air with the level-keeled lift of a liner, but shoots up rocket-fashion like the 'aeroplane' of our ancestors, and finds her level at top-speed from the first. That is why I found myself sitting suddenly on the large lap of Eustace Arnott, who commands the ABC Fleet. One knows vaguely that there is such a thing as a Fleet somewhere on the Planet, and that, theoretically, it exists for the purposes of what used to be known as 'war.' Only a week before, while visiting a glacier sanatorium behind Gothaven, I had seen some squadrons making false auroras far to the north while they manœuvred round the Pole, but, naturally, it had never occurred to me that the things could be used in earnest.

Said Arnott to De Forest as I staggered to a seat on the chartroom divan: 'We're tremendously grateful to 'em in Illinois. We've never had a chance of exercising all the Fleet together. I've turned in a General Call, and I expect we'll have at least two hundred keels aloft by evening.'

'Well aloft?' De Forest asked.

'Of course, sir. Out of sight till they're called for.'

Arnott laughed as he lolled over the transparent chart-table where the map of the summer-blue Atlantic slid along, degree by degree, in exact answer to our progress. Our dial already showed 320 m.p.h., and we were two thousand feet above the uppermost traffic lanes.

'Now, where is this Illinois District of yours?' said

Dragomiroff. 'One travels so much, one sees so little. Oh, I remember! It is in North America!'

De Forest, whose business it is to know his own responsibilities, told us that it lay at the foot of Lake Michigan, on the road to nowhere in particular, was about an hour's run from end to end, and, except in one corner, as flat as the sea. Like most flat countries nowadays, it was heavily guarded against invasion of privacy by forced timber – fifty-foot oak and tamarack, grown in five years. The population was close on two millions, largely migratory between Florida and California, with a backbone of small farms (they call a thousand acres a farm in Illinois), whose owners come into Chicago for amusements and society during the winter. They were, he said, noticeably kind, quiet folk, but a little exacting, as all flat countries must be, in their notions of privacy. There had, for instance, been no printed news-sheet in Illinois for twenty-seven years. Chicago argued that engines for printed news sooner or later developed into engines for invasion of privacy, which in turn might bring the old terror of crowds and blackmail back to the Planet. So news-sheets were not.

'And that's Illinois,' De Forest concluded. 'You see, in the Old Days, she was in the forefront of what they used to call "progress," and Chicago—'

'Chicago?' said Takahira. 'That's the little place where there is Salati's Statue of the Nigger in Flames? A fine bit of old work.'

'When did you see it?' asked De Forest quickly. 'They only unveil it once a year.'

'I know. At Thanksgiving. It was then,' said Takahira, with a shudder. 'And they sang MacDonough's Song too.'

'Whew!' De Forest whistled. 'I did not know that! I wish you'd told me before. MacDonough's Song may have had its uses when it was composed, but it was an infernal legacy for any man to leave behind.'

'It's protective instinct, my dear fellows,' said Pirolo, rolling a cigarette. 'The Planet, she has had her dose of popular government. She suffers from inherited agoraphobia. She has no – ah – use for crowds.'

Dragomiroff leaned forward to give him a light, 'Certainly,' said the white-bearded Russian, 'the Planet has taken all precautions against crowds for the past hundred years. What is our total population to-day? Six hundred million, we hope; five hundred, we think, but – but if next year's census shows more than four hundred and fifty I myself will eat all the extra little babies. We have cut the birth-rate out – right out! For a long time we have said to Almighty God: "Thank You, Sir, but we do not much like Your game of life. So we will not play."'

'Anyhow,' said Arnott defiantly, 'men live a century apiece on the average nowadays.'

'Oh, that is quite well! I am rich – you are rich – we are all rich and happy because we are so few and we live so long. Only *I* think Almighty God He will remember what the Planet was like in the time of the Crowds and the Plague. Perhaps He will send us nerves. Eh, Pirolo?'

The Italian blinked into space. 'Perhaps,' said he, 'he has sent them already. Anyhow, you cannot argue with the Planet. She does not forget the Old Days; and – what can you do?'

'For sure we can't remake the world.' De Forest glanced at the map flowing smoothly across the table from west to east. 'We ought to be over our ground by nine tonight. There won't be much sleep afterwards.'

On which hint we dispersed, and I slept till Takahira waked me for dinner. Our ancestors thought nine hours' sleep ample for their little lives. We, living thirty years longer, feel ourselves defrauded with less than eleven out of the twenty-four.

By ten o'clock we were over Lake Michigan. The west shore was lightless, except for a dull ground-glare at Chicago, and a single traffic-directing light – its leading beam pointing north – at Waukegan on our starboard bow. None of the Lake villages gave any sign of life; and inland, westward, so far as we could see, blackness lay unbroken on the level earth. We swooped down and skimmed low across the dark, throwing calls county by county. Now and again we picked up the faint glimmer of a house-light or heard the rasp and rend of a cultivator being played across the fields, but Northern Illinois as a whole was one inky, apparently uninhabited waste of high forced woods. Only our illuminated map, with its little pointer switching from county to county, as we wheeled and twisted, gave us any idea of our position. Our calls, urgent, pleading, coaxing or commanding, through the General Communicator, brought no answer. Illinois strictly maintained her own privacy in the timber she grew for that purpose.

'Oh, this is absurd!' said De Forest. 'We're like an owl trying to work a wheat-field. Is this Bureau Creek? Let's land, Arnott, and get hold of someone.'

We brushed over a belt of forced woodland – fifteen-year-old maple sixty feet high – grounded on a private meadow-dock, none too big, where we moored to our own grapnels, and hurried out through the warm, dark night towards a light in a verandah. As we neared the garden gate I could have sworn we had stepped knee-deep in quicksand, for we could scarcely drag our feet against the prickling currents that clogged them. After five paces we stopped, wiping our foreheads, as hopelessly stuck on dry, smooth turf as so many cows in a bog.

'Pest!' cried Pirolo angrily. 'We are ground-circuited. And it is my own system of ground-circuits, too! I know the feeling!'

'Good-evening,' said a girl's voice from the verandah. 'Oh, I'm sorry! We've locked up. Wait a minute.'

We heard the click of a switch, and almost fell forward as the currents round our knees were withdrawn.

The girl laughed and laid aside her knitting. An old-fashioned Controller stood at her elbow, which she reversed from time to time, and we could hear the snort and clank of the obedient cultivator half a mile away, behind the guardian woods.

'Come in and sit down,' she said. 'I'm only playing a plough. Dad's gone to Chicago to— Ah! Then it was *your* call I heard just now.'

She had caught sight of Arnott's Board uniform, leaped to the switch, and turned it full on.

We were checked, gasping, waist-deep in current this time, three yards from the verandah.

586

'We only want to know what's the matter with Illinois,' said De Forest placidly.

'Then hadn't you better go to Chicago and find out?' she answered. 'There's nothing wrong here. We own ourselves.'

'How can we go anywhere if you won't loose us?' De Forest went on while Arnott scowled. Admirals of Fleets are still quite human when their dignity is touched.

'Stop a minute – you don't know how funny you look!' She put her hands on her hips and laughed mercilessly.

'Don't worry about that,' said Arnott, and whistled. A voice answered from the *Victor Pirolo* in the meadow.

'Only a single-fuse ground-circuit!' Arnott called. 'Sort it out gently, please.'

We heard the ping of a breaking lamp; a fuse blew out somewhere in the verandah roof, frightening a nest full of birds. The ground-circuit was open. We stooped and rubbed our tingling ankles.

'How rude – how very rude of you!' the maiden cried.

'Sorry, but we haven't time to look funny,' said Arnott. 'We've got to go to Chicago; and if I were *you*, young lady, I'd go into the cellars for the next two hours, and take mother with me.'

Off he strode, with us at his heels, muttering indignantly, till the humour of the thing took and doubled him up with laughter at the foot of the gangway-ladder.

'The Board hasn't shown what you might call a fat spark on this occasion,' said De Forest, wiping his eyes. 'I hope I didn't look as big a fool as you did, Arnott! Hullo! What on the earth is that? Dad coming home from Chicago?'

There was a rattle and a rush, and a five-plough cultivator, blades in air like so many teeth, trundled itself at us round the edge of the timber, fuming and sparking furiously.

'Jump!' said Arnott, as we bundled ourselves through the none-too-wide door. 'Never mind about shutting it. Up!'

The *Victor Pirolo* lifted like a bubbly and the vicious machine shot just underneath us, clawing high as it passed.

'There's a nice little spit-kitten for you!' said Arnott, dusting his knees. 'We ask her a civil question. First she circuits us and then she plays a cultivator at us!'

'And then we fly,' said Dragomiroff. 'If I were forty years more young I would go back and kiss her. Ho! Ho!'

'I,' said Pirolo,' would smack her! My pet ship has been chased by a dirty plough; a – how do you say? – agricultural implement!'

'Oh, that is Illinois all over,' said De Forest. 'They don't content themselves with talking about privacy. They arrange to have it. And now where's your alleged fleet, Arnott? We must assert ourselves against this wench.'

Arnott pointed to the black heavens.

'Waiting on – up there,' said he. 'Shall I give them the whole installation, sir?'

'Oh, I don't think the young lady is quite worth all that,' said De Forest. 'Get over Chicago, and perhaps we'll see something.'

In a few minutes, we were hanging at two thousand feet over an oblong block of incandescence in the centre of the little town.

'That looks like the old City Hall. Yes, there is Salati's Statue in front of it,' said Takahira. 'But what on earth are they doing to the place? I thought they used it for a market nowadays? Drop a little, please.'

We could hear the sputter and crackle of road-surfacing machines – the cheap Western type which fuse stone and rubbish into lava-like ribbed glass for their rough country roads. Three or four surfacers worked on each side of a square of ruins. The brick and stone wreckage crumbled, slid forward, and presently spread out into white-hot pools of sticky slag, which the levelling-rods smoothed more or less flat. Already a third of the big block had been so treated, and was cooling to dull red before our astonished eyes.

'It is the Old Market,' said De Forest. 'Well, there's nothing to prevent Illinois from making a road through a market. It doesn't interfere with traffic, that I can see.'

'Hsh!' said Arnott, gripping me by the shoulder. 'Listen! They're singing. Why on the earth are they singing?'

We dropped again till we could see the black fringe of people at the edge of that glowing square.

At first they only roared against the roar of the surfacers and levellers. Then the words came up clearly – the words of the Forbidden Song that all men knew, and none let pass their lips – poor Pat Macdonough's Song, made in the days of the Crowds and the Plague – every silly word of it loaded to sparking point with the Planet's inherited memories of horror, panic, fear and cruelty. And Chicago – innocent, contented little Chicago – was singing it aloud to the infernal tune that carried riot, pestilence and lunacy round our Planet a few generations ago!

'Once there was The People – Terror gave it birth;
Once there was The People, and it made a hell of earth!

(Then the stamp and pause):

Earth arose and crushed it. Listen, oh, ye slain!
Once there was The People – it shall never be again!'

The levellers thrust in savagely against the ruins as the song renewed itself again, again and again, louder than the crash of the melting walls.

De Forest frowned.

'I don't like that,' he said. 'They've broken back to the Old Days! They'll be killing somebody soon. I think we'd better divert 'em, Arnott.'

'Ay, ay, sir!' Arnott's hand went to his cap, and we heard the hull of the *Victor Pirolo* ring to the command: 'Lamps! Both watches stand by! Lamps! Lamps! Lamps!'

'Keep still!' said Takahira to me. 'Blinkers, please, quartermaster.'

'It's all right – all right!' said Pirolo from behind, and to my horror slipped over my head some sort of rubber helmet that locked with a snap. I could feel thick colloid bosses before my eyes, but I stood in absolute darkness.

'To save the sight,' he explained, and pushed me on to the chartroom divan. 'You will see, in a minute.'

As he spoke, I became aware of a thin thread of almost

intolerable light, let down from heaven at an immense distance – one vertical hairsbreadth of frozen lightning.

'Those are our flanking ships,' said Arnott at my elbow, 'That one is over Galena. Look south – that other one's over Keithburg. Vincennes is behind us, and north yonder is Winthrop Woods. The Fleet's in position, sir' – this to De Forest. 'As soon as you give the word.'

'Ah, no! No!' cried Dragomiroff at my side. I could feel the old man tremble. 'I do not know all that you can do, but be kind! I ask you to be a little kind to them below! This is horrible – horrible!'

' "When a Woman kills a Chicken,
    Dynasties and Empires sicken," '

Takahira quoted. 'It is too late to be gentle now.'

'Then take off my helmet! Take off my helmet!' Dragomiroff began hysterically.

Pirolo must have put his arm round him.

'Hush,' he said, 'I am here. It is all right, Ivan, my dear fellow.'

'I'll just send our little girl in Bureau County a warning,' said Arnott. 'She don't deserve it, but we'll allow her a minute or two to take mamma to the cellar.'

In the utter hush that followed the growling spark after Arnott had linked up his Service Communicator with the invisible Fleet, we heard Macdonough's Song from the city beneath us grow fainter, as we rose to position. Then I clapped my hand before my mask lenses, for it was as though the floor of Heaven had been riddled, and all the inconceivable blaze of suns in the making was poured through the manholes.

'You needn't count,' said Arnott. I had had no thought of such a thing. 'There are two hundred and fifty keels up there, five miles apart. Full power, please, for another fifteen seconds.'

The firmament, as far as eye could reach, stood on pillars of white fire. One fell on the glowing square at Chicago, and turned it black.

'Oh! Oh! Oh! Can men be allowed to do such things?' Dragomiroff cried, and fell across our knees.

'Glass of water, please,' said Takahira, to a helmeted shape that leaped forward. 'He is a little faint.'

The lights switched off, and the darkness stunned like an avalanche. We could hear Dragomiroff's teeth on the glass edge.

Pirolo was comforting him.

'All right, all ra-ight,' he repeated.' Come and lie down. Come below and take off your mask. I give you my word, old friend, it is all right. They are my siege-lights. Little Victor Pirolo's leetle lights. You know me? I do not hurt people.'

'Pardon!' Dragomiroff moaned. 'I have never seen Death. I have never seen the Board take action. Shall we go down and burn them alive, or is that already done?'

'Oh, hush!' said Pirolo, and I think he rocked him in his arms.

'Do we repeat, sir?' Arnott asked De Forest.

'Give 'em a minute's break,' De Forest replied. 'They may need it.'

We waited a minute and then Macdonough's Song, broken but defiant, rose from undefeated Chicago.

'They seem fond of that tune,' said De Forest. 'I should let 'em have it, Arnott.'

'Very good, sir,' said Arnott, and felt his way to the Communicator keys.

No lights broke forth, but the hollow of the skies made herself the mouth for one note that touched the raw fibre of the brain. Men hear such sounds in delirium, advancing like tides from horizons beyond the ruled foreshores of space.

'That's our pitch-pipe,' said Arnott. 'We may be a bit ragged; I've never conducted two hundred and fifty performers before.' He pulled out the couplers, and struck a full chord on the Service Communicators.

The beams of light leaped down again, and danced, solemnly and awfully, a stilt-dance, sweeping thirty or forty miles left and right at each stiff-legged kick, while the darkness delivered itself – there is no scale to measure against that utterance – of the tune to which they kept time. Certain notes – one learnt to expect them with terror – cut through one's marrow, but, after three minutes, thought and emotion passed in indescribable agony.

We saw, we heard, but I think we were in some sort swooning. The two hundred and fifty beams shifted, re-formed, straddled and split, narrowed, widened, rippled in ribbons, broke into a thousand white-hot parallel lines, melted and revolved in interwoven rings like old-fashioned engine-turning, flung up to the zenith, made as if to descend and renew the torment, halted at the last instant, twizzled insanely round the horizon, and vanished, to bring back for the hundredth time darkness more shattering than their instantly renewed light over all Illinois. Then the tune and lights ceased together, and we heard one single, devastating wail that shook all the horizon as a rubbed wet finger shakes the rim of a bowl.

'Ah, that is my new siren,' said Pirolo. 'You can break an iceberg across, if you find the proper pitch. They will whistle by squadrons now. It is the wind through pierced shutters in the bows.'

I had collapsed beside Dragomiroff, broken and snivelling feebly, because I had been delivered before my time to all the terrors of Judgment Day, and the Archangels of the Resurrection were hailing me naked across the Universe to the sound of the music of the spheres.

Then I saw De Forest smacking Arnott's helmet with his open hand. The wailing died down in a long shriek as a black shadow swooped past us, and returned to her place above the lower clouds.

'I hate to interrupt a specialist when he's enjoying himself,' said De Forest, 'but, as a matter of fact, all Illinois has been asking us to stop for these last fifteen seconds.'

'What a pity!' Arnott slipped off his mask. 'I wanted you to hear us really hum. Our lower C can lift street-paving.'

'It is Hell – Hell!' cried Dragomiroff, and sobbed aloud.

Arnott looked away as he answered:

'It's a few thousand volts ahead of the old shoot-'em-and-sink-'em game, but I should scarcely call it *that*. What shall I tell the Fleet, sir?'

'Tell them we're very pleased and impressed. I don't think they need wait on any longer. There isn't a spark left down there.' De Forest pointed. 'They'll be deaf and blind.'

'Oh, I think not, sir. The demonstration lasted less than ten minutes.'

'Marvellous!' Takahira sighed. 'I should have said it was half a night. Now shall we go down and pick up the pieces?'

'But first a small drink,' said Pirolo. 'The Board must not arrive weeping at its own works.'

'I am an old fool – an old fool!' Dragomiroff began piteously. 'I did not know what would happen. It is all new to me. We reason with them in Little Russia.'

Chicago North landing-tower was unlighted, and Arnott worked his ship into the clips by her own lights. As soon as these broke out we heard groanings of horror and appeal from many people below.

'All right!' shouted Arnott into the darkness. 'We aren't beginning again!' We descended by the stairs, to find ourselves knee-deep in a grovelling crowd, some crying that they were blind, others beseeching us not to make any more noises, but the greater part writhing face downward, their hands or their caps before their eyes.

It was Pirolo who came to our rescue. He climbed the side of a surfacing-machine, and there, gesticulating as though they could see, made oration to those afflicted people of Illinois.

'You stchewpids!' he began. 'There is nothing to fuss for. Of *course*, your eyes will smart and be all red to-morrow. You will look as if you and your wives had drunk too much, but in a little while you will see again as well as before. I tell you this, and I – *I* am Pirolo! Victor Pirolo!'

The crowd with one accord shuddered, for many legends attach to Victor Pirolo of Foggia, deep in the secrets of God.

'Pirolo?' An unsteady voice lifted itself. 'Then tell us, was there anything except light in those lights of yours, just now?'

The question was repeated from every corner of the darkness.

Pirolo laughed.

'No!' he thundered. (Why have small men such large

voices?) 'I give you my word and the Board's word that there was nothing except light – just light! You stchewpids! Your birth-rate is too low already as it is. Some day I must invent something to send it up, but send it down – never!'

'Is that true? We thought – we heard – somebody said—'

One could feel the tension relax all round.

'You *too* big fools,' Pirolo cried. 'You could have sent us a call and we would have told you.'

'Send you a call!' a deep voice shouted. 'I wish you had been at *our* end of the wire.'

'I'm glad I wasn't,' said De Forest. 'It looked bad enough from behind the lamps. Never mind! It's over now. Is there anyone here I can talk business with? I'm De Forest, US – for the Board.'

'You might begin with me, for one – I'm Mayor,' the bass voice replied.

A big man rose unsteadily from the street, and staggered towards us, where we sat on the broad turf-edging, in front of the garden fences.

'I ought to be the first on my feet. Am I?' 'said he.

'Yes,' said De Forest, and steadied him as he dropped down beside us.

'Hello, Andy. Is that you?' a voice called.

'Excuse me,' said the Mayor; 'that sounds like my Chief of Police, Bluthner?'

'Bluthner it is; and here's Mulligan and Keefe – on their feet.'

'Bring 'em up, please, Blut. We're supposed to be the Four in charge of this hamlet. What we say, goes. And, De Forest, what do you say?'

'Nothing yet,' De Forest answered, as we made room for the panting, reeling men. '*You*'ve cut out of the system. Well?'

'Tell the steward to send down drinks, please,' Arnott whispered to an orderly at his side.

'Good!' said the Mayor, smacking his dry lips. 'Now I suppose we can take it, De Forest, that henceforward the Board will administer us direct?'

'Not if the Board can avoid it,' De Forest laughed. 'The ABC is responsible only for the planetary traffic.'

'*And all that that implies.*' The big Four who ran Chicago chanted their Magna Charta like children at school.

'Well, get on,' said De Forest wearily. 'What *is* your silly trouble, anyway?'

'Too much damn democracy,' said the Mayor, laying his hand on De Forest's knee.

'So? I thought Illinois had had her dose of that.'

'She has. That's why. Blut, what did you do with our prisoners last night?'

'Locked 'em in the water-tower to prevent the women killing 'em,' the Chief of Police replied. 'I'm too blind to move just yet, but—'

'Arnott, send some of your people, please, and fetch 'em along,' said De Forest.

'They're triple-circuited,' the Mayor called. 'You'll have to blow out three fuses.' He turned to De Forest, his large outline just visible in the paling darkness. 'I hate to throw any more work on the Board. I'm an administrator myself, but we've had a little fuss with our Serviles. What? In a big city there's bound to be a few men and women who can't live without listening to themselves, and who prefer drinking out of pipes they don't own both ends of. They inhabit flats and hotels all the year round. They say it saves 'em trouble. Anyway, it gives 'em more time to make trouble for their neighbours. We call 'em Serviles locally. And they are apt to be tuberculous.'

'Just so!' said the man called Mulligan. 'Transportation is Civilisation. Democracy is Disease. I've proved it by the blood-test, every time.'

'Mulligan's our Health Officer, and a one-cycle man,' said the Mayor, laughing. 'But it's true that most Serviles haven't much control. They *will* talk; and when people take to talking as a business, anything may arrive – mayn't it, De Forest?'

'Anything – except the facts of the case,' said De Forest, laughing.

'I'll give you those in a minute,' said the Mayor. 'Our Serviles got to talking – first in their houses, and then on the streets, telling men and women how to manage their own affairs. (You can't teach a Servile not to finger his neighbour's soul.) That's invasion of privacy, of course, but in Chicago we'll suffer anything sooner than make crowds. Nobody took much notice, and so I let 'em alone. My fault! I was warned there would be trouble, but there hasn't been a crowd or murder in Illinois for nineteen years.'

'Twenty-two,' said the Chief of Police.

'Likely. Anyway, we'd forgot such things. So, from talking in the houses and on the streets, our Serviles go to calling a meeting in the Old Market yonder.' He nodded across the square where the wrecked buildings heaved up grey in the dawn-glimmer behind the square-cased statue of The Negro in Flames. 'There's nothing to prevent anyone calling meetings except that it's against human nature to stand in a crowd, besides being bad for the health. I ought to have known by the way our men and women attended that first meeting that trouble was brewing. There were as many as a thousand in the market-place, touching each other. Touching! Then the Serviles turned in all tongue-switches and talked, and we—'

'What did they talk about?' said Takahira.

'First, how badly things were managed in the city. That pleased us Four – we were on the platform – because we hoped to catch one or two good men for City work. You know how rare executive capacity is. Even if we didn't, it's – it's refreshing to find anyone interested enough in our job to damn our eyes. *You* don't know what it means to work, year in, year out, without a spark of difference with a living soul.'

'Oh, don't we!' said De Forest. 'There are times on the Board when we'd give our positions if anyone would kick us out and take hold of things themselves.'

'But they don't,' said the Mayor ruefully. 'I assure you, sir, we Four have done things in Chicago, in the hope of rousing people, that would have discredited Nero. But what do they say? "Very good, Andy. Have it your own way. Anything's better than a crowd. I'll go back to my land." You *can't* do anything with folk who can go where they please, and don't want anything on God's earth except their own way. There isn't a kick or a kicker left on the Planet.'

'Then I suppose that little shed yonder fell down by itself?' said De Forest. We could see the bare and still smoking acre of ruins, and hear the slag-pools crackle as they hardened and set.

'Oh, that's only amusement. 'Tell you later. As I was saying, our Serviles held the meeting, and pretty soon we had to ground-circuit the platform to save 'em from being killed. And *that* didn't make our people any more pacific.'

'How d'you mean?' I ventured to ask.

'If you've ever been ground-circuited,' said the Mayor, 'you'll know it don't improve any man's temper to be held up straining against nothing. No, sir! Eight or nine hundred folk kept pawing and buzzing like flies in treacle for two hours, while a pack of perfectly safe Serviles invades their mental and spiritual privacy, may be amusing to watch, but they are not pleasant to handle afterwards.'

Pirolo chuckled.

'Our folk own themselves. They were of opinion things were going too far and too fiery. I warned the Serviles; but they're born house-dwellers. Unless a fact hits 'em on the head, they cannot see it. Would you believe me, they went on to talk of what they called "popular government"! They did! They wanted us to go back to the old Voodoo-business of voting with papers and wooden boxes, and word-drunk people and printed formulas, *and* news-sheets. They said they practised it among themselves about what they'd have to eat in their flats and hotels.

'Yes, sir! They stood up behind Bluthner's doubled ground-circuits, and they said *that*, in this present year of grace, to self-owning men and women, on that very spot! Then they finished' – he lowered his voice cautiously – 'by talking about "The People." And then Bluthner he had to sit up all night in charge of the circuits because he couldn't trust his men to keep 'em shut.'

'It was trying 'em too high,' said the Chief of Police. 'But we couldn't hold the crowd ground-circuited for ever. I gathered in all the Serviles on charge of crowd-making, and put 'em in the water-tower, and then I let things cut loose. I had to! The District lit like a sparked gas-tank!'

'The news was out over thirty degrees of country,' said the Mayor; 'and when once it's a question of invasion of privacy, goodbye to right and reason in Illinois! They began turning out traffic-lights and locking up landing-towers on Thursday night. Friday, they stopped all through traffic, and asked for the Board to take over. Then they wanted to clean Chicago off the side of the lake and rebuild elsewhere – just for a souvenir of "The People" that the Serviles talked about. I suggested that they should slag the Old Market where the meeting was held, while I turned in a call to you all on the Board. That kept 'em quiet till you came along. And – and now you can take hold of the situation.'

'Any chance of their quieting down?' De Forest asked.

'You can try,' said the Mayor.

De Forest raised his voice in the face of the reviving crowd that had edged in towards us. Day was come.

'Don't you think this business can be arranged?' he began. But there was a roar of angry voices:

'We've finished with crowds! We aren't going back to the Old Days! Take us over! Take the Serviles away! Administer direct, or we'll kill 'em! Down with The People!'

An attempt was made to begin Macdonough's Song. It got no further than the first line, for the *Victor Pirolo* sent down a warning drone on one stopped horn. A wrecked side-wall of the Old Market tottered and fell inwards on the slag-pools. None spoke or moved till the last of the dust had settled down again, turning the steel case of Salati's Statue ashy grey.

'You see, you'll just *have to* take us over,' the Mayor whispered.

De Forest shrugged his shoulders.

'You talk as if executive capacity could be snatched out of the air like so much horse-power. Can't you manage yourselves on any terms?' he said.

'We can, if you say so. It will cost those few lives to begin with.'

The Mayor pointed across the square, where Arnott's men guided a stumbling group of ten or twelve men and women to the lake front, and halted them under the Statue.

'Now I think,' said Takahira, under his breath, 'there will be trouble.'

The mass in front of us growled like beasts.

At that moment the sun rose clear, and revealed the blinking assembly to itself. As soon as it realised that it was a crowd, we saw the shiver of horror and mutual repulsion shoot across it precisely as the steely flaws shot across the lake outside. Nothing was said, and, being half blind, of course it moved but slowly. Yet in less than fifteen minutes most of that vast, multitude – five thousand, at the lowest count – melted away like frost on south eaves. The remnant stretched themselves on the grass, where a crowd feels and looks less like a crowd.

'*These* mean business,' the Mayor whispered to Takahira. 'There are a goodish few women there who've borne children. I don't like it.'

The morning draught off the lake stirred the trees round us with promise of a hot day; the sun reflected itself dazzlingly off the canister-shaped covering of Salati's Statue; cocks crew in the gardens, and we could hear gate-latches clicking in the distance as people stumblingly resought their homes.

'I'm afraid there won't be any morning deliveries,' said De Forest. 'We rather upset things in the country last night.'

'That makes no odds,' the Mayor returned. 'We're all provisioned for six months. *We* take no chances.'

Nor, when you come to think of it, does anyone else. It must be three-quarters of a generation since any house or city faced a food shortage. Yet is there house or city on the Planet to-day that has not half a year's provisions laid in? We are like the shipwrecked seamen in the old books, who, having once nearly starved to death, ever afterwards hide away bits of food and biscuit. Truly we trust no crowds, nor system based on crowds!

De Forest waited till the last footstep had died away. Meantime the prisoners at the base of the Statue shuffled, posed and fidgeted, with the shamelessness of quite little children. None of them were more than six feet high, and many of them were as grey-haired as the ravaged, harassed heads of old pictures. They huddled together in actual touch, while the crowd, spaced at large intervals, looked at them with congested eyes.

Suddenly a man among them began to talk. The Mayor had not in the least exaggerated. It appeared that our Planet lay sunk in slavery beneath the heel of the Aerial Board of Control. The orator urged us to arise in our might, burst our prison doors and break our fetters (all his metaphors, by the way, were of the most mediæval). Next he demanded that every matter of daily life, including most of the physical functions, should be submitted for decision at any time of the week, month, or year to, I gathered, anybody who happened to be passing by or residing within a certain radius, and that everybody should forthwith abandon his concerns to settle the matter, first by crowd-making, next by talking to the crowds made, and, lastly, by describing crosses on pieces of paper, which rubbish should later be counted with certain mystic ceremonies and oaths. Out of this amazing play, he assured us, would automatically rise a higher, nobler and kinder world, based – he demonstrated this with the awful lucidity of the insane – based on the sanctity of the Crowd and the villainy of the single person. In conclusion, he called loudly upon God to testify to his personal merits and integrity. When the flow ceased, I turned, bewildered, to Takahira, who was nodding solemnly.

'Quite correct,' said he. 'It is all in the old books. He has left out nothing, not even the war-talk.'

'But I don't see how this stuff can upset a child, much less a district,' I replied.

'Ah, you are too young!' said Dragomiroff. 'For another, you are not a mamma. Please look at the mammas.'

Ten or fifteen women who remained had separated themselves from the silent men, and were drawing in towards the prisoners. It reminded one of the stealthy encircling, before the rush in at the quarry, of wolves round musk-oxen in the North. The prisoners saw, and drew together more closely.

The Mayor covered his face with his hands for an instant. De Forest, bare-headed, stepped forward between the prisoners and the slowly, stiffly moving line.

'That's all very interesting,' he said to the dry-lipped orator. 'But the point seems that you've been making crowds and invading privacy.'

A woman stepped forward, and would have spoken, but there was a quick assenting murmur from the men, who realised that De Forest was trying to pull the situation down to ground-line.

'Yes! Yes!' they cried. 'We cut out because they made crowds and invaded privacy! Stick to that! Keep on that switch! Lift the Serviles out of this! The Board's in charge! Hsh!'

'Yes, the Board's in charge,' said De Forest. 'I'll take formal evidence of crowd-making if you like, but the Members of the Board can testify to it. Will that do?'

The women had moved in another pace, with hands that clenched and unclenched at their sides.

'Good! Good enough!' the men cried. 'We're content. Only take them away quickly.'

'Come along up!' said De Forest to the captives. 'Breakfast is quite ready.'

It appeared, however, that they did not wish to go. They intended to remain in Chicago and make crowds. They pointed out that De Forest's proposal was gross invasion of privacy.

'My dear fellow,' said Pirolo to the most voluble of the leaders, 'you hurry, or your crowd that can't be wrong will kill you!'

'But that would be murder,' answered the believer in crowds; and there was a roar of laughter from all sides that seemed to show the crisis had broken.

A woman stepped forward from the line of women, laughing, I protest, as merrily as any of the company. One hand, of course, shaded her eyes, the other was at her throat.

'Oh, they needn't be afraid of being killed!' she called.

'Not in the least,' said De Forest. 'But don't you think that now the Board's in charge you might go home while we get these people away?'

'I shall be home long before that. It – it has been rather a trying day.'

She stood up to her full height, dwarfing even De Forest's six-foot-eight, and smiled, with eyes closed against the fierce light.

'Yes, rather,' said De Forest. 'I'm afraid you feel the glare a little. We'll have the ship down.'

He motioned to the *Pirolo* to drop between us and the sun, and at the same time to loop-circuit the prisoners, who were a trifle unsteady. We saw them stiffen to the current where they stood. The woman's voice went on, sweet and deep and unshaken:

'I don't suppose you men realise how much this – this sort of thing means to a woman. I've borne three. We women don't want our children given to Crowds. It must be an inherited instinct. Crowds make trouble. They bring back the Old Days. Hate, fear, blackmail, publicity, "The People." *That! That! That!*' She pointed to the Statue, and the crowd growled once more.

'Yes, if they are allowed to go on,' said De Forest. 'But this little affair—'

'It means so much to us women that this little affair should never happen again. Of course, never's a long word, but one feels so strongly that it is important to stop crowds at the very beginning. Those creatures' – she pointed with her left hand at the prisoners swaying like seaweed in a tideway as the circuit pulled them – 'those people have friends and wives and children in the city and elsewhere. One doesn't want anything done to *them*, you know. It's terrible to force a human being out of fifty or sixty years of good life. I'm only forty myself. *I* know. But, at the same time, one feels no price is too heavy to pay if – if these people and *all that they imply* can be put an end to. Do you quite understand, or would you be kind enough to tell your men to take the casing off the Statue? It's worth looking at.'

'I understand perfectly. But I don't think anyone here wants to see the Statue on an empty stomach. Excuse me one moment.' De Forest called up to the ship. 'A flying loop ready on the port side, if you please.' Then to the woman he said with some stiffness: 'You might leave us a little discretion in the matter.'

'Oh, of course. Thank you for being so patient. I know my arguments are silly, but—' She half turned away, and went on in a changed voice: 'Perhaps this will help you to decide.'

She threw out her right arm, with a knife in it. Before the blade could be returned to her throat or bosom it was twitched from her grip, sparked as it flew out of the shadow of the ship above, and fell flashing in the sunshine at the foot of the Statue, fifty yards away. The outflung arm was arrested, rigid as a bar for an instant, till the releasing circuit permitted her to bring it slowly to her side. The other women shrank back silent among the men.

Pirolo rubbed his hands, and Takahira nodded.

'That was clever of you, De Forest,' said he.

'What a glorious pose!' Dragomiroff murmured, for the frightened woman was on the edge of tears.

'Why did you stop me? I would have done it!' she cried.

'I have no doubt you would,' said De Forest. 'But we can't waste a life like yours on these people. I hope the arrest didn't sprain your wrist; it's so hard to regulate a flying loop. But I think you are quite right about those persons' women and children. We'll take them all away with us if you promise not to do anything stupid to yourself.'

'I promised – I promise.' She controlled herself with an effort. 'But it is so important to us women. We know what it means; and I thought if you saw I was in earnest—'

'I saw you were, and you've gained your point. I shall take all your Serviles away with me at once. The Mayor will make lists of their friends and families in the city *and* the District, and he'll ship them after us this afternoon.'

'Sure,' said the Mayor, rising to his feet. 'Keefe, if you can see, hadn't you better finish levelling off the Old Market? It don't look sightly the way it is now, and we sha'n't use it for crowds any more.'

'I think you had better wipe out that Statue as well, Mr Mayor,' said De Forest. 'I don't question its merits as a work of art, but I believe it's a shade morbid.'

'Certainly, sir. Oh, Keefe! Slag the Nigger before you go on to fuse the market. I'll get to the Communicators and tell the District that the Board is in charge. Are you making any special appointments, sir?'

'None. We haven't men to waste on these backwoods. Carry on as before, but under the Board. Arnott, run your Serviles aboard, please. Ground ship and pass them through the bilge doors. We'll wait till we've finished with this work of art.'

The prisoners trailed past him, talking fluently, but unable to gesticulate in the drag of the current. Then the surfacers rolled up, two on each side of the Statue. With one accord the spectators looked elsewhere, but there was no need. Keefe turned on full power and the thing simply melted within its case. All I saw was a surge of white-hot metal pouring over the plinth, a glimpse of Salati's inscription, 'To the Eternal Memory of the Justice of the People,' ere the stone base itself cracked and powdered into finest lime. The crowd cheered.

'Thank you,' said De Forest,' but we want our breakfasts, and I expect you do too. Good-bye, Mr Mayor! Delighted to see you at any time, but I hope I sha'n't have to officially for the next thirty years. Good-bye, madam. Yes. We're all given to nerves, nowadays. I suffer from them myself. Good-bye, gentlemen all! You're under the tyrannous heel of the Board from this moment, but if ever you feel like breaking your fetters you've only to let us know. This is no treat to us. Good luck!'

We embarked amid shouts, and did not check our lift till they had dwindled into whispers. Then De Forest flung himself on the chartroom divan and mopped his forehead.

'I don't mind men,' he panted, 'but women are the devil!'

'Still the devil,' said Pirolo cheerfully. 'That one would have suicided.'

'I know it. That was why I signalled for the flying loop to be clapped on her. I owe you an apology for that, Arnott. I hadn't time to catch your eye, and you were busy with our caitiffs. By the way, who actually answered my signal? It was a smart piece of work.'

'Ilroy,' said Arnott. 'But he overloaded the wave. It may be pretty gallery-work to knock a knife out of a lady's hand, but – didn't you notice how she rubbed 'em? – he scorched her fingers. Slovenly, I call it.'

'Far be it from me to interfere with Fleet discipline, but don't be too hard on the boy. If that woman had killed herself, they would have killed every Servile and everything related to a Servile throughout the District by nightfall.'

'That was what she was playing for,' Takahira said, 'And with our Fleet gone we could have done nothing to hold them.'

'I may be ass enough to walk into a ground-circuit,' said Arnott, 'but I don't dismiss my fleet till I'm reasonably sure that trouble is over. They're in position still, and I intend to keep 'em there till the Serviles are shipped out of the district. That last little crowd meant murder, my friends.'

'Nerves! All nerves!' said Pirolo. 'You cannot argue with agoraphobia.'

'And it is not as if they had seen much dead – or *is* it?' said Takahira.

'In all my ninety years I have never seen death.' Dragomiroff spoke as one who would excuse himself. 'Perhaps that was why – last night.'

Then it came out, as we sat over breakfast, that, with the exception of Arnott and Pirolo, none of us had ever seen a corpse; or knew in what manner the spirit passes.

'We're a nice lot to flap about governing the Planet,' De Forest laughed. 'I confess, now it's all over, that my main fear was I mightn't be able to pull it off without losing a life.'

'I thought of that, too,' said Arnott. 'But there's no death reported, and I've inquired everywhere. What are we supposed to do with our passengers? I've fed 'em.'

'We're between two switches,' De Forest drawled. 'If we drop them in any place that isn't under the Board, the natives will make their presence an excuse for cutting out, same as Illinois did, and forcing the Board to take over. If we drop them in any place under the Board's control they'll be killed as soon as our backs are turned.'

'If you say so,' said Pirolo thoughtfully, 'I can guarantee that they will become extinct in process of time, quite happily. What is their birth-rate now?'

'Go down and ask 'em,' said De Forest.

'I think they might become nervous and tear me to bits,' the philosopher of Foggia replied.

'Not really? Well?'

'Open the bilge-doors,' said Tahakira with a downward jerk of the thumb.

'Scarcely – after all the trouble we've taken to save 'em,' said De Forest.

'Try London,' Arnott suggested. 'You could turn Satan himself loose there, and they'd only ask him to dinner.'

'Good man! You've given me an idea. Vincent! Oh, Vincent!' He threw the General Communicator open so that we could all hear, and in a few minutes the chartroom filled with the rich, fruity voice of Leopold Vincent, who has purveyed all London her choicest amusements for the last thirty years. We answered with expectant grins, as though we were actually in the stalls of, say, the Combination on a first night.

'We've picked up something in your line,' De Forest began.

'That's good, dear man. If it's old enough. There's nothing to beat the old things for business purposes. Have you seen *London, Chatham and Dover* at Earl's Court? No? I thought I missed you there. Im-mense! I've had the real steam loco-motive engines built from the old designs and the iron rails cast specially by hand. Cloth cushions in the carriages, too! Im-mense! And paper railway-tickets. *And* Polly Milton.'

'Polly Milton back again!' said Arnott rapturously. 'Book me two stalls for to-morrow night. What's she singing now, bless her?'

'The old songs. Nothing comes up to the old touch. Listen to this, dear men.' Vincent carolled with flourishes:

'Oh, cruel lamps of London
If tears your light could drown,

606

Your victims' eyes would weep them,
Oh, lights of London Town!

'Then they weep.'

'You see?' Pirolo waved his hands. 'The old world always weeped when it saw crowds together. It did not know why, but it weeped. We know why, but we do not weep, except when we pay to be made to by fat, wicked old Vincent.'

'Old, yourself!' Vincent laughed. 'I'm a public benefactor. I keep the world soft and united.'

'And I'm De Forest, of the Board,' said De Forest acidly. 'Trying to get a little business done. As I was saying, I've picked up a few people in Chicago.'

'I cut out. Chicago is—'

'*Do* listen! They're perfectly unique.'

'Do they build houses of baked mud-blocks while you wait – eh? That's an old contact.'

'They're an untouched, primitive community, with all the old ideas.'

'Sewing-machines and maypole dances? Cooking on coal-gas stoves, lighting pipes with matches and driving horses? Gerolstein tried that last year. An absolute blow-out!'

De Forest plugged him off wrathfully, and poured out the story of our doings for the last twenty-four hours on the top-note.

'And they do it *all* in public,' he concluded. 'You can't stop 'em. The more public, the better they are pleased. They'll talk for hours – like you! *Now* you can come in again.

'Do you really mean they know how to vote?' said Vincent. 'Can they act it?'

'Act? It's their life to 'em! And you never saw such faces! Scarred like volcanoes. Envy, hatred and malice in plain sight. Wonderfully flexible voices. They weep, too.'

'Aloud? In public?'

'I guarantee. Not a spark of shame or reticence in the entire installation. It's the chance of your career.'

'D'you say you've brought their voting props along – those papers and ballot-boxes things?'

'No, confound you! I'm not a luggage-lifter. Apply direct to the Mayor of Chicago. He'll forward you everything. Well?'

'Wait a minute. Did Chicago want to kill 'em? That 'ud look well on the Communicators.'

'Yes! They were only rescued with difficulty from a howling mob – if you know what that is.'

'But I don't,' answered the Great Vincent simply.

'Well, then, they'll tell you themselves. They can make speeches hours long.'

'How many are there?'

'By the time we ship 'em all over they'll be perhaps a hundred, counting children. An old world in miniature. Can't you see it?'

'M-yes; but I've got to pay for it if it's a blow-out, dear man.'

'They can sing the old war-songs in the streets. They can get word-drunk, and make crowds and invade privacy in the genuine old-fashioned way; and they'll do the voting act as often as you ask 'em a question.'

'Too good!' said Vincent.

'You unbelieving Jew! I've got a dozen head aboard here. I'll put you through direct. Sample 'em yourself.'

He lifted the switch, and we listened. Our passengers on the lower deck at once, but not less than five at a time, explained themselves to Vincent. They had been taken from the bosom of their families; stripped of their possessions; given food without finger-bowls, and cast into captivity in a noisome dungeon.

'But look here,' said Arnott, aghast. 'They're saying what isn't true. My lower deck isn't noisome, and I saw to the finger-bowls myself.'

'My people talk like that sometimes in Little Russia,' said Dragomiroff. 'We reason with them. We never kill. No!'

'But it's not *true*,' Arnott insisted. 'What can you do with people who don't tell facts? They're mad!'

'Hsh!' said Pirolo, his hand to his ear. 'It is such a little time since all the Planet told lies.'

We heard Vincent, silkily sympathetic. Would they, he asked, repeat their assertions in public – before a vast public? Only let Vincent give them a chance, and the Planet, they vowed, should ring with their wrongs. Their aim in life – two women and a man explained it together – was to reform the world. Oddly enough, this also had been Vincent's life-dream. He offered them an arena in which to explain, and by their living example to raise the Planet to loftier levels. He was eloquent on the moral uplift of a simple, old-world life presented in its entirety to a deboshed civilisation.

Could they – would they – for three months certain, devote themselves under his auspices, as missionaries, to the eleva-tion of mankind at a place called Earl's Court, which he said, with some truth, was one of the intellectual centres of the Planet? They thanked him, and demanded (we could hear his chuckle of delight) time to discuss and to vote on the matter. The vote, solemnly managed by counting heads – one head, one vote – was favourable. His offer, therefore, was accepted, and they moved a vote of thanks to him in two speeches – one by what they called the 'proposer,' and the other by the 'seconder.'

Vincent threw over to us, his voice shaking with gratitude:

'I've got 'em! Did you hear those speeches? That's Nature, dear men. Art can't teach *that*. And they voted as easily as lying. I've never had a troupe of natural liars before. Bless you, dear men! Remember, you're on my free lists for ever – anywhere – all of you. Oh, Gerolstein will be sick – sick!'

'Then you think they'll do?' said De Forest.

'Do? The Little Village'll go crazy! I'll knock up a series of old-world plays for 'em. Their voices alone will make you laugh and cry. My God, dear men, where *do* you suppose they picked up all their misery from, on this sweet earth? I'll have a pageant of the world's beginning, and Mosenthal shall do the music. I'll—'

'Go and knock up a village for 'em by to-night. We'll meet you at No. 15, West Landing Tower,' said De Forest. 'Remember, the rest will be coming along tomorrow.'

'Let 'em all come!' said Vincent. 'You don't know how hard it is nowadays, even for *me*, to find something that really gets under the public's damned iridium-plated hide. But I've got it at last. Good-bye!'

'Well,' said De Forest, when we had finished laughing, 'if anyone understood corruption in London I might have played off Vincent against Gerolstein, and sold my captives at enormous prices. As it is, I shall have to be their legal adviser to-night when the contracts are signed. And they won't exactly press any commission on me, either.'

'Meantime,' said Takahira, 'we cannot, of course, confine members of Leopold Vincent's last-engaged company. Chairs for the ladies, please, Arnott.'

'Then I go to bed,' said De Forest. '*I* can't face any more women!' And he vanished.

When our passengers were released and given another meal {finger-bowls came first this time), they told us what they thought of us and the Board; and, like Vincent, we all marvelled how they had contrived to extract and secrete so much bitter poison and unrest out of the good life God gives us. They raged, they stormed, they palpitated, flushed and exhausted their poor, torn nerves, panted themselves into silence, and renewed the senseless, shameless attacks.

'But *can't* you understand,' said Pirolo pathetically to a shrieking woman, 'that if we'd left you in Chicago you'd have been killed?'

'No. We shouldn't. You were bound to save us from being murdered.'

'Then we should have had to kill a lot of other people.'

'*That* doesn't matter. We were preaching the truth. You can't stop us. We shall go on preaching in London; and *then* you'll see!'

'You can see now,' said Pirolo, and opened a lower shutter.

We were closing on the Little Village, with her three million people spread out at ease inside her ring of girdling Main-Traffic Lights – those eight fixed beams at Chatham, Tonbridge, Redhill, Dorking, Woking, St Albans, Chipping Ongar and Southend.

Leopold Vincent's new company looked, with small, pale faces, at the silence, the size, and the separated houses.

Then some began to weep aloud, shamelessly – always without shame.

SWEPT AND GARNISHED

When the first waves of feverish cold stole over Frau Ebermann, she very wisely telephoned for the doctor and went to bed. He diagnosed the attack as mild influenza, prescribed the appropriate remedies, and left her to the care of her one servant in her comfortable Berlin flat. Frau Ebermann, beneath the thick coverlet, curled up with what patience she could until the aspirin should begin to act, and Anna should come back from the chemist with the formamint, the ammoniated quinine, the eucalyptus, and the little tin steam inhaler. Meantime every bone in her body ached; her head throbbed; her hot, dry hands would not stay the same size for a minute together; and her body, tucked into the smallest possible compass, shrank from the chill of the well-warmed sheets.

Of a sudden she noticed that an imitation-lace cover which should have lain mathematically square with the imitation-marble top of the radiator behind the green plush sofa had slipped away so that one corner hung over the bronze-painted steam-pipes. She recalled that she must have rested her poor head against the radiator top while she was taking off her boots. She tried to get up and set the thing straight, but the radiator at once receded toward the horizon, which, unlike true horizons, slanted diagonally, exactly parallel with the dropped lace edge of the cover. Frau Ebermann groaned through sticky lips and lay still.

'Certainly I have a temperature,' she said. 'Certainly, I have a grave temperature. I should have been warned by that chill after dinner.'

She resolved to shut her hot-lidded eyes, but opened them in a little while to torture herself with the knowledge of that ungeometrical outrage against the far wall. Then she saw a child – an untidy, thin-faced little girl of about ten, who must have strayed in from the adjoining flat. This proved – Frau Ebermann groaned again at the way the world falls to bits when one is sick – proved that Anna had forgotten to shut the outer door of the flat when she went to the chemist. Frau Ebermann had had children of her own, but they were all grown-up now, and she had never been a child-lover in any sense. Yet the intruder might be made to serve her scheme of things.

'Make – put,' she muttered thickly – 'that white thing straight on the top of that yellow thing.'

The child paid no attention, but moved about the room, investigating everything that came in her way – the yellow cut-glass handles of the chest of drawers, the stamped bronze hook to hold back the heavy puce curtains, and the mauve enamel, new-art finger-plates on the door. Frau Ebermann watched indignantly.

'Aie! That is bad and rude. Go away!' she cried, though it hurt to raise her voice. 'Go away by the road you came.' The child passed behind the bedfoot, where she could not see her. 'Shut the door as you go. I will speak to Anna, but – first put that white thing straight.'

She closed her eyes in misery of body and soul. The outer door clicked, and Anna entered, very penitent that she had stayed so long at the chemist's. But it had been difficult to find the proper type of inhaler, and—

'Where did the child go,' moaned Frau Ebermann – 'the child that was here?'

'There was no child,' said startled Anna. 'How should any child come in when I shut the door behind me after I go out? All the keys of the flats are different.'

'No, no; you forgot this time. But my back is aching, and up my legs also. Besides, who knows what it may have fingered and upset? Look and see.'

'Nothing is fingered, nothing is upset,' Anna replied as she took the inhaler from its paper box.

'Yes, there is. Now I remember all about it. But – put that

613

white thing, with the open edge – the lace, I mean – quite straight on that—' She pointed. Anna, accustomed to her ways, understood and went to it.

'Now is it quite straight?' Frau Ebermann demanded.

'Perfectly,' said Anna. 'In fact, in the very centre of the radiator.' Anna measured the equal margins with her knuckle, as she had been told to do when she first took service.

'And my tortoise-shell hair brushes?' Frau Ebermann could not command her dressing-table from where she lay.

'Perfectly straight, side by side in the big tray, and the comb laid across them. Your watch also in the coralline watch-holder. Everything—' she moved round the room to make sure '—everything is as you have it when you are well.' Frau Ebermann sighed with relief. It seemed to her that the room and her head had suddenly grown cooler.

'Good!' said she. 'Now warm my nightgown in the kitchen, so it will be ready when I have perspired. And the towels also. Make the inhaler steam, and put in the eucalyptus; that is good for the larynx. Then sit you in the kitchen, and come when I ring. But first my hot-water bottle.'

It was brought and scientifically tucked in.

'What news?' said Frau Ebermann, drowsily. She had not been out that day.

'Another victory,' said Anna. 'Many more prisoners and guns.'

Frau Ebermann purred; one might almost say grunted contentedly.

'That is good, too,' she said, and Anna, after lighting the inhaler-lamp, went out.

Frau Ebermann reflected that in an hour or so the aspirin would begin to work, and all would be well. To-morrow – no, the day after – she would take up life with something to talk over with her friends at coffee. It was rare – every one knew it – that she should be overcome by any ailment. Yet in all her distress she had not allowed the minutest deviation from daily routine and ritual. She would tell her friends – she ran over their names one by one – exactly what measures she had taken against the lace-cover on the radiator top and in regard to her two tortoise-shell hair brushes and the comb at right angles. How she had set everything in order – everything in order. She roved further afield as she wriggled her toes luxuriously on the hot-water bottle. If it pleased our dear God to take her to Himself, and she was not so young as she had been, – there was that plate of four lower ones in the blue tooth-glass, for instance, – He should find all her belongings fit to meet His eye. 'Swept and garnished' were the words that shaped themselves in her intent brain. 'Swept and garnished for—'

No, it was certainly not for the dear Lord that she had swept; she would have her room swept out to-morrow or the day after, and garnished. Her hands began to swell again into huge pillows of nothingness. Then they shrank, and so did her head, to minute dots. It occurred her that she was waiting for some event, some tremendously important event, to come to pass. She lay with shut eyes for a long time till her head and hands should return to their proper size.

She opened her eyes with a jerk.

'How stupid of me,' she said aloud, 'to set the room in order for a parcel of dirty little children!'

They were there, – five of them, two little boys and three girls, – headed by the anxious-eyed ten-year-old whom she had seen before. They must have entered by the outer door, which Anna had neglected to shut behind her when she returned with the inhaler. She counted them backward and forward as one counts scales – one, two, three, four, five.

They took no notice of her, but hung about first on one foot then on the other, like strayed chickens, the smaller ones holding by the larger. They had the air of utterly wearied passengers in a railway waiting-room, and their clothes were disgracefully dirty.

'Go away!' cried Frau Ebermann at last, after she had struggled, it seemed to her, for years to shape the words.

'You called?' said Anna at the living-room door.

'No,' said her mistress. 'Did you shut the flat door when you came in?'

'Assuredly,' said Anna. 'Besides, it is made to catch shut of itself.'

'Then go away,' said she, very little above a whisper. If Anna pretended not to see the children, she would speak to Anna later on.

'And now,' she said, turning toward them as soon as the door closed. The smallest of the crowd smiled at her, and shook his head before he buried it in his sister's skirts.

'Why – don't – you – go – away?' she whispered earnestly.

Again they took no notice, but, guided by the elder girl, set themselves to climb, boots and all, on to the green plush sofa in front of the radiator. The little boys had to be pushed, as they could not compass the stretch unaided. They settled themselves in a row, with small gasps of relief, and pawed the plush approvingly.

'I ask you – I ask you why do you not go away – why do you not go away?' Frau Ebermann found herself repeating the question twenty times. It seemed to her that everything in the world hung on the answer. 'You know you should not come into houses and rooms unless you are invited. Not houses and bedrooms, you know.'

'No,' a solemn little six-year-old repeated; 'not houses, nor bedrooms, nor dining-rooms, nor churches, nor all those places. Shouldn't come in. It's rude.'

'Yes, he said so,' the younger girl put in proudly. 'He said it. He told them only pigs would do that,' The line nodded and dimpled one to another with little explosive giggles, such as children use when they tell deeds of great daring against their elders.

'If you *know* it is wrong, that makes it much worse,' said Frau Ebermann.

'Oh, yes; much worse,' they assented cheerfully, till the smallest boy changed his smile to a baby wail of weariness.

'When will they come for us?' he asked, and the girl at the head of the row hauled him bodily into her square little capable lap.

'He's tired,' she explained. 'He is only four. He only had his first breeches this spring.' They came almost under his armpits, and were held up by broad linen braces, which, his sorrow diverted for the moment, he patted proudly.

'Yes, beautiful, dear,' said both girls.

'Go away!' said Frau Ebermann. 'Go home to your father and mother!'

Their faces grew grave at once.

'H'sh! We *can't*,' whispered the eldest. 'There isn't anything left.'

'All gone,' a boy echoed, and he puffed through pursed lips. 'Like *that*, uncle told me. Both cows, too.'

'*And* my own three ducks,' the boy on the girl's lap said sleepily.

'*So*, you see, we came here.' The elder girl leaned forward a little, caressing the child she rocked.

'I – I don't understand,' said Frau Ebermann. 'Are you lost, then? You must tell our police.'

'Oh, no; we are only waiting.'

'But what are you waiting *for*?'

'We are waiting for our people to come for us. They told us to come here and wait for them. So we are waiting till they come,' the eldest girl replied.

'Yes. We are waiting till our people come for us,' said all the others in chorus.

'But,' said Frau Ebermann very patiently – 'but now tell me, for I tell you that I am not in the least angry, where do you come from? Where do you come from?'

The five gave the names of two villages of which she had read in the papers.

'That is silly,' said Frau Ebermann. 'The people fired on us, and they were punished. Those places are wiped out, stamped flat.'

'Yes, yes, wiped out, stamped flat. That is why and – I have lost the ribbon off my pigtail,' said the younger girl. She looked behind her over the sofa-back.

'It is not here,' said the elder. 'It was lost before. Don't you remember?'

'Now, if you are lost, you must go and tell our police. They will take care of you and give you food,' said Frau Ebermann. 'Anna will show you the way there.'

'No,' – this was the six-year-old, with the smile, 'we must wait here till our people come for us. Mustn't we, sister?'

'Of *course*; we wait here till our people come for us. All the world knows that,' said the eldest girl.

'Yes,' The boy in her lap had waked again. 'Little children, too – as little as Henri, and *he* doesn't wear trousers yet. As little as all that.'

'I don't understand,' said Frau Ebermann shivering. In spite of the heat of the room and the damp breath of the steam-inhaler, the aspirin was not doing its duty.

The girl raised her blue eyes and looked at the woman for an instant.

'You see,' she said, ticking off her statements on her fingers, '*they* told *us* to wait *here* till *our* people came for us. So we came. We wait till our people come for us.'

'That is silly again,' said Frau Ebermann. 'It is no good for you to wait here. Do you know what this place is? You have been to school? It is Berlin, the capital of Germany.'

'Yes, yes,' they all cried; 'Berlin, capital of Germany. *We* know that. That is why we came.'

'So, you see, it is no good,' she said triumphantly; 'because your people can never come for you here.'

'They told us to come here and wait till our people came for us.' They delivered this as if it were a lesson in school. Then they sat still, their hands orderly folded on their laps, smiling as sweetly as ever.

'Go away! Go away!' Frau Ebermann shrieked.

'You called?' said Anna, entering.

'No, Go away! Go away!'

'Very good, old cat,' said the maid under her breath. 'Next time you *may* call,' and she returned to her friend in the kitchen.

'I ask you – I ask you, *please* to go away,' Frau Ebermann pleaded. 'Go to my Anna through that door, and she will give you cakes and sweeties. It is not kind of you to come into my room and behave so badly.'

'Where else shall we go now?' the elder girl demanded, turning to her little company. They fell into discussion. One preferred the broad street with trees, another the railway station; but when she suggested the emperor's palace, they agreed with her.

'We will go, then,' she said, and added half apologetically to Frau Ebermann, 'You see, they are so little they like to meet all the others.'

'What others?' said Frau Ebermann.

'The others – hundreds and hundreds and thousands and thousands of the others.'

'That is a lie. There cannot be a hundred even, much less a thousand,' cried Frau Ebermann.

'So?' said the girl, politely.

'Yes. *I* tell you; and I have very good information. I know how it happened. You should have been more careful. You should not have run out to see the horses and guns passing. That is how it is done when our troops pass through. My son has written me so.'

They had clambered down from the sofa and gathered round the bed with eager, interested eyes.

'Horses and guns going by – how fine!' some one whispered.

'Yes, yes; believe me, *that* is how the accidents to the children happen. You must know yourself that it is true. One runs out to look—'

'But I never saw any at all,' a boy cried sorrowfully. 'Only one noise I heard. That was when Aunt Emmeline's house fell down.'

'But listen to me. *I* am telling you. One runs out to look, because one is little and cannot see well. So one peeps between the man's legs, and then – you know how close those big horses and guns turn the corners – then one's foot slips and one gets run over. That's how it happens. Several times it has happened, but not many times; certainly not a hundred, per-haps not twenty. So, you see, you must be all. Tell me now that you are all that there are, and Anna shall give you the cakes.'

'Thousands,' a boy repeated montonously. 'Then we all come here to wait till our people come for us.'

'But now we will go away from here. The poor lady is tired,' said the elder girl, plucking his sleeve.

'Oh, you hurt, you hurt!' he cried, and burst into tears.

'What is that for?' said Frau Ebermann. 'To cry in a room where a poor lady is sick is very inconsiderate.'

'Oh, but look, lady!' said the elder girl.

Frau Ebermann looked and saw.

'*Au revoir*, lady.' They made their little smiling bows and curtsies undisturbed by her loud cries. '*Au revoir*, lady; we will wait till our people come for us.'

When Anna at last ran, she found her mistress on her knees, busily cleaning the floor with the lace-cover from the radiator, because, she explained, it was all spotted with the blood of five children, – she was perfectly certain there could not be more than five, – who had gone away for the moment, but were now waiting round the corner, and Anna was to find them and give them cakes to stop the bleeding, while her mistress swept and garnished that our dear Lord when He came might find everything as it should be.

MARY POSTGATE

Of Miss Mary Postgate, Lady McCausland wrote that she was 'thoroughly conscientious, tidy, companionable, and ladylike. I am very sorry to part with her, and shall always be interested in her welfare.'

Miss Fowler engaged her on this recommendation, and to her surprise, for she had had experience of companions, found that it was true. Miss Fowler was nearer sixty than fifty at the time, but though she needed care she did not exhaust her attendant's vitality. On the contrary, she gave out, stimulatingly and with reminiscences. Her father had been a minor Court official in the days when the Great Exhibition of 1851 had just set its seal on Civilisation made perfect. Some of Miss Fowler's tales, none the less, were not always for the young. Mary was not young, and though her speech was as colourless as her eyes or her hair, she was never shocked. She listened unflinchingly to every one; said at the end, 'How interesting!' or 'How shocking!' as the case might be, and never again referred to it, for she prided herself on a trained mind, which 'did not dwell on these things'. She was, too, a treasure at domestic accounts, for which the village tradesmen, with their weekly books, loved her not. Otherwise she had no enemies; provoked no jealousy even among the plainest; neither gossip nor slander had ever been traced to her; she supplied the odd place at the Rector's or the Doctor's table at half an hour's notice; she was a sort of public aunt to very many small children of the village street, whose parents, while accepting everything, would have been swift to resent what they called 'patronage'; she served on the Village Nursing Committee as Miss Fowler's nominee when Miss Fowler was crippled by rheumatoid arthritis, and came out of six months' fortnightly meetings equally respected by all the cliques.

And when Fate threw Miss Fowler's nephew, an unlovely orphan of eleven, on Miss Fowler's hands, Mary Postgate stood to her share of the business of education as practised in private and public schools. She checked printed clothes-lists, and unitemised bills of extras; wrote to Head and House masters, matrons, nurses and doctors, and grieved or rejoiced over half-term reports. Young Wyndham Fowler repaid her in his holidays by calling her 'Gatepost', 'Postey', or 'Packthread', by thumping her between her narrow shoulders, or by chasing her bleating, round the garden, her large mouth open, her large nose high in air, at a stiff-necked shamble very like a camel's. Later on he filled the house with clamour, argument, and harangues as to his personal needs, likes and dislikes, and the limitations of 'you women', reducing Mary to tears of physical fatigue, or, when he chose to be humorous, of helpless laughter. At crises, which multiplied as he grew older, she was his ambassadress and his interpretress to Miss Fowler, who had no large sympathy with the young; a vote in his interest at the councils on his future; his sewing-woman, strictly accountable for mislaid boots and garments; always his butt and his slave.

And when he decided to become a solicitor, and had entered an office in London; when his greeting had changed from 'Hullo, Postey, you old beast', to 'Mornin', Packthread', there came a war which, unlike all wars that Mary could remember, did not stay decently outside England and in the newspapers, but intruded on the lives of people whom she knew. As she said to Miss Fowler, it was 'most vexatious'. It took the Rector's son who was going into business with his elder brother; it took the Colonel's nephew on the eve of fruit-farming in Canada; it took Mrs Grant's son who, his mother said, was devoted to the ministry; and, very early indeed, it took Wynn Fowler, who announced on a postcard that he had joined the Flying Corps and wanted a cardigan waistcoat.

'He must go, and he must have the waistcoat,' said Miss Fowler, So Mary got the proper-sized needles and wool, while

Miss Fowler told the men of her establishment – two gardeners and an odd man, aged sixty – that those who could join the Army had better do so. The gardeners left. Cheape, the odd man, stayed on, and was promoted to the gardener's cottage. The cook, scorning to be limited in luxuries, also left, after a spirited scene with Miss Fowler, and took the housemaid with her. Miss Fowler gazetted Nellie, Cheape's seventeen-year-old daughter, to the vacant post; Mrs Cheape to the rank of cook, with occasional cleaning bouts; and the reduced establishment moved forward smoothly.

Wynn demanded an increase in his allowance. Miss Fowler, who always looked facts in the face, said, 'He must have it. The chances are he won't live long to draw it, and if three hundred makes him happy—'

Wynn was grateful, and came over, in his tight-buttoned uniform, to say so. His training centre was not thirty miles away, and his talk was so technical that it had to be explained by charts of the various types of machines. He gave Mary such a chart.

'And you'd better study it, Postey,' he said. 'You'll be seeing a lot of 'em soon.' So Mary studied the chart, but when Wynn next arrived to swell and exalt himself before his womenfolk, she failed badly in cross-examination, and he rated her as in the old days.

'You *look* more or less like a human being,' he said in his new Service voice. 'You *must* have had a brain at some time in your past. What have you done with it? Where d'you keep it? A sheep would know more than you do, Postey. You're lamentable. You are less use than an empty tin can, you dowey old cassowary.'

'I suppose that's how your superior officer talks to *you*?' said Miss Fowler from her chair.

'But Postey doesn't mind,' Wynn replied. 'Do you, Packthread?'

'Why? Was Wynn saying anything? I shall get this right next time you come,' she muttered, and knitted her pale brows again over the diagrams of Taubes, Farmans, and Zeppelins.

In a few weeks the mere land and sea battles which she

read to Miss Fowler after breakfast passed her like idle breath. Her heart and her interest were high in the air with Wynn, who had finished 'rolling' (whatever that might be) and had gone on from a 'taxi' to a machine more or less his own. One morning it circled over their very chimneys, alighted on Vegg's Heath, almost outside the garden gate, and Wynn came in, blue with cold, shouting for food. He and she drew Miss Fowler's bath-chair, as they had often done, along the Heath footpath to look at the biplane. Mary observed that 'it smelt very badly'.

'Postey, I believe you think with your nose,' said Wynn. 'I know you don't with your mind. Now, what type's that?'

'I'll go and get the chart,' said Mary.

'You're hopeless! You haven't the mental capacity of a white mouse,' he cried, and explained the dials and the sockets for bomb-dropping till it was time to mount and ride the wet clouds once more.

'Ah!' said Mary, as the stinking thing flared upward. 'Wait till our Flying Corps gets to work! Wynn says it's much safer than in the trenches.'

'I wonder,' said Miss Fowler. 'Tell Cheape to come and tow me home again.'

'It's all downhill. I can do it,' said Mary, 'if you put the brake on.' She laid her lean self against the pushing-bar and home they trundled.

'Now, be careful you aren't heated and catch a chill,' said overdressed Miss Fowler.

'Nothing makes me perspire,' said Mary. As she bumped the chair under the porch she straightened her long back. The exertion had given her a colour, and the wind had loosened a wisp of hair across her forehead. Miss Fowler glanced at her.

'What do you ever think of, Mary?' she demanded suddenly.

'Oh, Wynn says he wants another three pairs of stockings – as thick as we can make them.'

'Yes. But I mean the things that women think about. Here you are, more than forty—'

'Forty-four,' said truthful Mary.

'Well?'

'Well?' Mary offered Miss Fowler her shoulder as usual.

'And you've been with me ten years now.'

'Let's see,' said Mary. 'Wynn was eleven when he came. He's twenty now, and I came two years before that. It must be eleven.'

'Eleven! And you've never told me anything that matters in all that while. Looking back, it seems to me that I've done all the talking.'

'I'm afraid I'm not much of a conversationalist. As Wynn says, I haven't the mind. Let me take your hat.'

Miss Fowler, moving stiffly from the hip, stamped her rubber-tipped stick on the tiled hall floor. 'Mary, aren't you *anything* except a companion? Would you *ever* have been anything except a companion?'

Mary hung up the garden hat on its proper peg. 'No,' she said after consideration. 'I don't imagine I ever should. But I've no imagination, I'm afraid.'

She fetched Miss Fowler her eleven-o'clock glass of Contrexeville.

That was the wet December when it rained six inches to the month, and the women went abroad as little as might be. Wynn's flying chariot visited them several times, and for two mornings (he had warned her by postcard) Mary heard the thresh of his propellers at dawn. The second time she ran to the window, and stared at the whitening sky. A little blur passed overhead. She lifted her lean arms towards it.

That evening at six o'clock there came an announcement in an official envelope that Second Lieutenant W. Fowler had been killed during a trial flight. Death was instantaneous. She read it and carried it to Miss Fowler.

'I never expected anything else,' said Miss Fowler; 'but I'm sorry it happened before he had done anything.'

The room was whirling round Mary Postgate, but she found herself quite steady in the midst of it.

'Yes,' she said. 'It's a great pity he didn't die in action after he had killed somebody.'

'He was killed instantly. That's one comfort,' Miss Fowler went on.

'But Wynn says the shock of a fall kills a man at once – whatever happens to the tanks,' quoted Mary.

The room was coming to rest now. She heard Miss Fowler say impatiently, 'But why can't we cry, Mary?' and herself replying, 'There's nothing to cry for. He has done his duty as much as Mrs Grant's son did.'

'And when he died, *she* came and cried all the morning,' said Miss Fowler. 'This only makes me feel tired – terribly tired. Will you help me to bed, please, Mary? – And I think I'd like the hot-water bottle.'

So Mary helped her and sat beside, talking of Wynn in his riotous youth.

'I believe,' said Miss Fowler suddenly, 'that old people and young people slip from under a stroke like this. The aged feel it most.'

'I expect that's true,' said Mary, rising. 'I'm going to put away the things in his room now. Shall we wear mourning?'

'Certainly not,' said Miss Fowler. 'Except, of course, at the funeral. I can't go. You will. I want you to arrange about his being buried here. What a blessing it didn't happen at Salisbury!'

Everyone, from the Authorities of the Flying Corps to the Rector, was most kind and sympathetic. Mary found herself for the moment in a world where bodies were in the habit of being despatched by all sorts of conveyances to all sorts of places. And at the funeral two young men in buttoned-up uniforms stood beside the grave and spoke to her afterwards.

'You're Miss Postgate, aren't you?' said one. 'Fowler told me about you. He was a good chap – a first-class fellow – a great loss.'

'Great loss!' growled his companion. 'We're all awfully sorry.'

'How high did he fall from?' Mary whispered.

'Pretty nearly four thousand feet, I should think, didn't he? You were up that day, Monkey?'

'All of that,' the other child replied. 'My bar made three thousand, and I wasn't as high as him by a lot.'

'Then *that's* all right,' said Mary. 'Thank you very much.'

They moved away as Mrs Grant flung herself weeping on Mary's flat chest, under the lych-gate, and cried, '*I* know how it feels! *I* know how it feels!'

'But both his parents are dead,' Mary returned, as she fended her off. 'Perhaps they've all met by now,' she added vaguely as she escaped towards the coach.

'I've thought of that too,' wailed Mrs Grant; 'but then he'll be practically a stranger to them. Quite embarrassing!'

Mary faithfully reported every detail of the ceremony to Miss Fowler, who, when she described Mrs Grant's outburst, laughed aloud.

'Oh, how Wynn would have enjoyed it! He was always utterly unreliable at funerals. D'you remember—' And they talked of him again, each piecing out the other's gaps. 'And now,' said Miss Fowler, 'we'll pull up the blinds and we'll have a general tidy. That always does us good. Have you seen to Wynn's things?'

'Everything – since he first came,' said Mary. 'He was never destructive – even with his toys.'

They faced that neat room.

'It can't be natural not to cry,' Mary said at last. 'I'm *so* afraid you'll have a reaction.'

'As I told you, we old people slip from under the stroke. It's you I'm afraid for. Have you cried yet?'

'I can't. It only makes me angry with the Germans.'

'That's sheer waste of vitality,' said Miss Fowler. 'We must live till the war's finished.' She opened a full wardrobe. 'Now, I've been thinking things over. This is my plan. All his civilian clothes can be given away – Belgian refugees, and so on.'

Mary nodded. 'Boots, collars, and gloves?'

'Yes. We don't need to keep anything except his cap and belt.'

'They came back yesterday with his Flying Corps clothes' – Mary pointed to a roll on the little iron bed.

'Ah, but keep his Service things. Someone may be glad of them later. Do you remember his size?'

'Five feet eight and a half; thirty-six inches round the chest.

But he told me he's just put on an inch and a half. I'll mark it on a label and tie it on his sleeping-bag.'

'So that disposes of *that*,' said Miss Fowler, tapping the palm of one hand with the ringed third finger of the other. 'What waste it all is! We'll get his old school trunk tomorrow and pack his civilian clothes.'

'And the rest?' said Mary. 'His books and pictures and the games and the toys – and – and the rest?'

'My plan is to burn every single thing,' said Miss Fowler. 'Then we shall know where they are and no one can handle them afterwards. What do you think?'

'I think that would be much the best,' said Mary. 'But there's such a lot of them.'

'We'll burn them in the destructor,' said Miss Fowler.

This was an open-air furnace for the consumption of refuse; a little circular four-foot tower of pierced brick over an iron grating. Miss Fowler had noticed the design in a gardening journal years ago, and had had it built at the bottom of the garden. It suited her tidy soul, for it saved unsightly rubbish-heaps, and the ashes lightened the stiff clay soil.

Mary considered for a moment, saw her way clear, and nodded again. They spent the evening putting away well-remembered civilian suits, underclothes that Mary had marked, and the regiments of very gaudy socks and ties. A second trunk was needed, and, after that, a little packing-case, and it was late next day when Cheape and the local carrier lifted them to the cart. The Rector luckily knew of a friend's son, about five feet eight and a half inches high, to whom a complete Flying Corps outfit would be most acceptable, and sent his gardener's son down with a barrow to take delivery of it. The cap was hung up in Miss Fowler's bedroom, the belt in Miss Postgate's; for, as Miss Fowler said, they had no desire to make tea-party talk of them.

'That disposes of *that*,' said Miss Fowler. 'I'll leave the rest to you, Mary. I can't run up and down the garden. You'd better take the big clothes-basket and get Nellie to help you.'

'I shall take the wheel-barrow and do it myself,' said Mary, and for once in her life closed her mouth.

Miss Fowler, in moments of irritation, had called Mary deadly methodical. She put on her oldest waterproof and gardening-hat and her ever-slipping goloshes, for the weather was on the edge of more rain. She gathered fire-lighters from the kitchen, a half-scuttle of coals, and a faggot of brushwood. These she wheeled in the barrow down the mossed paths to the dank little laurel shrubbery where the destructor stood under the drip of three oaks. She climbed the wire fence into the Rector's glebe just behind, and from his tenant's rick pulled two large armfuls of good hay, which she spread neatly on the fire-bars. Next, journey by journey, passing Miss Fowler's white face at the morning-room window each time, she brought down in the towel-covered clothes-basket, on the wheelbarrow, thumbed and used Hentys, Marryats, Levers, Stevensons, Baroness Orczys, Garvices, schoolbooks, and atlases, unrelated piles of the *Motor Cyclist*, the *Light Car*, and catalogues of Olympia Exhibitions; the remnants of a fleet of sailing-ships from ninepenny cutters to a three-guinea yacht; a prep-school dressing-gown; bats from three-and-sixpence to twenty-four shillings; cricket and tennis balls; disintegrated steam and clockwork locomotives with their twisted rails; a grey and red tin model of a submarine; a dumb gramophone and cracked records; golf-clubs that had to be broken across the knee, like his walking-sticks, and an assegai; photographs of private and public school cricket and football elevens, and his OTC on the line of march; kodaks, and film-rolls; some pewters, and one real silver cup, for boxing competitions and Junior Hurdles; sheaves of school photographs; Miss Fowler's photograph; her own which he had borne off in fun and (good care she took not to ask!) had never returned; a playbox with a secret drawer; a load of flannels, belts, and jerseys, and a pair of spiked shoes unearthed in the attic; a packet of all the letters that Miss Fowler and she had ever written to him, kept for some absurd reason through all these years; a five-day attempt at a diary; framed pictures of racing motors in full Brooklands career, and load upon load of undistinguishable wreckage of tool-boxes, rabbit-hutches, electric batteries, tin soldiers, fret-saw outfits, and jig-saw puzzles.

Miss Fowler at the window watched her come and go, and said to herself, 'Mary's an old woman. I never realised it before.'

After lunch she recommended her to rest.

'I'm not in the least tired,' said Mary. 'I've got it all arranged. I'm going to the village at two o'clock for some paraffin. Nellie hasn't enough, and the walk will do me good.'

She made one last quest round the house before she started, and found that she had overlooked nothing. It began to mist as soon as she had skirted Vegg's Heath, where Wynn used to descend – it seemed to her that she could almost hear the beat of his propellers overhead, but there was nothing to see. She hoisted her umbrella and lunged into the blind wet till she had reached the shelter of the empty village. As she came out of Mr Kidd's shop with a bottle full of paraffin in her string shopping-bag, she met Nurse Eden, the village nurse, and fell into talk with her, as usual, about the village children. They were just parting opposite the 'Royal Oak', when a gun, they fancied, was fired immediately behind the house. It was followed by a child's shriek dying into a wail.

'Accident!' said Nurse Eden promptly, and dashed through the empty bar, followed by Mary. They found Mrs Gerritt, the publican's wife, who could only gasp and point to the yard, where a little cart-lodge was sliding sideways amid a clatter of tiles. Nurse Eden snatched up a sheet drying before the fire, ran out, lifted something from the ground, and flung the sheet round it. The sheet turned scarlet and half her uniform too, as she bore the load into the kitchen. It was little Edna Gerritt, aged nine, whom Mary had known since her perambulator days.

'Am I hurted bad?' Edna asked, and died between Nurse Eden's dripping hands. The sheet fell aside and for an instant, before she could shut her eyes, Mary saw the ripped and shredded body.

'It's a wonder she spoke at all,' said Nurse Eden. 'What in God's name was it?'

'A bomb,' said Mary.

'One o' the Zeppelins?'

'No. An aeroplane. I thought I heard it on the Heath, but I fancied it was one of ours. It must have shut off its engines as it came down. That's why we didn't notice it.'

'The filthy pigs!' said Nurse Eden, all white and shaken. 'See the pickle I'm in! Go and tell Dr Hennis, Miss Postgate.' Nurse looked at the mother, who had dropped face down on the floor. 'She's only in a fit. Turn her over.'

Mary heaved Mrs Gerritt right side up, and hurried off for the doctor. When she told her tale, he asked her to sit down in the surgery till he got her something.

'But I don't need it, I assure you,' said she. 'I don't think it would be wise to tell Miss Fowler about it, do you? Her heart is so irritable in this weather.'

Dr Hennis looked at her admiringly as he packed up his bag.

'No. Don't tell anybody till we're sure,' he said, and hastened to the 'Royal Oak', while Mary went on with the paraffin. The village behind her was as quiet as usual, for the news had not yet spread. She frowned a little to herself, her large nostrils expanded uglily, and from time to time she muttered a phrase which Wynn, who never restrained himself before his womenfolk, had applied to the enemy. 'Bloody pagans! They *are* bloody pagans. But,' she continued, falling back on the teaching that had made her what she was, 'one mustn't let one's mind dwell on these things.'

Before she reached the house Dr Hennis, who was also a special constable, overtook her in his car.

'Oh, Miss Postgate,' he said, 'I wanted to tell you that that accident at the "Royal Oak" was due to Gerritt's stable tumbling down. It's been dangerous for a long time. It ought to have been condemned.'

'I thought I heard an explosion too,' said Mary.

'You might have been misled by the beams snapping. I've been looking at 'em. They were dry-rotted through and through. Of course, as they broke, they would make a noise just like a gun.'

'Yes?' said Mary politely.

'Poor little Edna was playing underneath it,' he went on,

still holding her with his eyes, 'and that and the tiles cut her to pieces, you see?'

'I saw it,' said Mary, shaking her head. 'I heard it too.'

'Well, we cannot be sure.' Dr Hennis changed his tone completely. 'I know both you and Nurse Eden (I've been speaking to her) are perfectly trustworthy, and I can rely on you not to say anything – yet at least. It is no good to stir up people unless—'

'Oh, I never do – anyhow,' said Mary, and Dr Hennis went on to the county town.

After all, she told herself, it might, just possibly, have been the collapse of the old stable that had done all those things to poor little Edna. She was sorry she had even hinted at other things, but Nurse Eden was discretion itself. By the time she reached home the affair seemed increasingly remote by its very monstrosity. As she came in, Miss Fowler told her that a couple of aeroplanes had passed half an hour ago.

'I thought I heard them,' she replied. 'I'm going down to the garden now. I've got the paraffin.'

'Yes, but – what *have* you got on your boots? They're soaking wet. Change them at once.'

Not only did Mary obey but she wrapped the boots in a newspaper, and put them into the string bag with the bottle. So, armed with the longest kitchen poker, she left.

'It's raining again,' was Miss Fowler's last word, 'but – I know you won't be happy till that's disposed of.'

'It won't take long. I've got everything down there, and I've put the lid on the destructor to keep the wet out.'

The shrubbery was filling with twilight by the time she had completed her arrangements and sprinkled the sacrificial oil. As she lit the match that would burn her heart to ashes, she heard a groan or a grunt behind the dense Portugal laurels.

'Cheape?' she called impatiently, but Cheape, with his ancient lumbago, in his comfortable cottage would be the last man to profane the sanctuary. 'Sheep,' she concluded, and threw in the fusee. The pyre went up in a roar, and the immediate flame hastened night around her.

'How Wynn would have loved this!' she thought, stepping back from the blaze.

By its light she saw, half hidden behind a laurel not five paces away, a bareheaded man sitting very stiffly at the foot of one of the oaks. A broken branch lay across his lap – one booted leg protruding from beneath it. His head moved ceaselessly from side to side, but his body was as still as the tree's trunk. He was dressed – she moved sideways to look more closely – in a uniform something like Wynn's, with a flap buttoned across the chest. For an instant, she had some idea that it might be one of the young flying men she had met at the funeral. But their heads were dark and glossy. This man's was as pale as a baby's, and so closely cropped that she could see the disgusting pinky skin beneath. His lips moved.

'What do you say?' Mary moved towards him and stooped.

'Laty! Laty! Laty!' he muttered, while his hands picked at the dead wet leaves. There was no doubt as to his nationality. It made her so angry that she strode back to the destructor, though it was still too hot to use the poker there. Wynn's books seemed to be catching well. She looked up at the oak behind the man; several of the light upper and two or three rotten lower branches had broken and scattered their rubbish on the shrubbery path. On the lowest fork a helmet with dependent strings, showed like a bird's-nest in the light of a long-tongued flame. Evidently this person had fallen through the tree. Wynn had told her that it was quite possible for people to fall out of aeroplanes. Wynn told her too, that trees were useful things to break an aviator's fall, but in this case the aviator must have been broken or he would have moved from his queer position. He seemed helpless except for his horrible rolling head. On the other hand, she could see a pistol case at his belt – and Mary loathed pistols. Months ago, after reading certain Belgian reports together, she and Miss Fowler had had dealings with one – a huge revolver with flat-nosed bullets, which latter, Wynn said, were forbidden by the rules of war to be used against civilised enemies. 'They're good enough for us,' Miss Fowler had replied. 'Show Mary how it works.' And Wynn, laughing at the mere possibility of any such need, had

633

led the craven winking Mary into the Rector's disused quarry, and had shown her how to fire the terrible machine. It lay now in the top-left-hand drawer of her toilet-table – a memento not included in the burning. Wynn would be pleased to see how she was not afraid.

She slipped up to the house to get it. When she came through the rain, the eyes in the head were alive with expectation. The mouth even tried to smile. But at sight of the revolver its corners went down just like Edna Gerritt's. A tear trickled from one eye, and the head rolled from shoulder to shoulder as though trying to point out something.

'Cassée. Tout cassée,' it whimpered.

'What do you say?' said Mary disgustedly, keeping well to one side, though only the head moved.

'Cassée,' it repeated. 'Che me rends. Le médicin! Toctor!'

'Nein!' said she, bringing all her small German to bear with the big pistol. 'Ich haben der todt Kinder gesehn.'

The head was still. Mary's hand dropped. She had been careful to keep her finger off the trigger for fear of accidents. After a few moments' waiting, she returned to the destructor, where the flames were falling, and churned up Wynn's charring books with the poker. Again the head groaned for the doctor.

'Stop that!' said Mary, and stamped her foot. 'Stop that, you bloody pagan!'

The words came quite smoothly and naturally. They were Wynn's own words, and Wynn was a gentleman who for no consideration on earth would have torn little Edna into those vividly coloured strips and strings. But this thing hunched under the oak-tree had done that thing. It was no question of reading horrors out of newspapers to Miss Fowler. Mary had seen it with her own eyes on the 'Royal Oak' kitchen table. She must not allow her mind to dwell upon it. Now Wynn was dead, and everything connected with him was lumping and rustling and tinkling under her busy poker into red black dust and grey leaves of ash. The thing beneath the oak would die too. Mary had seen death more than once. She came of a family that had a knack of dying under, as she told Miss

Fowler, 'most distressing circumstances'. She would stay where she was till she was entirely satisfied that It was dead – dead as dear papa in the late 'eighties; aunt Mary in 'eighty-nine; mamma in 'ninety-one; cousin Dick in 'ninety-five; Lady McCausland's housemaid in 'ninety-nine; Lady McCausland's sister in nineteen hundred and one; Wynn buried five days ago; and Edna Gerritt still waiting for decent earth to hide her. As she thought – her under-lip caught up by one faded canine, brows knit and nostrils wide – she wielded the poker with lunges that jarred the grating at the bottom, and careful scrapes round the brick work above. She looked at her wrist-watch. It was getting on to half-past four, and the rain was coming down in earnest. Tea would be at five. If It did not die before that time, she would be soaked and would have to change. Meantime, and this occupied her, Wynn's things were burning well in spite of the hissing wet, though now and again a book-back with a quite distinguishable title would be heaved up out of the mass. The exercise of stoking had given her a glow which seemed to reach to the marrow of her bones. She hummed – Mary never had a voice – to herself. She had never believed in all those advanced views – though Miss Fowler herself leaned a little that way – of woman's work in the world; but now she saw there was much to be said for them. This, for instance, was *her* work – work which no man, least of all Dr Hennis, would ever have done. A man, at such a crisis, would be what Wynn called a 'sportsman'; would leave everything to fetch help, and would certainly bring It into the house. Now a woman's business was to make a happy home for – for a husband and children. Failing these – it was not a thing one should allow one's mind to dwell upon – but—

'Stop it!' Mary cried once more across the shadows. 'Nein, I tell you! Ich haben der todt Kinder gesehn.'

But it was a fact. A woman who had missed these things could still be useful – more useful than a man in certain respects. She thumped like a pavior through the settling ashes at the secret thrill of it. The rain was damping the fire, but she could feel – it was too dark to see – that her work was done. There was a dull red glow at the bottom of the destructor, not enough to char the wooden lid if she slipped it half over against the driving wet. This arranged, she leaned on the poker and waited, while an increasing rapture laid hold on her. She ceased to think. She gave herself up to feel. Her long pleasure was broken by a sound that she had waited for in agony several times in her life. She leaned forward and listened, smiling. There could be no mistake. She closed her eyes and drank it in. Once it ceased abruptly.

'Go on,' she murmured, half aloud. 'That isn't the end.'

Then the end came very distinctly in a lull between two rain-gusts. Mary Postgate drew her breath short between her teeth and shivered from head to foot. '*That's* all right,' said she contentedly, and went up to the house, where she scandalised the whole routine by taking a luxurious hot bath before tea, and came down looking, as Miss Fowler said when she saw her lying all relaxed on the other sofa, 'quite handsome!'

THE VILLAGE THAT VOTED THE EARTH WAS FLAT

Our drive till then had been quite a success. The other men in the car were my friend Woodhouse, young Ollyett, a distant connection of his, and Pallant, the MP. Woodhouse's business was the treatment and cure of sick journals. He knew by instinct the precise moment in a newspaper's life when the impetus of past good management is exhausted and it fetches up on the dead-centre between slow and expensive collapse and the new start which can be given by gold injections – and genius. He was wisely ignorant of journalism; but when he stooped on a carcass there was sure to be meat. He had that week added a half-dead, halfpenny evening paper to his collection, which consisted of a prosperous London daily, one provincial ditto, and a limp-bodied weekly of commercial leanings. He had also, that very hour, planted me with a large block of the evening paper's common shares, and was explaining the whole art of editorship to Ollyett, a young man three years from Oxford, with coir-matting-coloured hair and a face harshly modelled by harsh experiences, who, I understood, was assisting in the new venture. Pallant, the long, wrinkled MP, whose voice is more like a crane's than a peacock's, took no shares, but gave us all advice.

'You'll find it rather a knacker's yard,' Woodhouse was saying. 'Yes, I know they call me The Knacker; but it will pay inside a year. All my papers do. I've only one motto: Back your luck and back your staff. It'll come out all right.'

Then the car stopped, and a policeman asked our names and addresses for exceeding the speed-limit. We pointed out that the road ran absolutely straight for half a mile ahead without even a sidelane. That's just what we depend on,' said the policeman unpleasantly.

'The usual swindle,' said Woodhouse under his breath 'What's the name of this place?'

'Huckley,' said the policeman. 'H-u-c-k-l-e-y,' and wrote something in his note-book at which young Ollyett protested. A large red man on a grey horse who had been watching us from the other side of the hedge shouted an order we could not catch. The policeman laid his hand on the rim of the right driving-door (Woodhouse carries his spare tyres aft), and it closed on the button of the electric horn. The grey horse at once bolted, and we could hear the rider swearing all across the landscape.

'Damn it, man, you've got your silly fist on it! Take it off!' Woodhouse shouted.

'Ho!' said the constable, looking carefully at his fingers as though we had trapped them. 'That won't do you any good either,' and he wrote once more in his note-book before he allowed us to go.

This was Woodhouse's first brush with motor law, and since I expected no ill consequences to myself, I pointed out that it was very serious. I took the same view myself when in due time I found that I, too, was summonsed on charges ranging from the use of obscene language to endangering traffic.

Judgment was done in a little pale-yellow market-town with a small Jubilee clock-tower and a large corn-exchange. Woodhouse drove us there in his car. Pallant, who had not been included in the summons, came with us as moral support. While we waited outside, the fat man on the grey horse rode up and entered into loud talk with his brother magistrates. He said to one of them – for I took the trouble to note it down – 'It falls away from my lodge-gates, dead straight, three-quarters of a mile. I'd defy any one to resist it. We rooked seventy pounds out of 'em last month. No car can resist the temptation. You ought to have one your side of the county, Mike. They simply can't resist it.'

'Whew!' said Woodhouse. 'We're in for trouble. Don't you

say a word – or Ollyett either! I'll pay the fines and we'll get it over as soon as possible. Where's Pallant?'

'At the back of the court somewhere,' said Ollyett. 'I saw him slip in just now.'

The fat man then took his seat on the Bench, of which he was chairman, and I gathered from a bystander that his name was Sir Thomas Ingell, Bart, MP, of Ingell Park, Huckley. He began with an allocution pitched in a tone that would have justified revolt throughout empires. Evidence, when the crowded little court did not drown it with applause, was given in the pauses of the address. They were all very proud of their Sir Thomas, and looked from him to us, wondering why we did not applaud too.

Taking its time from the chairman, the Bench rollicked with us for seventeen minutes. Sir Thomas explained that he was sick and tired of processions of cads of our type, who would be better employed breaking stones on the road than in frightening horses worth more than themselves or their ancestors. This was after it had been proved that Woodhouse's man had turned on the horn purposely to annoy Sir Thomas, who 'happened to be riding by'! There were other remarks too – primitive enough – but it was the unspeakable brutality of the tone, even more than the quality of the justice, or the laughter of the audience, that stung our souls out of all reason. When we were dismissed – to the tune of twenty-three pounds, twelve shillings and sixpence – we waited for Pallant to join us, while we listened to the next case – one of driving without a licence. Ollyett with an eye to his evening paper, had already taken very full notes of our own, but we did not wish to seem prejudiced.

'It's all right,' said the reporter of the local paper soothingly. 'We never report Sir Thomas *in extenso*. Only the fines and charges.'

'Oh, thank you,' Ollyett replied, and I heard him ask who every one in court might be. The local reporter was very communicative.

The new victim, a large, flaxen-haired man in somewhat striking clothes, to which Sir Thomas, now thoroughly warmed, drew public attention, said that he had left his licence at home. Sir Thomas asked him if he expected the police to go to his home address at Jerusalem to find it for him; and the court roared. Nor did Sir Thomas approve of the man's name, but insisted on calling him 'Mr Masquerader,' and every time he did so, all his people shouted. Evidently this was their established *auto-da fé*.

'He didn't summons me – because I'm in the House, I suppose. I think I shall have to ask a Question,' said Pallant, reappearing at the close of the case.

'I think *I* shall have to give it a little publicity too,' said Woodhouse. 'We can't have this kind of thing going on, you know.' His face was set and quite white. Pallant's, on the other hand, was black, and I know that my very stomach had turned with rage. Ollyett was dumb.

'Well, let's have lunch,' Woodhouse said at last. 'Then we can get away before the show breaks up.'

We drew Ollyett from the arms of the local reporter, crossed the Market Square to the Red Lion and found Sir Thomas's 'Mr Masquerader' just sitting down to beer, beef and pickles.

'Ah!' said he, in a large voice. 'Companions in misfortune. Won't you gentlemen join me?'

'Delighted,' said Woodhouse. 'What did you get?'

'I haven't decided. It might make a good turn, but – the public aren't educated up to it yet. It's beyond 'em. If it wasn't, that red dub on the Bench would be worth fifty a week.'

'Where?' said Woodhouse. The man looked at him with unaffected surprise.

'At any one of My places,' he replied. 'But perhaps you live here?'

'Good heavens!' cried young Ollyett suddenly. 'You *are* Masquerier, then? I thought you were!'

'Bat Masquerier.' He let the words fall with the weight of an international ultimatum. 'Yes, that's all I am. But you have the advantage of me, gentlemen.'

For the moment, while we were introducing ourselves, I was puzzled. Then I recalled prismatic music-hall posters – of enormous acreage – that had been the unnoticed background of my visits to London for years past. Posters of men and women, singers, jongleurs, impersonators and audacities of every draped and undraped brand, all moved on and off in London and the Provinces by Bat Masquerier – with the long wedge-tailed flourish following the final 'r.'

'*I* knew you at once,' said Pallant, the trained MP, and I promptly backed the lie. Woodhouse mumbled excuses. Bat Masquerier was not moved for or against us any more than the frontage of one of his own palaces.

'I always tell My people there's a limit to the size of the lettering,' he said. 'Overdo that and the ret'na doesn't take it in. Advertisin' is the most delicate of all the sciences.'

'There's one man in the world who is going to get a little of it if I live for the next twenty-four hours,' said Woodhouse, and explained how this would come about.

Masquerier stared at him lengthily with gunmetal-blue eyes.

'You mean it?' he drawled; the voice was as magnetic as the look.

'*I* do,' said Ollyett. 'That business of the horn alone ought to have him off the Bench in three months.' Masquerier looked at him even longer than he had looked at Woodhouse.

'He told *me*,' he said suddenly, 'that my home-address was Jerusalem. You heard that?'

'But it was the tone – the tone,' Ollyett cried.

'You noticed that, too, did you?' said Masquerier. That's the artistic temperament. You can do a lot with it. And I'm Bat Masquerier,' he went on. He dropped his chin in his fists and scowled straight in front of him . . . 'I made the Silhouettes – I made the Trefoil and the Jocunda. I made 'Dal Benzaguen.' Here Ollyett sat straight up, for in common with the youth of that year he worshipped Miss Vidal Benzaguen of the Trefoil immensely and unreservedly. ' "*Is* that a dressing-gown or an ulster you're supposed to be wearing?" You heard *that*? . . . "And I suppose you hadn't time to brush your hair either?" You heard *that*? . . . Now, you hear *me*!' His voice filled the coffee-room, then dropped to a whisper as dreadful as a surgeon's before an operation. He spoke for several minutes.

Pallant muttered 'Hear! Hear!' I saw Ollyett's eye flash – it was to Ollyett that Masquerier addressed himself chiefly – and Woodhouse leaned forward with joined hands.

'Are you *with* me?' he went on, gathering us all up in one sweep of the arm. 'When I begin a thing I see it through, gentlemen. What Bat can't break, breaks him! But I haven't struck that thing yet. This is no one-turn turn-it-down show. This is business to the dead finish. Are you with me, gentlemen? Good! Now, we'll pool our assets. One London morning, and one provincial daily, didn't you say? One weekly commercial ditto and one MP.'

'Not much use, I'm afraid,' Pallant smirked.

'But privileged. *But* privileged,' he returned. 'And we have also my little team – London, Blackburn, Liverpool, Leeds – I'll tell you about Manchester later – and Me! Bat Masquerier.' He breathed the name reverently into his tankard. 'Gentlemen, when our combination has finished with Sir Thomas Ingell, Bart, MP, and everything else that is his, Sodom and Gomorrah will be a winsome bit of Merrie England beside 'em. I must go back to town now, but I trust you gentlemen will give me the pleasure of your company at dinner to-night at the Chop Suey – the Red Amber Room – and we'll block out the scenario.' He laid his hand on young Ollyett's shoulder and added: 'It's your brains I want.'

Then he left, in a good deal of astrachan collar and nickel-plated limousine, and the place felt less crowded.

We ordered our car a few minutes later. As Woodhouse, Ollyett and I were getting in, Sir Thomas Ingell, Bart, MP, came out of the Hall of Justice across the square and mounted his horse. I have sometimes thought that if he had gone in silence he might even then have been saved, but as he settled himself in the saddle he caught sight of us and must needs shout: 'Not off yet? You'd better get away and you'd better be careful.' At that moment Pallant, who had been buying picture-postcards, came out of the inn, took Sir Thomas's eye and very leisurely entered the car. It seemed to me that for one instant there was a shade of uneasiness on the baronet's grey-whiskered face.

'I hope,' said Woodhouse after several miles, 'I hope he's a widower.'

'Yes,' said Pallant. 'For his poor, dear wife's sake I hope that, very much indeed. I suppose he didn't see me in Court. Oh, here's the parish history of Huckley written by the Rector and here's your share of the picture-postcards. Are we all dining with this Mr Masquerier to-night?'

'Yes!' said we all.

If Woodhouse knew nothing of journalism, young Ollyett, who had graduated in a hard school, knew a good deal. Our halfpenny evening paper, which we will call *The Bun* to distinguish her from her prosperous morning sister, *The Cake*, was not only diseased but corrupt. We found this out when a man brought us the prospectus of a new oil-field and demanded sub-leaders on its prosperity. Ollyett talked pure Brasenose to him for three minutes. Otherwise he spoke and wrote trade-English – a toothsome amalgam of Americanisms and epigrams. But though the slang changes the game never alters, and Ollyett and I and, in the end, some others enjoyed it immensely. It was weeks ere we could see the wood for the trees, but so soon as the staff realised that they had proprietors who backed them right or wrong, and specially when they were wrong (which is the sole secret of journalism), and that their fate did not hang on any passing owner's passing mood, they did miracles.

But we did not neglect Huckley. As Ollyett said, our first care was to create an 'arresting atmosphere' round it. He used to visit the village of week-ends, on a motor-bicycle with a side-car; for which reason I left the actual place alone and dealt with it in the abstract. Yet it was I who drew first blood. Two inhabitants of Huckley wrote to contradict a small, quite solid paragraph in *The Bun* that a hoopoe had been seen at Huckley and had, 'of course, been shot by the local sportsmen.' There was some heat in their letters, both of which we published. Our version of how the hoopoe got his crest from King Solomon was, I grieve to say, so inaccurate that the Rector himself – no sportsman as he pointed out, but a lover of accuracy – wrote to us to correct it. We gave his letter good space and thanked him.

'This priest is going to be useful,' said Ollyett. 'He has the impartial mind. I shall vitalise him.'

Forthwith he created M. L. Sigden, a recluse of refined tastes who in *The Bun* demanded to know whether this Huckley-of-the-Hoopoe was the Hugly of his boyhood and whether, by any chance, the fell change of name had been wrought by collusion between a local magnate and the railway, in the mistaken interests of spurious refinement. 'For I knew it and loved it with the maidens of my day – *eheu ab angulo!* – as Hugly,' wrote M. L. Sigden from Oxford.

Though other papers scoffed, *The Bun* was gravely sympathetic. Several people wrote to deny that Huckley had been changed at birth. Only the Rector – no philosopher as he pointed out, but a lover of accuracy – had his doubts, which he laid publicly before Mr M. L. Sigden, who suggested, through *The Bun*, that the little place might have begun life in Anglo-Saxon days as 'Hogslea' or among the Normans as 'Argilé,' on account of its much clay. The Rector had his own ideas too (he said it was mostly gravel), and M. L. Sigden had a fund of reminiscences. Oddly enough – which is seldom the case with free reading-matter – our subscribers rather relished the correspondence, and contemporaries quoted freely.

'The secret of power,' said Ollyett, 'is not the big stick. It's the liftable stick.' (This means the 'arresting' quotation of six or seven lines.) 'Did you see the *Spec.* had a middle on "Rural Tenacities" last week. That was all Huckley. I'm doing a "Mobiquity" on Huckley next week.'

Our 'Mobiquities' were Friday evening accounts of easy motor-bike-*cum*-side-car trips round London, illustrated (we could never get that machine to work properly) by smudgy maps. Ollyett wrote the stuff with a fervour and a delicacy which I always ascribed to the side-car. His account of Epping Forest, for instance, was simply young love with its soul at its lips. But his Huckley 'Mobiquity' would have sickened a soapboiler. It chemically combined loathsome familiarity, leering suggestion, slimy piety and rancid 'social service' in one fuming compost that fairly lifted me off my feet.

'Yes,' said he, after compliments. 'It's the most vital, arresting and dynamic bit of tump I've done up to date. *Non nobis gloria!* I met Sir Thomas Ingell in his own park. He talked to me again. He inspired most of it.'

'Which? The "glutinous native drawl," or "the neglected adenoids of the village children"?' I demanded.

'Oh, no! That's only to bring in the panel doctor. It's the last flight we— I'm proudest of.'

This dealt with 'the crepuscular penumbra spreading her dim limbs over the boskage'; with jolly rabbits'; with a herd of 'gravid polled Angus'; and with the 'arresting, gipsy-like face of their swart, scholarly owner – as well known at the Royal Agricultural Shows as that of our late King-Emperor.'

' "Swart" is good and so's "gravid," said I, but the panel doctor will be annoyed about the adenoids.'

'Not half as much as Sir Thomas will about his face,' said Ollyett. 'And if you only knew what I've left out!'

He was right. The panel doctor spent his week-end (this is the advantage of Friday articles) in overwhelming us with a professional counterblast of no interest whatever to our subscribers. We told him so, and he, then and there, battered his way with it into the *Lancet* where they are keen on glands, and forgot us altogether. But Sir Thomas Ingell was of sterner stuff. He must have spent a happy week-end too. The letter which we received from him on Monday proved him to be a kinless loon of upright life, for no woman, however remotely interested in a man would have let it pass the home wastepaper-basket. He objected to our references to his own herd, to his own labours in his own village, which he said was a Model Village, and to our infernal insolence; but he objected most to our invoice of his features. We wrote him courteously to ask whether the letter was meant for publication. He, remembering, I presume, the Duke of Wellington, wrote back, 'publish and be damned.'

'Oh! This is too easy,' Ollyett said as he began heading the letter.

'Stop a minute,' I said. 'The game is getting a little beyond us. Tonight's the Bat dinner.' (I may have forgotten to tell you that our dinner with Bat Masquerier in the Red Amber Room of the Chop Suey had come to be a weekly affair.)

'Hold it over till they've all seen it.'

'Perhaps you're right,' he said. 'You might waste it.'

At dinner, then, Sir Thomas's letter was handed round. Bat seemed to be thinking of other matters, but Pallant was very interested.

'I've got an idea,' he said presently. 'Could you put something into *The Bun* to-morrow about foot-and-mouth disease in that fellow's herd?'

'Oh, plague if you like,' Ollyett replied. 'They're only five measly Shorthorns. I saw one lying down in the park. She'll serve as a substratum of fact.'

'Then, do that; and hold the letter over meanwhile. I think *I* come in here,' said Pallant.

'Why?' said I.

'Because there's something coming up in the House about foot-and-mouth, and because he wrote me a letter after that little affair when he fined you. 'Took ten days to think it over. Here you are,' said Pallant. 'House of Commons paper, you see.'

We read

Dear Pallant – Although in the past our paths have not lain much together, I am sure you will agree with me that on the floor of the House all members are on a footing of equality. I make bold, therefore, to approach you in a matter which I think capable of a very different interpretation from that which perhaps was put upon it by your friends. Will you let them know that that was the case and that I was in no way swayed by animus in the exercise of my magisterial duties, which as you, as a brother magistrate, can imagine are frequently very distasteful to – Yours very sincerely,
    T. Ingell.
P.S. – I have seen to it that the motor vigilance to which your friends took exception has been considerably relaxed in my district.

'What did you answer?' said Ollyett, when all our opinions had been expressed.

'I told him I couldn't do anything in the matter. And I couldn't – then. But you'll remember to put in that foot-and-mouth paragraph. I want something to work upon.'

'It seems to me *The Bun* has done all the work up to date,' I suggested. 'When does *The Cake* come in?'

'*The Cake*,' said Woodhouse, and I remembered afterwards that he spoke like a Cabinet Minister on the eve of a Budget, 'reserves to itself the fullest right to deal with situations as they arise.'

'Ye-eh!' Bat Masquerier shook himself out of his thoughts. ' "Situations as they arise." I ain't idle either. But there's no use fishing till the swim's baited. You' – he turned to Ollyett – 'manufacture very good ground-bait . . . I always tell My people— What the deuce is that?'

There was a burst of song from another private dining-room across the landing. 'It ees some ladies from the Trefoil,' the waiter began.

'Oh, I know that. What are they singing, though?'

He rose and went out, to be greeted by shouts of applause from that merry company. Then there was silence, such as one hears in the form-room after a master's entry. Then a voice that we loved began again: 'Here we go gathering nuts in May – nuts in May – nuts in May!'

'It's only 'Dal – and some nuts,' he explained when he returned. 'She says she's coming in to dessert.' He sat down, humming the old tune to himself, and till Miss Vidal Benzaguen entered, he held us speechless with tales of the artistic temperament.

We obeyed Pallant to the extent of slipping into *The Bun* a wary paragraph about cows lying down and dripping at the mouth, which might be read either as an unkind libel or, in the hands of a capable lawyer, as a piece of faithful nature-study.

'And besides,' said Ollyett, 'we allude to "gravid polled Angus." I am advised that no action can lie in respect of virgin Shorthorns. Pallant wants us to come to the House to-night. He's got us places for the Strangers' Gallery. I'm beginning to like Pallant.'

'Masquerier seems to like you,' I said.

'Yes, but I'm afraid of him,' Ollyett answered with perfect sincerity. 'I am. He's the Absolutely Amoral Soul. I've never met one yet.'

We went to the House together. It happened to be an Irish afternoon, and as soon as I had got the cries and the faces a little sorted out, I gathered there were grievances in the air, but how many of them was beyond me.

'It's all right,' said Ollyett of the trained ear. 'They've shut their ports against – oh yes – export of Irish cattle! Foot-and-mouth disease at Ballyhellion. *I* see Pallant's idea!'

The House was certainly all mouth for the moment, but, as I could feel, quite in earnest. A Minister with a piece of typewritten paper seemed to be fending off volleys of insults. He reminded me somehow of a nervous huntsman breaking up a fox in the face of rabid hounds.

'It's question-time. They're asking questions,' said Ollyett. 'Look! Pallant's up.'

There was no mistaking it. His voice, which his enemies said was his one parliamentary asset, silenced the hubbub as tooth-ache silences mere singing in the ears. He said:

'Arising out of that, may I ask if any special consideration has recently been shown in regard to any suspected outbreak of this disease on *this* side of the Channel?'

He raised his hand; it held a noon edition of *The Bun*. We had thought it best to drop the paragraph out of the later ones. He would have continued, but something in a grey frock-coat roared and bounded on a bench opposite, and waved another *Bun*. It was Sir Thomas Ingell.

'As the owner of the herd so dastardly implicated—' His voice was drowned in shouts of 'Order!' – the Irish leading.

'What's wrong?' I asked Ollyett. 'He's got his hat on his head, hasn't he?'

'Yes, but his wrath should have been put as a question.'

'Arising out of that, Mr Speaker, Sirrr!' Sir Thomas bel-lowed through a lull, 'are you aware that – that all this is a conspiracy – part of a dastardly conspiracy to make Huckley ridiculous – to make *us* ridiculous? Part of a deep-laid plot to make *me* ridiculous, Mr Speaker, Sir!'

The man's face showed almost black against his white whiskers, and he struck out swimmingly with his arms. His vehemence puzzled and held the House for an instant, and the Speaker took advantage of it to lift his pack from Ireland to a new scent. He addressed Sir Thomas Ingell in tones of measured rebuke, meant also, I imagine, for the whole House, which lowered its hackles at the word. Then Pallant, shocked and pained: 'I can only express my profound surprise that in response to my simple question the honourable member should have thought fit to indulge in a personal attack. If I have in any way offended—'

Again the Speaker intervened, for it appeared that he regulated these matters.

He, too, expressed surprise, and Sir Thomas sat back in a hush of reprobation that seemed to have the chill of the centuries behind it. The Empire's work was resumed.

'Beautiful!' said I, and I felt hot and cold up my back.

'And now we'll publish his letter,' said Ollyett. We did – on the heels of his carefully reported outburst. We made no comment.

With that rare instinct for grasping the heart of a situation which is the mark of the Anglo-Saxon, all our contemporaries and, I should say, two-thirds of our correspondents demanded how such a person could be made more ridiculous than he had already proved himself to be. But beyond spelling his name 'Injle,' we alone refused to hit a man when he was down.

'There's no need,' said Ollyett. 'The whole press is on the huckle from end to end.'

Even Woodhouse was a little astonished at the ease with which it had come about, and said as much.

'Rot!' said Ollyett. 'We haven't really begun. Huckley isn't news yet.'

'What do you mean?' said Woodhouse, who had grown to have great respect for his young but by no means distant connection.

'Mean? By the grace of God, Master Ridley, I mean to have it so that when Huckley turns over in its sleep, Reuters and the Press Association jump out of bed to cable.' Then he went off at score about certain restorations in Huckley Church which, he said – and he seemed to spend his every week-end there – had been perpetrated by the Rector's predecessor, who had abolished a 'leper-window' or a 'squinch-hole' (whatever these may be) to institute a lavatory in the vestry. It did not strike me as stuff for which Reuters or the Press Association would lose much sleep, and I left him declaiming to Woodhouse about a fourteenth-century font which, he said, he had unearthed in the sexton's tool-shed.

My methods were more on the lines of peaceful penetration. An odd copy, in *The Bun*'s rag-and-bone library, of Hone's *Every-Day Book* had revealed to me the existence of a village dance founded, like all village dances, on Druidical mysteries connected with the Solar Solstice (which is always unchallengeable) and Midsummer Morning, which is dewy and refreshing to the London eye. For this I take no credit – Hone being a mine any one can work – but that I rechristened that dance, after I had revised it, 'The Gubby' is my title to immortal fame. It was still to be witnessed, I wrote, 'In all its poignant purity at Huckley, that last home of significant mediaeval survivals'; and I fell so in love with my creation that I kept it back for days, enamelling and burnishing.

'You's better put it in,' said Ollyett at last. 'It's time we asserted ourselves again. The other fellows are beginning to poach. You saw that thing in the *Pinnacle* about Sir Thomas's Model Village? He must have got one of their chaps down to do it.'

'Nothing like the wounds of a friend,' I said. 'That account of the non-alcoholic pub alone was—'

'I liked the bit best about the white-tiled laundry and the Fallen Virgins who wash Sir Thomas's dress shirts. Our side couldn't come within a mile of that, you know. We haven't the proper flair for sexual slobber.'

'That's what I'm always saying,' I retorted. 'Leave 'em

alone. The other fellows are doing our work for us now. Besides I want to touch up my "Gubby Dance" a little more.'

'No. You'll spoil it. Let's shove it in to-day. For one thing it's Literature. I don't go in for compliments as you know, but, etc. etc.'

I had a healthy suspicion of young Ollyett in every aspect, but though I knew that I should have to pay for it, I fell to his flattery, and my priceless article on the 'Gubby Dance' appeared. Next Saturday he asked me to bring out *The Bun* in his absence, which I naturally assumed would be connected with the little maroon side-car. I was wrong.

On the following Monday I glanced at *The Cake* at breakfast-time to make sure, as usual, of her inferiority to my beloved but unremunerative *Bun*. I opened on a heading: 'The Village that Voted the Earth was Flat.' I read . . . I read that the Geoplanarian Society – a society devoted to the proposition that the earth is flat – had held its Annual Banquet and Exercises at Huckley on Saturday, when after convincing addresses, amid scenes of the greatest enthusiasm, Huckley village had decided by an unanimous vote of 438 that the earth was flat. I do not remember that I breathed again till I had finished the two columns of description that followed. Only one man could have written them. They were flawless – crisp, nervous, austere yet human, poignant, vital, arresting – most distinctly arresting – dynamic enough to shift a city – and quotable by whole sticks at a time. And there was a leader, a grave and poised leader, which tore me in two with mirth, until I remembered that I had been left out – infamously and unjustifiably dropped. I went to Ollyett's rooms. He was breakfasting, and, to do him justice, looked conscience-stricken.

It wasn't my fault,' he began. 'It was Bat Masquerier. I swear *I* would have asked you to come if—'

'Never mind that,' I said. 'It's the best bit of work you've ever done or will do. Did any of it happen?'

'Happen? Heavens! D'you think even I could have invented it?'

'Is it exclusive to *The Cake?*' I cried.

'It cost Bat Masquerier two thousand,' Ollyett replied. 'D'you think he'd let any one else in on that? But I give you my sacred word I knew nothing about it till he asked me to come down and cover it. He had Huckley posted in three colours, "The Geoplanarians' Annual Banquet and Exercises." Yes, he invented "Geoplanarians". He wanted Huckley to think it meant aeroplanes. Yes, I know that there is a real Society that thinks the world's flat – they ought to be grateful for the lift – but Bat made his own. He did! He created the whole show, I tell you. He swept out half his Halls for the job. Think of that – on a Saturday! They – we went down in motor char-à-bancs – three of 'em – one pink, one primrose, and one forget-me-not-blue – twenty people in each one and "The Earth *is* Flat" on each side and across the back. I went with Teddy Rickets and Lafone from the Trefoil, and both the Silhouette Sisters, and – wait a minute! – the Crossleigh Trio. You know the Every-Day Dramas Trio at the Jocunda – Ada Crossleigh, "Bunt" Crossleigh, and little Victorine? Them. And there was Hoke Ramsden, the lightning-change chap in *Morgiana and Drexel* – and there was Billy Turpeen. Yes, you know him! The North London Star. "I'm the Referee that got himself disliked at Blackheath." *That* chap! And there was Mackaye – that one-eyed Scotch fellow that all Glasgow is crazy about. Talk of subordinating yourself for Art's sake! Mackaye was the earnest inquirer who got converted at the end of the meeting. And there was quite a lot of girls I didn't know, and – oh, yes – there was 'Dal! Dal Benzaguen herself! We sat together, going and coming. She's all the darling there ever was. She sent you her love, and she told me to tell you that she won't forget about Nellie Farren. She says you've given her an ideal to work for. She? Oh, she was the Lady Secretary to the Geoplanarians, of course. I forget who were in the other brakes – provincial stars mostly – but they played up gorgeously. The art of the music-hall's changed since your day. They didn't overdo it a bit. You see, people who believe the earth is flat don't dress quite like other people. You may have noticed that I hinted at that in my account. It's a rather flat-fronted Ionic style – neo-Victorian, except for the bustles,

'Dal told me – but 'Dal looked heavenly in it! So did little Victorine. And there was a girl in the blue brake – she's a provincial – but she's coming to town this winter and she'll knock 'em – Winnie Deans. Remember that! She told Huckley how she had suffered for the Cause as a governess in a rich family where they believed that the world is round, and how she threw up her job sooner than teach immoral geography. That was at the overflow meeting outside the Baptist chapel. She knocked 'em to sawdust! We must look out for Winnie . . . But Lafone! Lafone was beyond everything. Impact, personality – conviction – the whole bag o' tricks! He sweated conviction. Gad, he convinced *me* while he was speaking! (Him? He was President of the Geoplanarians, of course. Haven't you read my account?) It *is* an infernally plausible theory. After all, no one has actually proved the earth is round, have they?'

'Never mind the earth. What about Huckley?'

'Oh, Huckley got tight. That's the worst of these model villages if you let 'em smell fire-water. There's one alcoholic pub in the place that Sir Thomas can't get rid of. Bat made it his base, He sent down the banquet in two motor lorries – dinner for five hundred and drinks for ten thousand. Huckley voted all right. Don't you make any mistake about that. No vote, no dinner. A unanimous vote – exactly as I've said. At least, the Rector and the Doctor were the only dissentients. We didn't count them. Oh yes, Sir Thomas was there. He came and grinned at us through his park gates. He'll grin worse to-day. There's an aniline dye that you rub through a stencil-plate that eats about a foot into any stone and wears good to the last. Bat had both the lodge-gates stencilled "The Earth is flat!" and all the barns and walls they could get at . . . Oh Lord, but Huckley was drunk! We had to fill 'em up to make 'em forgive us for not being aeroplanes. Unthankful yokels! D'you realise that Emperors couldn't have commanded the talent Bat decanted on 'em? Why, 'Dal alone was . . . And by eight o'clock not even a bit of paper left! The whole show packed up and gone, and Huckley hoo-raying for the earth being flat.'

'Very good,' I began. 'I am, as you know, a one-third proprietor of *The Bun*.'

'I didn't forget that,' Ollyett interrupted. 'That was uppermost in my mind all the time. I've got a special account for *The Bun* to-day – it's an idyll – and just to show how I thought of you, I told 'Dal, coming home, about your Gubby Dance, and she told Winnie. Winnie came back in our char-à-banc. After a bit we had to get out and dance it in a field. It's quite a dance the way we did it – and Lafone invented a sort of gorilla lockstep procession at the end. Bat had sent down a film-chap on the chance of getting something. He was the son of a clergyman – a most dynamic personality. He said there isn't anything for the cinema in meetings *qua* meetings – they lack action. Films are a branch of art by themselves. But he went wild over the Gubby. He said it was like Peter's vision at Joppa. He took about a million feet of it. Then I photoed it exclusive for *The Bun*. I've sent 'em in already, only remember we must eliminate Winnie's left leg in the first figure. It's too arresting . . . And there you are! But I tell you I'm afraid of Bat. That man's the Personal Devil. He did it all. He didn't even come down himself. He said he'd distract his people.'

'Why didn't he ask me to come?' I persisted.

'Because he said you'd distract me. He said he wanted my brains on ice. He got 'em. I believe it's the best thing I've ever done.' He reached for *The Cake* and re-read it luxuriously. 'Yes, out and away the best – supremely quotable,' he concluded, and – after another survey – 'By God, what a genius I was yesterday!'

I would have been angry, but I had not the time. That morning, Press agencies grovelled to me in *The Bun* office for leave to use certain photos, which, they understood, I controlled, of a certain village dance. When I had sent the fifth man away on the edge of tears, my self-respect came back a little. Then there was *The Bun*'s poster to get out. Art being elimination, I fined it down to two words (one too many, as it proved) – 'The Gubby!' in red, at which our manager protested; but by five o'clock he told me that I was the Napoleon of Fleet Street. Ollyett's account in *The Bun* of the

Geoplanarians' Exercises and Love Feast lacked the supreme shock of his version in *The Cake*, but it bruised more; while the photos of 'The Gubby' (which, with Winnie's left leg, was why I had set the doubtful press to work so early) were beyond praise and, next day, beyond price. But even then I did not understand.

A week later, I think it was, Bat Masquerier telephoned to me to come to the Trefoil.

'It's your turn now,' he said. 'I'm not asking Ollyett. Come to the stage-box.'

I went, and, as Bat's guest, was received as Royalty is not. We sat well back and looked out on the packed thousands. It was *Morgiana and Drexel*, that fluid and electric review which Bat – though he gave Lafone the credit – really created.

'Ye-es,' said Bat dreamily, after Morgiana had given 'the nasty jar' to the Forty Thieves in their forty oil 'combinations'. 'As you say, I've got 'em and I can hold 'em. What a man does doesn't matter much; and how he does it don't matter either. It's the *when* – the psychological moment. 'Press can't make up for it; money can't; brains can't. A lot's luck, but all the rest is genius. I'm not speaking about My people now. I'm talking of Myself.'

Then 'Dal – she was the only one who dared – knocked at the door and stood behind us all alive and panting as Morgiana. Lafone was carrying the police-court scene, and the house was ripped up crossways with laughter.

'Ah! Tell a fellow now,' she asked me for the twentieth time, 'did you love Nellie Farren when you were young?'

'Did we love her?' I answered. "If the earth and the sky and the sea" – There were three million of us, 'Dal, and we worshipped her.'

How did she get it across?' 'Dal went on.

'She was Nellie. The houses used to coo over her when she came on.'

'I've had a good deal, but I've never been cooed over yet,' said 'Dal wistfully.

'It isn't the how, it's the when,' Bat repeated. 'Ah!'

He leaned forward as the house began to rock and peal

full-throatedly. 'Dal fled. A sinuous and silent procession was filing into the police-court to a scarcely audible accompaniment. It was dressed – but the world and all its picture-palaces know how it was dressed. It danced and it danced, and it danced the dance which bit all humanity in the leg for half a year, and it wound up with the lockstep finale that mowed the house down in swathes, sobbing and aching. Somebody in the gallery moaned, 'Oh Gord, the Gubby!' and we heard the word run like a shudder, for they had not a full breath left among them. Then 'Dal came on, an electric star in her dark hair, the diamonds flashing in her three-inch heels – a vision that made no sign for thirty counted seconds while the police-court scene dissolved behind her into Morgiana's Manicure Palace, and they recovered themselves. The star on her forehead went out, and a soft light bathed her as she took – slowly, slowly to the croon of adoring strings – the eighteen paces forward. We saw her first as a queen alone; next as a queen for the first time conscious of her subjects, and at the end, when her hands fluttered, as a woman delighted, awed not a little, but transfigured and illuminated with sheer, compelling affection and goodwill. I caught the broken mutter of welcome – the coo which is more than tornadoes of applause. It died and rose and died again lovingly.

'She's got it across,' Bat whispered. 'I've never seen her like this. I told her to light up the star, but I was wrong, and she knew it. She's an artist.'

''Dal, you darling!' some one spoke, not loudly but it carried through the house.

'Thank *you*!' 'Dal answered, and in that broken tone one heard the last fetter riveted. 'Good evening, boys! I've just come from – now – where the dooce was it I have come from?' She turned to the impassive files of the Gubby dancers, and went on: 'Ah, so good of you to remind me, you dear, bunfaced things. I've just come from the village – The Village that Voted the Earth was Flat.'

She swept into that song with the full orchestra. It devastated the habitable earth for the next six months. Imagine, then, what its rage and pulse must have been at the incandescent hour of its birth! She only gave the chorus once. At the end of the second verse, 'Are you *with* me, boys?' she cried, and the house tore it clean away from her – '*Earth* was flat – *Earth* was flat. Flat as my hat – Flatter than that' – drowning all but the bassoons and double-basses that marked the word.

'Wonderful,' I said to Bat. 'And it's only "Nuts in May" with variations.'

'Yes – but I did the variations,' he replied.

At the last verse she gestured to Carlini the conductor, who threw her up his baton. She caught it with a boy's ease. 'Are you with me?' she cried once more, and – the maddened house behind her – abolished all the instruments except the guttural belch of the double-basses on '*Earth*' – The village that voted the *Earth* was Flat – *Earth* was flat!' It was delirium. Then she picked up the Gubby dancers and led them in a clattering improvised lockstep thrice round the stage till her last kick sent her diamond-hilted shoe Catherine-wheeling to the electrolier.

'I saw the forest of hands raised to catch it, heard the roaring and stamping pass through hurricanes to full typhoon; heard the song, pinned down by the faithful double-basses as the bull-dog pins down the bellowing bull, overbear even those; till at last the curtain fell and Bat took me round to her dressing-room, where she lay spent after her seventh call. Still the song, through all those white-washed walls, shook the reinforced concrete of the Trefoil as steam pile-drivers shake the flanks of a dock.

'I'm all out – first time in my life. Ah! Tell a fellow now, did I get it across?' she whispered huskily.

'You know you did,' I replied as she dipped her nose deep in a beaker of barley-water. 'They cooed over you.'

Bat nodded. 'And poor Nellie's dead – in Africa, ain't it?'

'I hope I'll die before they stop cooing,' said 'Dal.

' "*Earth* was flat – *Earth* was flat!" ' Now it was more like mine-pumps in flood.

'They'll have the house down if you don't take another,' some one called.

'Bless 'em!' said 'Dal, and went out for her eighth, when in the face of that cataract she said yawning, 'I don't know how *you* feel, children, but *I'm* dead. You be quiet.'

'Hold a minute,' said Bat to me. 'I've got to hear how it went in the provinces. Winnie Deans had it in Manchester, and Ramsden at Glasgow – and there are all the films too. I had rather a heavy week-end.'

The telephones presently reassured him.

'It'll do,' said he. 'And *he* said my home address was Jerusalem.' He left me humming the refrain of 'The Holy City.' Like Ollyett I found myself afraid of that man.

When I got out into the street and met the disgorging picture-palaces capering on the pavements and humming it (for he had put the gramophones on with the films), and when I saw far to the south the red electrics flash 'Gubby' across the Thames, I feared more than ever.

A few days passed which were like nothing except, perhaps, a suspense of fever in which the sick man perceives the search-lights of the world's assembled navies in act to converge on one minute fragment of wreckage – one only in all the black and agony-strewn sea. Then those beams focussed themselves. Earth as we knew it – the full circuit of our orb – laid the weight of its impersonal and searing curiosity on this Huckley which had voted that it was flat. It asked for news about Huckley – where and what it might be, and how it talked – it knew how it danced – and how it thought in its wonderful soul. And then, in all the zealous, merciless press, Huckley was laid out for it to look at, as a drop of pond water is exposed on the sheet of a magic-lantern show. But Huckley's sheet was only coterminous with the use of type among mankind. For the precise moment that was necessary, Fate ruled it that there should be nothing of first importance in the world's idle eye. One atrocious murder, a political crisis, an incautious or heady continental statesman, the mere catarrh of a king, would have wiped out the significance of our message, as a passing cloud annuls the urgent helio. But it was halcyon weather in every respect. Ollyett and I did not need to lift our little fingers any more than the Alpine climber whose last sentence has unkeyed the arch of the avalanche. The thing roared and pulverised and swept beyond eyesight all by itself-all by itself. And once well away, the fall of kingdoms could not have diverted it.

Ours is, after all, a kindly earth. While The Song ran and raped it with the cataleptic kick of 'Ta-ra-ra-boom-de-ay,' multiplied by the West African significance of 'Everybody's doing it,' plus twice the infernal elementality of a certain tune in *Dona et Gamma*; when for all practical purposes, literary, dramatic, artistic, social, municipal, political, commercial, and administrative, the Earth *was* flat, the Rector of Huckley wrote to us – again as a lover of accuracy – to point out that the Huckley vote on 'the alleged flatness of this scene of our labours here below' was *not* unanimous; he and the doctor having voted against it. And the great Baron Reuter himself (I am sure it could have been none other) flashed that letter in full to the front, back, and both wings of this scene of our labours. For Huckley was News. *The Bun* also contributed a photograph which cost me some trouble to fake.

'We are a vital nation,' said Ollyett while we were discussing affairs at a Bat dinner. 'Only an Englishman could have written that letter at this present juncture.'

'It reminded me of a tourist in the Cave of the Winds under Niagara. Just one figure in a mackintosh. But perhaps you saw our photo?' I said proudly.

'Yes,' Bat replied. 'I've been to Niagara, too. And how's Huckley taking it?'

'They don't quite understand, of course,' said Ollyett. 'But it's bringing pots of money into the place. Ever since the motor-bus excursions were started—'

'I didn't know they had been,' said Pallant.

'Oh yes. Motor char-à-bancs – uniformed guides and key-bugles included. They're getting a bit fed up with the tune there nowadays,' Ollyett added.

'They play it under his windows, don't they?' Bat asked. 'He can't stop the right of way across his park.'

'He cannot,' Ollyett answered. 'By the way, Woodhouse,

I've bought that font for you from the sexton. I paid fifteen pounds for it.'

'What am I supposed to do with it?' asked Woodhouse.

'You give it to the Victoria and Albert Museum. It is fourteenth-century work all right. You can trust me.'

'Is it worth it – now?' said Pallant. 'Not that I'm weakening, but merely as a matter of tactics?'

'But this is true,' said Ollyett. 'Besides, it is my hobby, I always wanted to be an architect. I'll attend to it myself. It's too serious for *The Bun* and miles too good for *The Cake*.'

He broke ground in a ponderous architectural weekly, which had never heard of Huckley. There was no passion in his statement, but mere fact backed by a wide range of authorities. He established beyond doubt that the old font at Huckley had been thrown out, on Sir Thomas's instigation, twenty years ago, to make room for a new one of Bath stone adorned with Limoges enamels; and that it had lain ever since in a corner of the sexton's shed. He proved, with learned men to support him, that there was only one other font in all England to compare with it. So Woodhouse bought it and presented it to a grateful South Kensington which said it would see the earth still flatter before it returned the treasure to purblind Huckley. Bishops by the benchful and most of the Royal Academy, not to mention 'Margaritas ante Porces,' wrote fervently to the papers. *Punch* based a political cartoon on it; the *Times* a third leader, 'The Lust of Newness'; and the *Spectator* a scholarly and delightful middle, 'Village Hausmania.' The vast amused outside world said in all its tongues and types: 'Of course! This is just what Huckley would do!' And neither Sir Thomas nor the Rector nor the sexton nor any one else wrote to deny it.

'You see,' said Ollyett, 'this is much more of a blow to Huckley than it looks – because every word of it's true. Your Gubby dance was inspiration, I admit, but it hadn't its roots in—'

'Two hemispheres and four continents so far,' I pointed out.

'Its roots in the hearts of Huckley was what I was going to

say. Why don't you ever come down and look at the place? You've never seen it since we were stopped there.'

'I've only my week-ends free,' I said, 'and you seem to spend yours there pretty regularly – with the side-car. I was afraid—'

'Oh, *that's* all right,' he said cheerily. 'We're quite an old engaged couple now. As a matter of fact, it happened after "the gravid polled Angus" business. Come along this Saturday. Woodhouse says he'll run us down after lunch. He wants to see Huckley too.'

Pallant could not accompany us, but Bat took his place.

'It's odd,' said Bat, 'that none of us except Ollyett has ever set eyes on Huckley since that time. That's what I always tell My people. Local colour is all right after you've got your idea. Before that, it's a mere nuisance.' He regaled us on the way down with panoramic views of the success – geographical and financial – of 'The Gubby' and The Song.

'By the way,' said he, 'I've assigned 'Dal all the gramophone rights of "The Earth." She's a born artist. 'Hadn't sense enough to hit me for triple-dubs the morning after. She'd have taken it out in coos.'

'Bless her! And what'll she make out of the gramophone rights?' I asked.

'Lord knows!' he replied. 'I've made fifty-four thousand my little end of the business, and it's only just beginning. Hear *that*!'

A shell-pink motor-brake roared up behind us to the music on a key-bugle of 'The Village that Voted the Earth was Flat.' In a few minutes we overtook another, in natural wood, whose occupants were singing it through their noses.

'I don't know that agency. It must be Cook's,' said Ollyett. 'They do suffer.' We were never out of ear-shot of the tune the rest of the way to Huckley.

Though I knew it would be so, I was disappointed with the actual aspect of the spot we had – it is not too much to say – created in the face of the nations. The alcoholic pub; the village green; the Baptist chapel; the church; the sexton's shed; the Rectory whence the so-wonderful letters had come; Sir Thomas's park gate pillars still violently declaring 'The Earth *is* flat,' were as mean, as average, as ordinary as the photograph of a room where a murder has been committed. Ollyett, who, of course, knew the place specially well, made the most of it to us. Bat, who had employed it as a back-cloth to one of his own dramas, dismissed it as a thing used and emptied, but Woodhouse expressed my feelings when he said: 'Is that all – after all we've done?'

'*I* know,' said Ollyett soothingly. ' "Like that strange song I heard Apollo sing: When Ilion like a mist rose into towers." I've felt the same sometimes, though it has been Paradise for me. But they *do* suffer.'

The fourth brake in thirty minutes had just turned into Sir Thomas's park to tell the Hall that 'The *Earth* was flat'; a knot of obviously American tourists were kodaking his lodge gates; while the tea-shop opposite the lych-gate was full of people buying postcards of the old font as it had lain twenty years in the sexton's shed. We went to the alcoholic pub and congratulated the proprietor.

'It's bringin' money to the place,' said he. 'But in a sense you can buy money too dear. It isn't doin' us any good. People are laughin' at us. That's what they're doin' . . . Now, with regard to that Vote of ours you may have heard talk about . . .'

'For Gorze sake, chuck that votin' business,' cried an elderly man at the door. 'Money-gettin' or no money-gettin', we're fed up with it.'

'Well, I do think,' said the publican, shifting his ground, 'I do think Sir Thomas might ha' managed better in some things.'

'He *tole* me,' – the elderly man shouldered his way to the bar – 'he tole me twenty years ago to take an' lay that font in my tool-shed. He *tole* me so himself. An' now, after twenty years, me own wife makin' me out little better than the common 'angman!'

'That's the sexton,' the publican explained. 'His good lady sells the postcards – if you 'aven't got some. But we feel Sir Thomas might ha' done better.'

'What's he got to do with it?' said Woodhouse.

'There's nothin' we can trace 'ome to 'im in so many words,

but we think he might 'ave saved us the font business. Now, in regard to that votin' business—'

'Chuck it! Oh, chuck it!' the sexton roared, 'or you'll 'ave me cuttin' my throat at cock-crow. 'Ere's another parcel of fun-makers!'

A motor-brake had pulled up at the door and a multitude of men and women immediately descended. We went out to look. They bore rolled banners, a reading-desk in three pieces, and, I specially noticed, a collapsible harmonium, such as is used on ships at sea.

'Salvation Army?' I said, though I saw no uniforms.

Two of them unfurled a banner between poles which bore the legend: 'The Earth *is* flat,' Woodhouse and I turned to Bat. He shook his head. 'No, no! Not me . . . If I had only seen their costumes in advance!'

'Good Lord!' said Ollyett. 'It's the genuine Society!'

The company advanced on the green with the precision of people well broke to these movements. Scene-shifters could not have been quicker with the three-piece rostrum, nor stewards with the harmonium. Almost before its cross-legs had been kicked into their catches, certainly before the tourists by the lodge-gates had begun to move over, a woman sat down to it and struck up a hymn:

Hear the truth our tongues are telling,
  Spread the light from shore to shore,
God hath given man a dwelling
  Flat and flat for evermore.

When the Primal Dark retreated,
  When the deeps were undesigned,
He with rule and level meted
  Habitation for mankind!

I saw sick envy on Bat's face. 'Curse Nature,' he muttered. 'She gets ahead of you every time. To think I forgot hymns and a harmonium!'

  Then came the chorus

Hear the truth our tongues are telling,
　Spread the light from shore to shore –
Oh, be faithful! Oh, be truthful!
　Earth is flat for evermore.

They sang several verses with the fervour of Christians awaiting their lions. Then there were growlings in the air. The
sexton, embraced by the landlord, two-stepped out of the pub-
door. Each was trying to outroar the other. 'Apologising in
advarnce for what he says,' the landlord shouted: 'You'd better
go away' (here the sexton began to speak words). 'This isn't
the time nor yet the place for – for any more o' this chat.'

The crowd thickened. I saw the village police-sergeant
come out of his cottage buckling his belt.

'But surely,' said the woman at the harmonium, 'there must
be some mistake. We are not suffragettes.'

'Damn it! They'd be a change,' cried the sexton. 'You get
out of this! Don't talk! – *I* can't stand it for one! Get right out,
or we'll font you!'

The crowd which was being recruited from every house in
sight echoed the invitation. The sergeant pushed forward. A
man beside the reading-desk said: 'But surely we are among
dear friends and sympathisers. Listen to me for a moment.'

It was the moment that a passing char-à-banc chose to strike
into The Song. The effect was instantaneous. Bat, Ollyett, and
I, who by divers roads have learned the psychology of crowds,
retreated towards the tavern door. Woodhouse, the newspaper
proprietor, anxious, I presume, to keep touch with the public,
dived into the thick of it. Every one else told the Society to go
away at once. When the lady at the harmonium (I began to
understand why it is sometimes necessary to kill women)
pointed at the stencilled park pillars and called them 'the
cromlechs of our common faith,' there was a snarl and a rush.
The police-sergeant checked it, but advised the Society to
keep on going. The Society withdrew into the brake fighting,
as it were, a rearguard action of oratory up each step. The
collapsed harmonium was hauled in last, and with the perfect
unreason of crowds, they cheered it loudly, till the chauffeur

slipped in his clutch and sped away. Then the crowd broke up, congratulating all concerned except the sexton, who was held to have disgraced his office by having sworn at ladies. We strolled across the green towards Woodhouse, who was talking to the police-sergeant near the park-gates, We were not twenty yards from him when we saw Sir Thomas Ingell emerge from the lodge and rush furiously at Woodhouse with an uplifted stick, at the same time shrieking: 'I'll teach you to laugh, you—' but Ollyett has the record of the language. By the time we reached them, Sir Thomas was on the ground; Woodhouse, very white, held the walking-stick and was saying to the sergeant

'I give this person in charge for assault.'

'But, good Lord!' said the sergeant, whiter than Woodhouse. 'It's Sir Thomas.'

'Whoever it is, it isn't fit to be at large,' said Woodhouse. The crowd suspecting something wrong began to reassemble, and all the English horror of a row in public moved us, headed by the sergeant, inside the lodge. We shut both park-gates and lodge-door.

'You saw the assault, sergeant,' Woodhouse went on. 'You can testify I used no more force than was necessary to protect myself. You can testify that I have not even damaged this person's property. (Here! take your stick, you!) You heard the filthy language he used.'

'I – I can't say I did,' the sergeant stammered.

'Oh, but *we* did!' said Ollyett, and repeated it, to the apron-veiled horror of the lodge-keeper's wife.

Sir Thomas on a hard kitchen chair began to talk. He said he had 'stood enough of being photographed like a wild beast,' and expressed loud regret that he had not killed 'that man,' who was 'conspiring with the sergeant to laugh at him.'

''Ad you ever seen 'im before, Sir Thomas?' the sergeant asked.

'No! But it's time an example was made here. I've never seen the sweep in my life.'

I think it was Bat Masquerier's magnetic eye that recalled

the past to him, for his face changed and his jaw dropped. 'But I have!' he groaned. 'I remember now.'

Here a writhing man entered by the back door. He was, he said, the village solicitor. I do not assert that he licked Woodhouse's boots, but we should have respected him more if he had and been done with it. His notion was that the matter could be accommodated, arranged and compromised for gold, and yet more gold. The sergeant thought so too. Woodhouse undeceived them both. To the sergeant he said, 'Will you or will you not enter the charge?' To the village solicitor he gave the name of his lawyers, at which the man wrung his hands and cried, 'Oh, Sir T., Sir T.!' in a miserable falsetto, for it was a Bat Masquerier of a firm. They conferred together in tragic whispers.

'I don't dive after Dickens,' said Ollyett to Bat and me by the window, 'but every time *I* get into a row I notice the police-court always fills up with his characters.'

'I've noticed that too,' said Bat. 'But the odd thing is you mustn't give the public straight Dickens – not in My business. I wonder why that is.'

Then Sir Thomas got his second wind and cursed the day that he, or it may have been we, were born. I feared that though he was a Radical he might apologise and, since he was an MP, might lie his way out of the difficulty. But he was utterly and truthfully beside himself. He asked foolish questions – such as what we were doing in the village at all, and how much blackmail Woodhouse expected to make out of him. But neither Woodhouse nor the sergeant nor the writhing solicitor listened. The upshot of their talk, in the chimney-corner, was that Sir Thomas stood engaged to appear next Monday before his brother magistrates on charges of assault, disorderly conduct, and language calculated, etc. Ollyett was specially careful about the language.

Then we left. The village looked very pretty in the late light – pretty and tuneful as a nest of nightingales.

'You'll turn up on Monday, I hope,' said Woodhouse, when we reached town. That was his only allusion to the affair.

So we turned up – through a world still singing that the

Earth was flat – at the little clay-coloured market-town with the large Corn Exchange and the small jubilee memorial. We had some difficulty in getting seats in the court. Woodhouse's imported London lawyer was a man of commanding personality, with a voice trained to convey blasting imputations by tone. When the case was called, he rose and stated his client's intention not to proceed with the charge. His client, he went on to say, had not entertained, and, of course, in the circumstances could not have entertained, any suggestion of accepting on behalf of public charities any moneys that might have been offered to him on the part of Sir Thomas's estate. At the same time, no one acknowledged more sincerely than his client the spirit in which those offers had been made by those entitled to make them. But, as a matter of fact – here he became the man of the world colloguing with his equals – certain – er – details had come to his client's knowledge *since* the lamentable outburst, which . . . He shrugged his shoulders. Nothing was served by going into them, but he ventured to say that, had those painful circumstances only been known earlier, his client would – again 'of course' – never have dreamed— A gesture concluded the sentence, and the ensnared Bench looked at Sir Thomas with new and withdrawing eyes. Frankly, as they could see, it would be nothing less than cruelty to proceed further with this – er – unfortunate affair. He asked leave, therefore, to withdraw the charge *in toto*, and at the same time to express his client's deepest sympathy with all who had been in any way distressed, as his client had been, by the fact and the publicity of proceedings which he could, of course, again assure them that his client would never have dreamed of instituting if, as he hoped he had made plain, certain facts had been before his client at the time when . . . But he had said enough. For his fee it seemed to me that he had.

Heaven inspired Sir Thomas's lawyer – all of a sweat lest his client's language should come out – to rise up and thank him. Then, Sir Thomas – not yet aware what leprosy had been laid upon him, but grateful to escape on any terms – followed suit. He was heard in interested silence, and people drew back a pace as Gehazi passed forth.

'You hit hard,' said Bat to Woodhouse afterwards. 'His own people think he's mad.'

'You don't say so? I'll show you some of his letters to-night at dinner,' he replied.

He brought them to the Red Amber Room of the Chop Suey. We forgot to be amazed, as till then we had been amazed, over The Song or 'The Gubby,' or the full tide of Fate that seemed to run only for our sakes. It did not even interest Ollyett that the verb 'to huckle' had passed into the English leader-writers' language. We were studying the interior of a soul, flash-lighted to its grimiest corners by the dread of 'losing its position.'

And then it thanked you, didn't it, for dropping the case?' said Pallant.

'Yes, and it sent me a telegram to confirm.' Woodhouse turned to Bat. 'Now d'you think I hit too hard?' he asked.

'No-o!' said Bat. 'After all – I'm talking of every one's business now – one can't ever do anything in Art that comes up to Nature in any game in life. Just think how this thing has—'

'Just let me run through that little case of yours again,' said Pallant, and picked up *The Bun* which had it set out in full.

'Any chance of 'Dal looking in on us to-night?' Ollyett began.

'She's occupied with her Art too,' Bat answered bitterly. 'What's the use of Art? Tell me, someone!' A barrel-organ outside promptly pointed out that the *Earth* was flat. 'The gramophone's killing street organs, but I let loose a hundred-and-seventy-four of those hurdygurdys twelve hours after The Song,' said Bat. 'Not counting the Provinces.' His face brightened a little.

'Look here!' said Pallant over the paper. 'I don't suppose you or those asinine JPs knew it – but your lawyer ought to have known that you've all put your foot in it most confoundedly over this assault case.'

'What's the matter?' said Woodhouse.

'It's ludicrous. It's insane. There isn't two penn'orth of legality in the whole thing. Of course, you could have withdrawn the charge, but the way you went about it is childish – besides being illegal. What on earth was the Chief Constable thinking of?'

'Oh, he was a friend of Sir Thomas's. They all were for that matter,' I replied.

'He ought to be hanged. So ought the Chairman of the Bench. I'm talking as a lawyer now.'

'Why, what have we been guilty of? Misprision of treason or compounding a felony – or what?' said Ollyett.

'I'll tell you later.' Pallant went back to the paper with knitted brows, smiling unpleasantly from time to time. At last he laughed.

'Thank you!' he said to Woodhouse. 'It ought to be pretty useful – for us.'

'What d'you mean?' said Ollyett.

'For our side. They are all Rads who are mixed up in this – from the Chief Constable down. There must be a Question. There must be a Question.'

'Yes, but I wanted the charge withdrawn in my own way,' Woodhouse insisted.

'That's nothing to do with the case. It's the legality of your silly methods. You wouldn't understand if I talked till morning,' He began to pace the room, his hands behind him. 'I wonder if I can get it through our Whip's thick head that it's a chance . . . That comes of stuffing the Bench with radical tinkers,' he muttered.

'Oh, sit down!' said Woodhouse.

'Where's your lawyer to be found now?' he jerked out.

'At the Trefoil,' said Bat promptly. 'I gave him the stage-box for to-night. He's an artist too.'

'Then I'm going to see him,' said Pallant. 'Properly handled this ought to be a godsend for our side.' He withdrew without apology.

'Certainly, this thing keeps on opening up, and up,' I remarked inanely.

'It's beyond me!' said Bat. 'I don't think if I'd known I'd have ever . . . Yes, I would, though. He said my home address was—'

'It was his tone – his tone!' Ollyett almost shouted. Woodhouse said nothing, but his face whitened as he brooded.

'Well, any way,' Bat went on, 'I'm glad I always believed in God and Providence and all those things. Else I should lose my nerve. We've put it over the whole world – the full extent of the geographical globe. We couldn't stop it if we wanted to now. It's got to burn itself out. I'm not in charge any more. What d'you expect'll happen next. Angels?'

I expected nothing. Nothing that I expected approached what I got. Politics are not my concern, but, for the moment, since it seemed that they were going to 'huckle' with the rest, I took an interest in them. They impressed me as a dog's life without a dog's decencies, and I was confirmed in this when an unshaven and unwashen Pallant called on me at ten o'clock one morning, begging for a bath and a couch.

'Bail too?' I asked. He was in evening dress and his eyes were sunk feet in his head.

'No,' he said hoarsely. 'All night sitting. Fifteen divisions. 'Nother to-night. Your place was nearer than mine, so—' He began to undress in the hall.

When he awoke at one o'clock he gave me lurid accounts of what he said was history, but which was obviously collective hysteria.

There had been a political crisis. He and his fellow MPs had 'done things' – I never quite got at the things – for eighteen hours on end, and the pitiless Whips were even then at the telephones to herd 'em up to another dog-fight. So he snorted and grew hot all over again while he might have been resting.

'I'm going to pitch in my question about that miscarriage of justice at Huckley this afternoon, if you care to listen to it,' he said. 'It'll be absolutely thrown away – in our present state. I told 'em so; but it's my only chance for weeks. P'raps Woodhouse would like to come.'

'I'm sure he would. Anything to do with Huckley interests us,' I said.

'It'll miss fire, I'm afraid. Both sides are absolutely cooked. The present situation has been working up for some time. You see the row was bound to come, &c. &c.,' and he flew off the handle once more.

I telephoned to Woodhouse, and we went to the House together. It was a dull, sticky afternoon with thunder in the air. For some reason or other, each side was determined to prove its virtue and endurance to the utmost. I heard men snarling about it all round me. 'If they won't spare us, we'll show 'em no mercy.' 'Break the brutes up from the start. They can't stand late hours.' 'Come on! No shirking! I know *you've* had a Turkish bath,' were some of the sentences I caught on our way. The House was packed already, and one could feel the negative electricity of a jaded crowd wrenching at one's own nerves, and depressing the afternoon soul.

'This is bad!' Woodhouse whispered. 'There'll be a row before they've finished. Look at the Front Benches!' And he pointed out little personal signs by which I was to know that each man was on edge. He might have spared himself. The House was ready to snap before a bone had been thrown. A sullen minister rose to reply to a staccato question. His supporters cheered defiantly.

'None o' that! None o' that!' came from the Back Benches. I saw the Speaker's face stiffen like the face of a helmsman as he humours a hard-mouthed yacht after a sudden following sea. The trouble was barely met in time. There came a fresh, apparently causeless gust a few minutes later – savage, threatening, but futile. It died out – one could hear the sigh – in sudden wrathful realisation of the dreary hours ahead, and the ship of state drifted on.

Then Pallant – and the raw House winced at the torture of his voice – rose. It was a twenty-line question, studded with legal technicalities.

The gist of it was that he wished to know whether the appropriate Minister was aware that there had been a grave miscarriage of justice on such and such a date, at such and such a place, before such and such justices of the peace, in regard to a case which arose—

I heard one desperate, weary 'Damn!' float up from the pit of that torment. Pallant sawed on – 'out of certain events which occurred at the village of Huckley.'

The House came to attention with a parting of the lips like a hiccough, and it flashed through my mind . . . Pallant repeated, 'Huckley. The village—'

'That voted the *Earth* was flat.' A single voice from a back Bench sang it once like a lone frog in a far pool.

'*Earth* was flat,' croaked another voice opposite.

'*Earth* was flat.' There were several. Then several more.

It was, you understand, the collective, over-strained nerve of the House, snapping, strand by strand, to various notes, as the hawser parts from its moorings.

'The Village that voted the *Earth* was flat.' The tune was beginning to shape itself: More voices were raised and feet began to beat time. Even so it did not occur to me that the thing would—

The Village that voted the *Earth* was flat!' It was easier now to see who were not singing. There were still a few. Of a sudden (and this proves the fundamental instability of the crossbench mind) a cross-bencher leaped on his seat and there played an imaginary double-bass with tremendous maestro-like wagglings of the elbow.

The last strand parted. The ship of state drifted out helpless on the rocking tide of melody.

'The Village that voted the
Earth was flat!
The Village that voted the
Earth was flat!'

The Irish first conceived the idea of using their order-papers as funnels wherewith to reach the correct '*vroom – vroom*' on '*Earth*'.

Labour, always conservative and respectable at a crisis, stood out longer than any other section, but when it came in it was howling syndicalism. Then, without distinction of Party, fear of constituents, desire for office, or hope of emolument, the House sang at the tops and at the bottoms of their voices, swaying their stale bodies and epileptically beating with their swelled feet. They sang 'The Village that voted the *Earth* was flat': first, because they wanted to, and secondly – which is the terror of that song – because they could not stop. For no consideration could they stop.

Pallant was still standing up. Someone pointed at him and they laughed. Others began to point, lunging, as it were, in time with the tune. At this moment two persons came in practically abreast from behind the Speaker's chair, and halted, appalled. One happened to be the Prime Minister and the other a messenger. The House, with tears running down their cheeks, transferred their attention to the paralysed couple. They pointed six hundred forefingers at them. They rocked, they waved, and they rolled while they pointed, but still they sang. When they weakened for an instant, Ireland would yell: 'Are ye *with* me, bhoys?' and they all renewed their strength like Antaeus. No man could say afterwards what happened in the Press or the Strangers' Gallery. It was the House, the hysterical and abandoned House of Commons that held all eyes, as it deafened all ears. I saw both Front Benches bend forward, some with their foreheads on their despatch-boxes, the rest with their faces in their hands; and their moving shoulders jolted the House out of its last rag of decency. Only the Speaker remained unmoved. The entire press of Great Britain bore witness next day that he had not even bowed his head. The Angel of the Constitution, for vain was the help of man, foretold him the exact moment at which the House would have broken into 'The Gubby.' He is reported to have said: 'I heard the Irish beginning to shuffle it. So I adjourned.' Pallant's version is that he added: 'And I was never so grateful to a private member in all my life as I was to Mr Pallant.'

He made no explanation. He did not refer to orders or disorders. He simply adjourned the House till six that evening. And the House adjourned – some of it nearly on all fours.

I was not correct when I said that the Speaker was the only man who did not laugh. Woodhouse was beside me all the time. His face was set and quite white – as white, they told me, as Sir Thomas Ingell's when he went, by request, to a private interview with his Chief Whip.

A MADONNA OF THE TRENCHES

'Whatever a man of the sons of men
    Shall say to his heart of the lords above,
They have shown man, verily, once and again,
    Marvellous mercy and infinite love.

'O sweet one love, O my life's delight,
    Dear, though the days have divided us,
Lost beyond hope, taken far out of sight,
    Not twice in the world shall the Gods do thus.'

Swinburne, 'Les Noyades'

Seeing how many unstable ex-soldiers came to the Lodge of Instruction (attached to Faith and Works EC 5837) in the years after the war, the wonder is there was not more trouble from Brethren whom sudden meetings with old comrades jerked back into their still raw past. But our round, torpedo-bearded local Doctor – Brother Keede, Senior Warden – always stood ready to deal with hysteria before it got out of hand; and when I examined Brethren unknown or imperfectly vouched for on the Masonic side, I passed on to him anything that seemed doubtful. He had had his experience as medical officer of a South London Battalion, during the last two years of the war; and, naturally, often found friends and acquaintances among the visitors.

Brother C. Strangwick, a young, tallish, new-made Brother, hailed from some South London Lodge. His papers and his answers were above suspicion, but his red-rimmed eyes had a puzzled glare that might mean nerves. So I introduced him particularly to Keede, who discovered in him a Headquarters Orderly of his old Battalion, congratulated him on his return to fitness – he had been discharged from some infirmary or other – and plunged at once into Somme memories.

'I hope I did right, Keede,' I said when we were robing before Lodge.

'Oh, quite. He reminded me that I had him under my hands at Sampoux in 'Eighteen, when he went to bits. He was a Runner.'

'Was it shock?' I asked.

'Of sorts – but not what he wanted me to think it was. No, he wasn't shamming. He had Jumps to the limit – but he played up to mislead me about the reason of 'em . . . Well, if we could stop patients from lying, medicine would be too easy, I suppose.'

I noticed that, after Lodge-working, Keede gave him a seat a couple of rows in front of us, that he might enjoy a lecture on the Orientation of King Solomon's Temple, which an earnest Brother thought would be a nice interlude between labour and the high tea that we called our 'Banquet.' Even helped by tobacco it was a dreary performance. About halfway through, Strangwick, who had been fidgeting and twitching for some minutes, rose, drove back his chair grinding across the tessellated floor, and yelped: 'Oh, My Aunt! I can't stand this any longer.' Under cover of a general laugh of assent he brushed past us and stumbled towards the door.

'I thought so!' Keede whispered to me. 'Come along!' We overtook him in the passage, crowing hysterically and wringing his hands. Keede led him into the Tyler's Room, a small office where we stored odds and ends of regalia and furniture, and locked the door.

'I'm – I'm all right,' the boy began, piteously.

''Course you are.' Keede opened a small cupboard which I had seen called upon before, mixed sal volatile and water in a graduated glass, and, as Strangwick drank, pushed him gently onto an old sofa. 'There,' he went on. 'It's nothing to write home about. I've seen you ten times worse. I expect our talk has brought things back.'

He hooked up a chair behind him with one foot, held the patient's hands in his own, and sat down. The chair creaked.

'Don't!' Strangwick squealed. 'I can't stand it! There's nothing on earth creaks like they do! And – and when it thaws we – we've got to slap 'em back with a spa-ade! Remember those Frenchmen's little boots under the duckboards? . . . What'll I do? What'll I do about it?'

Someone knocked at the door, to know if all were well.

'Oh quite, thanks!' said Keede over his shoulder. 'But I shall need this room awhile. Draw the curtains, please.'

We heard the rings of the hangings that drape the passage from Lodge to Banquet Room click along their poles, and what sound there had been, of feet and voices, was shut off.

Strangwick, retching impotently, complained of the frozen dead who creak in the frost.

'He's playing up still,' Keede whispered. '*That's* not his real trouble – any more than 'twas last time.'

'But surely,' I replied, 'men get those things on the brain pretty badly. Remember in October—'

'This chap hasn't, though. I wonder what's really helling him. What are you thinking of?' said Keede peremptorily.

'French End an' Butcher's Row,' Strangwick muttered.

'Yes, there were a few there. But, suppose we face Bogey instead of giving him best every time.' Keede turned towards me with a hint in his eye that I was to play up to his leads.

'What was the trouble with French End?' I opened at a venture.

'It was a bit by Sampoux, that we had taken over from the French. They're tough, but you wouldn't call 'em tidy as a nation. They had faced both sides of it with dead to keep the mud back. All those trenches were like gruel in a thaw. Our people had to do the same sort of thing – elsewhere; but Butcher's Row in French End was the – er – show-piece. Luckily, we pinched a salient from Jerry just then, an' straightened things out – so we didn't need to use the Row after November. You remember, Strangwick?'

'My God, yes! When the duckboard-slats were missin' you'd tread on 'em, an' they'd creak.'

'They're bound to. Like leather,' said Keede. 'It gets on one's nerves a bit, but—'

'Nerves? It's real! It's real!' Strangwick gulped.

'But at your time of life, it'll all fall behind you in a year or

677

so. I'll give you another sip of – paregoric, an' we'll face it quietly. Shall we?'

Keede opened his cupboard again and administered a carefully dropped dark dose of something that was not sal volatile. 'This'll settle you in a few minutes,' he explained. 'Lie still, an' don't talk unless you feel like it.'

He faced me, fingering his beard.

'Ye-es. Butcher's Row wasn't pretty,' he volunteered. 'Seeing Strangwick here, has brought it all back to me again. 'Funny thing! We had a Platoon Sergeant of Number Two – what the deuce was his name? – an elderly bird who must have lied like a patriot to get out to the front at his age; but he was a first-class Non-Com., and the last person, you'd think, to make mistakes. Well, he was due for a fortnight's home leave in January, 'Eighteen. You were at BHQ then, Strangwick, weren't you?'

'Yes. I was Orderly. It was January twenty-first'; Strangwick spoke with a thickish tongue, and his eyes burned. Whatever drug it was, had taken hold.

'About then,' Keede said. 'Well, this Sergeant, instead of coming down from the trenches the regular way an' joinin' Battalion Details after dark, an' takin' that funny little train for Arras, thinks he'll warm himself first. So he gets into a dug-out, in Butcher's Row, that used to be an old French dressing-station, and fugs up between a couple of braziers of pure charcoal! As luck 'ud have it, that was the only dug-out with an inside door opening inwards – some French anti-gas fitting, I expect – and, by what we could make out, the door must have swung to while he was warming. Anyhow, he didn't turn up at the train. There was a search at once. We couldn't afford to waste Platoon Sergeants. We found him in the morning. He'd got his gas all right. A machine-gunner reported him, didn't he, Strangwick?'

'No, sir. Corporal Grant – o' the Trench Mortars.'

'So it was. Yes, Grant – the man with that little wen on his neck. 'Nothing wrong with your memory, at any rate. What was the Sergeant's name?'

'Godsoe – John Godsoe,' Strangwick answered.

'Yes, that was it. I had to see him next mornin' – frozen stiff between the two braziers – and not a scrap of private papers on him. *That* was the only thing that made me think it mightn't have been – quite an accident.'

Strangwick's relaxing face set, and he threw back at once to the Orderly Room manner.

'I give my evidence – at the time – to you, sir. He passed – overtook me, I should say – comin' down from supports, after I'd warned him for leaf. I thought he was goin' through Parrot Trench as usual; but 'e must 'ave turned off into French End where the old bombed barricade was.'

'Yes. I remember now. You were the last man to see him alive. That was on the twenty-first of January, you say? Now, *when* was it that Dearlove and Billings brought you to me – clean out of your head?' . . . Keede dropped his hand, in the style of magazine detectives, on Strangwick's shoulder. The boy looked at him with cloudy wonder, and muttered: 'I was took to you on the evenin' of the twenty-fourth of January. But you don't think I did him in, do you?'

I could not help smiling at Keede's discomfiture; but he recovered himself. 'Then what the dickens *was* on your mind that evening – before I gave you the hypodermic?'

'The – the things in Butcher's Row. They kept on comin' over me. You've seen me like this before, sir.'

'But I knew that it was a lie. You'd no more got stiffs on the brain then than you have now. You've got something, but you're hiding it.'

''Ow do *you* know, Doctor?' Strangwick whimpered.

'D'you remember what you said to me, when Dearlove and Billings were holding you down that evening?'

'About the things in Butcher's Row?'

'Oh, no! You spun me a lot of stuff about corpses creaking; but you let yourself go in the middle of it – when you pushed that telegram at me. What did you mean, f'rinstance, by asking what advantage it was for you to fight beasts of officers if the dead didn't rise?'

'Did I say "Beasts of Officers"?'

'You did. It's out of the Burial Service.'

'I suppose, then, I must have heard it. As a matter of fact, I 'ave.' Strangwick shuddered extravagantly.

'Probably. And there's another thing – that hymn you were shouting till I put you under. It was something about Mercy and Love. Remember it?'

'I'll try,' said the boy obediently, and began to paraphrase, as nearly as possible thus: ' "Whatever a man may say in his heart unto the Lord, yea verily I say unto you – Gawd hath shown man, again and again, marvellous mercy an' – an' somethin' or other love." ' He screwed up his eyes and shook.

'Now where did you get *that* from?' Keede insisted.

'From Godsoe – on the twenty-first Jan . . . 'Ow could *I* tell what 'e meant to do?' he burst out in a high, unnatural key – 'Any more than I knew *she* was dead.'

'Who was dead?' asked Keede.

'Me Auntie Armine.'

'The one the telegram came to you about, at Sampoux, that you wanted me to explain – the one that you were talking of in the passage out here just now when you began: "O Auntie," and changed it to "O Gawd," when I collared you?'

'That's her! I haven't a chance with you, Doctor. *I* didn't know there was anything wrong with those braziers. How could I? We're always usin' 'em. Honest to God, I thought at first go-off he might wish to warm himself before the leaf-train. I – I didn't know Uncle John meant to start – 'ouse-keepin'.' He laughed horribly, and then the dry tears came.

Keede waited for them to pass in sobs and hiccoughs before he continued: 'Why? Was Godsoe your Uncle?'

'No,' said Strangwick, his head between his hands. 'Only we'd known him ever since we were born. Dad 'ad known him before that. He lived almost next street to us. Him an' Dad an' Ma an' – an' the rest had always been friends. So we called him Uncle – like children do.'

'What sort of man was he?'

'One o' *the* best, sir. Pensioned Sergeant with a little money left him – quite independent – and very superior. They had a sittin'-room full o' Indian curios that him and his wife used to let sister an' me see when we'd been good."

'Wasn't he rather old to join up?'

'That made no odds to him. He joined up as Sergeant Instructor at the first go-off, an' when the Battalion was ready he got 'imself sent along. He wangled me into 'is Platoon when I went out – early in 'Seventeen. Because Ma wanted it, I suppose.'

'I'd no notion you knew him that well,' was Keede's comment.

'Oh, it made no odds to him. He 'ad no pets in the Platoon, but 'e'd write 'ome to Ma about me an' all the doin's. You see' – Strangwick stirred uneasily on the sofa – 'we'd known him all our lives – lived in the next street an' all . . . An' him well over fifty. Oh dear me! *Oh* dear me! What a bloody mix-up things are, when one's as young as me!' he wailed of a sudden.

But Keede held him to the point. 'He wrote to your Mother about you?'

'Yes. Ma's eyes had gone bad followin' on air-raids. Blood-vessels broke behind 'em from sittin' in cellars an' bein' sick. She had to 'ave 'er letters read to her by Auntie. Now I think of it, that was the only thing that you might have called anything at all—'

'Was that the Aunt that died, and that you got the wire about?' Keede drove on.

'Yes – Auntie Armine – Ma's younger sister an' she nearer fifty than forty. What a mix-up! An' if I'd been asked any time about it, I'd 'ave sworn there wasn't a single sol'tary item concernin' her that everybody didn't know an' hadn't known all along. No more conceal to her doin's than – than so much shop-front. She'd looked after sister an' me, when needful – hoopin' cough an' measles – just the same as Ma. We was in an' out of her house like rabbits. You see, Uncle Armine is a cabinet-maker, an' second-'and furniture, an' we liked playin' with the things. She 'ad no children, and when the war came, she said she was glad of it. But she never talked much of her feelin's. She kept herself to herself, you understand.' He stared most earnestly at us to help out our understandings.

'What was she like?' Keede inquired.

'A biggish woman, an' had been 'andsome, I believe, but,

bein' used to her, we two didn't notice much – except, per'aps, for one thing. Ma called her 'er proper name, which was Bella; but Sis an' me always called 'er Auntie Armine. See?'

'What for?'

'We thought it sounded more like her – like somethin' movin' slow, in armour.'

'Oh! And she read your letters to your mother, did she?'

'Every time the post came in she'd slip across the road from opposite an' read 'em. An' – an' I'll go bail for it that that was all there was to it for as far back as *I* remember. Was I to swing tomorrow, I'd go bail for *that*! 'Tisn't fair of 'em to 'ave unloaded it all on me, because – because – if the dead *do* rise, why, what in 'ell becomes of me an' all I've believed all me life? I want to know *that*! I – I—'

But Keede would not be put off. 'Did the Sergeant give you away at all in his letters?' he demanded, very quietly.

'There was nothin' to give away – we was too busy – but his letters about me were a great comfort to Ma. I'm no good at writin'. I saved it all up for my leafs. I got me fourteen days every six months an' one over . . . I was luckier than most, that way.'

'And when you came home, used you to bring 'em news about the Sergeant?' said Keede.

'I expect I must have; but I didn't think much of it at the time. I was took up with me own affairs – naturally. Uncle John always wrote to me once each leaf, tellin' me what was doin' an' what I was li'ble to expect to return, an' Ma 'ud 'ave that read to her. The o' course I had to slip over to his wife an' pass her the news. An' then there was the young lady that I'd thought of marryin' if I came through. We'd got as far as pricin' things in the windows together.'

'And you didn't marry her – after all?'

Another tremor shook the boy. '*No!*' he cried. ' 'Fore it ended, I knew what reel things reely mean! I – I never dreamed such things could be! . . . An' she nearer fifty than forty an' me own Aunt! . . . But there wasn't a sign nor a hint from first to last, so 'ow *could* I tell? Don't you *see* it? All she said to me after me Christmas leaf in '18 when I come to say

good-bye – all Auntie Armine said to me was: "You'll be seein'
Mister Godsoe soon?" "Too soon for my likings," I says.
"Well then, tell 'im from me," she says, "that I expect to be
through with my little trouble by the twenty-first of next
month, an' I'm dyin' to see him as soon as possible after that
date"'

'What sort of trouble was it?' Keede turned professional at
once.

'She'd 'ad a bit of a gatherin' in 'er breast, I believe. But she
never talked of 'er body much to any one.'

'*I* see,' said Keede. 'And she said to you?'

Strangwick repeated: ' "Tell Uncle John I hope to be
finished of my drawback by the twenty-first, an' I'm dying to
see 'im as soon as 'e can after that date." An' then she says,
laughin': "But you've a head like a sieve. I'll write it down, an'
you can give it him when you see 'im." So she wrote it on a bit
o' paper an' I kissed 'er good-bye – I was always her favourite,
you see – an' I went back to Sampoux. The thing hardly stayed
in my mind at all, d'you see. But the next time I was up in the
front line – I was a Runner, d'ye see – our platoon was in
North Bay Trench an' I was up with a message to the Trench
Mortar there that Corporal Grant was in charge of. Followin'
on receipt of it, he borrowed a couple of men off the platoon,
to slue 'er round or somethin'. I give Uncle John Auntie
Armine's paper, an' I give Grant a fag, an' we warmed up a
bit over a brazier. Then Grant says to me: "I don't like it"; an'
he jerks 'is thumb at Uncle John in the bay studyin' Auntie's
message. Well, *you* know, sir, you had to speak to Grant about
'is way of prophesyin' things – after Rankine shot himself with
the Very light.'

'I did,' said Keede, and he explained to me: 'Grant had the
Second Sight – confound him! It upset the men. I was glad
when he got pipped. What happened after that, Strangwick?'

'Grant whispers to me: "Look, you damned Englishman.
'E's for it." Uncle John was leanin' up against the bay, an'
hummin' that hymn I was tryin' to tell you just now. He
looked different all of a sudden – as if 'e'd got shaved. *I* don't
know anything of these things, but I cautioned Grant as to his

style of speakin', if an officer 'ad 'eard him, an' I went on. Passin' Uncle John in the bay, 'e nods an' smiles, which he didn't often, an' he says, pocketin' the paper: "This suits *me*. I'm for leaf on the twenty-first, too."'

'He said that to you, did he?' said Keede.

'*Pre*cisely the same as passin' the time o' day. O' course I returned the agreeable about hopin' he'd get it, an' in due course I returned to 'Eadquarters. The thing 'ardly stayed in my mind a minute. That was the eleventh January – three days after I'd come back from leaf. You remember, sir, there wasn't anythin' doin' either side round Sampoux the first part o' the month. Jerry was gettin' ready for his March Push, an' as long as he kept quiet, we didn't want to poke 'im up.'

'I remember that,' said Keede. 'But what about the Sergeant?'

I must have met him, on an' off, I expect, goin' up an' down, through the ensuin' days, but it didn't stay in me mind. Why needed it? And on the twenty-first Jan., his name was on the leaf-paper when I went up to warn the leaf-men. I noticed *that*, o' course. Now that very afternoon Jerry 'ad been tryin' a new trench-mortar, an' before our 'Eavies could out it, he'd got a stinker into a bay an' mopped up 'alf a dozen. They were bringin' 'em down when I went up to the supports, an' that blocked Little Parrot, same as it always did. *You* remember, sir?'

'Rather! And there was that big machine-gun behind the Half-House waiting for you if you got out,' said Keede.

'I remembered that too. But it was just on dark an' the fog was comin' off the Canal, so I hopped out of Little Parrot an' cut across the open to where those four dead Warwicks are heaped up. But the fog turned me round, an' the next thing I knew I was knee-over in that old 'alf-trench that runs west o' Little Parrot into French End. I dropped into it – almost atop o' the machine-gun platform by the side o' the old sugar boiler an' the two Zoo-ave skel'tons. That gave me my bearin's, an' so I went through French End, all up those missin' duck-boards, into Butcher's Row where the *poy-looz* was laid in six deep each side, an' stuffed under the duckboards. It had froze tight, an' the drippin's had stopped, an' the creakin's had begun.'

'Did that really worry you at the time?' Keede asked.

'No,' said the boy with professional scorn. 'If a Runner starts noticin' such things he'd better chuck. In the middle of the Row, just before the old dressin'-station you referred to, sir, it come over me that somethin' ahead on the duckboards was just like Auntie Armine, waitin' beside the door; an' I thought to meself 'ow truly comic it would be if she could be dumped where I was then. In 'alf a second I saw it was only the dark an' some rags o' gas-screen, 'angin' on a bit of board, 'ad played me the trick. So I went on up to the supports an' warned the leaf-men there, includin' Uncle John. Then I went up Rake Alley to warn 'em in the front line. I didn't hurry because I didn't want to get there till Jerry 'ad quieted down a bit. Well, then a Company Relief dropped in – an' the officer got the wind up over some lights on the flank an' tied 'em into knots, an' I 'ad to hunt up me leaf-men all over the blinkin' shop. What with one thing an' another, it must 'ave been 'alf-past eight before I got back to the supports. There I run across Uncle John, scrapin' mud off himself, havin' shaved – quite the dandy. He asked about the Arras train, an' I said, if Jerry was quiet, it might be ten o'clock. "Good!" says 'e, "I'll come with you." So we started back down the old trench that used to run across Halnaker, back of the support dug-outs. *You* know, sir.'

Keede nodded.

'Then Uncle John says something to me about seein' Ma an' the rest of 'em in a few days, an' had I any messages for 'em? Gawd knows what made me do it, but I told 'im to tell Auntie Armine I never expected to see anything like *her* up in our part of the world. And while I told him I laughed. That's the last time I *'ave* laughed. "Oh – you've seen 'er, 'ave you?" says he, quite natural-like. Then I told 'im about the sand-bags an' rags in the dark, playin' the trick. "Very likely," says he, brushin' the mud off his puttees. By this time, we'd got to the corner where the old barricade into French End was – before they bombed it down, sir. He turns right an' climbs across it. "No, thanks," says I. "I've been there once this evenin'." But he wasn't attendin' to me. He felt behind the rubbish an' bones just inside the barricade, an' when he straightened up, he had a full brazier in each hand.

' "Come on, Clem," he says, an' he very rarely give me me own name. "You aren't afraid, are you?" he says. "It's just as short, an' if Jerry starts up again he won't waste stuff here. He knows it's abandoned." "Who's afraid now?" I says. "Me for one," says he. "I don't want *my* leaf spoiled at the last minute." Then 'e wheels round an' speaks that bit you said come out o' the Burial Service.'

For some reason Keede repeated it in full, slowly: 'If, after the manner of men, I have fought with beasts at Ephesus, what advantageth it me if the dead rise not?'

'That's it,' said Strangwick. 'So we went down French End together – everything froze up an' quiet, except for their creakin's. I remember thinkin' – ' his eyes began to flicker.

'Don't think. Tell what happened,' Keede ordered.

'Oh! Beg y' pardon! He went on with his braziers, hummin' his hymn, down Butcher's Row. Just before we got to the old dressin'-station he stops and sets 'em down an' says: "Where did you say she was, Clem? Me eyes ain't as good as they used to be."

' "In 'er bed at 'ome," I says. "Come on down. It's perishin' cold, an' *I'm* not due for leaf."

' "Well, I am," 'e says. "*I* am . . ." An' then – give you me word I didn't recognise the voice – he stretches out 'is neck a bit, in a way 'e 'ad, an' he says: "Why Bella!" 'e says. "Oh, Bella!" 'e says. "Thank Gawd!" 'e says. Just like that! An' then I saw – I tell you I *saw* – Auntie Armine herself standin' by the old dressin'-station door where first I'd thought I'd seen her. He was lookin' at 'er an' she was lookin' at him. I saw it, an' me soul turned over inside me because – because it knocked out everything I'd believed in. I 'ad nothin' to lay 'old of, d'ye see? An' 'e was lookin' at 'er as though he could 'ave et 'er, an' she was lookin' at 'im the same way, out of 'er eyes. Then he says: "Why, Bella," 'e says, "this must be only the second time we've been alone together in all these years." An' I saw 'er half hold out her arms to 'im in that perishin' cold. An' she nearer fifty than forty an' me own Aunt! You can shop me for a lunatic to-morrow, but I saw it – I *saw* 'er answerin' to his spoken word! . . . Then 'e made a snatch to unsling 'is rifle. Then 'e cuts 'is hand away saying: "No! Don't tempt me, Bella. We've all Eternity ahead of us. An hour or two won't make any odds." Then he picks up the braziers an' goes on to the dug-out door. He'd finished with me. He pours petrol on 'em, an' lights it with a match, an' carries 'em inside, flarin'. All that time Auntie Armine stood with 'er arms out – an' a look in 'er face! *I* didn't know such things was or could be! Then he comes out an' says: "Come in, my dear"; an' she stoops an' goes into the dug-out with that look on her face – that look on her face! An' then 'e shuts the door from inside an' starts wedgin' it up. So 'elp me Gawd, I saw an' 'eard all these things with my own eyes an' ears!'

He repeated his oath several times. After a long pause Keede asked him if he recalled what happened next.

'It was a bit of a mix-up, for me, from then on. I must have carried on – they told me I did, but – but I was – I felt a – a long way inside of meself, like – if you've ever had that feelin'. I wasn't rightly on the spot at all. They woke me up sometime next morning, because 'e 'adn't showed up at the train; an' some one had seen him with me. I wasn't 'alf cross-examined by all an' sundry till dinner-time.

'Then, I think, I volunteered for Dearlove, who 'ad a sore toe, for a front-line message. I had to keep movin', you see, because I hadn't anything to hold *on* to. Whilst up there, Grant informed me how he'd found Uncle John with the door wedged an' sandbags stuffed in the cracks. I hadn't waited for that. The knockin' when e' wedged up was enough for me. 'Like Dad's coffin.'

'No one told *me* the door had been wedged.' Keede spoke severely.

'No need to black a dead man's name, sir.'

'What made Grant go to Butcher's Row?'

'Because he'd noticed Uncle John had been pinchin' char-coal for a week past an' layin' it up behind the old barricade there. So when the 'unt began, he went that way straight as a string, an' when he saw the door shut, he knew. He told me he picked the sand-bags out of the cracks an' shoved 'is hand through and shifted the wedges before any one come along. It looked all right. You said yourself, sir, the door must 'ave blown to.'

'Grant knew what Godsoe meant, then?' Keede snapped.

'Grant knew Godsoe was for it; an' nothin' early could 'elp or 'inder. He told me so.'

'And then what did you do?'

'I expect I must 'ave kept on carryin' on, till Headquarters give me that wire from Ma – about Auntie Armine dyin'.'

'When had your Aunt died?'

'On the mornin' of the twenty-first. The mornin' of the 21st! That tore it, d'ye see? As long as I could think, I had kep' tellin' myself it was like those things you lectured about at Arras when we was billeted in the cellars – the Angels of Mons, and so on. But that wire tore it.'

'Oh! Hallucinations! I remember. And that wire tore it?' said Keede.

'Yes! You see' – he half lifted himself off the sofa – 'there wasn't a single gor-dam thing left abidin' for me to take hold of, here or hereafter. If the dead *do* rise – and I saw 'em – why – why *anything* can 'appen. Don't you understand?'

He was on his feet now, gesticulating stiffly.

'For I saw 'er,' he repeated. 'I saw 'im an' 'er – she dead since mornin' time, an' he killin' 'imself before my livin' eyes so's to carry on with 'er for all Eternity – an' she 'oldin' out 'er arms for it! I want to know where I'm *at*! Look 'ere, you two – why stand *we* in jeopardy every hour?'

'God knows,' said Keede to himself.

'Hadn't we better ring for some one?' I suggested. 'He'll go off the handle in a second.'

'No, he won't. It's the last kick-up before it takes hold. I know how the stuff works. Hul-lo!'

Strangwick, his hands behind his back and his eyes set, gave tongue in the strained, cracked voice of a boy reciting. 'Not twice in the world shall the Gods do thus,' he cried again and again.

'And I'm damned if it's goin' to be even once for me!' he went on with sudden insane fury. '*I* don't care whether we *'ave* been pricin' things in the windows . . . *Let* 'er sue if she likes! She don't know what reel things mean. *I* do – I've 'ad occasion to notice 'em . . . *No*, I tell you! I'll 'ave 'em when I want 'em, an' be done with 'em; but not till I see that look on a face . . . that look . . . I'm not takin' any. The reel thing's life an' death. It *begins* at death, d'ye see. *She* can't understand . . . Oh, go on an' push off to Hell, you an' your lawyers. I'm fed up with it – fed up!'

He stopped as abruptly as he had started, and the drawn face broke back to its natural irresolute lines. Keede, holding both his hands, led him back to the sofa, where he dropped like a wet towel, took out some flamboyant robe from a press, and drew it neatly over him.

'Ye-es. *That's* the real thing at last,' said Keede. 'Now he's got it off his mind he'll sleep. By the way, who introduced him?'

'Shall I go and find out?' I suggested.

'Yes; and you might ask him to come here. There's no need for us to stand to all night.'

So I went to the Banquet which was in full swing, and was seized by an elderly, precise Brother from a South London Lodge who followed me, concerned and apologetic. Keede soon put him at his ease.

'The boy's had trouble,' our visitor explained. 'I'm most mortified he should have performed his bad turn here. I thought he'd put it be'ind him.'

'I expect talking about old days with me brought it all back,' said Keede. 'It does sometimes.'

'Maybe! Maybe! But over and above that, Clem's had post-war trouble, too.'

'Can't he get a job? He oughtn't to let that weigh on him, at his time of life,' said Keede cheerily.

' 'Tisn't that – he's provided for – but' – he coughed confidentially behind his dry hand – 'as a matter of fact. Worshipful Sir, he's – he's implicated for the present in a little breach of promise action.'

'Ah! That's a different thing,' said Keede.

'Yes. That's his reel trouble. No reason given, you understand. The young lady in every way suitable, an' she'd make him a good little wife too, if I'm any judge. But he says she ain't his ideel or something. 'No getting at what's in young people's minds these days, is there?'

'I'm afraid there isn't,' said Keede. 'But he's all right now. He'll sleep. You sit by him, and when he wakes, take him home quietly . . . Oh, we're used to men getting a little upset here. You've nothing to thank us for. Brother – Brother—'

'Armine,' said the old gentleman. 'He's my nephew by marriage.'

'That's all that's wanted!' said Keede.

Brother Armine looked a little puzzled. Keede hastened to explain. 'As I was saying, all he wants now is to be kept quiet till he wakes.'

THE WISH HOUSE

The new Church Visitor had just left after a twenty minutes' call. During that time, Mrs Ashcroft had used such English as an elderly, experienced, and pensioned cook should, who had seen life in London. She was the readier, therefore, to slip back into easy, ancient Sussex ('t's softening to 'd's as one warmed) when the 'bus brought Mrs Fettley from thirty miles away for a visit, that pleasant March Saturday. The two had been friends since childhood; but, of late, destiny had separated their meetings by long intervals.

Much was to be said, and many ends, loose since last time, to be ravelled up on both sides, before Mrs Fettley, with her bag of quilt-patches, took the couch beneath the window commanding the garden, and the football-ground in the valley below.

'Most folk got out at Bush Tye for the match there,' she explained, 'so there weren't no one for me to cushion agin, the last five mile. An' she *do* just-about bounce ye.'

'You've took no hurt,' said her hostess. 'You don't brittle by agein', Liz.'

Mrs Fettley chuckled and made to match a couple of patches to her liking. 'No, or I'd ha' broke twenty year back. You can't ever mind when I was so's to be called round, can ye?'

Mrs Ashcroft shook her head slowly – she never hurried – and went on stitching a sack-cloth lining into a list-bound rush tool-basket. Mrs Fettley laid out more patches in the Spring light through the geraniums on the window-sill, and they were silent awhile.

'What like's this new Visitor o' yourn?' Mrs Fettley inquired, with a nod towards the door. Being very short-sighted, she had, on her entrance, almost bumped into the lady.

Mrs Ashcroft suspended the big packing-needle judicially on high, ere she stabbed home. 'Settin' aside she don't bring much news with her yet, I dunno as I've anythin' special agin her.'

'Ourn, at Keyneslade,' said Mrs Fettley, 'she's full o' words an' pity, but she don't stay for answers. Ye can get on with your thoughts while she clacks.'

'This 'un don't clack. She's aimin' to be one o' those High Church nuns, like.'

'Ourn's married, but, by what they say, she've made no great gains of it . . .' Mrs Fettley threw up her sharp chin. 'Lord! How they dam' cherubim do shake the very bones o' the place!'

The tile-sided cottage trembled at the passage of two specially chartered forty-seat charabancs on their way to the Bush Tye match; a regular Saturday 'shopping' 'bus, for the county's capital, fumed behind them; while, from one of the crowded inns, a fourth car backed out to join the procession, and held up the stream of through pleasure-traffic.

'You're as free-tongued as ever, Liz,' Mrs Ashcroft observed.

'Only when I'm with you. Otherwhiles, I'm Granny – three times over. I lay that basket's for one o' your gran'chiller – ain't it?'

'' Tis for Arthur – my Jane's eldest.'

'But he ain't workin' nowhere, is he?'

'No. 'Tis a picnic-basket.'

'You're let off light. My Willie, he's allus at me for money for them aireated wash-poles folk puts up in their gardens to draw the music from Lunnon, like. An' I give it 'im – pore fool me!'

'An' he forgets to give you the promise-kiss after, don't he?' Mrs Ashcroft's heavy smile seemed to strike inwards.

'He do. 'No odds 'twixt boys now an' forty year back. 'Take all an' give naught – an' we to put up with it! Pore fool we! Three shillin' at a time Willie'll ask me for!'

'They don't make nothin' o' money these days,' Mrs Ashcroft said.

'An' on'y last week,' the other went on, 'me daughter, she ordered a quarter pound suet at the butchers's; an' she sent it back to 'im to be chopped. She said she couldn't bother with choppin' it.'

'I lay he charged her, then.'

'I lay he did. She told me there was a whisk-drive that afternoon at the Institute, an' she couldn't bother to do the choppin'.'

'Tck!'

Mrs Ashcroft put the last firm touches to the basket-lining. She had scarcely finished when her sixteen-year-old grandson, a maiden of the moment in attendance, hurried up the garden-path shouting to know if the thing were ready, snatched it, and made off without acknowledgment. Mrs Fettley peered at him closely.

'They're goin' picnickin' somewheres,' Mrs Ashcroft explained.

'Ah,' said the other, with narrowed eyes. 'I lay *he* won't show much mercy to any he comes across, either. Now 'oo the dooce do he remind me of, all a sudden?'

'They must look arter theirselves – 'same as we did,' Mrs Ashcroft began to set out the tea.

'No denyin' *you* could. Gracie,' said Mrs Fettley.

'What's in your head now?'

'Dunno . . . But it come over me, sudden-like – about dat woman from Rye – I've slipped the name – Barnsley, wadn't it?'

'Batten – Polly Batten, you're thinkin' of.'

'That's it – Polly Batten. That day she had it in for you with a hay-fork – 'time we was all hayin' at Smalldene – for stealin' her man.'

'But you heered me tell her she had my leave to keep him?' Mrs Ashcroft's voice and smile were smoother than ever.

'I did – an' we was all looking that she'd prod the fork spang through your breastes when you said it.'

'No-oo. She'd never go beyond bounds – Polly. She shruck too much for reel doin's.'

'Allus seems to *me*,' Mrs Fettley said after a pause, 'that a man 'twixt two fightin' women is the foolishest thing on earth. Like a dog bein' called two ways.'

'Mebbe. But what set ye off on those times, Liz?'

'That boy's fashion o' carryin' his head an' arms. I haven't rightly looked at him since he's growed. Your Jane never showed it, but – *him*! Why, 'tis Jim Batten and his tricks come to life again! . . . Eh?'

'Mebbe. There's some that would ha' made it out so – bein' barren-like, themselves.'

'Oho! Ah well! Dearie, dearie me, now! . . . An' Jim Batten's been dead this—'

'Seven and twenty year,' Mrs Ashcroft answered briefly. 'Won't ye draw up, Liz?'

Mrs Fettley drew up to buttered toast, currant bread, stewed tea, bitter as leather, some home-preserved pears, and a cold boiled pig's tail to help down the muffins. She paid all the proper compliments.

'Yes. I dunno as I've ever owed me belly much,' said Mrs Ashcroft thoughtfully. 'We only go through this world once.'

'But don't it lay heavy on ye, sometimes?' her guest suggested.

'Nurse says I'm a sight liker to die o' me indigestion than me leg.' For Mrs Ashcroft had a long-standing ulcer on her shin, which needed regular care from the Village Nurse, who boasted (or others did, for her) that she had dressed it one hundred and three times already during her term of office.

'An' you that *was* so able, too! It's all come on ye before your full time, like. *I've* watched ye goin'.' Mrs Fettley spoke with real affection.

'Somethin's bound to find ye sometime. I've me 'eart left me still,' Mrs Ashcroft returned.

'You was always big-hearted enough for three. That's somethin' to look back on at the day's eend.'

'I reckon you've *your* back-lookin's, too,' was Mrs Ashcroft's answer.

'You know it. But I don't think much regardin' such matters excep' when I'm along with you, Gra'. Takes two sticks to make a fire.'

Mrs Fettley stared, with jaw half-dropped, at the grocer's bright calendar on the wall. The cottage shook again to the roar of the motor-traffic, and the crowded football-ground below the garden roared almost as loudly; for the village was well set to its Saturday leisure.

Mrs Fettley had spoken very precisely for some time without interruption, before she wiped her eyes. 'And,' she concluded, 'they read 'is death-notice to me, out o' the paper last month. O' course it wasn't any o' *my* becomin' concerns – let be I 'adn't set eyes on him for so long. O' course *I* couldn't say nor show nothin'. Nor I've no rightful call to go to Eastbourne to see 'is grave, either. I've been schemin' to slip over there by the 'bus some day; but they'd ask questions at 'ome past endurance. So I 'aven't even *that* to stay me.'

'But you've 'ad your satisfactions?'

'Godd! Yess! Those four years 'e was workin' on the rail near us. An' the other drivers they gave him a brave funeral, too.'

'Then you've naught to cast-up about. 'Nother cup o' tea?'

The light and air had changed a little with the sun's descent, and the two elderly ladies closed the kitchen-door against chill. A couple of jays squealed and skirmished through the undraped apple-trees in the garden. This time, the word was with Mrs Ashcroft, her elbows on the tea-table, and her sick leg propped on a stool . . . .

'Well I never! But what did your 'usband say to that?'Mrs Fettley asked, when the deep-toned recital halted.

' 'E said I might go where I pleased for all of 'im. But seein' 'e was bedrid, I said I'd 'tend 'im out. 'E knowed I wouldn't take no advantage of 'im in that state. 'E lasted eight or nine week. Then he was took with a seizure-like; an' laid stone-still for days. Then 'e propped 'imself up abed an' says: "You pray no man'll ever deal with you like you've dealed with some."

"An' you?" I says, for *you* know, Liz, what a rover 'e was. "It cuts both ways," says 'e, "but *I'm* death-wise, an' I can see what's comin' to you." He died a-Sunday an' was buried a-Thursday . . . An' yet I'd set a heap by him – one time or – did I ever?'

'You never told me that before,' Mrs Fettley ventured.

'I'm payin' ye for what ye told me just now. Him bein' dead, I wrote up, sayin' I was free for good, to that Mrs Marshall in Lunnon – which gave me my first place as kitchen-maid – Lord, how long ago! She was well pleased, for they two was both gettin' on, an' I knowed their ways. You remember, Liz, I used to go to 'em in service between whiles, for years – when we wanted money, or – or my 'usband was away – on occasion.'

' 'E *did* get that six months at Chichester, didn't 'e?' Mrs Fettley whispered. 'We never rightly won to the bottom of it.'

' 'E'd ha' got more, but the man didn't die.'

' 'None o' your doin's, was it, Gra'?'

'No! 'Twas the woman's husband this time. An' so, my man bein' dead, I went back to them Marshalls, as cook, to get me legs under a gentleman's table again, and be called with a handle to me name. That was the year you shifted to Portsmouth.'

'Cosham,' Mrs Fettley corrected. 'There was a middlin' lot o' new buildin' bein' done there. My man went first, an' got the room, an' I follered.'

'Well, then, I was a year-abouts in Lunnon, all at a breath, like, four meals a day an' livin' easy. Then, 'long towards autumn, they two went travellin', like, to France; keepin' me on, for they couldn't go without me.' I put the house to rights for the caretaker, an' then I slipped down 'ere to me sister Bessie – me wages in me pockets, an' all 'ands glad to be'old of me.'

'That would be when I was at Cosham,' said Mrs Fettley.

'*You* know. Liz, there wasn't no cheap-dog pride to folk, those days, no more than there was cinemas nor whisk-drives. Man or woman 'ud lay hold o' any job that promised a shillin' to the backside of it, didn't they? I was all peaked up after

696

Lunnon, an' I thought the fresh airs 'ud serve me. So I took on at Smalldene, obligin' with a hand at the early potato-liftin', stubbin' hens, an' such-like. They'd ha' mocked me sore in my kitchen in Lunnon, to see me in men's boots, an' me petticoats all shorted.'

'Did it bring ye any good?' Mrs Fettley asked.

' 'Twadn't for that I went. You know, 's'well's me, that na'un happens to ye till it *'as* 'appened. Your mind don't warn ye before 'and of the road ye've took, till you're at the far eend of it. We've only a backwent view of our proceedin's.'

' 'Oo was it?'

' 'Arry Mockler.' Mrs Ashcroft's face puckered to the pain of her sick leg.

Mrs Fettley gasped. ' 'Arry? Bert Mockler's son! An' *I* never guessed!'

Mrs Ashcroft nodded. 'An' I told myself – *an*' I left it – that I wanted field-work.'

'What did ye get out of it?'

'The usuals. Everythin' at first – worse than naught after. I had signs an' warnings a-plenty, but I took no heed of 'em. For we was burnin' rubbish one day, just when we'd come to know how 'twas with – with both of us. 'Twas early in the year for burnin', an' I said so. "No!" says he. "The sooner dat old stuff's off an' done with," 'e says, "the better." 'Is face was harder'n rocks when he spoke. Then it come over me that I'd found me master, which I 'adn't ever before. I'd allus owned 'em like.'

'Yes! Yes! They're yourn or you're theirn,' the other sighed. 'I like the right way best.'

'I didn't. But 'Arry did . . . 'Long then, it come time for me to go back to Lunnon. I couldn't. I clean couldn't! So, I took an' tipped a dollop o' scaldin' water out o' the copper one Monday mornin' over me left 'and and arm. Dat stayed me where I was for another fortnight.'

'Was it worth it?' said Mrs Fettley, looking at the silvery scar on the wrinkled fore-arm.

Mrs Ashcroft nodded. 'An' after that, we two made it up 'twixt us so's 'e could come to Lunnon for a job in a liv'ry-stable not far from me. 'E got it. *I* 'tended to that. There wadn't no talk nowhere. His own mother never suspicioned how 'twas. He just slipped up to Lunnon, an' there we abode that winter, not 'alf a mile 'tother from each.'

'Ye paid 'is fare an' all, though'; Mrs Fettley spoke convincedly.

Again Mrs Ashcroft nodded. 'Dere wadn't much I didn't do for him. 'E was me master, an' – O God help us! – we'd laugh over it walkin' together after dark in them paved streets, an' me corns fair wrenchin' in me boots! I'd never been like that before. Ner he! Ner he!'

Mrs Fettley clucked sympathetically.

'An' when did ye come to the eend?' she asked.

'When 'e paid it all back again, every penny. Then I knowed, but I wouldn't *suffer* meself to know. "You've been mortal kind to me," he says. "Kind!" I said. " 'Twixt *us*?" But 'e kep' all on tellin' me 'ow kind I'd been an' 'e'd never forget it all his days. I held it from off o' me for three evenin's, because I would *not* believe. Then 'e talked about not bein' satisfied with 'is job in the stables, an' the men there puttin' tricks on 'im, an' all they lies which a man tells when 'e's leavin' ye. I heard 'im out, neither 'elpin' nor 'inderin'. At the last, I took off a liddle brooch which he'd give me an' I says: "Dat'll do. *I* ain't askin' na'un'." An' I turned me round an' walked off to me own sufferin's. 'E didn't make 'em worse. 'E didn't come nor write after that. 'E slipped off 'ere back 'ome to 'is mother again.'

'An' 'ow often did ye look for 'en to come back?' Mrs Fettley demanded mercilessly.

'More'n once – more'n once! Goin' over the streets we'd used, I thought de very pave-stones 'ud shruck out under me feet.'

'Yes,' said Mrs Fettley. 'I dunno but dat don't 'urt as much as aught else. An' dat was all yet got?'

'No. 'Twadn't. That's the curious part, if you'll believe it, Liz.'

'I do. I lay you're further off lyin' now than in all your life, Gra'.'

'I am . . . An' I suffered, like I'd not wish my most arrantest enemies to. God's Own Name! I went through the hoop that spring! One part of it was headaches which I'd never know all me days before. Think o' *me* with an 'eddick! But I come to be grateful for 'em. They kep' me from thinkin' . . .'

' 'Tis like a tooth,' Mrs Fettley commented. 'It must rage an' rugg till it tortures itself quiet on ye; an' then – then there's na'un left.'

'*I* got enough lef' to last me all *my* days on earth. It come about through our charwoman's liddle girl – Sophy Ellis was 'er name – all eyes an' elbers an' hunger. I used to give 'er vittles. Otherwhiles, I took no special notice of 'er, an' a sight less, o' course, when me trouble about 'Arry was on me. But – you know how liddle maids first feel it sometimes – she come to be crazy-fond o' me, pawin' an' cuddlin' all whiles; an' I 'adn't the 'eart to beat 'er off . . . One afternoon, early in spring 'twas, 'er mother 'ad sent 'er round to scutchel up what vittles she could off of us. I was settin' by the fire, me apern over me head, half-mad with the 'eddick, when she slips in. I reckon I was middlin' short with 'er. "Lor'!" she says. "Is *that* all? I'll take it off you in two-twos!" I told her not to lay a finger on me, for I thought she'd want to stroke my forehead; an'– I ain't that make. "*I* won't tech ye," she says, an' slips out again. She 'adn't been gone ten minutes 'fore me old 'eddick took off quick as bein' kicked. So I went about my work. Prasin'ly, Sophy comes back, an' creeps into my chair quiet as a mouse. 'Er eyes was deep in 'er 'ead an' 'er face all drawed. I asked 'er what 'ad 'appened. "Nothin'," she says. "On'y *I*'ve got it now." "Got what?" I says. "Your 'eddick," she says, all hoarse an' sticky-lipped. "I've took it on me." "Nonsense," I says, "it went of itself when you was out. Lay still an' I'll make ye a cup o' tea." " 'Twon't do no good," she says, "till your time's up. 'Ow long do *your* 'eddicks last?" "Don't talk silly," I says, "or I'll send for the Doctor." It looked to me like she might be hatchin' de measles. "Oh, Mrs Ashcroft," she says stretchin' out 'er liddle thin arms. "I *do* love ye." There wasn't any holdin' agin that. I took 'er into me lap an' made much of 'er. "Is it truly gone?" she says. "Yes," I says, "an' if 'twas you took it away, I'm truly grateful." " 'Twas me," she says, layin' 'er cheek to mine. "No one but me knows how." An' then she said she'd changed me 'eddick for me at a Wish 'Ouse.'

'Whatt?' Mrs Fettley spoke sharply.

'A Wish House. No! I 'adn't 'eard o' such things, either. I couldn't get it straight at first, but, puttin' all together, I made out that a Wish 'Ouse 'ad to be a house which 'ad stood unlet an' empty long enough for Some One, like, to come an in'abit there. She said, a liddle girl that she'd played with in the livery-stables where 'Arry worked 'ad told 'er so. She said the girl 'ad belonged in a caravan that laid up, o' winters, in Lunnon. Gipsy, I judge.'

'Ooh! There's no sayin' what Gippos know, but I've never 'eard of a Wish 'Ouse, an' I know – some things,' said Mrs Fettley.

'Sophy said there was a Wish 'Ouse in Wadloes Road – just a few streets off, on the way to our green-grocer's. All you 'ad to do, she said, was to ring the bell an' wish your wish through the slit o' the letter-box. I asked 'er if the fairies give it 'er? "Don't ye know," she says, "there's no fairies in a Wish 'Ouse? There's on'y a Token."

'Goo' Lord A'mighty! Where did she come by that word?' cried Mrs Fettley; for a Token is a wraith of the dead or, worse still, of the living.

'The caravan-girl 'ad told 'er, she said. Well, Liz, it troubled me to 'ear 'er, an' lyin' in me arms she must ha' felt it. "That's very kind o' you," I says, holdin' 'er tight, "to wish me 'eddick away. But why didn't ye ask somethin' nice for yourself?" "You can't do that," she says. "All you'll get at a Wish 'Ouse is leave to take some one else's trouble. I've took Ma's 'eadaches, when she's been kind to me; but this is the first time I've been able to do aught for you. Oh, Mrs Ashcroft, I do just-about love you." An' she goes on all like that. Liz, I tell you my 'air e'en a'most stood on end to 'ear 'er. I asked 'er what like a Token was. "I dunno," she says, "but after you've ringed the bell, you'll 'ear it run up from the basement, to the front door. Then say your wish," she says, "an' go away."

' "The Token don't open de door to ye, then?" I says. "Oh

no," she says. "You on'y 'ear gigglin', like, be'ind the front door. Then you say you'll take the trouble off of 'oo ever 'tis you've chose for your love; an' ye'll get it," she says. I didn't ask no more – she was too 'ot an' fevered. I made much of 'er till it come time to light de gas, an' a riddle after that, 'er 'eddick – mine, I suppose – took off, an' she got down an' played with the cat.'

'Well, I never!' said Mrs Fetlley. 'Did – did ye foller it up, anyways?'

'She askt me to, but I wouldn't 'ave no such dealin's with a child.'

'What *did* ye do, then?'

'Sat in me own room 'stid o' the kitchen when me 'eddicks come on. But it lay at de back o' me mind.'

''Twould. Did she tell ye more, ever?'

'No. Besides what the Gippo girl 'ad told 'er, she knew naught, 'cept that the charm worked. An', next after that – in May 'twas – I suffered the summer out in Lunnon. 'Twas hot an' windy for weeks, an' the streets stinkin' o' dried 'orse-dung blowin' from side to side an' lyin' level with the kerb. We don't get that nowadays. I 'ad my 'ol'day just before hoppin',[1] an' come down 'ere to stay with Bessie again. She noticed I'd lost flesh, an' was all poochy under the eyes.'

'Did ye see 'Arry?'

Mrs Ashcroft nodded. 'The fourth – no, the fifth day. Wednesday 'twas. I knowed 'e was workin' at Smalldene again. I asked 'is mother in the street, bold as brass. She 'adn't room to say much, for Bessie – you know 'er tongue – was talkin' full-clack. But that Wednesday, I was walkin' with one o' Bessie's chillern hangin' on me skirts, at de back o' Chanter's Tot. Pras'nly, I felt 'e was be'ind me on the footpath, an' I knowed by 'is tread 'e'd changed 'is nature. I slowed, an' I heard 'im slow. Then I fussed a piece with the child, to force him past me, like. So 'e *ad* to come past. 'E just says, "Good-evenin'," and goes on, tryin' to pull 'isself together.'

'Drunk, was he?' Mrs Fettley asked.

[1] Hop-picking.

'Never! S'runk an' wizen; 'is clothes 'angin' on 'im like bags, an' the back of 'is neck whiter'n chalk. 'Twas all I could do not to oppen my arms an' cry after him. But I swallered me spittle till I was back 'ome again an' the chillern a bed. Then I says to Bessie, after supper, "What in de world's come to 'Arry Mockler?" Bessie told me 'e'd been a-Hospital for two months, 'long o' cuttin' 'is foot wid a spade, muckin' out the old pond at Smalldene. There was poison in de dirt, an' it rooshed up 'is leg, like, an' come out all over him. 'E 'adn't been back to 'is job – carterin' at Smalldene – more'n a fortnight. She told me the Doctor said he'd go off, likely, with the November frostes; an' 'is mother 'ad told 'er that 'e didn't rightly eat nor sleep, an' sweated 'imself into pools, no odds 'ow chill 'e lay. An' spit terrible o' mornin's. "Dearie me," I says. "But, mebbe, hoppin' 'll set 'im right again," an' I licked me thread-point an' I fetched me needle's eye up to it an' I threads me needle under de lamp, steady as rocks. An' dat night (me bed was in de wash-house) I cried an' I cried. An' *you* know, Liz – for you've been with me in my throes – it takes summat to make me cry.'

'Yes; but chile-bearin' is on'y just pain,' said Mrs Fettley.

'I come round by cock-crow, an' dabbed cold tea on me eyes to take away the signs. Long towards nex' evenin' – I was settin' out to lay some flowers on me 'usband's grave, for the look o' the thing – I met' 'Arry over against where the War Memorial is now. 'E was comin' back from 'is 'orses, so 'e couldn't *not* see me. I looked 'im all over, an' "'Arry," I says twix' me teeth, "come back an' rest-up in Lunnon." "I won't take it," he says, "for I can give ye naught." "I don't ask it," I says. "By God's Own Name, I don't ask na'un! On'y come up an' see a Lunnon doctor." 'E lifts 'is two 'eavy eyes at me: "'Tis past that, Gra'," 'e says. "I've but a few months left." "'Arry!" I says. "*My* man!" I says. I couldn't say no more. 'Twas all up in me throat. "Thank ye kindly, Gra'," 'e says (but 'e never says "my woman"), an' 'e went on up-street an' 'is mother – Oh, damn 'er! – she was watchin' for 'im, an' she shut de door be'ind 'im.'

Mrs Fettley stretched an arm across the table, and made to

finger Mrs Ashcroft's sleeve at the wrist, but the other moved it out of reach.

'So I went on to the churchyard with my flowers, an' I remembered my 'usband's warnin' that night he spoke. 'E *was* death-wise, an' it *'ad* 'appened as 'e said. But as I was settin' down de jam-pot on the grave-mound, it come over me there was one thing I *could* do for 'Arry. Doctor or no Doctor, I thought I'd make a trial of it. So I did. Nex' mornin', a bill came down from our Lunnon green-grocer. Mrs Marshall, she'd lef' me petty cash for suchlike – o' course – but I tole Bess 'twas for me to come an' open the 'ouse. So I went up, afternoon train.'

'An' – but I know you 'adn't – 'adn't you no fear?'

'What for? There was nothin' front o' me but my own shame an' God's croolty. I couldn't ever get 'Arry – 'ow *could* I? I knowed it must go on burnin' till it burned me out.'

'Aie!' said Mrs Fettley, reaching for the wrist again, and this time Mrs Ashcroft permitted it.

'Yit 'twas a comfort to know I could try *this* for 'im. So I went an' I paid the green-grocer's bill, an' put 'is receipt in me hand-bag, an' then I stepped round to Mrs Ellis – our char – an' got the 'ouse-keys an' opened the 'ouse. First, I made me bed to come back to (God's Own Name! Me bed to lie upon!). Nex' I made me a cup o' tea an' sat down in the kitchen thinkin', till 'long towards dusk. Terrible close, 'twas. Then I dressed me an' went out with the receipt in me 'and-bag, feignin' to study it for an address, like. Fourteen, Wadloes Road, was the place – a liddle basement-kitchen 'ouse, in a row of twenty-thirty such, an' tiddy strips o' walled garden in front – the paint off the front doors, an' na'un done to na'un since ever so long. There wasn't 'ardly no one in the streets 'cept the cats. 'Twas 'ot, too! I turned into the gate bold as brass; up de steps I went an' I ringed the front-door bell. She pealed loud, like it do in an empty house. When she'd all ceased, I 'eard a cheer, like, pushed back on de floor o' the kitchen. Then I 'eard feet on de kitchen-stairs, like it might ha' been a heavy woman in slippers. They come up to de stairhead, acrost the hall – I 'eard the bare boards creak under 'em – an' at de front door dey stopped. I stooped me to the letter-box slit, an' I says: "Let me take everythin' bad that's in store for my man, 'Arry Mockler, for love's sake." Then, whatever it was 'tother side de door let its breath out, like, as if it 'ad been holdin' it for to 'ear better.'

'Nothin' was *said* to ye?' Mrs Fettley demanded.

'Na'un. She just breathed out – a sort of *A-ah*, like. Then the steps went back an' downstairs to the kitchen – all draggy – an' I heard the cheer drawed up again.'

'An' you abode on de doorstep, throughout all, Gra'?' Mrs Ashcroft nodded.

'Then I went away, an' a man passin' says to me: "Didn't you know that house was empty?" "No," I says. "I must ha' been give the wrong number." An' I went back to our 'ouse, an' I went to bed; for I was fair flogged out. 'Twas too 'ot to sleep more'n snatches, so I walked me about, lyin' down betweens, till crack o' dawn. Then I went to the kitchen to make me a cup o' tea, an' I hitted meself just above the ankle on an old roastin'-jack o' mine that Mrs Ellis had moved out from the corner, her last cleanin'. An' so – nex' after that – I waited till the Marshalls come back o' their holiday.'

'Alone there? I'd ha' thought you'd 'ad enough of empty houses,' said Mrs Fettley, horrified.

'Oh, Mrs Ellis an' Sophy was runnin' in an' out soon's I was back, an' 'twixt us we cleaned de house again top-to-bottom. There's allus a hand's turn more to do in every house. An' that's 'ow 'twas with me that autumn an' winter, in Lunnon.'

'Then na'un hap – overtook ye for your doin's?'

Mrs Ashcroft smiled. 'No. Not then. 'Long in November I sent Bessie ten shillin's.'

'You was allus free-'anded,' Mrs Fettley interrupted.

'An' I got what I paid for, with the rest o' the news. She said the hoppin' 'ad set 'im up wonderful. 'E'd 'ad six weeks of it, and now 'e was back again carterin' at Smalldene. No odds to me *'ow* it 'ad 'appened – 'slong's it *'ad*. But I dunno as my ten shillin's eased me much. 'Arry bein' *dead*, like, 'e'd ha' been mine, till Judgment 'Arry bein' alive, 'e'd like as not pick up with some woman middlin' quick. I raged over that. Come spring, I 'ad somethin' else to rage for. I'd growed a nasty little weepin' boil, like, on me shin, just above the boot-top, that wouldn't heal no shape. It made me sick to look at it, for I'm clean-fleshed by nature. Chop me all over with a spade, an' I'd heal like turf. Then Mrs Marshall she set 'er own doctor at me. 'E said I ought to ha' come to him at first go-off, 'stead o' drawin' all manner o' dyed stockin's over it for months. 'E said I'd stood up too much to me work, for it was settin' very close atop of a big swelled vein, like behither the small o' me ankle. "Slow come, slow go," 'e says. "Lay your leg up on high an' rest it," he says, "an' 'twill ease off. Don't let it close up too soon. You've got a very fine leg, Mrs Ashcroft," 'e says. An' he put wet dressin's on it.'

' 'E done right.' Mrs Fettley spoke firmly. 'Wet dressin's to wet wounds. They draw de humours, same's a lamp-wick draws de oil.'

'That's true. An' Mrs Marshall was allus at me to make me set down more, an' dat nigh healed it up. An' then after a while they packed me off down to Bessie's to finish the cure; for I ain't the sort to sit down when I ought to stand up. You was back in the village then, Liz.'

'I was. I was, but – never did I guess!'

'I didn't desire ye to.' Mrs Ashcroft smiled. 'I saw 'Arry once or twice in de street, wonnerful fleshed up an' restored back. Then, one day I didn't see 'im, an' 'is mother told me one of 'is 'orses 'ad lashed out an' caught 'im on the 'ip. So 'e was abed an' middlin' painful. An' Bessie, she says to his mother, 'twas a pity 'Arry 'adn't a woman of 'is own to take the nursin' off 'er. And the old lady *was* mad! She told us that 'Arry 'ad never looked after any woman in 'is born days, an' as long as she was atop the mowlds, she'd contrive for 'im till 'er two 'ands dropped off. So I knowed she'd do watch-dog on me, 'thout askin' for bones.'

Mrs Fettley rocked with small laughter.

'That day,' Mrs Ashcroft went on, 'I'd stood on me feet nigh all the time, watchin' the doctor go in an' out; for they thought it might be 'is ribs, too. That made my boil break again, issuin' an' weepin'. But it turned out 'twadn't ribs at all, an' 'Arry 'ad a good night. When I heard that, nex' mornin', I says to meself, "I won't lay two an' two together – *yit*. I'll keep me leg down a week, an' see what comes of it." It didn't hurt me that day, to speak of – 'seemed more to draw the strength out o' me like – an' 'Arry 'ad another good night. That made me persevere; but I didn't dare lay two an' two together till the week-end, an' then, 'Arry come forth e'en a'most 'imself again – na'un hurt outside ner in of him. I nigh fell on me knees in de wash-house when Bessie was up-street. "I've got ye now, my man," I says. "You'll take your good from me 'thout knowin' it till my life's end. O God send me long to live for 'Arry's sake!" I says. An' I dunno that didn't still me ragin's.'

'For good?' Mrs Fettley asked.

'They come back, plenty times, but, let be how 'twould, I knowed I was doin' for 'im. I *knowed* it. I took an' worked me pains on an' off, like regulatin' my own range, till I learned to 'ave 'em at my commandments. An' that was funny, too. There was times, Liz, when my trouble 'ud all s'rink an' dry up, like. First, I used to try an' fetch it on again; bein' fearful to leave 'Arry alone too long for anythin' to lay 'old of. Prasin'ly I come to see that was a sign he'd do all right awhile, an' so I saved myself.'

''Ow long for?' Mrs Fettley asked, with deepest interest.

'I've gone de better part of a year onct or twice with na'un more to show than the liddle weepin' core of it, like. *All* s'rinked up an' dried off. Then he'd inflame up – for a warnin' – an' I'd suffer it. When I couldn't no more – an' I *'ad* to keep on goin' with my Lunnon work – I'd lay me leg high on a cheer till it eased. Not too quick. I knowed by the feel of it, those times, dat 'Arry was in need. Then I'd send another five shillin's to Bess, or somethin' for the chillern, to find out if, mebbe, 'e'd took any hurt through my neglects. 'Twas *so*! Year in, year out, I worked it dat way, Liz, an' 'e got 'is good from me 'thout knowin' – for years and years.'

'But what did *you* get out of it, Gra'?' Mrs Fettley almost wailed. 'Did ye see 'im reg'lar?'

'Times – when I was 'ere on me 'ol'days. An' more, now that I'm 'ere for good. But 'e's never looked at me, ner any other woman 'cept 'is mother. 'Ow I used to watch an' listen! So did she.'

'Years an' years!' Mrs Fettley repeated. 'An' where's 'e workin' at now?'

'Oh, 'e's give up carterin' quite a while. He's workin' for one o' them big tractorisin' firms – plowin' sometimes, an' sometimes off with lorries – fur as Wales, I've 'eard. He comes 'ome to 'is mother 'tween whiles; but I don't set eyes on him now, fer weeks on end. No odds! 'Is job keeps 'im from continuin' in one stay anywheres.'

'But – just for de sake o' sayin' somethin' – s'pose 'Arry *did* get married?' said Mrs Fettley.

Mrs Ashcroft drew her breath sharply between her still even and natural teeth. '*Dat* ain't been required of me,' she answered. 'I reckon my pains 'ull be counted agin that. Don't *you*, Liz?'

'It ought to be, dearie. It ought to be.'

'It *do* 'urt sometimes. You shall see it when Nurse comes. She thinks I don't know it's turned.'

Mrs Fettley understood. Human nature seldom walks up to the word 'cancer.'

'Be ye certain sure, Gra'?' she asked.

'I was sure of it when old Mr Marshall 'ad me up to 'is study an' spoke a long piece about my faithful service. I've obliged 'em on an' off for a goodish time, but not enough for a pension. But they give me a weekly 'lowance for life. I knew what *that* sinnified – as long as three years ago.'

'Dat don't *prove* it, Gra'.'

'To give fifteen bob a week to a woman 'oo'd live twenty year in the course o' nature? It *do*!'

'You're mistook! You're mistook!' Mrs Fettley insisted.

'Liz, there's *no* mistakin' when the edges are all heaped up, like – same as a collar. You'll see it. An' I laid out Dora Wickwood, too. *She* 'ad it under the arm-pit, like.'

Mrs Fettley considered awhile, and bowed her head in finality.

' 'Ow long d'you reckon 'twill allow ye, countin' from now, dearie?'

'Slow come, slow go. But if I don't set eyes on ye 'fore next hoppin', this'll be good-bye, Liz.'

'Dunno as I'll be able to manage by then – not 'thout I have a liddle dog to lead me. For de chillern, dey won't be troubled an' – O Gra'! – I'm blindin' up – I'm blindin' up!'

'Oh, *dat* – was why you didn't more'n finger with your quilt-patches all this while! I was wonderin' . . . But the pain *do* count, don't ye think, Liz? The pain *do* count to keep 'Arry – where I want 'im. Say it can't be wasted, like.'

'I'm sure of it – sure of it, dearie. You'll 'ave your reward.'

'I don't want no more'n this – *if* de pain is taken into de reckonin'.'

' 'Twill be – 'twill be, Gra'.'

There was a knock on the door.

'That's Nurse. She's before 'er time,' said Mrs Ashcroft. 'Open to er.'

The young lady entered briskly, all the bottles in her bag clicking. 'Evenin', Mrs Ashcroft,' she began. 'I've come raound a little earlier than usual because of the Institute dance to-na-ite. You won't ma-ind, will you?'

'Oh, no. Me dancin' days are over.' Mrs Ashcroft was the self-contained domestic at once. 'My old friend, Mrs Fettley 'ere, has been settin' talkin' with me a while.'

'I hope she 'asn't been fatiguing you?' said the Nurse a little frostily.

'Quite the contrary. It 'as been a pleasure. Only – only – just at the end I felt a bit – a bit flogged out like.'

'Yes, yes.' The Nurse was on her knees already, with the washes to hand. 'When old ladies get together they talk a deal too much, I've noticed.'

'Mebbe we do,' said Mrs Fettley, rising. 'So, now, I'll make myself scarce.'

'Look at it first, though,' said Mrs Ashcroft feebly. 'I'd like ye to look at it.'

Mrs Fettley looked, and shivered. Then she leaned over, and kissed Mrs Ashcroft once on the waxy yellow forehead, and again on the faded grey eyes.

'It *do*, count, don't it – de pain?' The lips that still kept trace of their original moulding hardly more than breathed the words.

Mrs Fettley kissed them and moved towards the door.

THE GARDENER

One grave to me was given,
    One watch till Judgment Day;
And God looked down from Heaven
    And rolled the stone away.

One day in all the years,
    One hour in that one day,
His Angel saw my tears,
        And rolled the stone away!

Every one in the village knew that Helen Turrell did her duty
by all her world, and by none more honourably than by her
only brother's unfortunate child. The village knew, too, that
George Turrell had tried his family severely since early youth,
and were not surprised to be told that, after many fresh starts
given and thrown away, he, an Inspector of Indian Police,
had entangled himself with the daughter of a retired non-
commissioned officer, and had died of a fall from a horse a few
week's before his child was born. Mercifully, George's father
and mother were both dead, and though Helen, thirty-five and
independent, might well have washed her hands of the whole
disgraceful affair, she most nobly took charge, though she was,
at the time, under threat of lung trouble which had driven
her to the South of France. She arranged for the passage of
the child and a nurse from Bombay, met them at Marseilles,
nursed the baby through an attack of infantile dysentery due to
the carelessness of the nurse, whom she had had to dismiss,
and at last, thin and worn but triumphant, brought the boy late
in the autumn, wholly restored, to her Hampshire home.

All these details were public property, for Helen was as open
as the day, and held that scandals are only increased by
hushing them up. She admitted that George had always been
rather a black sheep, but things might have been much worse if

the mother had insisted on her right to keep the boy. Luckily, it seemed that people of that class would do almost anything for money, and, as George had always turned to her in his scrapes, she felt herself justified – her friends agreed with her – in cutting the whole non-commissioned officer connection, and giving the child every advantage. A christening, by the Rector, under the name of Michael, was the first step. So far as she knew herself, she was not, she said, a child-lover, but, for all his faults, she had been very fond of George, and she pointed out that little Michael had his father's mouth to a line; which made something to build upon.

As a matter of fact, it was the Turrell forehead, broad, low, and well-shaped, with the widely spaced eyes beneath it, that Michael had most faithfully reproduced. His mouth was somewhat better cut than the family type. But Helen, who would concede nothing good to his mother's side, vowed he was a Turrell all over, and, there being no one to contradict, the likeness was established.

In a few years Michael took his place, as accepted as Helen had always been – fearless, philosophical, and fairly good-looking. At six, he wished to know why he could not call her 'Mummy,' as other boys called their mothers. She explained that she was only his auntie, and that aunties were not quite the same as mummies, but that, if it gave him pleasure, he might call her 'Mummy' at bedtime, for a pet-name between themselves.

Michael kept his secret most loyally, but Helen, as usual, explained the fact to her friends; which when Michael heard, he raged.

'Why did you tell? *Why* did you tell?' came at the end of the storm.

'Because it's always best to tell the truth,' Helen answered, her arm round him as he shook in his cot.

'All right, but when the troof's ugly I don't think it's nice.'

'Don't you, dear?'

'No, I don't, and' – she felt the small body stiffen – 'now you've told, I won't call you "Mummy" any more – not even at bedtimes.'

'But isn't that rather unkind?' said Helen softly.

'I don't care! I don't care! You've hurted me in my insides and I'll hurt you back. I'll hurt you as long as I live!'

'Don't, oh, don't talk like that, dear! You don't know what—'

'I will! And when I'm dead I'll hurt you worse!'

'Thank goodness, I shall be dead long before you, darling.'

'Huh!' Emma says, ' "Never know your luck." ' (Michael had been talking to Helen's elderly, flat-faced maid.) 'Lots of little boys die quite soon. So'll I. *Then* you'll see!'

Helen caught her breath and moved towards the door, but the wail of 'Mummy! Mummy!' drew her back again, and the two wept together.

At ten years old, after two terms at a prep school, something or somebody gave him the idea that his civil status was not quite regular. He attacked Helen on the subject, breaking down her stammered defences with the family directness.

'Don't believe a word of it,' he said, cheerily, at the end. 'People wouldn't have talked like they did if my people had been married. But don't you bother, Auntie. I've found out all about my sort in English Hist'ry and the Shakespeare bits. There was William the Conqueror to begin with, and – oh, heaps more, and they all got on first-rate. 'Twon't make any difference to you, my being *that* – will it?'

'As if anything could—' she began.

'All right. We won't talk about it any more if it makes you cry.' He never mentioned the thing again of his own will, but when, two years later, he skilfully managed to have measles in the holidays, as his temperature went up to the appointed one hundred and four he muttered of nothing else, till Helen's voice, piercing at last his delirium, reached him with assurance that nothing on earth or beyond could make any difference between them.

The terms at his public school and the wonderful Christmas, Easter, and Summer holidays followed each other, variegated and glorious as jewels on a string; and as jewels Helen treasured them. In due time Michael developed his own interests, which ran their courses and gave way to others; but his interest in Helen was constant and increasing throughout. She repaid it with all that she had of affection or could command of counsel and money; and since Michael was no fool, the War took him just before what was like to have been a most promising career.

He was to have gone up to Oxford, with a scholarship, in October. At the end of August he was on the edge of joining the first holocaust of public-school boys who threw themselves into the Line; but the captain of his OTC, where he had been sergeant for nearly a year, headed him off and steered him directly to a commission in a battalion so new that half of it still wore the old Army red, and the other half was breeding meningitis through living overcrowdedly in damp tents. Helen had been shocked at the idea of direct enlistment.

'But it's in the family,' Michael laughed.

'You don't mean to tell me that you believed that old story all this time?' said Helen. (Emma, her maid, had been dead now several years.) 'I gave you my word of honour – and I give it again – that – that it's all right. It is indeed.'

'Oh, *that* doesn't worry me. It never did,' he replied valiantly. 'What I meant was, I should have got into the show earlier if I'd enlisted – like my grandfather.'

'Don't talk like that! Are you afraid of it's ending so soon, then?'

'No such luck. You know what K. says.'

'Yes. But my banker told me last Monday it couldn't *possibly* last beyond Christmas – for financial reasons.'

'Hope he's right, but our Colonel – and he's a Regular – says it's going to be a long job.'

Michael's battalion was fortunate in that, by some chance which meant several 'leaves,' it was used for coast-defence among shallow trenches on the Norfolk coast; thence sent north to watch the mouth of a Scotch estuary, and, lastly, held for weeks on a baseless rumour of distant service. But, the very day that Michael was to have met Helen for four whole hours at a railway-junction up the line, it was hurled out, to help make good the wastage of Loos, and he had only just time to send her a wire of farewell.

In France luck again helped the battalion. It was put down near the Salient, where it led a meritorious and unexacting life, while the Somme was being manufactured; and enjoyed the peace of the Armentières and Laventie sectors when that battle began. Finding that it had sound views on protecting its own flanks and could dig, a prudent Commander stole it out of its own Division, under pretence of helping to lay telegraphs, and used it round Ypres at large.

A month later, and just after Michael had written Helen that there was nothing special doing and therefore no need to worry, a shell-splinter dropping out of a wet dawn killed him at once. The next shell uprooted and laid down over the body what had been the foundation of a barn wall, so neatly that none but an expert would have guessed that anything unpleasant had happened.

By this time the village was old in experience of war, and, English fashion, had evolved a ritual to meet it. When the postmistress handed her seven-year-old daughter the official telegram to take to Miss Turrell, she observed the Rector's gardener: 'It's Miss Helen's turn now.' He replied, thinking of his own son: 'Well, he's lasted longer than some.' The child herself came to the front-door weeping aloud, because Master Michael had often given her sweets. Helen, presently, found herself pulling down the house-blinds one after one with great care, and saying earnest to each: 'Missing *always* means dead.' Then she took her place in the dreary procession that was impelled to go through an inevitable series of unprofitable emotions. The Rector, of course, preached hope and prophesied word, very soon, from a prison camp. Several friends, too, told her perfectly truthful tales, but always about other women, to whom, after months and months of silence, their missing had been miraculously restored. Other people urged her to communicate with infallible Secretaries of organisations who could communicate with benevolent neutrals, who could extract accurate information from the most secretive of Hun prison commandants. Helen did and wrote and signed everything that was suggested or put before her.

Once, on one of Michael's leaves, he had taken her over a munition factory, where she saw the progress of a shell from blank-iron to the all but finished article. It struck her at the time that the wretched thing was never left alone for a single second; and 'I'm being manufactured into a bereaved next of kin,' she told herself, as she prepared her documents.

In due course, when all the organisations had deeply or sincerely regretted their inability to trace, etc., something gave way within her and all sensation – save of thankfulness for the release – came to an end in blessed passivity. Michael had died and her world had stood still and she had been one with the full shock of that arrest. Now she was standing still and the world was going forward, but it did not concern here – in no way or relation did it touch her. She knew this by the ease with which she could slip Michael's name into talk and incline her head to the proper angle, at the proper murmur of sympathy.

In the blessed realisation of that relief, the Armistice with all its bells broke over her and passed unheeded. At the end of another year she had overcome her physical loathing of the living and returned young, so that she could take them by the hand and – almost sincerely wish them well. She had no interest in any aftermath, national or personal, of the war, but, moving at an immense distance, she sat on various relief committees and held strong views – she heard herself delivering them – about the site of the proposed village War Memorial.

Then there came to her, as next of kin, an official intimation, backed by a page of a letter to her in indelible pencil, a silver identity-disc, and a watch, to the effect that the body of Lieutenant Michael Turrell had been found, identified, and re-interred in Hagenzeele Third Military Cemetery – the letter of the row and the grave's number in that row duly given.

So Helen found herself moved on to another process of the manufacture – to a world full of exultant or broken relatives, now strong in the certainty that there was an altar upon earth where they might lay their love. These soon told her, and by means of time-tables made clear, how easy it was and how little it interfered with life's affairs to go and see one's grave.

'*So* different,' as the Rector's wife said, 'if he'd been killed in Mesopotamia, or even Gallipoli.'

The agony of being waked up to some sort of second life drove Helen across the Channel, where, in a new world of abbreviated titles, she learnt that Hagenzeele Third could be comfortably reached by an afternoon train which fitted in with the morning boat, and that there was a comfortable little hotel not three kilometres from Hagenzeele itself, where one could spend quite a comfortable night and see one's grave next morning. All this she had from a Central Authority who lived in a board and tar-paper shed on the skirts of a razed city full of whirling lime-dust and blown papers.

'By the way,' said he, 'you know your grave, of course?'

'Yes, thank you,' said Helen, and showed its row and number typed on Michael's own little typewriter. The officer would have checked it, out of one of his many books; but a large Lancashire woman thrust between them and bade him tell her where she might find her son, who had been corporal in the ASC. His proper name, she sobbed, was Anderson, but, coming of respectable folk, he had of course enlisted under the name of Smith; and had been killed at Dickiebush, in early 'Fifteen. She had not his number nor did she know which of his two Christian names he might have used with his alias; but her Cook's tourist ticket expired at the end of Easter week, and if by then she could not find her child she would go mad. Whereupon she fell forward on Helen's breast; but the officer's wife came out quickly from a little bedroom behind the office, and the three of them lifted the woman on to the cot.

'They are often like this,' said the officer's wife, loosening the tight bonnet-strings. 'Yesterday she said he'd been killed at Hooge. Are you sure you know your grave? It makes such a difference.'

'Yes, thank you,' said Helen, and hurried out before the woman on the bed should begin to lament again.

*

Tea in a crowded mauve and blue striped wooden structure, with a false front, carried her still further into the nightmare. She paid her bill beside a stolid, plain-featured Englishwoman, who, hearing her inquire about the train to Hagenzeele, volunteered to come with her.

'I'm going to Hagenzeele myself,' she explained. 'Not to Hagenzeele Third; mine is Sugar Factory, but they call it La Rosière now. It's just south of Hagenzeele Three. Have you got your room at the hotel there?'

'Oh yes, thank you. I've wired.'

'That's better. Sometimes the place is quite full, and at others there's hardly a soul. But they've put bathrooms into the old Lion d'Or – that's the hotel on the west side of Sugar Factory – and it draws off a lot of people, luckily.'

'It's all new to me. This is the first time I've been over.'

'Indeed! This is my ninth time since the Armistice. Not on my own account. *I* haven't lost any one, thank God – but, like every one else, I've a lot of friends at home who have. Coming over as often as I do, I find it helps them to have some one just look at the – the place and tell them about it afterwards. And one can take photos for them, too. I get quite a list of commissions to execute.' She laughed nervously and tapped her slung Kodak. 'There are two or three to see at Sugar Factory this time, and plenty of others in the cemeteries all about. My system is to save them up, and arrange them, you know. And when I've got enough commissions for one area to make it worth while, I pop over and execute them. It *does* comfort people.'

'I suppose so,' Helen answered, shivering as they entered the little train.

'Of course it does. (Isn't it lucky we've got window-seats?) It must do or they wouldn't ask one to do it, would they? I've a list of quite twelve or fifteen commissions here' – she tapped the Kodak again – 'I must sort them out to-night. Oh, I forgot to ask you. What's yours?'

'My nephew,' said Helen. 'But I was very fond of him.'

'Ah yes! I sometimes wonder whether *they* know after death? What do you think?'

'Oh, I don't – I haven't dared to think much about that sort of thing,' said Helen, almost lifting her hands to keep her off.

'Perhaps that's better,' the woman answered. 'The sense of loss must be enough, I expect. Well, I won't worry you any more.'

Helen was grateful, but when they reached the hotel Mrs Scarsworth (they had exchanged names) insisted on dining at the same table with her, and after the meal, in the little, hideous salon full of low-voiced relatives, took Helen through her 'commissions' with biographies of the dead, where she happened to know them, and sketches of their next of kin. Helen endured till nearly half-past nine, ere she fled to her room.

Almost at once there was a knock at her door and Mrs Scarsworth entered; her hands, holding the dreadful list, clasped before her.

'Yes – yes – *I* know,' she began. 'You're sick of me, but I want to tell you something. You – you aren't married, are you? Then perhaps you won't . . . But it doesn't matter. I've *got* to tell some one. I can't go on any longer like this.'

'But please—' Mrs Scarsworth had backed against the shut door, and her mouth worked dryly.

'In a minute,' she said. 'You – you know about these graves of mine I was telling you about downstairs, just now? They really *are* commissions. At least several of them are.' Her eye wandered round the room. 'What extraordinary wall-papers they have in Belgium, don't you think? . . . Yes. I swear they are commissions. But there's *one*, d'you see, and – and he was more to me than anything else in the world. Do you understand?'

Helen nodded.

'More than any one else. And, of course, he oughtn't to have been. He ought to have been nothing to me. But he *was*. He *is*. That's why I do the commissions, you see. That's all.'

'But why do you tell me?' Helen asked desperately.

'Because I'm *so* tired of lying. Tired of lying – always lying –

year in and year out. When I don't tell lies I've got to act 'em and I've got to think 'em, always. *You* don't know what that means. He was everything to me that he oughtn't to have been – the one real thing – the only thing that ever happened to me in all my life; and I've had to pretend he wasn't. I've had to watch every word I said, and think out what lie I'd tell next for years and years!'

'How many years?' Helen asked.

'Six years and four months before, and two and three-quarters after. I've gone to him eight times since. To-morrow'll make the ninth, and – and I can't – I *can't* go to him again with nobody in the world knowing. I want to be honest with some one before I go. Do you understand? It doesn't matter about *me*. I was never truthful, even as a girl. But it isn't worthy of *him*. So – so I – I had to tell you. I can't keep it up any longer. Oh, I can't!'

She lifted her joined hands almost to the level of her mouth, and brought them down sharply, still joined, to full arms' length below her waist. Helen reached forward, caught them, bowed her head over them, and murmured: 'Oh, my dear! My dear!' Mrs Scarsworth stepped back, her face all mottled.

'My God!' said she. 'Is *that* how you take it?'

Helen could not speak, and the woman went out; but it was a long while before Helen was able to sleep.

Next morning Mrs Scarsworth left early on her round of commissions, and Helen walked alone to Hagenzeele Third. The place was still in the making, and stood some five or six feet above the metalled road, which it flanked for hundreds of yards. Culverts across a deep ditch served for entrances through the unfinished boundary wall. She climbed a few wooden-faced earthen steps and then met the entire crowded level of the thing in one held breath. She did not know that Hagenzeele Third counted twenty-one thousand dead already. All she saw was a merciless sea of black crosses, bearing little strips of stamped tin at all angles cross their faces. She could distinguish no order or arrangement in their mass; nothing but a waist-high wilderness as of weeds stricken dead, rushing at her. She went forward, moved to the left and the right hopelessly wondering by what guidance she should ever come to her own. A great distance away there was a line of whiteness. It proved to be a block of some two or three hundred graves whose headstones had already been set, whose flowers were planted out, and whose new-sown grass showed green. Here she could see clear-cut letters at the ends of the rows, and, referring to her slip, realised that it was not here she must look.

A man knelt behind a line of headstones – evidently a gardener, for he was firming a young plant in the soft earth. She went towards him, her paper in her hand. He rose at her approach and without prelude or salutation asked: 'Who are you looking for?'

'Lieutenant Michael Turrell – my nephew,' said Helen slowly and word for word, as she had many thousands of times in her life.

The man lifted his eyes and looked at her with infinite compassion before he turned from the fresh-sown grass toward the naked black crosses.

'Come with me,' he said, 'and I will show you where your son lies.'

When Helen left the Cemetery she turned for a last look. In the distance she saw the man bending over his young plants; and she went away, supposing him to be the gardener.

THE EYE OF ALLAH

The Cantor of St Illod's being far too enthusiastic a musician to concern himself with its Library, the Sub-Cantor, who idolised every detail of the work, was tidying up, after two hours' writing and dictation in the Scriptorium. The copying-monks handed him in their sheets – it was a plain Four Gospels ordered by an Abbot at Evesham – and filed out to vespers. John Otho, better known as John of Burgos, took no heed. He was burnishing a tiny boss of gold in his miniature of the Annunciation for his Gospel of St Luke, which it was hoped that Cardinal Falcodi, the Papal Legate, might later be pleased to accept.

'Break off, John,' said the Sub-Cantor in an undertone.

'Eh? Gone, have they? I never heard. Hold a minute, Clement.'

'The Sub-Cantor waited patiently. He had known John more than a dozen years, coming and going at St Illod's, to which monastery John, when abroad, always said he belonged. The claim was gladly allowed for, more even than other Fitz Otho's, he seemed to carry all the Arts under his hand, and most of their practical receipts under his hood.

The Sub-Cantor looked over his shoulder at the pinned-down sheet where the first words of the Magnificat were built up in gold washed with red-lac for a background to the Virgin's hardly yet fired halo. She was shown, hands joined in wonder, at a lattice of infinitely intricate arabesque, round the edges of which sprays of orange-bloom seemed to load the blue hot air that carried back over the minute parched landscape in the middle distance.

'You've made her all Jewess,' said the Sub-Cantor, studying

the olive-flushed cheek and the eyes charged with foreknowledge.

'What else was Our Lady?' John slipped out the pins. 'Listen, Clement. If I do not come back, this goes into my Great Luke, whoever finishes it.' He slid the drawing between its guard-papers.

'Then you're for Burgos again – as I heard?'

'In two days. The new Cathedral yonder – but they're slower than the Wrath of God, those masons – is good for the soul.'

'*Thy* soul?' The Sub-Cantor seemed doubtful.

'Even mine, by your permission. And down south – on the edge of the Conquered Countries – Granada way – there's some Moorish diaper-work that's wholesome. It allays vain thought and draws it toward the picture – as you felt, just now, in my Annunciation.'

'She – it was very beautiful. No wonder you go. But you'll not forget your absolution, John?'

'Surely.' This was a precaution John no more omitted on the eve of his travels than he did the recutting of the tonsure which he had provided himself with in his youth, somewhere near Ghent. The mark gave him privilege of clergy at a pinch, and a certain consideration on the road always.

'You'll not forget, either, what we need in the Scriptorium. There's no more true ultramarine in this world now. They mix it with that German blue. And as for vermilion—'

'I'll do my best always.'

'And Brother Thomas' (this was the Infirmarian in charge of the monastery hospital) 'he needs—'

'He'll do his own asking. I'll go over his side now, and get me re-tonsured.'

John went down the stairs to the lane that divides the hospital and cook-house from the back-cloisters. While he was being barbered, Brother Thomas (St Illod's meek but deadly persistent Infirmarian) gave him a list of drugs that he was to bring back from Spain by hook, crook, or lawful purchase. Here they were surprised by the lame, dark Abbot Stephen, in his fur-lined night-boots. Not that Stephen de

Sautré was any spy; but as a young man he had shared an unlucky Crusade, which had ended, after a battle at Mansura, in two years' captivity among the Saracens at Cairo where men learn to walk softly. A fair huntsman and hawker, a reasonable disciplinarian, but a man of science above all, and a Doctor of Medicine under one Ranulphus, Canon of St Paul's, his heart was more in the monastery's hospital work than its religious. He checked their list interestedly, adding items of his own. After the Infirmarian had withdrawn, he gave John generous absolution, to cover lapses by the way; for he did not hold with chance-bought Indulgences.

'And what seek you *this* journey?' he demanded, sitting on the bench beside the mortar and scales in the little warm cell for stored drugs.

'Devils, mostly,' said John, grinning.

'In Spain? Are not Abana and Pharphar—?'

John, to whom men were but matter for drawings, and well-born to boot (since he was a de Sanford on his mother's side), looked the Abbot full in the face and – 'Did *you* find it so?' said he.

'No. They were in Cairo too. But what's your special need of 'em?'

'For my Great Luke. He's the masterhand of all Four when it comes to devils.'

'No wonder. He was a physician. You're not.'

'Heaven forbid! But I'm weary of our Church-pattern devils. They're only apes and goats and poultry conjoined. 'Good enough for plain red-and-black Hells and Judgment Days – but not for me.'

'What makes you so choice in them?'

'Because it stands to reason and Art that there are all musters of devils in Hell's dealings. Those Seven, for example, that were haled out of the Magdalene. They'd be she-devils – no kin at all to the beaked and horned and bearded devils-general.'

The Abbot laughed.

'And see again! The devil that came out of the dumb man.

What use is snout or bill to *him*? He'd be faceless as a leper.
Above all – God send I live to do it! – the devils that entered
the Gadarene swine. They'd be – they'd be – I know not yet
what they'd be, but they'd be surpassing devils. I'd have 'em
diverse as the Saints themselves. But now, they're all one
pattern, for wall, window, or picture-work.'

'Go on, John. You're deeper in this mystery than I.'

'Heaven forbid! But I say there's respect due to devils,
damned tho' they be.'

'Dangerous doctrine.'

'My meaning is that if the shape of anything be worth man's
thought to picture to man, it's worth his best thought.'

'That's safer. But I'm glad I've given you Absolution.'

'There's less risk for a craftsman who deals with the outside
shapes of things – for Mother Church's glory.'

'Maybe so, but John' – the Abbot's hand almost touched
John's sleeve – 'tell me, now, is – is she Moorish or – or
Hebrew?'

'She's mine,' John returned.

'Is that enough?'

'I have found it so.'

'Well – ah well! It's out of my jurisdiction, but – how do
they look at it down yonder?'

'Oh, they drive nothing to a head in Spain – neither Church
nor King, bless them! There's too many Moors and Jews to kill
them all, and if they chased 'em away there'd be no trade nor
farming. Trust me, in the Conquered Countries, from Seville
to Granada, we live lovingly enough together – Spaniard,
Moor, and Jew. Ye see, *we* ask no questions.'

'Yes – yes,' Stephen sighed. 'And always there's the hope,
she may be converted.'

'Oh yes, there's always hope.'

The Abbot went on into the hospital. It was an easy age
before Rome tightened the screw as to clerical connections. If
the lady were not too forward, or the son too much his father's
beneficiary in ecclesiastical preferments and levies, a good deal
was overlooked. But, as the Abbot had reason to recall, unions
between Christian and Infidel led to sorrow. None the less,

when John with mule, mails, and man, clattered off down the lane for Southampton and the sea, Stephen envied him.

He was back, twenty months later, in good hard case, and loaded down with fairings. A lump of richest lazuli, a bar of orange-hearted vermilion, and a small packet of dried beetles which make most glorious scarlet, for the Sub-Cantor. Besides that, a few cubes of milky marble, with yet a pink flush in them, which could be slaked and ground down to incomparable background-stuff. There were quite half the drugs that the Abbot and Thomas had demanded, and there was a long deep-red cornelian necklace for the Abbot's Lady – Anne of Norton. She received it graciously, and asked where John had come by it.

'Near Granada,' he said.

'You left all well there?' Anne asked. (Maybe the Abbot had told her something of John's confession.)

'I left all in the hands of God.'

'Ah me! How long since?'

'Four months less eleven days.'

'Were you – with her?'

'In my arms. Childbed.'

'And?'

'The boy too. There is nothing now.'

Anne of Norton caught her breath.

'I think you'll be glad of that,' she said after a while.

'Give me time, and maybe I'll compass it. But not now.'

'You have your handwork and your art and – John – remember there's no jealousy in the grave.'

'Ye-es! I have my Art, and Heaven knows I'm jealous of none.'

'Thank God for that at least,' said Anne of Norton, the always ailing woman who followed the Abbot with her sunk eyes. 'And be sure I shall treasure this' – she touched the beads – 'as long as I shall live.

'I brought – trusted – it to you for that,' he replied, and took leave. When she told the Abbot how she had come by it, he said nothing, but as he and Thomas were storing the drugs that John handed over in the cell which backs on to the hospital kitchen-chimney, he observed, of a cake of dried poppy-juice: 'This has power to cut off all pain from a man's body.'

'I have seen it,' said John.

'But for pain of the soul there is, outside God's Grace, but one drug; and that is a man's craft, learning, or other helpful motion of his own mind.'

'That is coming to me, too,' was the answer.

John spent the next fair May day out in the woods with the monastery swineherd and all the porkers; and returned loaded with flowers and sprays of spring, to his own carefully kept place in the north bay of the Scriptorium. There, with his travelling sketch-books under his left elbow, he sunk himself past all recollections in his Great Luke.

Brother Martin, Senior Copyist (who spoke about once a fortnight), ventured to ask, later, how the work was going.

'All here!' John tapped his forehead with his pencil. 'It has been only waiting these months to – ah God! – be born. Are ye free of your plain-copying, Martin?'

Brother Martin nodded. It was his pride that John of Burgos turned to him, in spite of his seventy years, for really good page-work.

'Then see!' John laid out a new vellum – thin but flawless. 'There's no better than this sheet from here to Paris. Yes! Smell it if you choose. Wherefore – give me the compasses and I'll set it out for you – if ye make one letter lighter or darker than its next, I'll stick ye like a pig.'

'Never, John!' the old man beamed happily.

'But I will! Now, follow! Here and here, as I prick, and in script of just this height to the hair's-breadth, ye'll scribe the thirty-first and thirty-second verses of Eighth Luke.'

'Yes, the Gadarene Swine! "*And they besought him that he would not command them to go out into the abyss. And there was a herd of many swine*"' – Brother Martin naturally knew all the Gospels by heart.

'Just so! Down to "*and he suffered them.*" Take your time to it. My Magdalene has to come off my heart first.'

Brother Martin achieved the work so perfectly that John stole some soft sweetmeats from the Abbot's kitchen for his reward. The old man ate them; then repented; then confessed and insisted on penance. At which, the Abbot, knowing there was but one way to reach the real sinner, set him a book called *De Virtutibus Herbarum* to fair-copy. St Illod's had borrowed it from the gloomy Cistercians, who do not hold with pretty things, and the crabbed text kept Martin busy just when John wanted him for some rather specially spaced letterings.

'See now,' said the Sub-Cantor improvingly. 'You should not do such things, John. Here's Brother Martin on penance for your sake—'

'No – for my Great Luke. But I've paid the Abbot's cook. I've drawn him till his own scullions cannot keep straight-faced. *He*'ll not tell again.'

'Unkindly done! And you're out of favour with the Abbot too. He's made no sign to you since you came back – never asked you to high table.'

'I've been busy. Having eyes in his head, Stephen knew it. Clement, there's no Librarian from Durham to Torre fit to clean up after you.'

The Sub-Cantor stood on guard; he knew where John's compliments generally ended.

'But outside the Scriptorium—'

'Where I never go.' The Sub-Cantor had been excused even digging in the garden, lest it should mar his wonderful book-binding hands.

'In all things outside the Scriptorium you are the master-fool of Christendie. Take it from me, Clement. I've met many.'

'I take everything from you,' Clement smiled benignly. 'You use me worse than a singing-boy.'

They could hear one of that suffering breed in the cloister below, squalling as the Cantor pulled his hair.

'God love you! So I do! But have you ever thought how I lie and steal daily on my travels – yes, and for aught you know, murder – to fetch you colours and earths?'

'True,' said just and conscience-stricken Clement. 'I have

often thought that were I in the world – which God forbid! – I might be a strong thief in some matters.'

Even Brother Martin, bent above his loathed *De Virtutibus*, laughed.

But about mid-summer, Thomas the Infirmarian conveyed to John the Abbot's invitation to supper in his house that night, with the request that he would bring with him anything that he had done for his Great Luke.

'What's toward?' said John, who had been wholly shut up in his work.

'Only one of his "wisdom" dinners. You've sat at a few since you were a man.'

'True: and mostly good. How would Stephen have us—?'

'Gown and hood over all. There will be a doctor from Salerno – one Roger, an Italian. Wise and famous with the knife on the body. He's been in the Infirmary some ten days, helping me — even me!'

''Never heard the name. But our Stephen's *physicus* before *sacerdos*, always.'

'And his Lady has a sickness of some time. Roger came hither in chief because of her.'

'Did he? Now I think of it, I have not seen the Lady Anne for a while.'

'Ye've seen nothing for a long while. She has been housed near a month – they have to carry her abroad now.'

'So bad as that, then?'

'Roger of Salerno will not yet say what he thinks. But—'

'God pity Stephen! . . . Who else at table, beside thee?'

'An Oxford friar. Roger is his name also. A learned and famous philosopher. And he holds his liquor too, valiantly.'

'Three doctors – counting Stephen. I've always found that means two atheists.'

Thomas looked uneasily down his nose. 'That's a wicked proverb,' he stammered. 'You should not use it.'

'Hoh! Never come you the monk over me, Thomas! You've been Infirmarian at St Illod's eleven year – and a lay-brother still. Why have you never taken orders, all this while?'

'I – I am not worthy.'

'Ten times worthier than that new fat swine – Henry Who's-his-name – that takes the Infirmary Masses. He bullocks in with the Viaticum, under your nose, when a sick man's only faint from being bled. So the man dies – of pure fear. Ye know it! I've watched your face at such times. Take Orders, Didymus. You'll have a little more medicine and a little less Mass with your sick then; and they'll live longer.'

'I am unworthy – unworthy,' Thomas repeated pitifully.

'Not you – but – to your own master you stand or fall.' And now that my work releases me for awhile, I'll drink with any philosopher out of any school. And Thomas,' he coaxed, 'a hot bath for me in the Infirmary before vespers.'

When the Abbot's perfectly cooked and served meal had ended, and the deep-fringed naperies were removed, and the Prior had sent in the keys with word that all was fast in the Monastery, and the keys had been duly returned with the word, 'Make it so till Prime,' the Abbot and his guests went out to cool themselves in an upper cloister that took them, by way of the leads, to the South Choir side of the Triforium. The summer sun was still strong, for it was barely six o'clock, but the Abbey Church, of course, lay in her wonted darkness. Lights were being lit for choir-practice thirty feet below.

'Our Cantor gives them no rest,' the Abbot whispered. 'Stand by this pillar and we'll hear what he's driving them at now.'

'Remember all!' the Cantor's hard voice came up. 'This is the soul of Bernard himself, attacking our evil world. Take it quicker than yesterday, and throw all your words clean-bitten from you. In the loft there! Begin!'

The organ broke out for an instant, alone and raging. Then the voices crashed together into that first fierce line of the *'De Contemptu Mundi.'*[1]

'Hora novissima – tempora pessima'[1] – a dead pause till the assenting *sunt* broke, like a sob, out of the darkness, and one boy's voice, clearer than silver trumpets, returned the long-drawn *vigilemus*.

[1] Hymn No. 226 A. and M., 'The world is very evil'.

'*Ecce minaciter, imminet Arbiter*' (organ and voices were leashed together in terror and warning, breaking away liquidly to the '*ille supremus*'). Then the tone-colours shifted for the prelude to – '*Imminet, imminet, ut mala terminet—*'

'Stop! Again!' cried the Cantor; and gave his reasons a little more roundly than was natural at choir-practice.

'Ah! Pity o' man's vanity! He's guessed we are here. Come away!' said the Abbot. Anne of Norton, in her carried chair, had been listening too, further along the dark Triforium, with Roger of Salerno. John heard her sob. On the way back, he asked Thomas how her health stood. Before Thomas could reply the sharp-featured Italian doctor pushed between them. 'Following on our talk together, I judged it best to tell her,' said he to Thomas.

'What?' John asked simply enough.

'What she knew already.' Roger of Salerno launched into a Greek quotation to the effect that every woman knows all about everything.

'I have no Greek,' said John stiffly. Roger of Salerno had been giving them a good deal of it, at dinner.

'Then I'll come to you in Latin. Ovid hath it neatly. "*Utque malum late solet immedicabile cancer—*" but doubtless you know the rest, worthy Sir.'

'Alas! My school-Latin's but what I've gathered by the way from fools professing to heal sick women. "*Hocus-pocus—*" but doubtless you know the rest, worthy Sir.'

Roger of Salerno was quite quiet till they regained the dining-room, where the fire had been comforted and the dates, raisins, ginger, figs, and cinnamon-scented sweetmeats set out, with the choicer wines, on the after-table. The Abbot seated himself, drew off his ring, dropped it, that all might hear the tinkle, into an empty silver cup, stretched his feet towards the hearth, and looked at the great gilt and carved rose in the barrel-roof. The silence that keeps from Compline to Matins had closed on their world. The bull-necked Friar watched a ray of sunlight split itself into colours on the rim of a crystal salt-cellar; Roger of Salerno had re-opened some discussion with Brother Thomas on a type of spotted fever that was baffling them both in England and abroad; John took note of the keen profile, and – it might serve as a note for the Great Luke – his hand moved to his bosom. The Abbot saw, and nodded permission. John whipped out silver-point and sketch-book.

'Nay – modesty is good enough – but deliver your own opinion,' the Italian was urging the Infirmarian. Out of courtesy to the foreigner nearly all the talk was in table-Latin; more formal and more copious than monk's patter. Thomas began with his meek stammer.

'I confess myself at a loss for the cause of the fever unless – as Varro saith in his *De Re Rustica* – certain small animals which the eye cannot follow enter the body by the nose and mouth, and set up grave diseases. On the other hand, this is not in Scripture.'

Roger of Salerno hunched head and shoulders like an angry cat. ' Always *that*!' he said, and John snatched down the twist of the thin lips.

'Never at rest, John,' the Abbot smiled at the artist. 'You should break off every two hours for prayers, as we do. St Benedict was no fool. Two hours is all that a man can carry the edge of his eye or hand.'

'For copyists – yes. Brother Martin is not sure after one hour. But when a man's work takes him, he must go on till it lets him go.'

'Yes, that is the Demon of Socrates,' the Friar from Oxford rumbled above his cup.

'The doctrine leans toward presumption,' said the Abbot. 'Remember, "Shall mortal man be more just than his Maker?"'

'There is no danger of justice'; the Friar spoke bitterly. 'But at least Man might be suffered to go forward in his Art or his thought. Yet if Mother Church sees or hears him move anyward, what says she? "No!" Always "No,"'

'But if the little animals of Varro be invisible' – this was Roger of Salerno to Thomas – 'how are we any nearer to a cure?'

'By experiment' – the Friar wheeled round on them

suddenly. 'By reason and experiment. The one is useless without the other. But Mother Church—'

'Ay!' Roger de Salerno dashed at the fresh bait like a pike. 'Listen, Sirs. Her bishops – our Prince – strew our roads in Italy with carcasses that they make for their pleasure or wrath. Beautiful corpses! Yet if I – if we doctors – so much as raise the skin of one of them to look at God's fabric beneath, what says Mother Church? "Sacrilege! Stick to your pigs and dogs, or you burn!"'

'And not Mother Church only!' the Friar chimed in. '*Every* way we are barred – barred by the words of some man, dead a thousand years, which are held final. Who is any son of Adam that his one say-so should close a door towards truth? I would not except even Peter Peregrinus, my own great teacher.'

'Nor I Paul of Aegina,' Roger of Salerno cried. ' Listen, Sirs! Here is a case to the very point. Apuleius affirmeth, if a man eat fasting of the juice of the cut-leaved buttercup – *sceleratus* we call it, which means "rascally"' – this with a condescending nod towards John – 'his soul will leave his body laughing. Now this is the lie more dangerous than truth, since truth of a sort is in it.'

'He's away!' whispered the Abbot despairingly.

'For the juice of that herb, I know by experiment, burns, blisters, and wries the mouth. I know also the *rictus*, or pseudo-laughter on the face of such as have perished by the strong poisons of herbs allied to this ranunculus. Certainly that spasm resembles laughter. It seems then, in my judgment, that Apuleius, having seen the body of one thus poisoned, went off at score and wrote that the man died laughing.'

'Neither staying to observe, nor to confirm observation by experiment,' added the Friar, frowning.

Stephen the Abbot cocked an eyebrow toward John.

'How think *you*?' said he.

'I'm no doctor,' John returned, 'but I'd say Apuleius in all these years might have been betrayed by his copyists. They take short-cuts to save 'emselves trouble. Put case that Apuleius wrote the soul *seems to* leave the body laughing, after this poison. There's not three copyists in five (*my* judgment) would not leave out the "seems to." For who'd question Apuleius? If it seemed so to him, so it must be. Otherwise any child knows cut-leaved buttercup.'

'Have you knowledge of herbs?' Roger of Salerno asked curtly.

'Only, that when I was a boy in convent, I've made tetters round my mouth and on my neck with buttercup-juice, to save going to prayer o' cold nights.'

'Ah!' said Roger. 'I profess no knowledge of tricks.' He turned aside, stiffly.

'No matter! Now for your own tricks, John,' the tactful Abbot broke in. 'You shall show the doctors your Magdalene and your Gadarene Swine and the devils.'

'Devils? Devils? *I* have produced devils by means of drugs; and have abolished them by the same means. Whether devils be external to mankind or immanent, I have not yet pronounced.' Roger of Salerno was still angry.

'Ye dare not,' snapped the Friar from Oxford. 'Mother Church makes Her own devils.'

'Not wholly! Our John has come back from Spain with brand-new ones.' Abbot Stephen took the vellum handed to him, and laid it tenderly on the table. They gathered to look. The Magdalene was drawn in palest, almost transparent, grisaille, against a raging, swaying background of woman-faced devils, each broke to and by her special sin, and each, one could see, frenziedly straining against the Power that compelled her.

'I've never seen the like of this grey shadow-work,' said the Abbot. 'How came you by it?'

'*Non nobis!* It came to me,' said John, not knowing he was a generation or so ahead of his time in the use of that medium.

'Why is she so pale?' the Friar demanded.

'Evil has all come out of her – she'd take any colour now.'

'Ay, like light through glass. *I* see.'

Roger of Salerno was looking in silence – his nose nearer and nearer the page. 'It is so,' he pronounced finally. 'Thus it is in epilepsy – mouth, eyes, and forehead – even to the droop other wrist there. Every sign of it! She will need restoratives, that woman, and, afterwards, sleep natural. No poppy-juice, or she will vomit on her waking. And thereafter – but I am not in my Schools.' He drew himself up. 'Sir,' said he, 'you should be of Our calling. For, by the Snakes of Aesculapius, you *see!*'

The two struck hands as equals.

'And how think you of the Seven Devils?' the Abbot went on.

These melted into convoluted flower- or flame-like bodies, ranging in colour from phosphorescent green to the black purple of outworn iniquity, whose hearts could be traced beating through their substance. But, for sign of hope and the sane workings of life, to be regained, the deep border was of conventionalised spring flowers and birds, all crowned by a kingfisher in haste, atilt through a clump of yellow iris.

Roger of Salerno identified the herbs and spoke largely of their virtues.

'And now, the Gadarene Swine,' said Stephen. John laid the picture on the table.

Here were devils dishoused, in dread of being abolished to the Void, huddling and hurtling together to force lodgment by every opening into the brute bodies offered. Some of the swine fought the invasion, foaming and jerking; some were surrendering to it, sleepily, as to a luxurious back-scratching; others, wholly possessed, whirled off in bucking droves for the lake beneath. In one corner the freed man stretched out his limbs all restored to his control, and Our Lord, seated, looked at him as questioning what he would make of his deliverance.

'Devils indeed!' was the Friar's comment. 'But wholly a new sort.'

Some devils were mere lumps, with lobes and protuberances – a hint of a fiend's face peering through jelly-like walls. And there was a family of impatient, globular devillings who had burst open the belly of their smirking parent, and were revolving desperately toward their prey. Others patterned themselves into rods, chains and ladders, single or conjoined, round the throat and jaws of a shrieking sow, from whose ear emerged the lashing, glassy tail of a devil that had made good his refuge. And there were granulated and conglomerate devils, mixed up with the foam and slaver where the attack was fiercest. Thence the eye carried on to the insanely active backs of the downward-racing swine, the swineherd's aghast face, and his dog's terror.

Said Roger of Salerno, 'I pronounce that these were begotten of drugs. They stand outside the rational mind.'

'Not these,' said Thomas the Infirmarian, who as a servant of the Monastery should have asked his Abbot's leave to speak. 'Not *these* – look! – in the bordure.'

The border to the picture was a diaper of irregular but balanced compartments or cellules, where sat, swam, or weltered, devils in blank, so to say – things as yet uninspired by Evil – indifferent, but lawlessly outside imagination. Their shapes resembled, again, ladders, chains, scourges, diamonds, aborted buds, or gravid phosphorescent globes – some well-nigh star-like.

Roger of Salerno compared them to the obsessions of a Churchman's mind.

'Malignant?' the Friar from Oxford questioned.

' "Count everything unknown for horrible," ' Roger quoted with scorn.

'Not I. But they are marvellous – marvellous. I think—'

The Friar drew back. Thomas edged in to see better, and half opened his mouth.

'Speak,' said Stephen, who had been watching him. 'We are all in a sort doctors here.'

'I would say then' – Thomas rushed at it as one putting out his life's belief at the stake – 'that these lower shapes in the bordure may not be so much hellish and malignant as models and patterns upon which John has tricked out and embellished his proper devils among the swine above there!'

'And that would signify?' said Roger of Salerno sharply.

'In my poor judgment, that he may have seen such shapes – without help of drugs.'

'Now who – *who*,' said John of Burgos, after a round and unregarded oath, 'has made thee so wise of a sudden, my Doubter?'

'I wise? God forbid! Only John, remember – one winter six

735

years ago – the snow-flakes melting on your sleeve at the cookhouse-door. You showed me them through a little crystal, that made small things larger.'

'Yes. The Moors call such a glass the Eye of Allah,' John confirmed.

'You showed me them melting – six-sided. You called them, then, your patterns.'

'True. Snow-flakes melt six-sided. I have used them for diaper-work often.'

'Melting snow-flakes as seen through a glass? By art optical?' the Friar asked.

'Art optical? *I* have never heard!' Roger of Salerno cried.

'John,' said the Abbot of St Illod's commandingly, 'was it – is it so?'

'In some sort,' John replied, 'Thomas has the right of it. Those shapes in the bordure were my workshop-patterns for the devils above. In *my* craft, Salerno, we dare not drug. It kills hand and eye. My shapes are to be seen honestly, in nature.'

The Abbot drew a bowl of rose-water, towards him. 'When I was prisoner with – with the Saracens after Mansura,' he began, turning up the fold of his long sleeve, 'there were certain magicians – physicians – who could show—' he dipped his third finger delicately in the water – 'all the firmament of Hell, as it were, in—' he shook off one drop from his polished nail on to the polished table – 'even such a supernaculum as this.'

'But it must be foul water – not clean,' said John.

'Show us then – all – all,' said Stephen. ' I would make sure – once more.' The Abbot's voice was official.

John drew from his bosom a stamped leather box, some six or eight inches long, wherein, bedded on faded velvet, lay what looked like silver-bound compasses of old box-wood, with a screw at the head which opened or closed the legs to minute fractions. The legs terminated, not in points, but spoon-shapedly, one spatula pierced with a metal-lined hole less than a quarter of an inch across, the other with a half-inch hole. Into this latter John, after carefully wiping with a silk rag, slipped a metal cylinder that carried glass or crystal, it seemed, at each end.

'Ah! Art optic!' said the Friar. 'But what is that beneath it?'

It was a small swivelling sheet of polished silver no bigger than a florin, which caught the light and concentrated it on the lesser hole. John adjusted it without the Friar's proffered help.

'And now to find a drop of water,' said he, picking up a small brush.

'Come to my upper cloister. The sun is on the leads still,' said the Abbot, rising.

They followed him there. Halfway along, a drip from a gutter had made a greenish puddle in a worn stone. Very carefully, John dropped a drop of it into the smaller hole of the compass-leg, and, steadying the apparatus on a coping, worked the screw in the compass-joint, screwed the cylinder, and swung the swivel of the mirror till he was satisfied.

'Good!' He peered through the thing. 'My Shapes are all here. Now look, Father! If they do not meet your eye at first, turn this nicked edge here, left- or right-handed.'

'I have not forgotten,' said the Abbot, taking his place. 'Yes! They are here – as they were in my time – my time past. There is no end to them, I was told . . . There *is* no end!'

'The light will go. Oh, let me look! Suffer me to see, also!' the Friar pleaded, almost shouldering Stephen from the eye-piece. The Abbot gave way. His eyes were on time past. But the Friar, instead of looking, turned the apparatus in his capable hands.

'Nay, nay.' John interrupted, for the man was already fiddling at the screws. 'Let the Doctor see.'

Roger of Salerno looked, minute after minute. John saw his blue-veined cheek-bones turn white. He stepped back at last, as though stricken.

'It is a new world – a new world and – Oh, God Unjust! – I am old!'

'And now Thomas,' Stephen ordered.

John manipulated the tube for the Infirmarian, whose hands shook, and he too looked long. 'It is Life,' he said presently in a breaking voice. 'No Hell! Life created and rejoicing – the work of the Creator. They live, even as I have dreamed. Then it was no sin for me to dream. No sin – O God – no sin!'

He flung himself on his knees and began hysterically the *Benedicite omnia Opera*.

'And now I will see how it is actuated,' said the Friar from Oxford, thrusting forward again.

'Bring it within. The place is all eyes and ears,' said Stephen.

They walked quietly back along the leads, three English counties laid out in evening sunshine around them; church upon church, monastery upon monastery, cell after cell, and the bulk of a vast cathedral moored on the edge of the banked shoals of sunset.

When they were at the after-table once more they sat down, all except the Friar who went to the window and huddled bat-like over the thing. 'I see! I see!' he was repeating to himself.

'He'll not hurt it,' said John. But the Abbot, staring in front of him, like Roger of Salerno, did not hear. The Infirmarian's head was on the table between his shaking arms.

John reached for a cup of wine.

'It was shown to me,' the Abbot was speaking to himself, 'in Cairo, that man stands ever between two Infinities – of greatness and littleness. Therefore, there is no end – either to life – or—'

'And *I* stand on the edge of the grave,' snarled Roger of Salerno. 'Who pities *me*?'

'Hush!' said Thomas the Infirmarian. 'The little creatures shall be sanctified – sanctified to the service of His sick.'

'What need?' John of Burgos wiped his lips. 'It shows no more than the shapes of things. It gives good pictures. I had it at Granada. It was brought from the East, they told me.'

Roger of Salerno laughed with an old man's malice. 'What of Mother Church? Most Holy Mother Church? If it comes to Her ears that we have spied into Her Hell without Her leave, where do we stand?'

'At the stake,' said the Abbot of St Illod's, and, raising his voice a trifle, 'You hear that? Roger Bacon, heard you that?'

The Friar turned from the window, clutching the compasses tighter.

'No, no!' he appealed. 'Not with Falcodi – not with our

English-hearted Foulkes made Pope. He's wise – he's learned. He reads what I have put forth. Foulkes would never suffer it.'

' "Holy Pope is one thing, Holy Church another," ' Roger quoted.

'But I – *I* can bear witness it is no Art Magic,' the Friar went on. 'Nothing is it, except Art optical – wisdom after trial and experiment, mark you. I can prove it, and – my name weighs with men who dare think.'

'Find them!' croaked Roger of Salerno. 'Five or six in all the world. That makes less than fifty pounds by weight of ashes at the stake. I have watched such men – reduced.'

'I will not give this up!' The Friar's voice cracked in passion and despair. 'It would be to sin against the Light.'

'No, no! Let us – let us sanctify the little animals of Varro,' said Thomas.

Stephen leaned forward, fished his ring out of the cup, and slipped it on his finger. 'My sons,' said he, 'we have seen what we have seen.'

'That it is no magic but simple Art,' the Friar persisted.

' 'Avails nothing. In the eyes of Mother Church we have seen more than is permitted to man.'

'But it was Life – created and rejoicing,' said Thomas.

'To look into Hell as we shall be judged – as we shall be proved – to have looked, is for priests only.'

'Or green-sick virgins on the road to sainthood who, for cause any mid-wife could give you—'

The Abbot's half-lifted hand checked Roger of Salerno's outpouring.

'Nor may even priests see more in Hell than Church knows to be there. John, there is respect due to Church as well as to Devils.'

'My trade's the outside of things,' said John quietly. 'I have my patterns.'

'But you may need to look again for more,' the Friar said.

'In my craft, a thing done is done with. We go on to new shapes after that.'

'And if we trespass beyond bounds, even in thought, we lie open to the judgment of the Church,' the Abbot continued.

'But thou knowest – *knowest!*' Roger of Salerno had returned to the attack. 'Here's all the world in darkness concerning the causes of things – from the fever across the lane to thy Lady's – thine own Lady's – eating malady. Think!'

'I have thought upon it, Salerno! I have thought indeed.'

Thomas the Infirmarian lifted his head again; and this time he did not stammer at all. 'As in the water, so in the blood must they rage and war with each other! I have dreamed these ten years – I thought it was a sin – but my dreams and Varro's are true! Think on it again! Here's the Light under our very hand!'

'Quench it! You'd no more stand to roasting than – any other. I'll give you the case as Church – as I myself – would frame it. Our John here returns from the Moors, and shows us a hell of devils contending in the compass of one drop of water. Magic past clearance! You can hear the faggots crackle.'

'But thou knowest! Thou hast seen it all before! For man's poor sake! For old friendship's sake – Stephen!' The Friar was trying to stuff the compasses into his bosom as he appealed.

'What Stephen de Sautré knows, you his friends know also. I would have you, now, obey the Abbot of St Illod's. Give to me!' He held out his ringed hand.

'May I – may John hcre – not even make a drawing of one – one screw?' said the broken Friar, in spite or himself.

'Nowise!' Stephen took it over. 'Your dagger, John. Sheathed will serve.'

He unscrewed the metal cylinder, laid it on the table, and with the dagger's hilt smashed some crystal to sparkling dust which he swept into a scooped hand and cast behind the hearth.

'It would seem,' said he, 'the choice lies between two sins. To deny the world a Light which is under our hand, or to enlighten the world before her time. What you have seen, I saw long since among the physicians at Cairo. And I know what doctrine they drew from it. Hast *thou* dreamed, Thomas? I also – with fuller knowledge. But this birth, my sons, is untimely. It will be but the mother of more death, more torture, more division, and greater darkness in this dark age.

Therefore I, who know both my world and the Church, take this Choice on my conscience. Go! It is finished.'

He thrust the wooden part of the compasses deep among the beech logs till all was burned.

ON THE GATE: A TALE OF '16

If the Order Above be but the reflection of the Order Below (as that Ancient affirms, who had some knowledge of the Order), it is not outside the Order of Things that there should have been confusion also in the Department of Death. The world's steadily falling death-rate, the rising proportion of scientifically prolonged fatal illnesses, which allowed months of warning to all concerned, had weakened initiative throughout the Necrological Departments. When the War came, these were as unprepared as civilised mankind; and, like mankind, they improvised and recriminated in the face of Heaven.

As Death himself observed to St Peter who had just come off The Gate for a rest: 'One does the best one can with the means at one's disposal but—'

'*I* know,' said the good Saint sympathetically. 'Even with what help I can muster, I'm on The Gate twenty-two hours out of the twenty-four.'

'Do you find your volunteer staff any real use?' Death went on. 'Isn't it easier to do the work oneself than—'

'One must guard against that point of view,' St Peter returned, 'but I know what you mean. Office officialises the best of us . . . What is it *now*?' He turned to a prim-lipped Seraph who had followed him with an expulsion-form for signature. St Peter glanced it over. 'Private R. M. Buckland,' he read, 'on the charge of saying that there is no God. 'That all?'

'He says he is prepared to prove it, sir, and – according to the Rules—'

'If you will make yourself acquainted with the Rules, you'll find they lay down that "the fool says in his heart, there is no God." That decides it; probably shell-shock. Have you tested his reflexes?'

'No, sir. He kept *on* saying that there—'

'Pass him in at once! Tell off some one to argue with him and give him the best of the argument till St Luke's free. Anything else?'

'A hospital-nurse's record, sir. She has been nursing for two years.'

'A long while,' St Peter spoke severely. 'She may very well have grown careless.'

'It's her civilian record, sir. I judged best to refer it to you.' The Seraph handed him a vivid scarlet docket.

'The next time,' said St Peter, folding it down and -- writing on one corner, 'that you get one of these – er – tinted forms, mark it QMA and pass bearer at once. Don't worry over trifles.' The Seraph flashed off and returned to the clamorous Gate.

'Which Department is QMA?' said Death. St Peter chuckled.

'It's not a department. It's a Ruling. "*Quia multum amavit.*" A most useful Ruling. I've stretched it to . . . Now, I wonder what that child actually did die of.'

'I'll ask,' said Death, and moved to a public telephone near by. 'Give me War Check and Audit: English side: non-combatant,' he began. 'Latest returns . . . Surely you've got them posted up to date by now! . . . Yes! Hospital Nurse in France . . . No! *Not* "nature and aliases." I said – what -- was nature – of – illness? . . . Thanks.' He turned to St Peter. 'Quite normal,' he said. 'Heart-failure after neglected pleurisy following overwork.'

'Good! 'St Peter rubbed his hands. 'That brings her under the higher allowance – GLH scale – "Greater love hath no man—" But *my* people ought to have known that from the first.'

'Who is that clerk of yours?' asked Death. 'He seems rather a stickler for the proprieties.'

'The usual type nowadays,' St Peter returned. 'A young

Power in charge of some half-baked Universe. Never having dealt with life yet, he's somewhat nebulous.'

Death sighed. 'It's the same with my old Departmental Heads. Nothing on earth will make my fossils on the Normal Civil Side realise that we are dying in a new age. Come and look at them. They might interest you.'

'Thanks, I will, but— Excuse me a minute! Here's my zealous young assistant on the wing once more.'

The Seraph had returned to report the arrival of overwhelmingly heavy convoys at The Gate, and to ask what the Saint advised.

'I'm just off on an inter-departmental inspection which will take me some time,' said St Peter. 'You *must* learn to act on your own initiative. So I shall leave you to yourself for the next hour or two, merely suggesting (I don't wish in any way to sway your judgment) that you invite St Paul, St Ignatius (Loyola, I mean) and – er – St Christopher to assist as Supervising Assessors on the Board of Admission. Ignatius is one of the subtlest intellects we have, and an officer and a gentleman to boot. I assure you' – the Saint turned towards Death – 'he revels in dialectics. If he's allowed to prove his case, he's quite capable of letting off the offender. St Christopher, of course, will pass anything that looks wet and muddy.'

'They are nearly all that now, sir,' said the Seraph.

'So much the better; and – as I was going to say – St Paul is an embarrass— a distinctly strong colleague. Still – we all have our weaknesses. Perhaps a well-timed reference to his seamanship in the Mediterranean – by the way, look up the name of his ship, will you? Alexandria register, I think – might be useful in some of those sudden maritime cases that crop up. I needn't tell *you* to be firm, of course. That's your besetting – er – I mean – reprimand 'em severely and publicly, but—' the Saint's voice broke – 'oh, my child, *you* don't know what it is to need forgiveness. Be gentle with 'em – be very gentle with 'em!'

Swiftly as a falling shaft of light the Seraph kissed the sandalled feet and was away.

'Aha!' said St Peter. 'He can't go far wrong with that Board of Admission as I've – er – arranged it.'

They walked towards the great central office of Normal Civil Death, which, buried to the knees in a flood of temporary structures, resembled a closed cribbage-board among spilt dominoes.

They entered an area of avenues and cross-avenues, flanked by long, low buildings, each packed with seraphs working wing to folded wing.

'Our temporary buildings,' Death explained. ''Always being added to. This is the War-side. You'll find nothing changed on the Normal Civil Side. They are more human than mankind.'

'It doesn't lie in *my* mouth to blame them,' said St Peter.

'No, I've yet to meet the soul you wouldn't find excuse for,' said Death tenderly; 'but then – *I* don't – er – arrange my Boards of Admission.'

'If one doesn't help one's Staff, one's Staff will never help itself,' St Peter laughed, as the shadow of the main porch of the Normal Civil Death Offices darkened above them.

'This façade rather recalls the Vatican, doesn't it?' said the Saint.

'They're quite as conservative. 'Notice how they still keep the old Holbein uniforms? 'Morning, Sergeant Fell. How goes it?' said Death as he swung the dusty doors and nodded at a Commissionaire, clad in the grim livery of Death, even as Hans Holbein has designed it.

'Sadly. Very sadly indeed, sir,' the Commissionaire replied. 'So many pore ladies and gentlemen, sir, 'oo might well 'ave lived another few years, goin' off, as you might say, in every direction with no time for the proper obsequities.'

'Too bad,' said Death sympathetically. 'Well, we're none of us as young as we were, Sergeant.'

They climbed a carved staircase, behung with the whole millinery of undertaking at large. Death halted on a dark Aberdeen granite landing and beckoned a messenger.

'We're rather busy to-day, sir,' the messenger whispered, 'but I think His Majesty will see *you*.'

'Who *is* the Head of this Department if it isn't you?' St Peter whispered in turn.

'You may well ask,' his companion replied. 'I'm only—' he checked himself and went on. 'The fact is, our Normal Civil Death side is controlled by a Being who considers himself all that I am and more. He's Death as men have made him – in their own image.' He pointed to a brazen plate, by the side of a black-curtained door, which read: 'Normal Civil Death, KG, KT, KP, PC, etc.' 'He's as human as mankind.'

'I guessed as much from those letters. What do they mean?'

'Titles conferred on him from time to time. King of Ghosts; King of Terrors; King of Phantoms; Pallid Conqueror, and so forth. There's no denying he's earned every one of them. A first-class mind, but just a leetle bit of a sn—'

'His Majesty is at liberty,' said the messenger.

Civil Death did not belie his name. No monarch on earth could have welcomed them more graciously; or, in St Peter's case, with more of that particularity of remembrance which is the gift of good kings. But when Death asked him how his office was working, he became at once the Departmental Head with a grievance.

'Thanks to this abominable war,' he began testily, 'my NCD has to spend all its time fighting for mere existence. Your new War-side seems to think that nothing matters *except* the war. I've been asked to give up two-thirds of my Archives Basement (E. 7–E. 64) to the Polish Civilian Casualty Check and Audit. Preposterous! Where am I to move my Archives? And they've just been cross-indexed, too!'

'As I understood it,' said Death, 'our War-side merely applied for desk-room in your basement. They were prepared to leave your Archives *in situ*.'

'Impossible! We may need to refer to them at any moment. There's a case now which is interesting Us all – a Mrs Ollerby. Worcestershire by extraction – dying of an internal hered-itary complaint. At any moment, We may wish to refer to her dossier, and how *can* We if Our basement is given up to people over whom We exercise no departmental control? This war has been made excuse for slackness in every direction.'

'Indeed!' said Death. 'You surprise me. I thought nothing made any difference to the NCD.'

'A few years ago I should have concurred,' Civil Death replied. 'But since this – this recent outbreak of unregulated mortality there has been a distinct lack of respect toward certain aspects of Our administration. The attitude is bound to reflect itself in the office. The official is, in a large measure, what the public makes him. Of course, it is only temporary reaction, but the merest outsider would notice what I mean. Perhaps *you* would like to see for yourself?' Civil Death bowed towards St Peter, who feared that he might be taking up his time.

'Not in the least. If I am not the servant of the public, what am I?' Civil Death said, and preceded them to the landing. 'Now, this' – he ushered them into an immense but badly lighted office – 'is our International Mortuary Department – the IMD as we call it. It works with the Check and Audit. I should be sorry to say offhand how many billion sterling it represents, invested in the funeral ceremonies of all the races of mankind.' He stopped behind a very bald-headed clerk at a desk. 'And yet We take cognizance of the minutest detail, do not We?' he went on. 'What have We here, for example?'

'Funeral expenses of the late Mr John Shenks Tanner,' the clerk stepped aside from the red-ruled book. 'Cut down by the executors on account of the War from £173 : 19 : 1 to £47 : 18 : 4. A sad falling off, if I may say so, Your Majesty.'

'And what was the attitude of the survivors?' Civil Death asked.

'Very casual. It was a motor-hearse funeral.'

'A pernicious example, spreading, I fear, even in the lowest classes,' his superior muttered. 'Haste, lack of respect for the Dread Summons, carelessness in the Subsequent Disposition of the Corpse and—'

'But as regards people's real feelings?' St Peter demanded of the clerk.

'That isn't within the terms of our reference, Sir,' was the answer. 'But we *do* know that as often as not, they don't even buy black-edged announcement-cards nowadays.'

'Good Heavens!' said Civil Death swellingly. 'No cards! I must look into this myself. Forgive me, St Peter, but we Servants of Humanity, as you know, are not our own masters. No cards, indeed!' He waved them off with an official hand, and immersed himself in the ledger.

'Oh, come along,' Death whispered to St Peter. 'This is a blessed relief!'

They two walked on till they reached the far end of the vast dim office. The clerks at the desks here scarcely pretended to work. A messenger entered and slapped down a small auto-phonic reel.

'Here you are!' he cried. 'Mister Wilbraham Lattimer's last dying speech and record. He made a shockin' end of it.'

'Good for Lattimer!' a young voice called from a desk. 'Chuck it over!'

'Yes,' the messenger went on. 'Lattimer said to his brother: "Bert, I haven't time to worry about a little thing like dying these days, and what's more important, *you* haven't either. You go back to your Somme doin's, and I'll put it through with Aunt Maria. It'll amuse her and it won't hinder you." That's nice stuff for your boss!' The messenger whistled and departed. A clerk groaned as he snatched up the reel.

'How the deuce am I to knock this into official shape?' he began. 'Pass us the edifying Gantry Tubnell. I'll have to crib from him again, I suppose.'

'Be careful!' a companion whispered, and shuffled a type-written form along the desk. 'I've used Tubby twice this morning already.'

The late Mr Gantry Tubnell must have demised on approved departmental lines, for his record was much thumbed. Death and St Peter watched the editing with interest.

'I can't bring in Aunt Maria *any* way,' the clerk broke out at last. 'Listen here, every one! She has heart-disease. She dies just as she's lifted the dropsical Lattimer to change his sheets. She says: " Sorry, Willy! I'd make a dam' pore 'ospital nurse!" Then she sits down and croaks. Now *I* call that good! I've a great mind to take it round to the War-side as an indirect asualty and get a breath of fresh air.'

'Then you'll be hauled over the coals,' a neighbour suggested.

'I'm used to that, too,' the clerk sniggered.

'Are you?' said Death, stepping forward suddenly from behind a high map-stand. 'Who are you?' The clerk cowered in his skeleton jacket.

'I'm not on the Regular Establishment, Sir,' he stammered. 'I'm a – Volunteer. I – I wanted to see how people behaved when they were in trouble.'

'Did you? Well, take the late Mr Wilbraham Lattimer's and Miss Maria Lattimer's papers to the War-side General Reference Office. When they have been passed upon, tell the Attendance Clerk that you are to serve as probationer in – let's see – in the Domestic Induced Casualty Side – 7 GS.'

The clerk collected himself a little and spoke through dry lips.

'But – but I'm – I slipped in from the Lower Establishment, Sir,' he breathed.

There was no need to explain. He shook from head to foot as with the palsy; and under all Heaven none tremble save those who come from that class which 'also believe and tremble.'

'Do you tell Me this officially, or as one created being to another?' Death asked after a pause.

'Oh, non-officially, Sir. Strictly non-officially, so long as you know all about it.'

His awe-stricken fellow-workers could not restrain a smile at Death having to be told about anything. Even Death bit his lips.

'I don't think you will find the War-side will raise any objection,' said he. 'By the way, they don't wear that uniform over there.'

Almost before Death ceased speaking, it was ripped off and flung on the floor, and that which had been a sober clerk of Normal Civil Death stood up an unmistakable, curly-haired, bat-winged, faun-eared Imp of the Pit. But where his wings joined his shoulders there was a patch of delicate dove-coloured feathering that gave promise to spread all up the pinion. St Peter saw it and smiled, for it was a known sign of grace.

'Thank Goodness!' the ex-clerk gasped as he snatched up the Lattimer records and sheered sideways through the skylight.

'Amen!' said Death and St Peter together, and walked through the door.

'Weren't you hinting something to me a little while ago about *my* lax methods?' St Peter demanded, innocently.

'Well, if one doesn't help one's Staff, one's Staff will never help itself,' Death retorted. 'Now, I shall have to pitch in a stiff demi-official asking how that young fiend came to be taken on in the NCD without examination. And I must do it before the NCD complain that I've been interfering with their departmental transfers. *Aren't* they human? If you want to go back to The Gate I think our shortest way will be through here and across the War-Sheds.'

They came out of a side-door into Heaven's full light. A phalanx of Shining Ones swung across a great square singing:

'To Him Who made the Heavens abide, yet cease not from their motion,
To Him Who drives the cleansing tide twice a day round ocean –
Let His Name be magnified in all poor folk's devotion!'

Death halted their leader, and asked a question.

'We're Volunteer Aid Serving Powers,' the Seraph explained, 'reporting for duty in the Domestic Induced Casualty Department – told off to help relatives, where we can.'

The shift trooped on – such an array of Powers, Honours, Glories, Toils, Patiences, Services, Faiths and Loves as no man may conceive even by favour of dreams. Death and St Peter followed them into a DICD Shed on the English side where, for the moment, work had slackened. Suddenly a name flashed on the telephone-indicator. 'Mrs Arthur Bedott, 317, Portsmouth Avenue, Brondesbury. Husband badly wounded. One child.' Her special weakness was appended.

A Seraph on the raised dais that overlooked the Volunteer Aids waiting at the entrance, nodded and crooked a finger. One of the new shift – a temporary Acting Glory – hurled himself from his place and vanished earthward.

'You may take it,' Death whispered to St Peter, 'there will be a sustaining epic built up round Private Bedott's wound for his wife and Baby Bedott to cling to. And here—' they heard wings that flapped wearily – 'here, I suspect, comes one of our failures.'

A Seraph entered and dropped, panting, on a form. His plumage was ragged, his sword splintered to the hilt; and his face still worked with the passions of the world he had left, as his soiled vesture reeked of alcohol.

'Defeat,' he reported hoarsely, when he had given in a woman's name. 'Utter defeat! Look!' He held up the stump of his sword. 'I broke this on her gin-bottle.'

'So? We try again,' said the impassive Chief Seraph. Again he beckoned, and there stepped forward that very Imp whom Death had transferred from the NCD.

'Go *you*!' said the Seraph. 'We must deal with a fool according to her folly. Have you pride enough?'

There was no need to ask. The messenger's face glowed and his nostrils quivered with it. Scarcely pausing to salute, he poised and dived, and the papers on the desks spun beneath the draught of his furious vans.

St Peter nodded high approval. '*I* see!' he said. 'He'll work on her pride to steady her. By all means – "if by all means," as my good Paul used to say. Only it ought to read "by any manner of possible means." Excellent!'

'It's difficult, though,' a soft-eyed Patience whispered. 'I fail again and again. I'm only fit for an old-maid's tea-party.'

Once more the record flashed – a multiple-urgent appeal on behalf of a few thousand men, worn-out body and soul. The Patience was detailed.

'Oh, me!' she sighed, with a comic little shrug of despair, and took the void softly as a summer breeze at dawning.

'But how does this come under the head of Domesti

Casualties? Those men were in the trenches. I heard the mud squelch,' said St Peter.

'Something wrong with the installation – as usual. Waves are always jamming here,' the Seraph replied.

'So it seems,' said St Peter as a wireless cut in with the muffled note of some one singing (sorely out of tune), to an accompaniment of desultory poppings:

'Unless you can love as the Angels love With the breadth of Heaven be—'

'*Twickt!*' It broke off. The record showed a name. The waiting Seraphs stiffened to attention with a click of tense quills.

'As you were!' said the Chief Seraph. 'He's met her.'

'Who is she?' said St Peter.

'His mother. You never get over your weakness for romance,' Death answered, and a covert smile spread through the Office.

'Thank Heaven, I don't. But I really ought to be going—'

'Wait one minute. Here's trouble coming through, I think,' Death interposed.

A recorder had sparked furiously in a broken run of SOS's that allowed no time for inquiry.

'Name! Name!' an impatient young Faith panted at last. 'It *can't* be blotted out.' No name came up. Only the reiterated appeal.

'False alarm!' said a hard-featured Toil, well used to mankind. 'Some fool has found out that he owns a soul. 'Wants work. *I*'d cure him! . . .'

'Hush!' said a Love in Armour, stamping his mailed foot. The office listened.

' 'Bad case?' Death demanded at last.

'Rank bad, Sir. They are holding back the name,' said the Chief Seraph. The SOS signals grew more desperate, and then ceased with an emphatic thump. The Love in Armour winced.

'Firing-party,' he whispered to St Peter. ' 'Can't mistake that noise!'

'What is it?' St Peter cried nervously.

'Deserter; spy; murderer,' was the Chief Seraph's weighed

answer. 'It's out of my department – now. No – hold the line ! The name's up at last.'

It showed for an instant, broken and faint as sparks on charred wadding, but in that instant a dozen pens had it written. St Peter with never a word gathered his robes about him and bundled through the door, headlong for The Gate.

'No hurry,' said Death at his elbow. 'With the present rush your man won't come up for ever so long.'

' 'Never can be sure these days. Anyhow, the Lower Establishment will be after him like sharks. He's the very type they'd want for propaganda. Deserter – traitor – murderer. Out of my way, please, babies!'

A group of children round a red-headed man who was telling them stories, scattered laughing. The man turned to St Peter.

'Deserter, traitor, murderer,' he repeated. 'Can *I* be of service?'

'You can!' St Peter gasped. 'Double on ahead to The Gate and tell them to hold up all expulsions till I come. Then,' he shouted as the man sped off at a long hound-like trot, 'go and picket the outskirts of the Convoys. Don't let any one break away on any account. Quick!'

But Death was right. They need not have hurried. The crowd at The Gate was far beyond the capacities of the Examining Board even though, as St Peter's Deputy informed him, it had been enlarged twice in his absence.

'We're doing our best,' the Seraph explained, 'but delay is inevitable, Sir. The Lower Establishment are taking advantage of it, as usual, at the tail of the Convoys. I've doubled all pickets there, and I'm sending more. Here's the extra list, Sir – Arc J., Bradlaugh C., Bunyan J., Calvin J., Iscariot J. reported to me just now, as under your orders, and took 'em with him. Also Shakespeare W. and—'

'Never mind the rest,' said St Peter. 'I'm going there myself. Meantime, carry on with the passes – don't fiddle over 'em – and give me a blank or two.' He caught up a thick block of Free Passes, nodded to a group in khaki at a passport table, initialled their Commanding Officer's personal pass as for

'Officer and Party,' and left the numbers to be filled in by a quite competent-looking Quarter-master-Sergeant. Then, Death beside him, he breasted his way out of The Gate against the incoming multitude of all races, tongues, and creeds that stretched far across the plain.

An old lady, firmly clutching a mottle-nosed, middle-aged Major by the belt, pushed across a procession of keen-faced *poilus*, and blocked his path, her captive held in that terrible mother-grip no Power has yet been able to unlock.

'I found him! I've got him! Pass him!' she ordered.

St Peter's jaw fell. Death politely looked elsewhere.

'There are a few formalities,' the Saint began.

'With Jerry in this state? Nonsense! How like a man! My boy never gave me a moment's anxiety in—'

'Don't, dear – don't!' The Major looked almost as uncomfortable as St Peter.

'Well, nothing compared with what he *would* give me if he weren't passed.'

'Didn't I hear you singing just now?' Death asked, seeing that his companion needed a breathing-space.

'Of course you did,' the mother intervened. 'He sings beautifully. And that's *another* reason! You're bass, aren't you now, darling?'

St Peter glanced at the agonised Major and hastily initialled him a pass. Without a word of thanks the Mother hauled him away.

'Now, under what conceivable Ruling do you justify that?' said Death.

'IW – the Importunate Widow. It's scandalous!' St Peter groaned. Then his face darkened as he looked across the great plain beyond The Gate. 'I don't like this,' he said. 'The Lower Establishment is out in full force to-night. I hope our pickets are strong enough—'

The crowd here had thinned to a disorderly queue flanked on both sides by a multitude of busy, discreet emissaries from the Lower Establishment who continually edged in to do business with them, only to be edged off again by a line of watchful pickets. Thanks to the khaki everywhere, the scene was not unlike that which one might have seen on earth, any evening of the old days outside the refreshment-room by the Arch at Victoria Station, when the Army trains started. St Peter's appearance was greeted by the usual outburst of cock-crowing from the Lower Establishment.

'Dirty work at the cross-roads,' said Death dryly.

'I deserve it! 'St Peter grunted, 'but think what it must mean for Judas.'

He shouldered into the thick of the confusion where the pickets coaxed, threatened, implored, and in extreme cases bodily shoved the wearied men and women past the voluble and insinuating spirits who strove to draw them aside.

A Shropshire Yeoman had just accepted, together with a forged pass, the assurance of a genial runner of the Lower Establishment that Heaven lay round the corner, and was being stealthily steered thither, when a large hand jerked him back, another took the runner in the chest, and some one thundered: 'Get out, you crimp!' The situation was then vividly explained to the soldier in the language of the barrack-room.

'Don't blame *me*, Guv'nor,' the man expostulated. 'I 'aven't seen a woman, let alone angels, for umpteen months. I'm from Joppa. Where 'you from?'

'Northampton,' was the answer. 'Rein back and keep by me.'

'What? You ain't ever Charley B. that my dad used to tell about? I thought you always said—'

'I shall say a deal more soon. Your Sergeant's talking to that woman in red. Fetch him in – quick!'

Meantime, a sunken-eyed Scots officer, utterly lost to the riot around, was being button-holed by a person of reverend aspect who explained to him that, by the logic of his own ancestral creed, not only was the Highlander irrevocably damned, but that his damnation had been predetermined before Earth was made.

'It's unanswerable – just unanswerable,' said the young man sorrowfully. 'I'll be with ye.' He was moving off, when a smallish figure interposed, not without dignity.

'Monsieur,' it said, 'would it be of any comfort to you to know that *I* am – I was – John Calvin?' At this the reverend one cursed and swore like the lost Soul he was, while the Highlander turned to discuss with Calvin, pacing towards The Gate, some alterations in the fabric of a work of fiction called the *Institutio*.

Others were not so easily held. A certain Woman, with loosened hair, bare arms, flashing eyes and dancing feet, shepherded her knot of waverers, hoarse and exhausted. When the taunt broke out against her from the opposing line: 'Tell 'em what you were! Tell 'em if you dare!' she answered unflinchingly, as did Judas, who, worming through the crowd like an Armenian carpet-vendor, peddled his shame aloud that it might give strength to others.

'Yes,' he would cry, 'I am everything they say, but if *I'm* here it must be a moral cert for *you*, gents. This way, please. Many mansions, gentlemen! Go-ood billets! Don't you notice these low people, Sar. *Plees* keep hope, gentlemen!'

When there were cases that cried to him from the ground – poor souls who could not stick it but had found their way out with a rifle and a boot-lace, he would tell them of his own end, till he made them contemptuous enough to rise up and curse him. Here St Luke's imperturbable bedside manner backed and strengthened the other's almost too oriental flux of words.

In this fashion and step by step, all the day's Convoy were piloted past that danger-point where the Lower Establishment are, for reasons not given us, allowed to ply their trade. The pickets dropped to the rear, relaxed, and compared notes.

'What always impresses me most,' said Death to St Peter, 'is the sheeplike simplicity of the intellectual mind.' He had been watching one of the pickets apparently overwhelmed by the arguments of an advanced atheist who – so hot in his argument that he was deaf to the offers of the Lower Establishment to make him a god – had stalked, talking hard – while the picket always gave ground before him – straight past the Broad Road.

'He was plaiting of long-tagged epigrams,' the sober-faced picket smiled. 'Give that sort only an ear and they'll follow ye gobbling like turkeys.'

'And John held his peace through it all,' a full fresh voice broke in. '"It may be so," says John. "Doubtless, in your belief, it *is* so," says John. "Your words move me mightily," says John, and gorges his own beliefs like a pike going backwards. And that young fool, so busy spinning words – words – words – that he trips past Hell Mouth without seeing it! . . . Who's yonder, Joan?'

'One of your English. 'Always late. Look!' A young girl with short-cropped hair pointed with her sword across the plain towards a single faltering figure which made at first as though to overtake the Convoy, but then turned left towards the Lower Establishment, who were enthusiastically cheering him as a leader of enterprise.

'That's my traitor,' said St Peter. 'He has no business to report to the Lower Establishment before reporting to Convoy.'

The figure's pace slackened as he neared the applauding line. He looked over his shoulder once or twice, and then fairly turned tail and fled again towards the still Convoy.

'Nobody ever gave me credit for anything I did,' he began, sobbing and gesticulating. 'They were all against me from the first. I only wanted a little encouragement. It was a regular conspiracy, but *I* showed 'em what I could do! *I* showed 'em! And – and—' he halted again. 'Oh, God! What are you going to do with *me*?'

'No one offered any suggestion. He ranged sideways like a doubtful dog, while across the plain the Lower Establishment murmured seductively. All eyes turned to St Peter.

'At this moment,' the Saint said half to himself, 'I can't recall any precise ruling under which—'

'My own case?' the ever-ready Judas suggested.

'No-o! That's making too much of it. And yet—'

'Oh, hurry up and get it over,' the man wailed, and told them all that he had done, ending with the cry that none had ever recognised his merits; neither his own narrow-minded people, his inefficient employers, nor the snobbish jumped-up officers of his battalion.

'You see,' said St Peter at the end. 'It's sheer vanity. It isn't even as if we had a woman to fall back upon.'

'Yet there was a woman or I'm mistaken,' said the picket with the pleasing voice who had praised John.

'Eh – what? When?' St Peter turned swiftly on the speaker. 'Who was the woman?'

'The wise woman of Tekoah,' came the smooth answer. 'I remember, because that verse was the private heart of my plays – some of 'em.'

But the Saint was not listening. 'You have it!' he cried. 'Samuel Two, Double Fourteen. To think that *I* should have forgotten! "For we must needs die and are as water spilled on the ground which cannot be gathered up again. Neither doth God respect any person, *yet*—" Here you! Listen to this!'

The man stepped forward and stood to attention. Some one took his cap as Judas and the picket John closed up beside him.

' "*Yet doth He devise means* (d'you understand that?) *devise means that His banished be not expelled from Him!*" This covers your case. I don't know what the means will be. That's for you to find out. They'll tell you yonder.' He nodded towards the now silent Lower Establishment as he scribbled on a pass. 'Take this paper over to them and report for duty there. You'll have a thin time of it; but they won't keep you a day longer than I've put down. Escort!'

'Does – does that mean there's any hope?' the man stammered.

'Yes – I'll show you the way,' Judas whispered. 'I've lived there – a very long time!'

'I'll bear you company a piece,' said John, on his left flank. 'There'll be Despair to deal with. Heart up, Mr Littlesoul!'

The three wheeled off, and the Convoy watched them grow smaller and smaller across the plain.

St Peter smiled benignantly and rubbed his hands.

'And now we're rested,' said he, 'I think we might make a push for billets this evening, gentlemen, eh?'

The pickets fell in, guardians no longer but friends and companions all down the line. There was a little burst of cheering and the whole Convoy strode away towards the not so distant Gate.

The Saint and Death stayed behind to rest awhile. It was a heavenly evening. They could hear the whistle of the low-flighting Cherubim, clear and sharp, under the diviner note of some released Seraph's wings, where, his errand accomplished, he plunged three or four stars deep into the cool Baths of Hercules; the steady dynamo-like hum of the nearer planets on their axes; and, as the hush deepened, the surprised little sigh of some new-born sun a universe of universes away. But their minds were with the Convoy that their eyes followed.

Said St Peter proudly at last: 'If those people of mine had seen that fellow stripped of all hope in front of 'em, I doubt if they could have marched another yard to-night. Watch 'em stepping out now, though! Aren't they human?'

'To whom do you say it?' Death answered, with something of a tired smile. 'I'm more than human. *I*'ve got to die some time or other. But all other created Beings – afterwards . . .'

'*I* know,' said St Peter softly. 'And that is why I love you, O Azrael!'

For now they were alone Death had, of course, returned to his true majestic shape – that only One of all created beings who is doomed to perish utterly, and knows it.

'Well, that's *that* – for me!' Death concluded as he rose. 'And yet—' he glanced towards the empty plain where the Lower Establishment had withdrawn with their prisoner. ' "Yet doth He devise means." '

THE APPEAL

If I have given you delight
   By aught that I have done,
Let me lie quiet in that night
   Which shall be yours anon:

And for the little, little span
   The dead are borne in mind,
Seek not to question other than
   The books I leave behind.

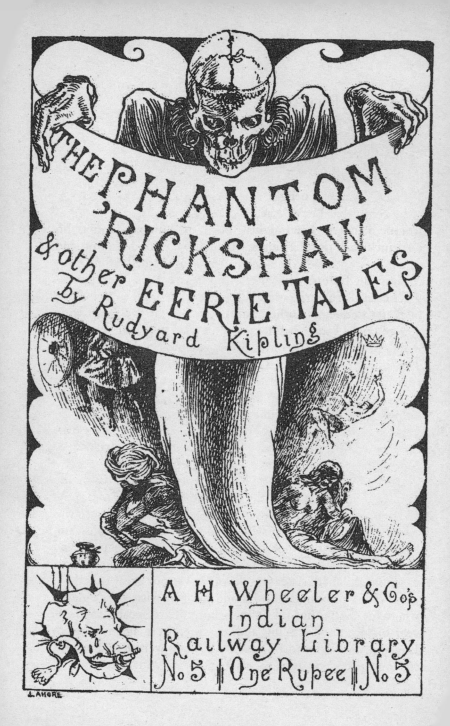

THE PHANTOM 'RICKSHAW & other EERIE TALES

by Rudyard Kipling

A H Wheeler & Co's Indian Railway Library

No. 5 One Rupee No. 5

LAHORE

AFTERWORD:
RUDYARD KIPLING:
A LIFE IN STORIES

by Stephen Jones

Joseph Rudyard Kipling was born in Bombay, India, on December 30, 1865. The son of John Lockwood Kipling and Alice Kipling (née Macdonald), he was named after Lake Rudyard in Staffordshire, where his parents became engaged.

Kipling's father, an author, artist and scholar who was Head of Department of Architectural Sculpture at the Jeejeebhoy School of Art, had considerable influence over his son's later work. Kipling's mother was also a talented writer and poet. Two of her sisters married the nineteenth-century painters Sir Edward Burne-Jones and Sir Edward Poynter, while a third married Alfred Baldwin and was the mother of Stanley Baldwin, who became Prime Minister of Great Britain.

With grandfathers who were both Methodist ministers, these familial connections would remain of importance to Kipling throughout his life.

During his first five years, Kipling led a blissfully happy life in India, then the jewel in the crown of the British Empire. As he later recalled: 'Far across green spaces round the house was a marvellous place filled with smells of paints and oils, and lumps of clay with which I played. That was the atelier of my Father's School of Art, and a Mr "Terry Sahib" his assistant, to whom my small sister was devoted, was our great friend.'

In 1868, the young boy made his first visit to England, where his sister Alice ('Trix') was born. Three years later, six-year-old Rudyard Kipling and his sister were again taken to England, this time to be educated. They were left there for six long years, boarded as paying guests with Captain and

Mrs P.A. Holloway at Lorne Lodge, a foster home in South-sea, near Portsmouth, while their parents returned to India. They gave their children no explanation.

Kipling described Captain Holloway as 'the only person in that house as far as I can remember who ever threw me a kind word'. However, after the Captain died, the deeply religious Mrs Holloway apparently took a dislike to the young Kipling and allowed her teenage son to bully him.

'I had never heard of Hell,' wrote Kipling, 'so I was intro-duced to it in all its terrors – I and whatever luckless little slavey might be in the house, whom severe rationing had led to steal food . . . Myself, I was regularly beaten.'

Because he kept this constant abuse to himself, much of Kipling's childhood was deeply miserable, and he wrote about these unhappy years with great bitterness in his 1888 story 'Baa Baa, Black Sheep'. He later described holidays spent each December in London with his mother's sister Georgiana Burne-Jones ('Aunt Georgy') and her husband Sir Edward Burne-Jones as 'a paradise which I verily believe saved me'.

Kipling took refuge in reading, 'So I read all that came within my reach,' he recalled. 'As soon as my pleasure in this was known, deprivation from reading was added to my punish-ments. I then read by stealth and the more earnestly.' It was also around this time that Kipling first began inventing stories and imaginary characters to entertain himself.

In 1877, after Kipling had suffered a nervous breakdown ('I imagined I saw shadows and things that were not there'), Alice Kipling arrived from India and took her son away from Mrs Holloway, although Trix remained in Southsea for a further three years.

Following a long recuperation, the sensitive and short-sighted Kipling was enrolled as a pupil at the United Services College, Westward Ho!, near Bideford in North Devon. It was a relatively new and inexpensive boarding school for the sons of impoverished Army officers and civil servants that specialised in training boys for entry into military academies. Conditions may have been basic, but the education was solid, and headmaster Cormell Price – a friend of Kipling's father –

fostered the young boy's literary ability by making him editor of the school magazine.

'Many of us loved the Head for what he had done for us,' wrote Kipling, 'but I owed him more than all of them put together.'

One of the thirteen-year-old Kipling's early stories, 'My First Adventure', involved a time-travelling 'ghost' and appeared in a hand-written magazine entitled *The Scribbler*, which he compiled with two fellow pupils in 1879.

While returning to Southsea the following year to collect his sister, Kipling met her fellow-boarder, Florence Garrard, with whom he fell in love. The relationship, which was always somewhat one-sided, vacillated for a number of years.

In 1881, back in India, his parents privately published Kipling's first booklet of poems, *Schoolboy Lyrics*, without his knowledge. Years later, he burned his original copy for fear of copyright theft.

After leaving school at the age of sixteen, Kipling returned to India in October to join his parents in Lahore, the principal city of the Punjab. Kipling's father Lockwood had become curator of the Lahore museum (later described as a 'wonder house' in the opening chapter of *Kim*). Outside the walled city, one of the oldest in Islam, were stationed a battalion of infantry and an artillery battery. Inside, around seventy British civilians lived in neat bungalows alongside 200,000 people from all the Asiatic races.

His father found him a job as an assistant editor on the *Civil and Military Gazette*, a local daily English-language newspaper for the British in northern India, where Kipling was paid 'one hundred silver rupees a month' and comprised fifty per cent of the editorial staff.

For the next seven years Kipling wrote journalism, working between ten and fifteen hours a day. Death, in the form of typhoid and cholera, was a constant companion, and he was often forced to work with a temperature of 104.

'The dead of all times were about us,' he later wrote, 'in the vast forgotten Moslem cemeteries round the Station, where one's horse's hoof of a morning might break through to the corpse below; skulls and bones tumbled out of our garden walls, and were turned up among the flowers by the Rains; and at every point were tombs of the dead.'

Kipling was fascinated by the contrasts between Lahore's various inhabitants and the ways in which they interacted with each other, and as a journalist he was able to move between the different classes unrestricted.

Suffering from insomnia, he would walk the streets until dawn. During these nocturnal excursions he had the opportunity to observe the highs and lows of the rich and poor of Anglo-Indian society. But although his love for the country of his birth was deep, Kipling was not uncritical. In his limited spare time, inspired by a novel he had read about a would-be author, he soon began filling the periodicals he worked for with prose sketches (which he described as 'penny-farthing yarns' because of the rate paid per line) and light verse.

Kipling's poems were published in *The Englishman of Calcutta* and the *Civil and Military Gazette* 'when and as padding was needed'. Soon turning his hand to fiction (or 'turnovers') to fill occasional columns in the newspaper, he once again called upon his keen observation of his Indian background for inspiration.

His first published story was entitled 'The Gate of a Hundred Sorrows', about a drug addict. It was written in the summer of 1894.

In his study, *Kipling, Auden and Co.* (1980), Randall Jarrell noted: 'Kipling is far closer to Gogol than to a normal realist or naturalist. In Kipling the pressure of the imagination has forced facts over into the supernatural.'

In fact, the second professional story Kipling ever wrote, 'The Dream of Duncan Parrenness', was a supernatural tale. Published anonymously in the *Civil and Military Gazette* on Christmas Day, 1884, it was basically an Anglo-Indian version of Charles Dickens' seminal ghost story 'A Christmas Carol' and took the author almost three months to complete.

The following Christmas, the newspaper produced a 126-page 'Christmas Annual' entitled *Quartette*, written by 'four

Anglo-Indian writers'. In fact, the stories and poems were by Kipling, his mother and father, and his sister Alice. Kipling contributed three supernatural tales: 'The Strange Ride of Morrowbie Jukes', 'The Unlimited Draw of Tick Boileau' and, most notably, The Phantom 'Rickshaw'.

Written when he was not quite twenty, 'The Phantom 'Rickshaw' was set in a milieu Kipling knew well and concerned a man who was eventually driven to his death by the ghost of a wronged lover. Despite being described by at least one critic as 'crudely material supernaturalism', Kipling later said of the story: 'Some of it was weak, much was bad and out of key; but it was my first serious attempt to think in another man's skin.'

However, Kipling was already a skilled enough writer to leave some doubt as to whether the supernatural manifestation was in fact a figment of his protagonist's fevered imagination.

'The Strange Ride of Morrowbie Jukes' was a *conte cruel*, about the eponymous English engineer held captive in a sand pit in a desert region beyond Lahore. It was perhaps inspired by reports Kipling had heard of 'The Village of the Dead' (the story's original title) which were well-known in India during the 1840s.

As Angus Wilson described the tale in his 1977 study *The Strange Ride of Rudyard Kipling*: 'It remains one of the most powerful nightmares of the precariousness of a ruling group, in this case haunted by memories of the Mutiny not yet twenty years old.'

The character of Tick Boileau in the third tale in the Christmas compendium subsequently turned up in two further Kipling stories: 'Only a Subaltern' (1888) and 'A Conference of the Powers' (1893).

In 1886, Kipling spent a month at Simla as a correspondent for the *Pioneer*, a major newspaper also owned by the proprietors of the *Civil and Military Gazette*. That same year, *Departmental Ditties and Other Verses*, his privately printed book of comic poems about Anglo-Indian life, sold out almost immediately and a second edition was rushed into print by Thacker, Spink & Co. of Calcutta.

No sooner had Kipling been promoted to the *Pioneer* at Allahabad, in the North-West Provinces, when he began contributing anonymous stories to a weekly edition of the newspaper on a regular basis. 'My pen took charge and I, greatly admiring, watched it write for me far into the nights,' he recalled.

According to editor Peter Haining in his 1987 collection *The Complete Supernatural Stories of Rudyard Kipling*, during his four years with the *Pioneer*, Kipling published nine articles, stories and verses, which he did sign with the single initial 'R'. Around the same time he became friends with Professor Alec Hill, a government employee, and his American wife Edmonia, who would later become another prevailing influence on Kipling's life and work. Meanwhile, the young Englishman was sent to Rajputana as a special correspondent. The articles he wrote during this period were later collected as *Letters of Marque* (1891).

Kipling continued to publish fiction in the *Civil and Military Gazette*, much of it apparently based on fact. 'The Recurring Smash' was credited to 'ST' while 'Bubbling Well Road' was signed 'The Traveller', although the latter was subsequently reprinted under the author's own by-line in the collection *Life's Handicap: Being Stories of Mine Own People* (1891).

'Mercifully, the mere act of writing was, and always has been, a physical pleasure to me,' Kipling later recalled. 'This made it easier to throw away anything that did not turn out well.'

Kipling obsessively read and re-read his work, editing it as often as he thought necessary until he had pared it down to a final draft that he was satisfied with. 'I have had tales by me for three or five years which shortened themselves almost yearly,' he revealed.

In 1888, Kipling became a boarder with the Hills at their house in Allahabad. Now editor of the supplement *Pioneer Weekly*, the twenty-two year-old Kipling's first short story collection which he had sold for £50, *Plain Tales from the Hills*, was published by Thacker Spink & Co. Along with the first appearance of the heroes of 'Soldiers Three' – Privates

Terence Mulvaney, Stanley Otheris and John Learoyd – the book also contained the supernatural tales 'In the House of Suddhoo', 'The Bisara of Pooree' and 'By Word of Mouth'.

However, another of the 'Plain Tales from India', the humorous 'Haunted Subalterns', originally published in the *Civil and Military Gazette* of May 27, 1887, was surprisingly not included in the collection.

'I have lived long enough in this India,' explained the author in his short introduction, 'to know that it is best to know nothing and can only write the story as it happened'.

Although Kipling was always sceptical of the supernatural, his writings reveal that he probably did have a belief in the existence of unexplained phenomena. 'There is a type of mind that dives after what it calls "psychical experiences," he wrote. 'And I am in no way "psychic".' However, he did admit to at least one case of clairvoyance, when he dreamt about a ceremony in Westminster Abbey before the event actually occurred in every detail.

The publication of *Plain Tales from the Hills* was followed by the Indian Railway Library series of short stories, published in Allahabad by AH Wheeler & Co. in six paper-covered volumes costing one rupee apiece: *Soldiers Three, The Story of the Gadsbys: A Tale Without a Plot* (a play), *In Black and White, Under the Deodars, Wee Willie Winkie and Other Child Stories* and his first collection entirely of weird fiction, *The Phantom 'Rickshaw and Other Eerie Tales*.

Actually the fifth volume in the series, *The Phantom 'Rickshaw* contained four stories – 'The Phantom 'Rickshaw', 'My Own True Ghost Story', 'The Strange Ride of Morrowbie Jukes' and 'The Man Who Would Be King' (a macabre adventure tale, considered by some reviewers to be the finest story in the English language).

As Kipling explained in his brief Preface: 'This is not exactly a book of real ghost-stories, as the cover makes believe, but rather a collection of facts that never quite explained themselves. All that the collector can be certain of is that one ma insisted upon dying because he believed himself to be haunt another man either made up a wonderful fiction, or vis a very strange place; while the third man was indubitably crucified by some person or persons unknown, and gave an extraordinary account of himself.

'Ghost-stories are very seldom told at first-hand. I have managed, with infinite trouble, to secure one exception to this rule. It is not a very good specimen, but you can credit it from beginning to end. The other three stories you must take on trust; as I did.'

In fact, despite the author's entreaty to 'credit' the events reported in 'My Own True Ghost Story', the supernatural element was basically explained away at the end.

Kipling had sold the rights for the six paperback books for £200 plus a small royalty. Each of the Indian Railway Library booklets featured a line drawing on the cover by an artist named Brownlow Fforde. His artwork of skull-headed figure for *The Phantom 'Rickshaw* was suitably macabre.

Encouraged by his parents and his editor-in-chief, Edward Kay Robinson, in the autumn of 1889 Kipling left India to become a roving correspondent and try to make a career for himself as an author.

'After all, there was no need for me to stay here for ever,' Kipling later recalled, 'and I could go away and measure myself against the doorsills of London as soon as I had money.'

He travelled with the Hills to Burma, Singapore, Hong Kong and Canton, Japan and San Francisco. While crossing the United States, they visited Mrs Hill's family home in Beaver, Pennsylvania, where he met her sister Caroline Taylor, to whom he became informally engaged.

The group finally arrived in London in September and took rooms in Villiers Street, off The Strand. Kipling's reputation had preceded him, and within a year he was already being acclaimed as one of the most brilliant authors of his time and a literary heir to Charles Dickens.

'There was an evident demand for my stuff,' Kipling ⹀served. 'I do not recall that I stirred a hand to help myself. ⹀ngs happened to me.'

Yet despite his new fame, Kipling soon found himself in debt. On the advice of Walter Besant, founder of the Authors' Society, he retained the services of AP Watt as his literary agent. 'In the course of forty odd years I do not recall any difference between us that three minutes' talk could not clear up,' Kipling later wrote about their very successful working relationship.

By the spring of 1890, Kipling had become so famous that his work was the subject of an editorial in *The Times* of March 25 which stated that the author had 'tapped a new vein'. Amongst the titles singled out for praise by the newspaper was 'that very grim story', 'In the House of Suddhoo' (1886).

'I am afraid that I was not much impressed by reviews,' said Kipling. 'As I got to know literary circles and their critical output, I was struck by the slenderness of some of the writers' equipment.'

Kipling found himself being praised by such contemporaries as Oscar Wilde, Lord Tennyson, Henry James and Andrew Lang, while Jerome K. Jerome observed that the author, 'must have felt like a comet trying to lose its tail'.

By now, all his earlier books had finally been published in English and American editions. However, despite his literary success, Kipling remained unlucky in love. While staying in London, his engagement to Caroline Taylor was broken off, and a chance meeting in the street with childhood sweetheart Florence Garrard ended unsuccessfully when he tried to resume their relationship.

The strain was too much, and Kipling suffered another nervous breakdown.

While Kipling was convalescing in London, he made a new friend, American writer and publisher Wolcott Balestier. He also met Balestier's mother and his sisters, Josephine and Caroline ('Carrie'). During his recovery, Kipling wrote his first novel, *The Light That Failed*, about a painter going blind who was spurned by the woman he loved. It was published in New York to great success the following year.

Meanwhile, an unauthorised collection of his articles for the *Pioneer* was published as *The City of Dreadful Night* fourteenth volume in AH Wheeler & Co.'s Indian Railway Library series. The title piece was an atmospheric prose-poem about death-like sleepers during the heat of an Indian night. Kipling attempted to have the book suppressed.

One of Kipling's best-known horror stories, 'The Mark of the Beast' appeared over two issues of the *Pioneer* in July 1890. It was about a man cursed by a native priest to apparently transform into a were-leopard. Kipling himself described the tale as 'a rather nasty story', while Andrew Lang declared it 'poisonous stuff.'

However, in his ground-breaking essay 'Supernatural Horror in Literature', American author HP Lovecraft wrote: 'The naked leper-priest who mewed like an otter, of the spots which appeared on the chest of the man that priest cursed, of the growing carnivorousness of the victim and of the fear which horses began to display towards him, and of the eventually half-accomplished transformation of that victim into a leopard, being things which no reader is ever likely to forget.'

The unconventional policeman Strickland who appeared in the story later turned up in a further five tales by Kipling, including 'The Recrudescence of Imray' (aka 'The Return of Imray', 1891), a murder mystery that revolved around a deadly curse and the decaying corpse of an Indian manservant. This latter tale appeared in another pirated volume of Kipling's fiction, *Life's Handicap*, published by Hurst & Company of New York in 1891.

That same year Kipling collaborated with Wolcott Balestier in writing the romantic novel *The Naulahka: A Story of West and East*. Balestier, who had now become Kipling's American agent, also helped his friend establish his copyrights in the United States, after many problems with unauthorised editions.

It was another busy year for Kipling, and the author suffered a further breakdown from overwork.

After setting off on a voyage to South Africa, Australia and ew Zealand, he returned one final time to India to spend istmas with his family. But no sooner had Kipling arrived he was informed by cable of Balestier's death from typhoid, and he rushed back to London, arriving on January 10, 1892.

Just eight days later, Kipling married Balestier's sister Caroline in a London gripped by an influenza epidemic. 'The undertakers had run out of black horses,' observed Kipling, 'and the dead had to be content with brown ones. The living were mostly abed.'

The newlyweds quickly left for a voyage around the world, stopping in Brattleboro, Vermont, to visit the bride's family. While there, Caroline's brother Beatty sold them a plot of land for a nominal sum.

The honeymooners then continued on to Japan. But when Kipling's bank failed, the couple were left with no assets but their travel tickets, which they exchanged for return fares to New England, where the Balestiers found them a house to rent for ten dollars (around £2.00) a month.

Written after his final visit to India the previous year, 'The Lost Legion' was one of the author's final supernatural stories set in his homeland. It shared the May 1892 issue of the then one-year-old *Strand Magazine* with the Sherlock Holmes mystery, 'The Adventure of the Beryl Coronet' by Arthur Conan Doyle. The two men would later become neighbours in Sussex, and Kipling paid tribute to the Great Detective in his 1909 story 'The House Surgeon'.

That same year saw the publication of *The Naulahka*, his collaboration with Wolcott Balestier, which was not a success. However, *Barrack-Room Ballads and Other Verses*, which included the poem 'Gunga Din', only added to Kipling's fame and, during this period, the author bought back the rights to some of his earlier books with the money he continued to earn in royalties.

With the death of the poet laureate Alfred, Lord Tennyson, it could be said that Kipling unofficially took his place in the public's estimation, although he reportedly turned down th and many other honours, including a knighthood and Order of Merit.

A daughter, Josephine, was born to the Kiplin

December 29 – her father's and mother's birthdays falling on the days either side. Perhaps inspired by the arrival of his first child, Kipling began writing for children.

Published in 1893, *Many Inventions* contained stories written both before and after his marriage to Caroline. It included the last story narrated by the Irish soldier Mulvaney (who, up until then, was his most popular character) and the first story about Mowgli, the feral child who would become the leading character in Kipling's classic collection of children's stories and poems, *The Jungle Book* (1894).

Many Inventions also featured 'The Finest Story in the World', one of Kipling's few fantastic stories not to be set in India, which concerns a poetic writer who suffers from a recurring dream of previous lives upon the sea.

Later that year, the Kiplings moved into 'Naulakha', a large wooden house they had had built on the land purchased from Beatty Balestier.

The Second Jungle Book was published in 1895 and was as equally successful as the first volume. 'When those books were finished they said so themselves with, almost, the water-hammer click of a tap turned off,' Kipling explained.

He also considered Edgar Rice Burroughs' *Tarzan of the Apes* to have been explicitly inspired by his own work: 'He had "jazzed" the motif of the *Jungle Books* and, I imagine, had thoroughly enjoyed himself,' said Kipling, with a trace of irony. 'He was reported to have said that he wanted to find out how bad a book he could write and "get away with", which is a legitimate ambition.'

On February 2, 1896, a second daughter was born to the Kiplings, who named her Elsie. Unfortunately, their happiness was shattered when the family's manners and attitudes were considered objectionable by Beatty Balestier and their neighbours. The dispute ended with a well-publicised court case after a confrontation on the road between Kipling and his coholic brother-in-law.

The idea seemed to be that I was "making money" out of rica,' explained Kipling, 'and was not sufficiently grateful privileges.'

From that time onwards, Kipling considered Americans – like the French – as 'foreigners', and he maintained his position that only 'lesser breeds' were born beyond the English Channel. As if to reinforce this xenophobic outlook, his collection of poems *The Seven Seas* (1896) included the popular patriotic cycle, 'A Song of the English'.

The family left Brattleboro, and in the spring of 1896 moved into a house in Torquay, England. Kipling admitted that the family's new home, 'seemed almost too good to be true' and despite the building's bright rooms and the fresh sea air, he revealed that he and his wife experienced 'the shape of a growing depression which enveloped us both – a gathering blackness of mind and sorrow of the heart, that each put down to the new, soft climate and, without telling the other, fought against for long weeks. It was the Feng-shui – the Spirit of the house itself – that darkened the sunshine and fell upon us every time we entered, checking the very words on our lips.'

He later wrote about the experience in his psychic detective story 'The House Surgeon', which was published in two parts in *Harper's Magazine* in September and October 1909.

In 1897, the family finally settled at 'The Elms' in Rottingdean, Sussex, near Kipling's cousin, Stanley Baldwin. A son, John, was born on August 17 in 'North End House', the holiday home of Kipling's aunt, Georgiana Burne-Jones.

That same year, Kipling published *Captains Courageous: A Story of the Grand Banks*, his novel about the New England cod-fishing fleet that was inspired by the author's American doctor and friend, Charles Eliot Conland. 'My part was the writing; his the details,' Kipling wrote. 'I wanted to see if I could catch and hold something of a rather beautiful localised American atmosphere that was already beginning to fade. Thanks to Conland I came near this.'

In America, Scribner's published a collection of Kipling work by subscription. The stories were rearranged by to and some uncollected material was added. At the age of th two, he was now the highest-paid writer in the world.

During the first of many winter holidays in South Africa, Kipling travelled to Rhodesia in 1898, where he struck up a friendship with the diamond magnate and statesman Cecil Rhodes, who presented him with a house near Cape Town.

This association only strengthened Kipling's imperialist and racist persuasions, which grew stronger with the passing of years. He genuinely believed that it was the duty of every Englishman – or, more likely, every white man – to bring European culture to the uncivilised natives who populated the rest of the world. This glorification of Britain as a colonial Empire reached its apogee in his poem 'The White Man's Burden' (1899).

However, Kipling's ideas were out of step with liberal thought of the age, and as he grew older he became an increasingly isolated figure. In 1924, the critic Alfred Ward wrote: 'Nearly all his Indian stories demand that the reader, shall, at the outset, grant certain large premises: such that the British are God's chosen race.'

That same year he published the short story collection *The Day's Work* which included 'The Maltese Cat', a story about polo ponies that would prove one of the most popular he ever wrote. He also published *A Fleet in Being*, a series of six articles on the navy reprinted from the *Morning Post*.

In the winter of 1899, the Kiplings paid their final visit to America. During the stormy sea crossing, Kipling and all the children became ill.

As newspapers around the world reported their condition on the front pages, Kipling and his beloved six-year-old daughter Josephine grew worse; and developed pneumonia in New York. Caroline Kipling, also unwell, was unable to care for both of them. She made the decision to take her daughter to a house across mid-winter Manhattan to be looked after by someone else.

Josephine died on March 6, and her father barely survived. Kipling was never the same again and wrote about the ␣t of his loss in 'They' (1904), a poignant story about a ␣ed father in a mysterious house filled with the laughter of ghostly children. It has justly been compared to Henry James' 'The Turn of the Screw' as a classic of supernatural fiction.

At the outbreak of the Boer War in South Africa, Kipling became involved in a campaign for service charities organised by the *Daily Mail* newspaper. 'The Absent-Minded Beggar' Fund, named after a poem Kipling wrote which became a popular song of the day, raised vast amounts of money for the benefit of British soldiers.

From Sea to Sea: Letters of Travel was published in 1899 in two volumes. It was an authorised version of travel sketches and uncollected articles from the *Pioneer* and *The Pioneer Post*. Meanwhile, Kipling featured himself as 'the egregious Beetle' in *Stalky & Co.*, a collection of public school stories with a strong autobiographical links to his time at the United Services College in Devon.

'*Stalky & Co.* became the illegitimate ancestor of several stories of school-life whose heroes lived through experiences mercifully denied to me,' the author later observed.

Kipling returned to South Africa for the first three months of 1900, where he continued war work and writing, including two weeks in Bloemfontein on the newspaper *The Friend*, published by the British Army. At the time, Kipling was criticised by many liberals for his support of the British military campaign against the Boers.

He was also working on the novel *Kim* (1901), the last – and thought by many to be the most important – of Kipling's Indian writings. It concerned the adventures of an orphaned boy of a sergeant in the Irish Guards and was written with help from Kipling's father.

'Under our united tobaccos it grew like the Djinn released from the brass bottle,' Kipling recalled, 'and the more we explored its possibilities the more opulence of detail did we discover.'

In 1902, the house in Vermont finally sold. The fam~ moved into their final home, a seventeenth-century i~ master's house near Burwash, Sussex. To maintain solitude, Kipling also purchased several acres of the surrounding countryside.

Built of local sandstone, 'Bateman's' had the atmosphere that Kipling had been looking for in a home. 'We entered and felt her Spirit – her Feng-shui – to be good,' he wrote. 'We went through every room and found no shadow of ancient regrets, stifled miseries, nor any menace though the "new" end of her was three hundred years old.'

However, Kipling's belief in the supernatural persisted as he listened to local folk-tales about magic, witchcraft and love-philtres. He came to believe that Gladwish Wood, close to his family's new home, was haunted by the ghost of a poacher, wrongly hanged for the death of a confederate: 'It is full of a sense of ancient ferocity and evil . . . there is a spirit of some kind there,' he revealed to ghost-hunter Robert Thurston Hopkins, author of *Rudyard Kipling's World* (1925). 'A very impolite fellow he is, too, for one evening something suddenly gripped me and despite my attempts to walk forward I was gradually forced back. I felt some unseen, unknown power just pushing against me and in the end I was compelled to turn around and leave the wood in a most undignified manner.'

Kipling also told his mother that he saw the figure of his deceased daughter, Josephine, in the house and gardens at 'Bateman's', and he used the building as the inspiration for the house in his story 'They'.

Just So Stories for Little Children (1902) was a collection of fables that had originally been written for his own children. Along with *The Jungle Book*, it has remained one of Kipling's most enduring works. *The Five Nations* (1903) was a great contrast; it collected together his poems about the Boer War and its aftermath.

Kipling enjoyed his seclusion amongst the Sussex Downs, and during the first decade of his new life there he wrote the collection *Traffics and Discoveries* (1904), plus the children's fantasies *Puck of Pook's Hill* (1906) – based on the hill that can be seen to the south-east of the lawn at 'Bateman's' – and *Rewards and Fairies* (1910).

The latter two titles featured Dan and Una, two children

who were transported back to specific moments in time by the supernatural Puck. They contained an innovative series of allegorical stories and poems primarily intended for children, inspired by the author's love of English history and his new home in the Sussex countryside.

Rewards and Fairies was also a belated attempt to put a cap on some of his 'imperialist' writings of the past. The book was nominally a sequel to *Puck of Pook's Hill* but, as Kipling later wrote, 'I worked the material in three or four overlaid tints and textures, which might or might not reveal themselves according to the shifting light of sex, youth and experience. The tales had to be read by children, before people realised that they were meant for grown-ups.' The book included perhaps his single most famous poem, 'If—', written for his son, John, when he was thirteen.

In 1907, Kipling was the first Englishman to be awarded the Nobel Prize for Literature. 'It was a very great honour,' revealed the author, 'in all ways unexpected'. He travelled to Stockholm, Sweden, to accept his prize from the new King.

That same year he journeyed to Canada for a speaking tour and to receive an honorary degree from the McGill University at Montreal. Years later, he recalled a story he was told in Canada about a body-snatching incident, 'perpetrated in some lonely prairie-town and culminating in purest horror'. Kipling wrote the story up and then put it aside. Months later, while glancing through a back-issue of *Harper's Magazine* in his dentist's parlour, he found the exact same story down to every detail. 'Had I published that tale,' he cautioned, 'what could have saved me from the charge of deliberate plagiarism?'

Another collection of stories, *Actions and Reactions*, appeared in 1909. It included Kipling's pioneering science fiction tale, 'With the Night Mail: A Story of 2000 AD', about flying-boats crossing the Atlantic. The story was originally published in *McClure's Magazine* in November 1905, but for its first British appearance the following month in *The Windsor Magazine* carried the subtitle 'From "The Windsor Magazine" Octob AD 2147'.

Abaft the Funnel was published in the United Stat

B. W. Dodge & Co. of New York without Kipling's permission. The book contained thirty uncollected stories and sketches from newspaper files in India, including the racing ghost story 'Sleipner, Late Thurinda' (1888), which Kipling had planned never to reprint. To secure copyright, the pirated printing was quickly followed by an authorised edition from his New York publishers, Doubleday, Page & Co.

'At first this annoyed me, but later I laughed,' wrote Kipling, 'and Frank Doubleday chased the pirates up with cheaper and cheaper editions, so that their thefts became less profitable.'

Kipling's mother, Alice, died in 1910, and his father followed her just a year later. Meanwhile, he collaborated on the textbook *A School History of England* (1911) with historian C. R. L. Fletcher.

Kipling visited Egypt in 1913. He also published *Songs from Books*, a collection of poems that had appeared in, or been used as introductions or afterwords to his previously published stories, some of which were expanded upon for this edition.

That same year, *The Harbour Watch*, a play written in collaboration with his teenage daughter Elsie, was performed in London but closed after only a few performances.

Around this time Kipling began work on a story about the dead of the Boer War 'flickerering and re-forming as the horizon flickered in the heat' during a summer day's military manoeuvres. However, he eventually decided that 'in cold blood it seemed more and more fantastic and absurd, unnecessary and hysterical,' and he later discarded the draft.

With the outbreak of the First World War, Kipling wrote 'Swept and Garnished' during the immediate aftermath of the German invasion of Belgium. A ghostly propaganda story, it appeared simultaneously in British and American magazines in January 1915.

After John was told that he could not enlist because of his ɔor eyesight, Kipling used his considerable influence and his ɔ was given a commission in the Irish Guards as a Second ·tenant. Not long after, the eighteen-year-old boy was ·ed missing in action, believed killed in the Battle of

Loos, his first conflict on the Western Front. Kipling did everything he could to trace his son, including travelling to France and even dropping leaflets behind enemy lines, but John's body was never recovered.

Perhaps exacerbated by worry for his missing son, from this period onwards Kipling was in constant pain from a duodenal ulcer, although at the time he feared it was cancer, which he thought was a family ailment.

He later explored his terror of the disease in the story 'The Wish House' (1924), which was published in the American *MacLean's Magazine* in October 1924, but did not appear in Britain until the December issue of *Pall Mall Magazine*.

Although a sense of bitter emptiness entered his work after his son's death, Kipling continued to publish articles on the war (much of it censored), and eighteen of these pieces from the *Daily Telegraph* were eventually collected in *The New Army in Training*, *France at War* and *Fringes of the Fleet* (all 1915).

Tales of the Trade (1916), *Sea Warfare* (1916) and *The Eyes of Asia* (1917) were further collections of war journalism from, amongst other sources, the *Daily Telegraph* and the *New York Times*.

In 1917, Kipling joined the War Graves Commission. That same year he published *A Diversity of Creatures*, a collection of stories mainly written before the outbreak of war, but including two 'Tales of '15'. One of these, 'Mary Postgate', apparently about a woman who refused to help a dying German pilot who had crashed in her garden, has been seen as among the most controversial and important of the author's later stories.

The book also included 'As Easy as ABC', a science fiction story that was a sequel-of-sorts to 'With the Night Mail: A Story of 2000 AD'. It had originally appeared over two issues of both *The Family Magazine* in America and *The London Magazine* in Britain in 1912, where it carried the subtitle 'A Tale c 2150 AD'.

Kipling also published in newspapers a series of war art about the Italian-Austrian front, five of which were col in *The War in the Mountains* (1917).

The Years Between (1919) was a collection of poems written during the period from just after the Boer War until the aftermath of the First World War and included 'Epitaphs of the War', while *Letters of Travel 1892-1913* (1920) collected old articles on Japan, the United States, Canada and Egypt.

The Irish Guards in The Great War, published in 1923, was a history of his late son's regiment that Kipling compiled from soldiers' letters and diaries, and the reminiscences of survivors. That same year, *Land and Sea Tales for Scouts and Guides* contained uncollected stories with two new additions and extra verse.

In 1924, Kipling's only surviving child, Elsie, married former Irish Guards Captain George Bambridge, MC.

Published in *Pall Mall Magazine* for September of that year, Kipling's story 'A Madonna of the Trenches' had its inspiration in the First World War. As its reference to 'the Angels of Mons' indicated, it also had its roots in Arthur Machen's totally fictitious tale 'The Bowmen', which had created great controversy almost a decade earlier when British troops returning from the first battle of Ypres had claimed to have seen the phantom archers featured in the story.

Debits and Credits (1926) was a collection of short stories that expanded upon some of the material Kipling collected while writing *The Irish Guards in The Great War*. It also included such tales as 'The Wish House', 'A Madonna of the Trenches' and 'The Eye of Allah'.

The latter tale caused its author some problems, as he revealed: 'Again and again it went dead under my hand, and for the life of me I could not see why. I put it away and waited.' He finally decided to treat it as 'an illuminated manuscript' rather than 'hard black-and-white decoration', and was able to finish it.

The final story in the book, 'The Gardener', was an enigmatic blend of religious symbolism and the supernatural. It s written after Kipling visited the war graves at the Rouen etery in France. 'One never gets over the shock of this sea of arrested lives,' he wrote to H. Rider Haggard two er on March 14, 1925.

The story was finished at Lourdes on March 22, and was originally published in the April 1925 edition of *McCall's Magazine* before Kipling spent a year revising it for its appearance in *Debits and Credits*.

'The Gardener' was Kipling's final supernatural story.

In 1927, Kipling took a voyage to Brazil and *Brazilian Sketches* reprinted his travel articles that had previously appeared in the *Morning Post*.

A Book of Words (1928) was a volume of collected speeches delivered between 1906 and 1927, while *Thy Servant a Dog* (1930) contained a series of tales 'Told by Boots', about a family living in an English country house as observed from the viewpoint of their dogs.

The Kiplings visited the West Indies in 1930 and were forced to stay for three months in Bermuda, due to Caroline's illness.

Kipling's final original story collection, *Limits and Renewals*, appeared in 1932. It contained 'Dayspring Mishandled' a tale concerning literary forgery that contained some scathing comments on the relationships between authors and critics.

'It must be nice to inspire affection at short notice,' Kipling had once written to H. Rider Haggard. 'I haven't the gift. Like olives and caviar and asafoetida, I'm an acquired taste stealing slowly on the senses.'

The largely autobiographical *Souvenirs of France* the following year covered Kipling's first visit to France in 1878, when his father took him to the Paris Exhibition.

Although it was initially thought to be gastritis, Kipling's gastric ulcer was finally diagnosed correctly in 1933.

Three years later he collapsed when his ulcer perforated. Kipling died in London on January 18, 1936 at the age of seventy-one. Although his death came two days before that of his friend and reigning sovereign, King George V, the countr no doubt thought it had lost a far more representative Er lishman with Kipling's passing. He was buried in P Corner at London's Westminster Abbey.

Kipling's reticent autobiography, *Something of Mysel*

Friends Known and Unknown, written in the last year of his life, was posthumously published in 1937. It was edited by his widow with help from Lord Webb-Johnson, Kipling's surgeon and friend. The book ended somewhat abruptly with the prophetic line '. . . which were well in use before my death'.

Over the next three years, the complete Sussex Editions of Kipling's works were published. Although they included the author's final revisions, they still had to be completed by others.

Following Kipling's death, Hollywood finally recognised the popularity of the author's tales of adventure, romance and selfless heroism.

Spencer Tracy gave an Oscar-winning performance as the Portuguese fisherman who rescued Freddie Bartholomew's spoiled brat in *Captains Courageous* (1937), ably supported by Melvyn Douglas, Lionel Barrymore, Mickey Rooney and John Carradine.

Ronald Coleman's artist was determined to finish Ida Lupino's portrait before he went blind in *The Light That Failed* (1939), and Shirley Temple was the cute little moppet befriended by Victor McLaglen's soft-hearted sergeant in John Ford's *Wee Willie Winkie* (1937).

McLaglen, Gary Grant and Douglas Fairbanks, Jr. played the three soldier comrades saved by Sam Jaffe's water boy in *Gunga Din* (1939), Errol Flynn befriended a young Dean Stockwell in *Kim* (1950), while Stuart Granger, Walter Pidgeon and David Niven were the *Soldiers Three* (1951).

Sean Connery and Michael Caine played the two loveable rogues who sought the hidden treasure of a lost empire in John Huston's *The Man Who Would Be King* (1975), which also featured Christopher Plummer as Kipling himself.

'They' was updated into a 1993 made-for-television movie starring Patrick Bergin and Vanessa Redgrave, while 'The Mark of the Beast' was adapted for a low budget anthology movie entitled *Things 3: Old Things* (1998).

Inspired by his cousin Philip Burne-Jones' 1897 painting of the name, Kipling's poem 'The Vampire' was first filmed It also formed the basis for a 1915 film starring Theda

Bara (the screen's first 'vamp') and a 1922 version, both retitled *A Fool There Was* (the first line of the verse).

The Jungle Book has, of course, been filmed several times, most notably in live-action with Sabu (1942) and Jason Scott Lee (1994), and by Walt Disney in 1967 as an animated musical that probably had the author spinning in his grave.

Caroline Kipling died in 1939. She bequeathed their home in Sussex to the National Trust for Places of Historic Interest and it is preserved as a memorial to Kipling's memory.

In 1976, Mrs Elsie Bambridge, Kipling's sole surviving child, died without an heir. His copyrights were bequeathed by her to the National Trust and lasted until 2006.

Although he fell out of favour with the public after the First World War and with the waning of British Imperialism, there are currently signs that a critical revaluation of Rudyard Kipling's work is underway.

Today it is difficult to imagine just how extraordinarily popular Kipling's fiction and verse was in the late nineteenth and early twentieth century. During his lifetime, he published around 550 poems (with at least as many again remaining unpublished), and seven million copies of his books were sold in Britain alone, with another eight million in the United States.

Despite his often jingoistic and imperialist views, his early tales conjure up the atmosphere of a colonial and often exotic India, while his verse precisely captures the colloquial speech of the common man.

'As of what Kipling wrote about nineteenth-century Anglo-India,' said George Orwell, '. . . it is not only the best but almost the only literary picture we have.'

It is hoped that this extensive collection of the author's fantastical tales will introduce his stories of a bygone era in British history to a whole new generation of readers.

Stephen Jones
London, England
June 2005